John Griffith London (born **John Griffith Chaney**; January 12, 1876 – November 22, 1916) was an American novelist, journalist, and social activist. A pioneer in the world of commercial magazine fiction, he was one of the first writers to become a worldwide celebrity and earn a large fortune from writing. He was also an innovator in the genre that would later become known as science fiction. His most famous works include The Call of the Wild and White Fang, both set in the Klondike Gold Rush, as well as the short stories "To Build a Fire", "An Odyssey of the North", and "Love of Life". He also wrote about the South Pacific in stories such as "The Pearls of Parlay" and "The Heathen". London was part of the radical literary group "The Crowd" in San Francisco and a passionate advocate of unionization, socialism, and the rights of workers. He wrote several powerful works dealing with these topics, such as his dystopian novel The Iron Heel, his non-fiction exposé The People of the Abyss, and The War of the Classes. (Source: Wikipedia)

Literary works:
The Cruise of the Dazzler (1902)
A Daughter of the Snows (1902)
The Call of the Wild (1903)
The Kempton-Wace Letters (1903)
The Sea-Wolf (1904)
The Game (1905)
White Fang (1906)
Before Adam (1907)
The Iron Heel (1908)
Martin Eden (1909)
Burning Daylight (1910)
Adventure (1911)
The Scarlet Plague (1912)
A Son of the Sun (1912)
The Abysmal Brute (1913)
The Valley of the Moon (1913)

ADVENTURE,

JERRY OF
THE ISLANDS
&
MARTIN EDEN

JACK LONDON

PRINCE CLASSICS

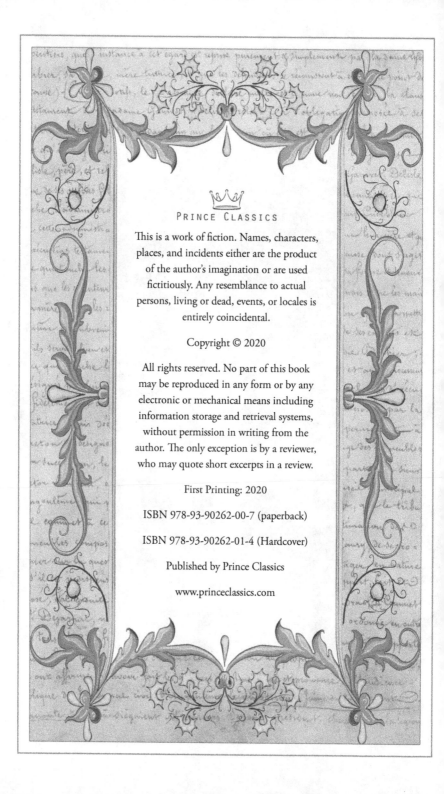

PRINCE CLASSICS

First Printing: 2020

ISBN 978-93-90262-00-7 (paperback)

ISBN 978-93-90262-01-4 (Hardcover)

Published by Prince Classics

www.princeclassics.com

Contents

ADVENTURE,
JERRY OF
THE ISLANDS
&
MARTIN EDEN

ADVENTURE

"We are those fools who could not rest

   In the dull earth we left behind,

But burned with passion for the West,

   And drank strange frenzy from its wind.

The world where wise men live at ease

   Fades from our unregretful eyes,

And blind across uncharted seas

   We stagger on our enterprise."

"THE SHIP OF FOOLS."

CHAPTER I—SOMETHING TO BE DONE

He was a very sick white man. He rode pick-a-back on a woolly-headed, black-skinned savage, the lobes of whose ears had been pierced and stretched until one had torn out, while the other carried a circular block of carved wood three inches in diameter. The torn ear had been pierced again, but this time not so ambitiously, for the hole accommodated no more than a short clay pipe. The man-horse was greasy and dirty, and naked save for an exceedingly narrow and dirty loin-cloth; but the white man clung to him closely and desperately. At times, from weakness, his head drooped and rested on the woolly pate. At other times he lifted his head and stared with swimming eyes at the cocoanut palms that reeled and swung in the shimmering heat. He was clad in a thin undershirt and a strip of cotton cloth, that wrapped about his waist and descended to his knees. On his head was a battered Stetson, known to the trade as a Baden-Powell. About his middle was strapped a belt, which carried a large-calibred automatic pistol and several spare clips, loaded and ready for quick work.

The rear was brought up by a black boy of fourteen or fifteen, who carried medicine bottles, a pail of hot water, and various other hospital appurtenances. They passed out of the compound through a small wicker gate, and went on under the blazing sun, winding about among new-planted cocoanuts that threw no shade. There was not a breath of wind, and the superheated, stagnant air was heavy with pestilence. From the direction they were going arose a wild clamour, as of lost souls wailing and of men in torment. A long, low shed showed ahead, grass-walled and grass-thatched, and it was from here that the noise proceeded. There were shrieks and screams, some unmistakably of grief, others unmistakably of unendurable pain. As the white man drew closer he could hear a low and continuous moaning and groaning. He shuddered at the thought of entering, and for a moment was quite certain that he was going to faint. For that most dreaded of Solomon Island scourges, dysentery, had struck Berande plantation, and he was all alone to cope with it. Also, he was afflicted himself.

By stooping close, still on man-back, he managed to pass through the low doorway. He took a small bottle from his follower, and sniffed strong ammonia to clear his senses for the ordeal. Then he shouted, "Shut up!" and the clamour stilled. A raised platform of forest slabs, six feet wide, with a slight pitch, extended the full length of the shed. Alongside of it was a yard-wide run-way. Stretched on the platform, side by side and crowded close, lay a score of blacks. That they were low in the order of human life was apparent at a glance. They were man-eaters. Their faces were asymmetrical, bestial; their bodies were ugly and ape-like. They wore nose-rings of clam-shell and turtle-shell, and from the ends of their noses which were also pierced, projected horns of beads strung on stiff wire. Their ears were pierced and distended to accommodate wooden plugs and sticks, pipes, and all manner of barbaric ornaments. Their faces and bodies were tattooed or scarred in hideous designs. In their sickness they wore no clothing, not even loin-cloths, though they retained their shell armlets, their bead necklaces, and their leather belts, between which and the skin were thrust naked knives. The bodies of many were covered with horrible sores. Swarms of flies rose and settled, or flew back and forth in clouds.

The white man went down the line, dosing each man with medicine. To some he gave chlorodyne. He was forced to concentrate with all his will in order to remember which of them could stand ipecacuanha, and which of them were constitutionally unable to retain that powerful drug. One who lay dead he ordered to be carried out. He spoke in the sharp, peremptory manner of a man who would take no nonsense, and the well men who obeyed his orders scowled malignantly. One muttered deep in his chest as he took the corpse by the feet. The white man exploded in speech and action. It cost him a painful effort, but his arm shot out, landing a back-hand blow on the black's mouth.

"What name you, Angara?" he shouted. "What for talk 'long you, eh? I knock seven bells out of you, too much, quick!"

With the automatic swiftness of a wild animal the black gathered himself to spring. The anger of a wild animal was in his eyes; but he saw the white man's hand dropping to the pistol in his belt. The spring was never made.

18

The tensed body relaxed, and the black, stooping over the corpse, helped carry it out. This time there was no muttering.

"Swine!" the white man gritted out through his teeth at the whole breed of Solomon Islanders.

He was very sick, this white man, as sick as the black men who lay helpless about him, and whom he attended. He never knew, each time he entered the festering shambles, whether or not he would be able to complete the round. But he did know in large degree of certainty that, if he ever fainted there in the midst of the blacks, those who were able would be at his throat like ravening wolves.

Part way down the line a man was dying. He gave orders for his removal as soon as he had breathed his last. A black stuck his head inside the shed door, saying,—

"Four fella sick too much."

Fresh cases, still able to walk, they clustered about the spokesman. The white man singled out the weakest, and put him in the place just vacated by the corpse. Also, he indicated the next weakest, telling him to wait for a place until the next man died. Then, ordering one of the well men to take a squad from the field-force and build a lean-to addition to the hospital, he continued along the run-way, administering medicine and cracking jokes in *bêche-de-mer* English to cheer the sufferers. Now and again, from the far end, a weird wail was raised. When he arrived there he found the noise was emitted by a boy who was not sick. The white man's wrath was immediate.

"What name you sing out alla time?" he demanded.

"Him fella my brother belong me," was the answer. "Him fella die too much."

"You sing out, him fella brother belong you die too much," the white man went on in threatening tones. "I cross too much along you. What name you sing out, eh? You fat-head make um brother belong you die dose up too much. You fella finish sing out, savvee? You fella no finish sing out I make finish damn quick."

He threatened the wailer with his fist, and the black cowered down, glaring at him with sullen eyes.

"Sing out no good little bit," the white man went on, more gently. "You no sing out. You chase um fella fly. Too much strong fella fly. You catch water, washee brother belong you; washee plenty too much, bime bye brother belong you all right. Jump!" he shouted fiercely at the end, his will penetrating the low intelligence of the black with dynamic force that made him jump to the task of brushing the loathsome swarms of flies away.

Again he rode out into the reeking heat. He clutched the black's neck tightly, and drew a long breath; but the dead air seemed to shrivel his lungs, and he dropped his head and dozed till the house was reached. Every effort of will was torture, yet he was called upon continually to make efforts of will. He gave the black he had ridden a nip of trade-gin. Viaburi, the house-boy, brought him corrosive sublimate and water, and he took a thorough antiseptic wash. He dosed himself with chlorodyne, took his own pulse, smoked a thermometer, and lay back on the couch with a suppressed groan. It was mid-afternoon, and he had completed his third round that day. He called the house-boy.

"Take um big fella look along *Jessie*," he commanded.

The boy carried the long telescope out on the veranda, and searched the sea.

"One fella schooner long way little bit," he announced. "One fella *Jessie*."

The white man gave a little gasp of delight.

"You make um *Jessie*, five sticks tobacco along you," he said.

There was silence for a time, during which he waited with eager impatience.

"Maybe *Jessie*, maybe other fella schooner," came the faltering admission.

20

The man wormed to the edge of the couch, and slipped off to the floor on his knees. By means of a chair he drew himself to his feet. Still clinging to the chair, supporting most of his weight on it, he shoved it to the door and out upon the veranda. The sweat from the exertion streamed down his face and showed through the undershirt across his shoulders. He managed to get into the chair, where he panted in a state of collapse. In a few minutes he roused himself. The boy held the end of the telescope against one of the veranda scantlings, while the man gazed through it at the sea. At last he picked up the white sails of the schooner and studied them.

"No *Jessie*," he said very quietly. "That's the *Malakula*."

He changed his seat for a steamer reclining-chair. Three hundred feet away the sea broke in a small surf upon the beach. To the left he could see the white line of breakers that marked the bar of the Balesuna River, and, beyond, the rugged outline of Savo Island. Directly before him, across the twelve-mile channel, lay Florida Island; and, farther to the right, dim in the distance, he could make out portions of Malaita—the savage island, the abode of murder, and robbery, and man-eating—the place from which his own two hundred plantation hands had been recruited. Between him and the beach was the cane-grass fence of the compound. The gate was ajar, and he sent the house-boy to close it. Within the fence grew a number of lofty cocoanut palms. On either side the path that led to the gate stood two tall flagstaffs. They were reared on artificial mounds of earth that were ten feet high. The base of each staff was surrounded by short posts, painted white and connected by heavy chains. The staffs themselves were like ships' masts, with topmasts spliced on in true nautical fashion, with shrouds, ratlines, gaffs, and flag-halyards. From the gaff of one, two gay flags hung limply, one a checkerboard of blue and white squares, the other a white pennant centred with a red disc. It was the international code signal of distress.

On the far corner of the compound fence a hawk brooded. The man watched it, and knew that it was sick. He wondered idly if it felt as bad as he felt, and was feebly amused at the thought of kinship that somehow penetrated his fancy. He roused himself to order the great bell to be rung as a signal for the plantation hands to cease work and go to their barracks. Then he mounted his man-horse and made the last round of the day.

In the hospital were two new cases. To these he gave castor-oil. He congratulated himself. It had been an easy day. Only three had died. He inspected the copra-drying that had been going on, and went through the barracks to see if there were any sick lying hidden and defying his rule of segregation. Returned to the house, he received the reports of the boss-boys and gave instructions for next day's work. The boat's crew boss also he had in, to give assurance, as was the custom nightly, that the whale-boats were hauled up and padlocked. This was a most necessary precaution, for the blacks were in a funk, and a whale-boat left lying on the beach in the evening meant a loss of twenty blacks by morning. Since the blacks were worth thirty dollars apiece, or less, according to how much of their time had been worked out, Berande plantation could ill afford the loss. Besides, whale-boats were not cheap in the Solomons; and, also, the deaths were daily reducing the working capital. Seven blacks had fled into the bush the week before, and four had dragged themselves back, helpless from fever, with the report that two more had been killed and *kai-kai*'d {1} by the hospitable bushmen. The seventh man was still at large, and was said to be working along the coast on the lookout to steal a canoe and get away to his own island.

Viaburi brought two lighted lanterns to the white man for inspection. He glanced at them and saw that they were burning brightly with clear, broad flames, and nodded his head. One was hoisted up to the gaff of the flagstaff, and the other was placed on the wide veranda. They were the leading lights to the Berande anchorage, and every night in the year they were so inspected and hung out.

He rolled back on his couch with a sigh of relief. The day's work was done. A rifle lay on the couch beside him. His revolver was within reach of his hand. An hour passed, during which he did not move. He lay in a state of half-slumber, half-coma. He became suddenly alert. A creak on the back veranda was the cause. The room was L-shaped; the corner in which stood his couch was dim, but the hanging lamp in the main part of the room, over the billiard table and just around the corner, so that it did not shine on him, was burning brightly. Likewise the verandas were well lighted. He waited without movement. The creaks were repeated, and he knew several men lurked outside.

"What name?" he cried sharply.

The house, raised a dozen feet above the ground, shook on its pile foundations to the rush of retreating footsteps.

"They're getting bold," he muttered. "Something will have to be done."

The full moon rose over Malaita and shone down on Berande. Nothing stirred in the windless air. From the hospital still proceeded the moaning of the sick. In the grass-thatched barracks nearly two hundred woolly-headed man-eaters slept off the weariness of the day's toil, though several lifted their heads to listen to the curses of one who cursed the white man who never slept. On the four verandas of the house the lanterns burned. Inside, between rifle and revolver, the man himself moaned and tossed in intervals of troubled sleep.

CHAPTER II—SOMETHING IS DONE

In the morning David Sheldon decided that he was worse. That he was appreciably weaker there was no doubt, and there were other symptoms that were unfavourable. He began his rounds looking for trouble. He wanted trouble. In full health, the strained situation would have been serious enough; but as it was, himself growing helpless, something had to be done. The blacks were getting more sullen and defiant, and the appearance of the men the previous night on his veranda—one of the gravest of offences on Berande—was ominous. Sooner or later they would get him, if he did not get them first, if he did not once again sear on their dark souls the flaming mastery of the white man.

He returned to the house disappointed. No opportunity had presented itself of making an example of insolence or insubordination—such as had occurred on every other day since the sickness smote Berande. The fact that none had offended was in itself suspicious. They were growing crafty. He regretted that he had not waited the night before until the prowlers had entered. Then he might have shot one or two and given the rest a new lesson, writ in red, for them to con. It was one man against two hundred, and he was horribly afraid of his sickness overpowering him and leaving him at their mercy. He saw visions of the blacks taking charge of the plantation, looting the store, burning the buildings, and escaping to Malaita. Also, one gruesome vision he caught of his own head, sun-dried and smoke-cured, ornamenting the canoe house of a cannibal village. Either the *Jessie* would have to arrive, or he would have to do something.

The bell had hardly rung, sending the labourers into the fields, when Sheldon had a visitor. He had had the couch taken out on the veranda, and he was lying on it when the canoes paddled in and hauled out on the beach. Forty men, armed with spears, bows and arrows, and war-clubs, gathered outside the gate of the compound, but only one entered. They knew the law of Berande, as every native knew the law of every white man's compound in all the thousand miles of the far-flung Solomons. The one man who came up the path, Sheldon recognized as Seelee, the chief of Balesuna village. The savage did not mount the steps, but stood beneath and talked to the white lord above.

Seelee was more intelligent than the average of his kind, but his intelligence only emphasized the lowness of that kind. His eyes, close together and small, advertised cruelty and craftiness. A gee-string and a cartridge-belt were all the clothes he wore. The carved pearl-shell ornament that hung from nose to chin and impeded speech was purely ornamental, as were the holes in his ears mere utilities for carrying pipe and tobacco. His broken-fanged teeth were stained black by betel-nut, the juice of which he spat upon the ground.

As he talked or listened, he made grimaces like a monkey. He said yes by dropping his eyelids and thrusting his chin forward. He spoke with childish arrogance strangely at variance with the subservient position he occupied beneath the veranda. He, with his many followers, was lord and master of Balesuna village. But the white man, without followers, was lord and master of Berande—ay, and on occasion, single-handed, had made himself lord and master of Balesuna village as well. Seelee did not like to remember that episode. It had occurred in the course of learning the nature of white men and of learning to abominate them. He had once been guilty of sheltering three runaways from Berande. They had given him all they possessed in return for the shelter and for promised aid in getting away to Malaita. This had given him a glimpse of a profitable future, in which his village would serve as the one depot on the underground railway between Berande and Malaita.

Unfortunately, he was ignorant of the ways of white men. This particular white man educated him by arriving at his grass house in the gray of dawn. In the first moment he had felt amused. He was so perfectly safe in the midst of his village. But the next moment, and before he could cry out, a pair of handcuffs on the white man's knuckles had landed on his mouth, knocking the cry of alarm back down his throat. Also, the white man's other fist had caught him under the ear and left him without further interest in what was happening. When he came to, he found himself in the white man's whale-

25

boat on the way to Berande. At Berande he had been treated as one of no consequence, with handcuffs on hands and feet, to say nothing of chains. When his tribe had returned the three runaways, he was given his freedom. And finally, the terrible white man had fined him and Balesuna village ten thousand cocoanuts. After that he had sheltered no more runaway Malaita men. Instead, he had gone into the business of catching them. It was safer. Besides, he was paid one case of tobacco per head. But if he ever got a chance at that white man, if he ever caught him sick or stood at his back when he stumbled and fell on a bush-trail—well, there would be a head that would fetch a price in Malaita.

Sheldon was pleased with what Seelee told him. The seventh man of the last batch of runaways had been caught and was even then at the gate. He was brought in, heavy-featured and defiant, his arms bound with cocoanut sennit, the dry blood still on his body from the struggle with his captors.

"Me savvee you good fella, Seelee," Sheldon said, as the chief gulped down a quarter-tumbler of raw trade-gin. "Fella boy belong me you catch short time little bit. This fella boy strong fella too much. I give you fella one case tobacco—my word, one case tobacco. Then, you good fella along me, I give you three fathom calico, one fella knife big fella too much."

The tobacco and trade goods were brought from the storeroom by two house-boys and turned over to the chief of Balesuna village, who accepted the additional reward with a non-committal grunt and went away down the path to his canoes. Under Sheldon's directions the house-boys handcuffed the prisoner, by hands and feet, around one of the pile supports of the house. At eleven o'clock, when the labourers came in from the field, Sheldon had them assembled in the compound before the veranda. Every able man was there, including those who were helping about the hospital. Even the women and the several pickaninnies of the plantation were lined up with the rest, two deep—a horde of naked savages a trifle under two hundred strong. In addition to their ornaments of bead and shell and bone, their pierced ears and nostrils were burdened with safety-pins, wire nails, metal hair-pins, rusty iron handles of cooking utensils, and the patent keys for opening corned beef tins. Some wore penknives clasped on their kinky locks for safety. On the chest of one a china door-knob was suspended, on the chest of another the brass wheel of an alarm clock.

Facing them, clinging to the railing of the veranda for support, stood the sick white man. Any one of them could have knocked him over with the blow of a little finger. Despite his firearms, the gang could have rushed him and delivered that blow, when his head and the plantation would have been theirs. Hatred and murder and lust for revenge they possessed to overflowing. But one thing they lacked, the thing that he possessed, the flame of mastery that would not quench, that burned fiercely as ever in the disease-wasted body, and that was ever ready to flare forth and scorch and singe them with its ire.

"Narada! Billy!" Sheldon called sharply.

Two men slunk unwillingly forward and waited.

Sheldon gave the keys of the handcuffs to a house-boy, who went under the house and loosed the prisoner.

"You fella Narada, you fella Billy, take um this fella boy along tree and make fast, hands high up," was Sheldon's command.

While this was being done, slowly, amidst mutterings and restlessness on the part of the onlookers, one of the house-boys fetched a heavy-handled, heavy-lashed whip. Sheldon began a speech.

"This fella Arunga, me cross along him too much. I no steal this fella Arunga. I no gammon. I say, 'All right, you come along me Berande, work three fella year.' He say, 'All right, me come along you work three fella year.' He come. He catch plenty good fella *kai-kai*, {2} plenty good fella money. What name he run away? Me too much cross along him. I knock what name outa him fella. I pay Seelee, big fella master along Balesuna, one case tobacco catch that fella Arunga. All right. Arunga pay that fella case tobacco. Six pounds that fella Arunga pay. Alle same one year more that fella Arunga work Berande. All right. Now he catch ten fella whip three times. You fella Billy catch whip, give that fella Arunga ten fella three times. All fella boys look see, all fella Marys {3} look see; bime bye, they like run away they think

27

strong fella too much, no run away. Billy, strong fella too much ten fella three times."

The house-boy extended the whip to him, but Billy did not take it. Sheldon waited quietly. The eyes of all the cannibals were fixed upon him in doubt and fear and eagerness. It was the moment of test, whereby the lone white man was to live or be lost.

"Ten fella three times, Billy," Sheldon said encouragingly, though there was a certain metallic rasp in his voice.

Billy scowled, looked up and looked down, but did not move.

"Billy!"

Sheldon's voice exploded like a pistol shot. The savage started physically. Grins overspread the grotesque features of the audience, and there was a sound of tittering.

"S'pose you like too much lash that fella Arunga, you take him fella Tulagi," Billy said. "One fella government agent make plenty lash. That um fella law. Me savvee um fella law."

It was the law, and Sheldon knew it. But he wanted to live this day and the next day and not to die waiting for the law to operate the next week or the week after.

"Too much talk along you!" he cried angrily. "What name eh? What name?"

"Me savvee law," the savage repeated stubbornly.

"Astoa!"

Another man stepped forward in almost a sprightly way and glanced insolently up. Sheldon was selecting the worst characters for the lesson.

"You fella Astoa, you fella Narada, tie up that fella Billy alongside other fella same fella way."

"Strong fella tie," he cautioned them.

"You fella Astoa take that fella whip. Plenty strong big fella too much ten fella three times. Savvee!"

"No," Astoa grunted.

Sheldon picked up the rifle that had leaned against the rail, and cocked it.

"I know you, Astoa," he said calmly. "You work along Queensland six years."

"Me fella missionary," the black interrupted with deliberate insolence.

"Queensland you stop jail one fella year. White fella master damn fool no hang you. You too much bad fella. Queensland you stop jail six months two fella time. Two fella time you steal. All right, you missionary. You savvee one fella prayer?"

"Yes, me savvee prayer," was the reply.

"All right, then you pray now, short time little bit. You say one fella prayer damn quick, then me kill you."

Sheldon held the rifle on him and waited. The black glanced around at his fellows, but none moved to aid him. They were intent upon the coming spectacle, staring fascinated at the white man with death in his hands who stood alone on the great veranda. Sheldon has won, and he knew it. Astoa changed his weight irresolutely from one foot to the other. He looked at the white man, and saw his eyes gleaming level along the sights.

"Astoa," Sheldon said, seizing the psychological moment, "I count three fella time. Then I shoot you fella dead, good-bye, all finish you."

And Sheldon knew that when he had counted three he would drop him in his tracks. The black knew it, too. That was why Sheldon did not have to do it, for when he had counted one, Astoa reached out his hand and took the whip. And right well Astoa laid on the whip, angered at his fellows for not supporting him and venting his anger with every stroke. From the veranda Sheldon egged him on to strike with strength, till the two triced savages screamed and howled while the blood oozed down their backs. The lesson was being well written in red.

When the last of the gang, including the two howling culprits, had passed out through the compound gate, Sheldon sank down half-fainting on his couch.

"You're a sick man," he groaned. "A sick man."

"But you can sleep at ease to-night," he added, half an hour later.

CHAPTER III—THE JESSIE

Two days passed, and Sheldon felt that he could not grow any weaker and live, much less make his four daily rounds of the hospital. The deaths were averaging four a day, and there were more new cases than recoveries. The blacks were in a funk. Each one, when taken sick, seemed to make every effort to die. Once down on their backs they lacked the grit to make a struggle. They believed they were going to die, and they did their best to vindicate that belief. Even those that were well were sure that it was only a mater of days when the sickness would catch them and carry them off. And yet, believing this with absolute conviction, they somehow lacked the nerve to rush the frail wraith of a man with the white skin and escape from the charnel house by the whale-boats. They chose the lingering death they were sure awaited them, rather than the immediate death they were very sure would pounce upon them if they went up against the master. That he never slept, they knew. That he could not be conjured to death, they were equally sure—they had tried it. And even the sickness that was sweeping them off could not kill him.

With the whipping in the compound, discipline had improved. They cringed under the iron hand of the white man. They gave their scowls or malignant looks with averted faces or when his back was turned. They saved their mutterings for the barracks at night, where he could not hear. And there were no more runaways and no more night-prowlers on the veranda.

Dawn of the third day after the whipping brought the *Jessie's* white sails in sight. Eight miles away, it was not till two in the afternoon that the light air-fans enabled her to drop anchor a quarter of a mile off the shore. The sight of her gave Sheldon fresh courage, and the tedious hours of waiting did not irk him. He gave his orders to the boss-boys and made his regular trips to the hospital. Nothing mattered now. His troubles were at an end. He could lie down and take care of himself and proceed to get well. The *Jessie* had arrived. His partner was on board, vigorous and hearty from six weeks' recruiting on Malaita. He could take charge now, and all would be well with Berande.

Sheldon lay in the steamer-chair and watched the *Jessie*'s whale-boat pull in for the beach. He wondered why only three sweeps were pulling, and he wondered still more when, beached, there was so much delay in getting out of the boat. Then he understood. The three blacks who had been pulling started up the beach with a stretcher on their shoulders. A white man, whom he recognized as the *Jessie*'s captain, walked in front and opened the gate, then dropped behind to close it. Sheldon knew that it was Hughie Drummond who lay in the stretcher, and a mist came before his eyes. He felt an overwhelming desire to die. The disappointment was too great. In his own state of terrible weakness he felt that it was impossible to go on with his task of holding Berande plantation tight-gripped in his fist. Then the will of him flamed up again, and he directed the blacks to lay the stretcher beside him on the floor. Hughie Drummond, whom he had last seen in health, was an emaciated skeleton. His closed eyes were deep-sunken. The shrivelled lips had fallen away from the teeth, and the cheek-bones seemed bursting through the skin. Sheldon sent a house-boy for his thermometer and glanced questioningly at the captain.

"Black-water fever," the captain said. "He's been like this for six days, unconscious. And we've got dysentery on board. What's the matter with you?"

"I'm burying four a day," Sheldon answered, as he bent over from the steamer-chair and inserted the thermometer under his partner's tongue.

Captain Oleson swore blasphemously, and sent a house-boy to bring whisky and soda. Sheldon glanced at the thermometer.

"One hundred and seven," he said. "Poor Hughie."

Captain Oleson offered him some whisky.

"Couldn't think of it—perforation, you know," Sheldon said.

He sent for a boss-boy and ordered a grave to be dug, also some of the packing-cases to be knocked together into a coffin. The blacks did not get coffins. They were buried as they died, being carted on a sheet of galvanized iron, in their nakedness, from the hospital to the hole in the ground. Having given the orders, Sheldon lay back in his chair with closed eyes.

"It's ben fair hell, sir," Captain Oleson began, then broke off to help himself to more whisky. "It's ben fair hell, Mr. Sheldon, I tell you. Contrary winds and calms. We've ben driftin' all about the shop for ten days. There's ten thousand sharks following us for the tucker we've ben throwin' over to them. They was snappin' at the oars when we started to come ashore. I wisht to God a nor'wester'd come along an' blow the Solomons clean to hell."

"We got it from the water—water from Owga creek. Filled my casks with it. How was we to know? I've filled there before an' it was all right. We had sixty recruits-full up; and my crew of fifteen. We've ben buryin' them day an' night. The beggars won't live, damn them! They die out of spite. Only three of my crew left on its legs. Five more down. Seven dead. Oh, hell! What's the good of talkin'?"

"How many recruits left?" Sheldon asked.

"Lost half. Thirty left. Twenty down, and ten tottering around."

Sheldon sighed.

"That means another addition to the hospital. We've got to get them ashore somehow.—Viaburi! Hey, you, Viaburi, ring big fella bell strong fella too much."

The hands, called in from the fields at that unwonted hour, were split into detachments. Some were sent into the woods to cut timber for house-beams, others to cutting cane-grass for thatching, and forty of them lifted a whale-boat above their heads and carried it down to the sea. Sheldon had gritted his teeth, pulled his collapsing soul together, and taken Berande plantation into his fist once more.

"Have you seen the barometer?" Captain Oleson asked, pausing at the bottom of the steps on his way to oversee the disembarkation of the sick.

"No," Sheldon answered. "Is it down?"

"It's going down."

"Then you'd better sleep aboard to-night," was Sheldon's judgment. "Never mind the funeral. I'll see to poor Hughie."

"A nigger was kicking the bucket when I dropped anchor."

The captain made the statement as a simple fact, but obviously waited for a suggestion. The other felt a sudden wave of irritation rush through him.

"Dump him over," he cried. "Great God, man! don't you think I've got enough graves ashore?"

"I just wanted to know, that was all," the captain answered, in no wise offended.

Sheldon regretted his childishness.

"Oh, Captain Oleson," he called. "If you can see your way to it, come ashore to-morrow and lend me a hand. If you can't, send the mate."

"Right O. I'll come myself. Mr. Johnson's dead, sir. I forgot to tell you—three days ago."

Sheldon watched the *Jessie's* captain go down the path, with waving arms and loud curses calling upon God to sink the Solomons. Next, Sheldon noted the Jessie rolling lazily on the glassy swell, and beyond, in the north-west, high over Florida Island, an alpine chain of dark-massed clouds. Then he turned to his partner, calling for boys to carry him into the house. But Hughie Drummond had reached the end. His breathing was imperceptible. By mere touch, Sheldon could ascertain that the dying man's temperature was going down. It must have been going down when the thermometer registered one hundred and seven. He had burned out. Sheldon knelt beside him, the house-boys grouped around, their white singlets and loin-cloths peculiarly at variance with their dark skins and savage countenances, their huge ear-plugs and carved and glistening nose-rings. Sheldon tottered to his feet at last, and half-fell into the steamer-chair. Oppressive as the heat had been, it was now even more oppressive. It was difficult to breathe. He panted for air. The faces and naked arms of the house-boys were beaded with sweat.

"Marster," one of them ventured, "big fella wind he come, strong fella too much."

Sheldon nodded his head but did not look. Much as he had loved Hughie Drummond, his death, and the funeral it entailed, seemed an intolerable burden to add to what he was already sinking under. He had a feeling—nay, it was a certitude—that all he had to do was to shut his eyes and let go, and that he would die, sink into immensity of rest. He knew it; it was very simple. All he had to do was close his eyes and let go; for he had reached the stage where he lived by will alone. His weary body seemed torn by the oncoming pangs of dissolution. He was a fool to hang on. He had died a score of deaths already, and what was the use of prolonging it to two-score deaths before he really died. Not only was he not afraid to die, but he desired to die. His weary flesh and weary spirit desired it, and why should the flame of him not go utterly out?

But his mind that could will life or death, still pulsed on. He saw the two whale-boats land on the beach, and the sick, on stretchers or pick-a-back, groaning and wailing, go by in lugubrious procession. He saw the wind making on the clouded horizon, and thought of the sick in the hospital. Here was something waiting his hand to be done, and it was not in his nature to lie down and sleep, or die, when any task remained undone.

The boss-boys were called and given their orders to rope down the hospital with its two additions. He remembered the spare anchor-chain, new and black-painted, that hung under the house suspended from the floor-beams, and ordered it to be used on the hospital as well. Other boys brought the coffin, a grotesque patchwork of packing-cases, and under his directions they laid Hughie Drummond in it. Half a dozen boys carried it down the beach, while he rode on the back of another, his arms around the black's neck, one hand clutching a prayer-book.

While he read the service, the blacks gazed apprehensively at the dark line on the water, above which rolled and tumbled the racing clouds. The first breath of the wind, faint and silken, tonic with life, fanned through his dry-baked body as he finished reading. Then came the second breath of the wind,

35

an angry gust, as the shovels worked rapidly, filling in the sand. So heavy was the gust that Sheldon, still on his feet, seized hold of his man-horse to escape being blown away. The *Jessie* was blotted out, and a strange ominous sound arose as multitudinous wavelets struck foaming on the beach. It was like the bubbling of some colossal cauldron. From all about could be heard the dull thudding of falling cocoanuts. The tall, delicate-trunked trees twisted and snapped about like whip-lashes. The air seemed filled with their flying leaves, any one of which, stem-on could brain a man. Then came the rain, a deluge, a straight, horizontal sheet that poured along like a river, defying gravitation. The black, with Sheldon mounted on him, plunged ahead into the thick of it, stooping far forward and low to the ground to avoid being toppled over backward.

"'He's sleeping out and far to-night,'" Sheldon quoted, as he thought of the dead man in the sand and the rainwater trickling down upon the cold clay.

So they fought their way back up the beach. The other blacks caught hold of the man-horse and pulled and tugged. There were among them those whose fondest desire was to drag the rider in the sand and spring upon him and mash him into repulsive nothingness. But the automatic pistol in his belt with its rattling, quick-dealing death, and the automatic, death-defying spirit in the man himself, made them refrain and buckle down to the task of hauling him to safety through the storm.

Wet through and exhausted, he was nevertheless surprised at the ease with which he got into a change of clothing. Though he was fearfully weak, he found himself actually feeling better. The disease had spent itself, and the mend had begun.

"Now if I don't get the fever," he said aloud, and at the same moment resolved to go to taking quinine as soon as he was strong enough to dare.

He crawled out on the veranda. The rain had ceased, but the wind, which had dwindled to a half-gale, was increasing. A big sea had sprung up, and the mile-long breakers, curling up to the over-fall two hundred yards from shore, were crashing on the beach. The *Jessie* was plunging madly to two anchors, and every second or third sea broke clear over her bow. Two flags were stiffly undulating from the halyards like squares of flexible sheet-iron. One was blue, the other red. He knew their meaning in the Berande private code—"What are your instructions? Shall I attempt to land boat?" Tacked on the wall, between the signal locker and the billiard rules, was the code itself, by which he verified the signal before making answer. On the flagstaff gaff a boy hoisted a white flag over a red, which stood for—"Run to Neal Island for shelter."

That Captain Oleson had been expecting this signal was apparent by the celerity with which the shackles were knocked out of both anchor-chains. He slipped his anchors, leaving them buoyed to be picked up in better weather. The *Jessie* swung off under her full staysail, then the foresail, double-reefed, was run up. She was away like a racehorse, clearing Balesuna Shoal with half a cable-length to spare. Just before she rounded the point she was swallowed up in a terrific squall that far out-blew the first.

All that night, while squall after squall smote Berande, uprooting trees, overthrowing copra-sheds, and rocking the house on its tall piles, Sheldon slept. He was unaware of the commotion. He never wakened. Nor did he change his position or dream. He awoke, a new man. Furthermore, he was hungry. It was over a week since food had passed his lips. He drank a glass of condensed cream, thinned with water, and by ten o'clock he dared to take a cup of beef-tea. He was cheered, also, by the situation in the hospital. Despite the storm there had been but one death, and there was only one fresh case, while half a dozen boys crawled weakly away to the barracks. He wondered if it was the wind that was blowing the disease away and cleansing the pestilential land.

By eleven a messenger arrived from Balesuna village, dispatched by Seelee. The *Jessie* had gone ashore half-way between the village and Neal Island. It was not till nightfall that two of the crew arrived, reporting the drowning of Captain Oleson and of the one remaining boy. As for the *Jessie*, from what they told him Sheldon could not but conclude that she was a total loss. Further to hearten him, he was taken by a shivering fit. In half an hour he was burning up. And he knew that at least another day must pass before he could undertake even the smallest dose of quinine. He crawled under a heap of blankets, and a little later found himself laughing aloud. He had surely reached the limit of disaster. Barring earthquake or tidal-wave, the worst had already befallen him. The *Flibberty-Gibbet* was certainly safe in Mboli Pass. Since nothing worse could happen, things simply had to mend. So it was, shivering under his blankets, that he laughed, until the house-boys, with heads together, marvelled at the devils that were in him.

CHAPTER IV—JOAN LACKLAND

By the second day of the northwester, Sheldon was in collapse from his fever. It had taken an unfair advantage of his weak state, and though it was only ordinary malarial fever, in forty-eight hours it had run him as low as ten days of fever would have done when he was in condition. But the dysentery had been swept away from Berande. A score of convalescents lingered in the hospital, but they were improving hourly. There had been but one more death—that of the man whose brother had wailed over him instead of brushing the flies away.

On the morning of the fourth day of his fever, Sheldon lay on the veranda, gazing dimly out over the raging ocean. The wind was falling, but a mighty sea was still thundering in on Berande beach, the flying spray reaching in as far as the flagstaff mounds, the foaming wash creaming against the gate-posts. He had taken thirty grains of quinine, and the drug was buzzing in his ears like a nest of hornets, making his hands and knees tremble, and causing a sickening palpitation of the stomach. Once, opening his eyes, he saw what he took to be an hallucination. Not far out, and coming in across the *Jessie's* anchorage, he saw a whale-boat's nose thrust skyward on a smoky crest and disappear naturally, as an actual whale-boat's nose should disappear, as it slid down the back of the sea. He knew that no whale-boat should be out there, and he was quite certain no men in the Solomons were mad enough to be abroad in such a storm.

But the hallucination persisted. A minute later, chancing to open his eyes, he saw the whale-boat, full length, and saw right into it as it rose on the face of a wave. He saw six sweeps at work, and in the stern, clearly outlined against the overhanging wall of white, a man who stood erect, gigantic, swaying with his weight on the steering-sweep. This he saw, and an eighth man who crouched in the bow and gazed shoreward. But what startled Sheldon was the sight of a woman in the stern-sheets, between the stroke-oar and the steersman. A woman she was, for a braid of her hair was flying, and she was just in the act of recapturing it and stowing it away beneath a hat that for all the world was like his own "Baden-Powell."

The boat disappeared behind the wave, and rose into view on the face of the following one. Again he looked into it. The men were dark-skinned, and larger than Solomon Islanders, but the woman, he could plainly see, was white. Who she was, and what she was doing there, were thoughts that drifted vaguely through his consciousness. He was too sick to be vitally interested, and, besides, he had a half feeling that it was all a dream; but he noted that the men were resting on their sweeps, while the woman and the steersman were intently watching the run of seas behind them.

"Good boatmen," was Sheldon's verdict, as he saw the boat leap forward on the face of a huge breaker, the sweeps plying swiftly to keep her on that front of the moving mountain of water that raced madly for the shore. It was well done. Part full of water, the boat was flung upon the beach, the men springing out and dragging its nose to the gate-posts. Sheldon had called vainly to the house-boys, who, at the moment, were dosing the remaining patients in the hospital. He knew he was unable to rise up and go down the path to meet the newcomers, so he lay back in the steamer-chair, and watched for ages while they cared for the boat. The woman stood to one side, her hand resting on the gate. Occasionally surges of sea water washed over her feet, which he could see were encased in rubber sea-boots. She scrutinized the house sharply, and for some time she gazed at him steadily. At last, speaking to two of the men, who turned and followed her, she started up the path.

Sheldon attempted to rise, got half up out of his chair, and fell back helplessly. He was surprised at the size of the men, who loomed like giants behind her. Both were six-footers, and they were heavy in proportion. He had never seen islanders like them. They were not black like the Solomon Islanders, but light brown; and their features were larger, more regular, and even handsome.

The woman—or girl, rather, he decided—walked along the veranda toward him. The two men waited at the head of the steps, watching curiously. The girl was angry; he could see that. Her gray eyes were flashing, and her lips were quivering. That she had a temper, was his thought. But the eyes were striking. He decided that they were not gray after all, or, at least, not all gray. They were large and wide apart, and they looked at him from under level brows. Her face was cameo-like, so clear cut was it. There were other striking things about her—the cowboy Stetson hat, the heavy braids of brown hair, and the long-barrelled 38 Colt's revolver that hung in its holster on her hip.

"Pretty hospitality, I must say," was her greeting, "letting strangers sink or swim in your front yard."

"I—I beg your pardon," he stammered, by a supreme effort dragging himself to his feet.

His legs wobbled under him, and with a suffocating sensation he began sinking to the floor. He was aware of a feeble gratification as he saw solicitude leap into her eyes; then blackness smote him, and at the moment of smiting him his thought was that at last, and for the first time in his life, he had fainted.

The ringing of the big bell aroused him. He opened his eyes and found that he was on the couch indoors. A glance at the clock told him that it was six, and from the direction the sun's rays streamed into the room he knew that it was morning. At first he puzzled over something untoward he was sure had happened. Then on the wall he saw a Stetson hat hanging, and beneath it a full cartridge-belt and a long-barrelled 38 Colt's revolver. The slender girth of the belt told its feminine story, and he remembered the whale-boat of the day before and the gray eyes that flashed beneath the level brows. She it must have been who had just rung the bell. The cares of the plantation rushed upon him, and he sat up in bed, clutching at the wall for support as the mosquito screen lurched dizzily around him. He was still sitting there, holding on, with eyes closed, striving to master his giddiness, when he heard her voice.

"You'll lie right down again, sir," she said.

It was sharply imperative, a voice used to command. At the same time one hand pressed him back toward the pillow while the other caught him from behind and eased him down.

"You've been unconscious for twenty-four hours now," she went on, "and I have taken charge. When I say the word you'll get up, and not until then. Now, what medicine do you take?—quinine? Here are ten grains. That's right. You'll make a good patient."

"My dear madame," he began.

"You musn't speak," she interrupted, "that is, in protest. Otherwise, you can talk."

"But the plantation—"

"A dead man is of no use on a plantation. Don't you want to know about *me*? My vanity is hurt. Here am I, just through my first shipwreck; and here are you, not the least bit curious, talking about your miserable plantation. Can't you see that I am just bursting to tell somebody, anybody, about my shipwreck?"

He smiled; it was the first time in weeks. And he smiled, not so much at what she said, as at the way she said it—the whimsical expression of her face, the laughter in her eyes, and the several tiny lines of humour that drew in at the corners. He was curiously wondering as to what her age was, as he said aloud:

"Yes, tell me, please."

"That I will not—not now," she retorted, with a toss of the head. "I'll find somebody to tell my story to who does not have to be asked. Also, I want information. I managed to find out what time to ring the bell to turn the hands to, and that is about all. I don't understand the ridiculous speech of your people. What time do they knock off?"

"At eleven—go on again at one."

"That will do, thank you. And now, where do you keep the key to the provisions? I want to feed my men."

"Your men!" he gasped. "On tinned goods! No, no. Let them go out and eat with my boys."

42

Her eyes flashed as on the day before, and he saw again the imperative expression on her face.

"That I won't; my men are *men*. I've been out to your miserable barracks and watched them eat. Faugh! Potatoes! Nothing but potatoes! No salt! Nothing! Only potatoes! I may have been mistaken, but I thought I understood them to say that that was all they ever got to eat. Two meals a day and every day in the week?"

He nodded.

"Well, my men wouldn't stand that for a single day, much less a whole week. Where is the key?"

"Hanging on that clothes-hook under the clock."

He gave it easily enough, but as she was reaching down the key she heard him say:

"Fancy niggers and tinned provisions."

This time she really was angry. The blood was in her cheeks as she turned on him.

"My men are not niggers. The sooner you understand that the better for our acquaintance. As for the tinned goods, I'll pay for all they eat. Please don't worry about that. Worry is not good for you in your condition. And I won't stay any longer than I have to—just long enough to get you on your feet, and not go away with the feeling of having deserted a white man."

"You're American, aren't you?" he asked quietly.

The question disconcerted her for the moment.

"Yes," she vouchsafed, with a defiant look. "Why?"

"Nothing. I merely thought so."

"Anything further?"

He shook his head.

43

"Why?" he asked.

"Oh, nothing. I thought you might have something pleasant to say."

"My name is Sheldon, David Sheldon," he said, with direct relevance, holding out a thin hand.

Her hand started out impulsively, then checked. "My name is Lackland, Joan Lackland." The hand went out. "And let us be friends."

"It could not be otherwise—" he began lamely.

"And I can feed my men all the tinned goods I want?" she rushed on.

"Till the cows come home," he answered, attempting her own lightness, then adding, "that is, to Berande. You see we don't have any cows at Berande."

She fixed him coldly with her eyes.

"Is that a joke?" she demanded.

"I really don't know—I—I thought it was, but then, you see, I'm sick."

"You're English, aren't you?" was her next query.

"Now that's too much, even for a sick man," he cried. "You know well enough that I am."

"Oh," she said absently, "then you are?"

He frowned, tightened his lips, then burst into laughter, in which she joined.

"It's my own fault," he confessed. "I shouldn't have baited you. I'll be careful in the future."

"In the meantime go on laughing, and I'll see about breakfast. Is there anything you would fancy?"

He shook his head.

"It will do you good to eat something. Your fever has burned out, and you are merely weak. Wait a moment."

44

She hurried out of the room in the direction of the kitchen, tripped at the door in a pair of sandals several sizes too large for her feet, and disappeared in rosy confusion.

"By Jove, those are my sandals," he thought to himself. "The girl hasn't a thing to wear except what she landed on the beach in, and she certainly landed in sea-boots."

CHAPTER V—SHE WOULD A PLANTER BE

Sheldon mended rapidly. The fever had burned out, and there was nothing for him to do but gather strength. Joan had taken the cook in hand, and for the first time, as Sheldon remarked, the chop at Berande was white man's chop. With her own hands Joan prepared the sick man's food, and between that and the cheer she brought him, he was able, after two days, to totter feebly out upon the veranda. The situation struck him as strange, and stranger still was the fact that it did not seem strange to the girl at all. She had settled down and taken charge of the household as a matter of course, as if he were her father, or brother, or as if she were a man like himself.

"It is just too delightful for anything," she assured him. "It is like a page out of some romance. Here I come along out of the sea and find a sick man all alone with two hundred slaves—"

"Recruits," he corrected. "Contract labourers. They serve only three years, and they are free agents when they enter upon their contracts."

"Yes, yes," she hurried on. "—A sick man alone with two hundred recruits on a cannibal island—they are cannibals, aren't they? Or is it all talk?"

"Talk!" he said, with a smile. "It's a trifle more than that. Most of my boys are from the bush, and every bushman is a cannibal."

"But not after they become recruits? Surely, the boys you have here wouldn't be guilty."

"They'd eat you if the chance afforded."

"Are you just saying so, on theory, or do you really know?" she asked.

"I know."

"Why? What makes you think so? Your own men here?"

"Yes, my own men here, the very house-boys, the cook that at the present moment is making such delicious rolls, thanks to you. Not more than three months ago eleven of them sneaked a whale-boat and ran for Malaita. Nine of them belonged to Malaita. Two were bushmen from San Cristoval. They were fools—the two from San Cristoval, I mean; so would any two Malaita men be who trusted themselves in a boat with nine from San Cristoval."

"Yes?" she asked eagerly. "Then what happened?"

"The nine Malaita men ate the two from San Cristoval, all except the heads, which are too valuable for mere eating. They stowed them away in the stern-locker till they landed. And those two heads are now in some bush village back of Langa Langa."

She clapped her hands and her eyes sparkled. "They are really and truly cannibals! And just think, this is the twentieth century! And I thought romance and adventure were fossilized!"

He looked at her with mild amusement.

"What is the matter now?" she queried.

"Oh, nothing, only I don't fancy being eaten by a lot of filthy niggers is the least bit romantic."

"No, of course not," she admitted. "But to be among them, controlling them, directing them, two hundred of them, and to escape being eaten by them—that, at least, if it isn't romantic, is certainly the quintessence of adventure. And adventure and romance are allied, you know."

"By the same token, to go into a nigger's stomach should be the quintessence of adventure," he retorted.

"I don't think you have any romance in you," she exclaimed. "You're just dull and sombre and sordid like the business men at home. I don't know why you're here at all. You should be at home placidly vegetating as a banker's clerk or—or—"

"A shopkeeper's assistant, thank you."

"Yes, that—anything. What under the sun are you doing here on the edge of things?"

"Earning my bread and butter, trying to get on in the world."

"'By the bitter road the younger son must tread, Ere he win to hearth and saddle of his own,'" she quoted. "Why, if that isn't romantic, then nothing is romantic. Think of all the younger sons out over the world, on a myriad of adventures winning to those same hearths and saddles. And here you are in the thick of it, doing it, and here am I in the thick of it, doing it."

"I—I beg pardon," he drawled.

"Well, I'm a younger daughter, then," she amended; "and I have no hearth nor saddle—I haven't anybody or anything—and I'm just as far on the edge of things as you are."

"In your case, then, I'll admit there is a bit of romance," he confessed.

He could not help but think of the preceding nights, and of her sleeping in the hammock on the veranda, under mosquito curtains, her bodyguard of Tahitian sailors stretched out at the far corner of the veranda within call. He had been too helpless to resist, but now he resolved she should have his couch inside while he would take the hammock.

"You see, I had read and dreamed about romance all my life," she was saying, "but I never, in my wildest fancies, thought that I should live it. It was all so unexpected. Two years ago I thought there was nothing left to me but. . . ." She faltered, and made a *moue* of distaste. "Well, the only thing that remained, it seemed to me, was marriage."

"And you preferred a cannibal isle and a cartridge-belt?" he suggested.

"I didn't think of the cannibal isle, but the cartridge-belt was blissful."

"You wouldn't dare use the revolver if you were compelled to. Or," noting the glint in her eyes, "if you did use it, to—well, to hit anything."

She started up suddenly to enter the house. He knew she was going for her revolver.

"Never mind," he said, "here's mine. What can you do with it?"

"Shoot the block off your flag-halyards."

He smiled his unbelief.

"I don't know the gun," she said dubiously.

"It's a light trigger and you don't have to hold down. Draw fine."

"Yes, yes," she spoke impatiently. "I know automatics—they jam when they get hot—only I don't know yours." She looked at it a moment. "It's cocked. Is there a cartridge in the chamber?"

She fired, and the block remained intact.

"It's a long shot," he said, with the intention of easing her chagrin.

But she bit her lip and fired again. The bullet emitted a sharp shriek as it ricochetted into space. The metal block rattled back and forth. Again and again she fired, till the clip was emptied of its eight cartridges. Six of them were hits. The block still swayed at the gaff-end, but it was battered out of all usefulness. Sheldon was astonished. It was better than he or even Hughie Drummond could have done. The women he had known, when they sporadically fired a rifle or revolver, usually shrieked, shut their eyes, and blazed away into space.

"That's really good shooting . . . for a woman," he said. "You only missed it twice, and it was a strange weapon."

"But I can't make out the two misses," she complained. "The gun worked beautifully, too. Give me another clip and I'll hit it eight times for anything you wish."

"I don't doubt it. Now I'll have to get a new block. Viaburi! Here you fella, catch one fella block along storeroom."

"I'll wager you can't do it eight out of eight . . . anything you wish," she challenged.

"No fear of my taking it on," was his answer. "Who taught you to shoot?"

"Oh, my father, at first, and then Von, and his cowboys. He was a shot—Dad, I mean, though Von was splendid, too."

Sheldon wondered secretly who Von was, and he speculated as to whether it was Von who two years previously had led her to believe that nothing remained for her but matrimony.

"What part of the United States is your home?" he asked. "Chicago or Wyoming? or somewhere out there? You know you haven't told me a thing about yourself. All that I know is that you are Miss Joan Lackland from anywhere."

"You'd have to go farther west to find my stamping grounds."

"Ah, let me see—Nevada?"

She shook her head.

"California?"

"Still farther west."

"It can't be, or else I've forgotten my geography."

"It's your politics," she laughed. "Don't you remember 'Annexation'?"

"The Philippines!" he cried triumphantly.

"No, Hawaii. I was born there. It is a beautiful land. My, I'm almost homesick for it already. Not that I haven't been away. I was in New York when the crash came. But I do think it is the sweetest spot on earth—Hawaii, I mean."

"Then what under the sun are you doing down here in this God-forsaken place?" he asked. "Only fools come here," he added bitterly.

"Nielsen wasn't a fool, was he?" she queried. "As I understand, he made three millions here."

"Only too true, and that fact is responsible for my being here."

"And for me, too," she said. "Dad heard about him in the Marquesas, and so we started. Only poor Dad didn't get here."

50

"He—your father—died?" he faltered.

She nodded, and her eyes grew soft and moist.

"I might as well begin at the beginning." She lifted her head with a proud air of dismissing sadness, after, the manner of a woman qualified to wear a Baden-Powell and a long-barrelled Colt's. "I was born at Hilo. That's on the island of Hawaii—the biggest and best in the whole group. I was brought up the way most girls in Hawaii are brought up. They live in the open, and they know how to ride and swim before they know what six-times-six is. As for me, I can't remember when I first got on a horse nor when I learned to swim. That came before my A B C's. Dad owned cattle ranches on Hawaii and Maui—big ones, for the islands. Hokuna had two hundred thousand acres alone. It extended in between Mauna Koa and Mauna Loa, and it was there I learned to shoot goats and wild cattle. On Molokai they have big spotted deer. Von was the manager of Hokuna. He had two daughters about my own age, and I always spent the hot season there, and, once, a whole year. The three of us were like Indians. Not that we ran wild, exactly, but that we were wild to run wild. There were always the governesses, you know, and lessons, and sewing, and housekeeping; but I'm afraid we were too often bribed to our tasks with promises of horses or of cattle drives.

"Von had been in the army, and Dad was an old sea-dog, and they were both stern disciplinarians; only the two girls had no mother, and neither had I, and they were two men after all. They spoiled us terribly. You see, they didn't have any wives, and they made chums out of us—when our tasks were done. We had to learn to do everything about the house twice as well as the native servants did it—that was so that we should know how to manage some day. And we always made the cocktails, which was too holy a rite for any servant. Then, too, we were never allowed anything we could not take care of ourselves. Of course the cowboys always roped and saddled our horses, but we had to be able ourselves to go out in the paddock and rope our horses—"

"What do you mean by *rope*?" Sheldon asked.

"To lariat them, to lasso them. And Dad and Von timed us in the saddling and made a most rigid examination of the result. It was the same way with our revolvers and rifles. The house-boys always cleaned them and greased them; but we had to learn how in order to see that they did it properly. More than once, at first, one or the other of us had our rifles taken away for a week just because of a tiny speck of rust. We had to know how to build fires in the driving rain, too, out of wet wood, when we camped out, which was the hardest thing of all—except grammar, I do believe. We learned more from Dad and Von than from the governesses; Dad taught us French and Von German. We learned both languages passably well, and we learned them wholly in the saddle or in camp.

"In the cool season the girls used to come down and visit me in Hilo, where Dad had two houses, one at the beach, or the three of us used to go down to our place in Puna, and that meant canoes and boats and fishing and swimming. Then, too, Dad belonged to the Royal Hawaiian Yacht Club, and took us racing and cruising. Dad could never get away from the sea, you know. When I was fourteen I was Dad's actual housekeeper, with entire power over the servants, and I am very proud of that period of my life. And when I was sixteen we three girls were all sent up to California to Mills Seminary, which was quite fashionable and stifling. How we used to long for home! We didn't chum with the other girls, who called us little cannibals, just because we came from the Sandwich Islands, and who made invidious remarks about our ancestors banqueting on Captain Cook—which was historically untrue, and, besides, our ancestors hadn't lived in Hawaii.

"I was three years at Mills Seminary, with trips home, of course, and two years in New York; and then Dad went smash in a sugar plantation on Maui. The report of the engineers had not been right. Then Dad had built a railroad that was called 'Lackland's Folly,'—it will pay ultimately, though. But it contributed to the smash. The Pelaulau Ditch was the finishing blow. And nothing would have happened anyway, if it hadn't been for that big money panic in Wall Street. Dear good Dad! He never let me know. But I read about the crash in a newspaper, and hurried home. It was before that, though, that people had been dinging into my ears that marriage was all any woman could get out of life, and good-bye to romance. Instead of which, with Dad's failure, I fell right into romance."

"How long ago was that?" Sheldon asked.

"Last year—the year of the panic."

"Let me see," Sheldon pondered with an air of gravity. "Sixteen plus five, plus one, equals twenty-two. You were born in 1887?"

"Yes; but it is not nice of you."

"I am really sorry," he said, "but the problem was so obvious."

"Can't you ever say nice things? Or is it the way you English have?" There was a snap in her gray eyes, and her lips quivered suspiciously for a moment. "I should recommend, Mr. Sheldon, that you read Gertrude Atherton's 'American Wives and English Husbands.'"

"Thank you, I have. It's over there." He pointed at the generously filled bookshelves. "But I am afraid it is rather partisan."

"Anything un-English is bound to be," she retorted. "I never have liked the English anyway. The last one I knew was an overseer. Dad was compelled to discharge him."

"One swallow doesn't make a summer."

"But that Englishman made lots of trouble—there! And now please don't make me any more absurd than I already am."

"I'm trying not to."

"Oh, for that matter—" She tossed her head, opened her mouth to complete the retort, then changed her mind. "I shall go on with my history. Dad had practically nothing left, and he decided to return to the sea. He'd always loved it, and I half believe that he was glad things had happened as they did. He was like a boy again, busy with plans and preparations from morning till night. He used to sit up half the night talking things over with me. That was after I had shown him that I was really resolved to go along.

"He had made his start, you know, in the South Seas—pearls and pearl shell—and he was sure that more fortunes, in trove of one sort and another, were to be picked up. Cocoanut-planting was his particular idea, with trading, and maybe pearling, along with other things, until the plantation should come into bearing. He traded off his yacht for a schooner, the *Miélé*, and away we went. I took care of him and studied navigation. He was his own skipper. We had a Danish mate, Mr. Ericson, and a mixed crew of Japanese and Hawaiians. We went up and down the Line Islands, first, until Dad was heartsick. Everything was changed. They had been annexed and divided by one power or another, while big companies had stepped in and gobbled land, trading rights, fishing rights, everything.

"Next we sailed for the Marquesas. They were beautiful, but the natives were nearly extinct. Dad was cut up when he learned that the French charged an export duty on copra—he called it medieval—but he liked the land. There was a valley of fifteen thousand acres on Nuka-hiva, half inclosing a perfect anchorage, which he fell in love with and bought for twelve hundred Chili dollars. But the French taxation was outrageous (that was why the land was so cheap), and, worst of all, we could obtain no labour. What kanakas there were wouldn't work, and the officials seemed to sit up nights thinking out new obstacles to put in our way.

"Six months was enough for Dad. The situation was hopeless. 'We'll go to the Solomons,' he said, 'and get a whiff of English rule. And if there are no openings there we'll go on to the Bismarck Archipelago. I'll wager the Admiraltys are not yet civilized.' All preparations were made, things packed on board, and a new crew of Marquesans and Tahitians shipped. We were just ready to start to Tahiti, where a lot of repairs and refitting for the *Miélé* were necessary, when poor Dad came down sick and died."

"And you were left all alone?"

Joan nodded.

"Very much alone. I had no brothers nor sisters, and all Dad's people were drowned in a Kansas cloud-burst. That happened when he was a little boy. Of course, I could go back to Von. There's always a home there waiting for me. But why should I go? Besides, there were Dad's plans, and I felt that it devolved upon me to carry them out. It seemed a fine thing to do. Also, I wanted to carry them out. And . . . here I am.

"Take my advice and never go to Tahiti. It is a lovely place, and so are the natives. But the white people! Now Barabbas lived in Tahiti. Thieves, robbers, and lairs—that is what they are. The honest men wouldn't require the fingers of one hand to count. The fact that I was a woman only simplified matters with them. They robbed me on every pretext, and they lied without pretext or need. Poor Mr. Ericson was corrupted. He joined the robbers, and O.K.'d all their demands even up to a thousand per cent. If they robbed me of ten francs, his share was three. One bill of fifteen hundred francs I paid, netted him five hundred francs. All this, of course, I learned afterward. But the *Miélé* was old, the repairs had to be made, and I was charged, not three prices, but seven prices.

"I never shall know how much Ericson got out of it. He lived ashore in a nicely furnished house. The shipwrights were giving it to him rent-free. Fruit, vegetables, fish, meat, and ice came to this house every day, and he paid for none of it. It was part of his graft from the various merchants. And all the while, with tears in his eyes, he bemoaned the vile treatment I was receiving from the gang. No, I did not fall among thieves. I went to Tahiti.

"But when the robbers fell to cheating one another, I got my first clues to the state of affairs. One of the robbed robbers came to me after dark, with facts, figures, and assertions. I knew I was ruined if I went to law. The judges were corrupt like everything else. But I did do one thing. In the dead of night I went to Ericson's house. I had the same revolver I've got now, and I made him stay in bed while I overhauled things. Nineteen hundred and odd francs was what I carried away with me. He never complained to the police, and he never came back on board. As for the rest of the gang, they laughed and snapped their fingers at me. There were two Americans in the place, and they warned me to leave the law alone unless I wanted to leave the *Miélé* behind as well.

"Then I sent to New Zealand and got a German mate. He had a master's certificate, and was on the ship's papers as captain, but I was a better navigator than he, and I was really captain myself. I lost her, too, but it's no reflection on my seamanship. We were drifting four days outside there in dead calms. Then the nor'wester caught us and drove us on the lee shore. We made sail and tried to clew off, when the rotten work of the Tahiti shipwrights became manifest. Our jib-boom and all our head-stays carried away. Our only chance was to turn and run through the passage between Florida and Ysabel. And when we were safely through, in the twilight, where the chart shows fourteen fathoms as the shoalest water, we smashed on a coral patch. The poor old *Miélé* struck only once, and then went clear; but it was too much for her, and we just had time to clear away in the boat when she went down. The German mate was drowned. We lay all night to a sea-drag, and next morning sighted your place here."

"I suppose you will go back to Von, now?" Sheldon queried.

"Nothing of the sort. Dad planned to go to the Solomons. I shall look about for some land and start a small plantation. Do you know any good land around here? Cheap?"

"By George, you Yankees are remarkable, really remarkable," said Sheldon. "I should never have dreamed of such a venture."

"Adventure," Joan corrected him.

"That's right—adventure it is. And if you'd gone ashore on Malaita instead of Guadalcanal you'd have been *kai-kai'd* long ago, along with your noble Tahitian sailors."

Joan shuddered.

"To tell the truth," she confessed, "we were very much afraid to land on Guadalcanal. I read in the 'Sailing Directions' that the natives were treacherous and hostile. Some day I should like to go to Malaita. Are there any plantations there?"

"Not one. Not a white trader even."

"Then I shall go over on a recruiting vessel some time."

"Impossible!" Sheldon cried. "It is no place for a woman."

"I shall go just the same," she repeated.

"But no self-respecting woman—"

"Be careful," she warned him. "I shall go some day, and then you may be sorry for the names you have called me."

CHAPTER VI—TEMPEST

It was the first time Sheldon had been at close quarters with an American girl, and he would have wondered if all American girls were like Joan Lackland had he not had wit enough to realize that she was not at all typical. Her quick mind and changing moods bewildered him, while her outlook on life was so different from what he conceived a woman's outlook should be, that he was more often than not at sixes and sevens with her. He could never anticipate what she would say or do next. Of only one thing was he sure, and that was that whatever she said or did was bound to be unexpected and unsuspected. There seemed, too, something almost hysterical in her make-up. Her temper was quick and stormy, and she relied too much on herself and too little on him, which did not approximate at all to his ideal of woman's conduct when a man was around. Her assumption of equality with him was disconcerting, and at times he half-consciously resented the impudence and bizarreness of her intrusion upon him—rising out of the sea in a howling nor'wester, fresh from poking her revolver under Ericson's nose, protected by her gang of huge Polynesian sailors, and settling down in Berande like any shipwrecked sailor. It was all on a par with her Baden-Powell and the long 38 Colt's.

At any rate, she did not look the part. And that was what he could not forgive. Had she been short-haired, heavy-jawed, large-muscled, hard-bitten, and utterly unlovely in every way, all would have been well. Instead of which she was hopelessly and deliciously feminine. Her hair worried him, it was so generously beautiful. And she was so slenderly and prettily the woman—the girl, rather—that it cut him like a knife to see her, with quick, comprehensive eyes and sharply imperative voice, superintend the launching of the whale-boat through the surf. In imagination he could see her roping a horse, and it always made him shudder. Then, too, she was so many-sided. Her knowledge of literature and art surprised him, while deep down was the feeling that a girl who knew such things had no right to know how to rig tackles, heave up anchors, and sail schooners around the South Seas. Such things in her brain were like so many oaths on her lips. While for such a girl to insist that she was going on a recruiting cruise around Malaita was positive self-sacrilege.

He always perturbedly harked back to her feminineness. She could play the piano far better than his sisters at home, and with far finer appreciation—the piano that poor Hughie had so heroically laboured over to keep in condition. And when she strummed the guitar and sang liquid, velvety Hawaiian *hulas*, he sat entranced. Then she was all woman, and the magic of sex kidnapped the irritations of the day and made him forget the big revolver, the Baden-Powell, and all the rest. But what right, the next thought in his brain would whisper, had such a girl to swagger around like a man and exult that adventure was not dead? Woman that adventured were adventuresses, and the connotation was not nice. Besides, he was not enamoured of adventure. Not since he was a boy had it appealed to him—though it would have driven him hard to explain what had brought him from England to the Solomons if it had not been adventure.

Sheldon certainly was not happy. The unconventional state of affairs was too much for his conservative disposition and training. Berande, inhabited by one lone white man, was no place for Joan Lackland. Yet he racked his brain for a way out, and even talked it over with her. In the first place, the steamer from Australia was not due for three weeks.

"One thing is evident: you don't want me here," she said. "I'll man the whale-boat to-morrow and go over to Tulagi."

"But as I told you before, that is impossible," he cried. "There is no one there. The Resident Commissioner is away in Australia. There is only one white man, a third assistant understrapper and ex-sailor—a common sailor. He is in charge of the government of the Solomons, to say nothing of a hundred or so niggers—prisoners. Besides, he is such a fool that he would fine you five pounds for not having entered at Tulagi, which is the port of entry, you know. He is not a nice man, and, I repeat, it is impossible."

"There is Guvutu," she suggested.

He shook his head.

"There's nothing there but fever and five white men who are drinking themselves to death. I couldn't permit it."

"Oh thank you," she said quietly. "I guess I'll start to-day.—Viaburi! You go along Noa Noah, speak 'm come along me."

Noa Noah was her head sailor, who had been boatswain of the *Miélé*.

"Where are you going?" Sheldon asked in surprise.—"Vlaburi! You stop."

"To Guvutu—immediately," was her reply.

"But I won't permit it."

"That is why I am going. You said it once before, and it is something I cannot brook."

"What?" He was bewildered by her sudden anger. "If I have offended in any way—"

"Viaburi, you fetch 'm one fella Noa Noah along me," she commanded.

The black boy started to obey.

"Viaburi! You no stop I break 'm head belong you. And now, Miss Lackland, I insist—you must explain. What have I said or done to merit this?"

"You have presumed, you have dared—"

She choked and swallowed, and could not go on.

Sheldon looked the picture of despair.

"I confess my head is going around with it all," he said. "If you could only be explicit."

"As explicit as you were when you told me that you would not permit me to go to Guvutu?"

"But what's wrong with that?"

"But you have no right—no man has the right—to tell me what he will permit or not permit. I'm too old to have a guardian, nor did I sail all the way to the Solomons to find one."

"A gentleman is every woman's guardian."

"Well, I'm not every woman—that's all. Will you kindly allow me to send your boy for Noa Noah? I wish him to launch the whale-boat. Or shall I go myself for him?"

Both were now on their feet, she with flushed cheeks and angry eyes, he, puzzled, vexed, and alarmed. The black boy stood like a statue—a plumb-black statue—taking no interest in the transactions of these incomprehensible whites, but dreaming with calm eyes of a certain bush village high on the jungle slopes of Malaita, with blue smoke curling up from the grass houses against the gray background of an oncoming mountain-squall.

"But you won't do anything so foolish—" he began.

"There you go again," she cried.

"I didn't mean it that way, and you know I didn't." He was speaking slowly and gravely. "And that other thing, that not permitting—it is only a manner of speaking. Of course I am not your guardian. You know you can go to Guvutu if you want to"—"or to the devil," he was almost tempted to add. "Only, I should deeply regret it, that is all. And I am very sorry that I should have said anything that hurt you. Remember, I am an Englishman."

Joan smiled and sat down again.

"Perhaps I have been hasty," she admitted. "You see, I am intolerant of restraint. If you only knew how I have been compelled to fight for my freedom. It is a sore point with me, this being told what I am to do or not do by you self-constituted lords of creation.-Viaburi I You stop along kitchen. No bring 'm Noa Noah.—And now, Mr. Sheldon, what am I to do? You don't want me here, and there doesn't seem to be any place for me to go."

"That is unfair. Your being wrecked here has been a godsend to me. I was very lonely and very sick. I really am not certain whether or not I should have pulled through had you not happened along. But that is not the point. Personally, purely selfishly personally, I should be sorry to see you go. But I am not considering myself. I am considering you. It—it is hardly the proper thing, you know. If I were married—if there were some woman of your own race here—but as it is—"

She threw up her hands in mock despair.

"I cannot follow you," she said. "In one breath you tell me I must go, and in the next breath you tell me there is no place to go and that you will not permit me to go. What is a poor girl to do?"

"That's the trouble," he said helplessly.

"And the situation annoys you."

"Only for your sake."

"Then let me save your feelings by telling you that it does not annoy me at all—except for the row you are making about it. I never allow what can't be changed to annoy me. There is no use in fighting the inevitable. Here is the situation. You are here. I am here. I can't go elsewhere, by your own account. You certainly can't go elsewhere and leave me here alone with a whole plantation and two hundred woolly cannibals on my hands. Therefore you stay, and I stay. It is very simple. Also, it is adventure. And furthermore, you needn't worry for yourself. I am not matrimonially inclined. I came to the Solomons for a plantation, not a husband."

Sheldon flushed, but remained silent.

"I know what you are thinking," she laughed gaily. "That if I were a man you'd wring my neck for me. And I deserve it, too. I'm so sorry. I ought not to keep on hurting your feelings."

"I'm afraid I rather invite it," he said, relieved by the signs of the tempest subsiding.

"I have it," she announced. "Lend me a gang of your boys for to-day. I'll build a grass house for myself over in the far corner of the compound—on piles, of course. I can move in to-night. I'll be comfortable and safe. The Tahitians can keep an anchor watch just as aboard ship. And then I'll study cocoanut planting. In return, I'll run the kitchen end of your household and give you some decent food to eat. And finally, I won't listen to any of your protests. I know all that you are going to say and offer—your giving the bungalow up to me and building a grass house for yourself. And I won't have it. You may as well consider everything settled. On the other hand, if you don't agree, I will go across the river, beyond your jurisdiction, and build a village for myself and my sailors, whom I shall send in the whale-boat to Guvutu for provisions. And now I want you to teach me billiards."

CHAPTER VII—A HARD-BITTEN GANG

Joan took hold of the household with no uncertain grip, revolutionizing things till Sheldon hardly recognized the place. For the first time the bungalow was clean and orderly. No longer the house-boys loafed and did as little as they could; while the cook complained that "head belong him walk about too much," from the strenuous course in cookery which she put him through. Nor did Sheldon escape being roundly lectured for his laziness in eating nothing but tinned provisions. She called him a muddler and a slouch, and other invidious names, for his slackness and his disregard of healthful food.

She sent her whale-boat down the coast twenty miles for limes and oranges, and wanted to know scathingly why said fruits had not long since been planted at Berande, while he was beneath contempt because there was no kitchen garden. Mummy apples, which he had regarded as weeds, under her guidance appeared as appetizing breakfast fruit, and, at dinner, were metamorphosed into puddings that elicited his unqualified admiration. Bananas, foraged from the bush, were served, cooked and raw, a dozen different ways, each one of which he declared was better than any other. She or her sailors dynamited fish daily, while the Balesuna natives were paid tobacco for bringing in oysters from the mangrove swamps. Her achievements with cocoanuts were a revelation. She taught the cook how to make yeast from the milk, that, in turn, raised light and airy bread. From the tip-top heart of the tree she concocted a delicious salad. From the milk and the meat of the nut she made various sauces and dressings, sweet and sour, that were served, according to preparation, with dishes that ranged from fish to pudding. She taught Sheldon the superiority of cocoanut cream over condensed cream, for use in coffee. From the old and sprouting nuts she took the solid, spongy centres and turned them into salads. Her forte seemed to be salads, and she astonished him with the deliciousness of a salad made from young bamboo shoots. Wild tomatoes, which had gone to seed or been remorselessly hoed out from the beginning of Berande, were foraged for salads, soups, and sauces.

The chickens, which had always gone into the bush and hidden their eggs, were given laying-bins, and Joan went out herself to shoot wild duck and wild pigeons for the table.

"Not that I like to do this sort of work," she explained, in reference to the cookery; "but because I can't get away from Dad's training."

Among other things, she burned the pestilential hospital, quarrelled with Sheldon over the dead, and, in anger, set her own men to work building a new, and what she called a decent, hospital. She robbed the windows of their lawn and muslin curtains, replacing them with gaudy calico from the trade-store, and made herself several gowns. When she wrote out a list of goods and clothing for herself, to be sent down to Sydney by the first steamer, Sheldon wondered how long she had made up her mind to stay.

She was certainly unlike any woman he had ever known or dreamed of. So far as he was concerned she was not a woman at all. She neither languished nor blandished. No feminine lures were wasted on him. He might have been her brother, or she his brother, for all sex had to do with the strange situation. Any mere polite gallantry on his part was ignored or snubbed, and he had very early given up offering his hand to her in getting into a boat or climbing over a log, and he had to acknowledge to himself that she was eminently fitted to take care of herself. Despite his warnings about crocodiles and sharks, she persisted in swimming in deep water off the beach; nor could he persuade her, when she was in the boat, to let one of the sailors throw the dynamite when shooting fish. She argued that she was at least a little bit more intelligent than they, and that, therefore, there was less liability of an accident if she did the shooting. She was to him the most masculine and at the same time the most feminine woman he had ever met.

A source of continual trouble between them was the disagreement over methods of handling the black boys. She ruled by stern kindness, rarely rewarding, never punishing, and he had to confess that her own sailors worshipped her, while the house-boys were her slaves, and did three times as much work for her as he had ever got out of them. She quickly saw the unrest of the contract labourers, and was not blind to the danger, always

65

imminent, that both she and Sheldon ran. Neither of them ever ventured out without a revolver, and the sailors who stood the night watches by Joan's grass house were armed with rifles. But Joan insisted that this reign of terror had been caused by the reign of fear practised by the white men. She had been brought up with the gentle Hawaiians, who never were ill-treated nor roughly handled, and she generalized that the Solomon Islanders, under kind treatment, would grow gentle.

One evening a terrific uproar arose in the barracks, and Sheldon, aided by Joan's sailors, succeeded in rescuing two women whom the blacks were beating to death. To save them from the vengeance of the blacks, they were guarded in the cook-house for the night. They were the two women who did the cooking for the labourers, and their offence had consisted of one of them taking a bath in the big cauldron in which the potatoes were boiled. The blacks were not outraged from the standpoint of cleanliness; they often took baths in the cauldrons themselves. The trouble lay in that the bather had been a low, degraded, wretched female; for to the Solomon Islander all females are low, degraded, and wretched.

Next morning, Joan and Sheldon, at breakfast, were aroused by a swelling murmur of angry voices. The first rule of Berande had been broken. The compound had been entered without permission or command, and all the two hundred labourers, with the exception of the boss-boys, were guilty of the offence. They crowded up, threatening and shouting, close under the front veranda. Sheldon leaned over the veranda railing, looking down upon them, while Joan stood slightly back. When the uproar was stilled, two brothers stood forth. They were large men, splendidly muscled, and with faces unusually ferocious, even for Solomon Islanders. One was Carin-Jama, otherwise The Silent; and the other was Bellin-Jama, The Boaster. Both had served on the Queensland plantations in the old days, and they were known as evil characters wherever white men met and gammed.

"We fella boy we want 'm them dam two black fella Mary," said Bellin-Jama.

"What you do along black fella Mary?" Sheldon asked.

"Kill 'm," said Bellin-Jama.

"What name you fella boy talk along me?" Sheldon demanded, with a show of rising anger. "Big bell he ring. You no belong along here. You belong along field. Bime by, big fella bell he ring, you stop along *kai-kai*, you come talk along me about two fella Mary. Now all you boy get along out of here."

The gang waited to see what Bellin-Jama would do, and Bellin-Jama stood still.

"Me no go," he said.

"You watch out, Bellin-Jama," Sheldon said sharply, "or I send you along Tulagi one big fella lashing. My word, you catch 'm strong fella."

Bellin-Jama glared up belligerently.

"You want 'm fight," he said, putting up his fists in approved, returned-Queenslander style.

Now, in the Solomons, where whites are few and blacks are many, and where the whites do the ruling, such an offer to fight is the deadliest insult. Blacks are not supposed to dare so highly as to offer to fight a white man. At the best, all they can look for is to be beaten by the white man.

A murmur of admiration at Bellin-Jama's bravery went up from the listening blacks. But Bellin-Jama's voice was still ringing in the air, and the murmuring was just beginning, when Sheldon cleared the rail, leaping straight downward. From the top of the railing to the ground it was fifteen feet, and Bellin-Jama was directly beneath. Sheldon's flying body struck him and crushed him to earth. No blows were needed to be struck. The black had been knocked helpless. Joan, startled by the unexpected leap, saw Carin-Jama, The Silent, reach out and seize Sheldon by the throat as he was half-way to his feet, while the five-score blacks surged forward for the killing. Her revolver was out, and Carin-Jama let go his grip, reeling backward with a bullet in his shoulder. In that fleeting instant of action she had thought to shoot him in the arm, which, at that short distance, might reasonably have been achieved. But the wave of savages leaping forward had changed her shot to the shoulder. It was a moment when not the slightest chance could be taken.

The instant his throat was released, Sheldon struck out with his fist, and Carin-Jama joined his brother on the ground. The mutiny was quelled, and five minutes more saw the brothers being carried to the hospital, and the mutineers, marshalled by the gang-bosses, on the way to the fields.

When Sheldon came up on the veranda, he found Joan collapsed on the steamer-chair and in tears. The sight unnerved him as the row just over could not possibly have done. A woman in tears was to him an embarrassing situation; and when that woman was Joan Lackland, from whom he had grown to expect anything unexpected, he was really frightened. He glanced down at her helplessly, and moistened his lips.

"I want to thank you," he began. "There isn't a doubt but what you saved my life, and I must say—"

She abruptly removed her hands, showing a wrathful and tear-stained face.

"You brute! You coward!" she cried. "You have made me shoot a man, and I never shot a man in my life before."

"It's only a flesh-wound, and he isn't going to die," Sheldon managed to interpolate.

"What of that? I shot him just the same. There was no need for you to jump down there that way. It was brutal and cowardly."

"Oh, now I say—" he began soothingly.

"Go away. Don't you see I hate you! hate you! Oh, won't you go away!"

Sheldon was white with anger.

"Then why in the name of common sense did you shoot?" he demanded.

"Be-be-because you were a white man," she sobbed. "And Dad would never have left any white man in the lurch. But it was your fault. You had no right to get yourself in such a position. Besides, it wasn't necessary."

"I am afraid I don't understand," he said shortly, turning away. "We will talk it over later on."

"Look how I get on with the boys," she said, while he paused in the doorway, stiffly polite, to listen. "There's those two sick boys I am nursing. They will do anything for me when they get well, and I won't have to keep them in fear of their life all the time. It is not necessary, I tell you, all this harshness and brutality. What if they are cannibals? They are human beings, just like you and me, and they are amenable to reason. That is what distinguishes all of us from the lower animals."

He nodded and went out.

"I suppose I've been unforgivably foolish," was her greeting, when he returned several hours later from a round of the plantation. "I've been to the hospital, and the man is getting along all right. It is not a serious hurt."

Sheldon felt unaccountably pleased and happy at the changed aspect of her mood.

"You see, you don't understand the situation," he began. "In the first place, the blacks have to be ruled sternly. Kindness is all very well, but you can't rule them by kindness only. I accept all that you say about the Hawaiians and the Tahitians. You say that they can be handled that way, and I believe you. I have had no experience with them. But you have had no experience with the blacks, and I ask you to believe me. They are different from your natives. You are used to Polynesians. These boys are Melanesians. They're blacks. They're niggers—look at their kinky hair. And they're a whole lot lower than the African niggers. Really, you know, there is a vast difference."

"They possess no gratitude, no sympathy, no kindliness. If you are kind to them, they think you are a fool. If you are gentle with them they think you are afraid. And when they think you are afraid, watch out, for they will get you. Just to show you, let me state the one invariable process in a black man's brain when, on his native heath, he encounters a stranger. His first thought is one of fear. Will the stranger kill him? His next thought, seeing that he is not killed, is: Can he kill the stranger? There was Packard, a Colonial trader, some twelve miles down the coast. He boasted that he ruled by kindness and never struck a blow. The result was that he did not rule at all. He used to come down in his whale-boat to visit Hughie and me. When his boat's crew decided to go home, he had to cut his visit short to accompany them. I remember one Sunday afternoon when Packard had accepted our invitation to stop to dinner. The soup was just served, when Hughie saw a nigger peering in through the door. He went out to him, for it was a violation of Berande custom. Any nigger has to send in word by the house-boys, and to keep outside the compound. This man, who was one of Packard's boat's-crew, was on the veranda. And he knew better, too. 'What name?' said Hughie. 'You tell 'm white man close up we fella boat's-crew go along. He no come now, we fella boy no wait. We go.' And just then Hughie fetched him a clout that knocked him clean down the stairs and off the veranda."

"But it was needlessly cruel," Joan objected. "You wouldn't treat a white man that way."

"And that's just the point. He wasn't a white man. He was a low black nigger, and he was deliberately insulting, not alone his own white master, but every white master in the Solomons. He insulted me. He insulted Hughie. He insulted Berande."

"Of course, according to your lights, to your formula of the rule of the strong—"

"Yes," Sheldon interrupted, "but it was according to the formula of the rule of the weak that Packard ruled. And what was the result? I am still alive. Packard is dead. He was unswervingly kind and gentle to his boys, and his boys waited till one day he was down with fever. His head is over on Malaita now. They carried away two whale-boats as well, filled with the loot of the store. Then there was Captain Mackenzie of the ketch *Minota*. He believed in kindness. He also contended that better confidence was established by carrying no weapons. On his second trip to Malaita, recruiting, he ran into Bina, which is near Langa Langa. The rifles with which the boat's-crew should have been armed, were locked up in his cabin. When the whale-boat went ashore after recruits, he paraded around the deck without even a revolver on him. He was tomahawked. His head remains in Malaita. It was suicide. So was Packard's finish suicide."

"I grant that precaution is necessary in dealing with them," Joan agreed; "but I believe that more satisfactory results can be obtained by treating them with discreet kindness and gentleness."

"And there I agree with *you*, but you must understand one thing. Berande, bar none, is by far the worst plantation in the Solomons so far as the labour is concerned. And how it came to be so proves your point. The previous owners of Berande were not discreetly kind. They were a pair of unadulterated brutes. One was a down-east Yankee, as I believe they are called, and the other was a guzzling German. They were slave-drivers. To begin with, they bought their labour from Johnny Be-blowed, the most notorious recruiter in the Solomons. He is working out a ten years' sentence in Fiji now, for the wanton killing of a black boy. During his last days here he had made himself so obnoxious that the natives on Malaita would have nothing to do with him. The only way he could get recruits was by hurrying to the spot whenever a murder or series of murders occurred. The murderers were usually only too willing to sign on and get away to escape vengeance. Down here they call such escapes, 'pier-head jumps.' There is suddenly a roar from the beach, and a nigger runs down to the water pursued by clouds of spears and arrows. Of course, Johnny Be-blowed's whale-boat is lying ready to pick him up. In his last days Johnny got nothing but pier-head jumps.

"And the first owners of Berande bought his recruits—a hard-bitten gang of murderers. They were all five-year boys. You see, the recruiter has the advantage over a boy when he makes a pier-head jump. He could sign him on for ten years did the law permit. Well, that's the gang of murderers we've got on our hands now. Of course some are dead, some have been killed, and there are others serving sentences at Tulagi. Very little clearing did those first owners do, and less planting. It was war all the time. They had one manager killed. One of the partners had his shoulder slashed nearly off by a cane-knife. The other was speared on two different occasions. Both were bullies, wherefore there was a streak of cowardice in them, and in the end they had to give up. They were chased away—literally chased away—by their own niggers. And along came poor Hughie and me, two new chums, to take hold of that hard-bitten gang. We did not know the situation, and we had bought Berande, and there was nothing to do but hang on and muddle through somehow.

"At first we made the mistake of indiscreet kindness. We tried to rule by persuasion and fair treatment. The niggers concluded that we were afraid. I blush to think of what fools we were in those first days. We were imposed on, and threatened and insulted; and we put up with it, hoping our square-dealing would soon mend things. Instead of which everything went from bad to worse. Then came the day when Hughie reprimanded one of the boys and was nearly killed by the gang. The only thing that saved him was the number on top of him, which enabled me to reach the spot in time.

"Then began the rule of the strong hand. It was either that or quit, and we had sunk about all our money into the venture, and we could not quit. And besides, our pride was involved. We had started out to do something, and we were so made that we just had to go on with it. It has been a hard fight, for we were, and are to this day, considered the worst plantation in the Solomons from the standpoint of labour. Do you know, we have been unable to get white men in. We've offered the managership to half a dozen. I won't say they were afraid, for they were not. But they did not consider it healthy—at least that is the way it was put by the last one who declined our offer. So Hughie and I did the managing ourselves."

"And when he died you were prepared to go on all alone!" Joan cried, with shining eyes.

"I thought I'd muddle through. And now, Miss Lackland, please be charitable when I seem harsh, and remember that the situation is unparalleled down here. We've got a bad crowd, and we're making them work. You've been over the plantation and you ought to know. And I assure you that there are no better three-and-four-years-old trees on any other plantation in the Solomons. We have worked steadily to change matters for the better. We've been slowly getting in new labour. That is why we bought the *Jessie*. We wanted to select our own labour. In another year the time will be up for most of the original gang. You see, they were recruited during the first year of Berande, and their contracts expire on different months. Naturally, they have contaminated the new boys to a certain extent; but that can soon be remedied, and then Berande will be a respectable plantation."

Joan nodded but remained silent. She was too occupied in glimpsing the vision of the one lone white man as she had first seen him, helpless from fever, a collapsed wraith in a steamer-chair, who, up to the last heart-beat, by some strange alchemy of race, was pledged to mastery.

"It is a pity," she said. "But the white man has to rule, I suppose."

"I don't like it," Sheldon assured her. "To save my life I can't imagine how I ever came here. But here I am, and I can't run away."

"Blind destiny of race," she said, faintly smiling. "We whites have been land robbers and sea robbers from remotest time. It is in our blood, I guess, and we can't get away from it."

"I never thought about it so abstractly," he confessed. "I've been too busy puzzling over why I came here."

CHAPTER VIII—LOCAL COLOUR

At sunset a small ketch fanned in to anchorage, and a little later the skipper came ashore. He was a soft-spoken, gentle-voiced young fellow of twenty, but he won Joan's admiration in advance when Sheldon told her that he ran the ketch all alone with a black crew from Malaita. And Romance lured and beckoned before Joan's eyes when she learned he was Christian Young, a Norfolk Islander, but a direct descendant of John Young, one of the original *Bounty* mutineers. The blended Tahitian and English blood showed in his soft eyes and tawny skin; but the English hardness seemed to have disappeared. Yet the hardness was there, and it was what enabled him to run his ketch single-handed and to wring a livelihood out of the fighting Solomons.

Joan's unexpected presence embarrassed him, until she herself put him at his ease by a frank, comradely manner that offended Sheldon's sense of the fitness of things feminine. News from the world Young had not, but he was filled with news of the Solomons. Fifteen boys had stolen rifles and run away into the bush from Lunga plantation, which was farther east on the Guadalcanal coast. And from the bush they had sent word that they were coming back to wipe out the three white men in charge, while two of the three white men, in turn, were hunting them through the bush. There was a strong possibility, Young volunteered, that if they were not caught they might circle around and tap the coast at Berande in order to steal or capture a whale-boat.

"I forgot to tell you that your trader at Ugi has been murdered," he said to Sheldon. "Five big canoes came down from Port Adams. They landed in the night-time, and caught Oscar asleep. What they didn't steal they burned. The *Flibberty-Gibbet* got the news at Mboli Pass, and ran down to Ugi. I was at Mboli when the news came."

"I think I'll have to abandon Ugi," Sheldon remarked.

"It's the second trader you've lost there in a year," Young concurred. "To make it safe there ought to be two white men at least. Those Malaita canoes are always raiding down that way, and you know what that Port Adams lot is. I've got a dog for you. Tommy Jones sent it up from Neal Island. He said he'd promised it to you. It's a first-class nigger-chaser. Hadn't been on board two minutes when he had my whole boat's-crew in the rigging. Tommy calls him Satan."

"I've wondered several times why you had no dogs here," Joan said.

"The trouble is to keep them. They're always eaten by the crocodiles."

"Jack Hanley was killed at Marovo Lagoon two months ago," Young announced in his mild voice. "The news just came down on the *Apostle*."

"Where is Marovo Lagoon?" Joan asked.

"New Georgia, a couple of hundred miles to the westward," Sheldon answered. "Bougainville lies just beyond."

"His own house-boys did it," Young went on; "but they were put up to it by the Marovo natives. His Santa Cruz boat's-crew escaped in the whale-boat to Choiseul, and Mather, in the *Lily*, sailed over to Marovo. He burned a village, and got Hanley's head back. He found it in one of the houses, where the niggers had it drying. And that's all the news I've got, except that there's a lot of new Lee-Enfields loose on the eastern end of Ysabel. Nobody knows how the natives got them. The government ought to investigate. And—oh yes, a war vessel's in the group, the *Cambrian*. She burned three villages at Bina—on account of the *Minota*, you know—and shelled the bush. Then she went to Sio to straighten out things there."

The conversation became general, and just before Young left to go on board Joan asked,—

"How can you manage all alone, Mr. Young?"

His large, almost girlish eyes rested on her for a moment before he replied, and then it was in the softest and gentlest of voices.

75

"Oh, I get along pretty well with them. Of course, there is a bit of trouble once in a while, but that must be expected. You must never let them think you are afraid. I've been afraid plenty of times, but they never knew it."

"You would think he wouldn't strike a mosquito that was biting him," Sheldon said when Young had gone on board. "All the Norfolk Islanders that have descended from the *Bounty* crowd are that way. But look at Young. Only three years ago, when he first got the *Minerva*, he was lying in Suu, on Malaita. There are a lot of returned Queenslanders there—a rough crowd. They planned to get his head. The son of their chief, old One-Eyed Billy, had recruited on Lunga and died of dysentery. That meant that a white man's head was owing to Suu—any white man, it didn't matter who so long as they got the head. And Young was only a lad, and they made sure to get his easily. They decoyed his whale-boat ashore with a promise of recruits, and killed all hands. At the same instant, the Suu gang that was on board the *Minerva* jumped Young. He was just preparing a dynamite stick for fish, and he lighted it and tossed it in amongst them. One can't get him to talk about it, but the fuse was short, the survivors leaped overboard, while he slipped his anchor and got away. They've got one hundred fathoms of shell money on his head now, which is worth one hundred pounds sterling. Yet he goes into Suu regularly. He was there a short time ago, returning thirty boys from Cape Marsh—that's the Fulcrum Brothers' plantation."

"At any rate, his news to-night has given me a better insight into the life down here," Joan said. "And it is colourful life, to say the least. The Solomons ought to be printed red on the charts—and yellow, too, for the diseases."

"The Solomons are not always like this," Sheldon answered. "Of course, Berande is the worst plantation, and everything it gets is the worst. I doubt if ever there was a worse run of sickness than we were just getting over when you arrived. Just as luck would have it, the *Jessie* caught the contagion as well. Berande has been very unfortunate. All the old-timers shake their heads at it. They say it has what you Americans call a *hoodoo* on it."

"Berande will succeed," Joan said stoutly. "I like to laugh at superstition. You'll pull through and come out the big end of the horn. The ill luck can't last for ever. I am afraid, though, the Solomons is not a white man's climate."

"It will be, though. Give us fifty years, and when all the bush is cleared off back to the mountains, fever will be stamped out; everything will be far healthier. There will be cities and towns here, for there's an immense amount of good land going to waste."

"But it will never become a white man's climate, in spite of all that," Joan reiterated. "The white man will always be unable to perform the manual labour."

"That is true."

"It will mean slavery," she dashed on.

"Yes, like all the tropics. The black, the brown, and the yellow will have to do the work, managed by the white men. The black labour is too wasteful, however, and in time Chinese or Indian coolies will be imported. The planters are already considering the matter. I, for one, am heartily sick of black labour."

"Then the blacks will die off?"

Sheldon shrugged his shoulders, and retorted,—

"Yes, like the North American Indian, who was a far nobler type than the Melanesian. The world is only so large, you know, and it is filling up—"

"And the unfit must perish?"

"Precisely so. The unfit must perish."

In the morning Joan was roused by a great row and hullabaloo. Her first act was to reach for her revolver, but when she heard Noa Noah, who was on guard, laughing outside, she knew there was no danger, and went out to see the fun. Captain Young had landed Satan at the moment when the bridge-building gang had started along the beach. Satan was big and black, short-haired and muscular, and weighed fully seventy pounds. He did not

77

love the blacks. Tommy Jones had trained him well, tying him up daily for several hours and telling off one or two black boys at a time to tease him. So Satan had it in for the whole black race, and the second after he landed on the beach the bridge-building gang was stampeding over the compound fence and swarming up the cocoanut palms.

"Good morning," Sheldon called from the veranda. "And what do you think of the nigger-chaser?"

"I'm thinking we have a task before us to train him in to the house-boys," she called back.

"And to your Tahitians, too. Look out, Noah! Run for it!"

Satan, having satisfied himself that the tree-perches were unassailable, was charging straight for the big Tahitian.

But Noah stood his ground, though somewhat irresolutely, and Satan, to every one's surprise, danced and frisked about him with laughing eyes and wagging tail.

"Now, that is what I might call a proper dog," was Joan's comment. "He is at least wiser than you, Mr. Sheldon. He didn't require any teaching to recognize the difference between a Tahitian and a black boy. What do you think, Noah? Why don't he bite you? He savvee you Tahitian eh?"

Noa Noah shook his head and grinned.

"He no savvee me Tahitian," he explained. "He savvee me wear pants all the same white man."

"You'll have to give him a course in 'Sartor Resartus,'" Sheldon laughed, as he came down and began to make friends with Satan.

It chanced just then that Adamu Adam and Matauare, two of Joan's sailors, entered the compound from the far side-gate. They had been down to the Balesuna making an alligator trap, and, instead of trousers, were clad in lava-lavas that flapped gracefully about their stalwart limbs. Satan saw them, and advertised his find by breaking away from Sheldon's hands and charging.

"No got pants," Noah announced with a grin that broadened as Adamu Adam took to flight.

He climbed up the platform that supported the galvanized iron tanks which held the water collected from the roof. Foiled here, Satan turned and charged back on Matauare.

"Run, Matauare! Run!" Joan called.

But he held his ground and waited the dog.

"He is the Fearless One—that is what his name means," Joan explained to Sheldon.

The Tahitian watched Satan coolly, and when that sanguine-mouthed creature lifted into the air in the final leap, the man's hand shot out. It was a fair grip on the lower jaw, and Satan described a half circle and was flung to the rear, turning over in the air and falling heavily on his back. Three times he leaped, and three times that grip on his jaw flung him to defeat. Then he contented himself with trotting at Matauare's heels, eyeing him and sniffing him suspiciously.

"It's all right, Satan; it's all right," Sheldon assured him. "That good fella belong along me."

But Satan dogged the Tahitian's movements for a full hour before he made up his mind that the man was an appurtenance of the place. Then he turned his attention to the three house-boys, cornering Ornfiri in the kitchen and rushing him against the hot stove, stripping the lava-lava from Lalaperu when that excited youth climbed a veranda-post, and following Viaburi on top the billiard-table, where the battle raged until Joan managed a rescue.

CHAPTER IX—AS BETWEEN A MAN AND A WOMAN

It was Satan's inexhaustible energy and good spirits that most impressed them. His teeth seemed perpetually to ache with desire, and in lieu of black legs he husked the cocoanuts that fell from the trees in the compound, kept the enclosure clear of intruding hens, and made a hostile acquaintance with every boss-boy who came to report. He was unable to forget the torment of his puppyhood, wherein everlasting hatred of the black had been woven into the fibres of consciousness; and such a terror did he make himself that Sheldon was forced to shut him up in the living room when, for any reason, strange natives were permitted in the compound. This always hurt Satan's feelings and fanned his wrath, so that even the house-boys had to watch out for him when he was first released.

Christian Young sailed away in the *Minerva*, carrying an invitation (that would be delivered nobody knew when) to Tommy Jones to drop in at Berande the next time he was passing.

"What are your plans when you get to Sydney?" Sheldon asked, that night, at dinner.

"First I've heard that I'm going to Sydney," Joan retorted. "I suppose you've received information, by bush-telegraph, that that third assistant understrapper and ex-sailorman at Tulagi is going to deport me as an undesirable immigrant."

"Oh, no, nothing of the sort, I assure you," Sheldon began with awkward haste, fearful of having offended, though he knew not how. "I was just wondering, that was all. You see, with the loss of the schooner and . . and all the rest . . . you understand . . I was thinking that if—a—if—hang it all, until you could communicate with your friends, my agents at Sydney could advance you a loan, temporary you see, why I'd be only too glad and all the rest, you know. The proper—"

But his jaw dropped and he regarded her irritably and with apprehension.

"What *is* the matter?" he demanded, with a show of heat. "What *have* I done now?"

Joan's eyes were bright with battle, the curve of her lips sharp with mockery.

"Certainly not the unexpected," she said quietly. "Merely ignored me in your ordinary, every-day, man-god, superior fashion. Naturally it counted for nothing, my telling you that I had no idea of going to Sydney. Go to Sydney I must, because you, in your superior wisdom, have so decreed."

She paused and looked at him curiously, as though he were some strange breed of animal.

"Of course I am grateful for your offer of assistance; but even that is no salve to wounded pride. For that matter, it is no more than one white man should expect from another. Shipwrecked mariners are always helped along their way. Only this particular mariner doesn't need any help. Furthermore, this mariner is not going to Sydney, thank you."

"But what do you intend to do?"

"Find some spot where I shall escape the indignity of being patronized and bossed by the superior sex."

"Come now, that is putting it a bit too strongly." Sheldon laughed, but the strain in his voice destroyed the effect of spontaneity. "You know yourself how impossible the situation is."

"I know nothing of the sort, sir. And if it is impossible, well, haven't I achieved it?"

"But it cannot continue. Really—"

"Oh, yes, it can. Having achieved it, I can go on achieving it. I intend to remain in the Solomons, but not on Berande. To-morrow I am going to take the whale-boat over to Pari-Sulay. I was talking with Captain Young about it. He says there are at least four hundred acres, and every foot of it good for planting. Being an island, he says I won't have to bother about wild

81

pigs destroying the young trees. All I'll have to do is to keep the weeds hoed until the trees come into bearing. First, I'll buy the island; next, get forty or fifty recruits and start clearing and planting; and at the same time I'll run up a bungalow; and then you'll be relieved of my embarrassing presence—now don't say that it isn't."

"It is embarrassing," he said bluntly. "But you refuse to see my point of view, so there is no use in discussing it. Now please forget all about it, and consider me at your service concerning this . . . this project of yours. I know more about cocoanut-planting than you do. You speak like a capitalist. I don't know how much money you have, but I don't fancy you are rolling in wealth, as you Americans say. But I do know what it costs to clear land. Suppose the government sells you Pari-Sulay at a pound an acre; clearing will cost you at least four pounds more; that is, five pounds for four hundred acres, or, say, ten thousand dollars. Have you that much?"

She was keenly interested, and he could see that the previous clash between them was already forgotten. Her disappointment was plain as she confessed:

"No; I haven't quite eight thousand dollars."

"Then here's another way of looking at it. You'll need, as you said, at least fifty boys. Not counting premiums, their wages are thirty dollars a year."

"I pay my Tahitians fifteen a month," she interpolated.

"They won't do on straight plantation work. But to return. The wages of fifty boys each year will come to three hundred pounds—that is, fifteen hundred dollars. Very well. It will be seven years before your trees begin to bear. Seven times fifteen hundred is ten thousand five hundred dollars— more than you possess, and all eaten up by the boys' wages, with nothing to pay for bungalow, building, tools, quinine, trips to Sydney, and so forth."

Sheldon shook his head gravely. "You'll have to abandon the idea."

"But I won't go to Sydney," she cried. "I simply won't. I'll buy in to the extent of my money as a small partner in some other plantation. Let me buy in in Berande!"

"Heaven forbid!" he cried in such genuine dismay that she broke into hearty laughter.

"There, I won't tease you. Really, you know, I'm not accustomed to forcing my presence where it is not desired. Yes, yes; I know you're just aching to point out that I've forced myself upon you ever since I landed, only you are too polite to say so. Yet as you said yourself, it was impossible for me to go away, so I had to stay. You wouldn't let me go to Tulagi. You compelled me to force myself upon you. But I won't buy in as partner with any one. I'll buy Pari-Sulay, but I'll put only ten boys on it and clear slowly. Also, I'll invest in some old ketch and take out a trading license. For that matter, I'll go recruiting on Malaita."

She looked for protest, and found it in Sheldon's clenched hand and in every line of his clean-cut face.

"Go ahead and say it," she challenged. "Please don't mind me. I'm— I'm getting used to it, you know. Really I am."

"I wish I were a woman so as to tell you how preposterously insane and impossible it is," he blurted out.

She surveyed him with deliberation, and said:

"Better than that, you are a man. So there is nothing to prevent your telling me, for I demand to be considered as a man. I didn't come down here to trail my woman's skirts over the Solomons. Please forget that I am accidentally anything else than a man with a man's living to make."

Inwardly Sheldon fumed and fretted. Was she making game of him? Or did there lurk in her the insidious unhealthfulness of unwomanliness? Or was it merely a case of blank, staring, sentimental, idiotic innocence?

"I have told you," he began stiffly, "that recruiting on Malaita is impossible for a woman, and that is all I care to say—or dare."

"And I tell you, in turn, that it is nothing of the sort. I've sailed the *Miélé* here, master, if you please, all the way from Tahiti—even if I did lose her, which was the fault of your Admiralty charts. I am a navigator, and that is more than your Solomons captains are. Captain Young told me all about it. And I am a seaman—a better seaman than you, when it comes right down to it, and you know it. I can shoot. I am not a fool. I can take care of myself. And I shall most certainly buy a ketch, run her myself, and go recruiting on Malaita."

Sheldon made a hopeless gesture.

"That's right," she rattled on. "Wash your hands of me. But as Von used to say, 'You just watch my smoke!'"

"There's no use in discussing it. Let us have some music."

He arose and went over to the big phonograph; but before the disc started, and while he was winding the machine, he heard her saying:

"I suppose you've been accustomed to Jane Eyres all your life. That's why you don't understand me. Come on, Satan; let's leave him to his old music."

He watched her morosely and without intention of speaking, till he saw her take a rifle from the stand, examine the magazine, and start for the door.

"Where are you going?" he asked peremptorily.

"As between man and woman," she answered, "it would be too terribly—er—indecent for you to tell me why I shouldn't go alligatoring. Good-night. Sleep well."

He shut off the phonograph with a snap, started toward the door after her, then abruptly flung himself into a chair.

"You're hoping a 'gator catches me, aren't you?" she called from the veranda, and as she went down the steps her rippling laughter drifted tantalizingly back through the wide doorway.

CHAPTER X—A MESSAGE FROM BOUCHER

The next day Sheldon was left all alone. Joan had gone exploring Pari-Sulay, and was not to be expected back until the late afternoon. Sheldon was vaguely oppressed by his loneliness, and several heavy squalls during the afternoon brought him frequently on to the veranda, telescope in hand, to scan the sea anxiously for the whale-boat. Betweenwhiles he scowled over the plantation account-books, made rough estimates, added and balanced, and scowled the harder. The loss of the *Jessie* had hit Berande severely. Not alone was his capital depleted by the amount of her value, but her earnings were no longer to be reckoned on, and it was her earnings that largely paid the running expenses of the plantation.

"Poor old Hughie," he muttered aloud, once. "I'm glad you didn't live to see it, old man. What a cropper, what a cropper!"

Between squalls the *Flibberty-Gibbet* ran in to anchorage, and her skipper, Pete Oleson (brother to the Oleson of the *Jessie*), ancient, grizzled, wild-eyed, emaciated by fever, dragged his weary frame up the veranda steps and collapsed in a steamer-chair. Whisky and soda kept him going while he made report and turned in his accounts.

"You're rotten with fever," Sheldon said. "Why don't you run down to Sydney for a blow of decent climate?"

The old skipper shook his head.

"I can't. I've ben in the islands too long. I'd die. The fever comes out worse down there."

"Kill or cure," Sheldon counselled.

"It's straight kill for me. I tried it three years ago. The cool weather put me on my back before I landed. They carried me ashore and into hospital. I was unconscious one stretch for two weeks. After that the doctors sent me back to the islands—said it was the only thing that would save me. Well, I'm still alive; but I'm too soaked with fever. A month in Australia would finish me."

"But what are you going to do?" Sheldon queried. "You can't stay here until you die."

"That's all that's left to me. I'd like to go back to the old country, but I couldn't stand it. I'll last longer here, and here I'll stay until I peg out; but I wish to God I'd never seen the Solomons, that's all."

He declined to sleep ashore, took his orders, and went back on board the cutter. A lurid sunset was blotted out by the heaviest squall of the day, and Sheldon watched the whale-boat arrive in the thick of it. As the spritsail was taken in and the boat headed on to the beach, he was aware of a distinct hurt at sight of Joan at the steering-oar, standing erect and swaying her strength to it as she resisted the pressures that tended to throw the craft broadside in the surf. Her Tahitians leaped out and rushed the boat high up the beach, and she led her bizarre following through the gate of the compound.

The first drops of rain were driving like hail-stones, the tall cocoanut palms were bending and writhing in the grip of the wind, while the thick cloud-mass of the squall turned the brief tropic twilight abruptly to night.

Quite unconsciously the brooding anxiety of the afternoon slipped from Sheldon, and he felt strangely cheered at the sight of her running up the steps laughing, face flushed, hair flying, her breast heaving from the violence of her late exertions.

"Lovely, perfectly lovely—Pari-Sulay," she panted. "I shall buy it. I'll write to the Commissioner to-night. And the site for the bungalow—I've selected it already—is wonderful. You must come over some day and advise me. You won't mind my staying here until I can get settled? Wasn't that squall beautiful? And I suppose I'm late for dinner. I'll run and get clean, and be with you in a minute."

And in the brief interval of her absence he found himself walking about the big living-room and impatiently and with anticipation awaiting her coming.

"Do you know, I'm never going to squabble with you again," he announced when they were seated.

"Squabble!" was the retort. "It's such a sordid word. It sounds cheap and nasty. I think it's much nicer to quarrel."

"Call it what you please, but we won't do it any more, will we?" He cleared his throat nervously, for her eyes advertised the immediate beginning of hostilities. "I beg your pardon," he hurried on. "I should have spoken for myself. What I mean is that I refuse to quarrel. You have the most horrible way, without uttering a word, of making me play the fool. Why, I began with the kindest intentions, and here I am now—"

"Making nasty remarks," she completed for him.

"It's the way you have of catching me up," he complained.

"Why, I never said a word. I was merely sitting here, being sweetly lured on by promises of peace on earth and all the rest of it, when suddenly you began to call me names."

"Hardly that, I am sure."

"Well, you said I was horrible, or that I had a horrible way about me, which is the same thing. I wish my bungalow were up. I'd move to-morrow."

But her twitching lips belied her words, and the next moment the man was more uncomfortable than ever, being made so by her laughter.

"I was only teasing you. Honest Injun. And if you don't laugh I'll suspect you of being in a temper with me. That's right, laugh. But don't—" she added in alarm, "don't if it hurts you. You look as though you had a toothache. There, there—don't say it. You know you promised not to quarrel, while I have the privilege of going on being as hateful as I please. And to begin with, there's the *Flibberty-Gibbet*. I didn't know she was so large a cutter; but she's in disgraceful condition. Her rigging is something queer, and the next sharp squall will bring her head-gear all about the shop. I watched Noa Noah's face as we sailed past. He didn't say anything. He just sneered. And I don't blame him."

"Her skipper's rotten bad with fever," Sheldon explained. "And he had to drop his mate off to take hold of things at Ugi—that's where I lost Oscar, my trader. And you know what sort of sailors the niggers are."

She nodded her head judicially, and while she seemed to debate a weighty judgment he asked for a second helping of tinned beef—not because he was hungry, but because he wanted to watch her slim, firm fingers, naked of jewels and banded metals, while his eyes pleasured in the swell of the forearm, appearing from under the sleeve and losing identity in the smooth, round wrist undisfigured by the netted veins that come to youth when youth is gone. The fingers were brown with tan and looked exceedingly boyish. Then, and without effort, the concept came to him. Yes, that was it. He had stumbled upon the clue to her tantalizing personality. Her fingers, sunburned and boyish, told the story. No wonder she had exasperated him so frequently. He had tried to treat with her as a woman, when she was not a woman. She was a mere girl—and a boyish girl at that—with sunburned fingers that delighted in doing what boys' fingers did; with a body and muscles that liked swimming and violent endeavour of all sorts; with a mind that was daring, but that dared no farther than boys' adventures, and that delighted in rifles and revolvers, Stetson hats, and a sexless *camaraderie* with men.

Somehow, as he pondered and watched her, it seemed as if he sat in church at home listening to the choir-boys chanting. She reminded him of those boys, or their voices, rather. The same sexless quality was there. In the body of her she was woman; in the mind of her she had not grown up. She had not been exposed to ripening influences of that sort. She had had no mother. Von, her father, native servants, and rough island life had constituted her training. Horses and rifles had been her toys, camp and trail her nursery. From what she had told him, her seminary days had been an exile, devoted to study and to ceaseless longing for the wild riding and swimming of Hawaii. A boy's training, and a boy's point of view! That explained her chafe at petticoats, her revolt at what was only decently conventional. Some day she would grow up, but as yet she was only in the process.

Well, there was only one thing for him to do. He must meet her on her own basis of boyhood, and not make the mistake of treating her as a woman. He wondered if he could love the woman she would be when her nature awoke; and he wondered if he could love her just as she was and himself wake her up. After all, whatever it was, she had come to fill quite a large place in his life, as he had discovered that afternoon while scanning the sea between the squalls. Then he remembered the accounts of Berande, and the cropper that was coming, and scowled.

He became aware that she was speaking.

"I beg pardon," he said. "What's that you were saying?"

"You weren't listening to a word—I knew it," she chided. "I was saying that the condition of the *Flibberty-Gibbet* was disgraceful, and that to-morrow, when you've told the skipper and not hurt his feelings, I am going to take my men out and give her an overhauling. We'll scrub her bottom, too. Why, there's whiskers on her copper four inches long. I saw it when she rolled. Don't forget, I'm going cruising on the *Flibberty* some day, even if I have to run away with her."

While at their coffee on the veranda, Satan raised a commotion in the compound near the beach gate, and Sheldon finally rescued a mauled and frightened black and dragged him on the porch for interrogation.

"What fella marster you belong?" he demanded. "What name you come along this fella place sun he go down?"

"Me b'long Boucher. Too many boy belong along Port Adams stop along my fella marster. Too much walk about."

The black drew a scrap of notepaper from under his belt and passed it over. Sheldon scanned it hurriedly.

"It's from Boucher," he explained, "the fellow who took Packard's place. Packard was the one I told you about who was killed by his boat's-crew. He says the Port Adams crowd is out—fifty of them, in big canoes—and camping on his beach. They've killed half a dozen of his pigs already, and seem to be looking for trouble. And he's afraid they may connect with the fifteen runaways from Lunga."

"In which case?" she queried.

"In which case Billy Pape will be compelled to send Boucher's successor. It's Pape's station, you know. I wish I knew what to do. I don't like to leave you here alone."

"Take me along then."

He smiled and shook his head.

"Then you'd better take my men along," she advised. "They're good shots, and they're not afraid of anything—except Utami, and he's afraid of ghosts."

The big bell was rung, and fifty black boys carried the whale-boat down to the water. The regular boat's-crew manned her, and Matauare and three other Tahitians, belted with cartridges and armed with rifles, sat in the stern-sheets where Sheldon stood at the steering-oar.

"My, I wish I could go with you," Joan said wistfully, as the boat shoved off.

Sheldon shook his head.

"I'm as good as a man," she urged.

"You really are needed here," he replied.

"There's that Lunga crowd; they might reach the coast right here, and with both of us absent rush the plantation. Good-bye. We'll get back in the morning some time. It's only twelve miles."

When Joan started to return to the house, she was compelled to pass among the boat-carriers, who lingered on the beach to chatter in queer, ape-like fashion about the events of the night. They made way for her, but there came to her, as she was in the midst of them, a feeling of her own helplessness. There were so many of them. What was to prevent them from dragging her down if they so willed? Then she remembered that one cry of hers would fetch Noa Noah and her remaining sailors, each one of whom was worth a dozen blacks in a struggle. As she opened the gate, one of the boys stepped up to her. In the darkness she could not make him out.

"What name?" she asked sharply. "What name belong you?"

"Me Aroa," he said.

She remembered him as one of the two sick boys she had nursed at the hospital. The other one had died.

"Me take 'm plenty fella medicine too much," Aroa was saying.

"Well, and you all right now," she answered.

"Me want 'm tobacco, plenty fella tobacco; me want 'm calico; me want 'm porpoise teeth; me want 'm one fella belt."

She looked at him humorously, expecting to see a smile, or at least a grin, on his face. Instead, his face was expressionless. Save for a narrow breech-clout, a pair of ear-plugs, and about his kinky hair a chaplet of white cowrie-shells, he was naked. His body was fresh-oiled and shiny, and his eyes glistened in the starlight like some wild animal's. The rest of the boys had crowded up at his back in a solid wall. Some one of them giggled, but the remainder regarded her in morose and intense silence.

"Well?" she said. "What for you want plenty fella things?"

"Me take 'm medicine," quoth Aroa. "You pay me."

And this was a sample of their gratitude, she thought. It looked as if Sheldon had been right after all. Aroa waited stolidly. A leaping fish splashed far out on the water. A tiny wavelet murmured sleepily on the beach. The shadow of a flying-fox drifted by in velvet silence overhead. A light air fanned coolly on her cheek; it was the land-breeze beginning to blow.

"You go along quarters," she said, starting to turn on her heel to enter the gate.

"You pay me," said the boy.

"Aroa, you all the same one big fool. I no pay you. Now you go."

But the black was unmoved. She felt that he was regarding her almost insolently as he repeated:

"I take 'm medicine. You pay me. You pay me now."

Then it was that she lost her temper and cuffed his ears so soundly as to drive him back among his fellows. But they did not break up. Another boy stepped forward.

"You pay me," he said.

His eyes had the querulous, troubled look such as she had noticed in monkeys; but while he was patently uncomfortable under her scrutiny, his thick lips were drawn firmly in an effort at sullen determination.

"What for?" she asked.

"Me Gogoomy," he said. "Bawo brother belong me."

Bawo, she remembered, was the sick boy who had died.

"Go on," she commanded.

"Bawo take 'm medicine. Bawo finish. Bawo my brother. You pay me. Father belong me one big fella chief along Port Adams. You pay me."

Joan laughed.

"Gogoomy, you just the same as Aroa, one big fool. My word, who pay me for medicine?"

She dismissed the matter by passing through the gate and closing it. But Gogoomy pressed up against it and said impudently:

"Father belong me one big fella chief. You no bang 'm head belong me. My word, you fright too much."

"Me fright?" she demanded, while anger tingled all through her.

"Too much fright bang 'm head belong me," Gogoomy said proudly.

And then she reached for him across the gate and got him. It was a sweeping, broad-handed slap, so heavy that he staggered sideways and nearly fell. He sprang for the gate as if to force it open, while the crowd surged forward against the fence. Joan thought rapidly. Her revolver was hanging on the wall of her grass house. Yet one cry would bring her sailors, and she knew she was safe. So she did not cry for help. Instead, she whistled for Satan, at the same time calling him by name. She knew he was shut up in the living room, but the blacks did not wait to see. They fled with wild yells through the darkness, followed reluctantly by Gogoomy; while she entered the bungalow, laughing at first, but finally vexed to the verge of tears by what had taken place. She had sat up a whole night with the boy who had died, and yet his brother demanded to be paid for his life.

"Ugh! the ungrateful beast!" she muttered, while she debated whether or not she would confess the incident to Sheldon.

CHAPTER XI—THE PORT ADAMS CROWD

"And so it was all settled easily enough," Sheldon was saying. He was on the veranda, drinking coffee. The whale-boat was being carried into its shed. "Boucher was a bit timid at first to carry off the situation with a strong hand, but he did very well once we got started. We made a play at holding a court, and Telepasse, the old scoundrel, accepted the findings. He's a Port Adams chief, a filthy beggar. We fined him ten times the value of the pigs, and made him move on with his mob. Oh, they're a sweet lot, I must say, at least sixty of them, in five big canoes, and out for trouble. They've got a dozen Sniders that ought to be confiscated."

"Why didn't you?" Joan asked.

"And have a row on my hands with the Commissioner? He's terribly touchy about his black wards, as he calls them. Well, we started them along their way, though they went in on the beach to *kai-kai* several miles back. They ought to pass here some time to-day."

Two hours later the canoes arrived. No one saw them come. The house-boys were busy in the kitchen at their own breakfast. The plantation hands were similarly occupied in their quarters. Satan lay sound asleep on his back under the billiard table, in his sleep brushing at the flies that pestered him. Joan was rummaging in the storeroom, and Sheldon was taking his siesta in a hammock on the veranda. He awoke gently. In some occult, subtle way a warning that all was not well had penetrated his sleep and aroused him. Without moving, he glanced down and saw the ground beneath covered with armed savages. They were the same ones he had parted with that morning, though he noted an accession in numbers. There were men he had not seen before.

He slipped from the hammock and with deliberate slowness sauntered to the railing, where he yawned sleepily and looked down on them. It came to him curiously that it was his destiny ever to stand on this high place, looking down on unending hordes of black trouble that required control, bullying, and cajolery. But while he glanced carelessly over them, he was keenly taking stock. The new men were all armed with modern rifles. Ah, he had thought so. There were fifteen of them, undoubtedly the Lunga runaways. In addition, a dozen old Sniders were in the hands of the original crowd. The rest were armed with spears, clubs, bows and arrows, and long-handled tomahawks. Beyond, drawn up on the beach, he could see the big war-canoes, with high and fantastically carved bows and sterns, ornamented with scrolls and bands of white cowrie shells. These were the men who had killed his trader, Oscar, at Ugi.

"What name you walk about this place?" he demanded.

At the same time he stole a glance seaward to where the *Flibberty-Gibbet* reflected herself in the glassy calm of the sea. Not a soul was visible under her awnings, and he saw the whale-boat was missing from alongside. The Tahitians had evidently gone shooting fish up the Balesuna. He was all alone in his high place above this trouble, while his world slumbered peacefully under the breathless tropic noon.

Nobody replied, and he repeated his demand, more of mastery in his voice this time, and a hint of growing anger. The blacks moved uneasily, like a herd of cattle, at the sound of his voice. But not one spoke. All eyes, however, were staring at him in certitude of expectancy. Something was about to happen, and they were waiting for it, waiting with the unanimous, unstable mob-mind for the one of them who would make the first action that would precipitate all of them into a common action. Sheldon looked for this one, for such was the one to fear. Directly beneath him he caught sight of the muzzle of a rifle, barely projecting between two black bodies, that was slowly elevating toward him. It was held at the hip by a man in the second row.

"What name you?" Sheldon suddenly shouted, pointing directly at the man who held the gun, who startled and lowered the muzzle.

Sheldon still held the whip hand, and he intended to keep it.

"Clear out, all you fella boys," he ordered. "Clear out and walk along salt water. Savvee!"

95

"Me talk," spoke up a fat and filthy savage whose hairy chest was caked with the unwashed dirt of years.

"Oh, is that you, Telepasse?" the white man queried genially. "You tell 'm boys clear out, and you stop and talk along me."

"Him good fella boy," was the reply. "Him stop along."

"Well, what do you want?" Sheldon asked, striving to hide under assumed carelessness the weakness of concession.

"That fella boy belong along me." The old chief pointed out Gogoomy, whom Sheldon recognized.

"White Mary belong you too much no good," Telepasse went on. "Bang 'm head belong Gogoomy. Gogoomy all the same chief. Bimeby me finish, Gogoomy big fella chief. White Mary bang 'm head. No good. You pay me plenty tobacco, plenty powder, plenty calico."

"You old scoundrel," was Sheldon's comment. An hour before, he had been chuckling over Joan's recital of the episode, and here, an hour later, was Telepasse himself come to collect damages.

"Gogoomy," Sheldon ordered, "what name you walk about here? You get along quarters plenty quick."

"Me stop," was the defiant answer.

"White Mary b'long you bang 'm head," old Telepasse began again. "My word, plenty big fella trouble you no pay."

"You talk along boys," Sheldon said, with increasing irritation. "You tell 'm get to hell along beach. Then I talk with you."

Sheldon felt a slight vibration of the veranda, and knew that Joan had come out and was standing by his side. But he did not dare glance at her. There were too many rifles down below there, and rifles had a way of going off from the hip.

96

Again the veranda vibrated with her moving weight, and he knew that Joan had gone into the house. A minute later she was back beside him. He had never seen her smoke, and it struck him as peculiar that she should be smoking now. Then he guessed the reason. With a quick glance, he noted the hand at her side, and in it the familiar, paper-wrapped dynamite. He noted, also, the end of fuse, split properly, into which had been inserted the head of a wax match.

"Telepasse, you old reprobate, tell 'm boys clear out along beach. My word, I no gammon along you."

"Me no gammon," said the chief. "Me want 'm pay white Mary bang 'm head b'long Gogoomy."

"I'll come down there and bang 'm head b'long you," Sheldon replied, leaning toward the railing as if about to leap over.

An angry murmur arose, and the blacks surged restlessly. The muzzles of many guns were rising from the hips. Joan was pressing the lighted end of the cigarette to the fuse. A Snider went off with the roar of a bomb-gun, and Sheldon heard a pane of window-glass crash behind him. At the same moment Joan flung the dynamite, the fuse hissing and spluttering, into the thick of the blacks. They scattered back in too great haste to do any more shooting. Satan, aroused by the one shot, was snarling and panting to be let out. Joan heard, and ran to let him out; and thereat the tragedy was averted, and the comedy began.

Rifles and spears were dropped or flung aside in a wild scramble for the protection of the cocoanut palms. Satan multiplied himself. Never had he been free to tear and rend such a quantity of black flesh before, and he bit and snapped and rushed the flying legs till the last pair were above his head. All were treed except Telepasse, who was too old and fat, and he lay prone and without movement where he had fallen; while Satan, with too great a heart to worry an enemy that did not move, dashed frantically from tree to tree, barking and springing at those who clung on lowest down.

"I fancy you need a lesson or two in inserting fuses," Sheldon remarked dryly.

Joan's eyes were scornful.

"There was no detonator on it," she said. "Besides, the detonator is not yet manufactured that will explode that charge. It's only a bottle of chlorodyne."

She put her fingers into her mouth, and Sheldon winced as he saw her blow, like a boy, a sharp, imperious whistle—the call she always used for her sailors, and that always made him wince.

"They're gone up the Balesuna, shooting fish," he explained. "But there comes Oleson with his boat's-crew. He's an old war-horse when he gets started. See him banging the boys. They don't pull fast enough for him."

"And now what's to be done?" she asked. "You've treed your game, but you can't keep it treed."

"No; but I can teach them a lesson."

Sheldon walked over to the big bell.

"It is all right," he replied to her gesture of protest. "My boys are practically all bushmen, while these chaps are salt-water men, and there's no love lost between them. You watch the fun."

He rang a general call, and by the time the two hundred labourers trooped into the compound Satan was once more penned in the living-room, complaining to high heaven at his abominable treatment. The plantation hands were dancing war-dances around the base of every tree and filling the air with abuse and vituperation of their hereditary enemies. The skipper of the *Flibberty-Gibbet* arrived in the thick of it, in the first throes of oncoming fever, staggering as he walked, and shivering so severely that he could scarcely hold the rifle he carried. His face was ghastly blue, his teeth clicked and chattered, and the violent sunshine through which he walked could not warm him.

"I'll s-s-sit down, and k-k-keep a guard on 'em," he chattered. "D-d-dash it all, I always g-get f-fever when there's any excitement. W-w-wh-what are you going to do?"

"Gather up the guns first of all."

Under Sheldon's direction the house-boys and gang-bosses collected the scattered arms and piled them in a heap on the veranda. The modern rifles, stolen from Lunga, Sheldon set aside; the Sniders he smashed into fragments; the pile of spears, clubs, and tomahawks he presented to Joan.

"A really unique addition to your collection," he smiled; "picked up right on the battlefield."

Down on the beach he built a bonfire out of the contents of the canoes, his blacks smashing, breaking, and looting everything they laid hands on. The canoes themselves, splintered and broken, filled with sand and coral-boulders, were towed out to ten fathoms of water and sunk.

"Ten fathoms will be deep enough for them to work in," Sheldon said, as they walked back to the compound.

Here a Saturnalia had broken loose. The war-songs and dances were more unrestrained, and, from abuse, the plantation blacks had turned to pelting their helpless foes with pieces of wood, handfuls of pebbles, and chunks of coral-rock. And the seventy-five lusty cannibals clung stoically to their tree-perches, enduring the rain of missiles and snarling down promises of vengeance.

"There'll be wars for forty years on Malaita on account of this," Sheldon laughed. "But I always fancy old Telepasse will never again attempt to rush a plantation."

"Eh, you old scoundrel," he added, turning to the old chief, who sat gibbering in impotent rage at the foot of the steps. "Now head belong you bang 'm too. Come on, Miss Lackland, bang 'm just once. It will be the crowning indignity."

"Ugh, he's too dirty. I'd rather give him a bath. Here, you, Adamu Adam, give this devil-devil a wash. Soap and water! Fill that wash-tub. Ornfiri, run and fetch 'm scrub-brush."

The Tahitians, back from their fishing and grinning at the bedlam of the compound, entered into the joke.

"*Tambo*! *Tambo*!" shrieked the cannibals from the trees, appalled at so awful a desecration, as they saw their chief tumbled into the tub and the sacred dirt rubbed and soused from his body.

Joan, who had gone into the bungalow, tossed down a strip of white calico, in which old Telepasse was promptly wrapped, and he stood forth, resplendent and purified, withal he still spat and strangled from the soap-suds with which Noa Noah had gargled his throat.

The house-boys were directed to fetch handcuffs, and, one by one, the Lunga runaways were haled down out of their trees and made fast. Sheldon ironed them in pairs, and ran a steel chain through the links of the irons. Gogoomy was given a lecture for his mutinous conduct and locked up for the afternoon. Then Sheldon rewarded the plantation hands with an afternoon's holiday, and, when they had withdrawn from the compound, permitted the Port Adams men to descend from the trees. And all afternoon he and Joan loafed in the cool of the veranda and watched them diving down and emptying their sunken canoes of the sand and rocks. It was twilight when they embarked and paddled away with a few broken paddles. A breeze had sprung up, and the *Flibberty-Gibbet* had already sailed for Lunga to return the runaways.

CHAPTER XII—MR. MORGAN AND MR. RAFF

Sheldon was back in the plantation superintending the building of a bridge, when the schooner *Malakula* ran in close and dropped anchor. Joan watched the taking in of sail and the swinging out of the boat with a sailor's interest, and herself met the two men who came ashore. While one of the house-boys ran to fetch Sheldon, she had the visitors served with whisky and soda, and sat and talked with them.

They seemed awkward and constrained in her presence, and she caught first one and then the other looking at her with secret curiosity. She felt that they were weighing her, appraising her, and for the first time the anomalous position she occupied on Berande sank sharply home to her. On the other hand, they puzzled her. They were neither traders nor sailors of any type she had known. Nor did they talk like gentlemen, despite the fact that there was nothing offensive in their bearing and that the veneer of ordinary social nicety was theirs. Undoubtedly, they were men of affairs—business men of a sort; but what affairs should they have in the Solomons, and what business on Berande? The elder one, Morgan, was a huge man, bronzed and moustached, with a deep bass voice and an almost guttural speech, and the other, Raff, was slight and effeminate, with nervous hands and watery, washed-out gray eyes, who spoke with a faint indefinable accent that was hauntingly reminiscent of the Cockney, and that was yet not Cockney of any brand she had ever encountered. Whatever they were, they were self-made men, she concluded; and she felt the impulse to shudder at thought of falling into their hands in a business way. There, they would be merciless.

She watched Sheldon closely when he arrived, and divined that he was not particularly delighted to see them. But see them he must, and so pressing was the need that, after a little perfunctory general conversation, he led the two men into the stuffy office. Later in the afternoon, she asked Lalaperu where they had gone.

"My word," quoth Lalaperu; "plenty walk about, plenty look 'm. Look 'm tree; look 'm ground belong tree; look 'm all fella bridge; look 'm copra-house; look 'm grass-land; look 'm river; look 'm whale-boat—my word, plenty big fella look 'm too much."

"What fella man them two fella?" she queried.

"Big fella marster along white man," was the extent of his description.

But Joan decided that they were men of importance in the Solomons, and that their examination of the plantation and of its accounts was of sinister significance.

At dinner no word was dropped that gave a hint of their errand. The conversation was on general topics; but Joan could not help noticing the troubled, absent expression that occasionally came into Sheldon's eyes. After coffee, she left them; and at midnight, from across the compound, she could hear the low murmur of their voices and see glowing the fiery ends of their cigars. Up early herself, she found they had already departed on another tramp over the plantation.

"What you think?" she asked Viaburi.

"Sheldon marster he go along finish short time little bit," was the answer.

"What you think?" she asked Ornfiri.

"Sheldon marster big fella walk about along Sydney. Yes, me t'ink so. He finish along Berande."

All day the examination of the plantation and the discussion went on; and all day the skipper of the *Malakula* sent urgent messages ashore for the two men to hasten. It was not until sunset that they went down to the boat, and even then a final talk of nearly an hour took place on the beach. Sheldon was combating something—that she could plainly see; and that his two visitors were not giving in she could also plainly see.

"What name?" she asked lightly, when Sheldon sat down to dinner.

He looked at her and smiled, but it was a very wan and wistful smile.

"My word," she went on. "One big fella talk. Sun he go down—talk-talk; sun he come up—talk-talk; all the time talk-talk. What name that fella talk-talk?

"Oh, nothing much." He shrugged his shoulders. "They were trying to buy Berande, that was all."

She looked at him challengingly.

"It must have been more than that. It was you who wanted to sell."

"Indeed, no, Miss Lackland; I assure you that I am far from desiring to sell."

"Don't let us fence about it," she urged. "Let it be straight talk between us. You're in trouble. I'm not a fool. Tell me. Besides, I may be able to help, to—to suggest something."

In the pause that followed, he seemed to debate, not so much whether he would tell her, as how to begin to tell her.

"I'm American, you see," she persisted, "and our American heritage is a large parcel of business sense. I don't like it myself, but I know I've got it—at least more than you have. Let us talk it over and find a way out. How much do you owe?"

"A thousand pounds, and a few trifles over—small bills, you know. Then, too, thirty of the boys finish their time next week, and their balances will average ten pounds each. But what is the need of bothering your head with it? Really, you know—"

"What is Berande worth?—right now?"

"Whatever Morgan and Raff are willing to pay for it." A glance at her hurt expression decided him. "Hughie and I have sunk eight thousand pounds in it, and our time. It is a good property, and worth more than that. But it has three years to run before its returns begin to come in. That is why

Hughie and I engaged in trading and recruiting. The *Jessie* and our stations came very near to paying the running expenses of Berande."

"And Morgan and Raff offered you what?"

"A thousand pounds clear, after paying all bills."

"The thieves!" she cried.

"No, they're good business men, that is all. As they told me, a thing is worth no more than one is willing to pay or to receive."

"And how much do you need to carry on Berande for three years?" Joan hurried on.

"Two hundred boys at six pounds a year means thirty-six hundred pounds—that's the main item."

"My, how cheap labour does mount up! Thirty-six hundred pounds, eighteen thousand dollars, just for a lot of cannibals! Yet the place is good security. You could go down to Sydney and raise the money."

He shook his head.

"You can't get them to look at plantations down there. They've been taken in too often. But I do hate to give the place up—more for Hughie's sake, I swear, than my own. He was bound up in it. You see, he was a persistent chap, and hated to acknowledge defeat. It—it makes me uncomfortable to think of it myself. We were running slowly behind, but with the *Jessie* we hoped to muddle through in some fashion."

"You were muddlers, the pair of you, without doubt. But you needn't sell to Morgan and Raff. I shall go down to Sydney on the next steamer, and I'll come back in a second-hand schooner. I should be able to buy one for five or six thousand dollars—"

He held up his hand in protest, but she waved it aside.

"I may manage to freight a cargo back as well. At any rate, the schooner will take over the *Jessie*'s business. You can make your arrangements accordingly, and have plenty of work for her when I get back. I'm going to become a partner in Berande to the extent of my bag of sovereigns—I've got over fifteen hundred of them, you know. We'll draw up an agreement right now—that is, with your permission, and I know you won't refuse it."

He looked at her with good-natured amusement.

"You know I sailed here all the way from Tahiti in order to become a planter," she insisted. "You know what my plans were. Now I've changed them, that's all. I'd rather be a part owner of Berande and get my returns in three years, than break ground on Pari-Sulay and wait seven years."

"And this—er—this schooner. . . . " Sheldon changed his mind and stopped.

"Yes, go on."

"You won't be angry?" he queried.

"No, no; this is business. Go on."

"You—er—you would run her yourself?—be the captain, in short?—and go recruiting on Malaita?"

"Certainly. We would save the cost of a skipper. Under an agreement you would be credited with a manager's salary, and I with a captain's. It's quite simple. Besides, if you won't let me be your partner, I shall buy Pari-Sulay, get a much smaller vessel, and run her myself. So what is the difference?"

"The difference?—why, all the difference in the world. In the case of Pari-Sulay you would be on an independent venture. You could turn cannibal for all I could interfere in the matter. But on Berande, you would be my partner, and then I would be responsible. And of course I couldn't permit you, as my partner, to be skipper of a recruiter. I tell you, the thing is what I would not permit any sister or wife of mine—"

"But I'm not going to be your wife, thank goodness—only your partner."

"Besides, it's all ridiculous," he held on steadily. "Think of the situation. A man and a woman, both young, partners on an isolated plantation. Why, the only practical way out would be that I'd have to marry you—"

"Mine was a business proposition, not a marriage proposal," she interrupted, coldly angry. "I wonder if somewhere in this world there is one man who could accept me for a comrade."

"But you are a woman just the same," he began, "and there are certain conventions, certain decencies—"

She sprang up and stamped her foot.

"Do you know what I'd like to say?" she demanded.

"Yes," he smiled, "you'd like to say, 'Damn petticoats!'"

She nodded her head ruefully.

"That's what I wanted to say, but it sounds different on your lips. It sounds as though you meant it yourself, and that you meant it because of me."

"Well, I am going to bed. But do, please, think over my proposition, and let me know in the morning. There's no use in my discussing it now. You make me so angry. You are cowardly, you know, and very egotistic. You are afraid of what other fools will say. No matter how honest your motives, if others criticized your actions your feelings would be hurt. And you think more about your own wretched feelings than you do about mine. And then, being a coward—all men are at heart cowards—you disguise your cowardice by calling it chivalry. I thank heaven that I was not born a man. Goodnight. Do think it over. And don't be foolish. What Berande needs is good American hustle. You don't know what that is. You are a muddler. Besides, you are enervated. I'm fresh to the climate. Let me be your partner, and you'll see me rattle the dry bones of the Solomons. Confess, I've rattled yours already."

"I should say so," he answered. "Really, you know, you have. I never received such a dressing-down in my life. If any one had ever told me that I'd be a party even to the present situation. . . . Yes, I confess, you have rattled my dry bones pretty considerably."

"But that is nothing to the rattling they are going to get," she assured him, as he rose and took her hand. "Good-night. And do, do give me a rational decision in the morning."

CHAPTER XIII—THE LOGIC OF YOUTH

"I wish I knew whether you are merely headstrong, or whether you really intend to be a Solomon planter," Sheldon said in the morning, at breakfast.

"I wish you were more adaptable," Joan retorted. "You have more preconceived notions than any man I ever met. Why in the name of common sense, in the name of . . . fair play, can't you get it into your head that I am different from the women you have known, and treat me accordingly? You surely ought to know I am different. I sailed my own schooner here— skipper, if you please. I came here to make my living. You know that; I've told you often enough. It was Dad's plan, and I'm carrying it out, just as you are trying to carry out your Hughie's plan. Dad started to sail and sail until he could find the proper islands for planting. He died, and I sailed and sailed until I arrived here. Well,"—she shrugged her shoulders—"the schooner is at the bottom of the sea. I can't sail any farther, therefore I remain here. And a planter I shall certainly be."

"You see—" he began.

"I haven't got to the point," she interrupted. "Looking back on my conduct from the moment I first set foot on your beach, I can see no false pretence that I have made about myself or my intentions. I was my natural self to you from the first. I told you my plans; and yet you sit there and calmly tell me that you don't know whether I really intend to become a planter, or whether it is all obstinacy and pretence. Now let me assure you, for the last time, that I really and truly shall become a planter, thanks to you, or in spite of you. Do you want me for a partner?"

"But do you realize that I would be looked upon as the most foolish jackanapes in the South Seas if I took a young girl like you in with me here on Berande?" he asked.

"No; decidedly not. But there you are again, worrying about what idiots and the generally evil-minded will think of you. I should have thought you had learned self-reliance on Berande, instead of needing to lean upon the moral support of every whisky-guzzling worthless South Sea vagabond."

He smiled, and said,—

"Yes, that is the worst of it. You are unanswerable. Yours is the logic of youth, and no man can answer that. The facts of life can, but they have no place in the logic of youth. Youth must try to live according to its logic. That is the only way to learn better."

"There is no harm in trying?" she interjected.

"But there is. That is the very point. The facts always smash youth's logic, and they usually smash youth's heart, too. It's like platonic friendships and . . . and all such things; they are all right in theory, but they won't work in practice. I used to believe in such things once. That is why I am here in the Solomons at present."

Joan was impatient. He saw that she could not understand. Life was too clearly simple to her. It was only the youth who was arguing with him, the youth with youth's pure-minded and invincible reasoning. Hers was only the boy's soul in a woman's body. He looked at her flushed, eager face, at the great ropes of hair coiled on the small head, at the rounded lines of the figure showing plainly through the home-made gown, and at the eyes—boy's eyes, under cool, level brows—and he wondered why a being that was so much beautiful woman should be no woman at all. Why in the deuce was she not carroty-haired, or cross-eyed, or hare-lipped?

"Suppose we do become partners on Berande," he said, at the same time experiencing a feeling of fright at the prospect that was tangled with a contradictory feeling of charm, "either I'll fall in love with you, or you with me. Propinquity is dangerous, you know. In fact, it is propinquity that usually gives the facer to the logic of youth."

"If you think I came to the Solomons to get married—" she began wrathfully. "Well, there are better men in Hawaii, that's all. Really, you know, the way you harp on that one string would lead an unprejudiced listener to conclude that you are prurient-minded—"

She stopped, appalled. His face had gone red and white with such abruptness as to startle her. He was patently very angry. She sipped the last of her coffee, and arose, saying,—

"I'll wait until you are in a better temper before taking up the discussion again. That is what's the matter with you. You get angry too easily. Will you come swimming? The tide is just right."

"If she were a man I'd bundle her off the plantation root and crop, whale-boat, Tahitian sailors, sovereigns, and all," he muttered to himself after she had left the room.

But that was the trouble. She was not a man, and where would she go, and what would happen to her?

He got to his feet, lighted a cigarette, and her Stetson hat, hanging on the wall over her revolver-belt, caught his eye. That was the devil of it, too. He did not want her to go. After all, she had not grown up yet. That was why her logic hurt. It was only the logic of youth, but it could hurt damnably at times. At any rate, he would resolve upon one thing: never again would he lose his temper with her. She was a child; he must remember that. He sighed heavily. But why in reasonableness had such a child been incorporated in such a woman's form?

And as he continued to stare at her hat and think, the hurt he had received passed away, and he found himself cudgelling his brains for some way out of the muddle—for some method by which she could remain on Berande. A chaperone! Why not? He could send to Sydney on the first steamer for one. He could—

Her trilling laughter smote upon his reverie, and he stepped to the screen-door, through which he could see her running down the path to the beach. At her heels ran two of her sailors, Papehara and Mahameme, in scarlet lava-lavas, with naked sheath-knives gleaming in their belts. It was another sample of her wilfulness. Despite entreaties and commands, and warnings of the danger from sharks, she persisted in swimming at any and all times, and by special preference, it seemed to him, immediately after eating.

He watched her take the water, diving cleanly, like a boy, from the end of the little pier; and he watched her strike out with single overhand stroke, her henchmen swimming a dozen feet on either side. He did not have much faith in their ability to beat off a hungry man-eater, though he did believe, implicitly, that their lives would go bravely before hers in case of an attack.

Straight out they swam, their heads growing smaller and smaller. There was a slight, restless heave to the sea, and soon the three heads were disappearing behind it with greater frequency. He strained his eyes to keep them in sight, and finally fetched the telescope on to the veranda. A squall was making over from the direction of Florida; but then, she and her men laughed at squalls and the white choppy sea at such times. She certainly could swim, he had long since concluded. That came of her training in Hawaii. But sharks were sharks, and he had known of more than one good swimmer drowned in a tide-rip.

The squall blackened the sky, beat the ocean white where he had last seen the three heads, and then blotted out sea and sky and everything with its deluge of rain. It passed on, and Berande emerged in the bright sunshine as the three swimmers emerged from the sea. Sheldon slipped inside with the telescope, and through the screen-door watched her run up the path, shaking down her hair as she ran, to the fresh-water shower under the house.

On the veranda that afternoon he broached the proposition of a chaperone as delicately as he could, explaining the necessity at Berande for such a body, a housekeeper to run the boys and the storeroom, and perform divers other useful functions. When he had finished, he waited anxiously for what Joan would say.

"Then you don't like the way I've been managing the house?" was her first objection. And next, brushing his attempted explanations aside, "One of two things would happen. Either I should cancel our partnership agreement and go away, leaving you to get another chaperone to chaperone your chaperone; or else I'd take the old hen out in the whale-boat and drown her. Do you imagine for one moment that I sailed my schooner down here to this raw edge of the earth in order to put myself under a chaperone?"

"But really . . . er . . . you know a chaperone is a necessary evil," he objected.

"We've got along very nicely so far without one. Did I have one on the *Miélé*? And yet I was the only woman on board. There are only three things I am afraid of—bumble-bees, scarlet fever, and chaperones. Ugh! the clucking, evil-minded monsters, finding wrong in everything, seeing sin in the most innocent actions, and suggesting sin—yes, causing sin—by their diseased imaginings."

"Phew!" Sheldon leaned back from the table in mock fear.

"You needn't worry about your bread and butter," he ventured. "If you fail at planting, you would be sure to succeed as a writer—novels with a purpose, you know."

"I didn't think there were persons in the Solomons who needed such books," she retaliated. "But you are certainly one—you and your custodians of virtue."

He winced, but Joan rattled on with the platitudinous originality of youth.

"As if anything good were worth while when it has to be guarded and put in leg-irons and handcuffs in order to keep it good. Your desire for a chaperone as much as implies that I am that sort of creature. I prefer to be good because it is good to be good, rather than because I can't be bad because some argus-eyed old frump won't let me have a chance to be bad."

"But it—it is not that," he put in. "It is what others will think."

"Let them think, the nasty-minded wretches! It is because men like you are afraid of the nasty-minded that you allow their opinions to rule you."

"I am afraid you are a female Shelley," he replied; "and as such, you really drive me to become your partner in order to protect you."

"If you take me as a partner in order to protect me . . . I . . . I shan't be your partner, that's all. You'll drive me into buying Pari-Sulay yet."

"All the more reason—" he attempted.

"Do you know what I'll do?" she demanded. "I'll find some man in the Solomons who won't want to protect me."

Sheldon could not conceal the shock her words gave him.

"You don't mean that, you know," he pleaded.

"I do; I really do. I am sick and tired of this protection dodge. Don't forget for a moment that I am perfectly able to take care of myself. Besides, I have eight of the best protectors in the world—my sailors."

"You should have lived a thousand years ago," he laughed, "or a thousand years hence. You are very primitive, and equally super-modern. The twentieth century is no place for you."

"But the Solomon Islands are. You were living like a savage when I came along and found you—eating nothing but tinned meat and scones that would have ruined the digestion of a camel. Anyway, I've remedied that; and since we are to be partners, it will stay remedied. You won't die of malnutrition, be sure of that."

"If we enter into partnership," he announced, "it must be thoroughly understood that you are not allowed to run the schooner. You can go down to Sydney and buy her, but a skipper we must have—"

"At so much additional expense, and most likely a whisky-drinking, irresponsible, and incapable man to boot. Besides, I'd have the business more at heart than any man we could hire. As for capability, I tell you I can sail all around the average broken captain or promoted able seaman you find in the South Seas. And you know I am a navigator."

"But being my partner," he said coolly, "makes you none the less a lady."

"Thank you for telling me that my contemplated conduct is unladylike."

She arose, tears of anger and mortification in her eyes, and went over to the phonograph.

"I wonder if all men are as ridiculous as you?" she said.

He shrugged his shoulders and smiled. Discussion was useless—he had learned that; and he was resolved to keep his temper. And before the day was out she capitulated. She was to go to Sydney on the first steamer, purchase the schooner, and sail back with an island skipper on board. And then she inveigled Sheldon into agreeing that she could take occasional cruises in the islands, though he was adamant when it came to a recruiting trip on Malaita. That was the one thing barred.

And after it was all over, and a terse and business-like agreement (by her urging) drawn up and signed, Sheldon paced up and down for a full hour, meditating upon how many different kinds of a fool he had made of himself. It was an impossible situation, and yet no more impossible than the previous one, and no more impossible than the one that would have obtained had she gone off on her own and bought Pari-Sulay. He had never seen a more independent woman who stood more in need of a protector than this boy-minded girl who had landed on his beach with eight picturesque savages, a long-barrelled revolver, a bag of gold, and a gaudy merchandise of imagined romance and adventure.

He had never read of anything to compare with it. The fictionists, as usual, were exceeded by fact. The whole thing was too preposterous to be true. He gnawed his moustache and smoked cigarette after cigarette. Satan, back from a prowl around the compound, ran up to him and touched his hand with a cold, damp nose. Sheldon caressed the animal's ears, then threw himself into a chair and laughed heartily. What would the Commissioner of the Solomons think? What would his people at home think? And in the one breath he was glad that the partnership had been effected and sorry that Joan Lackland had ever come to the Solomons. Then he went inside and looked at himself in a hand-mirror. He studied the reflection long and thoughtfully and wonderingly.

CHAPTER XIV—THE MARTHA

They were deep in a game of billiards the next morning, after the eleven o'clock breakfast, when Viaburi entered and announced,—

"Big fella schooner close up."

Even as he spoke, they heard the rumble of chain through hawse-pipe, and from the veranda saw a big black-painted schooner, swinging to her just-caught anchor.

"It's a Yankee," Joan cried. "See that bow! Look at that elliptical stern! Ah, I thought so—" as the Stars and Stripes fluttered to the mast-head.

Noa Noah, at Sheldon's direction, ran the Union Jack up the flagstaff.

"Now what is an American vessel doing down here?" Joan asked. "It's not a yacht, though I'll wager she can sail. Look! Her name! What is it?"

"*Martha,* San Francisco," Sheldon read, looking through the telescope. "It's the first Yankee I ever heard of in the Solomons. They are coming ashore, whoever they are. And, by Jove, look at those men at the oars. It's an all-white crew. Now what reason brings them here?"

"They're not proper sailors," Joan commented. "I'd be ashamed of a crew of black-boys that pulled in such fashion. Look at that fellow in the bow—the one just jumping out; he'd be more at home on a cow-pony."

The boat's-crew scattered up and down the beach, ranging about with eager curiosity, while the two men who had sat in the stern-sheets opened the gate and came up the path to the bungalow. One of them, a tall and slender man, was clad in white ducks that fitted him like a semi-military uniform. The other man, in nondescript garments that were both of the sea and shore, and that must have been uncomfortably hot, slouched and shambled like an overgrown ape. To complete the illusion, his face seemed to sprout in all directions with a dense, bushy mass of red whiskers, while his eyes were small and sharp and restless.

Sheldon, who had gone to the head of the steps, introduced them to Joan. The bewhiskered individual, who looked like a Scotsman, had the Teutonic name of Von Blix, and spoke with a strong American accent. The tall man in the well-fitting ducks, who gave the English name of Tudor—John Tudor—talked purely-enunciated English such as any cultured American would talk, save for the fact that it was most delicately and subtly touched by a faint German accent. Joan decided that she had been helped to identify the accent by the short German-looking moustache that did not conceal the mouth and its full red lips, which would have formed a Cupid's bow but for some harshness or severity of spirit that had moulded them masculinely.

Von Blix was rough and boorish, but Tudor was gracefully easy in everything he did, or looked, or said. His blue eyes sparkled and flashed, his clean-cut mobile features were an index to his slightest shades of feeling and expression. He bubbled with enthusiasms, and his faintest smile or lightest laugh seemed spontaneous and genuine. But it was only occasionally at first that he spoke, for Von Blix told their story and stated their errand.

They were on a gold-hunting expedition. He was the leader, and Tudor was his lieutenant. All hands—and there were twenty-eight—were shareholders, in varying proportions, in the adventure. Several were sailors, but the large majority were miners, culled from all the camps from Mexico to the Arctic Ocean. It was the old and ever-untiring pursuit of gold, and they had come to the Solomons to get it. Part of them, under the leadership of Tudor, were to go up the Balesuna and penetrate the mountainous heart of Guadalcanal, while the *Martha*, under Von Blix, sailed away for Malaita to put through similar exploration.

"And so," said Von Blix, "for Mr. Tudor's expedition we must have some black-boys. Can we get them from you?"

"Of course we will pay," Tudor broke in. "You have only to charge what you consider them worth. You pay them six pounds a year, don't you?"

"In the first place we can't spare them," Sheldon answered. "We are short of them on the plantation as it is."

"We?" Tudor asked quickly. "Then you are a firm or a partnership? I understood at Guvutu that you were alone, that you had lost your partner."

Sheldon inclined his head toward Joan, and as he spoke she felt that he had become a trifle stiff.

"Miss Lackland has become interested in the plantation since then. But to return to the boys. We can't spare them, and besides, they would be of little use. You couldn't get them to accompany you beyond Binu, which is a short day's work with the boats from here. They are Malaita-men, and they are afraid of being eaten. They would desert you at the first opportunity. You could get the Binu men to accompany you another day's journey, through the grass-lands, but at the first roll of the foothills look for them to turn back. They likewise are disinclined to being eaten."

"Is it as bad as that?" asked Von Blix.

"The interior of Guadalcanal has never been explored," Sheldon explained. "The bushmen are as wild men as are to be found anywhere in the world to-day. I have never seen one. I have never seen a man who has seen one. They never come down to the coast, though their scouting parties occasionally eat a coast native who has wandered too far inland. Nobody knows anything about them. They don't even use tobacco—have never learned its use. The Austrian expedition—scientists, you know—got part way in before it was cut to pieces. The monument is up the beach there several miles. Only one man got back to the coast to tell the tale. And now you have all I or any other man knows of the inside of Guadalcanal."

"But gold—have you heard of gold?" Tudor asked impatiently. "Do you know anything about gold?"

Sheldon smiled, while the two visitors hung eagerly upon his words.

"You can go two miles up the Balesuna and wash colours from the gravel. I've done it often. There is gold undoubtedly back in the mountains."

Tudor and Von Blix looked triumphantly at each other.

"Old Wheatsheaf's yarn was true, then," Tudor said, and Von Blix nodded. "And if Malaita turns out as well—"

117

Tudor broke off and looked at Joan.

"It was the tale of this old beachcomber that brought us here," he explained. "Von Blix befriended him and was told the secret." He turned and addressed Sheldon. "I think we shall prove that white men have been through the heart of Guadalcanal long before the time of the Austrian expedition."

Sheldon shrugged his shoulders.

"We have never heard of it down here," he said simply. Then he addressed Von Blix. "As to the boys, you couldn't use them farther than Binu, and I'll lend you as many as you want as far as that. How many of your party are going, and how soon will you start?"

"Ten," said Tudor; "nine men and myself."

"And you should be able to start day after to-morrow," Von Blix said to him. "The boats should practically be knocked together this afternoon. To-morrow should see the outfit portioned and packed. As for the *Martha*, Mr. Sheldon, we'll rush the stuff ashore this afternoon and sail by sundown."

As the two men returned down the path to their boat, Sheldon regarded Joan quizzically.

"There's romance for you," he said, "and adventure—gold-hunting among the cannibals."

"A title for a book," she cried. "Or, better yet, 'Gold-Hunting Among the Head-Hunters.' My! wouldn't it sell!"

"And now aren't you sorry you became a cocoanut planter?" he teased. "Think of investing in such an adventure."

"If I did," she retorted, "Von Blix wouldn't be finicky about my joining in the cruise to Malaita."

"I don't doubt but what he would jump at it."

"What do you think of them?" she asked.

"Oh, old Von Blix is all right, a solid sort of chap in his fashion; but Tudor is fly-away—too much on the surface, you know. If it came to being wrecked on a desert island, I'd prefer Von Blix."

"I don't quite understand," Joan objected. "What have you against Tudor?"

"You remember Browning's 'Last Duchess'?"

She nodded.

"Well, Tudor reminds me of her—"

"But she was delightful."

"So she was. But she was a woman. One expects something different from a man—more control, you know, more restraint, more deliberation. A man must be more solid, more solid and steady-going and less effervescent. A man of Tudor's type gets on my nerves. One demands more repose from a man."

Joan felt that she did not quite agree with his judgment; and, somehow, Sheldon caught her feeling and was disturbed. He remembered noting how her eyes had brightened as she talked with the newcomer—confound it all, was he getting jealous? he asked himself. Why shouldn't her eyes brighten? What concern was it of his?

A second boat had been lowered, and the outfit of the shore party was landed rapidly. A dozen of the crew put the knocked-down boats together on the beach. There were five of these craft—lean and narrow, with flaring sides, and remarkably long. Each was equipped with three paddles and several iron-shod poles.

"You chaps certainly seem to know river-work," Sheldon told one of the carpenters.

The man spat a mouthful of tobacco-juice into the white sand, and answered,—

119

"We use 'em in Alaska. They're modelled after the Yukon poling-boats, and you can bet your life they're crackerjacks. This creek'll be a snap alongside some of them Northern streams. Five hundred pounds in one of them boats, an' two men can snake it along in a way that'd surprise you."

At sunset the *Martha* broke out her anchor and got under way, dipping her flag and saluting with a bomb gun. The Union Jack ran up and down the staff, and Sheldon replied with his brass signal-cannon. The miners pitched their tents in the compound, and cooked on the beach, while Tudor dined with Joan and Sheldon.

Their guest seemed to have been everywhere and seen everything and met everybody, and, encouraged by Joan, his talk was largely upon his own adventures. He was an adventurer of adventurers, and by his own account had been born into adventure. Descended from old New England stock, his father a consul-general, he had been born in Germany, in which country he had received his early education and his accent. Then, still a boy, he had rejoined his father in Turkey, and accompanied him later to Persia, his father having been appointed Minister to that country.

Tudor had always been a wanderer, and with facile wit and quick vivid description he leaped from episode and place to episode and place, relating his experiences seemingly not because they were his, but for the sake of their bizarreness and uniqueness, for the unusual incident or the laughable situation. He had gone through South American revolutions, been a Rough Rider in Cuba, a scout in South Africa, a war correspondent in the Russo-Japanese war. He had *mushed* dogs in the Klondike, washed gold from the sands of Nome, and edited a newspaper in San Francisco. The President of the United States was his friend. He was equally at home in the clubs of London and the Continent, the Grand Hotel at Yokohama, and the selector's shanties in the Never-Never country. He had shot big game in Siam, pearled in the Paumotus, visited Tolstoy, seen the Passion Play, and crossed the Andes on mule-back; while he was a living directory of the fever holes of West Africa.

Sheldon leaned back in his chair on the veranda, sipping his coffee and listening. In spite of himself he felt touched by the charm of the man who had led so varied a life. And yet Sheldon was not comfortable. It seemed to him that the man addressed himself particularly to Joan. His words and smiles were directed impartially toward both of them, yet Sheldon was certain, had the two men of them been alone, that the conversation would have been along different lines. Tudor had seen the effect on Joan and deliberately continued the flow of reminiscence, netting her in the glamour of romance. Sheldon watched her rapt attention, listened to her spontaneous laughter, quick questions, and passing judgments, and felt grow within him the dawning consciousness that he loved her.

So he was very quiet and almost sad, though at times he was aware of a distinct irritation against his guest, and he even speculated as to what percentage of Tudor's tale was true and how any of it could be proved or disproved. In this connection, as if the scene had been prepared by a clever playwright, Utami came upon the veranda to report to Joan the capture of a crocodile in the trap they had made for her.

Tudor's face, illuminated by the match with which he was lighting his cigarette, caught Utami's eye, and Utami forgot to report to his mistress.

"Hello, Tudor," he said, with a familiarity that startled Sheldon.

The Polynesian's hand went out, and Tudor, shaking it, was staring into his face.

"Who is it?" he asked. "I can't see you."

"Utami."

"And who the dickens is Utami? Where did I ever meet you, my man?"

"You no forget the *Huahine*?" Utami chided. "Last time *Huahine* sail?"

Tudor gripped the Tahitian's hand a second time and shook it with genuine heartiness.

"There was only one kanaka who came out of the *Huahine* that last voyage, and that kanaka was Joe. The deuce take it, man, I'm glad to see you, though I never heard your new name before."

121

"Yes, everybody speak me Joe along the *Huahine*. Utami my name all the time, just the same."

"But what are you doing here?" Tudor asked, releasing the sailor's hand and leaning eagerly forward.

"Me sail along Missie Lackalanna her schooner *Miélé*. We go Tahiti, Raiatea, Tahaa, Bora-Bora, Manua, Tutuila, Apia, Savaii, and Fiji Islands—plenty Fiji Islands. Me stop along Missie Lackalanna in Solomons. Very soon she catch other schooner."

"He and I were the two survivors of the wreck of the *Huahine*," Tudor explained to the others. "Fifty-seven all told on board when we sailed from Huapa, and Joe and I were the only two that ever set foot on land again. Hurricane, you know, in the Paumotus. That was when I was after pearls."

"And you never told me, Utami, that you'd been wrecked in a hurricane," Joan said reproachfully.

The big Tahitian shifted his weight and flashed his teeth in a conciliating smile.

"Me no t'ink nothing 't all," he said.

He half-turned, as if to depart, by his manner indicating that he considered it time to go while yet he desired to remain.

"All right, Utami," Tudor said. "I'll see you in the morning and have a yarn."

"He saved my life, the beggar," Tudor explained, as the Tahitian strode away and with heavy softness of foot went down the steps. "Swim! I never met a better swimmer."

And thereat, solicited by Joan, Tudor narrated the wreck of the *Huahine*; while Sheldon smoked and pondered, and decided that whatever the man's shortcomings were, he was at least not a liar.

CHAPTER XV—A DISCOURSE ON MANNERS

The days passed, and Tudor seemed loath to leave the hospitality of Berande. Everything was ready for the start, but he lingered on, spending much time in Joan's company and thereby increasing the dislike Sheldon had taken to him. He went swimming with her, in point of rashness exceeding her; and dynamited fish with her, diving among the hungry ground-sharks and contesting with them for possession of the stunned prey, until he earned the approval of the whole Tahitian crew. Arahu challenged him to tear a fish from a shark's jaws, leaving half to the shark and bringing the other half himself to the surface; and Tudor performed the feat, a flip from the sandpaper hide of the astonished shark scraping several inches of skin from his shoulder. And Joan was delighted, while Sheldon, looking on, realized that here was the hero of her adventure-dreams coming true. She did not care for love, but he felt that if ever she did love it would be that sort of a man—"a man who exhibited," was his way of putting it.

He felt himself handicapped in the presence of Tudor, who had the gift of making a show of all his qualities. Sheldon knew himself for a brave man, wherefore he made no advertisement of the fact. He knew that just as readily as the other would he dive among ground-sharks to save a life, but in that fact he could find no sanction for the foolhardy act of diving among sharks for the half of a fish. The difference between them was that he kept the curtain of his shop window down. Life pulsed steadily and deep in him, and it was not his nature needlessly to agitate the surface so that the world could see the splash he was making. And the effect of the other's amazing exhibitions was to make him retreat more deeply within himself and wrap himself more thickly than ever in the nerveless, stoical calm of his race.

"You are so stupid the last few days," Joan complained to him. "One would think you were sick, or bilious, or something. You don't seem to have an idea in your head above black labour and cocoanuts. What is the matter?"

Sheldon smiled and beat a further retreat within himself, listening the while to Joan and Tudor propounding the theory of the strong arm by which the white man ordered life among the lesser breeds. As he listened Sheldon realized, as by revelation, that that was precisely what he was doing. While they philosophized about it he was living it, placing the strong hand of his race firmly on the shoulders of the lesser breeds that laboured on Berande or menaced it from afar. But why talk about it? he asked himself. It was sufficient to do it and be done with it.

He said as much, dryly and quietly, and found himself involved in a discussion, with Joan and Tudor siding against him, in which a more astounding charge than ever he had dreamed of was made against the very English control and reserve of which he was secretly proud.

"The Yankees talk a lot about what they do and have done," Tudor said, "and are looked down upon by the English as braggarts. But the Yankee is only a child. He does not know effectually how to brag. He talks about it, you see. But the Englishman goes him one better by not talking about it. The Englishman's proverbial lack of bragging is a subtler form of brag after all. It is really clever, as you will agree."

"I never thought of it before," Joan cried. "Of course. An Englishman performs some terrifically heroic exploit, and is very modest and reserved—refuses to talk about it at all—and the effect is that by his silence he as much as says, 'I do things like this every day. It is as easy as rolling off a log. You ought to see the really heroic things I could do if they ever came my way. But this little thing, this little episode—really, don't you know, I fail to see anything in it remarkable or unusual.' As for me, if I went up in a powder explosion, or saved a hundred lives, I'd want all my friends to hear about it, and their friends as well. I'd be prouder than Lucifer over the affair. Confess, Mr. Sheldon, don't you feel proud down inside when you've done something daring or courageous?"

Sheldon nodded.

"Then," she pressed home the point, "isn't disguising that pride under a mask of careless indifference equivalent to telling a lie?"

124

"Yes, it is," he admitted. "But we tell similar lies every day. It is a matter of training, and the English are better trained, that is all. Your countrymen will be trained as well in time. As Mr. Tudor said, the Yankees are young."

"Thank goodness we haven't begun to tell such lies yet!" was Joan's ejaculation.

"Oh, but you have," Sheldon said quickly. "You were telling me a lie of that order only the other day. You remember when you were going up the lantern-halyards hand over hand? Your face was the personification of duplicity."

"It was no such thing."

"Pardon me a moment," he went on. "Your face was as calm and peaceful as though you were reclining in a steamer-chair. To look at your face one would have inferred that carrying the weight of your body up a rope hand over hand was a very commonplace accomplishment—as easy as rolling off a log. And you needn't tell me, Miss Lackland, that you didn't make faces the first time you tried to climb a rope. But, like any circus athlete, you trained yourself out of the face-making period. You trained your face to hide your feelings, to hide the exhausting effort your muscles were making. It was, to quote Mr. Tudor, a subtler exhibition of physical prowess. And that is all our English reserve is—a mere matter of training. Certainly we are proud inside of the things we do and have done, proud as Lucifer—yes, and prouder. But we have grown up, and no longer talk about such things."

"I surrender," Joan cried. "You are not so stupid after all."

"Yes, you have us there," Tudor admitted. "But you wouldn't have had us if you hadn't broken your training rules."

"How do you mean?"

"By talking about it."

Joan clapped her hands in approval. Tudor lighted a fresh cigarette, while Sheldon sat on, imperturbably silent.

"He got you there," Joan challenged. "Why don't you crush him?"

125

"Really, I can't think of anything to say," Sheldon said. "I know my position is sound, and that is satisfactory enough."

"You might retort," she suggested, "that when an adult is with kindergarten children he must descend to kindergarten idioms in order to make himself intelligible. That was why you broke training rules. It was the only way to make us children understand."

"You've deserted in the heat of the battle, Miss Lackland, and gone over to the enemy," Tudor said plaintively.

But she was not listening. Instead, she was looking intently across the compound and out to sea. They followed her gaze, and saw a green light and the loom of a vessel's sails.

"I wonder if it's the *Martha* come back," Tudor hazarded.

"No, the sidelight is too low," Joan answered. "Besides, they've got the sweeps out. Don't you hear them? They wouldn't be sweeping a big vessel like the *Martha*."

"Besides, the *Martha* has a gasoline engine—twenty-five horse-power," Tudor added.

"Just the sort of a craft for us," Joan said wistfully to Sheldon. "I really must see if I can't get a schooner with an engine. I might get a second-hand engine put in."

"That would mean the additional expense of an engineer's wages," he objected.

"But it would pay for itself by quicker passages," she argued; "and it would be as good as insurance. I know. I've knocked about amongst reefs myself. Besides, if you weren't so mediaeval, I could be skipper and save more than the engineer's wages."

He did not reply to her thrust, and she glanced at him. He was looking out over the water, and in the lantern light she noted the lines of his face— strong, stern, dogged, the mouth almost chaste but firmer and thinner-lipped than Tudor's. For the first time she realized the quality of his strength, the calm and quiet of it, its simple integrity and reposeful determination. She glanced quickly at Tudor on the other side of her. It was a handsomer face, one that was more immediately pleasing. But she did not like the mouth. It was made for kissing, and she abhorred kisses. This was not a deliberately achieved concept; it came to her in the form of a faint and vaguely intangible repulsion. For the moment she knew a fleeting doubt of the man. Perhaps Sheldon was right in his judgment of the other. She did not know, and it concerned her little; for boats, and the sea, and the things and happenings of the sea were of far more vital interest to her than men, and the next moment she was staring through the warm tropic darkness at the loom of the sails and the steady green of the moving sidelight, and listening eagerly to the click of the sweeps in the rowlocks. In her mind's eye she could see the straining naked forms of black men bending rhythmically to the work, and somewhere on that strange deck she knew was the inevitable master-man, conning the vessel in to its anchorage, peering at the dim tree-line of the shore, judging the deceitful night-distances, feeling on his cheek the first fans of the land breeze that was even then beginning to blow, weighing, thinking, measuring, gauging the score or more of ever-shifting forces, through which, by which, and in spite of which he directed the steady equilibrium of his course. She knew it because she loved it, and she was alive to it as only a sailor could be.

Twice she heard the splash of the lead, and listened intently for the cry that followed. Once a man's voice spoke, low, imperative, issuing an order, and she thrilled with the delight of it. It was only a direction to the man at the wheel to port his helm. She watched the slight altering of the course, and knew that it was for the purpose of enabling the flat-hauled sails to catch those first fans of the land breeze, and she waited for the same low voice to utter the one word "Steady!" And again she thrilled when it did utter it. Once more the lead splashed, and "Eleven fadom" was the resulting cry. "Let go!" the low voice came to her through the darkness, followed by the surging rumble of the anchor-chain. The clicking of the sheaves in the blocks as the sails ran down, head-sails first, was music to her; and she detected on the instant the jamming of a jib-downhaul, and almost saw the impatient jerk with which the sailor must have cleared it. Nor did she take interest in the two men beside her till both lights, red and green, came into view as the anchor checked the onward way.

Sheldon was wondering as to the identity of the craft, while Tudor persisted in believing it might be the *Martha*.

"It's the *Minerva*," Joan said decidedly.

"How do you know?" Sheldon asked, sceptical of her certitude.

"It's a ketch to begin with. And besides, I could tell anywhere the rattle of her main peak-blocks—they're too large for the halyard."

A dark figure crossed the compound diagonally from the beach gate, where whoever it was had been watching the vessel.

"Is that you, Utami?" Joan called.

"No, Missie; me Matapuu," was the answer.

"What vessel is it?"

"Me t'ink *Minerva*."

Joan looked triumphantly at Sheldon, who bowed.

"If Matapuu says so it must be so," he murmured.

"But when Joan Lackland says so, you doubt," she cried, "just as you doubt her ability as a skipper. But never mind, you'll be sorry some day for all your unkindness. There's the boat lowering now, and in five minutes we'll be shaking hands with Christian Young."

Lalaperu brought out the glasses and cigarettes and the eternal whisky and soda, and before the five minutes were past the gate clicked and Christian Young, tawny and golden, gentle of voice and look and hand, came up the bungalow steps and joined them.

CHAPTER XVI—THE GIRL WHO HAD NOT GROWN UP

News, as usual, Christian Young brought—news of the drinking at Guvutu, where the men boasted that they drank between drinks; news of the new rifles adrift on Ysabel, of the latest murders on Malaita, of Tom Butler's sickness on Santa Ana; and last and most important, news that the *Matambo* had gone on a reef in the Shortlands and would be laid off one run for repairs.

"That means five weeks more before you can sail for Sydney," Sheldon said to Joan.

"And that we are losing precious time," she added ruefully.

"If you want to go to Sydney, the *Upolu* sails from Tulagi to-morrow afternoon," Young said.

"But I thought she was running recruits for the Germans in Samoa," she objected. "At any rate, I could catch her to Samoa, and change at Apia to one of the Weir Line freighters. It's a long way around, but still it would save time."

"This time the *Upolu* is going straight to Sydney," Young explained. "She's going to dry-dock, you see; and you can catch her as late as five to-morrow afternoon—at least, so her first officer told me."

"But I've got to go to Guvutu first." Joan looked at the men with a whimsical expression. "I've some shopping to do. I can't wear these Berande curtains into Sydney. I must buy cloth at Guvutu and make myself a dress during the voyage down. I'll start immediately—in an hour. Lalaperu, you bring 'm one fella Adamu Adam along me. Tell 'm that fella Ornfiri make 'm *kai-kai* take along whale-boat." She rose to her feet, looking at Sheldon. "And you, please, have the boys carry down the whale-boat—my boat, you know. I'll be off in an hour."

Both Sheldon and Tudor looked at their watches.

"It's an all-night row," Sheldon said. "You might wait till morning—"

"And miss my shopping? No, thank you. Besides, the *Upolu* is not a regular passenger steamer, and she is just as liable to sail ahead of time as on time. And from what I hear about those Guvutu sybarites, the best time to shop will be in the morning. And now you'll have to excuse me, for I've got to pack."

"I'll go over with you," Sheldon announced.

"Let me run you over in the *Minerva*," said Young.

She shook her head laughingly.

"I'm going in the whale-boat. One would think, from all your solicitude, that I'd never been away from home before. You, Mr. Sheldon, as my partner, I cannot permit to desert Berande and your work out of a mistaken notion of courtesy. If you won't permit me to be skipper, I won't permit your galivanting over the sea as protector of young women who don't need protection. And as for you, Captain Young, you know very well that you just left Guvutu this morning, that you are bound for Marau, and that you said yourself that in two hours you are getting under way again."

"But may I not see you safely across?" Tudor asked, a pleading note in his voice that rasped on Sheldon's nerves.

"No, no, and again no," she cried. "You've all got your work to do, and so have I. I came to the Solomons to work, not to be escorted about like a doll. For that matter, here's my escort, and there are seven more like him."

Adamu Adam stood beside her, towering above her, as he towered above the three white men. The clinging cotton undershirt he wore could not hide the bulge of his tremendous muscles.

"Look at his fist," said Tudor. "I'd hate to receive a punch from it."

"I don't blame you." Joan laughed reminiscently. "I saw him hit the captain of a Swedish bark on the beach at Levuka, in the Fijis. It was the captain's fault. I saw it all myself, and it was splendid. Adamu only hit him once, and he broke the man's arm. You remember, Adamu?"

The big Tahitian smiled and nodded, his black eyes, soft and deer-like, seeming to give the lie to so belligerent a nature.

"We start in an hour in the whale-boat for Guvutu, big brother," Joan said to him. "Tell your brothers, all of them, so that they can get ready. We catch the *Upolu* for Sydney. You will all come along, and sail back to the Solomons in the new schooner. Take your extra shirts and dungarees along. Plenty cold weather down there. Now run along, and tell them to hurry. Leave the guns behind. Turn them over to Mr. Sheldon. We won't need them."

"If you are really bent upon going—" Sheldon began.

"That's settled long ago," she answered shortly. "I'm going to pack now. But I'll tell you what you can do for me—issue some tobacco and other stuff they want to my men."

An hour later the three men had shaken hands with Joan down on the beach. She gave the signal, and the boat shoved off, six men at the oars, the seventh man for'ard, and Adamu Adam at the steering-sweep. Joan was standing up in the stern-sheets, reiterating her good-byes—a slim figure of a woman in the tight-fitting jacket she had worn ashore from the wreck, the long-barrelled Colt's revolver hanging from the loose belt around her waist, her clear-cut face like a boy's under the Stetson hat that failed to conceal the heavy masses of hair beneath.

"You'd better get into shelter," she called to them. "There's a big squall coming. And I hope you've got plenty of chain out, Captain Young. Good-bye! Good-bye, everybody!"

Her last words came out of the darkness, which wrapped itself solidly about the boat. Yet they continued to stare into the blackness in the direction in which the boat had disappeared, listening to the steady click of the oars in the rowlocks until it faded away and ceased.

"She is only a girl," Christian Young said with slow solemnity. The discovery seemed to have been made on the spur of the moment. "She is only a girl," he repeated with greater solemnity.

"A dashed pretty one, and a good traveller," Tudor laughed. "She certainly has spunk, eh, Sheldon?"

"Yes, she is brave," was the reluctant answer for Sheldon did not feel disposed to talk about her.

"That's the American of it," Tudor went on. "Push, and go, and energy, and independence. What do you think, skipper?"

"I think she is young, very young, only a girl," replied the captain of the *Minerva*, continuing to stare into the blackness that hid the sea.

The blackness seemed suddenly to increase in density, and they stumbled up the beach, feeling their way to the gate.

"Watch out for nuts," Sheldon warned, as the first blast of the squall shrieked through the palms. They joined hands and staggered up the path, with the ripe cocoanuts thudding in a monstrous rain all around them. They gained the veranda, where they sat in silence over their whisky, each man staring straight out to sea, where the wildly swinging riding-light of the *Minerva* could be seen in the lulls of the driving rain.

Somewhere out there, Sheldon reflected, was Joan Lackland, the girl who had not grown up, the woman good to look upon, with only a boy's mind and a boy's desires, leaving Berande amid storm and conflict in much the same manner that she had first arrived, in the stern-sheets of her whale-boat, Adamu Adam steering, her savage crew bending to the oars. And she was taking her Stetson hat with her, along with the cartridge-belt and the long-barrelled revolver. He suddenly discovered an immense affection for those fripperies of hers at which he had secretly laughed when first he saw them. He became aware of the sentimental direction in which his fancy was leading him, and felt inclined to laugh. But he did not laugh. The next moment he was busy visioning the hat, and belt, and revolver. Undoubtedly this was love, he thought, and he felt a tiny glow of pride in him in that the Solomons had not succeeded in killing all his sentiment.

An hour later, Christian Young stood up, knocked out his pipe, and prepared to go aboard and get under way.

"She's all right," he said, apropos of nothing spoken, and yet distinctly relevant to what was in each of their minds. "She's got a good boat's-crew, and she's a sailor herself. Good-night, Mr. Sheldon. Anything I can do for you down Marau-way?" He turned and pointed to a widening space of starry sky. "It's going to be a fine night after all. With this favouring bit of breeze she has sail on already, and she'll make Guvutu by daylight. Good-night."

"I guess I'll turn in, old man," Tudor said, rising and placing his glass on the table. "I'll start the first thing in the morning. It's been disgraceful the way I've been hanging on here. Good-night."

Sheldon, sitting on alone, wondered if the other man would have decided to pull out in the morning had Joan not sailed away. Well, there was one bit of consolation in it: Joan had certainly lingered at Berande for no man, not even Tudor. "I start in an hour"—her words rang in his brain, and under his eyelids he could see her as she stood up and uttered them. He smiled. The instant she heard the news she had made up her mind to go. It was not very flattering to man, but what could any man count in her eyes when a schooner waiting to be bought in Sydney was in the wind? What a creature! What a creature!

* * * * *

Berande was a lonely place to Sheldon in the days that followed. In the morning after Joan's departure, he had seen Tudor's expedition off on its way up the Balesuna; in the late afternoon, through his telescope, he had seen the smoke of the *Upolu* that was bearing Joan away to Sydney; and in the evening he sat down to dinner in solitary state, devoting more of his time to looking at her empty chair than to his food. He never came out on the veranda without glancing first of all at her grass house in the corner of the compound; and one evening, idly knocking the balls about on the billiard table, he came to himself to find himself standing staring at the nail upon which from the first she had hung her Stetson hat and her revolver-belt.

Why should he care for her? he demanded of himself angrily. She was certainly the last woman in the world he would have thought of choosing for himself. Never had he encountered one who had so thoroughly irritated him, rasped his feelings, smashed his conventions, and violated nearly every attribute of what had been his ideal of woman. Had he been too long away from the world? Had he forgotten what the race of women was like? Was it merely a case of propinquity? And she wasn't really a woman. She was a masquerader. Under all her seeming of woman, she was a boy, playing a boy's pranks, diving for fish amongst sharks, sporting a revolver, longing for adventure, and, what was more, going out in search of it in her whale-boat, along with her savage islanders and her bag of sovereigns. But he loved her— that was the point of it all, and he did not try to evade it. He was not sorry that it was so. He loved her—that was the overwhelming, astounding fact.

Once again he discovered a big enthusiasm for Berande. All the bubble-illusions concerning the life of the tropical planter had been pricked by the stern facts of the Solomons. Following the death of Hughie, he had resolved to muddle along somehow with the plantation; but this resolve had not been based upon desire. Instead, it was based upon the inherent stubbornness of his nature and his dislike to give over an attempted task.

But now it was different. Berande meant everything. It must succeed— not merely because Joan was a partner in it, but because he wanted to make that partnership permanently binding. Three more years and the plantation would be a splendid-paying investment. They could then take yearly trips to Australia, and oftener; and an occasional run home to England—or Hawaii, would come as a matter of course.

He spent his evenings poring over accounts, or making endless calculations based on cheaper freights for copra and on the possible maximum and minimum market prices for that staple of commerce. His days were spent out on the plantation. He undertook more clearing of bush; and clearing and planting went on, under his personal supervision, at a faster pace than ever before. He experimented with premiums for extra work performed by the black boys, and yearned continually for more of them to put to work. Not until Joan could return on the schooner would this be possible, for the professional recruiters were all under long contracts to the Fulcrum Brothers, Morgan and Raff, and the Fires, Philp Company; while the *Flibberty-Gibbet* was wholly occupied in running about among his widely scattered trading stations, which extended from the coast of New Georgia in one direction to Ulava and Sikiana in the other. Blacks he must have, and, if Joan were fortunate in getting a schooner, three months at least must elapse before the first recruits could be landed on Berande.

A week after the *Upolu's* departure, the *Malakula* dropped anchor and her skipper came ashore for a game of billiards and to gossip until the land breeze sprang up. Besides, as he told his super-cargo, he simply had to come ashore, not merely to deliver the large package of seeds with full instructions for planting from Joan, but to shock Sheldon with the little surprise born of information he was bringing with him.

Captain Auckland played the billiards first, and it was not until he was comfortably seated in a steamer-chair, his second whisky securely in his hand, that he let off his bomb.

"A great piece, that Miss Lackland of yours," he chuckled. "Claims to be a part-owner of Berande. Says she's your partner. Is that straight?"

Sheldon nodded coldly.

"You don't say? That is a surprise! Well, she hasn't convinced Guvutu or Tulagi of it. They're pretty used to irregular things over there, but—ha! ha!—" he stopped to have his laugh out and to mop his bald head with a trade handkerchief. "But that partnership yarn of hers was too big to swallow, though it gave them the excuse for a few more drinks."

"There is nothing irregular about it. It is an ordinary business transaction." Sheldon strove to act as though such transactions were quite the commonplace thing on plantations in the Solomons. "She invested something like fifteen hundred pounds in Berande—"

"So she said."

"And she has gone to Sydney on business for the plantation."

"Oh, no, she hasn't."

"I beg pardon?" Sheldon queried.

"I said she hasn't, that's all."

135

"But didn't the *Upolu* sail? I could have sworn I saw her smoke last Tuesday afternoon, late, as she passed Savo."

"The *Upolu* sailed all right." Captain Auckland sipped his whisky with provoking slowness. "Only Miss Lackland wasn't a passenger."

"Then where is she?"

"At Guvutu, last I saw of her. She was going to Sydney to buy a schooner, wasn't she?"

"Yes, yes."

"That's what she said. Well, she's bought one, though I wouldn't give her ten shillings for it if a nor'wester blows up, and it's about time we had one. This has been too long a spell of good weather to last."

"If you came here to excite my curiosity, old man," Sheldon said, "you've certainly succeeded. Now go ahead and tell me in a straightforward way what has happened. What schooner? Where is it? How did she happen to buy it?"

"First, the schooner *Martha*," the skipper answered, checking his replies off on his fingers. "Second, the *Martha* is on the outside reef at Poonga-Poonga, looted clean of everything portable, and ready to go to pieces with the first bit of lively sea. And third, Miss Lackland bought her at auction. She was knocked down to her for fifty-five quid by the third-assistant-resident-commissioner. I ought to know. I bid fifty myself, for Morgan and Raff. My word, weren't they hot! I told them to go to the devil, and that it was their fault for limiting me to fifty quid when they thought the chance to salve the *Martha* was worth more. You see, they weren't expecting competition. Fulcrum Brothers had no representative present, neither had Fires, Philp Company, and the only man to be afraid of was Nielsen's agent, Squires, and him they got drunk and sound asleep over in Guvutu.

"'Twenty,' says I, for my bid. 'Twenty-five,' says the little girl. 'Thirty,' says I. 'Forty,' says she. 'Fifty,' says I. 'Fifty-five,' says she. And there I was stuck. 'Hold on,' says I; 'wait till I see my owners.' 'No, you don't,' says she. 'It's customary,' says I. 'Not anywhere in the world,' says she. 'Then it's courtesy in the Solomons,' says I.

"And d'ye know, on my faith I think Burnett'd have done it, only she pipes up, sweet and pert as you please: 'Mr. Auctioneer, will you kindly proceed with the sale in the customary manner? I've other business to attend to, and I can't afford to wait all night on men who don't know their own minds.' And then she smiles at Burnett, as well—you know, one of those fetching smiles, and damme if Burnett doesn't begin singing out: 'Goin', goin', goin'—last bid—goin', goin' for fifty-five sovereigns—goin', goin', gone—to you, Miss—er—what name, please?'

"'Joan Lackland,' says she, with a smile to me; and that's how she bought the *Martha*."

Sheldon experienced a sudden thrill. The *Martha*!—a finer schooner than the *Malakula*, and, for that matter, the finest in the Solomons. She was just the thing for recruits, and she was right on the spot. Then he realized that for such a craft to sell at auction for fifty-five pounds meant that there was small chance for saving her.

"But how did it happen?" he asked. "Weren't they rather quick in selling the *Martha*?"

"Had to. You know the reef at Poonga-Poonga. She's not worth tuppence on it if any kind of a sea kicks up, and it's ripe for a nor'wester any moment now. The crowd abandoned her completely. Didn't even dream of auctioning her. Morgan and Raff persuaded them to put her up. They're a co-operative crowd, you know, an organized business corporation, fore and aft, all hands and the cook. They held a meeting and voted to sell."

"But why didn't they stand by and try to save her?"

"Stand by! You know Malaita. And you know Poonga-Poonga. That's where they cut off the *Scottish Chiefs* and killed all hands. There was nothing to do but take to the boats. The *Martha* missed stays going in, and inside five minutes she was on the reef and in possession. The niggers swarmed over her, and they just threw the crew into the boats. I talked with some of the men. They swear there were two hundred war canoes around her inside half an hour, and five thousand bushmen on the beach. Said you couldn't see Malaita for the smoke of the signal fires. Anyway, they cleared out for Tulagi."

"But why didn't they fight?" Sheldon asked.

"It was funny they didn't, but they got separated. You see, two-thirds of them were in the boats, without weapons, running anchors and never dreaming the natives would attack. They found out their mistake too late. The natives had charge. That's the trouble of new chums on the coast. It would never have happened with you or me or any old-timer."

"But what is Miss Lackland intending to do?" Captain Auckland grinned.

"She's going to try to get the *Martha* off, I should say. Or else why did she pay fifty-five quid for her? And if she fails, she'll try to get her money back by saving the gear—spars, you know, and patent steering-gear, and winches, and such things. At least that's what I'd do if I was in her place. When I sailed, the little girl had chartered the *Emily*—'I'm going recruiting,' says Munster—he's the skipper and owner now. 'And how much will you net on the cruise?' asks she. 'Oh, fifty quid,' says he. 'Good,' says she; 'you bring your *Emily* along with me and you'll get seventy-five.' You know that big ship's anchor and chain piled up behind the coal-sheds? She was just buying that when I left. She's certainly a hustler, that little girl of yours."

"She is my partner," Sheldon corrected.

"Well, she's a good one, that's all, and a cool one. My word! a white woman on Malaita, and at Poonga-Poonga of all places! Oh, I forgot to tell you—she palavered Burnett into lending her eight rifles for her men, and three cases of dynamite. You'd laugh to see the way she makes that Guvutu gang stand around. And to see them being polite and trying to give advice! Lord, Lord, man, that little girl's a wonder, a marvel, a—a—a catastrophe. That's what she is, a catastrophe. She's gone through Guvutu and Tulagi like a hurricane; every last swine of them in love with her—except Raff. He's sore over the auction, and he sprang his recruiting contract with Munster on her. And what does she do but thank him, and read it over, and point out that while Munster was pledged to deliver all recruits to Morgan and Raff, there was no clause in the document forbidding him from chartering the *Emily*."

"'There's your contract,' says she, passing it back. 'And a very good contract it is. The next time you draw one up, insert a clause that will fit emergencies like the present one.' And, Lord, Lord, she had him, too.

"But there's the breeze, and I'm off. Good-bye, old man. Hope the little girl succeeds. The *Martha*'s a whacking fine boat, and she'd take the place of the *Jessie*."

CHAPTER XVII—"YOUR" MISS LACKLAND

The next morning Sheldon came in from the plantation to breakfast, to find the mission ketch, *Apostle*, at anchor, her crew swimming two mares and a filly ashore. Sheldon recognized the animals as belonging to the Resident Commissioner, and he immediately wondered if Joan had bought them. She was certainly living up to her threat of rattling the dry bones of the Solomons, and he was prepared for anything.

"Miss Lackland sent them," said Welshmere, the missionary doctor, stepping ashore and shaking hands with him. "There's also a box of saddles on board. And this letter from her. And the skipper of the *Flibberty-Gibbet*."

The next moment, and before he could greet him, Oleson stepped from the boat and began.

"She's stolen the *Flibberty*, Mr. Sheldon. Run clean away with her. She's a wild one. She gave me the fever. Brought it on by shock. And got me drunk, as well—rotten drunk."

Dr. Welshmere laughed heartily.

"Nevertheless, she is not an unmitigated evil, your Miss Lackland. She's sworn three men off their drink, or, to the same purpose, shut off their whisky. You know them—Brahms, Curtis, and Fowler. She shipped them on the *Flibberty-Gibbet* along with her."

"She's the skipper of the *Flibberty* now," Oleson broke in. "And she'll wreck her as sure as God didn't make the Solomons."

Dr. Welshmere tried to look shocked, but laughed again.

"She has quite a way with her," he said. "I tried to back out of bringing the horses over. Said I couldn't charge freight, that the *Apostle* was under a yacht license, that I was going around by Savo and the upper end of Guadalcanal. But it was no use. 'Bother the charge,' said she. 'You take the horses like a good man, and when I float the *Martha* I'll return the service some day.'"

"And 'bother your orders,' said she to me," Oleson cried. "'I'm your boss now,' said she, 'and you take your orders from me.' 'Look at that load of ivory nuts,' I said. 'Bother them,' said she; 'I'm playin' for something bigger than ivory nuts. We'll dump them overside as soon as we get under way.'"

Sheldon put his hands to his ears.

"I don't know what has happened, and you are trying to tell me the tale backwards. Come up to the house and get in the shade and begin at the beginning."

"What I want to know," Oleson began, when they were seated, "is she your partner or ain't she? That's what I want to know."

"She is," Sheldon assured him.

"Well, who'd have believed it!" Oleson glanced appealingly at Dr. Welshmere, and back again at Sheldon. "I've seen a few unlikely things in these Solomons—rats two feet long, butterflies the Commissioner hunts with a shot-gun, ear-ornaments that would shame the devil, and head-hunting devils that make the devil look like an angel. I've seen them and got used to them, but this young woman of yours—"

"Miss Lackland is my partner and part-owner of Berande," Sheldon interrupted.

"So she said," the irate skipper dashed on. "But she had no papers to show for it. How was I to know? And then there was that load of ivory nuts-eight tons of them."

"For heaven's sake begin at the—" Sheldon tried to interrupt.

"And then she's hired them drunken loafers, three of the worst scoundrels that ever disgraced the Solomons—fifteen quid a month each—what d'ye think of that? And sailed away with them, too! Phew!—You might give me a drink. The missionary won't mind. I've been on his teetotal hooker four days now, and I'm perishing."

Dr. Welshmere nodded in reply to Sheldon's look of inquiry, and Viaburi was dispatched for the whisky and siphons.

"It is evident, Captain Oleson," Sheldon remarked to that refreshed mariner, "that Miss Lackland has run away with your boat. Now please give a plain statement of what occurred."

"Right O; here goes. I'd just come in on the *Flibberty*. She was on board before I dropped the hook—in that whale-boat of hers with her gang of Tahiti heathens—that big Adamu Adam and the rest. 'Don't drop the anchor, Captain Oleson,' she sang out. 'I want you to get under way for Poonga-Poonga.' I looked to see if she'd been drinking. What was I to think? I was rounding up at the time, alongside the shoal—a ticklish place—head-sails running down and losing way, so I says, 'Excuse me, Miss Lackland,' and yells for'ard, 'Let go!'

"'You might have listened to me and saved yourself trouble,' says she, climbing over the rail and squinting along for'ard and seeing the first shackle flip out and stop. 'There's fifteen fathom,' says she; 'you may as well turn your men to and heave up.'

"And then we had it out. I didn't believe her. I didn't think you'd take her on as a partner, and I told her as much and wanted proof. She got high and mighty, and I told her I was old enough to be her grandfather and that I wouldn't take gammon from a chit like her. And then I ordered her off the *Flibberty*. 'Captain Oleson,' she says, sweet as you please, 'I've a few minutes to spare on you, and I've got some good whisky over on the *Emily*. Come on along. Besides, I want your advice about this wrecking business. Everybody says you're a crackerjack sailor-man'—that's what she said, 'crackerjack.' And I went, in her whale-boat, Adamu Adam steering and looking as solemn as a funeral.

"On the way she told me about the *Martha*, and how she'd bought her, and was going to float her. She said she'd chartered the *Emily*, and was sailing as soon as I could get the *Flibberty* underway. It struck me that her gammon was reasonable enough, and I agreed to pull out for Berande right O, and get your orders to go along to Poonga-Poonga. But she said there wasn't a second to be lost by any such foolishness, and that I was to sail direct for Poonga-Poonga, and that if I couldn't take her word that she was your partner, she'd

142

get along without me and the *Flibberty*. And right there's where she fooled me.

"Down in the *Emily's* cabin was them three soaks—you know them—Fowler and Curtis and that Brahms chap. 'Have a drink,' says she. I thought they looked surprised when she unlocked the whisky locker and sent a nigger for the glasses and water-monkey. But she must have tipped them off unbeknownst to me, and they knew just what to do. 'Excuse me,' she says, 'I'm going on deck a minute.' Now that minute was half an hour. I hadn't had a drink in ten days. I'm an old man and the fever has weakened me. Then I took it on an empty stomach, too, and there was them three soaks setting me an example, they arguing for me to take the *Flibberty* to Poonga-Poonga, an' me pointing out my duty to the contrary. The trouble was, all the arguments were pointed with drinks, and me not being a drinking man, so to say, and weak from fever . . .

"Well, anyway, at the end of the half-hour down she came again and took a good squint at me. 'That'll do nicely,' I remember her saying; and with that she took the whisky bottles and hove them overside through the companionway. 'That's the last, she said to the three soaks, 'till the *Martha* floats and you're back in Guvutu. It'll be a long time between drinks.' And then she laughed.

"She looked at me and said—not to me, mind you, but to the soaks: 'It's time this worthy man went ashore'—me! worthy man! 'Fowler,' she said—you know, just like a straight order, and she didn't *mister* him—it was plain Fowler—'Fowler,' she said, 'just tell Adamu Adam to man the whale-boat, and while he's taking Captain Oleson ashore have your boat put me on the *Flibberty*. The three of you sail with me, so pack your dunnage. And the one of you that shows up best will take the mate's billet. Captain Oleson doesn't carry a mate, you know.'

"I don't remember much after that. All hands got me over the side, and it seems to me I went to sleep, sitting in the stern-sheets and watching that Adamu steer. Then I saw the *Flibberty's* mainsail hoisting, and heard the clank of her chain coming in, and I woke up. 'Here, put me on the *Flibberty*,'

I said to Adamu. 'I put you on the beach,' said he. 'Missie Lackalanna say beach plenty good for you.' Well, I let out a yell and reached for the steering-sweep. I was doing my best by my owners, you see. Only that Adamu gives me a shove down on the bottom-boards, puts one foot on me to hold me down, and goes on steering. And that's all. The shock of the whole thing brought on fever. And now I've come to find out whether I'm skipper of the *Flibberty*, or that chit of yours with her pirating, heathen boat's-crew."

"Never mind, skipper. You can take a vacation on pay." Sheldon spoke with more assurance than he felt. "If Miss Lackland, who is my partner, has seen fit to take charge of the *Flibberty-Gibbet*, why, it is all right. As you will agree, there was no time to be lost if the *Martha* was to be got off. It is a bad reef, and any considerable sea would knock her bottom out. You settle down here, skipper, and rest up and get the fever out of your bones. When the *Flibberty-Gibbet* comes back, you'll take charge again, of course."

After Dr. Welshmere and the *Apostle* departed and Captain Oleson had turned in for a sleep in a veranda hammock, Sheldon opened Joan's letter.

DEAR MR. SHELDON,—Please forgive me for stealing the *Flibberty-Gibbet.* I simply had to. The *Martha* means everything to us. Think of it, only fifty-five pounds for her, two hundred and seventy-five dollars. If I don't save her, I know I shall be able to pay all expenses out of her gear, which the natives will not have carried off. And if I do save her, it is the haul of a life-time. And if I don't save her, I'll fill the *Emily* and the *Flibberty-Gibbet* with recruits. Recruits are needed right now on Berande more than anything else.

And please, please don't be angry with me. You said I shouldn't go recruiting on the *Flibberty,* and I won't. I'll go on the *Emily.*

I bought two cows this afternoon. That trader at Nogi died of fever, and I bought them from his partner, Sam Willis his name is, who agrees to deliver them—most likely by the *Minerva* next time she is down that way. Berande has been long enough on tinned milk.

And Dr. Welshmere has agreed to get me some orange and lime trees from the mission station at Ulava. He will deliver them the next trip of the *Apostle*. If the Sydney steamer arrives before I get back, plant the sweet corn she will bring between the young trees on the high bank of the Balesuna. The current is eating in against that bank, and you should do something to save it.

I have ordered some fig-trees and loquats, too, from Sydney. Dr. Welshmere will bring some mango-seeds. They are big trees and require plenty of room.

The *Martha* is registered 110 tons. She is the biggest schooner in the Solomons, and the best. I saw a little of her lines and guess the rest. She will sail like a witch. If she hasn't filled with water, her engine will be all right. The reason she went ashore was because it was not working. The engineer had disconnected the feed-pipes to clean out the rust. Poor business, unless at anchor or with plenty of sea room.

Plant all the trees in the compound, even if you have to clean out the palms later on.

And don't plant the sweet corn all at once. Let a few days elapse between plantings.

JOAN LACKLAND.

He fingered the letter, lingering over it and scrutinizing the writing in a way that was not his wont. How characteristic, was his thought, as he studied the boyish scrawl—clear to read, painfully, clear, but none the less boyish. The clearness of it reminded him of her face, of her cleanly stencilled brows, her straightly chiselled nose, the very clearness of the gaze of her eyes, the firmly yet delicately moulded lips, and the throat, neither fragile nor robust, but—but just right, he concluded, an adequate and beautiful pillar for so shapely a burden.

He looked long at the name. Joan Lackland—just an assemblage of letters, of commonplace letters, but an assemblage that generated a subtle and heady magic. It crept into his brain and twined and twisted his mental processes until all that constituted him at that moment went out in love to that scrawled signature. A few commonplace letters—yet they caused him to know in himself a lack that sweetly hurt and that expressed itself in vague spiritual outpourings and delicious yearnings. Joan Lackland! Each time he looked at it there arose visions of her in a myriad moods and guises—coming in out of the flying smother of the gale that had wrecked her schooner; launching a whale-boat to go a-fishing; running dripping from the sea, with streaming hair and clinging garments, to the fresh-water shower; frightening four-score cannibals with an empty chlorodyne bottle; teaching Ornfiri how to make bread; hanging her Stetson hat and revolver-belt on the hook in the living-room; talking gravely about winning to hearth and saddle of her own, or juvenilely rattling on about romance and adventure, bright-eyed, her face flushed and eager with enthusiasm. Joan Lackland! He mused over the cryptic wonder of it till the secrets of love were made clear and he felt a keen sympathy for lovers who carved their names on trees or wrote them on the beach-sands of the sea.

Then he came back to reality, and his face hardened. Even then she was on the wild coast of Malaita, and at Poonga-Poonga, of all villainous and dangerous portions the worst, peopled with a teeming population of head-hunters, robbers, and murderers. For the instant he entertained the rash thought of calling his boat's-crew and starting immediately in a whale-boat for Poonga-Poonga. But the next instant the idea was dismissed. What could he do if he did go? First, she would resent it. Next, she would laugh at him and call him a silly; and after all he would count for only one rifle more, and she had many rifles with her. Three things only could he do if he went. He could command her to return; he could take the *Flibberty-Gibbet* away from her; he could dissolve their partnership;—any and all of which he knew would be foolish and futile, and he could hear her explain in terse set terms that she was legally of age and that nobody could say come or go to her. No, his pride would never permit him to start for Poonga-Poonga, though his heart whispered that nothing could be more welcome than a message from her asking him to come and lend a hand. Her very words—"lend a hand"; and in his fancy, he could see and hear her saying them.

There was much in her wilful conduct that caused him to wince in the heart of him. He was appalled by the thought of her shoulder to shoulder with the drunken rabble of traders and beachcombers at Guvutu. It was bad enough for a clean, fastidious man; but for a young woman, a girl at that, it was awful. The theft of the *Flibberty*-Gibbet was merely amusing, though the means by which the theft had been effected gave him hurt. Yet he found consolation in the fact that the task of making Oleson drunk had been turned over to the three scoundrels. And next, and swiftly, came the vision of her, alone with those same three scoundrels, on the *Emily*, sailing out to sea from Guvutu in the twilight with darkness coming on. Then came visions of Adamu Adam and Noa Noah and all her brawny Tahitian following, and his anxiety faded away, being replaced by irritation that she should have been capable of such wildness of conduct.

And the irritation was still on him as he got up and went inside to stare at the hook on the wall and to wish that her Stetson hat and revolver-belt were hanging from it.

CHAPTER XVIII—MAKING THE BOOKS COME TRUE

Several quiet weeks slipped by. Berande, after such an unusual run of visiting vessels, drifted back into her old solitude. Sheldon went on with the daily round, clearing bush, planting cocoanuts, smoking copra, building bridges, and riding about his work on the horses Joan had bought. News of her he had none. Recruiting vessels on Malaita left the Poonga-Poonga coast severely alone; and the *Clansman*, a Samoan recruiter, dropping anchor one sunset for billiards and gossip, reported rumours amongst the Sio natives that there had been fighting at Poonga-Poonga. As this news would have had to travel right across the big island, little dependence was to be placed on it.

The steamer from Sydney, the *Kammambo*, broke the quietude of Berande for an hour, while landing mail, supplies, and the trees and seeds Joan had ordered. The *Minerva*, bound for Cape Marsh, brought the two cows from Nogi. And the *Apostle*, hurrying back to Tulagi to connect with the Sydney steamer, sent a boat ashore with the orange and lime trees from Ulava. And these several weeks marked a period of perfect weather. There were days on end when sleek calms ruled the breathless sea, and days when vagrant wisps of air fanned for several hours from one direction or another. The land-breezes at night alone proved regular, and it was at night that the occasional cutters and ketches slipped by, too eager to take advantage of the light winds to drop anchor for an hour.

Then came the long-expected nor'wester. For eight days it raged, lulling at times to short durations of calm, then shifting a point or two and raging with renewed violence. Sheldon kept a precautionary eye on the buildings, while the Balesuna, in flood, so savagely attacked the high bank Joan had warned him about, that he told off all the gangs to battle with the river.

It was in the good weather that followed, that he left the blacks at work, one morning, and with a shot-gun across his pommel rode off after pigeons. Two hours later, one of the house-boys, breathless and scratched ran him down with the news that the *Martha*, the *Flibberty-Gibbet*, and the *Emily* were heading in for the anchorage.

Coming into the compound from the rear, Sheldon could see nothing until he rode around the corner of the bungalow. Then he saw everything at once—first, a glimpse at the sea, where the *Martha* floated huge alongside the cutter and the ketch which had rescued her; and, next, the ground in front of the veranda steps, where a great crowd of fresh-caught cannibals stood at attention. From the fact that each was attired in a new, snow-white lava-lava, Sheldon knew that they were recruits. Part way up the steps, one of them was just backing down into the crowd, while another, called out by name, was coming up. It was Joan's voice that had called him, and Sheldon reined in his horse and watched. She sat at the head of the steps, behind a table, between Munster and his white mate, the three of them checking long lists, Joan asking the questions and writing the answers in the big, red-covered, Berande labour-journal.

"What name?" she demanded of the black man on the steps.

"Tagari," came the answer, accompanied by a grin and a rolling of curious eyes; for it was the first white-man's house the black had ever seen.

"What place b'long you?"

"Bangoora."

No one had noticed Sheldon, and he continued to sit his horse and watch. There was a discrepancy between the answer and the record in the recruiting books, and a consequent discussion, until Munster solved the difficulty.

"Bangoora?" he said. "That's the little beach at the head of the bay out of Latta. He's down as a Latta-man—see, there it is, 'Tagari, Latta.'"

"What place you go you finish along white marster?" Joan asked.

"Bangoora," the man replied; and Joan wrote it down.

"Ogu!" Joan called.

The black stepped down, and another mounted to take his place. But Tagari, just before he reached the bottom step, caught sight of Sheldon. It was the first horse the fellow had ever seen, and he let out a frightened screech and dashed madly up the steps. At the same moment the great mass of blacks surged away panic-stricken from Sheldon's vicinity. The grinning house-boys shouted encouragement and explanation, and the stampede was checked, the new-caught head-hunters huddling closely together and staring dubiously at the fearful monster.

"Hello!" Joan called out. "What do you mean by frightening all my boys? Come on up."

"What do you think of them?" she asked, when they had shaken hands. "And what do you think of her?"—with a wave of the hand toward the *Martha*. "I thought you'd deserted the plantation, and that I might as well go ahead and get the men into barracks. Aren't they beauties? Do you see that one with the split nose? He's the only man who doesn't hail from the Poonga-Poonga coast; and they said the Poonga-Poonga natives wouldn't recruit. Just look at them and congratulate me. There are no kiddies and half-grown youths among them. They're men, every last one of them. I have such a long story I don't know where to begin, and I won't begin anyway till we're through with this and until you have told me that you are not angry with me."

"Ogu—what place b'long you?" she went on with her catechism.

But Ogu was a bushman, lacking knowledge of the almost universal bêche-de-mer English, and half a dozen of his fellows wrangled to explain.

"There are only two or three more," Joan said to Sheldon, "and then we're done. But you haven't told me that you are not angry."

Sheldon looked into her clear eyes as she favoured him with a direct, untroubled gaze that threatened, he knew from experience, to turn teasingly defiant on an instant's notice. And as he looked at her it came to him that he had never half-anticipated the gladness her return would bring to him.

"I was angry," he said deliberately. "I am still angry, very angry—" he noted the glint of defiance in her eyes and thrilled—"but I forgave, and I now forgive all over again. Though I still insist—"

"That I should have a guardian," she interrupted. "But that day will never come. Thank goodness I'm of legal age and able to transact business in my own right. And speaking of business, how do you like my forceful American methods?"

"Mr. Raff, from what I hear, doesn't take kindly to them," he temporized, "and you've certainly set the dry bones rattling for many a day. But what I want to know is if other American women are as successful in business ventures?"

"Luck, 'most all luck," she disclaimed modestly, though her eyes lighted with sudden pleasure; and he knew her boy's vanity had been touched by his trifle of tempered praise.

"Luck be blowed!" broke out the long mate, Sparrowhawk, his face shining with admiration. "It was hard work, that's what it was. We earned our pay. She worked us till we dropped. And we were down with fever half the time. So was she, for that matter, only she wouldn't stay down, and she wouldn't let us stay down. My word, she's a slave-driver—'Just one more heave, Mr. Sparrowhawk, and then you can go to bed for a week',—she to me, and me staggerin' 'round like a dead man, with bilious-green lights flashing inside my head, an' my head just bustin'. I was all in, but I gave that heave right O—and then it was, 'Another heave now, Mr. Sparrowhawk, just another heave.' An' the Lord lumme, the way she made love to old Kina-Kina!"

He shook his head reproachfully, while the laughter died down in his throat to long-drawn chuckles.

"He was older than Telepasse and dirtier," she assured Sheldon, "and I am sure much wickeder. But this isn't work. Let us get through with these lists."

She turned to the waiting black on the steps,—

"Ogu, you finish along big marster belong white man, you go Not-Not.—Here you, Tangari, you speak 'm along that fella Ogu. He finish he walk about Not-Not. Have you got that, Mr. Munster?"

151

"But you've broken the recruiting laws," Sheldon said, when the new recruits had marched away to the barracks. "The licenses for the *Flibberty* and the *Emily* don't allow for one hundred and fifty. What did Burnett say?"

"He passed them, all of them," she answered. "Captain Munster will tell you what he said—something about being blowed, or words to that effect. Now I must run and wash up. Did the Sydney orders arrive?"

"Yours are in your quarters," Sheldon said. "Hurry, for breakfast is waiting. Let me have your hat and belt. Do, please, allow me. There's only one hook for them, and I know where it is."

She gave him a quick scrutiny that was almost woman-like, then sighed with relief as she unbuckled the heavy belt and passed it to him.

"I doubt if I ever want to see another revolver," she complained. "That one has worn a hole in me, I'm sure. I never dreamed I could get so weary of one."

Sheldon watched her to the foot of the steps, where she turned and called back,—

"My! I can't tell you how good it is to be home again."

And as his gaze continued to follow her across the compound to the tiny grass house, the realization came to him crushingly that Berande and that little grass house was the only place in the world she could call "home."

* * * * *

"And Burnett said, 'Well, I'll be damned—I beg your pardon, Miss Lackland, but you have wantonly broken the recruiting laws and you know it,'" Captain Munster narrated, as they sat over their whisky, waiting for Joan to come back. "And says she to him, 'Mr. Burnett, can you show me any law against taking the passengers off a vessel that's on a reef?' 'That is not the point,' says he. 'It's the very, precise, particular point,' says she and you bear it in mind and go ahead and pass my recruits. You can report me to the Lord High Commissioner if you want, but I have three vessels here waiting on your convenience, and if you delay them much longer there'll be another report go in to the Lord High Commissioner.'

"'I'll hold you responsible, Captain Munster,' says he to me, mad enough to eat scrap-iron. 'No, you won't,' says she; 'I'm the charterer of the *Emily*, and Captain Munster has acted under my orders.'

"What could Burnett do? He passed the whole hundred and fifty, though the *Emily* was only licensed for forty, and the *Flibberty-Gibbet* for thirty-five."

"But I don't understand," Sheldon said.

"This is the way she worked it. When the *Martha* was floated, we had to beach her right away at the head of the bay, and whilst repairs were going on, a new rudder being made, sails bent, gear recovered from the niggers, and so forth, Miss Lackland borrows Sparrowhawk to run the *Flibberty* along with Curtis, lends me Brahms to take Sparrowhawk's place, and starts both craft off recruiting. My word, the niggers came easy. It was virgin ground. Since the *Scottish Chiefs*, no recruiter had ever even tried to work the coast; and we'd already put the fear of God into the niggers' hearts till the whole coast was quiet as lambs. When we filled up, we came back to see how the *Martha* was progressing."

"And thinking we was going home with our recruits," Sparrowhawk slipped in. "Lord lumme, that Miss Lackland ain't never satisfied. 'I'll take 'em on the *Martha*,' says she, 'and you can go back and fill up again.'"

"But I told her it couldn't be done," Munster went on. "I told her the *Martha* hadn't a license for recruiting. 'Oh,' she said, 'it can't be done, eh?' and she stood and thought a few minutes."

"And I'd seen her think before," cried Sparrowhawk, "and I knew at wunst that the thing was as good as done."

Munster lighted his cigarette and resumed.

"'You see that spit,' she says to me, 'with the little ripple breaking around it? There's a current sets right across it and on it. And you see them bafflin' little cat's-paws? It's good weather and a falling tide. You just start to beat out, the two of you, and all you have to do is miss stays in the same baffling puff and the current will set you nicely aground.'"

"'That little wash of sea won't more than start a sheet or two of copper,' says she, when Munster kicked," Sparrowhawk explained. "Oh, she's no green un, that girl."

"'Then I'll rescue your recruits and sail away—simple, ain't it?' says she," Munster continued. "'You hang up one tide,' says she; 'the next is the big high water. Then you kedge off and go after more recruits. There's no law against recruiting when you're empty.' 'But there is against starving 'em,' I said; 'you know yourself there ain't any *kai-kai* to speak of aboard of us, and there ain't a crumb on the *Martha*.'"

"We'd all been pretty well on native *kai-kai*, as it was," said Sparrowhawk.

"'Don't let the *kai-kai* worry you, Captain Munster,' says she; 'if I can find grub for eighty-four mouths on the *Martha*, the two of you can do as much by your two vessels. Now go ahead and get aground before a steady breeze comes up and spoils the manoeuvre. I'll send my boats the moment you strike. And now, good-day, gentlemen.'"

"And we went and did it," Sparrowhawk said solemnly, and then emitted a series of chuckling noises. "We laid over, starboard tack, and I pinched the *Emily* against the spit. 'Go about,' Captain Munster yells at me; 'go about, or you'll have me aground!' He yelled other things, much worse. But I didn't mind. I missed stays, pretty as you please, and the *Flibberty* drifted down on him and fouled him, and we went ashore together in as nice a mess as you ever want to see. Miss Lackland transferred the recruits, and the trick was done."

"But where was she during the nor'wester?" Sheldon asked.

"At Langa-Langa. Ran up there as it was coming on, and laid there the whole week and traded for grub with the niggers. When we got to Tulagi, there she was waiting for us and scrapping with Burnett. I tell you, Mr. Sheldon, she's a wonder, that girl, a perfect wonder."

Munster refilled his glass, and while Sheldon glanced across at Joan's house, anxious for her coming, Sparrowhawk took up the tale.

154

"Gritty! She's the grittiest thing, man or woman, that ever blew into the Solomons. You should have seen Poonga-Poonga the morning we arrived—Sniders popping on the beach and in the mangroves, war-drums booming in the bush, and signal-smokes raising everywhere. 'It's all up,' says Captain Munster."

"Yes, that's what I said," declared that mariner.

"Of course it was all up. You could see it with half an eye and hear it with one ear."

"'Up your granny,' she says to him," Sparrowhawk went on. "'Why, we haven't arrived yet, much less got started. Wait till the anchor's down before you get afraid.'"

"That's what she said to me," Munster proclaimed. "And of course it made me mad so that I didn't care what happened. We tried to send a boat ashore for a pow-wow, but it was fired upon. And every once and a while some nigger'd take a long shot at us out of the mangroves."

"They was only a quarter of a mile off," Sparrowhawk explained, "and it was damned nasty. 'Don't shoot unless they try to board,' was Miss Lackland's orders; but the dirty niggers wouldn't board. They just lay off in the bush and plugged away. That night we held a council of war in the *Flibberty*'s cabin. 'What we want,' says Miss Lackland, 'is a hostage.'"

"'That's what they do in books,' I said, thinking to laugh her away from her folly," Munster interrupted. "'True,' says she, 'and have you never seen the books come true?' I shook my head. 'Then you're not too old to learn,' says she. 'I'll tell you one thing right now,' says I, 'and that is I'll be blowed if you catch me ashore in the night-time stealing niggers in a place like this.'"

"You didn't say blowed," Sparrowhawk corrected. "You said you'd be damned."

"That's what I did, and I meant it, too."

"'Nobody asked you to go ashore,' says she, quick as lightning," Sparrowhawk grinned. "And she said more. She said, 'And if I catch you going ashore without orders there'll be trouble—understand, Captain Munster?'"

155

"Who in hell's telling this, you or me?" the skipper demanded wrathfully.

"Well, she did, didn't she?" insisted the mate.

"Yes, she did, if you want to make so sure of it. And while you're about it, you might as well repeat what she said to you when you said you wouldn't recruit on the Poonga-Poonga coast for twice your screw."

Sparrowhawk's sun-reddened face flamed redder, though he tried to pass the situation off by divers laughings and chucklings and face-twistings.

"Go on, go on," Sheldon urged; and Munster resumed the narrative.

"'What we need,' says she, 'is the strong hand. It's the only way to handle them; and we've got to take hold firm right at the beginning. I'm going ashore to-night to fetch Kina-Kina himself on board, and I'm not asking who's game to go for I've got every man's work arranged with me for him. I'm taking my sailors with me, and one white man.' 'Of course, I'm that white man,' I said; for by that time I was mad enough to go to hell and back again. 'Of course you're not,' says she. 'You'll have charge of the covering boat. Curtis stands by the landing boat. Fowler goes with me. Brahms takes charge of the *Flibberty*, and Sparrowhawk of the *Emily*. And we start at one o'clock.'

"My word, it was a tough job lying there in the covering boat. I never thought doing nothing could be such hard work. We stopped about fifty fathoms off, and watched the other boat go in. It was so dark under the mangroves we couldn't see a thing of it. D'ye know that little, monkey-looking nigger, Sheldon, on the *Flibberty*—the cook, I mean? Well, he was cabin-boy twenty years ago on the *Scottish Chiefs*, and after she was cut off he was a slave there at Poonga-Poonga. And Miss Lackland had discovered the fact. So he was the guide. She gave him half a case of tobacco for that night's work—"

"And scared him fit to die before she could get him to come along," Sparrowhawk observed.

"Well, I never saw anything so black as the mangroves. I stared at them till my eyes were ready to burst. And then I'd look at the stars, and listen to the surf sighing along the reef. And there was a dog that barked. Remember that dog, Sparrowhawk? The brute nearly gave me heart-failure when he first began. After a while he stopped—wasn't barking at the landing party at all; and then the silence was harder than ever, and the mangroves grew blacker, and it was all I could do to keep from calling out to Curtis in there in the landing boat, just to make sure that I wasn't the only white man left alive.

"Of course there was a row. It had to come, and I knew it; but it startled me just the same. I never heard such screeching and yelling in my life. The niggers must have just dived for the bush without looking to see what was up, while her Tahitians let loose, shooting in the air and yelling to hurry 'em on. And then, just as sudden, came the silence again—all except for some small kiddie that had got dropped in the stampede and that kept crying in the bush for its mother.

"And then I heard them coming through the mangroves, and an oar strike on a gunwale, and Miss Lackland laugh, and I knew everything was all right. We pulled on board without a shot being fired. And, by God! she had made the books come true, for there was old Kina-Kina himself being hoisted over the rail, shivering and chattering like an ape. The rest was easy. Kina-Kina's word was law, and he was scared to death. And we kept him on board issuing proclamations all the time we were in Poonga-Poonga.

"It was a good move, too, in other ways. She made Kina-Kina order his people to return all the gear they'd stripped from the *Martha*. And back it came, day after day, steering compasses, blocks and tackles, sails, coils of rope, medicine chests, ensigns, signal flags—everything, in fact, except the trade goods and supplies which had already been *kai-kai*'d. Of course, she gave them a few sticks of tobacco to keep them in good humour."

"Sure she did," Sparrowhawk broke forth. "She gave the beggars five fathoms of calico for the big mainsail, two sticks of tobacco for the chronometer, and a sheath-knife worth elevenpence ha'penny for a hundred fathoms of brand new five-inch manila. She got old Kina-Kina with that strong hand on the go off, and she kept him going all the time. She—here she comes now."

It was with a shock of surprise that Sheldon greeted her appearance. All the time, while the tale of happening at Poonga-Poonga had been going on, he had pictured her as the woman he had always known, clad roughly, skirt made out of window-curtain stuff, an undersized man's shirt for a blouse, straw sandals for foot covering, with the Stetson hat and the eternal revolver completing her costume. The ready-made clothes from Sydney had transformed her. A simple skirt and shirt-waist of some sort of wash-goods set off her trim figure with a hint of elegant womanhood that was new to him. Brown slippers peeped out as she crossed the compound, and he once caught a glimpse to the ankle of brown open-work stockings. Somehow, she had been made many times the woman by these mere extraneous trappings; and in his mind these wild Arabian Nights adventures of hers seemed thrice as wonderful.

As they went in to breakfast he became aware that Munster and Sparrowhawk had received a similar shock. All their air of *camaraderie* was dissipated, and they had become abruptly and immensely respectful.

"I've opened up a new field," she said, as she began pouring the coffee. "Old Kina-Kina will never forget me, I'm sure, and I can recruit there whenever I want. I saw Morgan at Guvutu. He's willing to contract for a thousand boys at forty shillings per head. Did I tell you that I'd taken out a recruiting license for the *Martha*? I did, and the *Martha* can sign eighty boys every trip."

Sheldon smiled a trifle bitterly to himself. The wonderful woman who had tripped across the compound in her Sydney clothes was gone, and he was listening to the boy come back again.

CHAPTER XIX—THE LOST TOY

"Well," Joan said with a sigh, "I've shown you hustling American methods that succeed and get somewhere, and here you are beginning your muddling again."

Five days had passed, and she and Sheldon were standing on the veranda watching the *Martha*, close-hauled on the wind, laying a tack off shore. During those five days Joan had never once broached the desire of her heart, though Sheldon, in this particular instance reading her like a book, had watched her lead up to the question a score of times in the hope that he would himself suggest her taking charge of the Martha. She had wanted him to say the word, and she had steeled herself not to say it herself. The matter of finding a skipper had been a hard one. She was jealous of the *Martha*, and no suggested man had satisfied her.

"Oleson?" she had demanded. "He does very well on the *Flibberty*, with me and my men to overhaul her whenever she's ready to fall to pieces through his slackness. But skipper of the *Martha*? Impossible!"

"Munster? Yes, he's the only man I know in the Solomons I'd care to see in charge. And yet, there's his record. He lost the *Umbawa*—one hundred and forty drowned. He was first officer on the bridge. Deliberate disobedience to instructions. No wonder they broke him.

"Christian Young has never had any experience with large boats. Besides, we can't afford to pay him what he's clearing on the *Minerva*. Sparrowhawk is a good man—to take orders. He has no initiative. He's an able sailor, but he can't command. I tell you I was nervous all the time he had charge of the *Flibberty* at Poonga-Poonga when I had to stay by the *Martha*."

And so it had gone. No name proposed was satisfactory, and, moreover, Sheldon had been surprised by the accuracy of her judgments. A dozen times she almost drove him to the statement that from the showing she made of Solomon Islands sailors, she was the only person fitted to command the

Martha. But each time he restrained himself, while her pride prevented her from making the suggestion.

"Good whale-boat sailors do not necessarily make good schooner-handlers," she replied to one of his arguments. "Besides, the captain of a boat like the *Martha* must have a large mind, see things in a large way; he must have capacity and enterprise."

"But with your Tahitians on board—" Sheldon had begun another argument.

"There won't be any Tahitians on board," she had returned promptly. "My men stay with me. I never know when I may need them. When I sail, they sail; when I remain ashore, they remain ashore. I'll find plenty for them to do right here on the plantation. You've seen them clearing bush, each of them worth half a dozen of your cannibals."

So it was that Joan stood beside Sheldon and sighed as she watched the *Martha* beating out to sea, old Kinross, brought over from Savo, in command.

"Kinross is an old fossil," she said, with a touch of bitterness in her voice. "Oh, he'll never wreck her through rashness, rest assured of that; but he's timid to childishness, and timid skippers lose just as many vessels as rash ones. Some day, Kinross will lose the *Martha* because there'll be only one chance and he'll be afraid to take it. I know his sort. Afraid to take advantage of a proper breeze of wind that will fetch him in in twenty hours, he'll get caught out in the calm that follows and spend a whole week in getting in. The *Martha* will make money with him, there's no doubt of it; but she won't make near the money that she would under a competent master."

She paused, and with heightened colour and sparkling eyes gazed seaward at the schooner.

"My! but she is a witch! Look at her eating up the water, and there's no wind to speak of. She's not got ordinary white metal either. It's man-of-war copper, every inch of it. I had them polish it with cocoanut husks when she was careened at Poonga-Poonga. She was a seal-hunter before this gold expedition got her. And seal-hunters had to sail. They've run away from second class Russian cruisers more than once up there off Siberia.

"Honestly, if I'd dreamed of the chance waiting for me at Guvutu when I bought her for less than three hundred dollars, I'd never have gone partners with you. And in that case I'd be sailing her right now."

The justice of her contention came abruptly home to Sheldon. What she had done she would have done just the same if she had not been his partner. And in the saving of the *Martha* he had played no part. Single-handed, unadvised, in the teeth of the laughter of Guvutu and of the competition of men like Morgan and Raff, she had gone into the adventure and brought it through to success.

"You make me feel like a big man who has robbed a small child of a lolly," he said with sudden contrition.

"And the small child is crying for it." She looked at him, and he noted that her lip was slightly trembling and that her eyes were moist. It was the boy all over, he thought; the boy crying for the wee bit boat with which to play. And yet it was a woman, too. What a maze of contradiction she was! And he wondered, had she been all woman and no boy, if he would have loved her in just the same way. Then it rushed in upon his consciousness that he really loved her for what she was, for all the boy in her and all the rest of her—for the total of her that would have been a different total in direct proportion to any differing of the parts of her.

"But the small child won't cry any more for it," she was saying. "This is the last sob. Some day, if Kinross doesn't lose her, you'll turn her over to your partner, I know. And I won't nag you any more. Only I do hope you know how I feel. It isn't as if I'd merely bought the *Martha*, or merely built her. I saved her. I took her off the reef. I saved her from the grave of the sea when fifty-five pounds was considered a big risk. She is mine, peculiarly mine. Without me she wouldn't exist. That big nor'wester would have finished her the first three hours it blew. And then I've sailed her, too; and she is a witch, a perfect witch. Why, do you know, she'll steer by the wind with half a spoke, give and take. And going about! Well, you don't have to baby her, starting head-sheets, flattening mainsail, and gentling her with the wheel. Put your wheel down, and around she comes, like a colt with the bit in its teeth. And you can back her like a steamer. I did it at Langa-Langa, between that shoal patch and the shore-reef. It was wonderful.

"But you don't love boats like I do, and I know you think I'm making a fool of myself. But some day I'm going to sail the *Martha* again. I know it. I know it."

In reply, and quite without premeditation, his hand went out to hers, covering it as it lay on the railing. But he knew, beyond the shadow of a doubt, that it was the boy that returned the pressure he gave, the boy sorrowing over the lost toy. The thought chilled him. Never had he been actually nearer to her, and never had she been more convincingly remote. She was certainly not acutely aware that his hand was touching hers. In her grief at the departure of the *Martha* it was, to her, anybody's hand—at the best, a friend's hand.

He withdrew his hand and walked perturbedly away.

"Why hasn't he got that big fisherman's staysail on her?" she demanded irritably. "It would make the old girl just walk along in this breeze. I know the sort old Kinross is. He's the skipper that lies three days under double-reefed topsails waiting for a gale that doesn't come. Safe? Oh, yes, he's safe—dangerously safe."

Sheldon retraced his steps.

"Never mind," he said. "You can go sailing on the *Martha* any time you please—recruiting on Malaita if you want to."

It was a great concession he was making, and he felt that he did it against his better judgment. Her reception of it was a surprise to him.

"With old Kinross in command?" she queried. "No, thank you. He'd drive me to suicide. I couldn't stand his handling of her. It would give me nervous prostration. I'll never step on the *Martha* again, unless it is to take charge of her. I'm a sailor, like my father, and he could never bear to see a vessel mishandled. Did you see the way Kinross got under way? It was disgraceful. And the noise he made about it! Old Noah did better with the Ark."

162

"But we manage to get somewhere just the same," he smiled.

"So did Noah."

"That was the main thing."

"For an antediluvian."

She took another lingering look at the *Martha*, then turned to Sheldon.

"You are a slovenly lot down here when it comes to boats—most of you are, any way. Christian Young is all right though, Munster has a slap-dash style about him, and they do say old Nielsen was a crackerjack. But with the rest I've seen, there's no dash, no go, no cleverness, no real sailor's pride. It's all humdrum, and podgy, and slow-going, any going so long as you get there heaven knows when. But some day I'll show you how the *Martha* should be handled. I'll break out anchor and get under way in a speed and style that will make your head hum; and I'll bring her alongside the wharf at Guvutu without dropping anchor and running a line."

She came to a breathless pause, and then broke into laughter, directed, he could see, against herself.

"Old Kinross is setting that fisherman's staysail," he remarked quietly.

"No!" she cried incredulously, swiftly looking, then running for the telescope.

She regarded the manoeuvre steadily through the glass, and Sheldon, watching her face, could see that the skipper was not making a success of it.

She finally lowered the glass with a groan.

"He's made a mess of it," she said, "and now he's trying it over again. And a man like that is put in charge of a fairy like the *Martha*! Well, it's a good argument against marriage, that's all. No, I won't look any more. Come on in and play a steady, conservative game of billiards with me. And after that I'm going to saddle up and go after pigeons. Will you come along?"

163

An hour later, just as they were riding out of the compound, Joan turned in the saddle for a last look at the *Martha*, a distant speck well over toward the Florida coast.

"Won't Tudor be surprised when he finds we own the *Martha*?" she laughed. "Think of it! If he doesn't strike pay-dirt he'll have to buy a steamer-passage to get away from the Solomons."

Still laughing gaily, she rode through the gate. But suddenly her laughter broke flatly and she reined in the mare. Sheldon glanced at her sharply, and noted her face mottling, even as he looked, and turning orange and green.

"It's the fever," she said. "I'll have to turn back."

By the time they were in the compound she was shivering and shaking, and he had to help her from her horse.

"Funny, isn't it?" she said with chattering teeth. "Like seasickness—not serious, but horribly miserable while it lasts. I'm going to bed. Send Noa Noah and Viaburi to me. Tell Ornfiri to make hot water. I'll be out of my head in fifteen minutes. But I'll be all right by evening. Short and sharp is the way it takes me. Too bad to lose the shooting. Thank you, I'm all right."

Sheldon obeyed her instructions, rushed hot-water bottles along to her, and then sat on the veranda vainly trying to interest himself in a two-months-old file of Sydney newspapers. He kept glancing up and across the compound to the grass house. Yes, he decided, the contention of every white man in the islands was right; the Solomons was no place for a woman.

He clapped his hands, and Lalaperu came running.

"Here, you!" he ordered; "go along barracks, bring 'm black fella Mary, plenty too much, altogether."

A few minutes later the dozen black women of Berande were ranged before him. He looked them over critically, finally selecting one that was young, comely as such creatures went, and whose body bore no signs of skin-disease.

"What name, you?" he demanded. "Sangui?"

"Me Mahua," was the answer.

"All right, you fella Mahua. You finish cook along boys. You stop along white Mary. All the time you stop along. You savvee?"

"Me savvee," she grunted, and obeyed his gesture to go to the grass house immediately.

"What name?" he asked Viaburi, who had just come out of the grass house.

"Big fella sick," was the answer. "White fella Mary talk 'm too much allee time. Allee time talk 'm big fella schooner."

Sheldon nodded. He understood. It was the loss of the *Martha* that had brought on the fever. The fever would have come sooner or later, he knew; but her disappointment had precipitated it. He lighted a cigarette, and in the curling smoke of it caught visions of his English mother, and wondered if she would understand how her son could love a woman who cried because she could not be skipper of a schooner in the cannibal isles.

CHAPTER XX—A MAN-TALK

The most patient man in the world is prone to impatience in love—and Sheldon was in love. He called himself an ass a score of times a day, and strove to contain himself by directing his mind in other channels, but more than a score of times each day his thoughts roved back and dwelt on Joan. It was a pretty problem she presented, and he was continually debating with himself as to what was the best way to approach her.

He was not an adept at love-making. He had had but one experience in the gentle art (in which he had been more wooed than wooing), and the affair had profited him little. This was another affair, and he assured himself continually that it was a uniquely different and difficult affair. Not only was here a woman who was not bent on finding a husband, but it was a woman who wasn't a woman at all; who was genuinely appalled by the thought of a husband; who joyed in boys' games, and sentimentalized over such things as adventure; who was healthy and normal and wholesome, and who was so immature that a husband stood for nothing more than an encumbrance in her cherished scheme of existence.

But how to approach her? He divined the fanatical love of freedom in her, the deep-seated antipathy for restraint of any sort. No man could ever put his arm around her and win her. She would flutter away like a frightened bird. Approach by contact—that, he realized, was the one thing he must never do. His hand-clasp must be what it had always been, the hand-clasp of hearty friendship and nothing more. Never by action must he advertise his feeling for her. Remained speech. But what speech? Appeal to her love? But she did not love him. Appeal to her brain? But it was apparently a boy's brain. All the deliciousness and fineness of a finely bred woman was hers; but, for all he could discern, her mental processes were sexless and boyish. And yet speech it must be, for a beginning had to be made somewhere, some time; her mind must be made accustomed to the idea, her thoughts turned upon the matter of marriage.

And so he rode overseeing about the plantation, with tightly drawn and puckered brows, puzzling over the problem, and steeling himself to the first attempt. A dozen ways he planned an intricate leading up to the first breaking of the ice, and each time some link in the chain snapped and the talk went off on unexpected and irrelevant lines. And then one morning, quite fortuitously, the opportunity came.

"My dearest wish is the success of Berande," Joan had just said, apropos of a discussion about the cheapening of freights on copra to market.

"Do you mind if I tell you the dearest wish of my heart?" he promptly returned. "I long for it. I dream about it. It is my dearest desire."

He paused and looked at her with intent significance; but it was plain to him that she thought there was nothing more at issue than mutual confidences about things in general.

"Yes, go ahead," she said, a trifle impatient at his delay.

"I love to think of the success of Berande," he said; "but that is secondary. It is subordinate to the dearest wish, which is that some day you will share Berande with me in a completer way than that of mere business partnership. It is for you, some day, when you are ready, to be my wife."

She started back from him as if she had been stung. Her face went white on the instant, not from maidenly embarrassment, but from the anger which he could see flaming in her eyes.

"This taking for granted!—this when I am ready!" she cried passionately. Then her voice swiftly became cold and steady, and she talked in the way he imagined she must have talked business with Morgan and Raff at Guvutu. "Listen to me, Mr. Sheldon. I like you very well, though you are slow and a muddler; but I want you to understand, once and for all, that I did not come to the Solomons to get married. That is an affliction I could have accumulated at home, without sailing ten thousand miles after it. I have my own way to make in the world, and I came to the Solomons to do it. Getting married is not making *my* way in the world. It may do for some women, but not for me, thank you. When I sit down to talk over the freight on copra, I don't care to have proposals of marriage sandwiched in. Besides—besides—"

Her voice broke for the moment, and when she went on there was a note of appeal in it that well-nigh convicted him to himself of being a brute.

"Don't you see?—it spoils everything; it makes the whole situation impossible . . . and . . . and I so loved our partnership, and was proud of it. Don't you see?—I can't go on being your partner if you make love to me. And I was so happy."

Tears of disappointment were in her eyes, and she caught a swift sob in her throat.

"I warned you," he said gravely. "Such unusual situations between men and women cannot endure. I told you so at the beginning."

"Oh, yes; it is quite clear to me what you did." She was angry again, and the feminine appeal had disappeared. "You were very discreet in your warning. You took good care to warn me against every other man in the Solomons except yourself."

It was a blow in the face to Sheldon. He smarted with the truth of it, and at the same time he smarted with what he was convinced was the injustice of it. A gleam of triumph that flickered in her eye because of the hit she had made decided him.

"It is not so one-sided as you seem to think it is," he began. "I was doing very nicely on Berande before you came. At least I was not suffering indignities, such as being accused of cowardly conduct, as you have just accused me. Remember—please remember, I did not invite you to Berande. Nor did I invite you to stay on at Berande. It was by staying that you brought about this—to you—unpleasant situation. By staying you made yourself a temptation, and now you would blame me for it. I did not want you to stay. I wasn't in love with you then. I wanted you to go to Sydney; to go back to Hawaii. But you insisted on staying. You virtually—"

He paused for a softer word than the one that had risen to his lips, and she took it away from him.

"Forced myself on you—that's what you meant to say," she cried, the flags of battle painting her cheeks. "Go ahead. Don't mind my feelings."

"All right; I won't," he said decisively, realizing that the discussion was in danger of becoming a vituperative, schoolboy argument. "You have insisted on being considered as a man. Consistency would demand that you talk like a man, and like a man listen to man-talk. And listen you shall. It is not your fault that this unpleasantness has arisen. I do not blame you for anything; remember that. And for the same reason you should not blame me for anything."

He noticed her bosom heaving as she sat with clenched hands, and it was all he could do to conquer the desire to flash his arms out and around her instead of going on with his coolly planned campaign. As it was, he nearly told her that she was a most adorable boy. But he checked all such wayward fancies, and held himself rigidly down to his disquisition.

"You can't help being yourself. You can't help being a very desirable creature so far as I am concerned. You have made me want you. You didn't intend to; you didn't try to. You were so made, that is all. And I was so made that I was ripe to want you. But I can't help being myself. I can't by an effort of will cease from wanting you, any more than you by an effort of will can make yourself undesirable to me."

"Oh, this desire! this want! want! want!" she broke in rebelliously. "I am not quite a fool. I understand some things. And the whole thing is so foolish and absurd—and uncomfortable. I wish I could get away from it. I really think it would be a good idea for me to marry Noa Noah, or Adamu Adam, or Lalaperu there, or any black boy. Then I could give him orders, and keep him penned away from me; and men like you would leave me alone, and not talk marriage and 'I want, I want.'"

Sheldon laughed in spite of himself, and far from any genuine impulse to laugh.

"You are positively soulless," he said savagely.

"Because I've a soul that doesn't yearn for a man for master?" she took up the gage. "Very well, then. I am soulless, and what are you going to do about it?"

169

"I am going to ask you why you look like a woman? Why have you the form of a woman? the lips of a woman? the wonderful hair of a woman? And I am going to answer: because you are a woman—though the woman in you is asleep—and that some day the woman will wake up."

"Heaven forbid!" she cried, in such sudden and genuine dismay as to make him laugh, and to bring a smile to her own lips against herself.

"I've got some more to say to you," Sheldon pursued. "I did try to protect you from every other man in the Solomons, and from yourself as well. As for me, I didn't dream that danger lay in that quarter. So I failed to protect you from myself. I failed to protect you at all. You went your own wilful way, just as though I didn't exist—wrecking schooners, recruiting on Malaita, and sailing schooners; one lone, unprotected girl in the company of some of the worst scoundrels in the Solomons. Fowler! and Brahms! and Curtis! And such is the perverseness of human nature—I am frank, you see—I love you for that too. I love you for all of you, just as you are."

She made a *moue* of distaste and raised a hand protestingly.

"Don't," he said. "You have no right to recoil from the mention of my love for you. Remember this is a man-talk. From the point of view of the talk, you are a man. The woman in you is only incidental, accidental, and irrelevant. You've got to listen to the bald statement of fact, strange though it is, that I love you."

"And now I won't bother you any more about love. We'll go on the same as before. You are better off and safer on Berande, in spite of the fact that I love you, than anywhere else in the Solomons. But I want you, as a final item of man-talk, to remember, from time to time, that I love you, and that it will be the dearest day of my life when you consent to marry me. I want you to think of it sometimes. You can't help but think of it sometimes. And now we won't talk about it any more. As between men, there's my hand."

He held out his hand. She hesitated, then gripped it heartily, and smiled through her tears.

"I wish—" she faltered, "I wish, instead of that black Mary, you'd given me somebody to swear for me."

And with this enigmatic utterance she turned away.

170

CHAPTER XXI—CONTRABAND

Sheldon did not mention the subject again, nor did his conduct change from what it had always been. There was nothing of the pining lover, nor of the lover at all, in his demeanour. Nor was there any awkwardness between them. They were as frank and friendly in their relations as ever. He had wondered if his belligerent love declaration might have aroused some womanly self-consciousness in Joan, but he looked in vain for any sign of it. She appeared as unchanged as he; and while he knew that he hid his real feelings, he was firm in his belief that she hid nothing. And yet the germ he had implanted must be at work; he was confident of that, though he was without confidence as to the result. There was no forecasting this strange girl's processes. She might awaken, it was true; and on the other hand, and with equal chance, he might be the wrong man for her, and his declaration of love might only more firmly set her in her views on single blessedness.

While he devoted more and more of his time to the plantation itself, she took over the house and its multitudinous affairs; and she took hold firmly, in sailor fashion, revolutionizing the system and discipline. The labour situation on Berande was improving. The *Martha* had carried away fifty of the blacks whose time was up, and they had been among the worst on the plantation—five-year men recruited by Billy Be-blowed, men who had gone through the old days of terrorism when the original owners of Berande had been driven away. The new recruits, being broken in under the new regime, gave better promise. Joan had joined with Sheldon from the start in the programme that they must be gripped with the strong hand, and at the same time be treated with absolute justice, if they were to escape being contaminated by the older boys that still remained.

"I think it would be a good idea to put all the gangs at work close to the house this afternoon," she announced one day at breakfast. "I've cleaned up the house, and you ought to clean up the barracks. There is too much stealing going on."

"A good idea," Sheldon agreed. "Their boxes should be searched. I've just missed a couple of shirts, and my best toothbrush is gone."

"And two boxes of my cartridges," she added, "to say nothing of handkerchiefs, towels, sheets, and my best pair of slippers. But what they want with your toothbrush is more than I can imagine. They'll be stealing the billiard balls next."

"One did disappear a few weeks before you came," Sheldon laughed. "We'll search the boxes this afternoon."

And a busy afternoon it was. Joan and Sheldon, both armed, went through the barracks, house by house, the boss-boys assisting, and half a dozen messengers, in relay, shouting along the line the names of the boys wanted. Each boy brought the key to his particular box, and was permitted to look on while the contents were overhauled by the boss-boys.

A wealth of loot was recovered. There were fully a dozen cane-knives—big hacking weapons with razor-edges, capable of decapitating a man at a stroke. Towels, sheets, shirts, and slippers, along with toothbrushes, wisp-brooms, soap, the missing billiard ball, and all the lost and forgotten trifles of many months, came to light. But most astonishing was the quantity of ammunition-cartridges for Lee-Metfords, for Winchesters and Marlins, for revolvers from thirty-two calibre to forty-five, shot-gun cartridges, Joan's two boxes of thirty-eight, cartridges of prodigious bore for the ancient Sniders of Malaita, flasks of black powder, sticks of dynamite, yards of fuse, and boxes of detonators. But the great find was in the house occupied by Gogoomy and five Port Adams recruits. The fact that the boxes yielded nothing excited Sheldon's suspicions, and he gave orders to dig up the earthen floor. Wrapped in matting, well oiled, free from rust, and brand new, two Winchesters were first unearthed. Sheldon did not recognize them. They had not come from Berande; neither had the forty flasks of black powder found under the corner-post of the house; and while he could not be sure, he could remember no loss of eight boxes of detonators. A big Colt's revolver he recognized as Hughie Drummond's; while Joan identified a thirty-two Ivor and Johnson as a loss reported by Matapuu the first week he landed at Berande. The absence of any cartridges made Sheldon persist in the digging up of the floor, and a fifty-pound flour tin was his reward. With glowering eyes Gogoomy looked on while Sheldon took from the tin a hundred rounds each for the two Winchesters and fully as many rounds more of nondescript cartridges of all sorts and makes and calibres.

The contraband and stolen property was piled in assorted heaps on the back veranda of the bungalow. A few paces from the bottom of the steps were grouped the forty-odd culprits, with behind them, in solid array, the several hundred blacks of the plantation. At the head of the steps Joan and Sheldon were seated, while on the steps stood the gang-bosses. One by one the culprits were called up and examined. Nothing definite could be extracted from them. They lied transparently, but persistently, and when caught in one lie explained it away with half a dozen others. One boy complacently announced that he had found eleven sticks of dynamite on the beach. Matapuu's revolver, found in the box of one Kapu, was explained away by that boy as having been given to him by Lervumie. Lervumie, called forth to testify, said he had got it from Noni; Noni had got it from Sulefatoi; Sulefatoi from Choka; Choka from Ngava; and Ngava completed the circle by stating that it had been given to him by Kapu. Kapu, thus doubly damned, calmly gave full details of how it had been given to him by Lervumie; and Lervumie, with equal wealth of detail, told how he had received it from Noni; and from Noni to Sulefatoi it went on around the circle again.

Divers articles were traced indubitably to the house-boys, each of whom steadfastly proclaimed his own innocence and cast doubts on his fellows. The boy with the billiard ball said that he had never seen it in his life before, and hazarded the suggestion that it had got into his box through some mysterious and occultly evil agency. So far as he was concerned it might have dropped down from heaven for all he knew how it got there. To the cooks and boats'-crews of every vessel that had dropped anchor off Berande in the past several years were ascribed the arrival of scores of the stolen articles and of the major portion of the ammunition. There was no tracing the truth in any of it, though it was without doubt that the unidentified weapons and unfamiliar cartridges had come ashore off visiting craft.

"Look at it," Sheldon said to Joan. "We've been sleeping over a volcano. They ought to be whipped—"

"No whip me," Gogoomy cried out from below. "Father belong me big fella chief. Me whip, too much trouble along you, close up, my word."

"What name you fella Gogoomy!" Sheldon shouted. "I knock seven bells out of you. Here, you Kwaque, put 'm irons along that fella Gogoomy."

Kwaque, a strapping gang-boss, plucked Gogoomy from out of his following, and, helped by the other gang-bosses; twisted his arms behind him and snapped on the heavy handcuffs.

"Me finish along you, close up, you die altogether," Gogoomy, with wrath-distorted face, threatened the boss-boy.

"Please, no whipping," Joan said in a low voice. "If whipping *is* necessary, send them to Tulagi and let the Government do it. Give them their choice between a fine or an official whipping."

Sheldon nodded and stood up, facing the blacks.

"Manonmie!" he called.

Manonmie stood forth and waited.

"You fella boy bad fella too much," Sheldon charged. "You steal 'm plenty. You steal 'm one fella towel, one fella cane-knife, two-ten fella cartridge. My word, plenty bad fella steal 'm you. Me cross along you too much. S'pose you like 'm, me take 'm one fella pound along you in big book. S'pose you no like 'm me take 'm one fella pound, then me send you fella along Tulagi catch 'm one strong fella government whipping. Plenty New Georgia boys, plenty Ysabel boys stop along jail along Tulagi. Them fella no like Malaita boys little bit. My word, they give 'm you strong fella whipping. What you say?"

"You take 'm one fella pound along me," was the answer.

And Manonmie, patently relieved, stepped back, while Sheldon entered the fine in the plantation labour journal.

174

Boy after boy, he called the offenders out and gave them their choice; and, boy by boy, each one elected to pay the fine imposed. Some fines were as low as several shillings; while in the more serious cases, such as thefts of guns and ammunition, the fines were correspondingly heavy.

Gogoomy and his five tribesmen were fined three pounds each, and at Gogoomy's guttural command they refused to pay.

"S'pose you go along Tulagi," Sheldon warned him, "you catch 'm strong fella whipping and you stop along jail three fella year. Mr. Burnett, he look 'm along Winchester, look 'm along cartridge, look 'm along revolver, look 'm along black powder, look 'm along dynamite—my word, he cross too much, he give you three fella year along jail. S'pose you no like 'm pay three fella pound you stop along jail. Savvee?"

Gogoomy wavered.

"It's true—that's what Burnett would give them," Sheldon said in an aside to Joan.

"You take 'm three fella pound along me," Gogoomy muttered, at the same time scowling his hatred at Sheldon, and transferring half the scowl to Joan and Kwaque. "Me finish along you, you catch 'm big fella trouble, my word. Father belong me big fella chief along Port Adams."

"That will do," Sheldon warned him. "You shut mouth belong you."

"Me no fright," the son of a chief retorted, by his insolence increasing his stature in the eyes of his fellows.

"Lock him up for to-night," Sheldon said to Kwaque. "Sun he come up put 'm that fella and five fella belong him along grass-cutting. Savvee?"

Kwaque grinned.

"Me savvee," he said. "Cut 'm grass, *ngari-ngari* {4} stop 'm along grass. My word!"

"There will be trouble with Gogoomy yet," Sheldon said to Joan, as the boss-boys marshalled their gangs and led them away to their work. "Keep an

175

eye on him. Be careful when you are riding alone on the plantation. The loss of those Winchesters and all that ammunition has hit him harder than your cuffing did. He is dead-ripe for mischief."

CHAPTER XXII—GOGOOMY FINISHES ALONG KWAQUE ALTOGETHER

"I wonder what has become of Tudor. It's two months since he disappeared into the bush, and not a word of him after he left Binu."

Joan Lackland was sitting astride her horse by the bank of the Balesuna where the sweet corn had been planted, and Sheldon, who had come across from the house on foot, was leaning against her horse's shoulder.

"Yes, it is along time for no news to have trickled down," he answered, watching her keenly from under his hat-brim and wondering as to the measure of her anxiety for the adventurous gold-hunter; "but Tudor will come out all right. He did a thing at the start that I wouldn't have given him or any other man credit for—persuaded Binu Charley to go along with him. I'll wager no other Binu nigger has ever gone so far into the bush unless to be *kai-kai*'d. As for Tudor—"

"Look! look!" Joan cried in a low voice, pointing across the narrow stream to a slack eddy where a huge crocodile drifted like a log awash. "My! I wish I had my rifle."

The crocodile, leaving scarcely a ripple behind, sank down and disappeared.

"A Binu man was in early this morning—for medicine," Sheldon remarked. "It may have been that very brute that was responsible. A dozen of the Binu women were out, and the foremost one stepped right on a big crocodile. It was by the edge of the water, and he tumbled her over and got her by the leg. All the other women got hold of her and pulled. And in the tug of war she lost her leg, below the knee, he said. I gave him a stock of antiseptics. She'll pull through, I fancy."

"Ugh—the filthy beasts," Joan gulped shudderingly. "I hate them! I hate them!"

"And yet you go diving among sharks," Sheldon chided.

"They're only fish-sharks. And as long as there are plenty of fish there is no danger. It is only when they're famished that they're liable to take a bite."

Sheldon shuddered inwardly at the swift vision that arose of the dainty flesh of her in a shark's many-toothed maw.

"I wish you wouldn't, just the same," he said slowly. "You acknowledge there is a risk."

"But that's half the fun of it," she cried.

A trite platitude about his not caring to lose her was on his lips, but he refrained from uttering it. Another conclusion he had arrived at was that she was not to be nagged. Continual, or even occasional, reminders of his feeling for her would constitute a tactical error of no mean dimensions.

"Some for the book of verse, some for the simple life, and some for the shark's belly," he laughed grimly, then added: "Just the same, I wish I could swim as well as you. Maybe it would beget confidence such as you have."

"Do you know, I think it would be nice to be married to a man such as you seem to be becoming," she remarked, with one of her abrupt changes that always astounded him. "I should think you could be trained into a very good husband—you know, not one of the domineering kind, but one who considered his wife was just as much an individual as himself and just as much a free agent. Really, you know, I think you are improving."

She laughed and rode away, leaving him greatly cast down. If he had thought there had been one bit of coyness in her words, one feminine flutter, one womanly attempt at deliberate lure and encouragement, he would have been elated. But he knew absolutely that it was the boy, and not the woman, who had so daringly spoken.

Joan rode on among the avenues of young cocoanut-palms, saw a hornbill, followed it in its erratic flights to the high forest on the edge of the plantation, heard the cooing of wild pigeons and located them in the deeper woods, followed the fresh trail of a wild pig for a distance, circled back, and took the narrow path for the bungalow that ran through twenty acres of uncleared cane. The grass was waist-high and higher, and as she rode along she remembered that Gogoomy was one of a gang of boys that had been detailed to the grass-cutting. She came to where they had been at work, but saw no signs of them. Her unshod horse made no sound on the soft, sandy footing, and a little further on she heard voices proceeding from out of the grass. She reined in and listened. It was Gogoomy talking, and as she listened she gripped her bridle-rein tightly and a wave of anger passed over her.

"Dog he stop 'm along house, night-time he walk about," Gogoomy was saying, perforce in *bêche-de-mer* English, because he was talking to others beside his own tribesmen. "You fella boy catch 'm one fella pig, put 'm *kai-kai* belong him along big fella fish-hook. S'pose dog he walk about catch 'm *kai-kai*, you fella boy catch 'm dog allee same one shark. Dog he finish close up. Big fella marster sleep along big fella house. White Mary sleep along pickaninny house. One fella Adamu he stop along outside pickaninny house. You fella boy finish 'm dog, finish 'm Adamu, finish 'm big fella marster, finish 'm White Mary, finish 'em altogether. Plenty musket he stop, plenty powder, plenty tomahawk, plenty knife-fee, plenty porpoise teeth, plenty tobacco, plenty calico—my word, too much plenty everything we take 'm along whale-boat, washee {5} like hell, sun he come up we long way too much."

"Me catch 'm pig sun he go down," spoke up one whose thin falsetto voice Joan recognized as belonging to Cosse, one of Gogoomy's tribesmen.

"Me catch 'm dog," said another.

"And me catch 'm white fella Mary," Gogoomy cried triumphantly. "Me catch 'm Kwaque he die along him damn quick."

This much Joan heard of the plan to murder, and then her rising wrath proved too much for her discretion. She spurred her horse into the grass, crying,—

"What name you fella boy, eh? What name?"

They arose, scrambling and scattering, and to her surprise she saw there were a dozen of them. As she looked in their glowering faces and noted the heavy, two-foot, hacking cane-knives in their hands, she became suddenly aware of the rashness of her act. If only she had had her revolver or a rifle, all would have been well. But she had carelessly ventured out unarmed, and she followed the glance of Gogoomy to her waist and saw the pleased flash in his eyes as he perceived the absence of the dreadful man-killing revolver.

The first article in the Solomon Islands code for white men was never to show fear before a native, and Joan tried to carry off the situation in cavalier fashion.

"Too much talk along you fella boy," she said severely. "Too much talk, too little work. Savvee?"

Gogoomy made no reply, but, apparently shifting weight, he slid one foot forward. The other boys, spread fan-wise about her, were also sliding forward, the cruel cane-knives in their hands advertising their intention.

"You cut 'm grass!" she commanded imperatively.

But Gogoomy slid his other foot forward. She measured the distance with her eye. It would be impossible to whirl her horse around and get away. She would be chopped down from behind.

And in that tense moment the faces of all of them were imprinted on her mind in an unforgettable picture—one of them, an old man, with torn and distended ear-lobes that fell to his chest; another, with the broad flattened nose of Africa, and with withered eyes so buried under frowning brows that nothing but the sickly, yellowish-looking whites could be seen; a third, thick-lipped and bearded with kinky whiskers; and Gogoomy—she had never realized before how handsome Gogoomy was in his mutinous and obstinate wild-animal way. There was a primitive aristocraticness about him that his fellows lacked. The lines of his figure were more rounded than theirs, the skin smooth, well oiled, and free from disease. On his chest, suspended from a single string of porpoise-teeth around his throat, hung a big crescent carved out of opalescent pearl-shell. A row of pure white cowrie shells banded his brow. From his hair drooped a long, lone feather. Above the swelling calf of one leg he wore, as a garter, a single string of white beads. The effect was dandyish in the extreme. A narrow gee-string completed his costume.

Another man she saw, old and shrivelled, with puckered forehead and a puckered face that trembled and worked with animal passion as in the past she had noticed the faces of monkeys tremble and work.

"Gogoomy," she said sharply, "you no cut 'm grass, my word, I bang 'm head belong you."

His expression became a trifle more disdainful, but he did not answer. Instead, he stole a glance to right and left to mark how his fellows were closing about her. At the same moment he casually slipped his foot forward through the grass for a matter of several inches.

Joan was keenly aware of the desperateness of the situation. The only way out was through. She lifted her riding-whip threateningly, and at the same moment drove in both spurs with her heels, rushing the startled horse straight at Gogoomy. It all happened in an instant. Every cane-knife was lifted, and every boy save Gogoomy leaped for her. He swerved aside to avoid the horse, at the same time swinging his cane-knife in a slicing blow that would have cut her in twain. She leaned forward under the flying steel, which cut through her riding-skirt, through the edge of the saddle, through the saddle cloth, and even slightly into the horse itself. Her right hand, still raised, came down, the thin whip whishing through the air. She saw the white, cooked mark of the weal clear across the sullen, handsome face, and still what was practically in the same instant she saw the man with the puckered face, overridden, go down before her, and she heard his snarling and grimacing chatter-for all the world like an angry monkey. Then she was free and away, heading the horse at top speed for the house.

Out of her sea-training she was able to appreciate Sheldon's executiveness when she burst in on him with her news. Springing from the steamer-chair in which he had been lounging while waiting for breakfast, he clapped his hands for the house-boys; and, while listening to her, he was buckling on his cartridge-belt and running the mechanism of his automatic pistol.

"Ornfiri," he snapped out his orders, "you fella ring big fella bell strong fella plenty. You finish 'm bell, you put 'm saddle on horse. Viaburi, you go quick house belong Seelee he stop, tell 'm plenty black fella run away—ten fella two fella black fella boy." He scribbled a note and handed it to Lalaperu. "Lalaperu, you go quick house belong white fella Marster Boucher."

"That will head them back from the coast on both sides," he explained to Joan. "And old Seelee will turn his whole village loose on their track as well."

In response to the summons of the big bell, Joan's Tahitians were the first to arrive, by their glistening bodies and panting chests showing that they had run all the way. Some of the farthest-placed gangs would be nearly an hour in arriving.

Sheldon proceeded to arm Joan's sailors and deal out ammunition and handcuffs. Adamu Adam, with loaded rifle, he placed on guard over the whale-boats. Noa Noah, aided by Matapuu, were instructed to take charge of the working-gangs as fast as they came in, to keep them amused, and to guard against their being stampeded into making a break themselves. The five other Tahitians were to follow Joan and Sheldon on foot.

"I'm glad we unearthed that arsenal the other day," Sheldon remarked as they rode out of the compound gate.

A hundred yards away they encountered one of the clearing gangs coming in. It was Kwaque's gang, but Sheldon looked in vain for him.

"What name that fella Kwaque he no stop along you?" he demanded.

A babel of excited voices attempted an answer.

"Shut 'm mouth belong you altogether," Sheldon commanded.

He spoke roughly, living up to the rôle of the white man who must always be strong and dominant.

"Here, you fella Babatani, you talk 'm mouth belong you."

Babatani stepped forward in all the pride of one singled out from among his fellows.

"Gogoomy he finish along Kwaque altogether," was Babatani's explanation. "He take 'm head b'long him run like hell."

In brief words, and with paucity of imagination, he described the murder, and Sheldon and Joan rode on. In the grass, where Joan had been attacked, they found the little shrivelled man, still chattering and grimacing, whom Joan had ridden down. The mare had plunged on his ankle, completely crushing it, and a hundred yards' crawl had convinced him of the futility of escape. To the last clearing-gang, from the farthest edge of the plantation, was given the task of carrying him in to the house.

A mile farther on, where the runaways' trail led straight toward the bush, they encountered the body of Kwaque. The head had been hacked off and was missing, and Sheldon took it on faith that the body was Kwaque's. He had evidently put up a fight, for a bloody trail led away from the body.

Once they were well into the thick bush the horses had to be abandoned. Papehara was left in charge of them, while Joan and Sheldon and the remaining Tahitians pushed ahead on foot. The way led down through a swampy hollow, which was overflowed by the Berande River on occasion, and where the red trail of the murderers was crossed by a crocodile's trail. They had apparently caught the creature asleep in the sun and desisted long enough from their flight to hack him to pieces. Here the wounded man had sat down and waited until they were ready to go on.

An hour later, following along a wild-pig trail, Sheldon suddenly halted. The bloody tracks had ceased. The Tahitians cast out in the bush on either side, and a cry from Utami apprised them of a find. Joan waited till Sheldon came back.

"It's Mauko," he said. "Kwaque did for him, and he crawled in there and died. That's two accounted for. There are ten more. Don't you think you've got enough of it?"

She nodded.

"It isn't nice," she said. "I'll go back and wait for you with the horses."

"But you can't go alone. Take two of the men."

"Then I'll go on," she said. "It would be foolish to weaken the pursuit, and I am certainly not tired."

The trail bent to the right as though the runaways had changed their mind and headed for the Balesuna. But the trail still continued to bend to the right till it promised to make a loop, and the point of intersection seemed to be the edge of the plantation where the horses had been left. Crossing one of the quiet jungle spaces, where naught moved but a velvety, twelve-inch butterfly, they heard the sound of shots.

"Eight," Joan counted. "It was only one gun. It must be Papehara."

They hurried on, but when they reached the spot they were in doubt. The two horses stood quietly tethered, and Papehara, squatted on his hams, was having a peaceful smoke. Advancing toward him, Sheldon tripped on a body that lay in the grass, and as he saved himself from falling his eyes lighted on a second. Joan recognized this one. It was Cosse, one of Gogoomy's tribesmen, the one who had promised to catch at sunset the pig that was to have baited the hook for Satan.

"No luck, Missie," was Papehara's greeting, accompanied by a disconsolate shake of the head. "Catch only two boy. I have good shot at Gogoomy, only I miss."

"But you killed them," Joan chided. "You must catch them alive."

The Tahitian smiled.

"How?" he queried. "I am have a smoke. I think about Tahiti, and breadfruit, and jolly good time at Bora Bora. Quick, just like that, ten boy he run out of bush for me. Each boy have long knife. Gogoomy have long knife one hand, and Kwaque's head in other hand. I no stop to catch 'm alive. I shoot like hell. How you catch 'm alive, ten boy, ten long knife, and Kwaque's head?"

The scattered paths of the different boys, where they broke back after the disastrous attempt to rush the Tahitian, soon led together. They traced it to the Berande, which the runaways had crossed with the clear intention of burying themselves in the huge mangrove swamp that lay beyond.

"There is no use our going any farther," Sheldon said. "Seelee will turn out his village and hunt them out of that. They'll never get past him. All we can do is to guard the coast and keep them from breaking back on the plantation and running amuck. Ah, I thought so."

Against the jungle gloom of the farther shore, coming from down stream, a small canoe glided. So silently did it move that it was more like an apparition. Three naked blacks dipped with noiseless paddles. Long-hafted, slender, bone-barbed throwing-spears lay along the gunwale of the canoe, while a quiverful of arrows hung on each man's back. The eyes of the man-hunters missed nothing. They had seen Sheldon and Joan first, but they gave no sign. Where Gogoomy and his followers had emerged from the river, the canoe abruptly stopped, then turned and disappeared into the deeper mangrove gloom. A second and a third canoe came around the bend from below, glided ghostlike to the crossing of the runaways, and vanished in the mangroves.

"I hope there won't be any more killing," Joan said, as they turned their horses homeward.

"I don't think so," Sheldon assured her. "My understanding with old Seelee is that he is paid only for live boys; so he is very careful."

CHAPTER XXIII—A MESSAGE FROM THE BUSH

Never had runaways from Berande been more zealously hunted. The deeds of Gogoomy and his fellows had been a bad example for the one hundred and fifty new recruits. Murder had been planned, a gang-boss had been killed, and the murderers had broken their contracts by fleeing to the bush. Sheldon saw how imperative it was to teach his new-caught cannibals that bad examples were disastrous things to pattern after, and he urged Seelee on night and day, while with the Tahitians he practically lived in the bush, leaving Joan in charge of the plantation. To the north Boucher did good work, twice turning the fugitives back when they attempted to gain the coast.

One by one the boys were captured. In the first man-drive through the mangrove swamp Seelee caught two. Circling around to the north, a third was wounded in the thigh by Boucher, and this one, dragging behind in the chase, was later gathered in by Seelee's hunters. The three captives, heavily ironed, were exposed each day in the compound, as good examples of what happened to bad examples, all for the edification of the seven score and ten half-wild Poonga-Poonga men. Then the *Minerva*, running past for Tulagi, was signalled to send a boat, and the three prisoners were carried away to prison to await trial.

Five were still at large, but escape was impossible. They could not get down to the coast, nor dared they venture too far inland for fear of the wild bushmen. Then one of the five came in voluntarily and gave himself up, and Sheldon learned that Gogoomy and two others were all that were at large. There should have been a fourth, but according to the man who had given himself up, the fourth man had been killed and eaten. It had been fear of a similar fate that had driven him in. He was a Malu man, from north-western Malaita, as likewise had been the one that was eaten. Gogoomy's two other companions were from Port Adams. As for himself, the black declared his preference for government trial and punishment to being eaten by his companions in the bush.

"Close up Gogoomy *kai-kai* me," he said. "My word, me no like boy *kai-kai* me."

Three days later Sheldon caught one of the boys, helpless from swamp fever, and unable to fight or run away. On the same day Seelee caught the second boy in similar condition. Gogoomy alone remained at large; and, as the pursuit closed in on him, he conquered his fear of the bushmen and headed straight in for the mountainous backbone of the island. Sheldon with four Tahitians, and Seelee with thirty of his hunters, followed Gogoomy's trail a dozen miles into the open grass-lands, and then Seelee and his people lost heart. He confessed that neither he nor any of his tribe had ever ventured so far inland before, and he narrated, for Sheldon's benefit, most horrible tales of the horrible bushmen. In the old days, he said, they had crossed the grass-lands and attacked the salt-water natives; but since the coming of the white men to the coast they had remained in their interior fastnesses, and no salt-water native had ever seen them again.

"Gogoomy he finish along them fella bushmen," he assured Sheldon. "My word, he finish close up, *kai-kai* altogether."

So the expedition turned back. Nothing could persuade the coast natives to venture farther, and Sheldon, with his four Tahitians, knew that it was madness to go on alone. So he stood waist-deep in the grass and looked regretfully across the rolling savannah and the soft-swelling foothills to the Lion's Head, a massive peak of rock that upreared into the azure from the midmost centre of Guadalcanal, a landmark used for bearings by every coasting mariner, a mountain as yet untrod by the foot of a white man.

That night, after dinner, Sheldon and Joan were playing billiards, when Satan barked in the compound, and Lalaperu, sent to see, brought back a tired and travel-stained native, who wanted to talk with the "big fella white marster." It was only the man's insistence that procured him admittance at such an hour. Sheldon went out on the veranda to see him, and at first glance at the gaunt features and wasted body of the man knew that his errand was likely to prove important. Nevertheless, Sheldon demanded roughly,—

"What name you come along house belong me sun he go down?"

"Me Charley," the man muttered apologetically and wearily. "Me stop along Binu."

"Ah, Binu Charley, eh? Well, what name you talk along me? What place big fella marster along white man he stop?"

Joan and Sheldon together listened to the tale Binu Charley had brought. He described Tudor's expedition up the Balesuna; the dragging of the boats up the rapids; the passage up the river where it threaded the grass-lands; the innumerable washings of gravel by the white men in search of gold; the first rolling foothills; the man-traps of spear-staked pits in the jungle trails; the first meeting with the bushmen, who had never seen tobacco, and knew not the virtues of smoking; their friendliness; the deeper penetration of the interior around the flanks of the Lion's Head; the bush-sores and the fevers of the white men, and their madness in trusting the bushmen.

"Allee time I talk along white fella marster," he said. "Me talk, 'That fella bushman he look 'm eye belong him. He savvee too much. S'pose musket he stop along you, that fella bushman he too much good friend along you. Allee time he look sharp eye belong him. S'pose musket he no stop along you, my word, that fella bushman he chop 'm off head belong you. He *kai-kai* you altogether.'"

But the patience of the bushmen had exceeded that of the white men. The weeks had gone by, and no overt acts had been attempted. The bushmen swarmed in the camp in increasing numbers, and they were always making presents of yams and taro, of pig and fowl, and of wild fruits and vegetables. Whenever the gold-hunters moved their camp, the bushmen volunteered to carry the luggage. And the white men waxed ever more careless. They grew weary prospecting, and at the same time carrying their rifles and the heavy cartridge-belts, and the practice began of leaving their weapons behind them in camp.

"I tell 'm plenty fella white marster look sharp eye belong him. And plenty fella white marster make 'm big laugh along me, say Binu Charley allee same pickaninny—my word, they speak along me allee same pickaninny."

188

Came the morning when Binu Charley noticed that the women and children had disappeared. Tudor, at the time, was lying in a stupor with fever in a late camp five miles away, the main camp having moved on those five miles in order to prospect an outcrop of likely quartz. Binu Charley was midway between the two camps when the absence of the women and children struck him as suspicious.

"My word," he said, "me t'ink like hell. Him black Mary, him pickaninny, walk about long way big bit. What name? Me savvee too much trouble close up. Me fright like hell. Me run. My word, me run."

Tudor, quite unconscious, was slung across his shoulder, and carried a mile down the trail. Here, hiding new trail, Binu Charley had carried him for a quarter of a mile into the heart of the deepest jungle, and hidden him in a big banyan tree. Returning to try to save the rifles and personal outfit, Binu Charley had seen a party of bushmen trotting down the trail, and had hidden in the bush. Here, and from the direction of the main camp, he had heard two rifle shots. And that was all. He had never seen the white men again, nor had he ventured near their old camp. He had gone back to Tudor, and hidden with him for a week, living on wild fruits and the few pigeons and cockatoos he had been able to shoot with bow and arrow. Then he had journeyed down to Berande to bring the news. Tudor, he said, was very sick, lying unconscious for days at a time, and, when in his right mind, too weak to help himself.

"What name you no kill 'm that big fella marster?" Joan demanded. "He have 'm good fella musket, plenty calico, plenty tobacco, plenty knife-fee, and two fella pickaninny musket shoot quick, bang-bang-bang—just like that."

The black smiled cunningly.

"Me savvee too much. S'pose me kill 'm big fella marster, bimeby plenty white fella marster walk about Binu cross like hell. 'What name this fellow musket?' those plenty fella white marster talk 'm along me. My word, Binu Charley finish altogether. S'pose me kill 'm him, no good along me. Plenty white fella marster cross along me. S'pose me no kill 'm him, bimeby he give me plenty tobacco, plenty calico, plenty everything too much."

"There is only the one thing to do," Sheldon said to Joan.

She drummed with her hand and waited, while Binu Charley gazed wearily at her with unblinking eyes.

"I'll start the first thing in the morning," Sheldon said.

"We'll start," she corrected. "I can get twice as much out of my Tahitians as you can, and, besides, one white should never be alone under such circumstances."

He shrugged his shoulders in token, not of consent, but of surrender, knowing the uselessness of attempting to argue the question with her, and consoling himself with the reflection that heaven alone knew what adventures she was liable to engage in if left alone on Berande for a week. He clapped his hands, and for the next quarter of an hour the house-boys were kept busy carrying messages to the barracks. A man was sent to Balesuna village to command old Seelee's immediate presence. A boat's-crew was started in a whale-boat with word for Boucher to come down. Ammunition was issued to the Tahitians, and the storeroom overhauled for a few days' tinned provisions. Viaburi turned yellow when told that he was to accompany the expedition, and, to everybody's surprise, Lalaperu volunteered to take his place.

Seelee arrived, proud in his importance that the great master of Berande should summon him in the night-time for council, and firm in his refusal to step one inch within the dread domain of the bushmen. As he said, if his opinion had been asked when the gold-hunters started, he would have foretold their disastrous end. There was only one thing that happened to any one who ventured into the bushmen's territory, and that was that he was eaten. And he would further say, without being asked, that if Sheldon went up into the bush he would be eaten too.

Sheldon sent for a gang-boss and told him to bring ten of the biggest, best, and strongest Poonga-Poonga men.

"Not salt-water boys," Sheldon cautioned, "but bush boys—leg belong him strong fella leg. Boy no savvee musket, no good. You bring 'm boy shoot musket strong fella."

190

They were ten picked men that filed up on the veranda and stood in the glare of the lanterns. Their heavy, muscular legs advertised that they were bushmen. Each claimed long experience in bush-fighting, most of them showed scars of bullet or spear-thrust in proof, and all were wild for a chance to break the humdrum monotony of plantation labour by going on a killing expedition. Killing was their natural vocation, not wood-cutting; and while they would not have ventured the Guadalcanal bush alone, with a white man like Sheldon behind them, and a white Mary such as they knew Joan to be, they could expect a safe and delightful time. Besides, the great master had told them that the eight gigantic Tahitians were going along.

The Poonga-Poonga volunteers stood with glistening eyes and grinning faces, naked save for their loin-cloths, and barbarously ornamented. Each wore a flat, turtle-shell ring suspended through his nose, and each carried a clay pipe in an ear-hole or thrust inside a beaded biceps armlet. A pair of magnificent boar tusks graced the chest of one. On the chest of another hung a huge disc of polished fossil clam-shell.

"Plenty strong fella fight," Sheldon warned them in conclusion.

They grinned and shifted delightedly.

"S'pose bushmen *kai-kai* along you?" he queried.

"No fear," answered their spokesman, one Koogoo, a strapping, thick-lipped Ethiopian-looking man. "S'pose Poonga-Poonga boy *kai-kai* bush-boy?"

Sheldon shook his head, laughing, and dismissed them, and went to overhaul the dunnage-room for a small shelter tent for Joan's use.

CHAPTER XXIV—IN THE BUSH

It was quite a formidable expedition that departed from Berande at break of day next morning in a fleet of canoes and dinghies. There were Joan and Sheldon, with Binu Charley and Lalaperu, the eight Tahitians, and the ten Poonga-Poonga men, each proud in the possession of a bright and shining modern rifle. In addition, there were two of the plantation boat's-crews of six men each. These, however, were to go no farther than Carli, where water transportation ceased and where they were to wait with the boats. Boucher remained behind in charge of Berande.

By eleven in the morning the expedition arrived at Binu, a cluster of twenty houses on the river bank. And from here thirty odd Binu men accompanied them, armed with spears and arrows, chattering and grimacing with delight at the warlike array. The long quiet stretches of river gave way to swifter water, and progress was slower and more dogged. The Balesuna grew shallow as well, and oftener were the loaded boats bumped along and half-lifted over the bottom. In places timber-falls blocked the passage of the narrow stream, and the boats and canoes were portaged around. Night brought them to Carli, and they had the satisfaction of knowing that they had accomplished in one day what had required two days for Tudor's expedition.

Here at Carli, next morning, half-way through the grass-lands, the boat's-crews were left, and with them the horde of Binu men, the boldest of which held on for a bare mile and then ran scampering back. Binu Charley, however, was at the fore, and led the way onward into the rolling foothills, following the trail made by Tudor and his men weeks before. That night they camped well into the hills and deep in the tropic jungle. The third day found them on the run-ways of the bushmen—narrow paths that compelled single file and that turned and twisted with endless convolutions through the dense undergrowth. For the most part it was a silent forest, lush and dank, where only occasionally a wood-pigeon cooed or snow-white cockatoos laughed harshly in laborious flight.

Here, in the mid-morning, the first casualty occurred. Binu Charley had dropped behind for a time, and Koogoo, the Poonga-Poonga man who had boasted that he would eat the bushmen, was in the lead. Joan and Sheldon heard the twanging thrum and saw Koogoo throw out his arms, at the same time dropping his rifle, stumble forward, and sink down on his hands and knees. Between his naked shoulders, low down and to the left, appeared the bone-barbed head of an arrow. He had been shot through and through. Cocked rifles swept the bush with nervous apprehension. But there was no rustle, no movement; nothing but the humid oppressive silence.

"Bushmen he no stop," Binu Charley called out, the sound of his voice startling more than one of them. "Allee same damn funny business. That fella Koogoo no look 'm eye belong him. He no savvee little bit."

Koogoo's arms had crumpled under him, and he lay quivering where he had fallen. Even as Binu Charley came to the front the stricken black's breath passed from him, and with a final convulsive stir he lay still.

"Right through the heart," Sheldon said, straightening up from the stooping examination. "It must have been a trap of some sort."

He noticed Joan's white, tense face, and the wide eyes with which she stared at the wreck of what had been a man the minute before.

"I recruited that boy myself," she said in a whisper. "He came down out of the bush at Poonga-Poonga and right on board the *Martha* and offered himself. And I was proud. He was my very first recruit—"

"My word! Look 'm that fella," Binu Charley interrupted, brushing aside the leafy wall of the run-way and exposing a bow so massive that no one bushman could have bent it.

The Binu man traced out the mechanics of the trap, and exposed the hidden fibre in the tangled undergrowth that at contact with Koogoo's foot had released the taut bow.

They were deep in the primeval forest. A dim twilight prevailed, for no random shaft of sunlight broke through the thick roof of leaves and creepers overhead. The Tahitians were plainly awed by the silence and gloom and mystery of the place and happening, but they showed themselves doggedly unafraid, and were for pushing on. The Poonga-Poonga men, on the contrary, were not awed. They were bushmen themselves, and they were used to this silent warfare, though the devices were different from those employed by them in their own bush. Most awed of all were Joan and Sheldon, but, being whites, they were not supposed to be subject to such commonplace emotions, and their task was to carry the situation off with careless bravado as befitted "big fella marsters" of the dominant breed.

Binu Charley took the lead as they pushed on, and trap after trap yielded its secret lurking-place to his keen scrutiny. The way was beset with a thousand annoyances, chiefest among which were thorns, cunningly concealed, that penetrated the bare feet of the invaders. Once, during the afternoon, Binu Charley barely missed being impaled in a staked pit that undermined the trail. There were times when all stood still and waited for half an hour or more while Binu Charley prospected suspicious parts of the trail. Sometimes he was compelled to leave the trail and creep and climb through the jungle so as to approach the man-traps from behind; and on one occasion, in spite of his precaution, a spring-bow was discharged, the flying arrow barely clipping the shoulder of one of the waiting Poonga-Poonga boys.

Where a slight run-way entered the main one, Sheldon paused and asked Binu Charley if he knew where it led.

"Plenty bush fella garden he stop along there short way little bit," was the answer. "All right you like 'm go look 'm along."

"'Walk 'm easy," he cautioned, a few minutes later. "Close up, that fella garden. S'pose some bush fella he stop, we catch 'm."

Creeping ahead and peering into the clearing for a moment, Binu Charley beckoned Sheldon to come on cautiously. Joan crouched beside him, and together they peeped out. The cleared space was fully half an acre in extent and carefully fenced against the wild pigs. Paw-paw and banana-trees were just ripening their fruit, while beneath grew sweet potatoes and yams. On one edge of the clearing was a small grass house, open-sided, a mere rain-shelter. In front of it, crouched on his hams before a fire, was a gaunt and bearded bushman. The fire seemed to smoke excessively, and in the thick of the smoke a round dark object hung suspended. The bushman seemed absorbed in contemplation of this object.

Warning them not to shoot unless the man was successfully escaping, Sheldon beckoned the Poonga-Poonga men forward. Joan smiled appreciatively to Sheldon. It was head-hunters against head-hunters. The blacks trod noiselessly to their stations, which were arranged so that they could spring simultaneously into the open. Their faces were keen and serious, their eyes eloquent with the ecstasy of living that was upon them—for this was living, this game of life and death, and to them it was the only game a man should play, withal they played it in low and cowardly ways, killing from behind in the dim forest gloom and rarely coming out into the open.

Sheldon whispered the word, and the ten runners leaped forward—for Binu Charley ran with them. The bushman's keen ears warned him, and he sprang to his feet, bow and arrow in hand, the arrow fixed in the notch and the bow bending as he sprang. The man he let drive at dodged the arrow, and before he could shoot another his enemies were upon him. He was rolled over and over and dragged to his feet, disarmed and helpless.

"Why, he's an ancient Babylonian!" Joan cried, regarding him. "He's an Assyrian, a Phoenician! Look at that straight nose, that narrow face, those high cheek-bones—and that slanting, oval forehead, and the beard, and the eyes, too."

"And the snaky locks," Sheldon laughed.

The bushman was in mortal fear, led by all his training to expect nothing less than death; yet he did not cower away from them. Instead, he returned their looks with lean self-sufficiency, and finally centred his gaze upon Joan, the first white woman he had ever seen.

"My word, bush fella *kai-kai* along that fella boy," Binu Charley remarked.

195

So stolid was his manner of utterance that Joan turned carelessly to see what had attracted his attention, and found herself face to face with Gogoomy. At least, it was the head of Gogoomy—the dark object they had seen hanging in the smoke. It was fresh—the smoke-curing had just begun—and, save for the closed eyes, all the sullen handsomeness and animal virility of the boy, as Joan had known it, was still to be seen in the monstrous thing that twisted and dangled in the eddying smoke.

Nor was Joan's horror lessened by the conduct of the Poonga-Poonga boys. On the instant they recognized the head, and on the instant rose their wild hearty laughter as they explained to one another in shrill falsetto voices. Gogoomy's end was a joke. He had been foiled in his attempt to escape. He had played the game and lost. And what greater joke could there be than that the bushmen should have eaten him? It was the funniest incident that had come under their notice in many a day. And to them there was certainly nothing unusual nor bizarre in the event. Gogoomy had completed the life-cycle of the bushman. He had taken heads, and now his own head had been taken. He had eaten men, and now he had been eaten by men.

The Poonga-Poonga men's laughter died down, and they regarded the spectacle with glittering eyes and gluttonous expressions. The Tahitians, on the other hand, were shocked, and Adamu Adam was shaking his head slowly and grunting forth his disgust. Joan was angry. Her face was white, but in each cheek was a vivid spray of red. Disgust had been displaced by wrath, and her mood was clearly vengeful.

Sheldon laughed.

"It's nothing to be angry over," he said. "You mustn't forget that he hacked off Kwaque's head, and that he ate one of his own comrades that ran away with him. Besides, he was born to it. He has but been eaten out of the same trough from which he himself has eaten."

Joan looked at him with lips that trembled on the verge of speech.

"And don't forget," Sheldon added, "that he is the son of a chief, and that as sure as fate his Port Adams tribesmen will take a white man's head in payment."

196

"It is all so ghastly ridiculous," Joan finally said.

"And—er—romantic," he suggested slyly.

She did not answer, and turned away; but Sheldon knew that the shaft had gone home.

"That fella boy he sick, belly belong him walk about," Binu Charley said, pointing to the Poonga-Poonga man whose shoulder had been scratched by the arrow an hour before.

The boy was sitting down and groaning, his arms clasping his bent knees, his head drooped forward and rolling painfully back and forth. For fear of poison, Sheldon had immediately scarified the wound and injected permanganate of potash; but in spite of the precaution the shoulder was swelling rapidly.

"We'll take him on to where Tudor is lying," Joan said. "The walking will help to keep up his circulation and scatter the poison. Adamu Adam, you take hold that boy. Maybe he will want to sleep. Shake him up. If he sleep he die."

The advance was more rapid now, for Binu Charley placed the captive bushman in front of him and made him clear the run-way of traps. Once, at a sharp turn where a man's shoulder would unavoidably brush against a screen of leaves, the bushman displayed great caution as he spread the leaves aside and exposed the head of a sharp-pointed spear, so set that the casual passer-by would receive at the least a nasty scratch.

"My word," said Binu Charley, "that fella spear allee same devil-devil."

He took the spear and was examining it when suddenly he made as if to stick it into the bushman. It was a bit of simulated playfulness, but the bushman sprang back in evident fright. Poisoned the weapon was beyond any doubt, and thereafter Binu Charley carried it threateningly at the prisoner's back.

The sun, sinking behind a lofty western peak, brought on an early but lingering twilight, and the expedition plodded on through the evil forest—

the place of mystery and fear, of death swift and silent and horrible, of brutish appetite and degraded instinct, of human life that still wallowed in the primeval slime, of savagery degenerate and abysmal. No slightest breezes blew in the gloomy silence, and the air was stale and humid and suffocating. The sweat poured unceasingly from their bodies, and in their nostrils was the heavy smell of rotting vegetation and of black earth that was a-crawl with fecund life.

They turned aside from the run-way at a place indicated by Binu Charley, and, sometimes crawling on hands and knees through the damp black muck, at other times creeping and climbing through the tangled undergrowth a dozen feet from the ground, they came to an immense banyan tree, half an acre in extent, that made in the innermost heart of the jungle a denser jungle of its own. From out of its black depths came the voice of a man singing in a cracked, eerie voice.

"My word, that big fella marster he no die!"

The singing stopped, and the voice, faint and weak, called out a hello. Joan answered, and then the voice explained.

"I'm not wandering. I was just singing to keep my spirits up. Have you got anything to eat?"

A few minutes saw the rescued man lying among blankets, while fires were building, water was being carried, Joan's tent was going up, and Lalaperu was overhauling the packs and opening tins of provisions. Tudor, having pulled through the fever and started to mend, was still frightfully weak and very much starved. So badly swollen was he from mosquito-bites that his face was unrecognizable, and the acceptance of his identity was largely a matter of faith. Joan had her own ointments along, and she prefaced their application by fomenting his swollen features with hot cloths. Sheldon, with an eye to the camp and the preparations for the night, looked on and felt the pangs of jealousy at every contact of her hands with Tudor's face and body. Somehow, engaged in their healing ministrations, they no longer seemed to him boy's hands, the hands of Joan who had gazed at Gogoomy's head with pale cheeks sprayed with angry flame. The hands were now a woman's hands, and Sheldon grinned to himself as his fancy suggested that some night he must lie outside the mosquito-netting in order to have Joan apply soothing fomentations in the morning.

CHAPTER XXV—THE HEAD-HUNTERS

The morning's action had been settled the night before. Tudor was to stay behind in his banyan refuge and gather strength while the expedition proceeded. On the far chance that they might rescue even one solitary survivor of Tudor's party, Joan was fixed in her determination to push on; and neither Sheldon nor Tudor could persuade her to remain quietly at the banyan tree while Sheldon went on and searched. With Tudor, Adamu Adam and Arahu were to stop as guards, the latter Tahitian being selected to remain because of a bad foot which had been brought about by stepping on one of the thorns concealed by the bushmen. It was evidently a slow poison, and not too strong, that the bushmen used, for the wounded Poonga-Poonga man was still alive, and though his swollen shoulder was enormous, the inflammation had already begun to go down. He, too, remained with Tudor.

Binu Charley led the way, by proxy, however, for, by means of the poisoned spear, he drove the captive bushman ahead. The run-way still ran through the dank and rotten jungle, and they knew no villages would be encountered till rising ground was gained. They plodded on, panting and sweating in the humid, stagnant air. They were immersed in a sea of wanton, prodigal vegetation. All about them the huge-rooted trees blocked their footing, while coiled and knotted climbers, of the girth of a man's arm, were thrown from lofty branch to lofty branch, or hung in tangled masses like so many monstrous snakes. Lush-stalked plants, larger-leaved than the body of a man, exuded a sweaty moisture from all their surfaces. Here and there, banyan trees, like rocky islands, shouldered aside the streaming riot of vegetation between their crowded columns, showing portals and passages wherein all daylight was lost and only midnight gloom remained. Tree-ferns and mosses and a myriad other parasitic forms jostled with gay-coloured fungoid growths for room to live, and the very atmosphere itself seemed to afford clinging space to airy fairy creepers, light and delicate as gem-dust, tremulous with microscopic blooms. Pale-golden and vermilion orchids flaunted their unhealthy blossoms in the golden, dripping sunshine that filtered through the matted roof. It was the mysterious, evil forest, a charnel house of silence, wherein naught moved save strange tiny birds—the strangeness of them making the mystery more profound, for they flitted on noiseless wings, emitting neither song nor chirp, and they were mottled with morbid colours, having all the seeming of orchids, flying blossoms of sickness and decay.

He was caught by surprise, fifteen feet in the air above the path, in the forks of a many-branched tree. All saw him as he dropped like a shadow, naked as on his natal morn, landing springily on his bent knees, and like a shadow leaping along the run-way. It was hard for them to realize that it was a man, for he seemed a weird jungle spirit, a goblin of the forest. Only Binu Charley was not perturbed. He flung his poisoned spear over the head of the captive at the flitting form. It was a mighty cast, well intended, but the shadow, leaping, received the spear harmlessly between the legs, and, tripping upon it, was flung sprawling. Before he could get away, Binu Charley was upon him, clutching him by his snow-white hair. He was only a young man, and a dandy at that, his face blackened with charcoal, his hair whitened with wood-ashes, with the freshly severed tail of a wild pig thrust through his perforated nose, and two more thrust through his ears. His only other ornament was a necklace of human finger-bones. At sight of their other prisoner he chattered in a high querulous falsetto, with puckered brows and troubled, wild-animal eyes. He was disposed of along the middle of the line, one of the Poonga-Poonga men leading him at the end of a length of bark-rope.

The trail began to rise out of the jungle, dipping at times into festering hollows of unwholesome vegetation, but rising more and more over swelling, unseen hill-slopes or climbing steep hog-backs and rocky hummocks where the forest thinned and blue patches of sky appeared overhead.

"Close up he stop," Binu Charley warned them in a whisper.

Even as he spoke, from high overhead came the deep resonant boom of a village drum. But the beat was slow, there was no panic in the sound. They were directly beneath the village, and they could hear the crowing of roosters, two women's voices raised in brief dispute, and, once, the crying of a child.

The run-way now became a deeply worn path, rising so steeply that several times the party paused for breath. The path never widened, and in places the feet and the rains of generations had scoured it till it was sunken twenty feet beneath the surface.

"One man with a rifle could hold it against a thousand," Sheldon whispered to Joan. "And twenty men could hold it with spears and arrows."

They came out on the village, situated on a small, upland plateau, grass-covered, and with only occasional trees. There was a wild chorus of warning cries from the women, who scurried out of the grass houses, and like frightened quail dived over the opposite edge of the clearing, gathering up their babies and children as they ran. At the same time spears and arrows began to fall among the invaders. At Sheldon's command, the Tahitians and Poonga-Poonga men got into action with their rifles. The spears and arrows ceased, the last bushman disappeared, and the fight was over almost as soon as it had begun. On their own side no one had been hurt, while half a dozen bushmen had been killed. These alone remained, the wounded having been carried off. The Tahitians and Poonga-Poonga men had warmed up and were for pursuit, but this Sheldon would not permit. To his pleased surprise, Joan backed him up in the decision; for, glancing at her once during the firing, he had seen her white face, like a glittering sword in its fighting intensity, the nostrils dilated, the eyes bright and steady and shining.

"Poor brutes," she said. "They act only according to their natures. To eat their kind and take heads is good morality for them."

"But they should be taught not to take white men's heads," Sheldon argued.

She nodded approval, and said, "If we find one head we'll burn the village. Hey, you, Charley! What fella place head he stop?"

"S'pose he stop along devil-devil house," was the answer. "That big fella house, he devil-devil."

It was the largest house in the village, ambitiously ornamented with fancy-plaited mats and king-posts carved into obscene and monstrous forms half-human and half-animal. Into it they went, in the obscure light stumbling across the sleeping-logs of the village bachelors and knocking their heads against strings of weird votive-offerings, dried and shrivelled, that hung from the roof-beams. On either side were rude gods, some grotesquely carved, others no more than shapeless logs swathed in rotten and indescribably filthy matting. The air was mouldy and heavy with decay, while strings of fish-tails and of half-cleaned dog and crocodile skulls did not add to the wholesomeness of the place.

In the centre, crouched before a slow-smoking fire, in the littered ashes of a thousand fires, was an old man who blinked apathetically at the invaders. He was extremely old—so old that his withered skin hung about him in loose folds and did not look like skin. His hands were bony claws, his emaciated face a sheer death's-head. His task, it seemed, was to tend the fire, and while he blinked at them he added to it a handful of dead and mouldy wood. And hung in the smoke they found the object of their search. Joan turned and stumbled out hastily, deathly sick, reeling into the sunshine and clutching at the air for support.

"See if all are there," she called back faintly, and tottered aimlessly on for a few steps, breathing the air in great draughts and trying to forget the sight she had seen.

Upon Sheldon fell the unpleasant task of tallying the heads. They were all there, nine of them, white men's heads, the faces of which he had been familiar with when their owners had camped in Berande compound and set up the poling-boats. Binu Charley, hugely interested, lent a hand, turning the heads around for identification, noting the hatchet-strokes, and remarking the distorted expressions. The Poonga-Poonga men gloated as usual, and as usual the Tahitians were shocked and angry, several of them cursing and muttering in undertones. So angry was Matapuu, that he strode suddenly over to the fire-tender and kicked him in the ribs, whereupon the old savage emitted an appalling squeal, pig-like in its wild-animal fear, and fell face downward in the ashes and lay quivering in momentary expectation of death.

Other heads, thoroughly sun-dried and smoke-cured, were found in abundance, but, with two exceptions, they were the heads of blacks. So this was the manner of hunting that went on in the dark and evil forest, Sheldon thought, as he regarded them. The atmosphere of the place was sickening, yet he could not forbear to pause before one of Binu Charley's finds.

"Me savvee black Mary, me savvee white Mary," quoth Binu Charley. "Me no savvee that fella Mary. What name belong him?"

Sheldon looked. Ancient and withered, blackened by many years of the smoke of the devil-devil house, nevertheless the shrunken, mummy-like face was unmistakably Chinese. How it had come there was the mystery. It was a woman's head, and he had never heard of a Chinese woman in the history of the Solomons. From the ears hung two-inch-long ear-rings, and at Sheldon's direction the Binu man rubbed away the accretions of smoke and dirt, and from under his fingers appeared the polished green of jade, the sheen of pearl, and the warm red of Oriental gold. The other head, equally ancient, was a white man's, as the heavy blond moustache, twisted and askew on the shrivelled upper lip, gave sufficient advertisement; and Sheldon wondered what forgotten bêche-de-mer fisherman or sandalwood trader had gone to furnish that ghastly trophy.

Telling Binu Charley to remove the ear-rings, and directing the Poonga-Poonga men to carry out the old fire-tender, Sheldon cleared the devil-devil house and set fire to it. Soon every house was blazing merrily, while the ancient fire-tender sat upright in the sunshine blinking at the destruction of his village. From the heights above, where were evidently other villages, came the booming of drums and a wild blowing of war-conchs; but Sheldon had dared all he cared to with his small following. Besides, his mission was accomplished. Every member of Tudor's expedition was accounted for; and it was a long, dark way out of the head-hunters' country. Releasing their two prisoners, who leaped away like startled deer, they plunged down the steep path into the steaming jungle.

Joan, still shocked by what she had seen, walked on in front of Sheldon, subdued and silent. At the end of half an hour she turned to him with a wan smile and said,—

"I don't think I care to visit the head-hunters any more. It's adventure, I know; but there is such a thing as having too much of a good thing. Riding around the plantation will henceforth be good enough for me, or perhaps salving another *Martha*; but the bushmen of Guadalcanal need never worry for fear that I shall visit them again. I shall have nightmares for months to come, I know I shall. Ugh!—the horrid beasts!"

That night found them back in camp with Tudor, who, while improved, would still have to be carried down on a stretcher. The swelling of the Poonga-Poonga man's shoulder was going down slowly, but Arahu still limped on his thorn-poisoned foot.

Two days later they rejoined the boats at Carli; and at high noon of the third day, travelling with the current and shooting the rapids, the expedition arrived at Berande. Joan, with a sigh, unbuckled her revolver-belt and hung it on the nail in the living-room, while Sheldon, who had been lurking about for the sheer joy of seeing her perform that particular home-coming act, sighed, too, with satisfaction. But the home-coming was not all joy to him, for Joan set about nursing Tudor, and spent much time on the veranda where he lay in the hammock under the mosquito-netting.

CHAPTER XXVI—BURNING DAYLIGHT

The ten days of Tudor's convalescence that followed were peaceful days on Berande. The work of the plantation went on like clock-work. With the crushing of the premature outbreak of Gogoomy and his following, all insubordination seemed to have vanished. Twenty more of the old-time boys, their term of service up, were carried away by the *Martha*, and the fresh stock of labour, treated fairly, was proving of excellent quality. As Sheldon rode about the plantation, acknowledging to himself the comfort and convenience of a horse and wondering why he had not thought of getting one himself, he pondered the various improvements for which Joan was responsible— the splendid Poonga-Poonga recruits; the fruits and vegetables; the *Martha* herself, snatched from the sea for a song and earning money hand over fist despite old Kinross's slow and safe method of running her; and Berande, once more financially secure, approaching each day nearer the dividend-paying time, and growing each day as the black toilers cleared the bush, cut the cane-grass, and planted more cocoanut palms.

In these and a thousand ways Sheldon was made aware of how much he was indebted for material prosperity to Joan—to the slender, level-browed girl with romance shining out of her gray eyes and adventure shouting from the long-barrelled Colt's on her hip, who had landed on the beach that piping gale, along with her stalwart Tahitian crew, and who had entered his bungalow to hang with boy's hands her revolver-belt and Baden-Powell hat on the nail by the billiard table. He forgot all the early exasperations, remembering only her charms and sweetnesses and glorying much in the traits he at first had disliked most—her boyishness and adventurousness, her delight to swim and risk the sharks, her desire to go recruiting, her love of the sea and ships, her sharp authoritative words when she launched the whale-boat and, with firestick in one hand and dynamite-stick in the other, departed with her picturesque crew to shoot fish in the Balesuna; her super-innocent disdain for the commonest conventions, her juvenile joy in argument, her fluttering, wild-bird love of freedom and mad passion for independence. All this he now loved, and he no longer desired to tame and hold her, though the paradox was the winning of her without the taming and the holding.

There were times when he was dizzy with thought of her and love of her, when he would stop his horse and with closed eyes picture her as he had seen her that first day, in the stern-sheets of the whale-boat, dashing madly in to shore and marching belligerently along his veranda to remark that it was pretty hospitality this letting strangers sink or swim in his front yard. And as he opened his eyes and urged his horse onward, he would ponder for the ten thousandth time how possibly he was ever to hold her when she was so wild and bird-like that she was bound to flutter out and away from under his hand.

It was patent to Sheldon that Tudor had become interested in Joan. That convalescent visitor practically lived on the veranda, though, while preposterously weak and shaky in the legs, he had for some time insisted on coming in to join them at the table at meals. The first warning Sheldon had of the other's growing interest in the girl was when Tudor eased down and finally ceased pricking him with his habitual sharpness of quip and speech. This cessation of verbal sparring was like the breaking off of diplomatic relations between countries at the beginning of war, and, once Sheldon's suspicions were aroused, he was not long in finding other confirmations. Tudor too obviously joyed in Joan's presence, too obviously laid himself out to amuse and fascinate her with his own glorious and adventurous personality. Often, after his morning ride over the plantation, or coming in from the store or from inspection of the copra-drying, Sheldon found the pair of them together on the veranda, Joan listening, intent and excited, and Tudor deep in some recital of personal adventure at the ends of the earth.

Sheldon noticed, too, the way Tudor looked at her and followed her about with his eyes, and in those eyes he noted a certain hungry look, and on the face a certain wistful expression; and he wondered if on his own face he carried a similar involuntary advertisement. He was sure of several things: first, that Tudor was not the right man for Joan and could not possibly make her permanently happy; next, that Joan was too sensible a girl really to fall in love with a man of such superficial stamp; and, finally, that Tudor would blunder his love-making somehow. And at the same time, with true lover's anxiety, Sheldon feared that the other might somehow fail to blunder, and win the girl with purely fortuitous and successful meretricious show. But of the one thing Sheldon was sure: Tudor had no intimate knowledge of her and was unaware of how vital in her was her wildness and love of independence. That was where he would blunder—in the catching and the holding of her. And then, in spite of all his certitude, Sheldon could not forbear wondering if his theories of Joan might not be wrong, and if Tudor was not going the right way about after all.

The situation was very unsatisfactory and perplexing. Sheldon played the difficult part of waiting and looking on, while his rival devoted himself energetically to reaching out and grasping at the fluttering prize. Then, again, Tudor had such an irritating way about him. It had become quite elusive and intangible, now that he had tacitly severed diplomatic relations; but Sheldon sensed what he deemed a growing antagonism and promptly magnified it through the jealous lenses of his own lover's eyes. The other was an interloper. He did not belong to Berande, and now that he was well and strong again it was time for him to go. Instead of which, and despite the calling in of the mail steamer bound for Sydney, Tudor had settled himself down comfortably, resumed swimming, went dynamiting fish with Joan, spent hours with her hunting pigeons, trapping crocodiles, and at target practice with rifle and revolver.

But there were certain traditions of hospitality that prevented Sheldon from breathing a hint that it was time for his guest to take himself off. And in similar fashion, feeling that it was not playing the game, he fought down the temptation to warn Joan. Had he known anything, not too serious, to Tudor's detriment, he would have been unable to utter it; but the worst of it was that he knew nothing at all against the man. That was the confounded part of it, and sometimes he was so baffled and overwrought by his feelings that he assumed a super-judicial calm and assured himself that his dislike of Tudor was a matter of unsubstantial prejudice and jealousy.

Outwardly, he maintained a calm and smiling aspect. The work of the plantation went on. The *Martha* and the *Flibberty-Gibbet* came and went,

208

as did all the miscellany of coasting craft that dropped in to wait for a breeze and have a gossip, a drink or two, and a game of billiards. Satan kept the compound free of niggers. Boucher came down regularly in his whale-boat to pass Sunday. Twice a day, at breakfast and dinner, Joan and Sheldon and Tudor met amicably at table, and the evenings were as amicably spent on the veranda.

And then it happened. Tudor made his blunder. Never divining Joan's fluttering wildness, her blind hatred of restraint and compulsion, her abhorrence of mastery by another, and mistaking the warmth and enthusiasm in her eyes (aroused by his latest tale) for something tender and acquiescent, he drew her to him, laid a forcible detaining arm about her waist, and misapprehended her frantic revolt for an exhibition of maidenly reluctance. It occurred on the veranda, after breakfast, and Sheldon, within, pondering a Sydney wholesaler's catalogue and making up his orders for next steamer-day, heard the sharp exclamation of Joan, followed by the equally sharp impact of an open hand against a cheek. Jerking free from the arm that was all distasteful compulsion, Joan had slapped Tudor's face resoundingly and with far more vim and weight than when she had cuffed Gogoomy.

Sheldon had half-started up, then controlled himself and sunk back in his chair, so that by the time Joan entered the door his composure was recovered. Her right forearm was clutched tightly in her left hand, while the white cheeks, centred with the spots of flaming red, reminded him of the time he had first seen her angry.

"He hurt my arm," she blurted out, in reply to his look of inquiry.

He smiled involuntarily. It was so like her, so like the boy she was, to come running to complain of the physical hurt which had been done her. She was certainly not a woman versed in the ways of man and in the ways of handling man. The resounding slap she had given Tudor seemed still echoing in Sheldon's ears, and as he looked at the girl before him crying out that her arm was hurt, his smile grew broader.

It was the smile that did it, convicting Joan in her own eyes of the silliness of her cry and sending over her face the most amazing blush he had ever seen. Throat, cheeks, and forehead flamed with the rush of the shamed blood.

"He—he—" she attempted to vindicate her deeper indignation, then whirled abruptly away and passed out the rear door and down the steps.

Sheldon sat and mused. He was a trifle angry, and the more he dwelt upon the happening the angrier he grew. If it had been any woman except Joan it would have been amusing. But Joan was the last woman in the world to attempt to kiss forcibly. The thing smacked of the back stairs anyway—a sordid little comedy perhaps, but to have tried it on Joan was nothing less than sacrilege. The man should have had better sense. Then, too, Sheldon was personally aggrieved. He had been filched of something that he felt was almost his, and his lover's jealousy was rampant at thought of this forced familiarity.

It was while in this mood that the screen door banged loudly behind the heels of Tudor, who strode into the room and paused before him. Sheldon was unprepared, though it was very apparent that the other was furious.

"Well?" Tudor demanded defiantly.

And on the instant speech rushed to Sheldon's lips.

"I hope you won't attempt anything like it again, that's all—except that I shall be only too happy any time to extend to you the courtesy of my whale-boat. It will land you in Tulagi in a few hours."

"As if that would settle it," was the retort.

"I don't understand," Sheldon said simply.

"Then it is because you don't wish to understand."

"Still I don't understand," Sheldon said in steady, level tones. "All that is clear to me is that you are exaggerating your own blunder into something serious."

Tudor grinned maliciously and replied,—

210

"It would seem that you are doing the exaggerating, inviting me to leave in your whale-boat. It is telling me that Berande is not big enough for the pair of us. Now let me tell you that the Solomon Islands is not big enough for the pair of us. This thing's got to be settled between us, and it may as well be settled right here and now."

"I can understand your fire-eating manners as being natural to you," Sheldon went on wearily, "but why you should try them on me is what I can't comprehend. You surely don't want to quarrel with me."

"I certainly do."

"But what in heaven's name for?"

Tudor surveyed him with withering disgust.

"You haven't the soul of a louse. I suppose any man could make love to your wife—"

"But I have no wife," Sheldon interrupted.

"Then you ought to have. The situation is outrageous. You might at least marry her, as I am honourably willing to do."

For the first time Sheldon's rising anger boiled over.

"You—" he began violently, then abruptly caught control of himself and went on soothingly, "you'd better take a drink and think it over. That's my advice to you. Of course, when you do get cool, after talking to me in this fashion you won't want to stay on any longer, so while you're getting that drink I'll call the boat's-crew and launch a boat. You'll be in Tulagi by eight this evening."

He turned toward the door, as if to put his words into execution, but the other caught him by the shoulder and twirled him around.

"Look here, Sheldon, I told you the Solomons were too small for the pair of us, and I meant it."

"Is that an offer to buy Berande, lock, stock, and barrel?" Sheldon queried.

"No, it isn't. It's an invitation to fight."

"But what the devil do you want to fight with me for?" Sheldon's irritation was growing at the other's persistence. "I've no quarrel with you. And what quarrel can you have with me? I have never interfered with you. You were my guest. Miss Lackland is my partner. If you saw fit to make love to her, and somehow failed to succeed, why should you want to fight with me? This is the twentieth century, my dear fellow, and duelling went out of fashion before you and I were born."

"You began the row," Tudor doggedly asserted. "You gave me to understand that it was time for me to go. You fired me out of your house, in short. And then you have the cheek to want to know why I am starting the row. It won't do, I tell you. You started it, and I am going to see it through."

Sheldon smiled tolerantly and proceeded to light a cigarette. But Tudor was not to be turned aside.

"You started this row," he urged.

"There isn't any row. It takes two to make a row, and I, for one, refuse to have anything to do with such tomfoolery."

"You started it, I say, and I'll tell you why you started it."

"I fancy you've been drinking," Sheldon interposed. "It's the only explanation I can find for your unreasonableness."

"And I'll tell you why you started it. It wasn't silliness on your part to exaggerate this little trifle of love-making into something serious. I was poaching on your preserves, and you wanted to get rid of me. It was all very nice and snug here, you and the girl, until I came along. And now you're jealous—that's it, jealousy—and want me out of it. But I won't go."

"Then stay on by all means. I won't quarrel with you about it. Make yourself comfortable. Stay for a year, if you wish."

"She's not your wife," Tudor continued, as though the other had not spoken. "A fellow has the right to make love to her unless she's your—well,

212

perhaps it was an error after all, due to ignorance, perfectly excusable, on my part. I might have seen it with half an eye if I'd listened to the gossip on the beach. All Guvutu and Tulagi were laughing about it. I was a fool, and I certainly made the mistake of taking the situation on its assumed innocent face-value."

So angry was Sheldon becoming that the face and form of the other seemed to vibrate and oscillate before his eyes. Yet outwardly Sheldon was calm and apparently weary of the discussion.

"Please keep her out of the conversation," he said.

"But why should I?" was the demand. "The pair of you trapped me into making a fool of myself. How was I to know that everything was not all right? You and she acted as if everything were on the square. But my eyes are open now. Why, she played the outraged wife to perfection, slapped the transgressor and fled to you. Pretty good proof of what all the beach has been saying. Partners, eh?—a business partnership? Gammon my eye, that's what it is."

Then it was that Sheldon struck out, coolly and deliberately, with all the strength of his arm, and Tudor, caught on the jaw, fell sideways, crumpling as he did so and crushing a chair to kindling wood beneath the weight of his falling body. He pulled himself slowly to his feet, but did not offer to rush.

"Now will you fight?" Tudor said grimly.

Sheldon laughed, and for the first time with true spontaneity. The intrinsic ridiculousness of the situation was too much for his sense of humour. He made as if to repeat the blow, but Tudor, white of face, with arms hanging resistlessly at his sides, offered no defence.

"I don't mean a fight with fists," he said slowly. "I mean to a finish, to the death. You're a good shot with revolver and rifle. So am I. That's the way we'll settle it."

"You have gone clean mad. You are a lunatic."

"No, I'm not," Tudor retorted. "I'm a man in love. And once again I ask you to go outside and settle it, with any weapons you choose."

Sheldon regarded him for the first time with genuine seriousness, wondering what strange maggots could be gnawing in his brain to drive him to such unusual conduct.

"But men don't act this way in real life," Sheldon remarked.

"You'll find I'm pretty real before you're done with me. I'm going to kill you to-day."

"Bosh and nonsense, man." This time Sheldon had lost his temper over the superficial aspects of the situation. "Bosh and nonsense, that's all it is. Men don't fight duels in the twentieth century. It's—it's antediluvian, I tell you."

"Speaking of Joan—"

"Please keep her name out of it," Sheldon warned him.

"I will, if you'll fight."

Sheldon threw up his arms despairingly.

"Speaking of Joan—"

"Look out," Sheldon warned again.

"Oh, go ahead, knock me down. But that won't close my mouth. You can knock me down all day, but as fast as I get to my feet I'll speak of Joan again. Now will you fight?"

"Listen to me, Tudor," Sheldon began, with an effort at decisiveness. "I am not used to taking from men a tithe of what I've already taken from you."

"You'll take a lot more before the day's out," was the answer. "I tell you, you simply must fight. I'll give you a fair chance to kill me, but I'll kill you before the day's out. This isn't civilization. It's the Solomon Islands, and a pretty primitive proposition for all that. King Edward and law and order are represented by the Commissioner at Tulagi and an occasional visiting gunboat. And two men and one woman is an equally primitive proposition. We'll settle it in the good old primitive way."

214

As Sheldon looked at him the thought came to his mind that after all there might be something in the other's wild adventures over the earth. It required a man of that calibre, a man capable of obtruding a duel into orderly twentieth century life, to find such wild adventures.

"There's only one way to stop me," Tudor went on. "I can't insult you directly, I know. You are too easy-going, or cowardly, or both, for that. But I can narrate for you the talk of the beach—ah, that grinds you, doesn't it? I can tell you what the beach has to say about you and this young girl running a plantation under a business partnership."

"Stop!" Sheldon cried, for the other was beginning to vibrate and oscillate before his eyes. "You want a duel. I'll give it to you." Then his common-sense and dislike for the ridiculous asserted themselves, and he added, "But it's absurd, impossible."

"Joan and David—partners, eh? Joan and David—partners," Tudor began to iterate and reiterate in a malicious and scornful chant.

"For heaven's sake keep quiet, and I'll let you have your way," Sheldon cried. "I never saw a fool so bent on his folly. What kind of a duel shall it be? There are no seconds. What weapons shall we use?"

Immediately Tudor's monkey-like impishness left him, and he was once more the cool, self-possessed man of the world.

"I've often thought that the ideal duel should be somewhat different from the conventional one," he said. "I've fought several of that sort, you know—"

"French ones," Sheldon interrupted.

"Call them that. But speaking of this ideal duel, here it is. No seconds, of course, and no onlookers. The two principals alone are necessary. They may use any weapons they please, from revolvers and rifles to machine guns and pompoms. They start a mile apart, and advance on each other, taking advantage of cover, retreating, circling, feinting—anything and everything permissible. In short, the principals shall hunt each other—"

"Like a couple of wild Indians?"

"Precisely," cried Tudor, delighted. "You've got the idea. And Berande is just the place, and this is just the right time. Miss Lackland will be taking her siesta, and she'll think we are. We've got two hours for it before she wakes. So hurry up and come on. You start out from the Balesuna and I start from the Berande. Those two rivers are the boundaries of the plantation, aren't they? Very well. The field of the duel will be the plantation. Neither principal must go outside its boundaries. Are you satisfied?"

"Quite. But have you any objections if I leave some orders?"

"Not at all," Tudor acquiesced, the pink of courtesy now that his wish had been granted.

Sheldon clapped his hands, and the running house-boy hurried away to bring back Adamu Adam and Noa Noah.

"Listen," Sheldon said to them. "This man and me, we have one big fight to-day. Maybe he die. Maybe I die. If he die, all right. If I die, you two look after Missie Lackalanna. You take rifles, and you look after her daytime and night-time. If she want to talk with Mr. Tudor, all right. If she not want to talk, you make him keep away. Savvee?"

They grunted and nodded. They had had much to do with white men, and had learned never to question the strange ways of the strange breed. If these two saw fit to go out and kill each other, that was their business and not the business of the islanders, who took orders from them. They stepped to the gun-rack, and each picked a rifle.

"Better all Tahitian men have rifles," suggested Adamu Adam. "Maybe big trouble come."

"All right, you take them," Sheldon answered, busy with issuing the ammunition.

They went to the door and down the steps, carrying the eight rifles to their quarters. Tudor, with cartridge-belts for rifle and pistol strapped around him, rifle in hand, stood impatiently waiting.

"Come on, hurry up; we're burning daylight," he urged, as Sheldon searched after extra clips for his automatic pistol.

216

Together they passed down the steps and out of the compound to the beach, where they turned their backs to each other, and each proceeded toward his destination, their rifles in the hollows of their arms, Tudor walking toward the Berande and Sheldon toward the Balesuna.

CHAPTER XXVII—MODERN DUELLING

Barely had Sheldon reached the Balesuna, when he heard the faint report of a distant rifle and knew it was the signal of Tudor, giving notice that he had reached the Berande, turned about, and was coming back. Sheldon fired his rifle into the air in answer, and in turn proceeded to advance. He moved as in a dream, absent-mindedly keeping to the open beach. The thing was so preposterous that he had to struggle to realize it, and he reviewed in his mind the conversation with Tudor, trying to find some clue to the common-sense of what he was doing. He did not want to kill Tudor. Because that man had blundered in his love-making was no reason that he, Sheldon, should take his life. Then what was it all about? True, the fellow had insulted Joan by his subsequent remarks and been knocked down for it, but because he had knocked him down was no reason that he should now try to kill him.

In this fashion he covered a quarter of the distance between the two rivers, when it dawned upon him that Tudor was not on the beach at all. Of course not. He was advancing, according to the terms of the agreement, in the shelter of the cocoanut trees. Sheldon promptly swerved to the left to seek similar shelter, when the faint crack of a rifle came to his ears, and almost immediately the bullet, striking the hard sand a hundred feet beyond him, ricochetted and whined onward on a second flight, convincing him that, preposterous and unreal as it was, it was nevertheless sober fact. It had been intended for him. Yet even then it was hard to believe. He glanced over the familiar landscape and at the sea dimpling in the light but steady breeze. From the direction of Tulagi he could see the white sails of a schooner laying a tack across toward Berande. Down the beach a horse was grazing, and he idly wondered where the others were. The smoke rising from the copra-drying caught his eyes, which roved on over the barracks, the tool-houses, the boat-sheds, and the bungalow, and came to rest on Joan's little grass house in the corner of the compound.

Keeping now to the shelter of the trees, he went forward another quarter of a mile. If Tudor had advanced with equal speed they should have come together at that point, and Sheldon concluded that the other was circling. The difficulty was to locate him. The rows of trees, running at right angles, enabled him to see along only one narrow avenue at a time. His enemy might be coming along the next avenue, or the next, to right or left. He might be a hundred feet away or half a mile. Sheldon plodded on, and decided that the old stereotyped duel was far simpler and easier than this protracted hide-and-seek affair. He, too, tried circling, in the hope of cutting the other's circle; but, without catching a glimpse of him, he finally emerged upon a fresh clearing where the young trees, waist-high, afforded little shelter and less hiding. Just as he emerged, stepping out a pace, a rifle cracked to his right, and though he did not hear the bullet in passing, the thud of it came to his ears when it struck a palm-trunk farther on.

He sprang back into the protection of the larger trees. Twice he had exposed himself and been fired at, while he had failed to catch a single glimpse of his antagonist. A slow anger began to burn in him. It was deucedly unpleasant, he decided, this being peppered at; and nonsensical as it really was, it was none the less deadly serious. There was no avoiding the issue, no firing in the air and getting over with it as in the old-fashioned duel. This mutual man-hunt must keep up until one got the other. And if one neglected a chance to get the other, that increased the other's chance to get him. There could be no false sentiment about it. Tudor had been a cunning devil when he proposed this sort of duel, Sheldon concluded, as he began to work along cautiously in the direction of the last shot.

When he arrived at the spot, Tudor was gone, and only his foot-prints remained, pointing out the course he had taken into the depths of the plantation. Once, ten minutes later, he caught a glimpse of Tudor, a hundred yards away, crossing the same avenue as himself but going in the opposite direction. His rifle half-leaped to his shoulder, but the other was gone. More in whim than in hope of result, grinning to himself as he did so, Sheldon raised his automatic pistol and in two seconds sent eight shots scattering through the trees in the direction in which Tudor had disappeared. Wishing

219

he had a shot-gun, Sheldon dropped to the ground behind a tree, slipped a fresh clip up the hollow butt of the pistol, threw a cartridge into the chamber, shoved the safety catch into place, and reloaded the empty clip.

It was but a short time after that that Tudor tried the same trick on him, the bullets pattering about him like spiteful rain, thudding into the palm trunks, or glancing off in whining ricochets. The last bullet of all, making a double ricochet from two different trees and losing most of its momentum, struck Sheldon a sharp blow on the forehead and dropped at his feet. He was partly stunned for the moment, but on investigation found no greater harm than a nasty lump that soon rose to the size of a pigeon's egg.

The hunt went on. Once, coming to the edge of the grove near the bungalow, he saw the house-boys and the cook, clustered on the back veranda and peering curiously among the trees, talking and laughing with one another in their queer falsetto voices. Another time he came upon a working-gang busy at hoeing weeds. They scarcely noticed him when he came up, though they knew thoroughly well what was going on. It was no affair of theirs that the enigmatical white men should be out trying to kill each other, and whatever interest in the proceedings might be theirs they were careful to conceal it from Sheldon. He ordered them to continue hoeing weeds in a distant and out-of-the-way corner, and went on with the pursuit of Tudor.

Tiring of the endless circling, Sheldon tried once more to advance directly on his foe, but the latter was too crafty, taking advantage of his boldness to fire a couple of shots at him, and slipping away on some changed and continually changing course. For an hour they dodged and turned and twisted back and forth and around, and hunted each other among the orderly palms. They caught fleeting glimpses of each other and chanced flying shots which were without result. On a grassy shelter behind a tree, Sheldon came upon where Tudor had rested and smoked a cigarette. The pressed grass showed where he had sat. To one side lay the cigarette stump and the charred match which had lighted it. In front lay a scattering of bright metallic fragments. Sheldon recognized their significance. Tudor was notching his steel-jacketed bullets, or cutting them blunt, so that they would spread on striking—in short, he was making them into the vicious dum-dum prohibited in modern warfare.

Sheldon knew now what would happen to him if a bullet struck his body. It would leave a tiny hole where it entered, but the hole where it emerged would be the size of a saucer.

He decided to give up the pursuit, and lay down in the grass, protected right and left by the row of palms, with on either hand the long avenue extending. This he could watch. Tudor would have to come to him or else there would be no termination of the affair. He wiped the sweat from his face and tied the handkerchief around his neck to keep off the stinging gnats that lurked in the grass. Never had he felt so great a disgust for the thing called "adventure." Joan had been bad enough, with her Baden-Powell and long-barrelled Colt's; but here was this newcomer also looking for adventure, and finding it in no other way than by lugging a peace-loving planter into an absurd and preposterous bush-whacking duel. If ever adventure was well damned, it was by Sheldon, sweating in the windless grass and fighting gnats, the while he kept close watch up and down the avenue.

Then Tudor came. Sheldon happened to be looking in his direction at the moment he came into view, peering quickly up and down the avenue before he stepped into the open. Midway he stopped, as if debating what course to pursue. He made a splendid mark, facing his concealed enemy at two hundred yards' distance. Sheldon aimed at the centre of his chest, then deliberately shifted the aim to his right shoulder, and, with the thought, "That will put him out of business," pulled the trigger. The bullet, driving with momentum sufficient to perforate a man's body a mile distant, struck Tudor with such force as to pivot him, whirling him half around by the shock of its impact and knocking him down.

"'Hope I haven't killed the beggar," Sheldon muttered aloud, springing to his feet and running forward.

A hundred feet away all anxiety on that score was relieved by Tudor, who made shift with his left hand, and from his automatic pistol hurled a rain of bullets all around Sheldon. The latter dodged behind a palm trunk, counting the shots, and when the eighth had been fired he rushed in on the wounded man. He kicked the pistol out of the other's hand, and then sat down on him in order to keep him down.

"Be quiet," he said. "I've got you, so there's no use struggling."

Tudor still attempted to struggle and to throw him off.

"Keep quiet, I tell you," Sheldon commanded. "I'm satisfied with the outcome, and you've got to be. So you might as well give in and call this affair closed."

Tudor reluctantly relaxed.

"Rather funny, isn't it, these modern duels?" Sheldon grinned down at him as he removed his weight. "Not a bit dignified. If you'd struggled a moment longer I'd have rubbed your face in the earth. I've a good mind to do it anyway, just to teach you that duelling has gone out of fashion. Now let us see to your injuries."

"You only got me that last," Tudor grunted sullenly, "lying in ambush like—"

"Like a wild Indian. Precisely. You've caught the idea, old man." Sheldon ceased his mocking and stood up. "You lie there quietly until I send back some of the boys to carry you in. You're not seriously hurt, and it's lucky for you I didn't follow your example. If you had been struck with one of your own bullets, a carriage and pair would have been none too large to drive through the hole it would have made. As it is, you're drilled clean—a nice little perforation. All you need is antiseptic washing and dressing, and you'll be around in a month. Now take it easy, and I'll send a stretcher for you."

CHAPTER XXVIII—CAPITULATION

When Sheldon emerged from among the trees he found Joan waiting at the compound gate, and he could not fail to see that she was visibly gladdened at the sight of him.

"I can't tell you how glad I am to see you," was her greeting. "What's become of Tudor? That last flutter of the automatic wasn't nice to listen to. Was it you or Tudor?"

"So you know all about it," he answered coolly. "Well, it was Tudor, but he was doing it left-handed. He's down with a hole in his shoulder." He looked at her keenly. "Disappointing, isn't it?" he drawled.

"How do you mean?"

"Why, that I didn't kill him."

"But I didn't want him killed just because he kissed me," she cried.

"Oh, he did kiss you!" Sheldon retorted, in evident surprise. "I thought you said he hurt your arm."

"One could call it a kiss, though it was only on the end of the nose." She laughed at the recollection. "But I paid him back for that myself. I boxed his face for him. And he did hurt my arm. It's black and blue. Look at it."

She pulled up the loose sleeve of her blouse, and he saw the bruised imprints of two fingers.

Just then a gang of blacks came out from among the trees carrying the wounded man on a rough stretcher.

"Romantic, isn't it?" Sheldon sneered, following Joan's startled gaze. "And now I'll have to play surgeon and doctor him up. Funny, this twentieth-century duelling. First you drill a hole in a man, and next you set about plugging the hole up."

They had stepped aside to let the stretcher pass, and Tudor, who had heard the remark, lifted himself up on the elbow of his sound arm and said with a defiant grin,—

"If you'd got one of mine you'd have had to plug with a dinner-plate."

"Oh, you wretch!" Joan cried. "You've been cutting your bullets."

"It was according to agreement," Tudor answered. "Everything went. We could have used dynamite if we wanted to."

"He's right," Sheldon assured her, as they swung in behind. "Any weapon was permissible. I lay in the grass where he couldn't see me, and bushwhacked him in truly noble fashion. That's what comes of having women on the plantation. And now it's antiseptics and drainage tubes, I suppose. It's a nasty mess, and I'll have to read up on it before I tackle the job."

"I don't see that it's my fault," she began. "I couldn't help it because he kissed me. I never dreamed he would attempt it."

"We didn't fight for that reason. But there isn't time to explain. If you'll get dressings and bandages ready I'll look up 'gun-shot wounds' and see what's to be done."

"Is he bleeding seriously?" she asked.

"No; the bullet seems to have missed the important arteries. But that would have been a pickle."

"Then there's no need to bother about reading up," Joan said. "And I'm just dying to hear what it was all about. The *Apostle* is lying becalmed inside the point, and her boats are out to wing. She'll be at anchor in five minutes, and Doctor Welshmere is sure to be on board. So all we've got to do is to make Tudor comfortable. We'd better put him in your room under the mosquito-netting, and send a boat off to tell Dr. Welshmere to bring his instruments."

An hour afterward, Dr. Welshmere left the patient comfortable and attended to, and went down to the beach to go on board, promising to come back to dinner. Joan and Sheldon, standing on the veranda, watched him depart.

"I'll never have it in for the missionaries again since seeing them here in the Solomons," she said, seating herself in a steamer-chair.

She looked at Sheldon and began to laugh.

"That's right," he said. "It's the way I feel, playing the fool and trying to murder a guest."

"But you haven't told me what it was all about."

"You," he answered shortly.

"Me? But you just said it wasn't."

"Oh, it wasn't the kiss." He walked over to the railing and leaned against it, facing her. "But it was about you all the same, and I may as well tell you. You remember, I warned you long ago what would happen when you wanted to become a partner in Berande. Well, all the beach is gossiping about it; and Tudor persisted in repeating the gossip to me. So you see it won't do for you to stay on here under present conditions. It would be better if you went away."

"But I don't want to go away," she objected with rueful countenance.

"A chaperone, then—"

"No, nor a chaperone."

"But you surely don't expect me to go around shooting every slanderer in the Solomons that opens his mouth?" he demanded gloomily.

"No, nor that either," she answered with quick impulsiveness. "I'll tell you what we'll do. We'll get married and put a stop to it all. There!"

He looked at her in amazement, and would have believed that she was making fun of him had it not been for the warm blood that suddenly suffused her cheeks.

"Do you mean that?" he asked unsteadily. "Why?"

"To put a stop to all the nasty gossip of the beach. That's a pretty good reason, isn't it?"

The temptation was strong enough and sudden enough to make him waver, but all the disgust came back to him that was his when he lay in the grass fighting gnats and cursing adventure, and he answered,—

"No; it is worse than no reason at all. I don't care to marry you as a matter of expedience—"

"You are the most ridiculous creature!" she broke in, with a flash of her old-time anger. "You talk love and marriage to me, very much against my wish, and go mooning around over the plantation week after week because you can't have me, and look at me when you think I'm not noticing and when all the time I'm wondering when you had your last square meal because of the hungry look in your eyes, and make eyes at my revolver-belt hanging on a nail, and fight duels about me, and all the rest—and—and now, when I say I'll marry you, you do yourself the honour of refusing me."

"You can't make me any more ridiculous than I feel," he answered, rubbing the lump on his forehead reflectively. "And if this is the accepted romantic programme—a duel over a girl, and the girl rushing into the arms of the winner—why, I shall not make a bigger ass of myself by going in for it."

"I thought you'd jump at it," she confessed, with a naïveté he could not but question, for he thought he saw a roguish gleam in her eyes.

"My conception of love must differ from yours then," he said. "I should want a woman to marry me for love of me, and not out of romantic admiration because I was lucky enough to drill a hole in a man's shoulder with smokeless powder. I tell you I am disgusted with this adventure tomfoolery and rot. I don't like it. Tudor is a sample of the adventure-kind—picking a quarrel with me and behaving like a monkey, insisting on fighting with me—'to the death,' he said. It was like a penny dreadful."

She was biting her lip, and though her eyes were cool and level-looking as ever, the tell-tale angry red was in her cheeks.

226

"Of course, if you don't want to marry me—"

"But I do," he hastily interposed.

"Oh, you do—"

"But don't you see, little girl, I want you to love me," he hurried on. "Otherwise, it would be only half a marriage. I don't want you to marry me simply because by so doing a stop is put to the beach gossip, nor do I want you to marry me out of some foolish romantic notion. I shouldn't want you . . . that way."

"Oh, in that case," she said with assumed deliberateness, and he could have sworn to the roguish gleam, "in that case, since you are willing to consider my offer, let me make a few remarks. In the first place, you needn't sneer at adventure when you are living it yourself; and you were certainly living it when I found you first, down with fever on a lonely plantation with a couple of hundred wild cannibals thirsting for your life. Then I came along—"

"And what with your arriving in a gale," he broke in, "fresh from the wreck of the schooner, landing on the beach in a whale-boat full of picturesque Tahitian sailors, and coming into the bungalow with a Baden-Powell on your head, sea-boots on your feet, and a whacking big Colt's dangling on your hip—why, I am only too ready to admit that you were the quintessence of adventure."

"Very good," she cried exultantly. "It's mere simple arithmetic—the adding of your adventure and my adventure together. So that's settled, and you needn't jeer at adventure any more. Next, I don't think there was anything romantic in Tudor's attempting to kiss me, nor anything like adventure in this absurd duel. But I do think, now, that it was romantic for you to fall in love with me. And finally, and it is adding romance to romance, I think . . . I think I do love you, Dave—oh, Dave!"

The last was a sighing dove-cry as he caught her up in his arms and pressed her to him.

"But I don't love you because you played the fool to-day," she whispered on his shoulder. "White men shouldn't go around killing each other."

"Then why do you love me?" he questioned, enthralled after the manner of all lovers in the everlasting query that for ever has remained unanswered.

"I don't know—just because I do, I guess. And that's all the satisfaction you gave me when we had that man-talk. But I have been loving you for weeks—during all the time you have been so deliciously and unobtrusively jealous of Tudor."

"Yes, yes, go on," he urged breathlessly, when she paused.

"I wondered when you'd break out, and because you didn't I loved you all the more. You were like Dad, and Von. You could hold yourself in check. You didn't make a fool of yourself."

"Not until to-day," he suggested.

"Yes, and I loved you for that, too. It was about time. I began to think you were never going to bring up the subject again. And now that I have offered myself you haven't even accepted."

With both hands on her shoulders he held her at arm's-length from him and looked long into her eyes, no longer cool but seemingly pervaded with a golden flush. The lids drooped and yet bravely did not droop as she returned his gaze. Then he fondly and solemnly drew her to him.

"And how about that hearth and saddle of your own?" he asked, a moment later.

"I well-nigh won to them. The grass house is my hearth, and the *Martha* my saddle, and—and look at all the trees I've planted, to say nothing of the sweet corn. And it's all your fault anyway. I might never have loved you if you hadn't put the idea into my head."

"There's the *Nongassla* coming in around the point with her boats out," Sheldon remarked irrelevantly. "And the Commissioner is on board. He's going down to San Cristoval to investigate that missionary killing. We're in luck, I must say."

"I don't see where the luck comes in," she said dolefully. "We ought to have this evening all to ourselves just to talk things over. I've a thousand questions to ask you."

"And it wouldn't have been a man-talk either," she added.

"But my plan is better than that." He debated with himself a moment. "You see, the Commissioner is the one official in the islands who can give us a license. And—there's the luck of it—Doctor Welshmere is here to perform the ceremony. We'll get married this evening."

Joan recoiled from him in panic, tearing herself from his arms and going backward several steps. He could see that she was really frightened.

"I . . . I thought . . ." she stammered.

Then, slowly, the change came over her, and the blood flooded into her face in the same amazing blush he had seen once before that day. Her cool, level-looking eyes were no longer level-looking nor cool, but warmly drooping and just unable to meet his, as she came toward him and nestled in the circle of his arms, saying softly, almost in a whisper,—

"I am ready, Dave."

FOOTNOTES

{1} Eaten.

{2} Food.

{3} Mary—bêche-de-mer English for woman.

{4} *Ngari-ngari*—literally "scratch-scratch"—a vegetable skin-poisoning that, while not serious, is decidedly uncomfortable.

{5} Paddle

JERRY OF THE ISLANDS

FOREWORD

It is a misfortune to some fiction-writers that fiction and unveracity in the average person's mind mean one and the same thing. Several years ago I published a South Sea novel. The action was placed in the Solomon Islands. The action was praised by the critics and reviewers as a highly creditable effort of the imagination. As regards reality—they said there wasn't any. Of course, as every one knew, kinky-haired cannibals no longer obtained on the earth's surface, much less ran around with nothing on, chopping off one another's heads, and, on occasion, a white man's head as well.

Now listen. I am writing these lines in Honolulu, Hawaii. Yesterday, on the beach at Waikiki, a stranger spoke to me. He mentioned a mutual friend, Captain Kellar. When I was wrecked in the Solomons on the blackbirder, the *Minota*, it was Captain Kellar, master of the blackbirder, the *Eugénie*, who rescued me. The blacks had taken Captain Kellar's head, the stranger told me. He knew. He had represented Captain Kellar's mother in settling up the estate.

Listen. I received a letter the other day from Mr. C. M. Woodford, Resident Commissioner of the British Solomons. He was back at his post, after a long furlough to England, where he had entered his son into Oxford. A search of the shelves of almost any public library will bring to light a book entitled, "A Naturalist Among the Head Hunters." Mr. C. M. Woodford is the naturalist. He wrote the book.

To return to his letter. In the course of the day's work he casually and briefly mentioned a particular job he had just got off his hands. His absence in England had been the cause of delay. The job had been to make a punitive expedition to a neighbouring island, and, incidentally, to recover the heads of some mutual friends of ours—a white-trader, his white wife and children, and his white clerk. The expedition was successful, and Mr. Woodford concluded his account of the episode with a statement to the effect: "What especially struck me was the absence of pain and terror in their faces, which seemed to express, rather, serenity and repose"—this, mind you, of men and women of his own race whom he knew well and who had sat at dinner with him in his own house.

Other friends, with whom I have sat at dinner in the brave, rollicking days in the Solomons have since passed out—by the same way. My goodness! I sailed in the teak-built ketch, the *Minota*, on a blackbirding cruise to Malaita, and I took my wife along. The hatchet-marks were still raw on the door of our tiny stateroom advertising an event of a few months before. The event was the taking of Captain Mackenzie's head, Captain Mackenzie, at that time, being master of the Minota. As we sailed in to Langa-Langa, the British cruiser, the *Cambrian*, steamed out from the shelling of a village.

It is not expedient to burden this preliminary to my story with further details, which I do make asseveration I possess a-plenty. I hope I have given some assurance that the adventures of my dog hero in this novel are real adventures in a very real cannibal world. Bless you!—when I took my wife along on the cruise of the *Minota*, we found on board a nigger-chasing, adorable Irish terrier puppy, who was smooth-coated like Jerry, and whose name was Peggy. Had it not been for Peggy, this book would never have been written. She was the chattel of the *Minota*'s splendid skipper. So much did Mrs. London and I come to love her, that Mrs. London, after the wreck of the *Minota*, deliberately and shamelessly stole her from the *Minota*'s skipper. I do further admit that I did, deliberately and shamelessly, compound my wife's felony. We loved Peggy so! Dear royal, glorious little dog, buried at sea off the east coast of Australia!

I must add that Peggy, like Jerry, was born at Meringe Lagoon, on Meringe Plantation, which is of the Island of Ysabel, said Ysabel Island lying next north of Florida Island, where is the seat of government and where dwells the Resident Commissioner, Mr. C. M. Woodford. Still further and finally, I knew Peggy's mother and father well, and have often known the warm surge in the heart of me at the sight of that faithful couple running side by side along the beach. Terrence was his real name. Her name was Biddy.

JACK LONDON

WAIKIKI BEACH,

HONOLULU, OAHU, T.H.

June 5, 1915

CHAPTER I

Not until *Mister* Haggin abruptly picked him up under one arm and stepped into the sternsheets of the waiting whaleboat, did Jerry dream that anything untoward was to happen to him. *Mister* Haggin was Jerry's beloved master, and had been his beloved master for the six months of Jerry's life. Jerry did not know *Mister* Haggin as "master," for "master" had no place in Jerry's vocabulary, Jerry being a smooth-coated, golden-sorrel Irish terrier.

But in Jerry's vocabulary, "*Mister* Haggin" possessed all the definiteness of sound and meaning that the word "master" possesses in the vocabularies of humans in relation to their dogs. "*Mister* Haggin" was the sound Jerry had always heard uttered by Bob, the clerk, and by Derby, the foreman on the plantation, when they addressed his master. Also, Jerry had always heard the rare visiting two-legged man-creatures such as came on the *Arangi*, address his master as *Mister* Haggin.

But dogs being dogs, in their dim, inarticulate, brilliant, and heroic-worshipping ways misappraising humans, dogs think of their masters, and love their masters, more than the facts warrant. "Master" means to them, as "*Mister*" Haggin meant to Jerry, a deal more, and a great deal more, than it means to humans. The human considers himself as "master" to his dog, but the dog considers his master "God."

Now "God" was no word in Jerry's vocabulary, despite the fact that he already possessed a definite and fairly large vocabulary. "*Mister* Haggin" was the sound that meant "God." In Jerry's heart and head, in the mysterious centre of all his activities that is called consciousness, the sound, "*Mister* Haggin," occupied the same place that "God" occupies in human consciousness. By word and sound, to Jerry, "*Mister* Haggin" had the same connotation that "God" has to God-worshipping humans. In short, *Mister* Haggin was Jerry's God.

And so, when *Mister* Haggin, or God, or call it what one will with the limitations of language, picked Jerry up with imperative abruptness, tucked him under his arm, and stepped into the whaleboat, whose black crew immediately bent to the oars, Jerry was instantly and nervously aware that the unusual had begun to happen. Never before had he gone out on board the *Arangi*, which he could see growing larger and closer to each lip-hissing stroke of the oars of the blacks.

Only an hour before, Jerry had come down from the plantation house to the beach to see the *Arangi* depart. Twice before, in his half-year of life, had he had this delectable experience. Delectable it truly was, running up and down the white beach of sand-pounded coral, and, under the wise guidance of Biddy and Terrence, taking part in the excitement of the beach and even adding to it.

There was the nigger-chasing. Jerry had been born to hate niggers. His first experiences in the world as a puling puppy, had taught him that Biddy, his mother, and his father Terrence, hated niggers. A nigger was something to be snarled at. A nigger, unless he were a house-boy, was something to be attacked and bitten and torn if he invaded the compound. Biddy did it. Terrence did it. In doing it, they served their God—*Mister* Haggin. Niggers were two-legged lesser creatures who toiled and slaved for their two-legged white lords, who lived in the labour barracks afar off, and who were so much lesser and lower that they must not dare come near the habitation of their lords.

And nigger-chasing was adventure. Not long after he had learned to sprawl, Jerry had learned that. One took his chances. As long as *Mister* Haggin, or Derby, or Bob, was about, the niggers took their chasing. But there were times when the white lords were not about. Then it was "'Ware niggers!" One must dare to chase only with due precaution. Because then, beyond the white lord's eyes, the niggers had a way, not merely of scowling and muttering, but of attacking four-legged dogs with stones and clubs. Jerry had seen his mother so mishandled, and, ere he had learned discretion, alone in the high grass had been himself club-mauled by Godarmy, the black who wore a china door-knob suspended on his chest from his neck on a string

240

of sennit braided from cocoanut fibre. More. Jerry remembered another high-grass adventure, when he and his brother Michael had fought Owmi, another black distinguishable for the cogged wheels of an alarm clock on his chest. Michael had been so severely struck on his head that for ever after his left ear had remained sore and had withered into a peculiar wilted and twisted upward cock.

Still more. There had been his brother Patsy, and his sister Kathleen, who had disappeared two months before, who had ceased and no longer were. The great god, *Mister* Haggin, had raged up and down the plantation. The bush had been searched. Half a dozen niggers had been whipped. And *Mister* Haggin had failed to solve the mystery of Patsy's and Kathleen's disappearance. But Biddy and Terrence knew. So did Michael and Jerry. The four-months' old Patsy and Kathleen had gone into the cooking-pot at the barracks, and their puppy-soft skins had been destroyed in the fire. Jerry knew this, as did his father and mother and brother, for they had smelled the unmistakable burnt-meat smell, and Terrence, in his rage of knowledge, had even attacked Mogom the house-boy, and been reprimanded and cuffed by *Mister* Haggin, who had not smelled and did not understand, and who had always to impress discipline on all creatures under his roof-tree.

But on the beach, when the blacks, whose terms of service were up came down with their trade-boxes on their heads to depart on the *Arangi*, was the time when nigger-chasing was not dangerous. Old scores could be settled, and it was the last chance, for the blacks who departed on the *Arangi* never came back. As an instance, this very morning Biddy, remembering a secret mauling at the hands of Lerumie, laid teeth into his naked calf and threw him sprawling into the water, trade-box, earthly possessions and all, and then laughed at him, sure in the protection of *Mister* Haggin who grinned at the episode.

Then, too, there was usually at least one bush-dog on the *Arangi* at which Jerry and Michael, from the beach, could bark their heads off. Once, Terrence, who was nearly as large as an Airedale and fully as lion-hearted—Terrence the Magnificent, as Tom Haggin called him—had caught such a bush-dog trespassing on the beach and given him a delightful thrashing, in

241

which Jerry and Michael, and Patsy and Kathleen, who were at the time alive, had joined with many shrill yelps and sharp nips. Jerry had never forgotten the ecstasy of the hair, unmistakably doggy in scent, which had filled his mouth at his one successful nip. Bush-dogs were dogs—he recognized them as his kind; but they were somehow different from his own lordly breed, different and lesser, just as the blacks were compared with *Mister* Haggin, Derby, and Bob.

But Jerry did not continue to gaze at the nearing *Arangi*. Biddy, wise with previous bitter bereavements, had sat down on the edge of the sand, her fore-feet in the water, and was mouthing her woe. That this concerned him, Jerry knew, for her grief tore sharply, albeit vaguely, at his sensitive, passionate heart. What it presaged he knew not, save that it was disaster and catastrophe connected with him. As he looked back at her, rough-coated and grief-stricken, he could see Terrence hovering solicitously near her. He, too, was rough-coated, as was Michael, and as Patsy and Kathleen had been, Jerry being the one smooth-coated member of the family.

Further, although Jerry did not know it and Tom Haggin did, Terrence was a royal lover and a devoted spouse. Jerry, from his earliest impressions, could remember the way Terrence had of running with Biddy, miles and miles along the beaches or through the avenues of cocoanuts, side by side with her, both with laughing mouths of sheer delight. As these were the only dogs, besides his brothers and sisters and the several eruptions of strange bush-dogs that Jerry knew, it did not enter his head otherwise than that this was the way of dogs, male and female, wedded and faithful. But Tom Haggin knew its unusualness. "Proper affinities," he declared, and repeatedly declared, with warm voice and moist eyes of appreciation. "A gentleman, that Terrence, and a four-legged proper man. A man-dog, if there ever was one, four-square as the legs on the four corners of him. And prepotent! My word! His blood'd breed true for a thousand generations, and the cool head and the kindly brave heart of him."

Terrence did not voice his sorrow, if sorrow he had; but his hovering about Biddy tokened his anxiety for her. Michael, however, yielding to the contagion, sat beside his mother and barked angrily out across the increasing stretch of water as he would have barked at any danger that crept and rustled in the jungle. This, too, sank to Jerry's heart, adding weight to his sure intuition that dire fate, he knew not what, was upon him.

For his six months of life, Jerry knew a great deal and knew very little. He knew, without thinking about it, without knowing that he knew, why Biddy, the wise as well as the brave, did not act upon all the message that her heart voiced to him, and spring into the water and swim after him. She had protected him like a lioness when the big *puarka* (which, in Jerry's vocabulary, along with grunts and squeals, was the combination of sound, or word, for "pig") had tried to devour him where he was cornered under the high-piled plantation house. Like a lioness, when the cook-boy had struck him with a stick to drive him out of the kitchen, had Biddy sprung upon the black, receiving without wince or whimper one straight blow from the stick, and then downing him and mauling him among his pots and pans until dragged (for the first time snarling) away by the unchiding *Mister* Haggin, who; however, administered sharp words to the cook-boy for daring to lift hand against a four-legged dog belonging to a god.

Jerry knew why his mother did not plunge into the water after him. The salt sea, as well as the lagoons that led out of the salt sea, were taboo. "Taboo," as word or sound, had no place in Jerry's vocabulary. But its definition, or significance, was there in the quickest part of his consciousness. He possessed a dim, vague, imperative knowingness that it was not merely not good, but supremely disastrous, leading to the mistily glimpsed sense of utter endingness for a dog, for any dog, to go into the water where slipped and slid and noiselessly paddled, sometimes on top, sometimes emerging from the depths, great scaly monsters, huge-jawed and horribly-toothed, that snapped down and engulfed a dog in an instant just as the fowls of *Mister* Haggin snapped and engulfed grains of corn.

Often he had heard his father and mother, on the safety of the sand, bark and rage their hatred of those terrible sea-dwellers, when, close to the beach, they appeared on the surface like logs awash. "Crocodile" was no word in Jerry's vocabulary. It was an image, an image of a log awash that was different from any log in that it was alive. Jerry, who heard, registered, and recognized many words that were as truly tools of thought to him as they were to humans, but who, by inarticulateness of birth and breed, could not utter these many words, nevertheless in his mental processes, used images just as articulate men use words in their own mental processes. And after all, articulate men, in the act of thinking, willy nilly use images that correspond to words and that amplify words.

Perhaps, in Jerry's brain, the rising into the foreground of consciousness of an image of a log awash connoted more intimate and fuller comprehension of the thing being thought about, than did the word "crocodile," and its accompanying image, in the foreground of a human's consciousness. For Jerry really did know more about crocodiles than the average human. He could smell a crocodile farther off and more differentiatingly than could any man, than could even a salt-water black or a bushman smell one. He could tell when a crocodile, hauled up from the lagoon, lay without sound or movement, and perhaps asleep, a hundred feet away on the floor mat of jungle.

He knew more of the language of crocodiles than did any man. He had better means and opportunities of knowing. He knew their many noises that were as grunts and slubbers. He knew their anger noises, their fear noises, their food noises, their love noises. And these noises were as definitely words in his vocabulary as are words in a human's vocabulary. And these crocodile noises were tools of thought. By them he weighed and judged and determined his own consequent courses of action, just like any human; or, just like any human, lazily resolved upon no course of action, but merely noted and registered a clear comprehension of something that was going on about him that did not require a correspondence of action on his part.

And yet, what Jerry did not know was very much. He did not know the size of the world. He did not know that this Meringe Lagoon, backed by high, forested mountains and fronted and sheltered by the off-shore coral islets, was anything else than the entire world. He did not know that it was a mere fractional part of the great island of Ysabel, that was again one island of a thousand, many of them greater, that composed the Solomon Islands that men marked on charts as a group of specks in the vastitude of the far-western South Pacific.

It was true, there was a somewhere else or a something beyond of which he was dimly aware. But whatever it was, it was mystery. Out of it, things that had not been, suddenly were. Chickens and puarkas and cats, that he had never seen before, had a way of abruptly appearing on Meringe Plantation. Once, even, had there been an eruption of strange four-legged, horned and hairy creatures, the images of which, registered in his brain, would have been identifiable in the brains of humans with what humans worded "goats."

It was the same way with the blacks. Out of the unknown, from the somewhere and something else, too unconditional for him to know any of the conditions, instantly they appeared, full-statured, walking about Meringe Plantation with loin-cloths about their middles and bone bodkins through their noses, and being put to work by *Mister* Haggin, Derby, and Bob. That their appearance was coincidental with the arrival of the *Arangi* was an association that occurred as a matter of course in Jerry's brain. Further, he did not bother, save that there was a companion association, namely, that their occasional disappearances into the beyond was likewise coincidental with the *Arangi*'s departure.

Jerry did not query these appearances and disappearances. It never entered his golden-sorrel head to be curious about the affair or to attempt to solve it. He accepted it in much the way he accepted the wetness of water and the heat of the sun. It was the way of life and of the world he knew. His hazy awareness was no more than an awareness of something—which, by the way, corresponds very fairly with the hazy awareness of the average human of the mysteries of birth and death and of the beyondness about which they have no definiteness of comprehension.

For all that any man may gainsay, the ketch *Arangi*, trader and blackbirder in the Solomon Islands, may have signified in Jerry's mind as much the mysterious boat that traffics between the two worlds, as, at one time, the boat that Charon sculled across the Styx signified to the human mind. Out of the nothingness men came. Into the nothingness they went. And they came and went always on the *Arangi*.

And to the *Arangi*, this hot-white tropic morning, Jerry went on the whaleboat under the arm of his *Mister* Haggin, while on the beach Biddy moaned her woe, and Michael, not sophisticated, barked the eternal challenge of youth to the Unknown.

CHAPTER II

From the whaleboat, up the low side of the *Arangi*, and over her six-inch rail of teak to her teak deck, was but a step, and Tom Haggin made it easily with Jerry still under his arm. The deck was cluttered with an exciting crowd. Exciting the crowd would have been to untravelled humans of civilization, and exciting it was to Jerry; although to Tom Haggin and Captain Van Horn it was a mere commonplace of everyday life.

The deck was small because the *Arangi* was small. Originally a teak-built, gentleman's yacht, brass-fitted, copper-fastened, angle-ironed, sheathed in man-of-war copper and with a fin-keel of bronze, she had been sold into the Solomon Islands' trade for the purpose of blackbirding or nigger-running. Under the law, however, this traffic was dignified by being called "recruiting."

The *Arangi* was a labour-recruit ship that carried the new-caught, cannibal blacks from remote islands to labour on the new plantations where white men turned dank and pestilential swamp and jungle into rich and stately cocoanut groves. The *Arangi's* two masts were of Oregon cedar, so scraped and hot-paraffined that they shone like tan opals in the glare of sun. Her excessive sail plan enabled her to sail like a witch, and, on occasion, gave Captain Van Horn, his white mate, and his fifteen black boat's crew as much as they could handle. She was sixty feet over all, and the cross beams of her crown deck had not been weakened by deck-houses. The only breaks— and no beams had been cut for them—were the main cabin skylight and companionway, the booby hatch for'ard over the tiny forecastle, and the small hatch aft that let down into the store-room.

And on this small deck, in addition to the crew, were the "return" niggers from three far-flung plantations. By "return" was meant that their three years of contract labour was up, and that, according to contract, they were being returned to their home villages on the wild island of Malaita. Twenty of them—familiar, all, to Jerry—were from Meringe; thirty of them came from the Bay of a Thousand Ships, in the Russell Isles; and the remaining twelve were from Pennduffryn on the east coast of Guadalcanar. In addition to these—and they were all on deck, chattering and piping in queer, almost elfish, falsetto voices—were the two white men, Captain Van Horn and his Danish mate, Borckman, making a total of seventy-nine souls.

"Thought your heart 'd failed you at the last moment," was Captain Van Horn's greeting, a quick pleasure light glowing into his eyes as they noted Jerry.

"It was sure near to doin' it," Tom Haggin answered. "It's only for you I'd a done it, annyways. Jerry's the best of the litter, barrin' Michael, of course, the two of them bein' all that's left and no better than them that was lost. Now that Kathleen was a sweet dog, the spit of Biddy if she'd lived.— Here, take 'm."

With a jerk of abruptness, he deposited Jerry in Van Horn's arms and turned away along the deck.

"An' if bad luck comes to him I'll never forgive you, Skipper," he flung roughly over his shoulder.

"They'll have to take my head first," the skipper chuckled.

"An' not unlikely, my brave laddy buck," Haggin growled. "Meringe owes Somo four heads, three from the dysentery, an' another wan from a tree fallin' on him the last fortnight. He was the son of a chief at that."

"Yes, and there's two heads more that the *Arangi* owes Somo," Van Horn nodded. "You recollect, down to the south'ard last year, a chap named Hawkins was lost in his whaleboat running the Arli Passage?" Haggin, returning along the deck, nodded. "Two of his boat's crew were Somo boys. I'd recruited them for Ugi Plantation. With your boys, that makes six heads the *Arangi* owes. But what of it? There's one salt-water village, acrost on the weather coast, where the *Arangi* owes eighteen. I recruited them for Aolo, and being salt-water men they put them on the *Sandfly* that was lost on the way to the Santa Cruz. They've got a jack-pot over there on the weather coast— my word, the boy that could get my head would be a second Carnegie! A hundred and fifty pigs and shell money no end the village's collected for the chap that gets me and delivers."

"And they ain't—yet," Haggin snorted.

"No fear," was the cheerful retort.

"You talk like Arbuckle used to talk," Haggin censured. "Manny's the time I've heard him string it off. Poor old Arbuckle. The most sure and most precautious chap that ever handled niggers. He never went to sleep without spreadin' a box of tacks on the floor, and when it wasn't them it was crumpled newspapers. I remember me well, bein' under the same roof at the time on Florida, when a big tomcat chased a cockroach into the papers. And it was blim, blam, blim, six times an' twice over, with his two big horse-pistols, an' the house perforated like a cullender. Likewise there was a dead tom-cat. He could shoot in the dark with never an aim, pullin' trigger with the second finger and pointing with the first finger laid straight along the barrel.

"No, sir, my laddy buck. He was the bully boy with the glass eye. The nigger didn't live that'd lift his head. But they got 'm. They got 'm. He lasted fourteen years, too. It was his cook-boy. Hatcheted 'm before breakfast. An' it's well I remember our second trip into the bush after what was left of 'm."

"I saw his head after you'd turned it over to the Commissioner at Tulagi," Van Horn supplemented.

"An' the peaceful, quiet, everyday face of him on it, with almost the same old smile I'd seen a thousand times. It dried on 'm that way over the smokin' fire. But they got 'm, if it did take fourteen years. There's manny's the head that goes to Malaita, manny's the time untooken; but, like the old pitcher, it's tooken in the end."

"But I've got their goat," the captain insisted. "When trouble's hatching, I go straight to them and tell them what. They can't get the hang of it. Think I've got some powerful devil-devil medicine."

Tom Haggin thrust out his hand in abrupt good-bye, resolutely keeping his eyes from dropping to Jerry in the other's arms.

"Keep your eye on my return boys," he cautioned, as he went over the side, "till you land the last mother's son of 'm. They've got no cause to love

Jerry or his breed, an' I'd hate ill to happen 'm at a nigger's hands. An' in the dark of the night 'tis like as not he can do a fare-you-well overside. Don't take your eye off 'm till you're quit of the last of 'm."

At sight of big *Mister* Haggin deserting him and being pulled away in the whaleboat, Jerry wriggled and voiced his anxiety in a low, whimpering whine. Captain Van Horn snuggled him closer in his arm with a caress of his free hand.

"Don't forget the agreement," Tom Haggin called back across the widening water. "If aught happens you, Jerry's to come back to me."

"I'll make a paper to that same and put it with the ship's articles," was Van Horn's reply.

Among the many words possessed by Jerry was his own name; and in the talk of the two men he had recognised it repeatedly, and he was aware, vaguely, that the talk was related to the vague and unguessably terrible thing that was happening to him. He wriggled more determinedly, and Van Horn set him down on the deck. He sprang to the rail with more quickness than was to be expected of an awkward puppy of six months, and not the quick attempt of Van Horn to cheek him would have succeeded. But Jerry recoiled from the open water lapping the *Arangi's* side. The taboo was upon him. It was the image of the log awash that was not a log but that was alive, luminous in his brain, that checked him. It was not reason on his part, but inhibition which had become habit.

He plumped down on his bob tail, lifted golden muzzle skyward, and emitted a long puppy-wail of dismay and grief.

"It's all right, Jerry, old man, brace up and be a man-dog," Van Horn soothed him.

But Jerry was not to be reconciled. While this indubitably was a white-skinned god, it was not his god. *Mister* Haggin was his god, and a superior god at that. Even he, without thinking about it at all, recognized that. His *Mister* Haggin wore pants and shoes. This god on the deck beside him was more like a black. Not only did he not wear pants, and was barefooted and barelegged, but about his middle, just like any black, he wore a brilliant-coloured loin-cloth, that, like a kilt, fell nearly to his sunburnt knees.

Captain Van Horn was a handsome man and a striking man, although Jerry did not know it. If ever a Holland Dutchman stepped out of a Rembrandt frame, Captain Van Horn was that one, despite the fact that he was New York born, as had been his knickerbocker ancestors before him clear back to the time when New York was not New York but New Amsterdam. To complete his costume, a floppy felt hat, distinctly Rembrandtish in effect, perched half on his head and mostly over one ear; a sixpenny, white cotton undershirt covered his torso; and from a belt about his middle dangled a tobacco pouch, a sheath-knife, filled clips of cartridges, and a huge automatic pistol in a leather holster.

On the beach, Biddy, who had hushed her grief, lifted it again when she heard Jerry's wail. And Jerry, desisting a moment to listen, heard Michael beside her, barking his challenge, and saw, without being conscious of it, Michael's withered ear with its persistent upward cock. Again, while Captain Van Horn and the mate, Borckman, gave orders, and while the *Arangi's* mainsail and spanker began to rise up the masts, Jerry loosed all his heart of woe in what Bob told Derby on the beach was the "grandest vocal effort" he had ever heard from any dog, and that, except for being a bit thin, Caruso didn't have anything on Jerry. But the song was too much for Haggin, who, as soon as he had landed, whistled Biddy to him and strode rapidly away from the beach.

At sight of her disappearing, Jerry was guilty of even more Caruso-like effects, which gave great joy to a Pennduffryn return boy who stood beside him. He laughed and jeered at Jerry with falsetto chucklings that were more like the jungle-noises of tree-dwelling creatures, half-bird and half-man, than of a man, all man, and therefore a god. This served as an excellent counter-irritant. Indignation that a mere black should laugh at him mastered Jerry, and the next moment his puppy teeth, sharp-pointed as needles, had scored the astonished black's naked calf in long parallel scratches from each of which leaped the instant blood. The black sprang away in trepidation, but the blood of Terrence the Magnificent was true in Jerry, and, like his father before him, he followed up, slashing the black's other calf into a ruddy pattern.

251

At this moment, anchor broken out and headsails running up, Captain Van Horn, whose quick eye had missed no detail of the incident, with an order to the black helmsman turned to applaud Jerry.

"Go to it, Jerry!" he encouraged. "Get him! Shake him down! Sick him! Get him! Get him!"

The black, in defence, aimed a kick at Jerry, who, leaping in instead of away—another inheritance from Terrence—avoided the bare foot and printed a further red series of parallel lines on the dark leg. This was too much, and the black, afraid more of Van Horn than of Jerry, turned and fled for'ard, leaping to safety on top of the eight Lee-Enfield rifles that lay on top of the cabin skylight and that were guarded by one member of the boat's crew. About the skylight Jerry stormed, leaping up and falling back, until Captain Van Horn called him off.

"Some nigger-chaser, that pup, *some* nigger-chaser!" Van Horn confided to Borckman, as he bent to pat Jerry and give him due reward of praise.

And Jerry, under this caressing hand of a god, albeit it did not wear pants, forgot for a moment longer the fate that was upon him.

"He's a lion-dog—more like an Airedale than an Irish terrier," Van Horn went on to his mate, still petting. "Look at the size of him already. Look at the bone of him. Some chest that. He's got the endurance. And he'll be some dog when he grows up to those feet of his."

Jerry had just remembered his grief and was starting a rush across the deck to the rail to gaze at Meringe growing smaller every second in the distance, when a gust of the South-east Trade smote the sails and pressed the *Arangi* down. And down the deck, slanted for the moment to forty-five degrees, Jerry slipped and slid, vainly clawing at the smooth surface for a hold. He fetched up against the foot of the mizzenmast, while Captain Van Horn, with the sailor's eye for the coral patch under his bow, gave the order "Hard a-lee!"

Borckman and the black steersman echoed his words, and, as the wheel spun down, the *Arangi*, with the swiftness of a witch, rounded into the wind and attained a momentary even keel to the flapping of her headsails and a shifting of headsheets.

Jerry, still intent on Meringe, took advantage of the level footing to recover himself and scramble toward the rail. But he was deflected by the crash of the mainsheet blocks on the stout deck-traveller, as the mainsail, emptied of the wind and feeling the wind on the other side, swung crazily across above him. He cleared the danger of the mainsheet with a wild leap (although no less wild had been Van Horn's leap to rescue him), and found himself directly under the mainboom with the huge sail looming above him as if about to fall upon him and crush him.

It was Jerry's first experience with sails of any sort. He did not know the beasts, much less the way of them, but, in his vivid recollection, when he had been a tiny puppy, burned the memory of the hawk, in the middle of the compound, that had dropped down upon him from out of the sky. Under that colossal threatened impact he crouched down to the deck. Above him, falling upon him like a bolt from the blue, was a winged hawk unthinkably vaster than the one he had encountered. But in his crouch was no hint of cower. His crouch was a gathering together, an assembling of all the parts of him under the rule of the spirit of him, for the spring upward to meet in mid career this monstrous, menacing thing.

But, the succeeding fraction of a moment, so that Jerry, leaping, missed even the shadow of it, the mainsail, with a second crash of blocks on traveller, had swung across and filled on the other tack.

Van Horn had missed nothing of it. Before, in his time, he had seen young dogs frightened into genuine fits by their first encounters with heaven-filling, sky-obscuring, down-impending sails. This was the first dog he had seen leap with bared teeth, undismayed, to grapple with the huge unknown.

With spontaneity of admiration, Van Horn swept Jerry from the deck and gathered him into his arms.

CHAPTER III

Jerry quite forgot Meringe for the time being. As he well remembered, the hawk had been sharp of beak and claw. This air-flapping, thunder-crashing monster needed watching. And Jerry, crouching for the spring and ever struggling to maintain his footing on the slippery, heeling deck, kept his eyes on the mainsail and uttered low growls at any display of movement on its part.

The *Arangi* was beating out between the coral patches of the narrow channel into the teeth of the brisk trade wind. This necessitated frequent tacks, so that, overhead, the mainsail was ever swooping across from port tack to starboard tack and back again, making air-noises like the swish of wings, sharply rat-tat-tatting its reef points and loudly crashing its mainsheet gear along the traveller. Half a dozen times, as it swooped overhead, Jerry leaped for it, mouth open to grip, lips writhed clear of the clean puppy teeth that shone in the sun like gems of ivory.

Failing in every leap, Jerry achieved a judgment. In passing, it must be noted that this judgment was only arrived at by a definite act of reasoning. Out of a series of observations of the thing, in which it had threatened, always in the same way, a series of attacks, he had found that it had not hurt him nor come in contact with him at all. Therefore—although he did not stop to think that he was thinking—it was not the dangerous, destroying thing he had first deemed it. It might be well to be wary of it, though already it had taken its place in his classification of things that appeared terrible but were not terrible. Thus, he had learned not to fear the roar of the wind among the palms when he lay snug on the plantation-house veranda, nor the onslaught of the waves, hissing and rumbling into harmless foam on the beach at his feet.

Many times, in the course of the day, alertly and nonchalantly, almost with a quizzical knowingness, Jerry cocked his head at the mainsail when it made sudden swooping movements or slacked and tautened its crashing sheet-gear. But he no longer crouched to spring for it. That had been the first lesson, and quickly mastered.

Having settled the mainsail, Jerry returned in mind to Meringe. But there was no Meringe, no Biddy and Terrence and Michael on the beach; no *Mister* Haggin and Derby and Bob; no beach: no land with the palm-trees near and the mountains afar off everlastingly lifting their green peaks into the sky. Always, to starboard or to port, at the bow or over the stern, when he stood up resting his fore-feet on the six-inch rail and gazing, he saw only the ocean, broken-faced and turbulent, yet orderly marching its white-crested seas before the drive of the trade.

Had he had the eyes of a man, nearly two yards higher than his own from the deck, and had they been the trained eyes of a man, sailor-man at that, Jerry could have seen the low blur of Ysabel to the north and the blur of Florida to the south, ever taking on definiteness of detail as the *Arangi* sagged close-hauled, with a good full, port-tacked to the south-east trade. And had he had the advantage of the marine glasses with which Captain Van Horn elongated the range of his eyes, he could have seen, to the east, the far peaks of Malaita lifting life-shadowed pink cloud-puffs above the sea-rim.

But the present was very immediate with Jerry. He had early learned the iron law of the immediate, and to accept what *was* when it was, rather than to strain after far other things. The sea was. The land no longer was. The *Arangi* certainly was, along with the life that cluttered her deck. And he proceeded to get acquainted with what was—in short, to know and to adjust himself to his new environment.

His first discovery was delightful—a wild-dog puppy from the Ysabel bush, being taken back to Malaita by one of the Meringe return boys. In age they were the same, but their breeding was different. The wild-dog was what he was, a wild-dog, cringing and sneaking, his ears for ever down, his tail for ever between his legs, for ever apprehending fresh misfortune and ill-treatment to fall on him, for ever fearing and resentful, fending off threatened hurt with lips curling malignantly from his puppy fangs, cringing under a blow, squalling his fear and his pain, and ready always for a treacherous slash if luck and safety favoured.

The wild-dog was maturer than Jerry, larger-bodied, and wiser in wickedness; but Jerry was blue-blooded, right-selected, and valiant. The wild-dog had come out of a selection equally rigid; but it was a different sort of selection. The bush ancestors from whom he had descended had survived by being fear-selected. They had never voluntarily fought against odds. In the open they had never attacked save when the prey was weak or defenceless. In place of courage, they had lived by creeping, and slinking, and hiding from danger. They had been selected blindly by nature, in a cruel and ignoble environment, where the prize of living was to be gained, in the main, by the cunning of cowardice, and, on occasion, by desperateness of defence when in a corner.

But Jerry had been love-selected and courage-selected. His ancestors had been deliberately and consciously chosen by men, who, somewhere in the forgotten past, had taken the wild-dog and made it into the thing they visioned and admired and desired it to be. It must never fight like a rat in a corner, because it must never be rat-like and slink into a corner. Retreat must be unthinkable. The dogs in the past who retreated had been rejected by men. They had not become Jerry's ancestors. The dogs selected for Jerry's ancestors had been the brave ones, the up-standing and out-dashing ones, who flew into the face of danger and battled and died, but who never gave ground. And, since it is the way of kind to beget kind, Jerry was what Terrence was before him, and what Terrence's forefathers had been for a long way back.

So it was that Jerry, when he chanced upon the wild-dog stowed shrewdly away from the wind in the lee-corner made by the mainmast and the cabin skylight, did not stop to consider whether the creature was bigger or fiercer than he. All he knew was that it was the ancient enemy—the wild-dog that had not come in to the fires of man. With a wild paean of joy that attracted Captain Van Horn's all-hearing ears and all-seeing eyes, Jerry sprang to the attack. The wild puppy gained his feet in full retreat with incredible swiftness, but was caught by the rush of Jerry's body and rolled over and over on the sloping deck. And as he rolled, and felt sharp teeth pricking him, he snapped and snarled, alternating snarls with whimperings and squallings of terror, pain, and abject humility.

256

And Jerry was a gentleman, which is to say he was a gentle dog. He had been so selected. Because the thing did not fight back, because it was abject and whining, because it was helpless under him, he abandoned the attack, disengaging himself from the top of the tangle into which he had slid in the lee scuppers. He did not think about it. He did it because he was so made. He stood up on the reeling deck, feeling excellently satisfied with the delicious, wild-doggy smell of hair in his mouth and consciousness, and in his ears and consciousness the praising cry of Captain Van Horn: "Good boy, Jerry! You're the goods, Jerry! *Some* dog, eh! Some dog!"

As he stalked away, it must be admitted that Jerry displayed pride in himself, his gait being a trifle stiff-legged, the cocking of his head back over his shoulder at the whining wild-dog having all the articulateness of: "Well, I guess I gave you enough this time. You'll keep out of my way after this."

Jerry continued the exploration of his new and tiny world that was never at rest, for ever lifting, heeling, and lunging on the rolling face of the sea. There were the Meringe return boys. He made it a point to identify all of them, receiving, while he did so, scowls and mutterings, and reciprocating with cocky bullyings and threatenings. Being so trained, he walked on his four legs superior to them, two-legged though they were; for he had moved and lived always under the aegis of the great two-legged and be-trousered god, *Mister* Haggin.

Then there were the strange return boys, from Pennduffryn and the Bay of a Thousand Ships. He insisted on knowing them all. He might need to know them in some future time. He did not think this. He merely equipped himself with knowledge of his environment without any awareness of provision or without bothering about the future.

In his own way of acquiring knowledge, he quickly discovered, just as on the plantation house-boys were different from field-boys, that on the *Arangi* there was a classification of boys different from the return boys. This was the boat's crew. The fifteen blacks who composed it were closer than the others to Captain Van Horn. They seemed more directly to belong to the *Arangi* and to him. They laboured under him at word of command, steering at the wheel, pulling and hauling on ropes, healing water upon the deck from overside and scrubbing with brooms.

Just as Jerry had learned from *Mister* Haggin that he must be more tolerant of the house-boys than of the field-boys if they trespassed on the compound, so, from Captain Van Horn, he learned that he must be more tolerant of the boat's crew than of the return boys. He had less license with them, more license with the others. As long as Captain Van Horn did not want his boat's crew chased, it was Jerry's duty not to chase. On the other hand he never forgot that he was a white-god's dog. While he might not chase these particular blacks, he declined familiarity with them. He kept his eye on them. He had seen blacks as tolerated as these, lined up and whipped by *Mister* Haggin. They occupied an intermediate place in the scheme of things, and they were to be watched in case they did not keep their place. He accorded them room, but he did not accord them equality. At the best, he could be stand-offishly considerate of them.

He made thorough examination of the galley, a rude affair, open on the open deck, exposed to wind and rain and storm, a small stove that was not even a ship's stove, on which somehow, aided by strings and wedges, commingled with much smoke, two blacks managed to cook the food for the four-score persons on board.

Next, he was interested by a strange proceeding on the part of the boat's crew. Upright pipes, serving as stanchions, were being screwed into the top of the *Arangi's* rail so that they served to support three strands of barbed wire that ran completely around the vessel, being broken only at the gangway for a narrow space of fifteen inches. That this was a precaution against danger, Jerry sensed without a passing thought to it. All his life, from his first impressions of life, had been passed in the heart of danger, ever-impending, from the blacks. In the plantation house at Meringe, always the several white men had looked askance at the many blacks who toiled for them and belonged to them. In the living-room, where were the eating-table, the billiard-table, and the phonograph, stood stands of rifles, and in each bedroom, beside each bed, ready to hand, had been revolvers and rifles. As well, *Mister* Haggin and Derby and Bob had always carried revolvers in their belts when they left the house to go among their blacks.

Jerry knew these noise-making things for what they were—instruments of destruction and death. He had seen live things destroyed by them, such as puarkas, goats, birds, and crocodiles. By means of such things the white-gods by their will crossed space without crossing it with their bodies, and destroyed live things. Now he, in order to damage anything, had to cross space with his body to get to it. He was different. He was limited. All impossible things were possible to the unlimited, two-legged white-gods. In a way, this ability of theirs to destroy across space was an elongation of claw and fang. Without pondering it, or being conscious of it, he accepted it as he accepted the rest of the mysterious world about him.

Once, even, had Jerry seen his *Mister* Haggin deal death at a distance in another noise-way. From the veranda he had seen him fling sticks of exploding dynamite into a screeching mass of blacks who had come raiding from the Beyond in the long war canoes, beaked and black, carved and inlaid with mother-of-pearl, which they had left hauled up on the beach at the door of Meringe.

Many precautions by the white-gods had Jerry been aware of, and so, sensing it almost in intangible ways, as a matter of course he accepted this barbed-wire fence on the floating world as a mark of the persistence of danger. Disaster and death hovered close about, waiting the chance to leap upon life and drag it down. Life had to be very alive in order to live was the law Jerry had learned from the little of life he knew.

Watching the rigging up of the barbed wire, Jerry's next adventure was an encounter with Lerumie, the return boy from Meringe, who, only that morning, on the beach embarking, had been rolled by Biddy, along with his possessions into the surf. The encounter occurred on the starboard side of the skylight, alongside of which Lerumie was standing as he gazed into a cheap trade-mirror and combed his kinky hair with a hand-carved comb of wood.

Jerry, scarcely aware of Lerumie's presence, was trotting past on his way aft to where Borckman, the mate, was superintending the stringing of the barbed wire to the stanchions. And Lerumie, with a side-long look to see if the deed meditated for his foot was screened from observation, aimed a kick at the son of his four-legged enemy. His bare foot caught Jerry on the sensitive end of his recently bobbed tail, and Jerry, outraged, with the sense of sacrilege committed upon him, went instantly wild.

Captain Van Horn, standing aft on the port quarter, gauging the slant of the wind on the sails and the inadequate steering of the black at the wheel, had not seen Jerry because of the intervening skylight. But his eyes had taken in the shoulder movement of Lerumie that advertised the balancing on one foot while the other foot had kicked. And from what followed, he divined what had already occurred.

Jerry's outcry, as he sprawled, whirled, sprang, and slashed, was a veritable puppy-scream of indignation. He slashed ankle and foot as he received the second kick in mid-air; and, although he slid clear down the slope of deck into the scuppers, he left on the black skin the red tracery of his puppy-needle teeth. Still screaming his indignation, he clawed his way back up the steep wooden hill.

Lerumie, with another side-long look, knew that he was observed and that he dare not go to extremes. He fled along the skylight to escape down the companionway, but was caught by Jerry's sharp teeth in his calf. Jerry, attacking blindly, got in the way of the black's feet. A long, stumbling fall, accelerated by a sudden increase of wind in the sails, ensued, and Lerumie, vainly trying to catch his footing, fetched up against the three strands of barbed wire on the lee rail.

The deck-full of blacks shrieked their merriment, and Jerry, his rage undiminished, his immediate antagonist out of the battle, mistaking himself as the object of the laughter of the blacks, turned upon them, charging and slashing the many legs that fled before him. They dropped down the cabin and forecastle companionways, ran out the bowsprit, and sprang into the rigging till they were perched everywhere in the air like monstrous birds. In the end, the deck belonged to Jerry, save for the boat's crew; for he had already learned to differentiate. Captain Van Horn was hilariously vocal of his praise, calling Jerry to him and giving him man-thumps of joyful admiration. Next, the captain turned to his many passengers and orated in *bêche-de-mer* English.

"Hey! You fella boy! I make 'm big fella talk. This fella dog he belong along me. One fella boy hurt 'm that fella dog—my word!—me cross too much along that fella boy. I knock 'm seven bells outa that fella boy. You take 'm care leg belong you. I take 'm care dog belong me. Savve?"

And the passengers, still perched in the air, with gleaming black eyes and with querulerus chirpings one to another, accepted the white man's law. Even Lerumie, variously lacerated by the barbed wire, did not scowl nor mutter threats. Instead, and bringing a roar of laughter from his fellows and a twinkle into the skipper's eyes, he rubbed questing fingers over his scratches and murmured: "My word! Some big fella dog that fella!"

It was not that Jerry was unkindly. Like Biddy and Terrence, he was fierce and unafraid; which attributes were wrapped up in his heredity. And, like Biddy and Terrence, he delighted in nigger-chasing, which, in turn, was a matter of training. From his earliest puppyhood he had been so trained. Niggers were niggers, but white men were gods, and it was the white-gods who had trained him to chase niggers and keep them in their proper lesser place in the world. All the world was held in the hollow of the white man's hands. The niggers—well, had not he seen them always compelled to remain in their lesser place? Had he not seen them, on occasion, triced up to the palm-trees of the Meringe compound and their backs lashed to ribbons by the white-gods? Small wonder that a high-born Irish terrier, in the arms of love of the white-god, should look at niggers through white-god's eyes, and act toward niggers in the way that earned the white-god's reward of praise.

It was a busy day for Jerry. Everything about the *Arangi* was new and strange, and so crowded was she that exciting things were continually happening. He had another encounter with the wild-dog, who treacherously attacked him in flank from ambuscade. Trade boxes belonging to the blacks had been irregularly piled so that a small space was left between two boxes in the lower tier. From this hole, as Jerry trotted past in response to a call from the skipper, the wild-dog sprang, scratched his sharp puppy-teeth into Jerry's yellow-velvet hide, and scuttled back into his lair.

Again Jerry's feelings were outraged. He could understand flank attack. Often he and Michael had played at that, although it had only been playing. But to retreat without fighting from a fight once started was alien to Jerry's ways and nature. With righteous wrath he charged into the hole after his enemy. But this was where the wild-dog fought to best advantage—in a corner. When Jerry sprang up in the confined space he bumped his head on the box above, and the next moment felt the snarling impact of the other's teeth against his own teeth and jaw.

There was no getting at the wild-dog, no chance to rush against him whole heartedly, with generous full weight in the attack. All Jerry could do was to crawl and squirm and belly forward, and always he was met by a snarling mouthful of teeth. Even so, he would have got the wild-dog in the end, had not Borckman, in passing, reached in and dragged Jerry out by a hind-leg. Again came Captain Van Horn's call, and Jerry, obedient, trotted on aft.

A meal was being served on deck in the shade of the spanker, and Jerry, sitting between the two men received his share. Already he had made the generalization that of the two, the captain was the superior god, giving many orders that the mate obeyed. The mate, on the other hand, gave orders to the blacks, but never did he give orders to the captain. Furthermore, Jerry was developing a liking for the captain, so he snuggled close to him. When he put his nose into the captain's plate, he was gently reprimanded. But once, when he merely sniffed at the mate's steaming tea-cup, her received a snub on the nose from the mate's grimy forefinger. Also, the mate did not offer him food.

Captain Van Horn gave him, first of all, a pannikin of oatmeal mush, generously flooded with condensed cream and sweetened with a heaping spoonful of sugar. After that, on occasion, he gave him morsels of buttered bread and slivers of fried fish from which he first carefully picked the tiny bones.

His beloved *Mister* Haggin had never fed him from the table at meal time, and Jerry was beside himself with the joy of this delightful experience. And, being young, he allowed his eagerness to take possession of him, so that soon he was unduly urging the captain for more pieces of fish and of bread and butter. Once, he even barked his demand. This put the idea into the captain's head, who began immediately to teach him to "speak."

At the end of five minutes he had learned to speak softly, and to speak only once—a low, mellow, bell-like bark of a single syllable. Also, in this first five minutes, he had learned to "sit down," as distinctly different from "lie down"; and that he must sit down whenever he spoke, and that he must speak without jumping or moving from the sitting position, and then must wait until the piece of food was passed to him.

Further, he had added three words to his vocabulary. For ever after, "speak" would mean to him "speak," and "sit down" would mean "sit down" and would not mean "lie down." The third addition to his vocabulary was "Skipper." That was the name he had heard the mate repeatedly call Captain Van Horn. And just as Jerry knew that when a human called "Michael," that the call referred to Michael and not to Biddy, or Terrence, or himself, so he knew that *Skipper* was the name of the two-legged white master of this new floating world.

"That isn't just a dog," was Van Horn's conclusion to the mate. "There's a sure enough human brain there behind those brown eyes. He's six months old. Any boy of six years would be an infant phenomenon to learn in five minutes all that he's just learned. Why, Gott-fer-dang, a dog's brain has to be like a man's. If he does things like a man, he's got to think like a man."

CHAPTER IV

The companionway into the main cabin was a steep ladder, and down this, after his meal, Jerry was carried by the captain. The cabin was a long room, extending for the full width of the *Arangi* from a lazarette aft to a tiny room for'ard. For'ard of this room, separated by a tight bulkhead, was the forecastle where lived the boat's crew. The tiny room was shared between Van Horn and Borckman, while the main cabin was occupied by the three-score and odd return boys. They squatted about and lay everywhere on the floor and on the long low bunks that ran the full length of the cabin along either side.

In the little stateroom the captain tossed a blanket on the floor in a corner, and he did not find it difficult to get Jerry to understand that that was his bed. Nor did Jerry, with a full stomach and weary from so much excitement, find it difficult to fall immediately asleep.

An hour later he was awakened by the entrance of Borckman. When he wagged his stub of a tail and smiled friendly with his eyes, the mate scowled at him and muttered angrily in his throat. Jerry made no further overtures, but lay quietly watching. The mate had come to take a drink. In truth, he was stealing the drink from Van Horn's supply. Jerry did not know this. Often, on the plantation, he had seen the white men take drinks. But there was something somehow different in the manner of Borckman's taking a drink. Jerry was aware, vaguely, that there was something surreptitious about it. What was wrong he did not know, yet he sensed the wrongness and watched suspiciously.

After the mate departed, Jerry would have slept again had not the carelessly latched door swung open with a bang. Opening his eyes, prepared for any hostile invasion from the unknown, he fell to watching a large cockroach crawling down the wall. When he got to his feet and warily stalked toward it, the cockroach scuttled away with a slight rustling noise and disappeared into a crack. Jerry had been acquainted with cockroaches all his life, but he was destined to learn new things about them from the particular breed that dwelt on the *Arangi*.

After a cursory examination of the stateroom he wandered out into the cabin. The blacks, sprawled about everywhere, but, conceiving it to be his duty to his *Skipper*, Jerry made it a point to identify each one. They scowled and uttered low threatening noises when he sniffed close to them. One dared to menace him with a blow, but Jerry, instead of slinking away, showed his teeth and prepared to spring. The black hastily dropped the offending hand to his side and made soothing, penitent noises, while others chuckled; and Jerry passed on his way. It was nothing new. Always a blow was to be expected from blacks when white men were not around. Both the mate and the captain were on deck, and Jerry, though unafraid, continued his investigations cautiously.

But at the doorless entrance to the lazarette aft, he threw caution to the winds and darted in in pursuit of the new scent that came to his nostrils. A strange person was in the low, dark space whom he had never smelled. Clad in a single shift and lying on a coarse grass-mat spread upon a pile of tobacco cases and fifty-pound tins of flour, was a young black girl.

There was something furtive and lurking about her that Jerry did not fail to sense, and he had long since learned that something was wrong when any black lurked or skulked. She cried out with fear as he barked an alarm and pounced upon her. Even though his teeth scratched her bare arm, she did not strike at him. Not did she cry out again. She cowered down and trembled and did not fight back. Keeping his teeth locked in the hold he had got on her flimsy shift, he shook and dragged at her, all the while growling and scolding for her benefit and yelping a high clamour to bring Skipper or the mate.

In the course of the struggle the girl over-balanced on the boxes and tins and the entire heap collapsed. This caused Jerry to yelp a more frenzied alarm, while the blacks, peering in from the cabin, laughed with cruel enjoyment.

When Skipper arrived, Jerry wagged his stump tail and, with ears laid back, dragged and tugged harder than ever at the thin cotton of the girl's

265

garment. He expected praise for what he had done, but when Skipper merely told him to let go, he obeyed with the realization that this lurking, fear-struck creature was somehow different, and must be treated differently, from other lurking creatures.

Fear-struck she was, as it is given to few humans to be and still live. Van Horn called her his parcel of trouble, and he was anxious to be rid of the parcel, without, however, the utter annihilation of the parcel. It was this annihilation which he had saved her from when he bought her in even exchange for a fat pig.

Stupid, worthless, spiritless, sick, not more than a dozen years old, no delight in the eyes of the young men of her village, she had been consigned by her disappointed parents to the cooking-pot. When Captain Van Horn first encountered her had been when she was the central figure in a lugubrious procession on the banks of the Balebuli River.

Anything but a beauty—had been his appraisal when he halted the procession for a pow-wow. Lean from sickness, her skin mangy with the dry scales of the disease called *bukua*, she was tied hand and foot and, like a pig, slung from a stout pole that rested on the shoulders of the bearers, who intended to dine off of her. Too hopeless to expect mercy, she made no appeal for help, though the horrible fear that possessed her was eloquent in her wild-staring eyes.

In the universal bêche-de-mer English, Captain Van Horn had learned that she was not regarded with relish by her companions, and that they were on their way to stake her out up to her neck in the running water of the Balebuli. But first, before they staked her, their plan was to dislocate her joints and break the big bones of the arms and legs. This was no religious rite, no placation of the brutish jungle gods. Merely was it a matter of gastronomy. Living meat, so treated, was made tender and tasty, and, as her companions pointed out, she certainly needed to be put through such a process. Two days in the water, they told the captain, ought to do the business. Then they would kill her, build the fire, and invite in a few friends.

After half an hour of bargaining, during which Captain Van Horn had insisted on the worthlessness of the parcel, he had bought a fat pig worth five dollars and exchanged it for her. Thus, since he had paid for the pig in trade goods, and since trade goods were rated at a hundred per cent. profit, the girl had actually cost him two dollars and fifty cents.

And then Captain Van Horn's troubles had begun. He could not get rid of the girl. Too well he knew the natives of Malaita to turn her over to them anywhere on the island. Chief Ishikola of Su'u had offered five twenties of drinking coconuts for her, and Bau, a bush chief, had offered two chickens on the beach at Malu. But this last offer had been accompanied by a sneer, and had tokened the old rascal's scorn of the girl's scrawniness. Failing to connect with the missionary brig, the *Western Cross*, on which she would not have been eaten, Captain Van Horn had been compelled to keep her in the cramped quarters of the *Arangi* against a problematical future time when he would be able to turn her over to the missionaries.

But toward him the girl had no heart of gratitude because she had no brain of understanding. She, who had been sold for a fat pig, considered her pitiful rôle in the world to be unchanged. Eatee she had been. Eatee she remained. Her destination merely had been changed, and this big fella white marster of the *Arangi* would undoubtedly be her destination when she had sufficiently fattened. His designs on her had been transparent from the first, when he had tried to feed her up. And she had outwitted him by resolutely eating no more than would barely keep her alive.

As a result, she, who had lived in the bush all her days and never so much as set foot in a canoe, rocked and rolled unendingly over the broad ocean in a perpetual nightmare of fear. In the bêche-de-mer that was current among the blacks of a thousand islands and ten thousand dialects, the *Arangi's* procession of passengers assured her of her fate. "My word, you fella Mary," one would say to her, "short time little bit that big fella white marster kai-kai along you." Or, another: "Big fella white marster kai-kai along you, my word, belly belong him walk about too much."

267

Kai-kai was the bêche-de-mer for "eat." Even Jerry knew that. "Eat" did not obtain in his vocabulary; but kai-kai did, and it meant all and more than "eat," for it served for both noun and verb.

But the girl never replied to the jeering of the blacks. For that matter, she never spoke at all, not even to Captain Van Horn, who did not so much as know her name.

It was late afternoon, after discovering the girl in the lazarette, when Jerry again came on deck. Scarcely had Skipper, who had carried him up the steep ladder, dropped him on deck than Jerry made a new discovery— land. He did not see it, but he smelled it. His nose went up in the air and quested to windward along the wind that brought the message, and he read the air with his nose as a man might read a newspaper—the salt smells of the seashore and of the dank muck of mangrove swamps at low tide, the spicy fragrances of tropic vegetation, and the faint, most faint, acrid tingle of smoke from smudgy fires.

The trade, which had laid the *Arangi* well up under the lee of this outjutting point of Malaita, was now failing, so that she began to roll in the easy swells with crashings of sheets and tackles and thunderous flappings of her sails. Jerry no more than cocked a contemptuous quizzical eye at the mainsail anticking above him. He knew already the empty windiness of its threats, but he was careful of the mainsheet blocks, and walked around the traveller instead of over it.

While Captain Van Horn, taking advantage of the calm to exercise the boat's crew with the fire-arms and to limber up the weapons, was passing out the Lee-Enfields from their place on top the cabin skylight, Jerry suddenly crouched and began to stalk stiff-legged. But the wild-dog, three feet from his lair under the trade-boxes, was not unobservant. He watched and snarled threateningly. It was not a nice snarl. In fact, it was as nasty and savage a snarl as all his life had been nasty and savage. Most small creatures were afraid of that snarl, but it had no deterrent effect on Jerry, who continued his steady stalking. When the wild-dog sprang for the hole under the boxes, Jerry sprang after, missing his enemy by inches. Tossing overboard bits of wood, bottles and empty tins, Captain Van Horn ordered the eight eager boat's crew with rifles to turn loose. Jerry was excited and delighted with the fusillade, and added his puppy yelpings to the noise. As the empty brass cartridges were ejected, the return boys scrambled on the deck for them, esteeming them as very precious objects and thrusting them, still warm, into the empty holes in their ears. Their ears were perforated with many of these holes, the smallest capable of receiving a cartridge, while the larger ones contained-clay pipes, sticks of tobacco, and even boxes of matches. Some of the holes in the ear-lobes were so huge that they were plugged with carved wooden cylinders three inches in diameter.

Mate and captain carried automatics in their belts, and with these they turned loose, shooting away clip after clip to the breathless admiration of the blacks for such marvellous rapidity of fire. The boat's crew were not even fair shots, but Van Horn, like every captain in the Solomons, knew that the bush natives and salt-water men were so much worse shots, and knew that the shooting of his boat's crew could be depended upon—if the boat's crew itself did not turn against the ship in a pinch.

At first, Borckman's automatic jammed, and he received a caution from Van Horn for his carelessness in not keeping it clean and thin-oiled. Also, Borckman was twittingly asked how many drinks he had taken, and if that was what accounted for his shooting being under his average. Borckman explained that he had a touch of fever, and Van Horn deferred stating his doubts until a few minutes later, squatting in the shade of the spanker with Jerry in his arms, he told Jerry all about it.

"The trouble with him is the schnapps, Jerry," he explained. "Gott-fer-dang, it makes me keep all my watches and half of his. And he says it's the fever. Never believe it, Jerry. It's the schnapps—just the plain s-c-h-n-a-p-p-s schnapps. An' he's a good sailor-man, Jerry, when he's sober. But when he's schnappy he's sheer lunatic. Then his noddle goes pinwheeling and he's a blighted fool, and he'd snore in a gale and suffer for sleep in a dead calm.— Jerry, you're just beginning to pad those four little soft feet of yours into the world, so take the advice of one who knows and leave the schnapps alone. Believe me, Jerry, boy—listen to your father—schnapps will never buy you anything."

269

Whereupon, leaving Jerry on deck to stalk the wild-dog, Captain Van Horn went below into the tiny stateroom and took a long drink from the very bottle from which Borckman was stealing.

The stalking of the wild-dog became a game, at least to Jerry, who was so made that his heart bore no malice, and who hugely enjoyed it. Also, it gave him a delightful consciousness of his own mastery, for the wild-dog always fled from him. At least so far as dogs were concerned, Jerry was cock of the deck of the *Arangi*. It did not enter his head to query how his conduct affected the wild-dog, though, in truth, he led that individual a wretched existence. Never, except when Jerry was below, did the wild one dare venture more than several feet from his retreat, and he went about in fear and trembling of the fat roly-poly puppy who was unafraid of his snarl.

In the late afternoon, Jerry trotted aft, after having administered another lesson to the wild-dog, and found Skipper seated on the deck, back against the low rail, knees drawn up, and gazing absently off to leeward. Jerry sniffed his bare calf—not that he needed to identify it, but just because he liked to, and in a sort of friendly greeting. But Van Horn took no notice, continuing to stare out across the sea. Nor was he aware of the puppy's presence.

Jerry rested the length of his chin on Skipper's knee and gazed long and earnestly into Skipper's face. This time Skipper knew, and was pleasantly thrilled; but still he gave no sign. Jerry tried a new tack. Skipper's hand drooped idly, half open, from where the forearm rested on the other knee. Into the part-open hand Jerry thrust his soft golden muzzle to the eyes and remained quite still. Had he been situated to see, he would have seen a twinkle in Skipper's eyes, which had been withdrawn from the sea and were looking down upon him. But Jerry could not see. He kept quiet a little longer, and then gave a prodigious sniff.

This was too much for Skipper, who laughed with such genial heartiness as to lay Jerry's silky ears back and down in self-deprecation of affection and pleadingness to bask in the sunshine of the god's smile. Also, Skipper's laughter set Jerry's tail wildly bobbing. The half-open hand closed in a firm grip that gathered in the slack of the skin of one side of Jerry's head and jowl.

270

Then the hand began to shake him back and forth with such good will that he was compelled to balance back and forth on all his four feet.

It was bliss to Jerry. Nay, more, it was ecstasy. For Jerry knew there was neither anger nor danger in the roughness of the shake, and that it was play of the sort that he and Michael had indulged in. On occasion, he had so played with Biddy and lovingly mauled her about. And, on very rare occasion, *Mister* Haggin had lovingly mauled him about. It was speech to Jerry, full of unmistakable meaning.

As the shake grew rougher, Jerry emitted his most ferocious growl, which grew more ferocious with the increasing violence of the shaking. But that, too, was play, a making believe to hurt the one he liked too well to hurt. He strained and tugged at the grip, trying to twist his jowl in the slack of skin so as to reach a bite.

When Skipper, with a quick thrust, released him and shoved him clear, he came back, all teeth and growl, to be again caught and shaken. The play continued, with rising excitement to Jerry. Once, too quick for Skipper, he caught his hand between teeth; but he did not bring them together. They pressed lovingly, denting the skin, but there was no bite in them.

The play grew rougher, and Jerry lost himself in the play. Still playing, he grew so excited that all that had been feigned became actual. This was battle a struggle against the hand that seized and shook him and thrust him away. The make-believe of ferocity passed out of his growls; the ferocity in them became real. Also, in the moments when he was shoved away and was springing back to the attack, he yelped in high-pitched puppy hysteria. And Captain Van Horn, realizing, suddenly, instead of clutching, extended his hand wide open in the peace sign that is as ancient as the human hand. At the same time his voice rang out the single word, "Jerry!" In it was all the imperativeness of reproof and command and all the solicitous insistence of love.

Jerry knew and was checked back to himself. He was instantly contrite, all soft humility, ears laid back with pleadingness for forgiveness and protestation of a warm throbbing heart of love. Instantly, from an open-mouthed, fang-bristling dog in full career of attack, he melted into a bundle of softness and silkiness, that trotted to the open hand and kissed it with a tongue that flashed out between white gleaming teeth like a rose-red jewel. And the next moment he was in Skipper's arms, jowl against cheek, and the tongue was again flashing out in all the articulateness possible for a creature denied speech. It was a veritable love-feast, as dear to one as to the other.

"Gott-fer-dang!" Captain Van Horn crooned. "You're nothing but a bunch of high-strung sensitiveness, with a golden heart in the middle and a golden coat wrapped all around. Gott-fer-dang, Jerry, you're gold, pure gold, inside and out, and no dog was ever minted like you in all the world. You're heart of gold, you golden dog, and be good to me and love me as I shall always be good to you and love you for ever and for ever."

And Captain Van Horn, who ruled the *Arangi* in bare legs, a loin cloth, and a sixpenny under-shirt, and ran cannibal blacks back and forth in the blackbird trade with an automatic strapped to his body waking and sleeping and with his head forfeit in scores of salt-water villages and bush strongholds, and who was esteemed the toughest skipper in the Solomons where only men who are tough may continue to live and esteem toughness, blinked with sudden moisture in his eyes, and could not see for the moment the puppy that quivered all its body of love in his arms and kissed away the salty softness of his eyes.

CHAPTER V

And swift tropic night smote the *Arangi*, as she alternately rolled in calms and heeled and plunged ahead in squalls under the lee of the cannibal island of Malaita. It was a stoppage of the south-east trade wind that made for variable weather, and that made cooking on the exposed deck galley a misery and sent the return boys, who had nothing to wet but their skins, scuttling below.

The first watch, from eight to twelve, was the mate's; and Captain Van Horn, forced below by the driving wet of a heavy rain squall, took Jerry with him to sleep in the tiny stateroom. Jerry was weary from the manifold excitements of the most exciting day in his life; and he was asleep and kicking and growling in his sleep, ere Skipper, with a last look at him and a grin as he turned the lamp low, muttered aloud: "It's that wild-dog, Jerry. Get him. Shake him. Shake him hard."

So soundly did Jerry sleep, that when the rain, having robbed the atmosphere of its last breath of wind, ceased and left the stateroom a steaming, suffocating furnace, he did not know when Skipper, panting for air, his loin cloth and undershirt soaked with sweat, arose, tucked blanket and pillow under his arm, and went on deck.

Jerry only awakened when a huge three-inch cockroach nibbled at the sensitive and hairless skin between his toes. He awoke kicking the offended foot, and gazed at the cockroach that did not scuttle, but that walked dignifiedly away. He watched it join other cockroaches that paraded the floor. Never had he seen so many gathered together at one time, and never had he seen such large ones. They were all of a size, and they were everywhere. Long lines of them poured out of cracks in the walls and descended to join their fellows on the floor.

The thing was indecent—at least, in Jerry's mind, it was not to be tolerated. *Mister* Haggin, Derby, and Bob had never tolerated cockroaches, and their rules were his rules. The cockroach was the eternal tropic enemy. He sprang at the nearest, pouncing to crush it to the floor under his paws. But the thing did what he had never known a cockroach to do. It arose in the air strong-flighted as a bird. And as if at a signal, all the multitude of cockroaches took wings of flight and filled the room with their flutterings and circlings.

He attacked the winged host, leaping into the air, snapping at the flying vermin, trying to knock them down with his paws. Occasionally he succeeded and destroyed one; nor did the combat cease until all the cockroaches, as if at another signal, disappeared into the many cracks, leaving the room to him.

Quickly, his next thought was: Where is Skipper? He knew he was not in the room, though he stood up on his hind-legs and investigated the low bunk, his keen little nose quivering delightedly while he made little sniffs of delight as he smelled the recent presence of Skipper. And what made his nose quiver and sniff, likewise made his stump of a tail bob back and forth.

But where was Skipper? It was a thought in his brain that was as sharp and definite as a similar thought would be in a human brain. And it similarly preceded action. The door had been left hooked open, and Jerry trotted out into the cabin where half a hundred blacks made queer sleep-moanings, and sighings, and snorings. They were packed closely together, covering the floor as well as the long sweep of bunks, so that he was compelled to crawl over their naked legs. And there was no white god about to protect him. He knew it, but was unafraid.

Having made sure that Skipper was not in the cabin, Jerry prepared for the perilous ascent of the steep steps that were almost a ladder, then recollected the lazarette. In he trotted and sniffed at the sleeping girl in the cotton shift who believed that Van Horn was going to eat her if he could succeed in fattening her.

Back at the ladder-steps, he looked up and waited in the hope that Skipper might appear from above and carry him up. Skipper had passed that way, he knew, and he knew for two reasons. It was the only way he could have passed, and Jerry's nose told him that he had passed. His first attempt to climb the steps began well. Not until a third of the way up, as the *Arangi* rolled in a sea and recovered with a jerk, did he slip and fall. Two or three boys awoke and watched him while they prepared and chewed betel nut and lime wrapped in green leaves.

Twice, barely started, Jerry slipped back, and more boys, awakened by their fellows, sat up and enjoyed his plight. In the fourth attempt he managed to gain half way up before he fell, coming down heavily on his side. This was hailed with low laughter and querulous chirpings that might well have come from the throats of huge birds. He regained his feet, absurdly bristled the hair on his shoulders and absurdly growled his high disdain of these lesser, two-legged things that came and went and obeyed the wills of great, white-skinned, two-legged gods such as Skipper and *Mister* Haggin.

Undeterred by his heavy fall, Jerry essayed the ladder again. A temporary easement of the *Arangi's* rolling gave him his opportunity, so that his forefeet were over the high combing of the companion when the next big roll came. He held on by main strength of his bent forelegs, then scrambled over and out on deck.

Amidships, squatting on the deck near the sky-light, he investigated several of the boat's crew and Lerumie. He identified them circumspectly, going suddenly stiff-legged as Lerumie made a low, hissing, menacing noise. Aft, at the wheel, he found a black steering, and, near him, the mate keeping the watch. Just as the mate spoke to him and stooped to pat him, Jerry whiffed Skipper somewhere near at hand. With a conciliating, apologetic bob of his tail, he trotted on up wind and came upon Skipper on his back, rolled in a blanket so that only his head stuck out, and sound asleep.

First of all Jerry needs must joyfully sniff him and joyfully wag his tail. But Skipper did not awake and a fine spray of rain, almost as thin as mist, made Jerry curl up and press closely into the angle formed by Skipper's head and shoulder. This did awake him, for he uttered "Jerry" in a low, crooning voice, and Jerry responded with a touch of his cold damp nose to the other's cheek. And then Skipper went to sleep again. But not Jerry. He lifted the edge of the blanket with his nose and crawled across the shoulder until he

275

was altogether inside. This roused Skipper, who, half-asleep, helped him to curl up.

Still Jerry was not satisfied, and he squirmed around until he lay in the hollow of Skipper's arm, his head resting on Skipper's shoulder, when, with a profound sigh of content, he fell asleep.

Several times the noises made by the boat's crew in trimming the sheets to the shifting draught of air roused Van Horn, and each time, remembering the puppy, he pressed him caressingly with his hollowed arm. And each time, in his sleep, Jerry stirred responsively and snuggled cosily to him.

For all that he was a remarkable puppy, Jerry had his limitations, and he could never know the effect produced on the hard-bitten captain by the soft warm contact of his velvet body. But it made the captain remember back across the years to his own girl babe asleep on his arm. And so poignantly did he remember, that he became wide awake, and many pictures, beginning, with the girl babe, burned their torment in his brain. No white man in the Solomons knew what he carried about with him, waking and often sleeping; and it was because of these pictures that he had come to the Solomons in a vain effort to erase them.

First, memory-prodded by the soft puppy in his arm, he saw the girl and the mother in the little Harlem flat. Small, it was true, but tight-packed with the happiness of three that made it heaven.

He saw the girl's flaxen-yellow hair darken to her mother's gold as it lengthened into curls and ringlets until finally it became two thick long braids. From striving not to see these many pictures he came even to dwelling upon them in the effort so to fill his consciousness as to keep out the one picture he did not want to see.

He remembered his work, the wrecking car, and the wrecking crew that had toiled under him, and he wondered what had become of Clancey, his right-hand man. Came the long day, when, routed from bed at three in the morning to dig a surface car out of the wrecked show windows of a drug store and get it back on the track, they had laboured all day clearing up a half-dozen smash-ups and arrived at the car house at nine at night just as another call came in.

"Glory be!" said Clancey, who lived in the next block from him. He could see him saying it and wiping the sweat from his grimy face. "Glory be, 'tis a small matter at most, an' right in our neighbourhood—not a dozen blocks away. Soon as it's done we can beat it for home an' let the down-town boys take the car back to the shop."

"We've only to jack her up for a moment," he had answered.

"What is it?" Billy Jaffers, another of the crew, asked.

"Somebody run over—can't get them out," he said, as they swung on board the wrecking-car and started.

He saw again all the incidents of the long run, not omitting the delay caused by hose-carts and a hook-and-ladder running to a cross-town fire, during which time he and Clancey had joked Jaffers over the dates with various fictitious damsels out of which he had been cheated by the night's extra work.

Came the long line of stalled street-cars, the crowd, the police holding it back, the two ambulances drawn up and waiting their freight, and the young policeman, whose beat it was, white and shaken, greeting him with: "It's horrible, man. It's fair sickening. Two of them. We can't get them out. I tried. One was still living, I think."

But he, strong man and hearty, used to such work, weary with the hard day and with a pleasant picture of the bright little flat waiting him a dozen blocks away when the job was done, spoke cheerfully, confidently, saying that he'd have them out in a jiffy, as he stooped and crawled under the car on hands and knees.

Again he saw himself as he pressed the switch of his electric torch and looked. Again he saw the twin braids of heavy golden hair ere his thumb relaxed from the switch, leaving him in darkness.

"Is the one alive yet?" the shaken policeman asked.

And the question was repeated, while he struggled for will power sufficient to press on the light.

He heard himself reply, "I'll tell you in a minute."

Again he saw himself look. For a long minute he looked.

"Both dead," he answered quietly. "Clancey, pass in a number three jack, and get under yourself with another at the other end of the truck."

He lay on his back, staring straight up at one single star that rocked mistily through a thinning of cloud-stuff overhead. The old ache was in his throat, the old harsh dryness in mouth and eyes. And he knew—what no other man knew—why he was in the Solomons, skipper of the teak-built yacht *Arangi*, running niggers, risking his head, and drinking more Scotch whiskey than was good for any man.

Not since that night had he looked with warm eyes on any woman. And he had been noted by other whites as notoriously cold toward pickanninnies white or black.

But, having visioned the ultimate horror of memory, Van Horn was soon able to fall asleep again, delightfully aware, as he drowsed off, of Jerry's head on his shoulder. Once, when Jerry, dreaming of the beach at Meringe and of *Mister* Haggin, Biddy, Terrence, and Michael, set up a low whimpering, Van Horn roused sufficiently to soothe him closer to him, and to mutter ominously: "Any nigger that'd hurt that pup. . . "

At midnight when the mate touched him on the shoulder, in the moment of awakening and before he was awake Van Horn did two things automatically and swiftly. He darted his right hand down to the pistol at his hip, and muttered: "Any nigger that'd hurt that pup . . ."

"That'll be Kopo Point abreast," Borckman explained, as both men stared to windward at the high loom of the land. "She hasn't made more than ten miles, and no promise of anything steady."

"There's plenty of stuff making up there, if it'll ever come down," Van Horn said, as both men transferred their gaze to the clouds drifting with many breaks across the dim stars.

278

Scarcely had the mate fetched a blanket from below and turned in on deck, than a brisk steady breeze sprang up from off the land, sending the *Arangi* through the smooth water at a nine-knot clip. For a time Jerry tried to stand the watch with Skipper, but he soon curled up and dozed off, partly on the deck and partly on Skipper's bare feet.

When Skipper carried him to the blanket and rolled him in, he was quickly asleep again; and he was quickly awake, out of the blanket, and padding after along the deck as Skipper paced up and down. Here began another lesson, and in five minutes Jerry learned it was the will of Skipper that he should remain in the blanket, that everything was all right, and that Skipper would be up and down and near him all the time.

At four the mate took charge of the deck.

"Reeled off thirty miles," Van Horn told him. "But now it is baffling again. Keep an eye for squalls under the land. Better throw the halyards down on deck and make the watch stand by. Of course they'll sleep, but make them sleep on the halyards and sheets."

Jerry roused to Skipper's entrance under the blanket, and, quite as if it were a long-established custom, curled in between his arm and side, and, after one happy sniff and one kiss of his cool little tongue, as Skipper pressed his cheek against him caressingly, dozed off to sleep.

Half an hour later, to all intents and purposes, so far as Jerry could or could not comprehend, the world might well have seemed suddenly coming to an end. What awoke him was the flying leap of Skipper that sent the blanket one way and Jerry the other. The deck of the *Arangi* had become a wall, down which Jerry slipped through the roaring dark. Every rope and shroud was thrumming and screeching in resistance to the fierce weight of the squall.

"Stand by main halyards!—Jump!" he could hear Skipper shouting loudly; also he heard the high note of the mainsheet screaming across the sheaves as Van Horn, bending braces in the dark, was swiftly slacking the sheet through his scorching palms with a single turn on the cleat.

While all this, along with many other noises, squealings of boat-boys and shouts of Borckman, was impacting on Jerry's ear-drums, he was still sliding down the steep deck of his new and unstable world. But he did not bring up against the rail where his fragile ribs might well have been broken. Instead, the warm ocean water, pouring inboard across the buried rail in a flood of pale phosphorescent fire, cushioned his fall. A raffle of trailing ropes entangled him as he struck out to swim.

And he swam, not to save his life, not with the fear of death upon him. There was but one idea in his mind. *Where was Skipper?* Not that he had any thought of trying to save Skipper, nor that he might be of assistance to him. It was the heart of love that drives one always toward the beloved. As the mother in catastrophe tries to gain her babe, as the Greek who, dying, remembered sweet Argos, as soldiers on a stricken field pass with the names of their women upon their lips, so Jerry, in this wreck of a world, yearned toward Skipper.

The squall ceased as abruptly as it had struck. The *Arangi* righted with a jerk to an even keel, leaving Jerry stranded in the starboard scuppers. He trotted across the level deck to Skipper, who, standing erect on wide-spread legs, the bight of the mainsheet still in his hand, was exclaiming:

"Gott-fer-dang! Wind he go! Rain he no come!"

He felt Jerry's cool nose against his bare calf, heard his joyous sniff, and bent and caressed him. In the darkness he could not see, but his heart warmed with knowledge that Jerry's tail was surely bobbing.

Many of the frightened return boys had crowded on deck, and their plaintive, querulous voices sounded like the sleepy noises of a roost of birds. Borckman came and stood by Van Horn's shoulder, and both men, strung to their tones in the tenseness of apprehension, strove to penetrate the surrounding blackness with their eyes, while they listened with all their ears for any message of the elements from sea and air.

"Where's the rain?" Borckman demanded peevishly. "Always wind first, the rain follows and kills the wind. There is no rain."

Van Horn still stared and listened, and made no answer.

The anxiety of the two men was sensed by Jerry, who, too, was on his toes. He pressed his cool nose to Skipper's leg, and the rose-kiss of his tongue brought him the salt taste of sea-water.

Skipper bent suddenly, rolled Jerry with quick toughness into the blanket, and deposited him in the hollow between two sacks of yams lashed on deck aft of the mizzenmast. As an afterthought, he fastened the blanket with a piece of rope yarn, so that Jerry was as if tied in a sack.

Scarcely was this finished when the spanker smashed across overhead, the headsails thundered with a sudden filling, and the great mainsail, with all the scope in the boom-tackle caused by Van Horn's giving of the sheet, came across and fetched up to tautness on the tackle with a crash that shook the vessel and heeled her violently to port. This second knock-down had come from the opposite direction, and it was mightier than the first.

Jerry heard Skipper's voice ring out, first, to the mate: "Stand by main-halyards! Throw off the turns! I'll take care of the tackle!"; and, next, to some of the boat's crew: "Batto! you fella slack spanker tackle quick fella! Ranga! you fella let go spanker sheet!"

Here Van Horn was swept off his legs by an avalanche of return boys who had cluttered the deck with the first squall. The squirming mass, of which he was part, slid down into the barbed wire of the port rail beneath the surface of the sea.

Jerry was so secure in his nook that he did not roll away. But when he heard Skipper's commands cease, and, seconds later, heard his cursings in the barbed wire, he set up a shrill yelping and clawed and scratched frantically at the blanket to get out. Something had happened to Skipper. He knew that. It was all that he knew, for he had no thought of himself in the chaos of the ruining world.

But he ceased his yelping to listen to a new noise—a thunderous slatting of canvas accompanied by shouts and cries. He sensed, and sensed wrongly, that it boded ill, for he did not know that it was the mainsail being lowered on the run after Skipper had slashed the boom-tackle across with his sheath-knife.

As the pandemonium grew, he added his own yelping to it until he felt a fumbling hand without the blanket. He stilled and sniffed. No, it was not Skipper. He sniffed again and recognized the person. It was Lerumie, the black whom he had seen rolled on the beach by Biddy only the previous morning, who, still were recently, had kicked him on his stub of a tail, and who not more than a week before he had seen throw a rock at Terrence.

The rope yarn had been parted, and Lerumie's fingers were feeling inside the blanket for him. Jerry snarled his wickedest. The thing was sacrilege. He, as a white man's dog, was taboo to all blacks. He had early learned the law that no nigger must ever touch a white-god's dog. Yet Lerumie, who was all of evil, at this moment when the world crashed about their ears, was daring to touch him.

And when the fingers touched him, his teeth closed upon them. Next, he was clouted by the black's free hand with such force as to tear his clenched teeth down the fingers through skin and flesh until the fingers went clear.

Raging like a tiny fiend, Jerry found himself picked up by the neck, half-throttled, and flung through the air. And while flying through the air, he continued to squall his rage. He fell into the sea and went under, gulping a mouthful of salt water into his lungs, and came up strangling but swimming. Swimming was one of the things he did not have to think about. He had never had to learn to swim, any more than he had had to learn to breathe. In fact, he had been compelled to learn to walk; but he swam as a matter of course.

The wind screamed about him. Flying froth, driven on the wind's breath, filled his mouth and nostrils and beat into his eyes, stinging and blinding him. In the struggle to breathe he, all unlearned in the ways of the sea, lifted his muzzle high in the air to get out of the suffocating welter. As a result, off the horizontal, the churning of his legs no longer sustained him, and he went down and under perpendicularly. Again he emerged, strangling with more salt water in his windpipe. This time, without reasoning it out, merely moving along the line of least resistance, which was to him the line of greatest comfort, he straightened out in the sea and continued so to swim as to remain straightened out.

Through the darkness, as the squall spent itself, came the slatting of the half-lowered mainsail, the shrill voices of the boat's crew, a curse of Borckman's, and, dominating all, Skipper's voice, shouting:

"Grab the leech, you fella boys! Hang on! Drag down strong fella! Come in mainsheet two blocks! Jump, damn you, jump!"

CHAPTER VI

At recognition of Skipper's voice, Jerry, floundering in the stiff and crisping sea that sprang up with the easement of the wind, yelped eagerly and yearningly, all his love for his new-found beloved eloquent in his throat. But quickly all sounds died away as the *Arangi* drifted from him. And then, in the loneliness of the dark, on the heaving breast of the sea that he recognized as one more of the eternal enemies, he began to whimper and cry plaintively like a lost child.

Further, by the dim, shadowy ways of intuition, he knew his weakness in that merciless sea with no heart of warmth, that threatened the unknowable thing, vaguely but terribly guessed, namely, death. As regarded himself, he did not comprehend death. He, who had never known the time when he was not alive, could not conceive of the time when he would cease to be alive.

Yet it was there, shouting its message of warning through every tissue cell, every nerve quickness and brain sensitivity of him—a totality of sensation that foreboded the ultimate catastrophe of life about which he knew nothing at all, but which, nevertheless, he *felt* to be the conclusive supreme disaster. Although he did not comprehend it, he apprehended it no less poignantly than do men who know and generalize far more deeply and widely than mere four-legged dogs.

As a man struggles in the throes of nightmare, so Jerry struggled in the vexed, salt-suffocating sea. And so he whimpered and cried, lost child, lost puppy-dog that he was, only half a year existent in the fair world sharp with joy and suffering. And he *wanted Skipper*. Skipper was a god.

* * * * *

On board the *Arangi*, relieved by the lowering of her mainsail, as the fierceness went out of the wind and the cloudburst of tropic rain began to fall, Van Horn and Borckman lurched toward each other in the blackness.

"A double squall," said Van Horn. "Hit us to starboard and to port."

"Must a-split in half just before she hit us," the mate concurred.

"And kept all the rain in the second half—"

Van Horn broke off with an oath.

"Hey! What's the matter along you fella boy?" he shouted to the man at the wheel.

For the ketch, under her spanker which had just then been flat-hauled, had come into the wind, emptying her after-sail and permitting her headsails to fill on the other tack. The *Arangi* was beginning to work back approximately over the course she had just traversed. And this meant that she was going back toward Jerry floundering in the sea. Thus, the balance, on which his life titubated, was inclined in his favour by the blunder of a black steersman.

Keeping the *Arangi* on the new tack, Van Horn set Borckman clearing the mess of ropes on deck, himself, squatting in the rain, undertaking to long-splice the tackle he had cut. As the rain thinned, so that the crackle of it on deck became less noisy, he was attracted by a sound from out over the water. He suspended the work of his hands to listen, and, when he recognized Jerry's wailing, sprang to his feet, galvanized into action.

"The pup's overboard!" he shouted to Borckman. "Back your jib to wind'ard!"

He sprang aft, scattering a cluster of return boys right and left.

"Hey! You fella boat's crew! Come in spanker sheet! Flatten her down good fella!"

He darted a look into the binnacle and took a hurried compass bearing of the sounds Jerry was making.

"Hard down your wheel!" he ordered the helmsman, then leaped to the wheel and put it down himself, repeating over and over aloud, "Nor'east by east a quarter, nor'east by east a quarter."

Back and peering into the binnacle, he listened vainly for another wail from Jerry in the hope of verifying his first hasty bearing. But not long he waited. Despite the fact that by his manoeuvre the *Arangi* had been hove to, he knew that windage and sea-driftage would quickly send her away from the swimming puppy. He shouted Borckman to come aft and haul in the whaleboat, while he hurried below for his electric torch and a boat compass.

The ketch was so small that she was compelled to tow her one whaleboat astern on long double painters, and by the time the mate had it hauled in under the stern, Van Horn was back. He was undeterred by the barbed wire, lifting boy after boy of the boat's crew over it and dropping them sprawling into the boat, following himself, as the last, by swinging over on the spanker boom, and calling his last instructions as the painters were cast off.

"Get a riding light on deck, Borckman. Keep her hove to. Don't hoist the mainsail. Clean up the decks and bend the watch tackle on the main boom."

He took the steering-sweep and encouraged the rowers with: "Washee-washee, good fella, washee-washee!"—which is the bêche-de-mer for "row hard."

As he steered, he kept flashing the torch on the boat compass so that he could keep headed north-east by east a quarter east. Then he remembered that the boat compass, on such course, deviated two whole points from the *Arangi's* compass, and altered his own course accordingly.

Occasionally he bade the rowers cease, while he listened and called for Jerry. He had them row in circles, and work back and forth, up to windward and down to leeward, over the area of dark sea that he reasoned must contain the puppy.

"Now you fella boy listen ear belong you," he said, toward the first. "Maybe one fella boy hear 'm pickaninny dog sing out, I give 'm that fella boy five fathom calico, two ten sticks tobacco."

At the end of half an hour he was offering "Two ten fathoms calico and ten ten sticks tobacco" to the boy who first heard "pickaninny dog sing out."

* * * * *

286

Jerry was in bad shape. Not accustomed to swimming, strangled by the salt water that lapped into his open mouth, he was getting loggy when first he chanced to see the flash of the captain's torch. This, however, he did not connect with Skipper, and so took no more notice of it than he did of the first stars showing in the sky. It never entered his mind that it might be a star nor even that it might not be a star. He continued to wail and to strangle with more salt water. But when he at length heard Skipper's voice he went immediately wild. He attempted to stand up and to rest his forepaws on Skipper's voice coming out of the darkness, as he would have rested his forepaws on Skipper's leg had he been near. The result was disastrous. Out of the horizontal, he sank down and under, coming up with a new spasm of strangling.

This lasted for a short time, during which the strangling prevented him from answering Skipper's cry, which continued to reach him. But when he could answer he burst forth in a joyous yelp. Skipper was coming to take him out of the stinging, biting sea that blinded his eyes and hurt him to breathe. Skipper was truly a god, his god, with a god's power to save.

Soon he heard the rhythmic clack of the oars on the thole-pins, and the joy in his own yelp was duplicated by the joy in Skipper's voice, which kept up a running encouragement, broken by objurgations to the rowers.

"All right, Jerry, old man. All right, Jerry. All right.—Washee-washee, you fella boy!—Coming, Jerry, coming. Stick it out, old man. Stay with it.—Washee-washee like hell!—Here we are, Jerry. Stay with it. Hang on, old boy, we'll get you.—Easy . . . easy. 'Vast washee."

And then, with amazing abruptness, Jerry saw the whaleboat dimly emerge from the gloom close upon him, was blinded by the stab of the torch full in his eyes, and, even as he yelped his joy, felt and recognized Skipper's hand clutching him by the slack of the neck and lifting him into the air.

He landed wet and soppily against Skipper's rain-wet chest, his tail bobbing frantically against Skipper's containing arm, his body wriggling, his tongue dabbing madly all over Skipper's chin and mouth and cheeks and nose. And Skipper did not know that he was himself wet, and that he was in the first shock of recurrent malaria precipitated by the wet and the excitement. He knew only that the puppy-dog, given him only the previous morning, was safe back in his arms.

While the boat's crew bent to the oars, he steered with the sweep between his arm and his side in order that he might hold Jerry with the other arm.

"You little son of a gun," he crooned, and continued to croon, over and over. "You little son of a gun."

And Jerry responded with tongue-kisses, whimpering and crying as is the way of lost children immediately after they are found. Also, he shivered violently. But it was not from the cold. Rather was it due to his over-strung, sensitive nerves.

Again on board, Van Horn stated his reasoning to the mate.

"The pup didn't just calmly walk overboard. Nor was he washed overboard. I had him fast and triced in the blanket with a rope yarn."

He walked over, the centre of the boat's crew and of the three-score return boys who were all on deck, and flashed his torch on the blanket still lying on the yams.

"That proves it. The rope-yarn's cut. The knot's still in it. Now what nigger is responsible?"

He looked about at the circle of dark faces, flashing the light on them, and such was the accusation and anger in his eyes, that all eyes fell before his or looked away.

"If only the pup could speak," he complained. "He'd tell who it was."

He bent suddenly down to Jerry, who was standing as close against his legs as he could, so close that his wet forepaws rested on Skipper's bare feet.

"You know 'm, Jerry, you known the black fella boy," he said, his words quick and exciting, his hand moving in questing circles toward the blacks.

Jerry was all alive on the instant, jumping about, barking with short yelps of eagerness.

288

"I do believe the dog could lead me to him," Van Horn confided to the mate. "Come on, Jerry, find 'm, sick 'm, shake 'm down. Where is he, Jerry? Find 'm. Find 'm."

All that Jerry knew was that Skipper wanted something. He must find something that Skipper wanted, and he was eager to serve. He pranced about aimlessly and willingly for a space, while Skipper's urging cries increased his excitement. Then he was struck by an idea, and a most definite idea it was. The circle of boys broke to let him through as he raced for'ard along the starboard side to the tight-lashed heap of trade-boxes. He put his nose into the opening where the wild-dog laired, and sniffed. Yes, the wild-dog was inside. Not only did he smell him, but he heard the menace of his snarl.

He looked up to Skipper questioningly. Was it that Skipper wanted him to go in after the wild-dog? But Skipper laughed and waved his hand to show that he wanted him to search in other places for something else.

He leaped away, sniffing in likely places where experience had taught him cockroaches and rats might be. Yet it quickly dawned on him that it was not such things Skipper was after. His heart was wild with desire to serve, and, without clear purpose, he began sniffing legs of black boys.

This brought livelier urgings and encouragements from Skipper, and made him almost frantic. That was it. He must identify the boat's crew and the return boys by their legs. He hurried the task, passing swiftly from boy to boy, until he came to Lerumie.

And then he forgot that Skipper wanted him to do something. All he knew was that it was Lerumie who had broken the taboo of his sacred person by laying hands on him, and that it was Lerumie who had thrown him overboard.

With a cry of rage, a flash of white teeth, and a bristle of short neck-hair, he sprang for the black. Lerumie fled down the deck, and Jerry pursued amid the laughter of all the blacks. Several times, in making the circuit of the deck, he managed to scratch the flying calves with his teeth. Then Lerumie took to the main rigging, leaving Jerry impotently to rage on the deck beneath him.

About this point the blacks grouped in a semi-circle at a respectful distance, with Van Horn to the fore beside Jerry. Van Horn centred his electric torch on the black in the rigging, and saw the long parallel scratches on the fingers of the hand that had invaded Jerry's blanket. He pointed them out significantly to Borckman, who stood outside the circle so that no black should be able to come at his back.

Skipper picked Jerry up and soothed his anger with:

"Good boy, Jerry. You marked and sealed him. Some dog, you, some big man-dog."

He turned back to Lerumie, illuminating him as he clung in the rigging, and his voice was harsh and cold as he addressed him.

"What name belong along you fella boy?" he demanded.

"Me fella Lerumie," came the chirping, quavering answer.

"You come along Pennduffryn?"

"Me come along Meringe."

Captain Van Horn debated the while he fondled the puppy in his arms. After all, it was a return boy. In a day, in two days at most, he would have him landed and be quit of him.

"My word," he harangued, "me angry along you. Me angry big fella too much along you. Me angry along you any amount. What name you fella boy make 'm pickaninny dog belong along me walk about along water?"

Lerumie was unable to answer. He rolled his eyes helplessly, resigned to receive a whipping such as he had long since bitterly learned white masters were wont to administer.

Captain Van Horn repeated the question, and the black repeated the helpless rolling of his eyes.

"For two sticks tobacco I knock 'm seven bells outa you," the skipper bullied. "Now me give you strong fella talk too much. You look 'm eye belong you one time along this fella dog belong me, I knock 'm seven bells and whole starboard watch outa you. Savve?"

"Me savve," Lerumie, plaintively replied; and the episode was closed.

The return boys went below to sleep in the cabin. Borckman and the boat's crew hoisted the mainsail and put the *Arangi* on her course. And Skipper, under a dry blanket from below, lay down to sleep with Jerry, head on his shoulder, in the hollow of his arm.

CHAPTER VII

At seven in the morning, when Skipper rolled him out of the blanket and got up, Jerry celebrated the new day by chasing the wild-dog back into his hole and by drawing a snicker from the blacks on deck, when, with a growl and a flash of teeth, he made Lerumie side-step half a dozen feet and yield the deck to him.

He shared breakfast with Skipper, who, instead of eating, washed down with a cup of coffee fifty grains of quinine wrapped in a cigarette paper, and who complained to the mate that he would have to get under the blankets and sweat out the fever that was attacking him. Despite his chill, and despite his teeth that were already beginning to chatter while the burning sun extracted the moisture in curling mist-wreaths from the deck planking, Van Horn cuddled Jerry in his arms and called him princeling, and prince, and a king, and a son of kings.

For Van Horn had often listened to the recitals of Jerry's pedigree by Tom Haggin, over Scotch-and-sodas, when it was too pestilentially hot to go to bed. And the pedigree was as royal-blooded as was possible for an Irish terrier to possess, whose breed, beginning with the ancient Irish wolf-hound, had been moulded and established by man in less than two generations of men.

There was Terrence the Magnificent—descended, as Van Horn remembered, from the American-bred Milton Droleen, out of the Queen of County Antrim, Breda Muddler, which royal bitch, as every one who is familiar with the stud book knows, goes back as far as the almost mythical Spuds, with along the way no primrose dallyings with black-and-tan Killeney Boys and Welsh nondescripts. And did not Biddy trace to Erin, mother and star of the breed, through a long descendant out of Breda Mixer, herself an ancestress of Breda Muddler? Nor could be omitted from the purple record the later ancestress, Moya Doolen.

So Jerry knew the ecstasy of loving and of being loved in the arms of his love-god, although little he knew of such phrases as "king's son" and "son of kings," save that they connoted love for him in the same way that Lerumie's hissing noises connoted hate. One thing Jerry knew without knowing that he knew, namely, that in the few hours he had been with Skipper he loved him more than he had loved Derby and Bob, who, with the exception of *Mister* Haggin, were the only other white-gods he had ever known. He was not conscious of this. He merely loved, merely acted on the prompting of his heart, or head, or whatever organic or anatomical part of him that developed the mysterious, delicious, and insatiable hunger called "love."

Skipper went below. He went all unheeding of Jerry, who padded softly at his heels until the companionway was reached. Skipper was unheeding of Jerry because of the fever that wrenched his flesh and chilled his bones, that made his head seem to swell monstrously, that glazed the world to his swimming eyes and made him walk feebly and totteringly like a drunken man or a man very aged. And Jerry sensed that something was wrong with Skipper.

Skipper, beginning the babblings of delirium which alternated with silent moments of control in order to get below and under blankets, descended the ladder-like stairs, and Jerry, all-yearning, controlled himself in silence and watched the slow descent with the hope that when Skipper reached the bottom he would raise his arms and lift him down. But Skipper was too far gone to remember that Jerry existed. He staggered, with widespread arms to keep from falling, along the cabin floor for'ard to the bunk in the tiny stateroom.

Jerry was truly of a kingly line. He wanted to call out and beg to be taken down. But he did not. He controlled himself, he knew not why, save that he was possessed by a nebulous awareness that Skipper must be considered as a god should be considered, and that this was no time to obtrude himself on Skipper. His heart was torn with desire, although he made no sound, and he continued only to yearn over the companion combing and to listen to the faint sounds of Skipper's progress for'ard.

But even kings and their descendants have their limitations, and at the end of a quarter of an hour Jerry was ripe to cease from his silence. With the going below of Skipper, evidently in great trouble, the light had gone out of the day for Jerry. He might have stalked the wild-dog, but no inducement lay there. Lerumie passed by unnoticed, although he knew he could bully him and make him give deck space. The myriad scents of the land entered his keen nostrils, but he made no note of them. Not even the flopping, bellying mainsail overhead, as the *Arangi* rolled becalmed, could draw a glance of quizzical regard from him.

Just as it was tremblingly imperative that Jerry must suddenly squat down, point his nose at the zenith, and vocalize his heart-rending woe, an idea came to him. There is no explaining how this idea came. No more can it be explained than can a human explain why, at luncheon to-day, he selects green peas and rejects string beans, when only yesterday he elected to choose string beans and to reject green peas. No more can it be explained than can a human judge, sentencing a convicted criminal and imposing eight years imprisonment instead of the five or nine years that also at the same time floated upward in his brain, explain why he categorically determined on eight years as the just, adequate punishment. Since not even humans, who are almost half-gods, can fathom the mystery of the genesis of ideas and the dictates of choice, appearing in their consciousness as ideas, it is not to be expected of a more dog to know the why of the ideas that animate it to definite acts toward definite ends.

And so Jerry. Just as he must immediately howl, he was aware that the idea, an entirely different idea, was there, in the innermost centre of the quick-thinkingness of him, with all its compulsion. He obeyed the idea as a marionette obeys the strings, and started forthwith down the deck aft in quest of the mate.

He had an appeal to make to Borckman. Borckman was also a two-legged white-god. Easily could Borckman lift him down the precipitous ladder, which was to him, unaided, a taboo, the violation of which was pregnant with disaster. But Borckman had in him little of the heart of love, which is understanding. Also, Borckman was busy. Besides overseeing the continuous adjustment, by trimming of sails and orders to the helmsman, of the *Arangi* to her way on the sea, and overseeing the boat's crew at its task of washing deck and polishing brasswork, he was engaged in steadily nipping from a stolen bottle of his captain's whiskey which he had stowed away in the hollow between the two sacks of yams lashed on deck aft the mizzenmast.

Borckman was on his way for another nip, after having thickly threatened to knock seven bells and the ten commandments out of the black at the wheel for faulty steering, when Jerry appeared before him and blocked the way to his desire. But Jerry did not block him as he would have blocked Lerumie, for instance. There was no showing of teeth, no bristling of neck hair. Instead, Jerry was all placation and appeal, all softness of pleading in a body denied speech that nevertheless was articulate, from wagging tail and wriggling sides to flat-laid ears and eyes that almost spoke, to any human sensitive of understanding.

But Borckman saw in his way only a four-legged creature of the brute world, which, in his arrogant brutalness he esteemed more brute than himself. All the pretty picture of the soft puppy, instinct with communicativeness, bursting with tenderness of petition, was veiled to his vision. What he saw was merely a four-legged animal to be thrust aside while he continued his lordly two-legged progress toward the bottle that could set maggots crawling in his brain and make him dream dreams that he was prince, not peasant, that he was a master of matter rather than a slave of matter.

And thrust aside Jerry was, by a rough and naked foot, as harsh and unfeeling in its impact as an inanimate breaking sea on a beach-jut of insensate rock. He half-sprawled on the slippery deck, regained his balance, and stood still and looked at the white-god who had treated him so cavalierly. The meanness and unfairness had brought from Jerry no snarling threat of retaliation, such as he would have offered Lerumie or any other black. Nor in his brain was any thought of retaliation. This was no Lerumie. This was a superior god, two-legged, white-skinned, like Skipper, like *Mister* Haggin and the couple of other superior gods he had known. Only did he know hurt, such as any child knows under the blow of a thoughtless or unloving mother.

In the hurt was mingled a resentment. He was keenly aware that there were two sorts of roughness. There was the kindly roughness of love, such as when Skipper gripped him by the jowl, shook him till his teeth rattled, and thrust him away with an unmistakable invitation to come back and be so shaken again. Such roughness, to Jerry, was heaven. In it was the intimacy of contact with a beloved god who in such manner elected to express a reciprocal love.

But this roughness of Borckman was different. It was the other kind of roughness in which resided no warm affection, no heart-touch of love. Jerry did not quite understand, but he sensed the difference and resented, without expressing in action, the wrongness and unfairness of it. So he stood, after regaining balance, and soberly regarded, in a vain effort to understand, the mate with a bottle-bottom inverted skyward, the mouth to his lips, the while his throat made gulping contractions and noises. And soberly he continued to regard the mate when he went aft and threatened to knock the "Song of Songs" and the rest of the Old Testament out of the black helmsman whose smile of teeth was as humbly gentle and placating as Jerry's had been when he made his appeal.

Leaving this god as a god unliked and not understood, Jerry sadly trotted back to the companionway and yearned his head over the combing in the direction in which he had seen Skipper disappear. What bit at his consciousness and was a painful incitement in it, was his desire to be with Skipper who was not right, and who was in trouble. He wanted Skipper. He wanted to be with him, first and sharply, because he loved him, and, second and dimly, because he might serve him. And, wanting Skipper, in his helplessness and youngness in experience of the world, he whimpered and cried his heart out across the companion combing, and was too clean and direct in his sorrow to be deflected by an outburst of anger against the niggers, on deck and below, who chuckled at him and derided him.

From the crest of the combing to the cabin floor was seven feet. He had, only a few hours before, climbed the precipitous stairway; but it was impossible, and he knew it, to descend the stairway. And yet, at the last, he dared it. So compulsive was the prod of his heart to gain to Skipper at any cost, so clear was his comprehension that he could not climb down the ladder head first, with no grippingness of legs and feet and muscles such as were possible in the ascent, that he did not attempt it. He launched outward and down, in one magnificent and love-heroic leap. He knew that he was violating a taboo of life, just as he knew he was violating a taboo if he sprang into Meringe Lagoon where swam the dreadful crocodiles. Great love is always capable of expressing itself in sacrifice and self-immolation. And only for love, and for no lesser reason, could Jerry have made the leap.

He struck on his side and head. The one impact knocked the breath out of him; the other stunned him. Even in his unconsciousness, lying on his side and quivering, he made rapid, spasmodic movements of his legs as if running for'ard to Skipper. The boys looked on and laughed, and when he no longer quivered and churned his legs they continued to laugh. Born in savagery, having lived in savagery all their lives and known naught else, their sense of humour was correspondingly savage. To them, the sight of a stunned and possibly dead puppy was a side-splitting, ludicrous event.

Not until the fourth minute ticked off did returning consciousness enable Jerry to crawl to his feet and with wide-spread legs and swimming eyes adjust himself to the *Arangi*'s roll. Yet with the first glimmerings of consciousness persisted the one idea that he must gain to Skipper. Blacks? In his anxiety and solicitude and love they did not count. He ignored the chuckling, grinning, girding black boys, who, but for the fact that he was under the terrible aegis of the big fella white marster, would have delighted to kill and eat the puppy who, in the process of training, was proving a most capable nigger-chaser. Without a turn of head or roll of eye, aristocratically positing their non-existingness to their faces, he trotted for'ard along the cabin floor and into the stateroom where Skipper babbled maniacally in the bunk.

Jerry, who had never had malaria, did not understand. But in his heart he knew great trouble in that Skipper was in trouble. Skipper did not recognize him, even when he sprang into the bunk, walked across Skipper's heaving chest, and licked the acrid sweat of fever from Skipper's face. Instead, Skipper's wildly-thrashing arms brushed him away and flung him violently against the side of the bunk.

This was roughness that was not love-roughness. Nor was it the roughness of Borckman spurning him away with his foot. It was part of Skipper's trouble. Jerry did not reason this conclusion. But, and to the point, he acted upon it as if he had reasoned it. In truth, through inadequacy of one of the most adequate languages in the world, it can only be said that Jerry *sensed* the new difference of this roughness.

He sat up, just out of range of one restless, beating arm, yearned to come closer and lick again the face of the god who knew him not, and who, he knew, loved him well, and palpitatingly shared and suffered all Skipper's trouble.

"Eh, Clancey," Skipper babbled. "It's a fine job this day, and no better crew to clean up after the dubs of motormen. . . . Number three jack, Clancey. Get under the for'ard end." And, as the spectres of his nightmare metamorphosed: "Hush, darling, talking to your dad like that, telling him the combing of your sweet and golden hair. As if I couldn't, that have combed it these seven years—better than your mother, darling, better than your mother. I'm the one gold-medal prize-winner in the combing of his lovely daughter's lovely hair. . . . She's broken out! Give her the wheel aft there! Jib and fore-topsail halyards! Full and by, there! A good full! . . . Ah, she takes it like the beauty fairy boat that she is upon the sea. . . I'll just lift that—sure, the limit. Blackey, when you pay as much to see my cards as I'm going to pay to see yours, you're going to see some cards, believe *me*!"

And so the farrago of unrelated memories continued to rise vocal on Skipper's lips to the heave of his body and the beat of his arms, while Jerry, crouched against the side of the bunk mourned and mourned his grief and inability to be of help. All that was occurring was beyond him. He knew no more of poker hands than did he know of getting ships under way, of clearing up surface car wrecks in New York, or of combing the long yellow hair of a loved daughter in a Harlem flat.

"Both dead," Skipper said in a change of delirium. He said it quietly, as if announcing the time of day, then wailed: "But, oh, the bonnie, bonnie braids of all the golden hair of her!"

298

He lay motionlessly for a space and sobbed out a breaking heart. This was Jerry's chance. He crept inside the arm that tossed, snuggled against Skipper's side, laid his head on Skipper's shoulder, his cool nose barely touching Skipper's cheek, and felt the arm curl about him and press him closer. The hand bent from the wrist and caressed him protectingly, and the warm contact of his velvet body put a change in Skipper's sick dreams, for he began to mutter in cold and bitter ominousness: "Any nigger that as much as bats an eye at that puppy. . ."

CHAPTER VIII

When, in half an hour, Van Horn's sweat culminated in profusion, it marked the breaking of the malarial attack. Great physical relief was his, and the last mists of delirium ebbed from his brain. But he was left limply weak, and, after tossing off the blankets and recognizing Jerry, he fell into a refreshing natural sleep.

Not till two hours later did he awake and start to go on deck. Halfway up the companion, he deposited Jerry on deck and went back to the stateroom for a forgotten bottle of quinine. But he did not immediately return to Jerry. The long drawer under Borckman's bunk caught his eye. The wooden button that held it shut was gone, and it was far out and hanging at an angle that jammed it and prevented it from falling to the floor. The matter was serious. There was little doubt in his mind, had the drawer, in the midst of the squall of the previous night, fallen to the floor, that no *Arangi* and no soul of the eighty souls on board would have been left. For the drawer was filled with a heterogeneous mess of dynamite sticks, boxes of fulminating caps, coils of fuses, lead sinkers, iron tools, and many boxes of rifle, revolver and pistol cartridges. He sorted and arranged the varied contents, and with a screwdriver and a longer screw reattached the button.

In the meantime, Jerry was encountering new adventure not of the pleasantest. While waiting for Skipper to return, Jerry chanced to see the wild-dog brazenly lying on deck a dozen feet from his lair in the trade-boxes. Instantly stiffly crouching, Jerry began to stalk. Success seemed assured, for the wild-dog, with closed eyes, was apparently asleep.

And at this moment the mate, two-legging it along the deck from for'ard in the direction of the bottle stored between the yam sacks, called, "Jerry," in a remarkably husky voice. Jerry flattened his filbert-shaped ears and wagged his tail in acknowledgment, but advertised his intention of continuing to stalk his enemy. And at sound of the mate's voice the wild-dog flung quick-opened eyes in Jerry's direction and flashed into his burrow, where he immediately turned around, thrust his head out with a show of teeth, and snarled triumphant defiance.

Baulked of his quarry by the inconsiderateness of the mate, Jerry trotted back to the head of the companion to wait for Skipper. But Borckman, whose brain was well a-crawl by virtue of the many nips, clung to a petty idea after the fashion of drunken men. Twice again, imperatively, he called Jerry to him, and twice again, with flattened ears of gentleness and wagging tail, Jerry good-naturedly expressed his disinclination. Next, he yearned his head over the coming and into the cabin after Skipper.

Borckman remembered his first idea and continued to the bottle, which he generously inverted skyward. But the second idea, petty as it was, persisted; and, after swaying and mumbling to himself for a time, after unseeingly making believe to study the crisp fresh breeze that filled the *Arangi*'s sails and slanted her deck, and, after sillily attempting on the helmsman to portray eagle-like vigilance in his drink-swimming eyes, he lurched amidships toward Jerry.

Jerry's first intimation of Borckman's arrival was a cruel and painful clutch on his flank and groin that made him cry out in pain and whirl around. Next, as the mate had seen Skipper do in play, Jerry had his jowls seized in a tooth-clattering shake that was absolutely different from the Skipper's rough love-shake. His head and body were shaken, his teeth clattered painfully, and with the roughest of roughness he was flung part way down the slippery slope of deck.

Now Jerry was a gentleman. All the soul of courtesy was in him, for equals and superiors. After all, even in an inferior like the wild-dog, he did not consciously press an advantage very far—never extremely far. In his stalking and rushing of the wild-dog, he had been more sound and fury than an overbearing bully. But with a superior, with a two-legged white-god like Borckman, there was more a demand upon his control, restraint, and inhibition of primitive promptings. He did not want to play with the mate a game that he ecstatically played with Skipper, because he had experienced no similar liking for the mate, two-legged white-god that he was.

And still Jerry was all gentleness. He came back in a feeble imitation rush of the whole-hearted rush that he had learned to make on Skipper. He was, in truth, acting, play-acting, attempting to do what he had no heart-prompting to do. He made believe to play, and uttered simulated growls that failed of the verity of simulation.

He bobbed his tail good-naturedly and friendly, and growled ferociously and friendly; but the keenness of the drunkenness of the mate discerned the difference and aroused in him, vaguely, the intuition of difference, of play-acting, of cheating. Jerry was cheating—out of his heart of consideration. Borckman drunkenly recognized the cheating without crediting the heart of good behind it. On the instant he was antagonistic. Forgetting that he was only a brute, he posited that this was no more than a brute with which he strove to play in the genial comradely way that the Skipper played.

Red war was inevitable—not first on Jerry's part, but on Borckman's part. Borckman felt the abysmal urgings of the beast, as a beast, to prove himself master of this four-legged beast. Jerry felt his jowl and jaw clutched still more harshly and hardly and, with increase of harshness and hardness, he was flung farther down the deck, which, on account of its growing slant due to heavier gusts of wind, had become a steep and slippery hill.

He came back, clawing frantically up the slope that gave him little footing; and he came back, no longer with poorly attempted simulation of ferocity, but impelled by the first flickerings of real ferocity. He did not know this. If he thought at all, he was under the impression that he was playing the game as he had played it with Skipper. In short, he was taking an interest in the game, although a radically different interest from what he had taken with Skipper.

This time his teeth flashed quicker and with deeper intent at the jowl-clutching hand, and, missing, he was seized and flung down the smooth incline harder and farther than before. He was growing angry, as he clawed back, though he was not conscious of it. But the mate, being a man, albeit a drunken one, sensed the change in Jerry's attack ere Jerry dreamed there was any change in it. And not only did Borckman sense it, but it served as a spur to drive him back into primitive beastliness, and to fight to master this puppy as a primitive man, under dissimilar provocation, might have fought with the members of the first litter stolen from a wolf-den among the rocks.

True, Jerry could trace as far back. His ancient ancestors had been Irish wolf-hounds, and, long before that, the ancestors of the wolf-hounds had been wolves. The note in Jerry's growls changed. The unforgotten and ineffaceable past strummed the fibres of his throat. His teeth flashed with fierce intent, in the desire of sinking as deep in the man's hand as passion could drive. For Jerry by this time was all passion. He had leaped back into the dark stark rawness of the early world almost as swiftly as had Borckman. And this time his teeth scored, ripping the tender and sensitive and flesh of all the inside of the first and second joints of Borckman's right hand. Jerry's teeth were needles that stung, and Borckman, gaining the grasp on Jerry's jaw, flung him away and down so that almost he hit the *Arangi's* tiny-rail ere his clawing feet stopped him.

And Van Horn, having finished his rearrangement and repair of the explosive-filled drawer under the mate's bunk, climbed up the companion steps, saw the battle, paused, and quietly looked on.

But he looked across a million years, at two mad creatures who had slipped the leach of the generations and who were back in the darkness of spawning life ere dawning intelligence had modified the chemistry of such life to softness of consideration. What stirred in the brain crypts of Borckman's heredity, stirred in the brain-crypts of Jerry's heredity. Time had gone backward for both. All the endeavour and achievement of the ten thousand generations was not, and, as wolf-dog and wild-man, the combat was between Jerry and the mate. Neither saw Van Horn, who was inside the companionway hatch, his eyes level with the combing.

To Jerry, Borckman was now no more a god than was he himself a mere, smooth-coated Irish terrier. Both had forgotten the million years stamped into their heredity more feebly, less eraseably, than what had been stamped in prior to the million years. Jerry did not know drunkenness, but he did know unfairness; and it was with raging indignation that he knew it. Borckman fumbled his next counter to Jerry's attack, missed, and had both hands slashed in quick succession ere he managed to send the puppy sliding.

And still Jerry came back. As any screaming creature of the jungle, he hysterically squalled his indignation. But he made no whimper. Nor did he wince or cringe to the blows. He bored straight in, striving, without avoiding a blow, to beat and meet the blow with his teeth. So hard was he flung down the last time that his side smashed painfully against the rail, and Van Horn cried out:

"Cut that out, Borckman! Leave the puppy alone!"

The mate turned in the startle of surprise at being observed. The sharp, authoritative words of Van Horn were a call across the million years. Borckman's anger-convulsed face ludicrously attempted a sheepish, deprecating grin, and he was just mumbling, "We was only playing," when Jerry arrived back, leaped in the air, and sank his teeth into the offending hand.

Borckman immediately and insanely went back across the million years. An attempted kick got his ankle scored for his pains. He gibbered his own rage and hurt, and, stooping, dealt Jerry a tremendous blow alongside the head and neck. Being in mid-leap when he received the blow Jerry was twistingly somersaulted sidewise before he struck the deck on his back. As swiftly as he could scramble to footing and charge, he returned to the attack, but was checked by Skipper's:

"Jerry! Stop it! Come here!"

He obeyed, but only by prodigious effort, his neck bristling and his lips writhing clear of his teeth as he passed the mate. For the first time there was a whimper in his throat; but it was not the whimper of fear, nor of pain, but of outrage, and of desire to continue the battle which he struggled to control at Skipper's behest.

Stepping out on deck, Skipper picked him up and patted and soothed him the while he expressed his mind to the mate.

"Borckman, you ought to be ashamed. You ought to be shot or have your block knocked off for this. A puppy, a little puppy scarcely weaned. For two cents I'd give you what-for myself. The idea of it. A little puppy, a weanling little puppy. Glad your hands are ripped. You deserved it. Hope you get blood-poisoning in them. Besides, you're drunk. Go below and turn in, and don't you dare come on deck until you're sober. Savve?"

And Jerry, far-journeyer across life and across the history of all life that goes to make the world, strugglingly mastering the abysmal slime of the prehistoric with the love that had come into existence and had become warp and woof of him in far later time, his wrath of ancientness still faintly reverberating in his throat like the rumblings of a passing thunder-storm, knew, in the wide warm ways of feeling, the augustness and righteousness of Skipper. Skipper was in truth a god who did right, who was fair, who protected, and who imperiously commanded this other and lesser god that slunk away before his anger.

CHAPTER IX

Jerry and Skipper shared the long afternoon-watch together, the latter being guilty of recurrent chuckles and exclamations such as: "Gott-fer-dang, Jerry, believe *me*, you're some fighter and all dog"; or, "You're a proper man's dog, you are, a lion dog. I bet the lion don't live that could get your goat."

And Jerry, understanding none of the words, with the exception of his own name, nevertheless knew that the sounds made by Skipper were broad of praise and warm of love. And when Skipper stooped and rubbed his ears, or received a rose-kiss on extended fingers, or caught him up in his arms, Jerry's heart was nigh to bursting. For what greater ecstasy can be the portion of any creature than that it be loved by a god? This was just precisely Jerry's ecstasy. This was a god, a tangible, real, three-dimensioned god, who went about and ruled his world in a loin-cloth and on two bare legs, and who loved him with crooning noises in throat and mouth and with two wide-spread arms that folded him in.

At four o'clock, measuring a glance at the afternoon sun and gauging the speed of the *Arangi* through the water in relation to the closeness of Su'u, Van Horn went below and roughly shook the mate awake. Until both returned, Jerry held the deck alone. But for the fact that the white-gods were there below and were certain to be back at any moment, not many moments would Jerry have held the deck, for every lessened mile between the return boys and Malaita contributed a rising of their spirits, and under the imminence of their old-time independence, Lerumie, as an instance of many of them, with strong gustatory sensations and a positive drooling at the mouth, regarded Jerry in terms of food and vengeance that were identical.

Flat-hauled on the crisp breeze, the *Arangi* closed in rapidly with the land. Jerry peered through the barbed wire, sniffing the air, Skipper beside him and giving orders to the mate and helmsman. The heap of trade-boxes was now unlashed, and the boys began opening and shutting them. What gave them particular delight was the ringing of the bell with which each box was equipped and which rang whenever a lid was raised. Their pleasure in the toy-like contrivance was that of children, and each went back again and again to unlock his own box and make the bell ring.

Fifteen of the boys were to be landed at Su'u and with wild gesticulations and cries they began to recognize and point out the infinitesimal details of the landfall of the only spot they had known on earth prior to the day, three years before, when they had been sold into slavery by their fathers, uncles, and chiefs.

A narrow neck of water, scarcely a hundred yards across, gave entrance to a long and tiny bay. The shore was massed with mangroves and dense, tropical vegetation. There was no sign of houses nor of human occupancy, although Van Horn, staring at the dense jungle so close at hand, knew as a matter of course that scores, and perhaps hundreds, of pairs of human eyes were looking at him.

"Smell 'm, Jerry, smell 'm," he encouraged.

And Jerry's hair bristled as he barked at the mangrove wall, for truly his keen scent informed him of lurking niggers.

"If I could smell like him," the captain said to the mate, "there wouldn't be any risk at all of my ever losing my head."

But Borckman made no reply and sullenly went about his work. There was little wind in the bay, and the *Arangi* slowly forged in and dropped anchor in thirty fathoms. So steep was the slope of the harbour bed from the beach that even in such excessive depth the *Arangi*'s stern swung in within a hundred feet of the mangroves.

Van Horn continued to cast anxious glances at the wooded shore. For Su'u had an evil name. Since the schooner *Fair Hathaway*, recruiting labour for the Queensland plantations, had been captured by the natives and all hands slain fifteen years before, no vessel, with the exception of the *Arangi*, had dared to venture into Su'u. And most white men condemned Van Horn's recklessness for so venturing.

Far up the mountains, that towered many thousands of feet into the trade-wind clouds, arose many signal smokes that advertised the coming of the vessel. Far and near, the *Arangi's* presence was known; yet from the jungle so near at hand only shrieks of parrots and chatterings of cockatoos could be heard.

The whaleboat, manned with six of the boat's crew, was drawn alongside, and the fifteen Su'u boys and their boxes were loaded in. Under the canvas flaps along the thwarts, ready to hand for the rowers, were laid five of the Lee-Enfields. On deck, another of the boat's crew, rifle in hand, guarded the remaining weapons. Borckman had brought up his own rifle to be ready for instant use. Van Horn's rifle lay handy in the stern sheets where he stood near Tambi, who steered with a long sweep. Jerry raised a low whine and yearned over the rail after Skipper, who yielded and lifted him down.

The place of danger was in the boat; for there was little likelihood, at this particular time, of a rising of the return boys on the *Arangi*. Being of Somo, No-ola, Langa-Langa, and far Malu they were in wholesome fear, did they lose the protection of their white masters, of being eaten by the Su'u folk, just as the Su'u boys would have feared being eaten by the Somo and Langa-Langa and No-ola folk.

What increased the danger of the boat was the absence of a covering boat. The invariable custom of the larger recruiting vessels was to send two boats on any shore errand. While one landed on the beach, the other lay off a short distance to cover the retreat of the shore party, if trouble broke out. Too small to carry one boat on deck, the *Arangi* could not conveniently tow two astern; so Van Horn, who was the most daring of the recruiters, lacked this essential safeguard.

Tambi, under Van Horn's low-uttered commands, steered a parallel course along the shore. Where the mangroves ceased, and where high ground and a beaten runway came down to the water's edge, Van Horn motioned the rowers to back water and lay on their oars. High palms and lofty, wide-branched trees rose above the jungle at this spot, and the runway showed like the entrance of a tunnel into the dense, green wall of tropical vegetation.

Van Horn, regarding the shore for some sign of life, lighted a cigar and put one hand to the waist-line of his loin-cloth to reassure himself of the presence of the stick of dynamite that was tucked between the loin-cloth and his skin. The lighted cigar was for the purpose, if emergency arose, of igniting the fuse of the dynamite. And the fuse was so short, with its end split to accommodate the inserted head of a safety match, that between the time of touching it off with the live cigar to the time of the explosion not more than three seconds could elapse. This required quick cool work on Van Horn's part, in case need arose. In three seconds he would have to light the fuse and throw the sputtering stick with directed aim to its objective. However, he did not expect to use it, and had it ready merely as a precautionary measure.

Five minutes passed, and the silence of the shore remained profound. Jerry sniffed Skipper's bare leg as if to assure him that he was beside him no matter what threatened from the hostile silence of the land, then stood up with his forepaws on the gunwale and continued to sniff eagerly and audibly, to prick his neck hair, and to utter low growls.

"They're there, all right," Skipper confided to him; and Jerry, with a sideward glance of smiling eyes, with a bobbing of his tail and a quick love-flattening of his ears, turned his nose shoreward again and resumed his reading of the jungle tale that was wafted to him on the light fans of the stifling and almost stagnant air.

"Hey!" Van Horn suddenly shouted. "Hey, you fella boy stick 'm head out belong you!"

As if in a transformation scene, the apparently tenantless jungle spawned into life. On the instant a hundred stark savages appeared. They broke forth everywhere from the vegetation. All were armed, some with Snider rifles and ancient horse pistols, others with bows and arrows, with long throwing spears, with war-clubs, and with long-handled tomahawks. In a flash, one of them leaped into the sunlight in the open space where runway and water met. Save for decorations, he was naked as Adam before the Fall. A solitary white feather uprose from his kinky, glossy, black hair. A polished bodkin of white petrified shell, with sharp-pointed ends, thrust through a hole in the partition

309

of his nostrils, extended five inches across his face. About his neck, from a cord of twisted coconut sennit, hung an ivory-white necklace of wild-boar's tusks. A garter of white cowrie shells encircled one leg just below the knee. A flaming scarlet flower was coquettishly stuck over one ear, and through a hole in the other ear was threaded a pig's tail so recently severed that it still bled.

As this dandy of Melanesia leaped into the sunshine, the Snider rifle in his hands came into position, aimed from his hip, the generous muzzle bearing directly on Van Horn. No less quick was Van Horn. With equal speed he had snatched his rifle and brought it to bear from his hip. So they stood and faced each other, death in their finger-tips, forty feet apart. The million years between barbarism and civilization also yawned between them across that narrow gulf of forty feet. The hardest thing for modern, evolved man to do is to forget his ancient training. Easiest of all things is it for him to forget his modernity and slip back across time to the howling ages. A lie in the teeth, a blow in the face, a love-thrust of jealousy to the heart, in a fraction of an instant can turn a twentieth-century philosopher into an ape-like arborean pounding his chest, gnashing his teeth, and seeing red.

So Van Horn. But with a difference. He straddled time. He was at one and the same instant all modern, all imminently primitive, capable of fighting in redness of tooth and claw, desirous of remaining modern for as long as he could with his will master the study of ebon black of skin and dazzling white of decoration that confronted him.

A long ten seconds of silence endured. Even Jerry, he knew not why, stilled the growl in his throat. Five score of head-hunting cannibals on the fringe of the jungle, fifteen Su'u return blacks in the boat, seven black boat's crew, and a solitary white man with a cigar in his mouth, a rifle at his hip, and an Irish terrier bristling against his bare calf, kept the solemn pact of those ten seconds, and no one of them knew or guessed what the outcome would be.

One of the return boys, in the bow of the whaleboat, made the peace sign with his palm extended outward and weaponless, and began to chirp in the unknown Su'u dialect. Van Horn held his aim and waited. The dandy lowered his Snider, and breath came more easily to the chests of all who composed the picture.

310

"Me good fella boy," the dandy piped, half bird-like and half elf.

"You big fella fool too much," Van Horn retorted harshly, dropping his gun into the stern-sheets, motioning to rowers and steersman to turn the boat around, and puffing his cigar as carelessly casual as if, the moment before, life and death had not been the debate.

"My word," he went on with fine irritable assumption. "What name you stick 'm gun along me? Me no kai-kai (eat) along you. Me kai-kai along you, stomach belong me walk about. You kai-kai along me, stomach belong you walk about. You no like 'm kai-kai Su'u boy belong along you? Su'u boy belong you all the same brother along you. Long time before, three monsoon before, me speak 'm true speak. Me say three monsoon boy come back. My word, three monsoon finish, boy stop along me come back."

By this time the boat had swung around, reversing bow and stern, Van Horn pivoting so as to face the Snider-armed dandy. At another signal from Van Horn the rowers backed water and forced the boat, stern in, up to the solid ground of the runway. And each rower, his oar in position in case of attack, privily felt under the canvas flap to make sure of the exact location of his concealed Lee-Enfield.

"All right boy belong you walk about?" Van Horn queried of the dandy, who signified the affirmative in the Solomon Islands fashion by half-closing his eyes and nodding his head upward, in a queer, perky way;

"No kai-kai 'm Su'u fella boy suppose walk about along you?"

"No fear," the dandy answered. "Suppose 'm Su'u fella boy, all right. Suppose 'm no fella Su'u boy, my word, big trouble. Ishikola, big fella black marster along this place, him talk 'm me talk along you. Him say any amount bad fella boy stop 'm along bush. Him say big fella white marster no walk about. Him say jolly good big fella white marster stop 'm along ship."

Van Horn nodded in an off-hand way, as if the information were of little value, although he knew that for this time Su'u would furnish him no fresh recruits. One at a time, compelling the others to remain in their places, he directed the return boys astern and ashore. It was Solomon Islands tactics.

Crowding was dangerous. Never could the blacks be risked to confusion in numbers. And Van Horn, smoking his cigar in lordly indifferent fashion, kept his apparently uninterested eyes glued to each boy who made his way aft, box on shoulder, and stepped out on the land. One by one they disappeared into the runway tunnel, and when the last was ashore he ordered the boat back to the ship.

"Nothing doing here this trip," he told the mate. "We'll up hook and out in the morning."

The quick tropic twilight swiftly blent day and darkness. Overhead all stars were out. No faintest breath of air moved over the water, and the humid heat beaded the faces and bodies of both men with profuse sweat. They ate their deck-spread supper languidly and ever and anon used their forearms to wipe the stinging sweat from their eyes.

"Why a man should come to the Solomons—beastly hole," the mate complained.

"Or stay on," the captain rejoined.

"I'm too rotten with fever," the mate grumbled. "I'd die if I left. Remember, I tried it two years ago. It takes the cold weather to bring out the fever. I arrived in Sydney on my back. They had to take me to hospital in an ambulance. I got worse and worse. The doctors told me the only thing to do was to head back where I got the fever. If I did I might live a long time. If I hung on in Sydney it meant a quick finish. They packed me on board in another ambulance. And that's all I saw of Australia for my holiday. I don't want to stay in the Solomons. It's plain hell. But I got to, or croak."

He rolled, at a rough estimate, thirty grains of quinine in a cigarette paper, regarded the result sourly for a moment, then swallowed it at a gulp. This reminded Van Horn, who reached for the bottle and took a similar dose.

"Better put up a covering cloth," he suggested.

Borckman directed several of the boat's crew in the rigging up of a thin tarpaulin, like a curtain along the shore side of the *Arangi*. This was

312

a precaution against any bushwhacking bullet from the mangroves only a hundred feet away.

Van Horn sent Tambi below to bring up the small phonograph and run off the dozen or so scratchy, screechy records that had already been under the needle a thousand times. Between records, Van Horn recollected the girl, and had her haled out of her dark hole in the lazarette to listen to the music. She obeyed in fear, apprehensive that her time had come. She looked dumbly at the big fella white master, her eyes large with fright; nor did the trembling of her body cease for a long time after he had made her lie down. The phonograph meant nothing to her. She knew only fear—fear of this terrible white man that she was certain was destined to eat her.

Jerry left the caressing hand of Skipper for a moment to go over and sniff her. This was an act of duty. He was identifying her once again. No matter what happened, no matter what months or years might elapse, he would know her again and for ever know her again. He returned to the free hand of Skipper that resumed its caressing. The other hand held the cigar which he was smoking.

The wet sultry heat grew more oppressive. The air was nauseous with the dank mucky odour that cooked out of the mangrove swamp. Rowelled by the squeaky music to recollection of old-world ports and places, Borckman lay on his face on the hot planking, beat a tattoo with his naked toes, and gutturally muttered an unending monologue of curses. But Van Horn, with Jerry panting under his hand, placidly and philosophically continued to smoke, lighting a fresh cigar when the first gave out.

He roused abruptly at the faint wash of paddles which he was the first on board to hear. In fact, it was Jerry's low growl and neck-rippling of hair that had keyed Van Horn to hear. Pulling the stick of dynamite out from the twist of his loin cloth and glancing at the cigar to be certain it was alight, he rose to his feet with leisurely swiftness and with leisurely swiftness gained the rail.

"What name belong you?" was his challenge to the dark.

"Me fella Ishikola," came the answer in the quavering falsetto of age.

Van Horn, before speaking again, loosened his automatic pistol half out of its holster, and slipped the holster around from his hip till it rested on his groin conveniently close to his hand.

"How many fella boy stop along you?" he demanded.

"One fella ten-boy altogether he stop," came the aged voice.

"Come alongside then." Without turning his head, his right hand unconsciously dropping close to the butt of the automatic, Van Horn commanded: "You fella Tambi. Fetch 'm lantern. No fetch 'm this place. Fetch 'm aft along mizzen rigging and look sharp eye belong you."

Tambi obeyed, exposing the lantern twenty feet away from where his captain stood. This gave Van Horn the advantage over the approaching canoe-men, for the lantern, suspended through the barbed wire across the rail and well down, would clearly illuminate the occupants of the canoe while he was left in semi-darkness and shadow.

"Washee-washee!" he urged peremptorily, while those in the invisible canoe still hesitated.

Came the sound of paddles, and, next, emerging into the lantern's area of light, the high, black bow of a war canoe, curved like a gondola, inlaid with silvery-glistening mother-of-pearl; the long lean length of the canoe which was without outrigger; the shining eyes and the black-shining bodies of the stark blacks who knelt in the bottom and paddled; Ishikola, the old chief, squatting amidships and not paddling, an unlighted, empty-bowled, short-stemmed clay pipe upside-down between his toothless gums; and, in the stern, as coxswain, the dandy, all nakedness of blackness, all whiteness of decoration, save for the pig's tail in one ear and the scarlet hibiscus that still flamed over the other ear.

Less than ten blacks had been known to rush a blackbirder officered by no more than two white men, and Van Horn's hand closed on the butt of his automatic, although he did not pull it clear of the holster, and although, with his left hand, he directed the cigar to his mouth and puffed it lively alight.

"Hello, Ishikola, you blooming old blighter," was Van Horn's greeting to the old chief, as the dandy, with a pry of his steering-paddle against the side of the canoe and part under its bottom, brought the dug-out broadside-on to the *Arangi* so that the sides of both crafts touched.

Ishikola smiled upward in the lantern light. He smiled with his right eye, which was all he had, the left having been destroyed by an arrow in a youthful jungle-skirmish.

"My word!" he greeted back. "Long time you no stop eye belong me."

Van Horn joked him in understandable terms about the latest wives he had added to his harem and what price he had paid for them in pigs.

"My word," he concluded, "you rich fella too much together."

"Me like 'm come on board gammon along you," Ishikola meekly suggested.

"My word, night he stop," the captain objected, then added, as a concession against the known rule that visitors were not permitted aboard after nightfall: "You come on board, boy stop 'm along boat."

Van Horn gallantly helped the old man to clamber to the rail, straddle the barbed wire, and gain the deck. Ishikola was a dirty old savage. One of his tambos (tambo being bêche-de-mer and Melanesian for "taboo") was that water unavoidable must never touch his skin. He who lived by the salt sea, in a land of tropic downpour, religiously shunned contact with water. He never went swimming or wading, and always fled to shelter from a shower. Not that this was true of the rest of his tribe. It was the peculiar tambo laid upon him by the devil-devil doctors. Other tribesmen the devil-devil doctors tabooed against eating shark, or handling turtle, or contacting with crocodiles or the fossil remains of crocodiles, or from ever being smirched by the profanity of a woman's touch or of a woman's shadow cast across the path.

So Ishikola, whose tambo was water, was crusted with the filth of years. He was sealed like a leper, and, weazen-faced and age-shrunken, he hobbled horribly from an ancient spear-thrust to the thigh that twisted his

315

torso droopingly out of the vertical. But his one eye gleamed brightly and wickedly, and Van Horn knew that it observed as much as did both his own eyes.

Van Horn shook hands with him—an honour he accorded only chiefs—and motioned him to squat down on deck on his hams close to the fear-struck girl, who began trembling again at recollection of having once heard Ishikola offer five twenties of drinking coconuts for the meat of her for a dinner.

Jerry needs must sniff, for future identification purposes, this graceless, limping, naked, one-eyed old man. And, when he had sniffed and registered the particular odour, Jerry must growl intimidatingly and win a quick eye-glance of approval from Skipper.

"My word, good fella kai-kai dog," said Ishikola. "Me give 'm half-fathom shell money that fella dog."

For a mere puppy this offer was generous, because half a fathom of shell-money, strung on a thread of twisted coconut fibres, was equivalent in cash to half a sovereign in English currency, to two dollars and a half in American, or, in live-pig currency, to half of a fair-sized fat pig.

"One fathom shell-money that fella dog," Van Horn countered, in his heart knowing that he would not sell Jerry for a hundred fathoms, or for any fabulous price from any black, but in his head offering so small a price over par as not to arouse suspicion among the blacks as to how highly he really valued the golden-coated son of Biddy and Terrence.

Ishikola next averred that the girl had grown much thinner, and that he, as a practical judge of meat, did not feel justified this time in bidding more than three twenty-strings of drinking coconuts.

After these amenities, the white master and the black talked of many things, the one bluffing with the white-man's superiority of intellect and knowledge, the other feeling and guessing, primitive statesman that he was, in an effort to ascertain the balance of human and political forces that bore upon his Su'u territory, ten miles square, bounded by the sea and by landward lines of an inter-tribal warfare that was older than the oldest Su'u myth. Eternally, heads had been taken and bodies eaten, now on one side, now on the other, by the temporarily victorious tribes. The boundaries had remained the same. Ishikola, in crude bêche-de-mer, tried to learn the Solomon Islands general situation in relation to Su'u, and Van Horn was not above playing the unfair diplomatic game as it is unfairly played in all the chancellories of the world powers.

"My word," Van Horn concluded; "you bad fella too much along this place. Too many heads you fella take; too much kai-kai long pig along you." (Long pig, meaning barbecued human flesh.)

"What name, long time black fella belong Su'u take 'm heads, kai-kai along long pig?" Ishikola countered.

"My word," Van Horn came back, "too much along this place. Bime by, close up, big fella warship stop 'm along Su'u, knock seven balls outa Su'u."

"What name him big fella warship stop 'm along Solomons?" Ishikola demanded.

"Big fella *Cambrian*, him fella name belong ship," Van Horn lied, too well aware that no British cruiser had been in the Solomons for the past two years.

The conversation was becoming rather a farcical dissertation upon the relations that should obtain between states, irrespective of size, when it was broken off by a cry from Tambi, who, with another lantern hanging overside at the end of his arm had made a discovery.

"Skipper, gun he stop along canoe!" was his cry.

Van Horn, with a leap, was at the rail and peering down over the barbed wire. Ishikola, despite his twisted body, was only seconds behind him.

"What name that fella gun stop 'm along bottom?" Van Horn indignantly demanded.

The dandy, in the stern, with a careless look upward, tried with his foot to shove over the green leaves so as to cover the out-jutting butts of several

317

rifles, but made the matter worse by exposing them more fully. He bent to rake the leaves over with his hand, but sat swiftly upright when Van Horn roared at him:

"Stand clear! Keep 'm fella hand belong you long way big bit!"

Van Horn turned on Ishikola, and simulated wrath which he did not feel against the ancient and ever-recurrent trick.

"What name you come alongside, gun he stop along canoe belong you?" he demanded.

The old salt-water chief rolled his one eye and blinked a fair simulation of stupidity and innocence.

"My word, me cross along you too much," Van Horn continued. "Ishikola, you plenty bad fella boy. You get 'm to hell overside."

The old fellow limped across the deck with more agility than he had displayed coming aboard, straddled the barbed wire without assistance, and without assistance dropped into the canoe, cleverly receiving his weight on his uninjured leg. He blinked up for forgiveness and in reassertion of innocence. Van Horn turned his face aside to hide a grin, and then grinned outright when the old rascal, showing his empty pipe, wheedled up:

"Suppose 'm five stick tobacco you give 'm along me?"

While Borckman went below for the tobacco, Van Horn orated to Ishikola on the sacred solemnity of truth and promises. Next, he leaned across the barbed wire and handed down the five sticks of tobacco.

"My word," he threatened. "Somo day, Ishikola, I finish along you altogether. You no good friend stop along salt-water. You big fool stop along bush."

When Ishikola attempted protest, he shut him off with, "My word, you gammon along me too much."

Still the canoe lingered. The dandy's toe strayed privily to feel out the butts of the Sniders under the green leaves, and Ishikola was loth to depart.

"Washee-washee!" Van Horn cried with imperative suddenness.

The paddlers, without command from chief or dandy, involuntarily obeyed, and with deep, strong strokes sent the canoe into the encircling darkness. Just as quickly Van Horn changed his position on deck to the tune of a dozen yards, so that no hazarded bullet might reach him. He crouched low and listened to the wash of paddles fade away in the distance.

"All right, you fella Tambi," he ordered quietly. "Make 'm music he fella walk about."

And while "Red Wing" screeched its cheap and pretty rhythm, he reclined elbow on deck, smoked his cigar, and gathered Jerry into caressing inclosure.

As he smoked he watched the abrupt misting of the stars by a rain-squall that made to windward or to where windward might vaguely be configured. While he gauged the minutes ere he must order Tambi below with the phonograph and records, he noted the bush-girl gazing at him in dumb fear. He nodded consent with half-closed eyes and up-tilting face, clinching his consent with a wave of hand toward the companionway. She obeyed as a beaten dog, spirit-broken, might have obeyed, dragging herself to her feet, trembling afresh, and with backward glances of her perpetual terror of the big white master that she was convinced would some day eat her. In such fashion, stabbing Van Horn to the heart because of his inability to convey his kindness to her across the abyss of the ages that separated them, she slunk away to the companionway and crawled down it feet-first like some enormous, large-headed worm.

After he had sent Tambi to follow her with the precious phonograph, Van Horn continued to smoke on while the sharp, needle-like spray of the rain impacted soothingly on his heated body.

Only for five minutes did the rain descend. Then, as the stars drifted back in the sky, the smell of steam seemed to stench forth from deck and mangrove swamp, and the suffocating heat wrapped all about.

Van Horn knew better, but ill health, save for fever, had never concerned him; so he did not bother for a blanket to shelter him.

"Yours the first watch," he told Borckman. "I'll have her under way in the morning, before I call you."

He tucked his head on the biceps of his right arm, with the hollow of the left snuggling Jerry in against his chest, and dozed off to sleep.

And thus adventuring, white men and indigenous black men from day to day lived life in the Solomons, bickering and trafficking, the whites striving to maintain their heads on their shoulders, the blacks striving, no less single-heartedly, to remove the whites' heads from their shoulders and at the same time to keep their own anatomies intact.

And Jerry, who knew only the world of Meringe Lagoon, learning that these new worlds of the ship *Arangi* and of the island of Malaita were essentially the same, regarded the perpetual game between the white and the black with some slight sort of understanding.

CHAPTER X

Daylight saw the *Arangi* under way, her sails drooping heavily in the dead air while the boat's crew toiled at the oars of the whaleboat to tow her out through the narrow entrance. Once, when the ketch, swerved by some vagrant current, came close to the break of the shore-surf, the blacks on board drew toward one another in apprehension akin to that of startled sheep in a fold when a wild woods marauder howls outside. Nor was there any need for Van Horn's shout to the whaleboat: "Washee-washee! Damn your hides!" The boat's crew lifted themselves clear of the thwarts as they threw all their weight into each stroke. They knew what dire fate was certain if ever the sea-washed coral rock gripped the *Arangi*'s keel. And they knew fear precisely of the same sort as that of the fear-struck girl below in the lazarette. In the past more than one Langa-Langa and Somo boy had gone to make a Su'u feast day, just as Su'u boys, on occasion, had similarly served feasts at Langa-Langa and at Somo.

"My word," Tambi, at the wheel, addressed Van Horn as the period of tension passed and the *Arangi* went clear. "Brother belong my father, long time before he come boat's crew along this place. Big fella schooner brother belong my father he come along. All finish this place Su'u. Brother belong my father Su'u boys kai-kai along him altogether."

Van Horn recollected the *Fair Hathaway* of fifteen years before, looted and burned by the people of Su'u after all hands had been killed. Truly, the Solomons at this beginning of the twentieth century were savage, and truly, of the Solomons, this great island of Malaita was savagest of all.

He cast his eyes speculatively up the slopes of the island to the seaman's landmark, Mount Kolorat, green-forested to its cloud-capped summit four thousand feet in the air. Even as he looked, thin smoke-columns were rising along the slopes and lesser peaks, and more were beginning to rise.

"My word," Tambi grinned. "Plenty boy stop 'm bush lookout along you eye belong him."

Van Horn smiled understandingly. He knew, by the ancient telegraphy of smoke-signalling, the message was being conveyed from village to village and tribe to tribe that a labour-recruiter was on the leeward coast.

All morning, under a brisk beam wind which had sprung up with the rising of the sun, the *Arangi* flew north, her course continuously advertised by the increasing smoke-talk that gossiped along the green summits. At high noon, with Van Horn, ever-attended by Jerry, standing for'ard and conning, the *Arangi* headed into the wind to thread the passage between two palm-tufted islets. There was need for conning. Coral patches uprose everywhere from the turquoise depths, running the gamut of green from deepest jade to palest tourmaline, over which the sea filtered changing shades, creamed lazily, or burst into white fountains of sun-flashed spray.

The smoke columns along the heights became garrulous, and long before the *Arangi* was through the passage the entire leeward coast, from the salt-water men of the shore to the remotest bush villagers, knew that the labour recruiter was going in to Langa-Langa. As the lagoon, formed by the chain of islets lying off shore, opened out, Jerry began to smell the reef-villages. Canoes, many canoes, urged by paddles or sailed before the wind by the weight of the freshening South East trade on spread fronds of coconut palms, moved across the smooth surface of the lagoon. Jerry barked intimidatingly at those that came closest, bristling his neck and making a ferocious simulation of an efficient protector of the white god who stood beside him. And after each such warning, he would softly dab his cool damp muzzle against the sun-heated skin of Skipper's leg.

Once inside the lagoon, the *Arangi* filled away with the wind a-beam. At the end of a swift half-mile she rounded to, with head-sails trimming down and with a great flapping of main and mizzen, and dropped anchor in fifty feet of water so clear that every huge fluted clamshell was visible on the coral floor. The whaleboat was not necessary to put the Langa-Langa return boys ashore. Hundreds of canoes lay twenty deep along both sides of the *Arangi*, and each boy, with his box and bell, was clamoured for by scores of relatives and friends.

In such height of excitement, Van Horn permitted no one on board. Melanesians, unlike cattle, are as prone to stampede to attack as to retreat. Two of the boat's crew stood beside the Lee-Enfields on the skylight. Borckman, with half the boat's crew, went about the ship's work. Van Horn, Jerry at his heels, careful that no one should get at his back, superintended the departure of the Langa-Langa returns and kept a vigilant eye on the remaining half of the boat's crew that guarded the barbed-wire rails. And each Somo boy sat on his trade-box to prevent it from being tossed into the waiting canoes by some Langa-Langa boy.

In half an hour the riot departed ashore. Only several canoes lingered, and from one of these Van Horn beckoned aboard Nau-hau, the biggest chief of the stronghold of Langa-Langa. Unlike most of the big chiefs, Nau-hau was young, and, unlike most of the Melanesians, he was handsome, even beautiful.

"Hello, King o' Babylon," was Van Horn's greeting, for so he had named him because of fancied Semitic resemblance blended with the crude power that marked his visage and informed his bearing.

Born and trained to nakedness, Nau-hau trod the deck boldly and unashamed. His sole gear of clothing was a length of trunk strap buckled about his waist. Between this and his bare skin was thrust the naked blade of a ten-inch ripping knife. His sole decoration was a white China soup-plate, perforated and strung on coconut sennit, suspended from about his neck so that it rested flat on his chest and half-concealed the generous swell of muscles. It was the greatest of treasures. No man of Malaita he had ever heard of possessed an unbroken soup-plate.

Nor was he any more ridiculous because of the soup-plate than was he ludicrous because of his nakedness. He was royal. His father had been a king before him, and he had proved himself greater than his father. Life and death he bore in his hands and head. Often he had exercised it, chirping to his subjects in the tongue of Langa-Langa: "Slay here," and "Slay there"; "Thou shalt die," and "Thou shalt live." Because his father, a year abdicated, had chosen foolishly to interfere with his son's government, he had called two boys and had them twist a cord of coconut around his father's neck so that thereafter he never breathed again. Because his favourite wife, mother of his eldest born, had dared out of silliness of affection to violate one of his kingly tamboos, he had had her killed and had himself selfishly and religiously eaten the last of her even to the marrow of her cracked joints, sharing no morsel with his boonest of comrades.

Royal he was, by nature, by training, by deed. He carried himself with consciousness of royalty. He looked royal—as a magnificent stallion may look royal, as a lion on a painted tawny desert may look royal. He was as splendid a brute—an adumbration of the splendid human conquerors and rulers, higher on the ladder of evolution, who have appeared in other times and places. His pose of body, of chest, of shoulders, of head, was royal. Royal was the heavy-lidded, lazy, insolent way he looked out of his eyes.

Royal in courage was he, this moment on the *Arangi*, despite the fact that he knew he walked on dynamite. As he had long since bitterly learned, any white man was as much dynamite as was the mysterious death-dealing missile he sometimes employed. When a stripling, he had made one of the canoe force that attacked the sandalwood-cutter that had been even smaller than the *Arangi*. He had never forgotten that mystery. Two of the three white men he had seen slain and their heads removed on deck. The third, still fighting, had but the minute before fled below. Then the cutter, along with all her wealth of hoop-iron, tobacco, knives and calico, had gone up into the air and fallen back into the sea in scattered and fragmented nothingness. It had been dynamite—the MYSTERY. And he, who had been hurled uninjured through the air by a miracle of fortune, had divined that white men in themselves were truly dynamite, compounded of the same mystery as the substance with which they shot the swift-darting schools of mullet, or blow up, in extremity, themselves and the ships on which they voyaged the sea from far places. And yet on this unstable and death-terrific substance of which he was well aware Van Horn was composed, he trod heavily with his personality, daring, to the verge of detonation, to impact it with his insolence.

"My word," he began, "what name you make 'm boy belong me stop along you too much?" Which was a true and correct charge that the boys which Van Horn had just returned had been away three years and a half instead of three years.

"You talk that fella talk I get cross too much along you," Van Horn bristled back, and then added, diplomatically, dipping into a half-case of tobacco sawed across and proffering a handful of stick tobacco: "Much better you smoke 'm up and talk 'm good fella talk."

But Nau-hau grandly waved aside the gift for which he hungered.

"Plenty tobacco stop along me," he lied. "What name one fella boy go way no come back?" he demanded.

Van Horn pulled the long slender account book out of the twist of his loin-cloth, and, while he skimmed its pages, impressed Nau-hau with the dynamite of the white man's superior powers which enabled him to remember correctly inside the scrawled sheets of a book instead of inside his head.

"Sati," Van Horn read, his finger marking the place, his eyes alternating watchfully between the writing and the black chief before him, while the black chief himself speculated and studied the chance of getting behind him and, with the single knife-thrust he knew so well, of severing the other's spinal cord at the base of the neck.

"Sati," Van Horn read. "Last monsoon begin about this time, him fella Sati get 'm sick belly belong him too much; bime by him fella Sati finish altogether," he translated into bêche-de-mer the written information: *Died of dysentery July 4th*, 1901.

"Plenty work him fella Sati, long time," Nau-hau drove to the point. "What come along money belong him?"

Van Horn did mental arithmetic from the account.

"Altogether him make 'm six tens pounds and two fella pounds gold money," was his translation of sixty-two pounds of wages. "I pay advance father belong him one ten pounds and five fella pounds. Him finish altogether four tens pounds and seven fella pounds."

"What name stop four tens pounds and seven fella pounds?" Nau-hau demanded, his tongue, but not his brain, encompassing so prodigious a sum.

Van Horn held up his hand.

"Too much hurry you fella Nau-hau. Him fella Sati buy 'm slop chest along plantation two tens pounds and one fella pound. Belong Sati he finish altogether two tens pounds and six fella pounds."

"What name stop two tens pounds and six fella pounds?" Nau-hau continued inflexibly.

"Stop 'm along me," the captain answered curtly.

"Give 'm me two tens pounds and six fella pounds."

"Give 'm you hell," Van Horn refused, and in the blue of his eyes the black chief sensed the impression of the dynamite out of which white men seemed made, and felt his brain quicken to the vision of the bloody day he first encountered an explosion of dynamite and was hurled through the air.

"What name that old fella boy stop 'm along canoe?" Van Horn asked, pointing to an old man in a canoe alongside. "Him father belong Sati?"

"Him father belong Sati," Nau-hau affirmed.

Van Horn motioned the old man in and on board, beckoned Borckman to take charge of the deck and of Nau-hau, and went below to get the money from his strong-box. When he returned, cavalierly ignoring the chief, he addressed himself to the old man.

"What name belong you?"

"Me fella Nino," was the quavering response. "Him fella Sati belong along me."

Van Horn glanced for verification to Nau-hau, who nodded affirmation in the reverse Solomon way; whereupon Van Horn counted twenty-six gold sovereigns into the hand of Sati's father.

Immediately thereafter Nau-hau extended his hand and received the sum. Twenty gold pieces the chief retained for himself, returning to the old man the remaining six. It was no quarrel of Van Horn's. He had fulfilled his duty and paid properly. The tyranny of a chief over a subject was none of his business.

Both masters, white and black, were fairly contented with themselves. Van Horn had paid the money where it was due; Nau-hau, by virtue of kingship, had robbed Sati's father of Sati's labour before Van Horn's eyes. But Nau-hau was not above strutting. He declined a proffered present of tobacco, bought a case of stick tobacco from Van Horn, paying him five pounds for it, and insisted on having it sawed open so that he could fill his pipe.

"Plenty good boy stop along Langa-Langa?" Van Horn, unperturbed, politely queried, in order to make conversation and advertise nonchalance.

The King o' Babylon grinned, but did not deign to reply.

"Maybe I go ashore and walk about?" Van Horn challenged with tentative emphasis.

"Maybe too much trouble along you," Nau-hau challenged back. "Maybe plenty bad fella boy kai-kai along you."

Although Van Horn did not know it, at this challenge he experienced the hair-pricking sensations in his scalp that Jerry experienced when he bristled his back.

"Hey, Borckman," he called. "Man the whaleboat."

When the whaleboat was alongside, he descended into it first, superiorly, then invited Nau-hau to accompany him.

"My word, King o' Babylon," he muttered in the chief's ears as the boat's crew bent to the oars, "one fella boy make 'm trouble, I shoot 'm hell outa you first thing. Next thing I shoot 'm hell outa Langa-Langa. All the time you me fella walk about, you walk about along me. You no like walk about along me, you finish close up altogether."

And ashore, a white man alone, attended by an Irish terrier puppy with a heart flooded with love and by a black king resentfully respectful of the dynamite of the white man, Van Horn went, swashbuckling barelegged through a stronghold of three thousand souls, while his white mate, addicted to schnapps, held the deck of the tiny craft at anchor off shore, and while his black boat's crew, oars in hands, held the whaleboat stern-on to the beach to receive the expected flying leap of the man they served but did not love, and whose head they would eagerly take any time were it not for fear of him.

Van Horn had had no intention of going ashore, and that he went ashore at the black chief's insolent challenge was merely a matter of business. For an hour he strolled about, his right hand never far from the butt of the automatic that lay along his groin, his eyes never too far from the unwilling Nau-hau beside him. For Nau-hau, in sullen volcanic rage, was ripe to erupt at the slightest opportunity. And, so strolling, Van Horn was given to see what few white men have seen, for Langa-Langa and her sister islets, beautiful beads strung along the lee coast of Malaita, were as unique as they were unexplored.

Originally these islets had been mere sand-banks and coral reefs awash in the sea or shallowly covered by the sea. Only a hunted, wretched creature, enduring incredible hardship, could have eked out a miserable existence upon them. But such hunted, wretched creatures, survivors of village massacres, escapes from the wrath of chiefs and from the long-pig fate of the cooking-pot, did come, and did endure. They, who knew only the bush, learned the salt water and developed the salt-water-man breed. They learned the ways of the fish and the shell-fish, and they invented hooks and lines, nets and fish-traps, and all the diverse cunning ways by which swimming meat can be garnered from the shifting, unstable sea.

Such refugees stole women from the mainland, and increased and multiplied. With herculean labour, under the burning sun, they conquered the sea. They walled the confines of their coral reefs and sand-banks with coral-rock stolen from the mainland on dark nights. Fine masonry, without mortar or cutting chisel, they builded to withstand the ocean surge. Likewise stolen from the mainland, as mice steal from human habitations when humans sleep, they stole canoe-loads, and millions of canoe-loads, of fat, rich soil.

Generations and centuries passed, and, behold, in place of naked sandbanks half awash were walled citadels, perforated with launching-ways for the long canoes, protected against the mainland by the lagoons that were to them their narrow seas. Coconut palms, banana trees, and lofty breadfruit trees gave food and sun-shelter. Their gardens prospered. Their long, lean war-canoes ravaged the coasts and visited vengeance for their forefathers upon the descendants of them that had persecuted and desired to eat.

Like the refugees and renegades who slunk away in the salt marshes of the Adriatic and builded the palaces of powerful Venice on her deep-sunk piles, so these wretched hunted blacks builded power until they became masters of the mainland, controlling traffic and trade-routes, compelling the bushmen for ever after to remain in the bush and never to dare attempt the salt-water.

And here, amidst the fat success and insolence of the sea-people, Van Horn swaggered his way, taking his chance, incapable of believing that he might swiftly die, knowing that he was building good future business in the matter of recruiting labour for the plantations of other adventuring white men on far islands who dared only less greatly than he.

And when, at the end of an hour, Van Horn passed Jerry into the sternsheets of the whaleboat and followed, he left on the beach a stunned and wondering royal black, who, more than ever before, was respectful of the dynamite-compounded white men who brought to him stick tobacco, calico, knives and hatchets, and inexorably extracted from such trade a profit.

CHAPTER XI

Back on board, Van Horn immediately hove short, hoisted sail, broke out the anchor, and filled away for the ten-mile beat up the lagoon to windward that would fetch Somo. On the way, he stopped at Binu to greet Chief Johnny and land a few Binu returns. Then it was on to Somo, and to the end of voyaging for ever of the *Arangi* and of many that were aboard of her.

Quite the opposite to his treatment at Langa-Langa was that accorded Van Horn at Somo. Once the return boys were put ashore, and this was accomplished no later than three-thirty in the afternoon, he invited Chief Bashti on board. And Chief Bashti came, very nimble and active despite his great age, and very good-natured—so good-natured, in fact, that he insisted on bringing three of his elderly wives on board with him. This was unprecedented. Never had he permitted any of his wives to appear before a white man, and Van Horn felt so honoured that he presented each of them with a gay clay pipe and a dozen sticks of tobacco.

Late as the afternoon was, trade was brisk, and Bashti, who had taken the lion's share of the wages due to the fathers of two boys who had died, bought liberally of the *Arangi*'s stock. When Bashti promised plenty of fresh recruits, Van Horn, used to the changeableness of the savage mind, urged signing them up right away. Bashti demurred, and suggested next day. Van Horn insisted that there was no time like the present, and so well did he insist that the old chief sent a canoe ashore to round up the boys who had been selected to go away to the plantations.

"Now, what do you think?" Van Horn asked of Borckman, whose eyes were remarkably fishy. "I never saw the old rascal so friendly. Has he got something up his sleeve?"

The mate stared at the many canoes alongside, noted the numbers of women in them, and shook his head.

"When they're starting anything they always send the Marys into the bush," he said.

"You never can tell about these niggers," the captain grumbled. "They may be short on imagination, but once in a while they do figure out something new. Now Bashti's the smartest old nigger I've ever seen. What's to prevent his figuring out that very bet and playing it in reverse? Just because they've never had their women around when trouble was on the carpet is no reason that they will always keep that practice."

"Not even Bashti's got the savvee to pull a trick like that," Borckman objected. "He's just feeling good and liberal. Why, he's bought forty pounds of goods from you already. That's why he wants to sign on a new batch of boys with us, and I'll bet he's hoping half of them die so's he can have the spending of their wages."

All of which was most reasonable. Nevertheless, Van Horn shook his head.

"All the same keep your eyes sharp on everything," he cautioned. "And remember, the two of us mustn't ever be below at the same time. And no more schnapps, mind, until we're clear of the whole kit and caboodle."

Bashti was incredibly lean and prodigiously old. He did not know how old he was himself, although he did know that no person in his tribe had been alive when he was a young boy in the village. He remembered the days when some of the old men, still alive, had been born; and, unlike him, they were now decrepit, shaken with palsy, blear-eyed, toothless of mouth, deaf of ear, or paralysed. All his own faculties remained unimpaired. He even boasted a dozen worn fangs of teeth, gum-level, on which he could still chew. Although he no longer had the physical endurance of youth, his thinking was as original and clear as it had always been. It was due to his thinking that he found his tribe stronger than when he had first come to rule it. In his small way he had been a Melanesian Napoleon. As a warrior, the play of his mind had enabled him to beat back the bushmen's boundaries. The scars on his withered body attested that he had fought to the fore. As a Law-giver, he had encouraged and achieved strength and efficiency within his tribe. As a statesman, he had always kept one thought ahead of the thoughts of the neighbouring chiefs in the making of treaties and the granting of concessions.

And with his mind, still keenly alive, he had but just evolved a scheme whereby he might outwit Van Horn and get the better of the vast British Empire about which he guessed little and know less.

For Somo had a history. It was that queer anomaly, a salt-water tribe that lived on the lagoon mainland where only bushmen were supposed to live. Far back into the darkness of time, the folk-lore of Somo cast a glimmering light. On a day, so far back that there was no way of estimating its distance, one, Somo, son of Loti, who was the chief of the island fortress of Umbo, had quarrelled with his father and fled from his wrath along with a dozen canoe-loads of young men. For two monsoons they had engaged in an odyssey. It was in the myth that they circumnavigated Malaita twice, and forayed as far as Ugi and San Cristobal across the wide seas.

Women they had inevitably stolen after successful combats, and, in the end, being burdened with women and progeny, Somo had descended upon the mainland shore, driven the bushmen back, and established the salt-water fortress of Somo. Built it was, on its sea-front, like any island fortress, with walled coral-rock to oppose the sea and chance marauders from the sea, and with launching ways through the walls for the long canoes. To the rear, where it encroached on the jungle, it was like any scattered bush village. But Somo, the wide-seeing father of the new tribe, had established his boundaries far up in the bush on the shoulders of the lesser mountains, and on each shoulder had planted a village. Only the greatly daring that fled to him had Somo permitted to join the new tribe. The weaklings and cowards they had promptly eaten, and the unbelievable tale of their many heads adorning the canoe-houses was part of the myth.

And this tribe, territory, and stronghold, at the latter end of time, Bashti had inherited, and he had bettered his inheritance. Nor was he above continuing to better it. For a long time he had reasoned closely and carefully in maturing the plan that itched in his brain for fulfilment. Three years before, the tribe of Ano Ano, miles down the coast, had captured a recruiter, destroyed her and all hands, and gained a fabulous store of tobacco, calico, beads, and all manner of trade goods, rifles and ammunition.

Little enough had happened in the way of price that was paid. Half a year after, a war vessel had poked her nose into the lagoon, shelled Ano Ano, and sent its inhabitants scurrying into the bush. The landing-party that followed had futilely pursued along the jungle runways. In the end it had contented itself with killing forty fat pigs and chopping down a hundred coconut trees. Scarcely had the war vessel passed out to open sea, when the people of Ano Ano were back from the bush to the village. Shell fire on flimsy grass houses is not especially destructive. A few hours' labour of the women put that little matter right. As for the forty dead pigs, the entire tribe fell upon the carcasses, roasted them under the ground with hot stones, and feasted. The tender tips of the fallen palms were likewise eaten, while the thousands of coconuts were husked and split and sun-dried and smoke-cured into copra to be sold to the next passing trader.

Thus, the penalty exacted had proved a picnic and a feast—all of which appealed to the thrifty, calculating brain of Bashti. And what was good for Ano Ano, in his judgment was surely good for Somo. Since such were white men's ways who sailed under the British flag and killed pigs and cut down coconuts in cancellation of blood-debts and headtakings, Bashti saw no valid reason why he should not profit as Ano Ano had profited. The price to be paid at some possible future time was absurdly disproportionate to the immediate wealth to be gained. Besides, it had been over two years since the last British war vessel had appeared in the Solomons.

And thus, Bashti, with a fine fresh idea inside his head, bowed his chief's head in consent that his people could flock aboard and trade. Very few of them knew what his idea was or that he even had an idea.

Trade grew still brisker as more canoes came alongside and black men and women thronged the deck. Then came the recruits, new-caught, young, savage things, timid as deer, yet yielding to stern parental and tribal law and going down into the *Arangi*'s cabin, one by one, their fathers and mothers and relatives accompanying them in family groups, to confront the big fella white marster, who wrote their names down in a mysterious book, had them ratify the three years' contract of their labour by a touch of the right hand to the pen with which he wrote, and who paid the first year's advance in trade goods to the heads of their respective families.

Old Bashti sat near, taking his customary heavy tithes out of each advance, his three old wives squatting humbly at his feet and by their mere presence giving confidence to Van Horn, who was elated by the stroke of business. At such rate his cruise on Malaita would be a short one, when he would sail away with a full ship.

On deck, where Borckman kept a sharp eye out against danger, Jerry prowled about, sniffing the many legs of the many blacks he had never encountered before. The wild-dog had gone ashore with the return boys, and of the return boys only one had come back. It was Lerumie, past whom Jerry repeatedly and stiff-leggedly bristled without gaining response of recognition. Lerumie coolly ignored him, went down below once and purchased a trade hand-mirror, and, with a look of the eyes, assured old Bashti that all was ready and ripe to break at the first favourable moment.

On deck, Borckman gave this favourable moment. Nor would he have so given it had he not been guilty of carelessness and of disobedience to his captain's orders. He did not leave the schnapps alone. Be did not sense what was impending all about him. Aft, where he stood, the deck was almost deserted. Amidships and for'ard, gamming with the boat's crew, the deck was crowded with blacks of both sexes. He made his way to the yam sacks lashed abaft the mizzenmast and got his bottle. Just before he drank, with a shred of caution, he cast a glance behind him. Near him stood a harmless Mary, middle-aged, fat, squat, asymmetrical, unlovely, a sucking child of two years astride her hip and taking nourishment. Surely no harm was to be apprehended there. Furthermore, she was patently a weaponless Mary, for she wore no stitch of clothing that otherwise might have concealed a weapon. Over against the rail, ten feet to one side, stood Lerumie, smirking into the trade mirror he had just bought.

It was in the trade mirror that Lerumie saw Borckman bend to the yam-sacks, return to the erect, throw his head back, the mouth of the bottle glued to his lips, the bottom elevated skyward. Lerumie lifted his right hand in signal to a woman in a canoe alongside. She bent swiftly for something that she tossed to Lerumie. It was a long-handled tomahawk, the head of it an ordinary shingler's hatchet, the haft of it, native-made, a black and polished piece of hard wood, inlaid in rude designs with mother-of-pearl and wrapped with coconut sennit to make a hand grip. The blade of the hatchet had been ground to razor-edge.

As the tomahawk flew noiselessly through the air to Lerumie's hand, just as noiselessly, the next instant, it flew through the air from his hand into the hand of the fat Mary with the nursing child who stood behind the mate. She clutched the handle with both hands, while the child, astride her hip, held on to her with both small arms part way about her.

Still she waited the stroke, for with Borckman's head thrown back was no time to strive to sever the spinal cord at the neck. Many eyes beheld the impending tragedy. Jerry saw, but did not understand. With all his hostility to niggers he had not divined the attack from the air. Tambi, who chanced to be near the skylight, saw, and, seeing, reached for a Lee-Enfield. Lerumie saw Tambi's action and hissed haste to the Mary.

Borckman, as unaware of this, his last second of life, as he had been of his first second of birth, lowered the bottle and straightened forward his head. The keen edge sank home. What, in that flash of instant when his brain was severed from the rest of his body, Borckman may have felt or thought, if he felt or thought at all, is a mystery unsolvable to living man. No man, his spinal cord so severed, has ever given one word or whisper of testimony as to what were his sensations and impressions. No less swift than the hatchet stroke was the limp placidity into which Borckman's body melted to the deck. He did not reel or pitch. He *melted*, as a sack of wind suddenly emptied, as a bladder of air suddenly punctured. The bottle fell from his dead hand upon the yams without breaking, although the remnant of its contents gurgled gently out upon the deck.

So quick was the occurrence of action, that the first shot from Tambi's musket missed the Mary ere Borckman had quite melted to the deck. There was no time for a second shot, for the Mary, dropping the tomahawk, holding her child in both her hands and plunging to the rail, was in the air and overboard, her fall capsizing the canoe which chanced to be beneath her.

Scores of actions were simultaneous. From the canoes on both sides uprose a glittering, glistening rain of mother-of-pearl-handled tomahawks that descended into the waiting hands of the Somo men on deck, while the Marys on deck crouched down and scrambled out of the fray. At the same time that the Mary who had killed Borckman leapt the rail, Lerumie bent for the tomahawk she had dropped, and Jerry, aware of red war, slashed the hand that reached for the tomahawk. Lerumie stood upright and loosed loudly, in a howl, all the pent rage and hatred, of months which he had cherished against the puppy. Also, as he gained the perpendicular and as Jerry flew at his legs, he launched a kick with all his might that caught and lifted Jerry squarely under the middle.

And in the next second, or fraction of second, as Jerry lifted and soared through the air, over the barbed wire of the rail and overboard, while Sniders were being passed up overside from the canoes, Tambi fired his next hasty shot. And Lerumie, the foot with which he had kicked not yet returned to the deck as again he was in mid-action of stooping to pick up the tomahawk, received the bullet squarely in the heart and pitched down to melt with Borckman into the softness of death.

Ere Jerry struck the water, the glory of Tambi's marvellously lucky shot was over for Tambi; for, at the moment he pressed trigger to the successful shot, a tomahawk bit across his skull at the base of the brain and darkened from his eyes for ever the bright vision of the sea-washed, sun-blazoned tropic world. As swiftly, all occurring almost simultaneously, did the rest of the boat's crew pass and the deck became a shambles.

It was to the reports of the Sniders and the noises of the death scuffle that Jerry's head emerged from the water. A man's hand reached over a canoe-side and dragged him in by the scruff of the neck, and, although he snarled and struggled to bite his rescuer, he was not so much enraged as was he torn by the wildest solicitude for Skipper. He knew, without thinking about it, that the *Arangi* had been boarded by the hazily sensed supreme disaster of life that all life intuitively apprehends and that only man knows and calls by the name of "death." Borckman he had seen struck down. Lerumie he had heard struck down. And now he was hearing the explosions of rifles and the yells and screeches of triumph and fear.

So it was, helpless, suspended in the air by the nape of the neck, that he bawled and squalled and choked and coughed till the black, disgusted, flung him down roughly in the canoe's bottom. He scrambled to his feet and made two leaps: one upon the gunwale of the canoe; the next, despairing and hopeless, without consideration of self, for the rail of the *Arangi*.

His forefeet missed the rail by a yard, and he plunged down into the sea. He came up, swimming frantically, swallowing and strangling salt water because he still yelped and wailed and barked his yearning to be on board with Skipper.

But a boy of twelve, in another canoe, having witnessed the first black's adventure with Jerry, treated him without ceremony, laying, first the flat, and next the edge, of a paddle upon his head while he still swam. And the darkness of unconsciousness welled over his bright little love-suffering brain, so that it was a limp and motionless puppy that the black boy dragged into his canoe.

In the meantime, down below in the *Arangi's* cabin, ere ever Jerry hit the water from Lerumie's kick, even while he was in the air, Van Horn, in one great flashing profound fraction of an instant, had known his death. Not for nothing had old Bashti lived longest of any living man in his tribe, and ruled wisest of all the long line of rulers since Somo's time. Had he been placed more generously in earth space and time, he might well have proved an Alexander, a Napoleon, or a swarthy Kahehameha. As it was, he performed well, and splendidly well, in his limited little kingdom on the leeward coast of the dark cannibal island of Malaita.

And such a performance! In cool good nature in rigid maintenance of his chiefship rights, he had smiled at Van Horn, given royal permission to his young men to sign on for three years of plantation slavery, and exacted his share of each year's advance. Aora, who might be described as his prime minister and treasurer, had received the tithes as fast as they were paid over, and filled them into large, fine-netted bags of coconut sennit. At Bashti's back, squatting on the bunk-boards, a slim and smooth-skinned maid of thirteen had flapped the flies away from his royal head with the royal fly-flapper. At his feet had squatted his three old wives, the oldest of them, toothless and somewhat palsied, ever presenting to his hand, at his head nod, a basket rough-woven of pandanus leaf.

And Bashti, his keen old ears pitched for the first untoward sound from on deck, had continually nodded his head and dipped his hand into the proffered basket—now for betel-nut, and lime-box, and the invariable green leaf with which to wrap the mouthful; now for tobacco with which to fill his short clay pipe; and, again, for matches with which to light the pipe which seemed not to draw well and which frequently went out.

Toward the last the basket had hovered constantly close to his hand, and, at the last, he made one final dip. It was at the moment when the Mary's axe, on deck, had struck Borckman down and when Tambi loosed the first shot at her from his Lee-Enfield. And Bashti's withered ancient hand, the back of it netted with a complex of large up-standing veins from which the flesh had shrunk away, dipped out a huge pistol of such remote vintage that one of Cromwell's round-heads might well have carried it or that it might well have voyaged with Quiros or La Perouse. It was a flint-lock, as long as a man's forearm, and it had been loaded that afternoon by no less a person than Bashti himself.

Quick as Bashti had been, Van Horn was almost as quick, but not quite quick enough. Even as his hand leapt to the modern automatic lying out of it's holster and loose on his knees, the pistol of the centuries went off. Loaded with two slugs and a round bullet, its effect was that of a sawed-off shotgun. And Van Horn knew the blaze and the black of death, even as "Gott fer dang!" died unuttered on his lips and as his fingers relaxed from the part-lifted automatic, dropping it to the floor.

Surcharged with black powder, the ancient weapon had other effect. It burst in Bashti's hand. While Aora, with a knife produced apparently from nowhere, proceeded to hack off the white master's head, Bashti looked quizzically at his right forefinger dangling by a strip of skin. He seized it with his left hand, with a quick pull and twist wrenched it off, and grinningly tossed it, as a joke, into the pandanus basket which still his wife with one hand held before him while with the other she clutched her forehead bleeding from a flying fragment of pistol.

Collaterally with this, three of the young recruits, joined by their fathers and uncles, had downed, and were finishing off the only one of the boat's crew that was below. Bashti, who had lived so long that he was a philosopher who minded pain little and the loss of a finger less, chuckled and chirped his satisfaction and pride of achievement in the outcome, while his three old wives, who lived only at the nod of his head, fawned under him on the floor in the abjectness of servile congratulation and worship. Long had they lived, and they had lived long only by his kingly whim. They floundered and gibbered and mowed at his feet, lord of life and death that he was, infinitely wise as he had so often proved himself, as he had this time proved himself again.

And the lean, fear-stricken girl, like a frightened rabbit in the mouth of its burrow, on hands and knees peered forth upon the scene from the lazarette and knew that the cooking-pot and the end of time had come for her.

CHAPTER XII

What happened aboard the *Arangi* Jerry never knew. He did know that it was a world destroyed, for he saw it destroyed. The boy who had knocked him on the head with the paddle, tied his legs securely and tossed him out on the beach ere he forgot him in the excitement of looting the *Arangi*.

With great shouting and song, the pretty teak-built yacht was towed in by the long canoes and beached close to where Jerry lay just beyond the confines of the coral-stone walls. Fires blazed on the beach, lanterns were lighted on board, and, amid a great feasting, the *Arangi* was gutted and stripped. Everything portable was taken ashore, from her pigs of iron ballast to her running gear and sails. No one in Somo slept that night. Even the tiniest of children toddled about the feasting fires or sprawled surfeited on the sands. At two in the morning, at Bashti's command, the shell of the boat was fired. And Jerry, thirsting for water, having whimpered and wailed himself to exhaustion, lying helpless, leg-tied, on his side, saw the floating world he had known so short a time go up in flame and smoke.

And by the light of her burning, old Bashti apportioned the loot. No one of the tribe was too mean to receive nothing. Even the wretched bush-slaves, who had trembled through all the time of their captivity from fear of being eaten, received each a clay pipe and several sticks of tobacco. The main bulk of the trade goods, which was not distributed, Bashti had carried up to his own large grass house. All the wealth of gear was stored in the several canoe houses. While in the devil devil houses the devil devil doctors set to work curing the many heads over slow smudges; for, along with the boat's crew there were a round dozen of No-ola return boys and several Malu boys which Van Horn had not yet delivered.

Not all these had been slain, however. Bashti had issued stern injunctions against wholesale slaughter. But this was not because his heart was kind. Rather was it because his head was shrewd. Slain they would all be in the end. Bashti had never seen ice, did not know it existed, and was unversed in the science of refrigeration. The only way he knew to keep meat was to keep it alive. And in the biggest canoe house, the club house of the stags, where no Mary might come under penalty of death by torture, the captives were stored.

Tied or trussed like fowls or pigs, they were tumbled on the hard-packed earthen floor, beneath which, shallowly buried, lay the remains of ancient chiefs, while, overhead, in wrappings of grass mats, swung all that was left of several of Bashti's immediate predecessors, his father latest among them and so swinging for two full generations. Here, too, since she was to be eaten and since the taboo had no bearing upon one condemned to be cooked, the thin little Mary from the lazarette was tumbled trussed upon the floor among the many blacks who had teased and mocked her for being fattened by Van Horn for the eating.

And to this canoe house Jerry was also brought to join the others on the floor. Agno, chief of the devil devil doctors, had stumbled across him on the beach, and, despite the protestations of the boy who claimed him as personal trove, had ordered him to the canoe house. Carried past the fires of the feasting, his keen nostrils had told him of what the feast consisted. And, new as the experience was, he had bristled and snarled and struggled against his bonds to be free. Likewise, at first, tossed down in the canoe house, he had bristled and snarled at his fellow captives, not realizing their plight, and, since always he had been trained to look upon niggers as the eternal enemy, considering them responsible for the catastrophe to the *Arangi* and to Skipper.

For Jerry was only a little dog, with a dog's limitations, and very young in the world. But not for long did he throat his rage at them. In vague ways it was borne in upon him that they, too, were not happy. Some had been cruelly wounded, and kept up a moaning and groaning. Without any clearness of concept, nevertheless Jerry had a realization that they were as painfully circumstanced as himself. And painful indeed was his own circumstance. He lay on his side, the cords that bound his legs so tight as to bite into his tender flesh and shut off the circulation. Also, he was perishing for water, and panted, dry-tongued, dry-mouthed, in the stagnant heat.

A dolorous place it was, this canoe house, filled with groans and sighs, corpses beneath the floor and composing the floor, creatures soon to be corpses upon the floor, corpses swinging in aerial sepulchre overhead, long black canoes, high-ended like beaked predatory monsters, dimly looming in the light of a slow fire where sat an ancient of the tribe of Somo at his interminable task of smoke-curing a bushman's head. He was withered, and blind, and senile, gibbering and mowing like some huge ape as ever he turned and twisted, and twisted back again, the suspended head in the pungent smoke, and handful by handful added rotten punk of wood to the smudge fire.

Sixty feet in the clear, the dim fire occasionally lighted, through shadowy cross-beams, the ridge-pole that was covered with sennit of coconut that was braided in barbaric designs of black and white and that was stained by the smoke of years almost to a monochrome of dirty brown. From the lofty cross-beams, on long sennit strings, hung the heads of enemies taken aforetime in jungle raid and sea foray. The place breathed the very atmosphere of decay and death, and the imbecile ancient, curing in the smoke the token of death, was himself palsiedly shaking into the disintegration of the grave.

Toward daylight, with great shouting and heaving and pull and haul, scores of Somo men brought in another of the big war canoes. They made way with foot and hand, kicking and thrusting dragging and shoving, the bound captives to either side of the space which the canoe was to occupy. They were anything but gentle to the meat with which they had been favoured by good fortune and the wisdom of Bashti.

For a time they sat about, all pulling at clay pipes and chirruping and laughing in queer thin falsettos at the events of the night and the previous afternoon. Now one and now another stretched out and slept without covering; for so, directly under the path of the sun, had they slept nakedly from the time they were born.

Remained awake, as dawn paled the dark, only the grievously wounded or the too-tightly bound, and the decrepit ancient who was not so old as Bashti. When the boy who had stunned Jerry with his paddle-blade and who claimed him as his own stole into the canoe house, the ancient did not hear him. Being blind, he did not see him. He continued gibbering and chuckling dementedly, to twist the bushman's head back and forth and to feed the smudge with punk-wood. This was no night-task for any man, nor even for him who had forgotten how to do aught else. But the excitement of cutting out the *Arangi* had been communicated to his addled brain, and, with vague reminiscent flashes of the strength of life triumphant, he shared deliriously in this triumph of Somo by applying himself to the curing of the head that was in itself the concrete expression of triumph.

But the twelve-year-old lad who stole in and cautiously stepped over the sleepers and threaded his way among the captives, did so with his heart in his mouth. He knew what taboos he was violating. Not old enough even to leave his father's grass roof and sleep in the youths' canoe house, much less to sleep with the young bachelors in their canoe house, he knew that he took his life, with all of its dimly guessed mysteries and arrogances, in his hand thus to trespass into the sacred precinct of the full-made, full-realized, full-statured men of Somo.

But he wanted Jerry and he got him. Only the lean little Mary, trussed for the cooking, staring through her wide eyes of fear, saw the boy pick Jerry up by his tied legs and carry him out and away from the booty of meat of which she was part. Jerry's heroic little heart of courage would have made him snarl and resent such treatment of handling had he not been too exhausted and had not his mouth and throat been too dry for sound. As it was, miserably and helplessly, not half himself, a puppet dreamer in a half-nightmare, he knew, as a restless sleeper awakening between vexing dreams, that he was being transported head-downward out of the canoe house that stank of death, through the village that was only less noisome, and up a path under lofty, wide-spreading trees that were beginning languidly to stir with the first breathings of the morning wind.

CHAPTER XIII

The boy's name, as Jerry was to learn, was Lamai, and to Lamai's house Jerry was carried. It was not much of a house, even as cannibal grass-houses go. On an earthen floor, hard-packed of the filth of years, lived Lamai's father and mother and a spawn of four younger brothers and sisters. A thatched roof that leaked in every heavy shower leaned to a wabbly ridge-pole over the floor. The walls were even more pervious to a driving rain. In fact, the house of Lamai, who was the father of Lumai, was the most miserable house in all Somo.

Lumai, the house-master and family head, unlike most Malaitans, was fat. And of his fatness it would seem had been begotten his good nature with its allied laziness. But as the fly in his ointment of jovial irresponsibility was his wife, Lenerengo—the prize shrew of Somo, who was as lean about the middle and all the rest of her as her husband was rotund; who was as remarkably sharp-spoken as he was soft-spoken; who was as ceaselessly energetic as he was unceasingly idle; and who had been born with a taste for the world as sour in her mouth as it was sweet in his.

The boy merely peered into the house as he passed around it to the rear, and he saw his father and mother, at opposite corners, sleeping without covering, and, in the middle of the floor, his four naked brothers and sisters curled together in a tangle like a litter of puppies. All about the house, which in truth was scarcely more than an animal lair, was an earthly paradise. The air was spicily and sweetly heavy with the scents of wild aromatic plants and gorgeous tropic blooms. Overhead three breadfruit trees interlaced their noble branches. Banana and plantain trees were burdened with great bunches of ripening fruit. And huge, golden melons of the papaia, ready for the eating, globuled directly from the slender-trunked trees not one-tenth the girth of the fruits they bore. And, for Jerry, most delightful of all, there was the gurgle and plash of a brooklet that pursued its invisible way over mossy stones under a garmenture of tender and delicate ferns. No conservatory of a king could compare with this wild wantonness of sun-generous vegetation.

Maddened by the sound of the water, Jerry had first to endure an embracing and hugging from the boy, who, squatted on his hams, rocked back and forth and mumbled a strange little crooning song. And Jerry, lacking articulate speech, had no way of telling him of the thirst of which he was perishing.

Next, Lamai tied him securely with a sennit cord about the neck and untied the cords that bit into his legs. So numb was Jerry from lack of circulation, and so weak from lack of water through part of a tropic day and all of a tropic night, that he stood up, tottered and fell, and, time and again, essaying to stand, floundered and fell. And Lamai understood, or tentatively guessed. He caught up a coconut calabash attached to the end of a stick of bamboo, dipped into the greenery of ferns, and presented to Jerry the calabash brimming with the precious water.

Jerry lay on his side at first as he drank, until, with the moisture, life flowed back into the parched channels of him, so that, soon, still weak and shaky, he was up and braced on all his four wide-spread legs and still eagerly lapping. The boy chuckled and chirped his delight in the spectacle, and Jerry found surcease and easement sufficient to enable him to speak with his tongue after the heart-eloquent manner of dogs. He took his nose out of the calabash and with his rose-ribbon strip of tongue licked Lamai's hand. And Lamai, in ecstasy over this establishment of common speech, urged the calabash back under Jerry's nose, and Jerry drank again.

He continued to drink. He drank until his sun-shrunken sides stood out like the walls of a balloon, although longer were the intervals from the drinking in which, with his tongue of gratefulness, he spoke against the black skin of Lamai's hand. And all went well, and would have continued to go well, had not Lamai's mother, Lenerengo, just awakened, stepped across her black litter of progeny and raised her voice in shrill protest against her eldest born's introducing of one more mouth and much more nuisance into the household.

A squabble of human speech followed, of which Jerry knew no word but of which he sensed the significance. Lamai was with him and for him. Lamai's mother was against him. She shrilled and shrewed her firm conviction that her son was a fool and worse because he had neither the consideration nor the silly sense of a fool's solicitude for a hard-worked mother. She appealed to the sleeping Lumai, who awoke heavily and fatly, who muttered and mumbled easy terms of Somo dialect to the effect that it was a most decent world, that all puppy dogs and eldest-born sons were right delightful things to possess, that he had never yet starved to death, and that peace and sleep were the finest things that ever befell the lot of mortal man—and, in token thereof, back into the peace of sleep, he snuggled his nose into the biceps of his arm for a pillow and proceeded to snore.

But Lamai, eyes stubbornly sullen, with mutinous foot-stampings and a perfect knowledge that all was clear behind him to leap and flee away if his mother rushed upon him, persisted in retaining his puppy dog. In the end, after an harangue upon the worthlessness of Lamai's father, she went back to sleep.

Ideas beget ideas. Lamai had learned how astonishingly thirsty Jerry had been. This engendered the idea that he might be equally hungry. So he applied dry branches of wood to the smouldering coals he dug out of the ashes of the cooking-fire, and built a large fire. Into this, as it gained strength, he placed many stones from a convenient pile, each fire-blackened in token that it had been similarly used many times. Next, hidden under the water of the brook in a netted hand-bag, he brought to light the carcass of a fat wood-pigeon he had snared the previous day. He wrapped the pigeon in green leaves, and, surrounding it with the hot stones from the fire, covered pigeon and stones with earth.

When, after a time, he removed the pigeon and stripped from it the scorched wrappings of leaves, it gave forth a scent so savoury as to prick up Jerry's ears and set his nostrils to quivering. When the boy had torn the steaming carcass across and cooled it, Jerry's meal began; nor did the meal cease till the last sliver of meat had been stripped and tongued from the bones and the bones crunched and crackled to fragments and swallowed. And throughout the meal Lamai made love to Jerry, crooning over and over his little song, and patting and caressing him.

346

On the other hand, refreshed by the water and the meat, Jerry did not reciprocate so heartily in the love-making. He was polite, and received his petting with soft-shining eyes, tail-waggings and the customary body-wrigglings; but he was restless, and continually listened to distant sounds and yearned away to be gone. This was not lost upon the boy, who, before he curled himself down to sleep, securely tied to a tree the end of the cord that was about Jerry's neck.

After straining against the cord for a time, Jerry surrendered and slept. But not for long. Skipper was too much with him. He knew, and yet he did not know, the irretrievable ultimate disaster to Skipper. So it was, after low whinings and whimperings, that he applied his sharp first-teeth to the sennit cord and chewed upon it till it parted.

Free, like a homing pigeon, he headed blindly and directly for the beach and the salt sea over which had floated the *Arangi*, on her deck Skipper in command. Somo was largely deserted, and those that were in it were sunk in sleep. So no one vexed him as he trotted through the winding pathways between the many houses and past the obscene kingposts of totemic heraldry, where the forms of men, carved from single tree trunks, were seated in the gaping jaws of carved sharks. For Somo, tracing back to Somo its founder, worshipped the shark-god and the salt-water deities as well as the deities of the bush and swamp and mountain.

Turning to the right until he was past the sea-wall, Jerry came on down to the beach. No *Arangi* was to be seen on the placid surface of the lagoon. All about him was the debris of the feast, and he scented the smouldering odours of dying fires and burnt meat. Many of the feasters had not troubled to return to their houses, but lay about on the sand, in the mid-morning sunshine, men, women, and children and entire families, wherever they had yielded to slumber.

Down by the water's edge, so close that his fore-feet rested in the water, Jerry sat down, his heart bursting for Skipper, thrust his nose heavenward at the sun, and wailed his woe as dogs have ever wailed since they came in from the wild woods to the fires of men.

And here Lamai found him, hushed his grief against his breast with cuddling arms, and carried him back to the grass house by the brook. Water he offered, but Jerry could drink no more. Love he offered, but Jerry could not forget his torment of desire for Skipper. In the end, disgusted with so unreasonable a puppy, Lamai forgot his love in his boyish savageness, clouted Jerry over the head, right side and left, and tied him as few whites men's dogs have ever been tied. For, in his way, Lamai was a genius. He had never seen the thing done with any dog, yet he devised, on the spur of the moment, the invention of tying Jerry with a stick. The stick was of bamboo, four feet long. One end he tied shortly to Jerry's neck, the other end, just as shortly to a tree. All that Jerry's teeth could reach was the stick, and dry and seasoned bamboo can defy the teeth of any dog.

CHAPTER XIV

For many days, tied by the stick, Jerry remained Lamai's prisoner. It was not a happy time, for the house of Lumai was a house of perpetual bickering and quarrelling. Lamai fought pitched battles with his brothers and sisters for teasing Jerry, and these battles invariably culminated in Lenerengo taking a hand and impartially punishing all her progeny.

After that, as a matter of course and on general principles, she would have it out with Lumai, whose soft voice always was for quiet and repose, and who always, at the end of a tongue-lashing, took himself off to the canoe house for a couple of days. Here, Lenerengo was helpless. Into the canoe house of the stags no Mary might venture. Lenerengo had never forgotten the fate of the last Mary who had broken the taboo. It had occurred many years before, when she was a girl, and the recollection was ever vivid of the unfortunate woman hanging up in the sun by one arm for all of a day, and for all of a second day by the other arm. After that she had been feasted upon by the stags of the canoe house, and for long afterward all women had talked softly before their husbands.

Jerry did discover liking for Lamai, but it was not strong nor passionate. Rather was it out of gratitude, for only Lamai saw to it that he received food and water. Yet this boy was no Skipper, no *Mister* Haggin. Nor was he even a Derby or a Bob. He was that inferior man-creature, a nigger, and Jerry had been thoroughly trained all his brief days to the law that the white men were the superior two-legged gods.

He did not fail to recognize, however, the intelligence and power that resided in the niggers. He did not reason it out. He accepted it. They had power of command over other objects, could propel sticks and stones through the air, could even tie him a prisoner to a stick that rendered him helpless. Inferior as they might be to the white-gods, still they were gods of a sort.

It was the first time in his life that Jerry had been tied up, and he did not like it. Vainly he hurt his teeth, some of which were loosening under the pressure of the second teeth rising underneath. The stick was stronger than he. Although he did not forget Skipper, the poignancy of his loss faded with the passage of time, until uppermost in his mind was the desire to be free.

But when the day came that he was freed, he failed to take advantage of it and scuttle away for the beach. It chanced that Lenerengo released him. She did it deliberately, desiring to be quit of him. But when she untied Jerry, he stopped to thank her, wagging his tail and smiling up at her with his hazel-brown eyes. She stamped her foot at him to be gone, and uttered a harsh and intimidating cry. This Jerry did not understand, and so unused was he to fear that he could not be frightened into running away. He ceased wagging his tail, and, though he continued to look up at her, his eyes no longer smiled. Her action and noise he identified as unfriendly, and he became alert and watchful, prepared for whatever hostile act she might next commit.

Again she cried out and stamped her foot. The only effect on Jerry was to make him transfer his watchfulness to the foot. This slowness in getting away, now that she had released him, was too much for her short temper. She launched the kick, and Jerry, avoiding it, slashed her ankle.

War broke on the instant, and that she might have killed Jerry in her rage was highly probable had not Lamai appeared on the scene. The stick untied from Jerry's neck told the tale of her perfidy and incensed Lamai, who sprang between and deflected the blow with a stone poi-pounder that might have brained Jerry.

Lamai was now the one in danger of grievous damage, and his mother had just knocked him down with a clout alongside the head when poor Lumai, roused from sleep by the uproar, ventured out to make peace. Lenerengo, as usual, forgot everything else in the fiercer pleasure of berating her spouse.

The conclusion of the affair was harmless enough. The children stopped their crying, Lamai retied Jerry with the stick, Lenerengo harangued herself breathless, and Lumai departed with hurt feelings for the canoe house where stags could sleep in peace and Marys pestered not.

That night, in the circle of his fellow stags, Lumai recited his sorrows and told the cause of them—the puppy dog which had come on the *Arangi*. It chanced that Agno, chief of the devil devil doctors, or high priest, heard the tale, and recollected that he had sent Jerry to the canoe house along with the rest of the captives. Half an hour later he was having it out with Lumai. Beyond doubt, the boy had broken the taboos, and privily he told him so, until Lamai trembled and wept and squirmed abjectly at his feet, for the penalty was death.

It was too good an opportunity to get a hold over the boy for Agno to misplay it. A dead boy was worth nothing to him, but a living boy whose life he carried in his hand would serve him well. Since no one else knew of the broken taboo, he could afford to keep quiet. So he ordered Lamai forthright down to live in the youths' canoe house, there to begin his novitiate in the long series of tasks, tests and ceremonies that would graduate him into the bachelors' canoe house and half way along toward being a recognized man.

* * * * *

In the morning, obeying the devil devil doctor's commands, Lenerengo tied Jerry's feet together, not without a struggle in which his head was banged about and her hands were scratched. Then she carried him down through the village on the way to deliver him at Agno's house. On the way, in the open centre of the village where stood the kingposts, she left him lying on the ground in order to join in the hilarity of the population.

Not only was old Bashti a stern law-giver, but he was a unique one. He had selected this day at the one time to administer punishment to two quarrelling women, to give a lesson to all other women, and to make all his subjects glad once again that they had him for ruler. Tiha and Wiwau, the two women, were squat and stout and young, and had long been a scandal because of their incessant quarrelling. Bashti had set them a race to run. But such a race. It was side-splitting. Men, women, and children, beholding, howled with delight. Even elderly matrons and greybeards with a foot in the grave screeched and shrilled their joy in the spectacle.

The half-mile course lay the length of the village, through its heart, from the beach where the *Arangi* had been burned to the beach at the other end of the sea-wall. It had to be covered once in each direction by Tiha and Wiwau, in each case one of them urging speed on the other and the other desiring speed that was unattainable.

Only the mind of Bashti could have devised the show. First, two round coral stones, weighing fully forty pounds each, were placed in Tiha's arms. She was compelled to clasp them tightly against her sides in order that they might not roll to the ground. Behind her, Bashti placed Wiwau, who was armed with a bristle of bamboo splints mounted on a light long shaft of bamboo. The splints were sharp as needles, being indeed the needles used in tattooing, and on the end of the pole they were intended to be applied to Tiha's back in the same way that men apply ox-goads to oxen. No serious damage, but much pain, could be inflicted, which was just what Bashti had intended.

Wiwau prodded with the goad, and Tiha stumbled and wabbled in gymnastic efforts to make speed. Since, when the farther beach had been reached, the positions would be reversed and Wiwau would carry the stones back while Tiha prodded, and since Wiwau knew that for what she gave Tiha would then try to give more, Wiwau exerted herself to give the utmost while yet she could. The perspiration ran down both their faces. Each had her partisans in the crowd, who encouraged and heaped ridicule with every prod.

Ludicrous as it was, behind it lay iron savage law. The two stones were to be carried the entire course. The woman who prodded must do so with conviction and dispatch. The woman who was prodded must not lose her temper and fight her tormentor. As they had been duly forewarned by Bashti, the penalty for infraction of the rules he had laid down was staking out on the reef at low tide to be eaten by the fish-sharks.

As the contestants came opposite where Bashti and Aora his prime minister stood, they redoubled their efforts, Wiwau goading enthusiastically, Tiha jumping with every thrust to the imminent danger of dropping the stones. At their heels trooped the children of the village and all the village dogs, whooping and yelping with excitement.

"Long time you fella Tiha no sit 'm along canoe," Aora bawled to the victim and set Bashti cackling again.

At an unusually urgent prod, Tiha dropped a stone and was duly goaded while she sank to her knees and with one arm scooped it in against her side, regained her feet, and waddled on.

Once, in stark mutiny at so much pain, she deliberately stopped and addressed her tormentor.

"Me cross along you too much," she told Wiwau. "Bime by, close—"

But she never completed the threat. A warmly administered prod broke through her stoicism and started her tottering along.

The shouting of the rabble ebbed away as the queer race ran on toward the beach. But in a few minutes it could be heard flooding back, this time Wiwau panting with the weight of coral stone and Tiha, a-smart with what she had endured, trying more than to even the score.

Opposite Bashti, Wiwau lost one of the stones, and, in the effort to recover it, lost the other, which rolled a dozen feet away from the first. Tiha became a whirlwind of avenging fury. And all Somo went wild. Bashti held his lean sides with merriment while tears of purest joy ran down his prodigiously wrinkled cheeks.

And when all was over, quoth Bashti to his people: "Thus shall all women fight when they desire over much to fight."

Only he did not say it in this way. Nor did he say it in the Somo tongue. What he did say was in bêche-de-mer, and his words were:

"Any fella Mary he like 'm fight, all fella Mary along Somo fight 'm this fella way."

CHAPTER XV

For some time after the conclusion of the race, Bashti stood talking with his head men, Agno among them. Lenerengo was similarly engaged with several old cronies. As Jerry lay off to one side where she had forgotten him, the wild-dog he had bullied on the *Arangi* came up and sniffed at him. At first he sniffed at a distance, ready for instant flight. Then he drew cautiously closer. Jerry watched him with smouldering eyes. At the moment wild-dog's nose touched him, he uttered a warning growl. Wild-dog sprang back and whirled away in headlong flight for a score of yards before he learned that he was not pursued.

Again he came back cautiously, as it was the instinct in him to stalk wild game, crouching so close to the ground that almost his belly touched. He lifted and dropped his feet with the lithe softness of a cat, and from time to time glanced to right and to left as if in apprehension of some flank attack. A noisy outburst of boys' laughter in the distance caused him to crouch suddenly down, his claws thrust into the ground for purchase, his muscles tense springs for the leap he knew not in what direction, from the danger he knew not what that might threaten him. Then he identified the noise, know that no harm impended, and resumed his stealthy advance on the Irish terrier.

What might have happened there is no telling, for at that moment Bashti's eyes chanced to rest on the golden puppy for the first time since the capture of the *Arangi*. In the rush of events Bashti had forgotten the puppy.

"What name that fella dog?" he cried out sharply, causing wild-dog to crouch down again and attracting Lenerengo's attention.

She cringed in fear to the ground before the terrible old chief and quavered a recital of the facts. Her good-for-nothing boy Lamai had picked the dog from the water. It had been the cause of much trouble in her house. But now Lamai had gone to live with the youths, and she was carrying the dog to Agno's house at Agno's express command.

"What name that dog stop along you?" Bashti demanded directly of Agno.

"Me kai-kai along him," came the answer. "Him fat fella dog. Him good fella dog kai-kai."

Into Bashti's alert old brain flashed an idea that had been long maturing.

"Him good fella dog too much," he announced. "Better you eat 'm bush fella dog," he advised, pointing at wild-dog.

Agno shook his head. "Bush fella dog no good kai-kai."

"Bush fella dog no good too much," was Bashti's judgment. "Bush fella dog too much fright. Plenty fella bush dog too much fright. White marster's dog no fright. Bush dog no fight. White marster's dog fight like hell. Bush dog run like hell. You look 'm eye belong you, you see."

Bashti stepped over to Jerry and cut the cords that tied his legs. And Jerry, upon his feet in a surge, was for once in too great haste to pause to give thanks. He hurled himself after wild-dog, caught him in mid-flight, and rolled him over and over in a cloud of dust. Ever wild-dog strove to escape, and ever Jerry cornered him, rolled him, and bit him, while Bashti applauded and called on his head men to behold.

By this time Jerry had become a raging little demon. Fired by all his wrongs, from the bloody day on the *Arangi* and the loss of Skipper down to this latest tying of his legs, he was avenging himself on wild-dog for everything. The owner of wild-dog, a return boy, made the mistake of trying to kick Jerry away. Jerry was upon him in a flash scratching his calves with his teeth, in the suddenness of his onslaught getting between the black's legs and tumbling him to the ground.

"What name!" Bashti cried in a rage at the offender, who lay fear-stricken where he had fallen, trembling for what next words might fall from his chief's lips.

But Bashti was already doubling with laughter at sight of wild-dog running for his life down the street with Jerry a hundred feet behind and tearing up the dust.

As they disappeared, Bashti expounded his idea. If men planted banana trees, it ran, what they would get would be bananas. If they planted yams, yams would be produced, not sweet potatoes or plantains, but yams, nothing but yams. The same with dogs. Since all black men's dogs were cowards, all the breeding of all black men's dogs would produce cowards. White men's dogs were courageous fighters. When they were bred they produced courageous fighters. Very well, and to the conclusion, namely, here was a white man's dog in their possession. The height of foolishness would be to eat it and to destroy for all time the courage that resided in it. The wise thing to do was to regard it as a seed dog, to keep it alive, so that in the coming generations of Somo dogs its courage would be repeated over and over and spread until all Somo dogs would be strong and brave.

Further, Bashti commanded his chief devil devil doctor to take charge of Jerry and guard him well. Also, he sent his word forth to all the tribe that Jerry was taboo. No man, woman, or child was to throw spear or stone at him, strike him with club or tomahawk, or hurt him in any way.

* * * * *

Thenceforth, and until Jerry himself violated one of the greatest of taboos, he had a happy time in Agno's gloomy grass house. For Bashti, unlike most chiefs, ruled his devil devil doctors with an iron hand. Other chiefs, even Nau-hau of Langa-Langa, were ruled by their devil devil doctors. For that matter, the population of Somo believed that Bashti was so ruled. But the Somo folk did not know what went on behind the scenes, when Bashti, a sheer infidel, talked alone now with one doctor and now with another.

In these private talks he demonstrated that he knew their game as well as they did, and that he was no slave to the dark superstitions and gross impostures with which they kept the people in submission. Also, he exposited the theory, as ancient as priests and rulers, that priests and rulers must work together in the orderly governance of the people. He was content that the people should believe that the gods, and the priests who were the mouth-pieces of the gods, had the last word, but he would have the priests know that in private the last word was his. Little as they believed in their trickery, he told them, he believed less.

He knew taboo, and the truth behind taboo. He explained his personal taboos, and how they came to be. Never must he eat clam-meat, he told Agno. It was so selected by himself because he did not like clam-meat. It was old Nino, high priest before Agno, with an ear open to the voice of the shark-god, who had so laid the taboo. But, he, Bashti, had privily commanded Nino to lay the taboo against clam-meat upon him, because he, Bashti, did not like clam-meat and had never liked clam-meat.

Still further, since he had lived longer than the oldest priest of them, his had been the appointing of every one of them. He knew them, had made them, had placed them, and they lived by his pleasure. And they would continue to take program from him, as they had always taken it, or else they would swiftly and suddenly pass. He had but to remind them of the passing of Kori, the devil devil doctor who had believed himself stronger than his chief, and who, for his mistake, had screamed in pain for a week ere what composed him had ceased to scream and for ever ceased to scream.

* * * * *

In Agno's large grass house was little light and much mystery. There was no mystery there for Jerry, who merely knew things, or did not know things, and who never bothered about what he did not know. Dried heads and other cured and mouldy portions of human carcasses impressed him no more than the dried alligators and dried fish that contributed to the festooning of Agno's dark abode.

Jerry found himself well cared for. No children nor wives cluttered the devil devil doctor's house. Several old women, a fly-flapping girl of eleven, and two young men who had graduated from the canoe house of the youths and who were studying priestcraft under the master, composed the household and waited upon Jerry. Food of the choicest was his. After Agno had eaten first-cut of pig, Jerry was served second. Even the two acolytes and the fly-flapping maid ate after him, leaving the debris for the several old women. And, unlike the mere bush dogs, who stole shelter from the rain under overhanging eaves, Jerry was given a dry place under the roof where the heads of bushmen and of forgotten sandalwood traders hung down from above in the midst of a dusty confusion of dried viscera of sharks, crocodile skulls, and skeletons of Solomons rats that measured two-thirds of a yard in length from bone-tip of nose to bone-tip of tail.

A number of times, all freedom being his, Jerry stole away across the village to the house of Lumai. But never did he find Lamai, who, since Skipper, was the only human he had met that had placed a bid to his heart. Jerry never appeared openly, but from the thick fern of the brookside observed the house and scented out its occupants. No scent of Lamai did he ever obtain, and, after a time, he gave up his vain visits and accepted the devil devil doctor's house as his home and the devil devil doctor as his master.

But he bore no love for this master. Agno, who had ruled by fear so long in his house of mystery, did not know love. Nor was affection any part of him, nor was geniality. He had no sense of humour, and was as frostily cruel as an icicle. Next to Bashti he stood in power, and all his days had been embittered in that he was not first in power. He had no softness for Jerry. Because he feared Bashti he feared to harm Jerry.

The months passed, and Jerry got his firm, massive second teeth and increased in weight and size. He came as near to being spoiled as is possible for a dog. Himself taboo, he quickly learned to lord it over the Somo folk and to have his way and will in all matters. No one dared to dispute with him with stick or stone. Agno hated him—he knew that; but also he gleaned the knowledge that Agno feared him and would not dare to hurt him. But Agno was a chill-blooded philosopher and bided his time, being different from Jerry in that he possessed human prevision and could adjust his actions to remote ends.

From the edge of the lagoon, into the waters of which, remembering the crocodile taboo he had learned on Meringe, he never ventured, Jerry ranged to the outlying bush villages of Bashti's domain. All made way for him. All fed him when he desired food. For the taboo was upon him, and he might unchidden invade their sleeping-mats or food calabashes. He might bully as he pleased, and be arrogant beyond decency, and there was no one to say him nay. Even had Bashti's word gone forth that if Jerry were attacked by the full-grown bush dogs, it was the duty of the Somo folk to take his part and kick and stone and beat the bush dogs. And thus his own four-legged cousins came painfully to know that he was taboo.

And Jerry prospered. Fat to stupidity he might well have become, had it not been for his high-strung nerves and his insatiable, eager curiosity. With the freedom of all Somo his, he was ever a-foot over it, learning its metes and bounds and the ways of the wild creatures that inhabited its swamps and forests and that did not acknowledge his taboo.

Many were his adventures. He fought two battles with the wood-rats that were almost of his size, and that, being mature and wild and cornered, fought him as he had never been fought before. The first he had killed, unaware that it was an old and feeble rat. The second, in prime of vigour, had so punished him that he crawled back, weak and sick to the devil devil doctor's house, where, for a week, under the dried emblems of death, he licked his wounds and slowly came back to life and health.

He stole upon the dugong and joyed to stampede that silly timid creature by sudden ferocious onslaughts which he knew himself to be all sound and fury, but which tickled him and made him laugh with the consciousness of playing a successful joke. He chased the unmigratory tropi-ducks from their shrewd-hidden nests, walked circumspectly among the crocodiles hauled out of water for slumber, and crept under the jungle-roof and spied upon the snow-white saucy cockatoos, the fierce ospreys, the heavy-flighted buzzards, the lories and kingfishers, and the absurdly garrulous little pygmy parrots.

Thrice, beyond the boundaries of Somo, he encountered the little black bushmen who were more like ghosts than men, so noiseless and unperceivable were they, and who, guarding the wild-pig runways of the jungle, missed spearing him on the three memorable occasions. As the wood-rats had taught him discretion, so did these two-legged lurkers in the jungle twilight. He had not fought with them, although they tried to spear him. He quickly came to know that these were other folk than Somo folk, that his taboo did not extend to them, and that, even of a sort, they were two-legged gods who carried flying death in their hands that reached farther than their hands and bridged distance.

As he ran the jungle, so Jerry ran the village. No place was sacred to him. In the devil devil houses, where, before the face of mystery men and women crawled in fear and trembling, he walked stiff-legged and bristling; for fresh heads were suspended there—heads his eyes and keen nostrils identified as those of once living blacks he had known on board the *Arangi*. In the biggest devil devil house he encountered the head of Borckman, and snarled at it, without receiving response, in recollection of the fight he had fought with the schnapps-addled mate on the deck of the *Arangi*.

Once, however, in Bashti's house, he chanced upon all that remained on earth of Skipper. Bashti had lived very long, had lived most wisely and thought much, and was thoroughly aware that, having lived far beyond the span of man his own span was very short. And he was curious about it all— the meaning and purpose of life. He loved the world and life, into which he had been fortunately born, both as to constitution and to place, which latter, for him, had been the high place over hie priests and people. He was not afraid to die, but he wondered if he might live again. He discounted the silly views of the tricky priests, and he was very much alone in the chaos of the confusing problem.

For he had lived so long, and so luckily, that he had watched the waning to extinction of all the vigorous appetites and desires. He had known wives and children, and the keen-edge of youthful hunger. He had seen his children grow to manhood and womanhood and become fathers and grandfathers, mothers and grandmothers. But having known woman, and love, and fatherhood, and the belly-delights of eating, he had passed on beyond. Food? Scarcely did he know its meaning, so little did he eat. Hunger, that bit him like a spur when he was young and lusty, had long since ceased to stir and prod him. He ate out of a sense of necessity and duty, and cared little for what he ate, save for one thing: the eggs of the megapodes that were, in season, laid in his private, personal, strictly tabooed megapode laying-yard. Here was left to him his last lingering flesh thrill. As for the rest, he lived in his intellect, ruling his people, seeking out data from which to induce laws that would make his people stronger and rivet his people's clinch upon life.

But he realized clearly the difference between that abstract thing, the tribe, and that most concrete of things, the individual. The tribe persisted. Its members passed. The tribe was a memory of the history and habits of all previous members, which the living members carried on until they passed and became history and memory in the intangible sum that was the tribe. He, as a member, soon or late, and late was very near, must pass. But pass to what? There was the rub. And so it was, on occasion, that he ordered all forth from his big grass house, and, alone with his problem, lowered from the roof-beams the matting-wrapped parcels of heads of men he had once seen live and who had passed into the mysterious nothingness of death.

Not as a miser had he collected these heads, and not as a miser counting his secret hoard did he ponder these heads, unwrapped, held in his two hands or lying on his knees. He wanted to know. He wanted to know what he guessed they might know, now that they had long since gone into the darkness that rounds the end of life.

Various were the heads Bashti thus interrogated—in his hands, on his knees, in his dim-lighted grasshouse, while the overhead sun blazed down and the fading south-east sighed through the palm-fronds and breadfruit branches. There was the head of a Japanese—the only one he had ever seen or heard of. Before he was born it had been taken by his father. Ill-cured it was, and battered and marred with ancientness and rough usage. Yet he studied its features, decided that it had once had two lips as live as his own and a mouth as vocal and hungry as his had often been in the past. Two eyes and a nose it had, a thatched crown of roof, and a pair of ears like to his own. Two legs and a body it must once have had, and desires and lusts. Heats of wrath and of love, so he decided, had also been its once on a time when it never thought to die.

A head that amazed him much, whose history went back before his father's and grandfather's time, was the head of a Frenchman, although Bashti knew it not. Nor did he know it was the head of La Perouse, the doughty old navigator, who had left his bones, the bones of his crews, and the bones of his two frigates, the *Astrolabe* and the *Boussole*, on the shores of the cannibal Solomons. Another head—for Bashti was a confirmed head-collector—went back two centuries before La Perouse to Alvaro de Mendana, the Spaniard. It was the head of one of Mendana's armourers, lost in a beach scrimmage to one of Bashti's remote ancestors.

Still another head, the history of which was vague, was a white woman's head. What wife of what navigator there was no telling. But earrings of gold and emerald still clung to the withered ears, and the hair, two-thirds of a fathom long, a shimmering silk of golden floss, flowed from the scalp that covered what had once been the wit and will of her that Bashti reasoned had in her ancient time been quick with love in the arms of man.

Ordinary heads, of bushmen and salt-water men, and even of schnapps-drinking white men like Borckman, he relegated to the canoe houses and devil devil houses. For he was a connoisseur in the matter of heads. There was a strange head of a German that lured him much. Red-bearded it was, and red-haired, but even in dried death there was an ironness of feature and a massive brow that hinted to him of mastery of secrets beyond his ken. No more than did he know it once had been a German, did he know it was a German professor's head, an astronomer's head, a head that in its time had carried within its content profound knowledge of the stars in the vasty heavens, of the way of star-directed ships upon the sea, and of the way of the earth on its starry course through space that was a myriad million times beyond the slight concept of space that he possessed.

Last of all, sharpest of bite in his thought, was the head of Van Horn. And it was the head of Van Horn that lay on his knees under his contemplation when Jerry, who possessed the freedom of Somo, trotted into Bashti's grass house, scented and identified the mortal remnant of Skipper, wailed first in woe over it, then bristled into rage.

Bashti did not notice at first, for he was deep in interrogation of Van Horn's head. Only short months before this head had been alive, he pondered, quick with wit, attached to a two-legged body that stood erect and that swaggered about, a loincloth and a belted automatic around its middle, more powerful, therefrom, than Bashti, but with less wit, for had not he, Bashti, with an ancient pistol, put darkness inside that skull where wit resided, and removed that skull from the soddenly relaxed framework of flesh and bone on which it had been supported to tread the earth and the deck of the *Arangi*?

What had become of that wit? Had that wit been all of the arrogant, upstanding Van Horn, and had it gone out as the flickering flame of a splinter of wood goes out when it is quite burnt to a powder-fluff of ash? Had all that made Van Horn passed like the flame of the splinter? Had he passed into the darkness for ever into which the beast passed, into which passed the speared crocodile, the hooked bonita, the netted mullet, the slain pig that was fat to eat? Was Van Horn's darkness as the darkness of the blue-bottle fly that his fly-flapping maid smashed and disrupted in mid-flight of the air?—as the darkness into which passed the mosquito that knew the secret of flying, and that, despite its perfectness of flight, with almost an unthought action, he squashed with the flat of his hand against the back of his neck when it bit him?

What was true of this white man's head, so recently alive and erectly dominant, Bashti knew was true of himself. What had happened to this white man, after going through the dark gate of death, would happen to him. Wherefore he questioned the head, as if its dumb lips might speak to him from out of the mystery and tell him the meaning of life, and the meaning of death that inevitably laid life by the heels.

Jerry's long-drawn howl of woe at sight and scent of all that was left of Skipper, roused Bashti from his reverie. He looked at the sturdy, golden-brown puppy, and immediately included it in his reverie. It was alive. It was like man. It knew hunger, and pain, anger and love. It had blood in its veins, like man, that a thrust of a knife could make redly gush forth and denude it to death. Like the race of man it loved its kind, and birthed and breast-nourished its young. And passed. Ay, it passed; for many a dog, as well as a human, had he, Bashti, devoured in his hey-dey of appetite and youth, when he knew only motion and strength, and fed motion and strength out of the calabashes of feasting.

But from woe Jerry went on into anger. He stalked stiff-legged, with a snarl writhen on his lips, and with recurrent waves of hair-bristling along

363

his back and up his shoulders and neck. And he stalked not the head of Skipper, where rested his love, but Bashti, who held the head on his knees. As the wild wolf in the upland pasture stalks the mare mother with her newly delivered colt, so Jerry stalked Bashti. And Bashti, who had never feared death all his long life and who had laughed a joke with his forefinger blown off by the bursting flint-lock pistol, smiled gleefully to himself, for his glee was intellectual and in admiration of this half-grown puppy whom he rapped on the nose with a short, hardwood stick and compelled to keep distance. No matter how often and fiercely Jerry rushed him, he met the rush with the stick, and chuckled aloud, understanding the puppy's courage, marvelling at the stupidity of life that impelled him continually to thrust his nose to the hurt of the stick, and that drove him, by passion of remembrance of a dead man to dare the pain of the stick again and again.

This, too, was life, Bashti meditated, as he deftly rapped the screaming puppy away from him. Four-legged life it was, young and silly and hot, heart-prompted, that was like any young man making love to his woman in the twilight, or like any young man fighting to the death with any other young man over a matter of passion, hurt pride, or thwarted desire. As much as in the dead head of Van Horn or of any man, he realized that in this live puppy might reside the clue to existence, the solution of the riddle.

So he continued to rap Jerry on the nose away from him, and to marvel at the persistence of the vital something within him that impelled him to leap forward always to the stick that hurt him and made him recoil. The valour and motion, the strength and the unreasoning of youth he knew it to be, and he admired it sadly, and envied it, willing to exchange for it all his lean grey wisdom if only he could find the way.

"Some dog, that dog, sure some dog," he might have uttered in Van Horn's fashion of speech. Instead, in bêche-de-mer, which was as habitual to him as his own Somo speech, he thought:

"My word, that fella dog no fright along me."

But age wearied sooner of the play, and Bashti put an end to it by rapping Jerry heavily behind the ear and stretching him out stunned. The spectacle of the puppy, so alive and raging the moment before, and, the moment after, lying as if dead, caught Bashti's speculative fancy. The stick, with a single sharp rap of it, had effected the change. Where had gone the anger and wit of the puppy? Was that all it was, the flame of the splinter that could be quenched by any chance gust of air? One instant Jerry had raged and suffered, snarled and leaped, willed and directed his actions. The next instant he lay limp and crumpled in the little death of unconsciousness. In a brief space, Bashti knew, consciousness, sensation, motion, and direction would flow back into the wilted little carcass. But where, in the meanwhile, at the impact of the stick, had gone all the consciousness, and sensitiveness, and will?

Bashti sighed wearily, and wearily wrapped the heads in their grass-mat coverings—all but Van Horn's; and hoisted them up in the air to hang from the roof-beams—to hang as he debated, long after he was dead and out if it, even as some of them had so hung from long before his father's and his grandfather's time. The head of Van Horn he left lying on the floor, while he stole out himself to peer in through a crack and see what next the puppy might do.

Jerry quivered at first, and in the matter of a minute struggled feebly to his feet where he stood swaying and dizzy; and thus Bashti, his eye to the crack, saw the miracle of life flow back through the channels of the inert body and stiffen the legs to upstanding, and saw consciousness, the mystery of mysteries, flood back inside the head of bone that was covered with hair, smoulder and glow in the opening eyes, and direct the lips to writhe away from the teeth and the throat to vibrate to the snarl that had been interrupted when the stick smashed him down into darkness.

And more Bashti saw. At first, Jerry looked about for his enemy, growling and bristling his neck hair. Next, in lieu of his enemy, he saw Skipper's head, and crept to it and loved it, kissing with his tongue the hard cheeks, the closed lids of the eyes that his love could not open, the immobile lips that would not utter one of the love-words they had been used to utter to the little dog.

Next, in profound desolation, Jerry set down before Skipper's head, pointed his nose toward the lofty ridge-pole, and howled mournfully and long. Finally, sick and subdued, he crept out of the house and away to the house of his devil devil master, where, for the round of twenty-four hours, he waked and slept and dreamed centuries of nightmares.

For ever after in Somo, Jerry feared that grass house of Bashti. He was not in fear of Bashti. His fear was indescribable and unthinkable. In that house was the nothingness of what once was Skipper. It was the token of the ultimate catastrophe to life that was wrapped and twisted into every fibre of his heredity. One step advanced beyond this, Jerry's uttermost, the folk of Somo, from the contemplation of death, had achieved concepts of the spirits of the dead still living in immaterial and supersensuous realms.

And thereafter Jerry hated Bashti intensely, as a lord of life who possessed and laid on his knees the nothingness of Skipper. Not that Jerry reasoned it out. All dim and vague it was, a sensation, an emotion, a feeling, an instinct, an intuition, name it mistily as one will in the misty nomenclature of speech wherein words cheat with the impression of definiteness and lie to the brain an understanding which the brain does not possess.

CHAPTER XVI

Three months more passed; the north-west monsoon, after its half-year of breath, had given way to the south-east trade; and Jerry still continued to live in the house of Agno and to have the run of the village. He had put on weight, increased in size, and, protected by the taboo, had become self-confident almost to lordliness. But he had found no master. Agno had never won a heart-throb from him. For that matter, Agno had never tried to win him. Nor, in his cold-blooded way, had he ever betrayed his hatred of Jerry.

Not even the several old women, the two acolytes, and the fly-flapping maid in Agno's house dreamed that the devil devil doctor hated Jerry. Nor did Jerry dream it. To him Agno was a neutral sort of person, a person who did not count. Those of the household Jerry recognized as slaves or servants to Agno, and he knew when they fed him that the food he ate proceeded from Agno and was Agno's food. Save himself, taboo protected, all of them feared Agno, and his house was truly a house of fear in which could bloom no love for a stray puppy dog. The eleven-years' maid might have placed a bid for Jerry's affection, had she not been deterred at the start by Agno, who reprimanded her sternly for presuming to touch or fondle a dog of such high taboo.

What delayed Agno's plot against Jerry for the half-year of the monsoon was the fact that the season of egg-laying for the megapodes in Bashti's private laying-yard did not begin until the period of the south-east trades. And Agno, having early conceived his plot, with the patience that was characteristic of him was content to wait the time.

Now the megapode of the Solomons is a distant cousin to the brush turkey of Australia. No larger than a large pigeon, it lays an egg the size of a domestic duck's. The megapode, with no sense of fear, is so silly that it would have been annihilated hundreds of centuries before had it not been preserved by the taboos of the chiefs and priests. As it was, the chiefs were compelled to keep cleared patches of sand for it, and to fence out the dogs. It buried its eggs two feet deep, depending on the heat of the sun for the hatching. And it would dig and lay, and continue to dig and lay, while a black dug out its eggs within two or three feet of it.

The laying-yard was Bashti's. During the season, he lived almost entirely on megapode eggs. On rare occasion he even had megapodes that were near to finishing their laying killed for his kai-kai. This was no more than a whim, however, prompted by pride in such exclusiveness of diet only possible to one in such high place. In truth, he cared no more for megapode meat than for any other meat. All meat tasted alike to him, for his taste for meat was one of the vanished pleasures in the limbo of memory.

But the eggs! He liked to eat them. They were the only article of food he liked to eat, They gave him reminiscent thrills of the ancient food-desires of his youth. Actually was he hungry when he had megapode eggs, and the well-nigh dried founts of saliva and of internal digestive juices were stimulated to flow again at contemplation of a megapode egg prepared for the eating. Wherefore, he alone of all Somo, barred rigidly by taboo, ate megapode eggs. And, since the taboo was essentially religious, to Agno was deputed the ecclesiastical task of guarding and cherishing and caring for the royal laying-yard.

But Agno was no longer young. The acid bite of belly desire had long since deserted him, and he, too, ate from a sense of duty, all meat tasting alike to him. Megapode eggs only stung his taste alive and stimulated the flow of his juices. Thus it was that he broke the taboos he imposed, and, privily, before the eyes of no man, woman, or child ate the eggs he stole from Bashti's private preserve.

So it was, as the laying season began, and when both Bashti and Agno were acutely egg-yearning after six months of abstinence, that Agno led Jerry along the taboo path through the mangroves, where they stepped from root to root above the muck that ever steamed and stank in the stagnant air where the wind never penetrated.

The path, which was not an ordinary path and which consisted, for a man, in wide strides from root to root, and for a dog in four-legged leaps and plunges, was new to Jerry. In all his ranging of Somo, because it was so unusual a path, he had never discovered it. The unbending of Agno, thus to lead him, was a surprise and a delight to Jerry, who, without reasoning about it, in a vague way felt the preliminary sensations that possibly Agno, in a small way, might prove the master which his dog's soul continually sought.

Emerging from the swamp of mangroves, abruptly they came upon a patch of sand, still so salt and inhospitable from the sea's deposit that no great trees rooted and interposed their branches between it and the sun's heat. A primitive gate gave entrance, but Agno did not take Jerry through it. Instead, with weird little chirrupings of encouragement and excitation, he persuaded Jerry to dig a tunnel beneath the rude palisade of fence. He helped with his own hands, dragging out the sand in quantities, but imposing on Jerry the leaving of the indubitable marks of a dog's paws and claws.

And, when Jerry was inside, Agno, passing through the gate, enticed and seduced him into digging out the eggs. But Jerry had no taste of the eggs. Eight of them Agno sucked raw, and two of them he tucked whole into his arm-pits to take back to his house of the devil devils. The shells of the eight he sucked he broke to fragments as a dog might break them, and, to build the picture he had long visioned, of the eighth egg he reserved a tiny portion which he spread, not on Jerry's jowls where his tongue could have erased it, but high up about his eyes and above them, where it would remain and stand witness against him according to the plot he had planned.

Even worse, in high priestly sacrilege, he encouraged Jerry to attack a megapode hen in the act of laying. And, while Jerry slew it, knowing that the lust of killing, once started, would lead him to continue killing the silly birds, Agno left the laying-yard to hot-foot it through the mangrove swamp and present to Bashti an ecclesiastical quandary. The taboo of the dog, as he expounded it, had prevented him from interfering with the taboo dog when it ate the taboo egg-layers. Which taboo might be the greater was beyond him. And Bashti, who had not tasted a megapode egg in half a year, and who was keen for the one recrudescent thrill of remote youth still left to him, led the way back across the mangrove swamp at so prodigious a pace as quite to wind his high priest who was many years younger than he.

And he arrived at the laying-yard and caught Jerry, red-pawed and red-mouthed, in the midst of his fourth kill of an egg-layer, the raw yellow yolk of the portion of one egg, plastered by Agno to represent many eggs, still about his eyes and above his eyes to the bulge of his forehead. In vain Bashti looked about for one egg, the six months' hunger stronger than ever upon him in the thick of the disaster. And Jerry, under the consent and encouragement of Agno, wagged his tail to Bashti in a bid for recognition, of prowess, and laughed with his red-dripping jowls and yellow plastered eyes.

Bashti did not rage as he would have done had he been alone. Before the eyes of his chief priest he disdained to lower himself to such commonness of humanity. Thus it is always with those in the high places, ever temporising with their natural desires, ever masking their ordinariness under a show of disinterest. So it was that Bashti displayed no vexation at the disappointment to his appetite. Agno was a shade less controlled, for he could not quite chase away the eager light in his eyes. Bashti glimpsed it and mistook it for simple curiosity of observation not guessing its real nature. Which goes to show two things of those in the high place: one, that they may fool those beneath them; the other, that they may be fooled by those beneath them.

Bashti regarded Jerry quizzically, as if the matter were a joke, and shot a careless side glance to note the disappointment in his priest's eyes. Ah, ha, thought Bashti; I have fooled him.

"Which is the high taboo?" Agno queried in the Somo tongue.

"As you should ask. Of a surety, the megapode."

"And the dog?" was Agno's next query.

"Must pay for breaking the taboo. It is a high taboo. It is my taboo. It was so placed by Somo, the ancient father and first ruler of all of us, and it has been ever since the taboo of the chiefs. The dog must die."

He paused and considered the matter, while Jerry returned to digging the sand where the scent was auspicious. Agno made to stop him, but Bashti interposed.

370

"Let be," he said. "Let the dog convict himself before my eyes."

And Jerry did, uncovering two eggs, breaking them and lapping that portion of their precious contents which was not spilled and wasted in the sand. Bashti's eyes were quite lack-lustre as he asked

"The feast of dogs for the men is to-day?"

"To-morrow, at midday," Agno answered. "Already are the dogs coming in. There will be at least fifty of them."

"Fifty and one," was Bashti's verdict, as he nodded at Jerry.

The priest made a quick movement of impulse to capture Jerry.

"Why now?" the chief demanded. "You will but have to carry him through the swamp. Let him trot back on his own legs, and when he is before the canoe house tie his legs there."

Across the swamp and approaching the canoe house, Jerry, trotting happily at the heels of the two men, heard the wailing and sorrowing of many dogs that spelt unmistakable woe and pain. He developed instant suspicion that was, however, without direct apprehension for himself. And at that moment, his ears cocked forward and his nose questing for further information in the matter, Bashti seized him by the nape of the neck and held him in the air while Agno proceeded to tie his legs.

No whimper, nor sound, nor sign of fear, came from Jerry—only choking growls of ferociousness, intermingled with snarls of anger, and a belligerent up-clawing of hind-legs. But a dog, clutched by the neck from the back, can never be a match for two men, gifted with the intelligence and deftness of men, each of them two-handed with four fingers and an opposable thumb to each hand.

His fore-legs and hind-legs tied lengthwise and crosswise, he was carried head-downward the short distance to the place of slaughter and cooking, and flung to the earth in the midst of the score or more of dogs similarly tied and helpless. Although it was mid-afternoon, a number of them had so lain since early morning in the hot sun. They were all bush dogs or wild-dogs, and so small was their courage that their thirst and physical pain from cords drawn too tight across veins and arteries, and their dim apprehension of the fate such treatment foreboded, led them to whimper and wail and howl their despair and suffering.

The next thirty hours were bad hours for Jerry. The word had gone forth immediately that the taboo on him had been removed, and of the men and boys none was so low as to do him reverence. About him, till night-fall, persisted a circle of teasers and tormentors. They harangued him for his fall, sneered and jeered at him, rooted him about contemptuously with their feet, made a hollow in the sand out of which he could not roll and desposited him in it on his back, his four tied legs sticking ignominiously in the air above him.

And all he could do was growl and rage his helplessness. For, unlike the other dogs, he would not howl or whimper his pain. A year old now, the last six months had gone far toward maturing him, and it was the nature of his breed to be fearless and stoical. And, much as he had been taught by his white masters to hate and despise niggers, he learned in the course of these thirty hours an especially bitter and undying hatred.

His torturers stopped at nothing. Even they brought wild-dog and set him upon Jerry. But it was contrary to wild-dog's nature to attack an enemy that could not move, even if the enemy was Jerry who had so often bullied him and rolled him on the deck. Had Jerry, with a broken leg or so, still retained power of movement, then he would have mauled him, perhaps to death. But this utter helplessness was different. So the expected show proved a failure. When Jerry snarled and growled, wild-dog snarled and growled back and strutted and bullied around him, him to persuasion of the blacks could induce but no sink his teeth into Jerry.

The killing-ground before the canoe house was a bedlam of horror. From time to time more bound dogs were brought in and flung down. There was a continuous howling, especially contributed to by those which had lain in the sun since early morning and had no water. At times, all joined in, the control of the quietest breaking down before the wave of excitement and fear that swept spasmodically over all of them. This howling, rising and falling, but never ceasing, continued throughout the night, and by morning all were suffering from the intolerable thirst.

The sun blazing down upon them in the white sand and almost parboiling them, brought anything but relief. The circle of torturers formed about Jerry again, and again was wreaked upon him all abusive contempt for having lost his taboo. What drove Jerry the maddest were not the blows and physical torment, but the laughter. No dog enjoys being laughed at, and Jerry, least of all, could restrain his wrath when they jeered him and cackled close in his face.

Although he had not howled once, his snarling and growling, combined with his thirst, had hoarsened his throat and dried the mucous membranes of his mouth so that he was incapable, except under the sheerest provocation, of further sound. His tongue hung out of his mouth, and the eight o'clock sun began slowly to burn it.

It was at this time that one of the boys cruelly outraged him. He rolled Jerry out of the hollow in which he had lain all night on his back, turned him over on his side, and presented to him a small calabash filled with water. Jerry lapped it so fanatically that not for half a minute did he become aware that the boy had squeezed into it many hot seeds of ripe red peppers. The circle shrieked with glee, and what Jerry's thirst had been before was as nothing compared with this new thirst to which had been added the stinging agony of pepper.

Next in event, and a most important event it was to prove, came Nalasu. Nalasu was an old man of three-score years, and he was blind, walking with a large staff with which he prodded his path. In his free hand he carried a small pig by its tied legs.

"They say the white master's dog is to be eaten," he said in the Somo speech. "Where is the white master's dog? Show him to me."

Agno, who had just arrived, stood beside him as he bent over Jerry and examined him with his fingers. Nor did Jerry offer to snarl or bite, although the blind man's hands came within reach of his teeth more than once. For Jerry sensed no enmity in the fingers that passed so softly over him. Next, Nalasu felt over the pig, and several times, as if calculating, alternated between Jerry and the pig.

Nalasu stood up and voiced judgment:

"The pig is as small as the dog. They are of a size, but the pig has more meat on it for the eating. Take the pig and I shall take the dog."

"Nay," said Agno. "The white master's dog has broken the taboo. It must be eaten. Take any other dog and leave the pig. Take a big dog."

"I will have the white master's dog," Nalasu persisted. "Only the white master's dog and no other."

The matter was at a deadlock when Bashti chanced upon the scene and stood listening.

"Take the dog, Nalasu," he said finally. "It is a good pig, and I shall myself eat it."

"But he has broken the taboo, your great taboo of the laying-yard, and must go to the eating," Agno interposed quickly.

Too quickly, Bashti thought, while a vague suspicion arose in his mind of he knew not what.

"The taboo must be paid in blood and cooking," Agno continued.

"Very well," said Bashti. "I shall eat the small pig. Let its throat be cut and its body know the fire."

"I but speak the law of the taboo. Life must pay for the breaking."

"There is another law," Bashti grinned. "Long has it been since ever Somo built these walls that life may buy life."

"But of life of man and life of woman," Agno qualified.

"I know the law," Bashti held steadily on. "Somo made the law. Never has it been said that animal life may not buy animal life."

"It has never been practised," was the devil devil doctor's fling.

"And for reason enough," the old chief retorted. "Never before has a man been fool enough to give a pig for a dog. It is a young pig, and it is fat and tender. Take the dog, Nalasu. Take the dog now."

But the devil devil doctor was not satisfied.

"As you said, O Bashti, in your very great wisdom, he is the seed dog of strength and courage. Let him be slain. When he comes from the fire, his body shall be divided into many small pieces so that every man may eat of him and thereby get his portion of strength and courage. Better is it for Somo that its men be strong and brave rather than its dogs."

But Bashti held no anger against Jerry. He had lived too long and too philosophically to lay blame on a dog for breaking a taboo which it did not know. Of course, dogs often were slain for breaking the taboos. But he allowed this to be done because the dogs themselves in nowise interested him, and because their deaths emphasized the sacredness of the taboo. Further, Jerry had more than slightly interested him. Often, since, Jerry had attacked him because of Van Horn's head, he had pondered the incident. Baffling as it was, as all manifestations of life were baffling, it had given him food for thought. Then there was his admiration for Jerry's courage and that inexplicable something in him that prevented him crying out from the pain of the stick. And, without thinking of it as beauty, the beauty of line and colour of Jerry had insensibly penetrated him with a sense of pleasantness. It was good to look upon.

There was another angle to Bashti's conduct. He wondered why his devil devil doctor so earnestly desired a mere dog's death. There were many dogs. Then why this particular dog? That the weight of something was on the other's mind was patent, although what it was Bashti could not gauge, guess—unless it might be revenge incubated the day he had prevented Agno from eating the dog. If such were the case, it was a state of mind he could not tolerate in any of his tribespeople. But whatever was the motive, guarding as he always did against the unknown, he thought it well to discipline his priest and demonstrate once again whose word was the last word in Somo. Wherefore Bashti replied:

"I have lived long and eaten many pigs. What man may dare say that the many pigs have entered into me and made me a pig?"

He paused and cast a challenging eye around the circle of his audience; but no man spoke. Instead, some men grinned sheepishly and were restless on their feet, while Agno's expression advertised sturdy unbelief that there was anything pig-like about his chief.

"I have eaten much fish," Bashti continued. "Never has one scale of a fish grown out on my skin. Never has a gill appeared on my throat. As you all know, by the looking, never have I sprouted one fin out of my backbone.—Nalasu, take the dog.—Aga, carry the pig to my house. I shall eat it to-day.—Agno, let the killing of the dogs begin so that the canoe-men shall eat at due time."

Then, as he turned to go, he lapsed into bêche-de-mer English and flung sternly over his shoulder, "My word, you make 'm me cross along you."

CHAPTER XVII

As blind Nalasu slowly plodded away, with one hand tapping the path before him and with the other carrying Jerry head-downward suspended by his tied legs, Jerry heard a sudden increase in the wild howling of the dogs as the killing began and they realized that death was upon them.

But, unlike the boy Lamai, who had known no better, the old man did not carry Jerry all the way to his house. At the first stream pouring down between the low hills of the rising land, he paused and put Jerry down to drink. And Jerry knew only the delight of the wet coolness on his tongue, all about his mouth, and down his throat. Nevertheless, in his subconsciousness was being planted the impression that, kinder than Lamai, than Agno, than Bashti, this was the kindest black he had encountered in Somo.

When he had drunk till for the moment he could drink no more, he thanked Nalasu with his tongue—not warmly nor ecstatically as had it been Skipper's hand, but with due gratefulness for the life-giving draught. The old man chuckled in a pleased way, rolled Jerry's parched body into the water, and, keeping his head above the surface, rubbed the water into his dry skin and let him lie there for long blissful minutes.

From the stream to Nalasu's house, a goodly distance, Nalasu still carried him with bound legs, although not head-downward but clasped in one arm against his chest. His idea was to love the dog to him. For Nalasu, having sat in the lonely dark for many years, had thought far more about the world around him and knew it far better than had he been able to see it. For his own special purpose he had need of a dog. Several bush dogs he had tried, but they had shown little appreciation of his kindness and had invariably run away. The last had remained longest because he had treated it with the greatest kindness, but run away it had before he had trained it to his purpose. But the white master's dog, he had heard, was different. It never ran away in fear, while it was said to be more intelligent than the dogs of Somo.

The invention Lamai had made of tying Jerry with a stick had been noised abroad in the village, and by a stick, in Nalasu's house, Jerry found himself again tied. But with a difference. Never once was the blind man impatient, while he spent hours each day in squatting on his hams and petting Jerry. Yet, had he not done this, Jerry, who ate his food and who was growing accustomed to changing his masters, would have accepted Nalasu for master. Further, it was fairly definite in Jerry's mind, after the devil devil doctor's tying him and flinging him amongst the other helpless dogs on the killing-ground, that all mastership of Agno had ceased. And Jerry, who had never been without a master since his first days in the world, felt the imperative need of a master.

So it was, when the day came that the stick was untied from him, that Jerry remained, voluntarily in Nalasu's house. When the old man was satisfied there would be no running away, he began Jerry's training. By slow degrees he advanced the training until hours a day were devoted to it.

First of all Jerry learned a new name for himself, which was Bao, and he was taught to respond to it from an ever-increasing distance no matter how softly it was uttered, and Nalasu continued to utter it more softly until it no longer was a spoken word, but a whisper. Jerry's ears were keen, but Nalasu's, from long use, were almost as keen.

Further, Jerry's own hearing was trained to still greater acuteness. Hours at a time, sitting by Nalasu or standing apart from him, he was taught to catch the slightest sounds or rustlings from the bush. Still further, he was taught to differentiate between the bush noises and between the ways he growled warnings to Nalasu. If a rustle took place that Jerry identified as a pig or a chicken, he did not growl at all. If he did not identify the noise, he growled fairly softly. But if the noise were made by a man or boy who moved softly and therefore suspiciously, Jerry learned to growl loudly; if the noise were loud and careless, then Jerry's growl was soft.

It never entered Jerry's mind to question why he was taught all this. He merely did it because it was this latest master's desire that he should. All this, and much more, at a cost of interminable time and patience, Nalasu taught him, and much more he taught him, increasing his vocabulary so that, at a distance, they could hold quick and sharply definite conversations.

Thus, at fifty feet away, Jerry would "Whuff!" softly the information that there was a noise he did not know; and Nalasu, with different sibilances, would hiss to him to stand still, to whuff more softly, or to keep silent, or to come to him noiselessly, or to go into the bush and investigate the source of the strange noise, or, barking loudly, to rush and attack it.

Perhaps, if from the opposite direction Nalasu's sharp ears alone caught a strange sound, he would ask Jerry if he had heard it. And Jerry, alert to his toes to listen, by an alteration in the quantity or quality of his whuff, would tell Nalasu that he did not hear; next, that he did hear; and, perhaps finally, that it was a strange dog, or a wood-rat, or a man, or a boy—all in the softest of sounds that were scarcely more than breath-exhalations, all monosyllables, a veritable shorthand of speech.

Nalasu was a strange old man. He lived by himself in a small grass house on the edge of the village. The nearest house was quite a distance away, while his own stood in a clearing in the thick jungle which approached no where nearer than sixty feet. Also, this cleared space he kept continually free from the fast-growing vegetation. Apparently he had no friends. At least no visitors ever came to his dwelling. Years had passed since he discouraged the last. Further, he had no kindred. His wife was long since dead, and his three sons, not yet married, in a foray behind the bounds of Somo had lost their heads in the jungle runways of the higher hills and been devoured by their bushman slayers.

For a blind man he was very busy. He asked favour of no one and was self-supporting. In his house-clearing he grew yams, sweet potatoes, and taro. In another clearing—because it was his policy to have no trees close to his house—he had plantains, bananas, and half a dozen coconut palms. Fruits and vegetables he exchanged down in the village for meat and fish and tobacco.

He spent a good portion of his time on Jerry's education, and, on occasion, would make bows and arrows that were so esteemed by his tribespeople as to command a steady sale. Scarcely a day passed in which he did not himself practise with bow and arrow. He shot only by direction of sound; and whenever a noise or rustle was heard in the jungle, and when Jerry had informed him of its nature, he would shoot an arrow at it. Then it was Jerry's duty cautiously to retrieve the arrow had it missed the mark.

A curious thing about Nalasu was that he slept no more than three hours in the twenty-four, that he never slept at night, and that his brief daylight sleep never took place in the house. Hidden in the thickest part of the neighbouring jungle was a sort of nest to which led no path. He never entered nor left by the same way, so that the tropic growth on the rich soil, being so rarely trod upon, ever obliterated the slightest sign of his having passed that way. Whenever he slept, Jerry was trained to remain on guard and never to go to sleep.

Reason enough there was and to spare for Nalasu's infinite precaution. The oldest of his three sons had slain one, Ao, in a quarrel. Ao had been one of six brothers of the family of Anno which dwelt in one of the upper villages. According to Somo law, the Anno family was privileged to collect the blood-debt from the Nalasu family, but had been balked of it by the deaths of Nalasu's three sons in the bush. And, since the Somo code was a life for a life, and since Nalasu alone remained alive of his family, it was well known throughout the tribe that the Annos would never be content until they had taken the blind man's life.

But Nalasu had been famous as a great fighter, as well as having been the progenitor of three such warlike sons. Twice had the Annos sought to collect, the first time while Nalasu still retained his eyesight. Nalasu had discovered their trap, circled about it, and in the rear encountered and slain Anno himself, the father, thus doubling the blood-debt.

Then had come his accident. While refilling many-times used Snider cartridges, an explosion of black powder put out both his eyes. Immediately thereafter, while he sat nursing his wounds, the Annos had descended upon him—just what he had expected. And for which he had made due preparation. That night two uncles and another brother stepped on poisoned thorns and died horribly. Thus the sum of lives owing the Annos had increased to five, with only a blind man from whom to collect.

Thenceforth the Annos had feared the thorns too greatly to dare again, although ever their vindictiveness smouldered and they lived in hope of the day when Nalasu's head should adorn their ridgepole. In the meantime the state of affairs was not that of a truce but of a stalemate. The old man could not proceed against them, and they were afraid to proceed against him. Nor did the day come until after Jerry's adoption, when one of the Annos made an invention the like of which had never been known in all Malaita.

CHAPTER XVIII

Meanwhile the months slipped by, the south-east trade blew itself out, the monsoon had begun to breathe, and Jerry added to himself six months of time, weight, stature, and thickness of bone. An easy time his half-year with the blind man had been, despite the fact that Nalasu was a rigid disciplinarian who insisted on training Jerry for longer hours, day in and day out, than falls to the lot of most dogs. Never did Jerry receive from him a blow, never a harsh word. This man, who had slain four of the Annos, three of them after he had gone blind, who had slain still more men in his savage youth, never raised his voice in anger to Jerry and ruled him by nothing severer than the gentlest of chidings.

Mentally, the persistent education Jerry received, in this period of late puppyhood, fixed in him increased brain power for all his life. Possibly no dog in all the world had ever been so vocal as he, and for three reasons: his own intelligence, the genius for teaching that was Nalasu's, and the long hours devoted to the teaching.

His shorthand vocabulary, for a dog, was prodigious. Almost might it be said that he and the man could talk by the hour, although few and simple were the abstractions they could talk; very little of the immediate concrete past, and scarcely anything of the immediate concrete future, entered into their conversations. Jerry could no more tell him of Meringe, nor of the *Arangi*, than could he tell him of the great love he had borne Skipper, or of his reason for hating Bashti. By the same token, Nalasu could not tell Jerry of the blood-feud with the Annos, nor of how he had lost his eyesight.

Practically all their conversation was confined to the instant present, although they could compass a little of the very immediate past. Nalasu would give Jerry a series of instructions, such as, going on a scout by himself, to go to the nest, then circle about it widely, to continue to the other clearing where were the fruit trees, to cross the jungle to the main path, to proceed down the main path toward the village till he came to the great banyan tree, and then to return along the small path to Nalasu and Nalasu's house. All of which Jerry would carry out to the letter, and, arrived back, would make report. As, thus: at the nest nothing unusual save that a buzzard was near it; in the other clearing three coconuts had fallen to the ground—for Jerry could count unerringly up to five; between the other clearing and the main path were four pigs; along the main path he had passed a dog, more than five women, and two children; and on the small path home he had noted a cockatoo and two boys.

But he could not tell Nalasu his states of mind and heart that prevented him from being fully contented in his present situation. For Nalasu was not a white-god, but only a mere nigger god. And Jerry hated and despised all niggers save for the two exceptions of Lamai and Nalasu. He tolerated them, and, for Nalasu, had even developed a placid and sweet affection. Love him he did not and could not.

At the best, they were only second-rate gods, and he could not forget the great white-gods such as Skipper and *Mister* Haggin, and, of the same breed, Derby and Bob. They were something else, something other, something better than all this black savagery in which he lived. They were above and beyond, in an unattainable paradise which he vividly remembered, for which he yearned, but to which he did not know the way, and which, dimly sensing the ending that comes to all things, might have passed into the ultimate nothingness which had already overtaken Skipper and the *Arangi*.

In vain did the old man play to gain Jerry's heart of love. He could not bid against Jerry's many reservations and memories, although he did win absolute faithfulness and loyalty. Not passionately, as he would have fought to the death for Skipper, but devotedly would he have fought to the death for Nalasu. And the old man never dreamed but what he had won all of Jerry's heart.

* * * * *

Came the day of the Annos, when one of them made the invention, which was thick-plaited sandals to armour the soles of their feet against the poisoned thorns with which Nalasu had taken three of their lives. The day, in truth, was the night, a black night, a night so black under a cloud-palled sky that a tree-trunk could not be seen an eighth of an inch beyond one's nose. And the Annos descended on Nalasu's clearing, a dozen of them, armed with Sniders, horse pistols, tomahawks and war clubs, walking gingerly, despite their thick sandals, because of fear of the thorns which Nalasu no longer planted.

Jerry, sitting between Nalasu's knees and nodding sleepily, gave the first warning to Nalasu, who sat outside his door, wide-eyed, ear-strung, as he had sat through all the nights of the many years. He listened still more tensely through long minutes in which he heard nothing, at the same time whispering to Jerry for information and commanding him to be soft-spoken; and Jerry, with whuffs and whiffs and all the short-hand breath-exhalations of speech he had been taught, told him that men approached, many men, more men than five.

Nalasu reached the bow beside him, strung an arrow, and waited. At last his own ears caught the slightest of rustlings, now here, now there, advancing upon him in the circle of the compass. Still speaking for softness, he demanded verification from Jerry, whose neck hair rose bristling under Nalasu's sensitive fingers, and who, by this time, was reading the night air with his nose as well as his ears. And Jerry, as softly as Nalasu, informed him again that it was men, many men, more men than five.

With the patience of age Nalasu sat on without movement, until, close at hand, on the very edge of the jungle, sixty feet away, he located a particular noise of a particular man. He stretched his bow, loosed the arrow, and was rewarded by a gasp and a groan strangely commingled. First he restrained Jerry from retrieving the arrow, which he knew had gone home; and next he fitted a fresh arrow to the bow string.

Fifteen minutes of silence passed, the blind man as if carven of stone, the dog, trembling with eagerness under the articulate touch of his fingers, obeying the bidding to make no sound. For Jerry, as well as Nalasu, knew that death rustled and lurked in the encircling dark. Again came a softness of movement, nearer than before; but the sped arrow missed. They heard its impact against a tree trunk beyond and a confusion of small sounds caused by the target's hasty retreat. Next, after a time of silence, Nalasu told Jerry silently to retrieve the arrow. He had been well trained and long trained, for with no sound even to Nalasu's ears keener than seeing men's ears, he followed the direction of the arrow's impact against the tree and brought the arrow back in his mouth.

Again Nalasu waited, until the rustlings of a fresh drawing-in of the circle could be heard, whereupon Nalasu, Jerry accompanying him, picked up all his arrows and moved soundlessly half-way around the circle. Even as they moved, a Snider exploded that was aimed in the general direction of the spot just vacated.

And the blind man and the dog, from midnight to dawn, successfully fought off twelve men equipped with the thunder of gunpowder and the wide-spreading, deep-penetrating, mushroom bullets of soft lead. And the blind man defended himself only with a bow and a hundred arrows. He discharged many hundreds of arrows which Jerry retrieved for him and which he discharged over and over. But Jerry aided valiantly and well, adding to Nalasu's acute hearing his own acuter hearing, circling noiselessly about the house and reporting where the attack pressed closest.

Much of their precious powder the Annos wasted, for the affair was like a game of invisible ghosts. Never was anything seen save the flashes of the rifles. Never did they see Jerry, although they became quickly aware of his movements close to them as he searched out the arrows. Once, as one of them felt for an arrow which had narrowly missed him, he encountered Jerry's back with his hand and acknowledged the sharp slash of Jerry's teeth with a wild yell of terror. They tried firing at the twang of Nalasu's bowstring, but every time Nalasu fired he instantly changed position. Several times, warned of Jerry's nearness, they fired at him, and, once even, was his nose slightly powder burned.

When day broke, in the quick tropic grey that marks the leap from dark to sun, the Annos retreated, while Nalasu, withdrawn from the light into his house, still possessed eighty arrows, thanks to Jerry. The net result to Nalasu was one dead man and no telling how many arrow-pricked wounded men who dragged themselves away.

And half the day Nalasu crouched over Jerry, fondling and caressing him for what he had done. Then he went abroad, Jerry with him, and told of the battle. Bashti paid him a visit ere the day was done, and talked with him earnestly.

"As an old man to an old man, I talk," was Bashti's beginning. "I am older than you, O Nalasu; I have ever been unafraid. Yet never have I been braver than you. I would that every man of the tribe were as brave as you. Yet do you give me great sorrow. Of what worth are your courage and cunning, when you have no seed to make your courage and cunning live again?"

"I am an old man," Nalasu began.

"Not so old as I am," Bashti interrupted. "Not too old to marry so that your seed will add strength to the tribe."

"I was married, and long married, and I fathered three brave sons. But they are dead. I shall not live so long as you. I think of my young days as pleasant dreams remembered after sleep. More I think of death, and the end. Of marriage I think not at all. I am too old to marry. I am old enough to make ready to die, and a great curiousness have I about what will happen to me when I am dead. Will I be for ever dead? Will I live again in a land of dreams—a shadow of a dream myself that will still remember the days when I lived in the warm world, the quick juices of hunger in my mouth, in the chest of the body of me the love of woman?"

Bashti shrugged his shoulders.

"I too, have thought much on the matter," he said. "Yet do I arrive nowhere. I do not know. You do not know. We will not know until we are dead, if it happens that we know anything when what we are we no longer are. But this we know, you and I: the tribe lives. The tribe never dies. Wherefore, if there be meaning at all to our living, we must make the tribe strong. Your work in the tribe is not done. You must marry so that your cunning and your courage live after you. I have a wife for you—nay, two wives, for your days are short and I shall surely live to see you hang with my fathers from the canoe-house ridgepole."

"I will not pay for a wife," Nalasu protested. "I will not pay for any wife. I would not pay a stick of tobacco or a cracked coconut for the best woman in Somo."

"Worry not," Bashti went on placidly. "I shall pay you for the price of the wife, of the two wives. There is Bubu. For half a case of tobacco shall I buy her for you. She is broad and square, round-legged, broad-hipped, with generous breasts of richness. There is Nena. Her father sets a stiff price upon her—a whole case of tobacco. I will buy her for you as well. Your time is short. We must hurry."

"I will not marry," the old blind man proclaimed hysterically.

"You will. I have spoken."

"No, I say, and say again, no, no, no, no. Wives are nuisances. They are young things, and their heads are filled with foolishness. Their tongues are loose with idleness of speech. I am old, I am quiet in my ways, the fires of life have departed from me, I prefer to sit alone in the dark and think. Chattering young things about me, with nothing but foam and spume in their heads, on their tongues, would drive me mad. Of a surety they would drive me mad— so mad that I will spit into every clam shell, make faces at the moon, and bite my veins and howl."

"And if you do, what of it? So long as your seed does not perish. I shall pay for the wives to their fathers and send them to you in three days."

"I will have nothing to do with them," Nalasu asserted wildly.

"You will," Bashti insisted calmly. "Because if you do not you will have to pay me. It will be a sore, hard debt. I will have every joint of you unhinged so that you will be like a jelly-fish, like a fat pig with the bones removed, and I will then stake you out in the midmost centre of the dog-killing ground to swell in pain under the sun. And what is left of you I shall fling to the dogs to eat. Your seed shall not perish out of Somo. I, Bashti, so tell you. In three days I shall send to you your two wives. . . ."

He paused, and a long silence fell upon them.

"Well?" Bashti reiterated. "It is wives or staking out unhinged in the sun. You choose, but think well before you choose the unhinging."

"At my age, with all the vexations of youngness so far behind me!" Nalasu complained.

"Choose. You will find there is vexation, and liveliness and much of it, in the centre of the dog-killing yard when the sun cooks your sore joints till the grease of the leanness of you bubbles like the tender fat of a cooked sucking-pig."

"Then send me the wives," Nalasu managed to utter after a long pause. "But send them in three days, not in two, nor to-morrow."

"It is well," Bashti nodded gravely. "You have lived at all only because of those before you, now long in the dark, who worked so that the tribe might live and you might come to be. You are. They paid the price for you. It is your debt. You came into being with this debt upon you. You will pay the debt before you pass out of being. It is the law. It is very well."

CHAPTER XIX

And had Bashti hastened delivery of the wives by one day, or by even two days, Nalasu would have entered the feared, purgatory of matrimony. But Bashti kept his word, and on the third day was too busy, with a more momentous problem, to deliver Bubu and Nena to the blind old man who apprehensively waited their coming. For the morning of the third day all the summits of leeward Malaita smoked into speech. A warship was on the coast—so the tale ran; a big warship that was heading in through the reef islands at Langa-Langa. The tale grew. The warship was not stopping at Langa-Langa. The warship was not stopping at Binu. It was directing its course toward Somo.

Nalasu, blind, could not see this smoke speech written in the air. Because of the isolation of his house, no one came and told him. His first warning was when shrill voices of women, cries of children, and wailings of babes in nameless fear came to him from the main path that led from the village to the upland boundaries of Somo. He read only fear and panic from the sounds, deduced that the village was fleeing to its mountain fastnesses, but did not know the cause of the flight.

He called Jerry to him and instructed him to scout to the great banyan tree, where Nalasu's path and the main path joined, and to observe and report. And Jerry sat under the banyan tree and observed the flight of all Somo. Men, women, and children, the young and the aged, babes at breast and patriarchs leaning on sticks and staffs passed before his eyes, betraying the greatest haste and alarm. The village dogs were as frightened, whimpering and whining as they ran. And the contagion of terror was strong upon Jerry. He knew the prod of impulse to join in this rush away from some unthinkably catastrophic event that impended and that stirred his intuitive apprehensions of death. But he mastered the impulse with his sense of loyalty to the blind man who had fed him and caressed him for a long six months.

Back with Nalasu, sitting between his knees, he made his report. It was impossible for him to count more than five, although he knew the fleeing population numbered many times more than five. So he signified five men, and more; five women, and more five children, and more; five babies, and more; five dogs, and more—even of pigs did he announce five and more. Nalasu's ears told him that it was many, many times more, and he asked for names. Jerry know the names of Bashti, of Agno, and of Lamai, and Lumai. He did not pronounce them with the slightest of resemblance to their customary soundings, but pronounced them in the whiff-whuff of shorthand speech that Nalasu had taught him.

Nalasu named over many other names that Jerry knew by ear but could not himself evoke in sound, and he answered yes to most of them by simultaneously nodding his head and advancing his right paw. To some names he remained without movement in token that he did not know them. And to other names, which he recognized, but the owners of which he had not seen, he answered no by advancing his left paw.

And Nalasu, beyond knowing that something terrible was impending—something horribly more terrible than any foray of neighbouring salt-water tribes, which Somo, behind her walls, could easily fend off, divined that it was the long-expected punitive man-of-war. Despite his three-score years, he had never experienced a village shelling. He had heard vague talk of what had happened in the matter of shell-fire in other villages, but he had no conception of it save that it must be, bullets on a larger scale than Snider bullets that could be fired correspondingly longer distances through the air.

But it was given to him to know shell-fire before he died. Bashti, who had long waited the cruiser that was to avenge the destruction of the *Arangi* and the taking of the heads of the two white men, and who had long calculated the damage to be wrought, had given the command to his people to flee to the mountains. First in the vanguard, borne by a dozen young men, went his mat-wrapped parcels of heads. The last slow trailers in the rear of the exodus were just passing, and Nalasu, his bow and his eighty arrows clutched to him, Jerry at his heels, made his first step to follow, when the air above him was rent by a prodigiousness of sound.

Nalasu sat down abruptly. It was his first shell, and it was a thousand times more terrible than he had imagined. It was a rip-snorting, sky-splitting sound as of a cosmic fabric being torn asunder between the hands of some powerful god. For all the world it was like the roughest tearing across of sheets that were thick as blankets, that were broad as the earth and wide as the sky.

Not only did he sit down just outside his door, but he crouched his head to his knees and shielded it with the arch of his arms. And Jerry, who had never heard shell-fire, much less imagined what it was like, was impressed with the awfulness of it. It was to him a natural catastrophe such as had happened to the *Arangi* when she was flung down reeling on her side by the shouting wind. But, true to his nature, he did not crouch down under the shriek of that first shell. On the contrary, he bristled his hair and snarled up with menacing teeth at whatever the thing was which was so enormously present and yet invisible to his eyes.

Nalasu crouched closer when the shell burst beyond, and Jerry snarled and rippled his hair afresh. Each repeated his actions with each fresh shell, for, while they screamed no more loudly, they burst in the jungle more closely. And Nalasu, who had lived a long life most bravely in the midst of perils he had known, was destined to die a coward out of his fear of the thing unknown, the chemically propelled missile of the white masters. As the dropping shells burst nearer and nearer, what final self-control he possessed left him. Such was his utter panic that he might well have bitten his veins and howled. With a lunatic scream, he sprang to his feet and rushed inside the house as if forsooth its grass thatch could protect his head from such huge projectiles. He collided with the door-jamb, and, ere Jerry could follow him, whirled around in a part circle into the centre of the floor just in time to receive the next shell squarely upon his head.

Jerry had just gained the doorway when the shell exploded. The house went into flying fragments, and Nalasu flew into fragments with it. Jerry, in the doorway, caught in the out-draught of the explosion, was flung a score of feet away. All in the same fraction of an instant, earthquake, tidal wave, volcanic eruption, the thunder of the heavens and the fire-flashing of an electric bolt from the sky smote him and smote consciousness out of him.

391

He had no conception of how long he lay. Five minutes passed before his legs made their first spasmodic movements, and, as he stumbled to his feet and rocked giddily, he had no thought of the passage of time. He had no thought about time at all. As a matter of course, his own idea, on which he proceeded to act without being aware of it, was that, a part of a second before, he had been struck a terrific blow magnified incalculable times beyond the blow of a stick at a nigger's hands.

His throat and lungs filled with the pungent stifling smoke of powder, his nostrils with earth and dust, he frantically wheezed and sneezed, leaping about, falling drunkenly, leaping into the air again, staggering on his hind-legs, dabbing with his forepaws at his nose head-downward between his forelegs, and even rubbing his nose into the ground. He had no thought for anything save to remove the biting pain from his nose and mouth, the suffocation from his lungs.

By a miracle he had escaped being struck by the flying splinters of iron, and, thanks to his strong heart, had escaped being killed by the shock of the explosion. Not until the end of five minutes of mad struggling, in which he behaved for all the world like a beheaded chicken, did he find life tolerable again. The maximum of stifling and of agony passed, and, although he was still weak and giddy, he tottered in the direction of the house and of Nalasu. And there was no house and no Nalasu—only a debris intermingled of both.

While the shells continued to shriek and explode, now near, now far, Jerry investigated the happening. As surely as the house was gone, just as surely was Nalasu gone. Upon both had descended the ultimate nothingness. All the immediate world seemed doomed to nothingness. Life promised only somewhere else, in the high hills and remote bush whither the tribe had already fled. Loyal he was to his salt, to the master whom he had obeyed so long, nigger that he was, who so long had fed him, and for whom he had entertained a true affection. But this master no longer was.

Retreat Jerry did, but he was not hasty in retreat. For a time he snarled at every shell-scream in the air and every shell-burst in the bush. But after a time, while the awareness of them continued uncomfortably with him, the hair on his neck remained laid down and he neither uttered a snarl nor bared his teeth.

And when he parted from what had been and which had ceased to be, not like the bush dogs did he whimper and run. Instead, he trotted along the path at a regular and dignified pace. When he emerged upon the main path, he found it deserted. The last refugee had passed. The path, always travelled from daylight to dark, and which he had so recently seen glutted with humans, now in its emptiness affected him profoundly with the impression of the endingness of all things in a perishing world. So it was that he did not sit down under the banyan tree, but trotted along at the far rear of the tribe.

With his nose he read the narrative of the flight. Only once did he encounter what advertised its terror. It was an entire group annihilated by a shell. There were: an old man of fifty, with a crutch because of the leg which had been slashed off by a shark when he was a young boy; a dead Mary with a dead babe at her breast and a dead child of three clutching her hand; and two dead pigs, huge and fat, which the woman had been herding to safety.

And Jerry's nose told him of how the stream of the fugitives had split and flooded past on each side and flowed together again beyond. Incidents of the flight he did encounter: a part-chewed joint of sugar-cane some child had dropped; a clay pipe, the stem short from successive breakages; a single feather from some young man's hair, and a calabash, full of cooked yams and sweet potatoes, deposited carefully beside the trail by some Mary for whom its weight had proved too great.

The shell-fire ceased as Jerry trotted along; next he heard the rifle-fire from the landing-party, as it shot down the domestic pigs on Somo's streets. He did not hear, however, the chopping down of the coconut trees, any more than did he ever return to behold what damage the axes had wrought.

For right here occurred with Jerry a wonderful thing that thinkers of the world have not explained. He manifested in his dog's brain the free agency of life, by which all the generations of metaphysicians have postulated God, and by which all the deterministic philosophers have been led by the nose despite their clear denouncement of it as sheer illusion. What Jerry did he did. He did not know how or why he did it any more than does the philosopher know how or why he decides on mush and cream for breakfast instead of two soft-boiled eggs.

What Jerry did was to yield in action to a brain impulse to do, not what seemed the easier and more usual thing, but to do what seemed the harder and more unusual thing. Since it is easier to endure the known than to fly to the unknown; since both misery and fear love company; the apparent easiest thing for Jerry to have done would have been to follow the tribe of Somo into its fastnesses. Yet what Jerry did was to diverge from the line of retreat and to start northward, across the bounds of Somo, and continue northward into a strange land of the unknown.

Had Nalasu not been struck down by the ultimate nothingness, Jerry would have remained. This is true, and this, perhaps, to the one who considers his action, might have been the way he reasoned. But he did not reason it, did not reason at all; he acted on impulse. He could count five objects, and pronounce them by name and number, but he was incapable of reasoning that he would remain in Somo if Nalasu lived, depart from Somo if Nalasu died. He merely departed from Somo because Nalasu was dead, and the terrible shell-fire passed quickly into the past of his consciousness, while the present became vivid after the way of the present. Almost on his toes did he tread the wild bushmen's trails, tense with apprehension of the lurking death he know infested such paths, his ears cocked alertly for jungle sounds, his eyes following his ears to discern what made the sounds.

No more doughty nor daring was Columbus, venturing all that he was to the unknown, than was Jerry in venturing this jungle-darkness of black Malaita. And this wonderful thing, this seeming great deed of free will, he performed in much the same way that the itching of feet and tickle of fancy have led the feet of men over all the earth.

Though Jerry never laid eyes on Somo again, Bashti returned with his tribe the same day, grinning and chuckling as he appraised the damage. Only a few grass houses had been damaged by the shells. Only a few coconuts had been chopped down. And as for the slain pigs, lest they spoil, he made of their carcasses a great feast. One shell had knocked a hole through his sea-wall. He enlarged it for a launching-ways, faced the sides of it with dry-fitted coral rock, and gave orders for the building of an additional canoe-house. The only vexation he suffered was the death of Nalasu and the disappearance of Jerry—his two experiments in primitive eugenics.

CHAPTER XX

A week Jerry spent in the bush, deterred always from penetrating to the mountains by the bushmen who ever guarded the runways. And it would have gone hard with him in the matter of food, had he not, on the second day, encountered a lone small pig, evidently lost from its litter. It was his first hunting adventure for a living, and it prevented him from travelling farther, for, true to his instinct, he remained by his kill until it was nearly devoured.

True, he ranged widely about the neighbourhood, finding no other food he could capture. But always, until it was gone, he returned to the slain pig. Yet he was not happy in his freedom. He was too domesticated, too civilized. Too many thousands of years had elapsed since his ancestors had run freely wild. He was lonely. He could not get along without man. Too long had he, and the generations before him, lived in intimate relationship with the two-legged gods. Too long had his kind loved man, served him for love, endured for love, died for love, and, in return, been partly appreciated, less understood, and roughly loved.

So great was Jerry's loneliness that even a two-legged black-god was desirable, since white-gods had long since faded into the limbo of the past. For all he might have known, had he been capable of conjecturing, the only white-gods in existence had perished. Acting on the assumption that a black-god was better than no god, when he had quite finished the little pig, he deflected his course to the left, down-hill, toward the sea. He did this, again without reasoning, merely because, in the subtle processes of his brain, experience worked. His experience had been to live always close by the sea; humans he had always encountered close by the sea; and down-hill had invariably led to the sea.

He came out upon the shore of the reef-sheltered lagoon where ruined grass houses told him men had lived. The jungle ran riot through the place. Six-inch trees, throated with rotten remnants of thatched roofs through which they had aspired toward the sun, rose about him. Quick-growing trees had shadowed the kingposts so that the idols and totems, seated in carved shark jaws, grinned greenly and monstrously at the futility of man through a rime of moss and mottled fungus. A poor little sea-wall, never much at its best, sprawled in ruin from the coconut roots to the placid sea. Bananas, plantains, and breadfruit lay rotting on the ground. Bones lay about, human bones, and Jerry nosed them out, knowing them for what they were, emblems of the nothingness of life. Skulls he did not encounter, for the skulls that belonged to the scattered bones ornamented the devil devil houses in the upland bush villages.

The salt tang of the sea gladdened his nostrils, and he snorted with the pleasure of the stench of the mangrove swamp. But, another Crusoe chancing upon the footprint of another man Friday, his nose, not his eyes, shocked him electrically alert as he smelled the fresh contact of a living man's foot with the ground. It was a nigger's foot, but it was alive, it was immediate; and, as he traced it a score of yards, he came upon another foot-scent, indubitably a white man's.

Had there been an onlooker, he would have thought Jerry had gone suddenly mad. He rushed frantically about, turning and twisting his course, now his nose to the ground, now up in the air, whining as frantically as he rushed, leaping abruptly at right angles as new scents reached him, scurrying here and there and everywhere as if in a game of tag with some invisible playfellow.

But he was reading the full report which many men had written on the ground. A white man had been there, he learned, and a number of blacks. Here a black had climbed a coconut tree and cast down the nuts. There a banana tree had been despoiled of its clustered fruit; and, beyond, it was evident that a similar event had happened to a breadfruit tree. One thing, however, puzzled him—a scent new to him that was neither black man's nor white man's. Had he had the necessary knowledge and the wit of eye-observance, he would have noted that the footprint was smaller than a man's and that the toeprints were different from a Mary's in that they were close together and did not press deeply into the earth. What bothered him in his smelling was his ignorance of talcum powder. Pungent it was in his nostrils, but never, since first he had smelled out the footprints of man, had he encountered such a scent. And with this were combined other and fainter scents that were equally strange to him.

Not long did he interest himself in such mystery. A white man's footprints he had smelled, and through the maze of all the other prints he followed the one print down through a breach of sea-wall to the sea-pounded coral sand lapped by the sea. Here the latest freshness of many feet drew together where the nose of a boat had rested on the beach and where men had disembarked and embarked again. He smelled up all the story, and, his forelegs in the water till it touched his shoulders, he gazed out across the lagoon where the disappearing trail was lost to his nose.

Had he been half an hour sooner he would have seen a boat, without oars, gasoline-propelled, shooting across the quiet water. What he did see was an *Arangi*. True, it was far larger than the *Arangi* he had known, but it was white, it was long, it had masts, and it floated on the surface of the sea. It had three masts, sky-lofty and all of a size; but his observation was not trained to note the difference between them and the one long and the one short mast of the *Arangi*. The one floating world he had known was the white-painted *Arangi*. And, since, without a quiver of doubt, this was the *Arangi*, then, on board, would be his beloved Skipper. If *Arangis* could resurrect, then could Skippers resurrect, and in utter faith that the head of nothingness he had last seen on Bashti's knees he would find again rejoined to its body and its two legs on the deck of the white-painted floating world, he waded out to his depth, and, swimming dared the sea.

He greatly dared, for in venturing the water he broke one of the greatest and earliest taboos he had learned. In his vocabulary was no word for "crocodile"; yet in his thought, as potent as any utterable word, was an image of dreadful import—an image of a log awash that was not a log and that was alive, that could swim upon the surface, under the surface, and haul out across the dry land, that was huge-toothed, mighty-mawed, and certain death to a swimming dog.

398

But he continued the breaking of the taboo without fear. Unlike a man who can be simultaneously conscious of two states of mind, and who, swimming, would have known both the fear and the high courage with which he overrode the fear, Jerry, as he swam, knew only one state of mind, which was that he was swimming to the *Arangi* and to Skipper. At the moment preceding the first stroke of his paws in the water out of his depth, he had known all the terribleness of the taboo he deliberately broke. But, launched out, the decision made, the line of least resistance taken, he knew, single-thoughted, single-hearted, only that he was going to Skipper.

Little practised as he was in swimming, he swam with all his strength, whimpering in a sort of chant his eager love for Skipper who indubitably must be aboard the white yacht half a mile away. His little song of love, fraught with keenness of anxiety, came to the ears of a man and woman lounging in deck-chairs under the awning; and it was the quick-eyed woman who first saw the golden head of Jerry and cried out what she saw.

"Lower a boat, Husband-Man," she commanded. "It's a little dog. He mustn't drown."

"Dogs don't drown that easily," was "Husband-Man's" reply. "He'll make it all right. But what under the sun a dog's doing out here . . . " He lifted his marine glasses to his eyes and stared a moment. "And a white man's dog at that!"

Jerry beat the water with his paws and moved steadily along, straining his eyes at the growing yacht until suddenly warned by a sensing of immediate danger. The taboo smote him. This that moved toward him was the log awash that was not a log but a live thing of peril. Part of it he saw above the surface moving sluggishly, and ere that projecting part sank, he had an awareness that somehow it was different from a log awash.

Next, something brushed past him, and he encountered it with a snarl and a splashing of his forepaws. He was half-whirled about in the vortex of the thing's passage caused by the alarmed flirt of its tail. Shark it was, and not crocodile, and not so timidly would it have sheered clear but for the fact that it was fairly full with a recent feed of a huge sea turtle too feeble with age to escape.

Although he could not see it, Jerry sensed that the thing, the instrument of nothingness, lurked about him. Nor did he see the dorsal fin break surface and approach him from the rear. From the yacht he heard rifle-shots in quick succession. From the rear a panic splash came to his ears. That was all. The peril passed and was forgotten. Nor did he connect the rifle-shots with the passing of the peril. He did not know, and he was never to know, that one, known to men as Harley Kennan, but known as "Husband-Man" by the woman he called "Wife-Woman," who owned the three-topmast schooner yacht *Ariel*, had saved his life by sending a thirty-thirty Marlin bullet through the base of a shark's fin.

But Jerry was to know Harley Kennan, and quickly, for it was Harley Kennan, a bowline around his body under his arm-pits, lowered by a couple of seamen down the generous freeboard of the *Ariel*, who gathered in by the nape of the neck the smooth-coated Irish terrier that, treading water perpendicularly, had no eyes for him so eagerly did he gaze at the line of faces along the rail in quest of the one face.

No pause for thanks did he make when he was dropped down upon the deck. Instead, shaking himself instinctively as he ran, he scurried along the deck for Skipper. The man and his wife laughed at the spectacle.

"He acts as if he were demented with delight at being rescued," Mrs. Kennan observed.

And Mr. Kennan: "It's not that. He must have a screw loose somewhere. Perhaps he's one of those creatures who've slipped the ratchet off the motion cog. Maybe he can't stop running till he runs down."

In the meantime Jerry continued to run, up port side and down starboard side, from stern to bow and back again, wagging his stump tail and laughing friendliness to the many two-legged gods he encountered. Had he been able to think to such abstraction he would have been astounded at the number of white-gods. Thirty there were at least of them, not counting other gods that were neither black nor white, but that still, two-legged, upright and garmented, were beyond all peradventure gods. Likewise, had he been capable of such generalization, he would have decided that the white-gods had not yet all of them passed into the nothingness. As it was, he realized all this without being aware that he realized it.

But there was no Skipper. He sniffed down the forecastle hatch, sniffed into the galley where two Chinese cooks jabbered unintelligibly to him, sniffed down the cabin companionway, sniffed down the engine-room skylight and for the first time knew gasoline and engine oil; but sniff as he would, wherever he ran, no scent did he catch of Skipper.

Aft, at the wheel, he would have sat down and howled his heartbreak of disappointment, had not a white-god, evidently of command, in gold-decorated white duck cap and uniform, spoken to him. Instantly, always a gentleman, Jerry smiled with flattened ears of courtesy, wagged his tail, and approached. The hand of this high god had almost caressed his head when the woman's voice came down the deck in speech that Jerry did not understand. The words and terms of it were beyond him. But he sensed power of command in it, which was verified by the quick withdrawal of the hand of the god in white and gold who had almost caressed him. This god, stiffened electrically and pointed Jerry along the deck, and, with mouth encouragements and urgings the import of which Jerry could only guess, directed him toward the one who so commanded by saying:

"Send him, please, along to me, Captain Winters."

Jerry wriggled his body in delight of obeying, and would loyally have presented his head to her outreaching caress of hand, had not the strangeness and difference of her deterred him. He broke off in mid-approach and with a show of teeth snarled himself back and away from the windblown skirt of her. The only human females he had known were naked Marys. This skirt, flapping in the wind like a sail, reminded him of the menacing mainsail of the *Arangi* when it had jarred and crashed and swooped above his head. The noises her mouth made were gentle and ingratiating, but the fearsome skirt still flapped in the breeze.

"You ridiculous dog!" she laughed. "I'm not going to bite you."

But her husband thrust out a rough, sure hand and drew Jerry in to him. And Jerry wriggled in ecstasy under the god's caress, kissing the hand with a red flicker of tongue. Next, Harley Kennan directed him toward the woman sitting up in the deck-chair and bending forward, with hovering hands of greeting. Jerry obeyed. He advanced with flattened ears and laughing mouth: but, just ere she could touch him, the wind fluttered the skirt again and he backed away with a snarl.

"It's not you that he's afraid of, Villa," he said. "But of your skirt. Perhaps he's never seen a skirt before."

"You mean," Villa Kennan challenged, "that these head-hunting cannibals ashore here keep records of pedigrees and maintain kennels; for surely this absurd adventurer of a dog is as proper an Irish terrier as the *Ariel* is an Oregon-pine-planked schooner."

Harley Kennan laughed in acknowledgment. Villa Kennan laughed too; and Jerry knew that these were a pair of happy gods, and himself laughed with them.

Of his own initiative, he approached the lady god again, attracted by the talcum powder and other minor fragrances he had already identified as the strange scents encountered on the beach. But the unfortunate trade wind again fluttered her skirt, and again he backed away—not so far, this time, with much less of a bristle of his neck and shoulder hair, and with no more of a snarl than a mere half-baring of his fangs.

"He's afraid of your skirt," Harley insisted. "Look at him! He wants to come to you, but the skirt keeps him away. Tuck it under you so that it won't flutter, and see what happens."

Villa Kennan carried out the suggestion, and Jerry came circumspectly, bent his head to her hand and writhed his back under it, the while he sniffed her feet, stocking-clad and shoe-covered, and knew them as the feet which had trod uncovered the ruined ways of the village ashore.

"No doubt of it," Harley agreed. "He's white-man selected, white-man bred and born. He has a history. He knows adventure from the ground-roots up. If he could tell his story, we'd sit listening entranced for days. Depend on it, he's not known blacks all his life. Let's try him on Johnny."

Johnny, whom Kennan beckoned up to him, was a loan from the Resident Commissioner of the British Solomons at Tulagi, who had come along as pilot and guide to Kennan rather than as philosopher and friend. Johnny approached grinning, and Jerry's demeanour immediately changed. His body stiffened under Villa Kennan's hand as he drew away from her and stalked stiff-legged to the black. Jerry's ears did not flatten, nor did he laugh fellowship with his mouth, as he inspected Johnny and smelt his calves for future reference. Cavalier he was to the extreme, and, after the briefest of inspection, he turned back to Villa Kennan.

"What did I say?" her husband exulted. "He knows the colour line. He's a white man's dog that has been trained to it."

"My word," spoke up Johnny. "Me know 'm that fella dog. Me know 'm papa and mamma belong along him. Big fella white marster *Mister* Haggin stop along Meringe, mamma and papa stop along him that fella place."

Harley Kennan uttered a sharp exclamation.

"Of course," he cried. "The Commissioner told me all about it. The *Arangi*, that the Somo people captured, sailed last from Meringe Plantation. Johnny recognizes the dog as the same breed as the pair Haggin, of Meringe, must possess. But that was a long time ago. He must have been a little puppy. Of course he's a white man's dog."

"And yet you've overlooked the crowning proof of it," Villa Kennan teased. "The dog carries the evidence around with him."

Harley looked Jerry over carefully.

"Indisputable evidence," she insisted.

After another prolonged scrutiny, Kennan shook his head.

"Blamed if I can see anything so indisputable as to leave conjecture out."

"The tail," his wife gurgled. "Surely the natives do not bob the tails of their dogs.—Do they, Johnny? Do black man stop along Malaita chop 'm off tail along dog."

"No chop 'm off," Johnny agreed. "*Mister* Haggin along Meringe he chop 'm off. My word, he chop 'm that fella tail, you bet."

"Then he's the sole survivor of the *Arangi*," Villa Kennan concluded. "Don't you agree, Mr. Sherlock Holmes Kennan?"

"I salute you, Mrs. S. Holmes," her husband acknowledged gallantly. "And all that remains is for you to lead me directly to the head of La Perouse himself. The sailing directions record that he left it somewhere in these islands."

Little did they guess that Jerry had lived on intimate terms with one Bashti, not many miles away along the shore, who, in Somo, at that very moment, sat in his grass house pondering over a head on his withered knees that had once been the head of the great navigator, the history of which had been forgotten by the sons of the chief who had taken it.

CHAPTER XXI

The fine, three-topmast schooner *Ariel*, on a cruise around the world, had already been out a year from San Francisco when Jerry boarded her. As a world, and as a white-god world, she was to him beyond compare. She was not small like the *Arangi*, nor was she cluttered fore and aft, on deck and below, with a spawn of niggers. The only black Jerry found on her was Johnny; while her spaciousness was filled principally with two-legged white-gods.

He met them everywhere, at the wheel, on lookout, washing decks, polishing brass-work, running aloft, or tailing on to sheets and tackles half a dozen at a time. But there was a difference. There were gods and gods, and Jerry was not long in learning that in the hierarchy of the heaven of these white-gods on the *Ariel*, the sailorizing, ship-working ones were far beneath the captain and his two white-and-gold-clad officers. These, in turn, were less than Harley Kennan and Villa Kennan; for them, it came quickly to him, Harley Kennan commanded. Nevertheless, there was one thing he did not learn and was destined never to learn, namely, the supreme god over all on the *Ariel*. Although he never tried to know, being unable to think to such a distance, he never came to know whether it was Harley Kennan who commanded Villa, or Villa Kennan who commanded Harley. In a way, without vexing himself with the problem, he accepted their over-lordship of the world as dual. Neither out-ranked the other. They seemed to rule co-equal, while all others bowed before them.

It is not true that to feed a dog is to win a dog's heart. Never did Harley or Villa feed Jerry; yet it was to them he elected to belong, them he elected to love and serve rather than to the Japanese steward who regularly fed him. For that matter, Jerry, like any dog, was able to differentiate between the mere direct food-giver and the food source. That is, subconsciously, he was aware that not alone his own food, but the food of all on board found its source in the man and woman. They it was who fed all and ruled all. Captain Winters might give orders to the sailors, but Captain Winters took orders from Harley Kennan. Jerry knew this as indubitably as he acted upon it, although all the while it never entered his head as an item of conscious knowledge.

And, as he had been accustomed, all his life, as with Mister Haggin, Skipper, and even with Bashti and the chief devil devil doctor of Somo, he attached himself to the high gods themselves, and from the gods under them received deference accordingly. As Skipper, on the *Arangi*, and Bashti in Somo, had promulgated taboos, so the man and the woman on the *Ariel* protected Jerry with taboos. From Sano, the Japanese steward, and from him alone, did Jerry receive food. Not from any sailor in whaleboat or launch could he accept, or would he be offered, a bit of biscuit or an invitation to go ashore for a run. Nor did they offer it. Nor were they permitted to become intimate, to the extent of romping and playing with him, nor even of whistling to him along the deck.

By nature a "one-man" dog, all this was very acceptable to Jerry. Differences of degree there were, of course; but no one more delicately and definitely knew those differences than did Jerry himself. Thus, it was permissible for the two officers to greet him with a "Hello," or a "Good morning," and even to touch a hand in a brief and friendly pat to his head. With Captain Winters, however, greater familiarity obtained. Captain Winters could rub his ears, shake hands with his, scratch his back, and even roughly catch him by the jowls. But Captain Winters invariably surrendered him up when the one man and the one woman appeared on deck.

When it came to liberties, delicious, wanton liberties, Jerry alone of all on board could take them with the man and woman, and, on the other hand, they were the only two to whom he permitted liberties. Any indignity that Villa Kennan chose to inflict upon him he was throbbingly glad to receive, such as doubling his ears inside out till they stuck, at the same time making him sit upright, with helpless forefeet paddling the air for equilibrium, while she blew roguishly in his face and nostrils. As bad was Harley Kennan's trick of catching him gloriously asleep on an edge of Villa's skirt and of tickling the hair between his toes and making him kick involuntarily in his sleep, until he kicked himself awake to hearing of gurgles and snickers of laughter at his expense.

406

In turn, at night on deck, wriggling her toes at him under a rug to simulate some strange and crawling creature of an invader, he would dare to simulate his own befoolment and quite disrupt Villa's bed with his frantic ferocious attack on the thing that he knew was only her toes. In gales of laughter, intermingled with half-genuine cries of alarm as almost his teeth caught her toes, she always concluded by gathering him into her arms and laughing the last of her laughter away into his flattened ears of joy and love. Who else, of all on board the *Ariel,* would have dared such devilishness with the lady-god's bed? This question it never entered his mind to ask himself; yet he was fully aware of how exclusively favoured he was.

Another of his deliberate tricks was one discovered by accident. Thrusting his muzzle to meet her in love, he chanced to encounter her face with his soft-hard little nose with such force as to make her recoil and cry out. When, another time, in all innocence this happened again, he became conscious of it and of its effect upon her; and thereafter, when she grew too wildly wild, too wantonly facetious in her teasing playful love of him, he would thrust his muzzle at her face and make her throw her head back to escape him. After a time, learning that if he persisted, she would settle the situation by gathering him into her arms and gurgling into his ears, he made it a point to act his part until such delectable surrender and joyful culmination were achieved.

Never, by accident, in this deliberate game, did he hurt her chin or cheek so severely as he hurt his own tender nose, but in the hurt itself he found more of delight than pain. All of fun it was, all through, and, in addition, it was love fun. Such hurt was more than fun. Such pain was heart-pleasure.

All dogs are god-worshippers. More fortunate than most dogs, Jerry won to a pair of gods that, no matter how much they commanded, loved more. Although his nose might threaten grievously to hurt the cheek of his adored god, rather than have it really hurt he would have spilled out all the love-tide of his heart that constituted the life of him. He did not live for food, for shelter, for a comfortable place between the darknesses that rounded existence. He lived for love. And as surely as he gladly lived for love, would he have died gladly for love.

Not quickly, in Somo, had Jerry's memory of Skipper and Mister Haggin faded. Life in the cannibal village had been too unsatisfying. There had been too little love. Only love can erase the memory of love, or rather, the hurt of lost love. And on board the *Ariel* such erasement occurred quickly. Jerry did not forget Skipper and Mister Haggin. But at the moments he remembered them the yearning that accompanied the memory grew less pronounced and painful. The intervals between the moments widened, nor did Skipper and Mister Haggin take form and reality so frequently in his dreams; for, after the manner of dogs, he dreamed much and vividly.

CHAPTER XXII

Northward, along the leeward coast of Malaita, the *Ariel* worked her leisurely way, threading the colour-riotous lagoon that lay between the shore-reefs and outer-reefs, daring passages so narrow and coral-patched that Captain Winters averred each day added a thousand grey hairs to his head, and dropping anchor off every walled inlet of the outer reef and every mangrove swamp of the mainland that looked promising of cannibal life. For Harley and Villa Kennan were in no hurry. So long as the way was interesting, they dared not how long it proved from anywhere to anywhere.

During this time Jerry learned a new name for himself—or, rather, an entire series of names for himself. This was because of an aversion on Harley Kennan's part against renaming a named thing.

"A name he must have had," he argued to Villa. "Haggin must have named him before he sailed on the *Arangi*. Therefore, nameless he must be until we get back to Tulagi and find out his real name."

"What's in a name?" Villa had begun to tease.

"Everything," her husband retorted. "Think of yourself, shipwrecked, called by your rescuers 'Mrs. Riggs,' or 'Mademoiselle de Maupin,' or just plain 'Topsy.' And think of me being called 'Benedict Arnold,' or ' Judas,' or . . . or . . . 'Haman.' No, keep him nameless, until we find out his original name."

"Must call him something," she objected. "Can't think of him without thinking something."

"Then call him many names, but never the same name twice. Call him 'Dog' to-day, and '*Mister* Dog' to-morrow, and the next day something else."

So it was, more by tone and emphasis and context of situation than by anything else, that Jerry came hazily to identify himself with names such as: Dog, *Mister* Dog, Adventurer, Strong Useful One, Sing Song Silly, Noname, and Quivering Love-Heart. These were a few of the many names lavished on him by Villa. Harley, in turn, addressed him as: Man-Dog, Incorruptible One, Brass Tacks, Then Some, Sin of Gold, South Sea Satrap, Nimrod, Young Nick, and Lion-Slayer. In brief, the man and woman competed with each other to name him most without naming him ever the same. And Jerry, less by sound and syllable than by what of their hearts vibrated in their throats, soon learned to know himself by any name they chose to address to him. He no longer thought of himself as Jerry, but, instead, as any sound that sounded nice or was love-sounded.

His great disappointment (if "disappointment" may be considered to describe an unconsciousness of failure to realize the expected) was in the matter of language. No one on board, not even Harley and Villa, talked Nalasu's talk. All Jerry's large vocabulary, all his proficiency in the use of it, which would have set him apart as a marvel beyond all other dogs in the mastery of speech, was wasted on those of the *Ariel*. They did not speak, much less guess, the existence of the whiff-whuff shorthand language which Nalasu had taught him, and which, Nalasu dead, Jerry alone knew of all living creatures in the world.

In vain Jerry tried it on the lady-god. Sitting squatted on his haunches, his head bowed forward and held between her hands, he would talk and talk and elicit never a responsive word from her. With tiny whines and thin whimperings, with whiffs and whuffs and growly sorts of noises down in his throat, he would try to tell her somewhat of his tale. She was all meltingness of sympathy; she would hold her ear so near to the articulate mouth of him as almost to drown him in the flowing fragrance of her hair; and yet her brain told her nothing of what he uttered, although her heart surely sensed his intent.

"Bless me, Husband-Man!" she would cry out. "The Dog is talking. I know he is talking. He is telling me all about himself. The story of his life is mine, could I but understand. It's right here pouring into my miserable inadequate ears, only I can't catch it."

Harley was sceptical, but her woman's intuition guessed aright.

"I know it!" she would assure her husband. "I tell you he could tell the tale of all his adventures if only we had understanding. No other dog has ever talked this way to me. There's a tale there. I feel its touches. Sometimes almost do I know he is telling of joy, of love, of high elation, and combat. Again, it is indignation, hurt of outrage, despair and sadness."

"Naturally," Harley agreed quietly. "A white man's dog, adrift among the anthropophagi of Malaita, would experience all such sensations and, just as naturally, a white man's woman, a Wife-Woman, a dear, delightful Villa Kennan woman, can of herself imagine such a dog's experiences and deem his silly noises a recital of them, failing to recognize them as projections of her own delicious, sensitive, sympathetic self. The song of the sea from the lips of the shell—Pshaw! The song oneself makes of the sea and puts into the shell."

"Just the same—"

"Always the same," he gallantly cut her off. "Always right, especially when most wrong. Not in navigation, of course, nor in affairs such as the multiplication table, where the brass tacks of reality stud the way of one's ship among the rocks and shoals of the sea; but right, truth beyond truth to truth higher than truth, namely, intuitional truth."

"Now you are laughing at me with your superior man-wisdom," she retorted. "But I know—" she paused for the strength of words she needed, and words forsook her, so that her quick sweeping gesture of hand-touch to heart named authority that overrode all speech.

"We agree—I salute," he laughed gaily. "It was just precisely what I was saying. Our hearts can talk our heads down almost any time, and, best all, our hearts are always right despite the statistic that they are mostly wrong."

Harley Kennan did not believe, and never did believe, his wife's report of the tales Jerry told. And through all his days to the last one of them, he considered the whole matter a pleasant fancy, all poesy of sentiment, on Villa's part.

But Jerry, four-legged, smooth-coated, Irish terrier that he was, had the gift of tongues. If he could not teach languages, at least he could learn

411

languages. Without effort, and quickly, practically with no teaching, he began picking up the language of the *Ariel*. Unfortunately, it was not a whiff-whuff, dog-possible language such as Nalasu had invented. While Jerry came to understand much that was spoken on the *Ariel*, he could speak none of it. Three names, at least, he had for the lady-god: "Villa," "Wife-Woman," "Missis Kennan," for so he heard her variously called. But he could not so call her. This was god-language entire, which only gods could talk. It was unlike the language of Nalasu's devising, which had been a compromise between god-talk and dog-talk, so that a god and a dog could talk in the common medium.

In the same way he learned many names for the one-man god: "*Mister Kennan*," "Harley," "Captain Kennan," and "Skipper." Only in the intimacy of the three of them alone did Jerry hear him called: "Husband-Man," "My Man," "Patient One," "Dear Man," "Lover," and "This Woman's Delight." But in no way could Jerry utter these names in address of the one-man nor the many names in address of the one-woman. Yet on a quiet night with no wind among the trees, often and often had he whispered to Nalasu, by whiff-whuff of name, from a hundred feet away.

One day, bending over him, her hair (drying from a salt-water swim) flying about him, the one-woman, her two hands holding his head and jowls so that his ribbon of kissing tongue just missed her nose in the empty air, sang to him: "'Don't know what to call him, but he's mighty lak' a rose!'"

On another day she repeated this, at the same time singing most of the song to him softly in his ear. In the midst of it Jerry surprised her. Equally true might be the statement that he surprised himself. Never, had he consciously done such a thing before. And he did it without volition. He never intended to do it. For that matter, the very thing he did was what mastered him into doing it. No more than could he refrain from shaking the water from his back after a swim, or from kicking in his sleep when his feet were tickled, could he have avoided doing this imperative thing.

As her voice, in the song, made soft vibrations in his ears, it seemed to him that she grew dim and vague before him, and that somehow, under the soft searching prod of her song, he was otherwhere. So much was he otherwhere that he did the surprising thing. He sat down abruptly, almost cataleptically, drew his head away from the clutch of her hands and out of the entanglement of her hair, and, his nose thrust upward at an angle of forty-five degrees, he began to quiver and to breathe audibly in rhythm to the rhythm of her singing. With a quick jerk, cataleptically, his nose pointed to the zenith, his mouth opened, and a flood of sound poured forth, running swiftly upward in crescendo and slowly falling as it died away.

This howl was the beginning, and it led to the calling him "Sing Song Silly." For Villa Kennan was quick to seize upon the howling her singing induced and to develop it. Never did he hang back when she sat down, extended her welcoming hands to him, and invited: "Come on, Sing Song Silly." He would come to her, sit down with the loved fragrance of her hair in his nostrils, lay the side of his head against hers, point his nose past her ear, and almost immediately follow her when she began her low singing. Minor strains were especially provocative in getting him started, and, once started, he would sing with her as long as she wished.

Singing it truly was. Apt in all ways of speech, he quickly learned to soften and subdue his howl till it was mellow and golden. Even could he manage it to die away almost to a whisper, and to rise and fall, accelerate and retard, in obedience to her own voice and in accord with it.

Jerry enjoyed the singing much in the same way the opium eater enjoys his dreams. For dream he did, vaguely and indistinctly, eyes wide open and awake, the lady-god's hair in a faint-scented cloud about him, her voice mourning with his, his consciousness drowning in the dreams of otherwhereness that came to him of the singing and that was the singing. Memories of pain were his, but of pain so long forgotten that it was no longer pain. Rather did it permeate him with a delicious sadness, and lift him away and out of the *Ariel* (lying at anchor in some coral lagoon) to that unreal place of Otherwhere.

For visions were his at such times. In the cold bleakness of night, it would seem he sat on a bare hill and raised his howl to the stars, while out of

413

the dark, from far away, would drift to him an answering howl. And other howls, near and far, would drift along until the night was vocal with his kind. His kind it was. Without knowing it he *knew* it, this camaraderie of the land of Otherwhere.

Nalasu, in teaching him the whiff-whuff language, deliberately had gone into the intelligence of him; but Villa, unwitting of what she was doing, went into the heart of him, and into the heart of his heredity, touching the profoundest chords of ancient memories and making them respond.

As instance: dim shapes and shadowy forms would sometimes appear to him out of the night, and as they flitted spectrally past he would hear, as in a dream, the hunting cries of the pack; and, as his pulse quickened, his own hunting instinct would rouse until his controlled soft-howling in the song broke into eager whinings. His head would lower out of the entanglement of the woman's hair; his feet would begin making restless, spasmodic movements as if running; and Presto, in a flash, he would be out and away, across the face of time, out of reality and into the dream, himself running in the midst of those shadowy forms in the hunting fellowship of the pack.

And as men have ever desired the dust of the poppy and the juice of the hemp, so Jerry desired the joys that were his when Villa Kennan opened her arms to him, embraced him with her hair, and sang him across time and space into the dream of his ancient kind.

Not always, however, were such experiences his when they sang together. Usually, unaccompanied by visions, he knew no more than vaguenesses of sensations, sadly sweet, ghosts of memories that they were. At other times, incited by such sadness, images of Skipper and *Mister* Haggin would throng his mind; images, too, of Terrence, and Biddy, and Michael, and the rest of the long-vanished life at Meringe Plantation.

"My dear," Harley said to Villa at the conclusion of one such singing, "it's fortunate for him that you are not an animal trainer, or, rather, I suppose, it would be better called 'trained animal show-woman'; for you'd be topping the bill in all the music-halls and vaudeville houses of the world."

414

"If I did," she replied, "I know he'd just love to do it with me—"

"Which would make it a very unusual turn," Harley caught her up.

"You mean . . .?"

"That in about one turn in a hundred does the animal love its work or is the animal loved by its trainer."

"I thought all the cruelty had been done away with long ago," she contended.

"So the audience thinks, and the audience is ninety-nine times wrong."

Villa heaved a great sigh of renunciation as she said, "Then I suppose I must abandon such promising and lucrative career right now in the very moment you have discovered it for me. Just the same the billboards would look splendid with my name in the hugest letters—"

"Villa Kennan the Thrush-throated Songstress, and Sing Song Silly the Irish-Terrier Tenor," her husband pictured the head-lines for her.

And with dancing eyes and lolling tongue Jerry joined in the laughter, not because he knew what it was about, but because it tokened they were happy and his love prompted him to be happy with them.

For Jerry had found, and in the uttermost, what his nature craved—the love of a god. Recognizing the duality of their lordship over the *Ariel*, he loved the pair of them; yet, somehow, perhaps because she had penetrated deepest into his heart with her magic voice that transported him to the land of Otherwhere, he loved the lady-god beyond all love he had ever known, not even excluding his love for Skipper.

CHAPTER XXIII

One thing Jerry learned early on the *Ariel*, namely, that nigger-chasing was not permitted. Eager to please and serve his new gods, he took advantage of the first opportunity to worry a canoe-load of blacks who came visiting on board. The quick chiding of Villa and the command of Harley made him pause in amazement. Fully believing he had been mistaken, he resumed his ragging of the particular black he had picked upon. This time Harley's voice was peremptory, and Jerry came to him, his wagging tail and wriggling body all eagerness of apology, as was his rose-strip of tongue that kissed the hand of forgiveness with which Harley patted him.

Next, Villa called him to her. Holding him close to her with her hands on his jowls, eye to eye and nose to nose, she talked to him earnestly about the sin of nigger-chasing. She told him that he was no common bush-dog, but a blooded Irish gentleman, and that no dog that was a gentleman ever did such things as chase unoffending black men. To all of which he listened with unblinking serious eyes, understanding little of what she said, yet comprehending all. "Naughty" was a word in the *Ariel* language he had already learned, and she used it several times. "Naughty," to him, meant "must not," and was by way of expressing a taboo.

Since it was their way and their will, who was he, he might well have asked himself, to disobey their rule or question it? If niggers were not to be chased, then chase them he would not, despite the fact that Skipper had encouraged him to chase them. Not in such set terms did Jerry consider the matter; but in his own way he accepted the conclusions.

Love of a god, with him, implied service. It pleased him to please with service. And the foundation-stone of service, in his case, was obedience. Yet it strained him sore for a time to refrain from snarl and snap when the legs of strange and presumptuous blacks passed near him along the *Ariel's* white deck.

But there were times and times, as he was to learn, and the time came when Villa Kennan wanted a bath, a real bath in fresh, rain-descended, running water, and when Johnny, the black pilot from Tulagi, made a mistake. The chart showed a mile of the Suli river where it emptied into the sea. Why it showed only a mile was because no white man had ever explored it farther. When Villa proposed the bath, her husband advised with Johnny. Johnny shook his head.

"No fella boy stop 'm along that place," he said. "No make 'm trouble along you. Bush fella boy stop 'm long way too much."

So it was that the launch went ashore, and, while its crew lolled in the shade of the beach coconuts, Villa, Harley, and Jerry followed the river inland a quarter of a mile to the first likely pool.

"One can never be too sure," Harley said, taking his automatic pistol from its holster and placing it on top his heap of clothes. "A stray bunch of blacks might just happen to surprise us."

Villa stepped into the water to her knees, looked up at the dark jungle roof high overhead through which only occasional shafts of sunlight penetrated, and shuddered.

"An appropriate setting for a dark deed," she smiled, then scooped a handful of chill water against her husband, who plunged in in pursuit.

For a time Jerry sat by their clothes and watched the frolic. Then the drifting shadow of a huge butterfly attracted his attention, and soon he was nosing through the jungle on the trail of a wood-rat. It was not a very fresh trail. He knew that well enough; but in the deeps of him were all his instincts of ancient training—instincts to hunt, to prowl, to pursue living things, in short, to play the game of getting his own meat though for ages man had got the meat for him and his kind.

So it was, exercising faculties that were no longer necessary, but that were still alive in him and clamorous for exercise, he followed the long-since passed wood-rat with all the soft-footed crouching craft of the meat-pursuer and with utmost fineness of reading the scent. The trail crossed a fresh trail, a trail very fresh, very immediately fresh. As if a rope had been attached to it, his head was jerked abruptly to right angles with his body. The unmistakable smell of a black was in his nostrils. Further, it was a strange black, for he did not identify it with the many he possessed filed away in the pigeon-holes of his brain.

Forgotten was the stale wood-rat as he followed the new trail. Curiosity and play impelled him. He had no thought of apprehension for Villa and Harley—not even when he reached the spot where the black, evidently startled by bearing their voices, had stood and debated, and so left a very strong scent. From this point the trail swerved off toward the pool. Nervously alert, strung to extreme tension, but without alarm, still playing at the game of tracking, Jerry followed.

From the pool came occasional cries and laughter, and each time they reached his ears Jerry experienced glad little thrills. Had he been asked, and had he been able to express the sensations of emotion in terms of thought, he would have said that the sweetest sound in the world was any sound of Villa Kennan's voice, and that, next sweetest, was any sound of Harley Kennan's voice. Their voices thrilled him, always, reminding him of his love for them and that he was beloved of them.

With the first sight of the strange black, which occurred close to the pool, Jerry's suspicions were aroused. He was not conducting himself as an ordinary black, not on evil intent, should conduct himself. Instead, he betrayed all the actions of one who lurked in the perpetration of harm. He crouched on the jungle floor, peering around a great root of a board tree. Jerry bristled and himself crouched as he watched.

Once, the black raised his rifle half-way to his shoulder; but, with an outburst of splashing and laughter, his unconscious victims evidently removed themselves from his field of vision. His rifle was no old-fashioned Snider, but a modern, repeating Winchester; and he showed habituation to firing it from his shoulder rather than from the hip after the manner of most Malaitans.

Not satisfied with his position by the board tree, he lowered his gun to his side and crept closer to the pool. Jerry crouched low and followed. So low did he crouch that his head, extended horizontally forward, was much lower than his shoulders which were humped up queerly and composed the highest part of him. When the black paused, Jerry paused, as if instantly frozen. When the black moved, he moved, but more swiftly, cutting down the distance between them. And all the while the hair of his neck and shoulders bristled in recurrent waves of ferocity and wrath. No golden dog this, ears flattened and tongue laughing in the arms of the lady-god, no Sing Song Silly chanting ancient memories in the cloud-entanglement of her hair; but a four-legged creature of battle, a fanged killer ripe to rend and destroy.

Jerry intended to attack as soon as he had crept sufficiently near. He was unaware of the *Ariel* taboo against nigger-chasing. At that moment it had no place in his consciousness. All he knew was that harm threatened the man and woman and that this nigger intended this harm.

So much had Jerry gained on his quarry, that when again the black squatted for his shot, Jerry deemed he was near enough to rush. The rifle was coming to shoulder when he sprang forward. Swiftly as he sprang, he made no sound, and his victim's first warning was when Jerry's body, launched like a projectile, smote the black squarely between the shoulders. At the same moment his teeth entered the back of the neck, but too near the base in the lumpy shoulder muscles to permit the fangs to penetrate to the spinal cord.

In the first fright of surprise, the black's finger pulled the trigger and his throat loosed an unearthly yell. Knocked forward on his face, he rolled over and grappled with Jerry, who slashed cheek-bone and cheek and ribboned an ear; for it is the way of an Irish terrier to bite repeatedly and quickly rather than to hold a bulldog grip.

When Harley Kennan, automatic in hand and naked as Adam, reached the spot, he found dog and man locked together and tearing up the forest mould in their struggle. The black, his face streaming blood, was throttling Jerry with both hands around his neck; and Jerry, snorting, choking, snarling, was scratching for dear life with the claws of his hind feet. No puppy claws were they, but the stout claws of a mature dog that were stiffened by a backing of hard muscles. And they ripped naked chest and abdomen full length again

419

and again until the whole front of the man was streaming red. Harley Kennan did not dare chance a shot, so closely were the combatants locked. Instead, stepping in close; he smashed down the butt of his automatic upon the side of the man's head. Released by the relaxing of the stunned black's hands, Jerry flung himself in a flash upon the exposed throat, and only Harley's hand on his neck and Harley's sharp command made him cease and stand clear. He trembled with rage and continued to snarl ferociously, although he would desist long enough to glance up with his eyes, flatten his ears, and wag his tail each time Harley uttered "Good boy."

"Good boy" he knew for praise; and he knew beyond any doubt, by Harley's repetition of it, that he had served him and served him well.

"Do you know the beggar intended to bush-whack us," Harley told Villa, who, half-dressed and still dressing, had joined him. "It wasn't fifty feet and he couldn't have missed. Look at the Winchester. No old smooth bore. And a fellow with a gun like that would know how to use it."

"But why didn't he?" she queried.

Her husband pointed to Jerry.

Villa's eyes brightened with quick comprehension. "You mean . . . ?" she began.

He nodded. "Just that. Sing Song Silly beat him to it." He bent, rolled the man over, and discovered the lacerated back of the neck. "That's where he landed on him first, and he must have had his finger on the trigger, drawing down on you and me, most likely me first, when Sing Song Silly broke up his calculations."

Villa was only half hearing, for she had Jerry in her arms and was calling him "Blessed Dog," the while she stilled his snarling and soothed down the last bristling hair.

But Jerry snarled again and was for leaping upon the black when he stirred restlessly and dizzily sat up. Harley removed a knife from between the bare skin and a belt.

420

"What name belong you?" he demanded.

But the black had eyes only for Jerry, staring at him in wondering amaze until he pieced the situation together in his growing clarity of brain and realized that such a small chunky animal had spoiled his game.

"My word," he grinned to Harley, "that fella dog put 'm crimp along me any amount."

He felt out the wounds of his neck and face, while his eyes embraced the fact that the white master was in possession of his rifle.

"You give 'm musket belong me," he said impudently.

"I give 'm you bang alongside head," was Harley's answer.

"He doesn't seem to me to be a regular Malaitan," he told Villa. "In the first place, where would he get a rifle like that? Then think of his nerve. He must have seen us drop anchor, and he must have known our launch was on the beach. Yet he played to take our heads and get away with them back into the bush—"

"What name belong you?" he again demanded.

But not until Johnny and the launch crew arrived breathless from their run, did he learn. Johnny's eyes gloated when he beheld the prisoner, and he addressed Kennan in evident excitement.

"You give 'm me that fella boy," he begged. "Eh? You give 'm me that fella boy."

"What name you want 'm?"

Not for some time would Johnny answer this question, and then only when Kennan told him that there was no harm done and that he intended to let the black go. At this Johnny protested vehemently.

"Maybe you fetch 'm that fella boy along Government House, Tulagi, Government House give 'm you twenty pounds. Him plenty bad fella boy too much. Makawao he name stop along him. Bad fella boy too much. Him Queensland boy—"

"What name Queensland?" Kennan interrupted. "He belong that fella place?"

Johnny shook his head.

"Him belong along Malaita first time. Long time before too much he recruit 'm along schooner go work along Queensland."

"He's a return Queenslander," Harley interpreted to Villa. "You know, when Australia went 'all white,' the Queensland plantations had to send all the black birds back. This Makawao is evidently one of them, and a hard case as well, if there's anything in Johnny's gammon about twenty pounds reward for him. That's a big price for a black."

Johnny continued his explanation which, reduced to flat and sober English, was to the effect that Makawao had always borne a bad character. In Queensland he had served a total of four years in jail for thefts, robberies, and attempted murder. Returned to the Solomons by the Australian government, he had recruited on Buli Plantation for the purpose—as was afterwards proved—of getting arms and ammunition. For an attempt to kill the manager he had received fifty lashes at Tulagi and served a year. Returned to Buli Plantation to finish his labour service, he had contrived to kill the owner in the manager's absence and to escape in a whaleboat.

In the whaleboat with him he had taken all the weapons and ammunition of the plantation, the owner's head, ten Malaita recruits, and two recruits from San Cristobal—the two last because they were salt-water men and could handle the whaleboat. Himself and the ten Malaitans, being bushmen, were too ignorant of the sea to dare the long passage from Guadalcanar.

On the way, he had raided the little islet of Ugi, sacked the store, and taken the head of the solitary trader, a gentle-souled half-caste from Norfolk Island who traced back directly to a Pitcairn ancestry straight from the loins of McCoy of the Bounty. Arrived safely at Malaita, he and his fellows, no longer having any use for the two San Cristobal boys, had taken their heads and eaten their bodies.

"My word, him bad fella boy any amount," Johnny finished his tale. "Government House, Tulagi, damn glad give 'm twenty pounds along that fella."

422

"You blessed Sing Song Silly," Villa, murmured in Jerry's ears. "If it hadn't been for you—"

"Your head and mine would even now be galumping through the bush as Makawao hit the high places for home," Harley concluded for her. "My word, some fella dog that, any amount," he added lightly. "And I gave him merry Ned just the other day for nigger-chasing, and he knew his business better than I did all the time."

"If anybody tries to claim him—" Villa threatened.

Harley confirmed her muttered sentiment with a nod.

"Any way," he said, with a smile, "there would have been one consolation if your head had gone up into the bush."

"Consolation!" she cried, throaty with indignation.

"Why, yes; because in that case my head would have gone along."

"You dear and blessed Husband-Man," she murmured, a quick cloudiness of moisture in her eyes, as with her eyes she embraced him, her arms still around Jerry, who, sensing the ecstasy of the moment, kissed her fragrant cheek with his ribbon-tongue of love.

CHAPTER XXIV

When the *Ariel* cleared from Malu, on the north-west coast of Malaita, Malaita sank down beneath the sea-rim astern and, so far as Jerry's life was concerned, remained sunk for ever—another vanished world, that, in his consciousness, partook of the ultimate nothingness that had befallen Skipper. For all Jerry might have known, though he pondered it not, Malaita was a universe, beheaded and resting on the knees of some brooding lesser god, himself vastly mightier than Bashti whose knees bore the brooding weight of Skipper's sun-dried, smoke-cured head, this lesser god vexed and questing, feeling and guessing at the dual twin-mysteries of time and space and of motion and matter, above, beneath, around, and beyond him.

Only, in Jerry's case, there was no pondering of the problem, no awareness of the existence of such mysteries. He merely accepted Malaita as another world that had ceased to be. He remembered it as he remembered dreams. Himself a live thing, solid and substantial, possessed of weight and dimension, a reality incontrovertible, he moved through the space and place of being, concrete, hard, quick, convincing, an absoluteness of something surrounded by the shades and shadows of the fluxing phantasmagoria of nothing.

He took his worlds one by one. One by one his worlds evaporated, rose beyond his vision as vapours in the hot alembic of the sun, sank for ever beneath sea-levels, themselves unreal and passing as the phantoms of a dream. The totality of the minute, simple world of the humans, microscopic and negligible as it was in the siderial universe, was as far beyond his guessing as is the siderial universe beyond the starriest guesses and most abysmal imaginings of man.

Jerry was never to see the dark island of savagery again, although often in his sleeping dreams it was to return to him in vivid illusion, as he relived his days upon it, from the destruction of the *Arangi* and the man-eating orgy on the beach to his flight from the shell-scattered house and flesh of Nalasu.

These dream episodes constituted for him another land of Otherwhere, mysterious, unreal, and evanescent as clouds drifting across the sky or bubbles taking iridescent form and bursting on the surface of the sea. Froth and foam it was, quick-vanishing as he awoke, non-existent as Skipper, Skipper's head on the withered knees of Bashti in the lofty grass house. Malaita the real, Malaita the concrete and ponderable, vanished and vanished for ever, as Meringe had vanished, as Skipper had vanished, into the nothingness.

From Malaita the *Ariel* steered west of north to Ongtong Java and to Tasman—great atolls that sweltered under the Line not quite awash in the vast waste of the West South Pacific. After Tasman was another wide sea-stretch to the high island of Bougainville. Thence, bearing generally south-east and making slow progress in the dead beat to windward, the *Ariel* dropped anchor in nearly every harbour of the Solomons, from Choiseul and Ronongo islands, to the islands of Kulambangra, Vangunu, Pavuvu, and New Georgia. Even did she ride to anchor, desolately lonely, in the Bay of a Thousand Ships.

Last of all, so far as concerned the Solomons, her anchor rumbled down and bit into the coral-sanded bottom of the harbour of Tulagi, where, ashore on Florida Island, lived and ruled the Resident Commissioner.

To the Commissioner, Harley Kennan duly turned over Makawao, who was committed to a grass-house jail, well guarded, to sit in leg-irons against the time of trial for his many crimes. And Johnny, the pilot, ere he returned to the service of the Commissioner, received a fair portion of the twenty pounds of head money that Kennan divided among the members of the launch crew who had raced through the jungle to the rescue the day Jerry had taken Makawao by the back of the neck and startled him into pulling the trigger of his unaimed rifle.

"I'll tell you his name," the Commissioner said, as they sat on the wide veranda of his bungalow. "It's one of Haggin's terriers—Haggin of Meringe Lagoon. The dog's father is Terrence, the mother is Biddy. The dog's own name is Jerry, for I was present at the christening before ever his eyes were open. Better yet, I'll show you his brother. His brother's name is Michael.

He's nigger-chaser on the *Eugénie,* the two-topmast schooner that rides abreast of you. Captain Kellar is the skipper. I'll have him bring Michael ashore. Beyond all doubt, this Jerry is the sole survivor of the *Arangi.*"

"When I get the time, and a sufficient margin of funds, I shall pay a visit to Chief Bashti—oh, no British cruiser program. I'll charter a couple of trading ketches, take my own black police force and as many white men as I cannot prevent from volunteering. There won't be any shelling of grass houses. I'll land my shore party down the coast and cut in and come down upon Somo from the rear, timing my vessels to arrive on Somo's sea-front at the same time."

"You will answer slaughter with slaughter?" Villa Kennan objected.

"I will answer slaughter with law," the Commissioner replied. "I will teach Somo law. I hope that no accidents will occur. I hope that no life will be lost on either side. I know, however, that I shall recover Captain Van Horn's head, and his mate Borckman's, and bring them back to Tulagi for Christian burial. I know that I shall get old Bashti by the scruff of the neck and sit him down while I pump law and square-dealing into him. Of course . . ."

The Commissioner, ascetic-looking, an Oxford graduate, narrow-shouldered and elderly, tired-eyed and bespectacled like the scholar he was, like the scientist he was, shrugged his shoulders. "Of course, if they are not amenable to reason, there may be trouble, and some of them and some of us will get hurt. But, one way or the other, the conclusion will be the same. Old Bashti will learn that it is expedient to maintain white men's heads on their shoulders."

"But how will he learn?" Villa Kennan asked. "If he is shrewd enough not to fight you, and merely sits and listens to your English law, it will be no more than a huge joke to him. He will no more than pay the price of listening to a lecture for any atrocity he commits."

"On the contrary, my dear Mrs. Kennan. If he listens peaceably to the lecture, I shall fine him only a hundred thousand coconuts, five tons of ivory nut, one hundred fathoms of shell money, and twenty fat pigs. If he refuses to listen to the lecture and goes on the war path, then, unpleasantly for me, I assure you, I shall be compelled to thrash him and his village, first: and, next, I shall triple the fine he must pay and lecture the law into him a trifle more compendiously."

"Suppose he doesn't fight, stops his ears to the lecture, and declines to pay?" Villa Kennan persisted.

"Then he shall be my guest, here in Tulagi, until he changes his mind and heart, and does pay, and listens to an entire course of lectures."

* * * * *

So it was that Jerry came to hear his old-time name on the lips of Villa and Harley, and saw once again his full-brother Michael.

"Say nothing," Harley muttered to Villa, as they made out, peering over the bow of the shore-coming whaleboat, the rough coat, red-wheaten in colour, of Michael. "We won't know anything about anything, and we won't even let on we're watching what they do."

Jerry, feigning interest in digging a hole in the sand as if he were on a fresh scent, was unaware of Michael's nearness. In fact, so well had Jerry feigned that he had forgotten it was all a game, and his interest was very real as he sniffed and snorted joyously in the bottom of the hole he had dug. So deep was it, that all he showed of himself was his hind-legs, his rump, and an intelligent and stiffly erect stump of a tail.

Little wonder that he and Michael failed to see each other. And Michael, spilling over with unused vitality from the cramped space of the *Eugénie's* deck, scampered down the beach in a hurly-burly of joy, scenting a thousand intimate land-scents as he ran, and describing a jerky and eccentric course as he made short dashes and good-natured snaps at the coconut crabs that scuttled across his path to the safety of the water or reared up and menaced him with formidable claws and a spluttering and foaming of the shell-lids of their mouths.

427

The beach was only so long. The end of it reached where rose the rugged wall of a headland, and while the Commissioner introduced Captain Kellar to Mr. and Mrs. Kennan, Michael came tearing back across the wet-hard sand. So interested was he in everything that he failed to notice the small rear-end portion of Jerry that was visible above the level surface of the beach. Jerry's ears had given him warning, and, the precise instant that he backed hurriedly up and out of the hole, Michael collided with him. As Jerry was rolled, and as Michael fell clear over him, both erupted into ferocious snarls and growls. They regained their legs, bristled and showed teeth at each other, and stalked stiff-leggedly, in a stately and dignified sort of way, as they drew intimidating semi-circles about each other.

But they were fooling all the while, and were more than a trifle embarrassed. For in each of their brains were bright identification pictures of the plantation house and compound and beach of Meringe. They knew, but they were reticent of recognition. No longer puppies, vaguely proud of the sedateness of maturity, they strove to be proud and sedate while all their impulse was to rush together in a frantic ecstasy.

Michael it was, less travelled in the world than Jerry, by nature not so self-controlled, who threw the play-acting of dignity to the wind, and, with shrill whinings of emotion, with body-wrigglings of delight, flashed out his tongue of love and shouldered his brother roughly in eagerness to get near to him.

Jerry responded as eagerly with kiss of tongue and contact of shoulder; then both, springing apart, looked at each other, alert and querying, almost in half challenge, Jerry's ears pricked into living interrogations, Michael's one good ear similarly questioning, his withered ear retaining its permanent queer and crinkly cock in the tip of it. As one, they sprang away in a wild scurry down the beach, side by side, laughing to each other and occasionally striking their shoulders together as they ran.

"No doubt of it," said the Commissioner. "The very way their father and mother run. I have watched them often."

* * * * *

But, after ten days of comradeship, came the parting. It was Michael's first visit on the *Ariel*, and he and Jerry had spent a frolicking half-hour on her white deck amid the sound and commotion of hoisting in boats, making sail, and heaving out anchor. As the *Ariel* began to move through the water and heeled to the filling of her canvas by the brisk trade-wind, the Commissioner and Captain Kellar shook last farewells and scrambled down the gang-plank to their waiting whaleboats. At the last moment Captain Kellar had caught Michael up, tucked him under an arm, and with him dropped into the, sternsheets of his whaleboat.

Painters were cast off, and in the sternsheets of each boat solitary white men were standing up, heads bared in graciousness of conduct to the furnace-stab of the tropic sun, as they waved additional and final farewells. And Michael, swept by the contagion of excitement, barked and barked again, as if it were a festival of the gods being celebrated.

"Say good-bye to your brother, Jerry," Villa Kennan prompted in Jerry's ear, as she held him, his quivering flanks between her two palms, on the rail where she had lifted him.

And Jerry, not understanding her speech, torn about with conflicting desires, acknowledged her speech with wriggling body, a quick back-toss of head, and a red flash of kissing tongue, and, the next moment, his head over the rail and lowered to see the swiftly diminishing Michael, was mouthing grief and woe very much akin to the grief and woe his mother, Biddy, had mouthed in the long ago, on the beach of Meringe, when he had sailed away with Skipper.

For Jerry had learned partings, and beyond all peradventure this was a parting, though little he dreamed that he would again meet Michael across the years and across the world, in a fabled valley of far California, where they would live out their days in the hearts and arms of the beloved gods.

Michael, his forefeet on the gunwale, barked to him in a puzzled, questioning sort of way, and Jerry whimpered back incommunicable understanding. The lady-god pressed his two flanks together reassuringly, and he turned to her, his cool nose touched questioningly to her cheek. She

429

gathered his body close against her breast in one encircling arm, her free hand resting on the rail, half-closed, a pink-and-white heart of flower, fragrant and seducing. Jerry's nose quested the way of it. The aperture invited. With snuggling, budging, and nudging-movements he spread the fingers slightly wider as his nose penetrated into the sheer delight and loveliness of her hand.

He came to rest, his golden muzzle soft-enfolded to the eyes, and was very still, all forgetful of the *Ariel* showing her copper to the sun under the press of the wind, all forgetful of Michael growing small in the distance as the whaleboat grew small astern. No less still was Villa. Both were playing the game, although to her it was new.

As long as he could possibly contain himself, Jerry maintained his stiffness. And then, his love bursting beyond the control of him, he gave a sniff—as prodigious a one as he had sniffed into the tunnel of Skipper's hand in the long ago on the deck of the *Arangi*. And, as Skipper had relaxed into the laughter of love, so did the lady-god now. She gurgled gleefully. Her fingers tightened, in a caress that almost hurt, on Jerry's muzzle. Her other hand and arm crushed him against her till he gasped. Yet all the while his stump of tail valiantly bobbed back and forth, and, when released from such blissful contact, his silky ears flattened back and down as, with first a scarlet slash of tongue to cheek, he seized her hand between his teeth and dented the soft skin with a love bite that did not hurt.

And so, for Jerry, vanished Tulagi, its Commissioner's bungalow on top of the hill, its vessels riding to anchor in the harbour, and Michael, his full blood-brother. He had grown accustomed to such vanishments. In such way had vanished as in the mirage of a dream, Meringe, Somo, and the *Arangi*. In such way had vanished all the worlds and harbours and roadsteads and atoll lagoons where the *Ariel* had lifted her laid anchor and gone on across and over the erasing sea-rim.

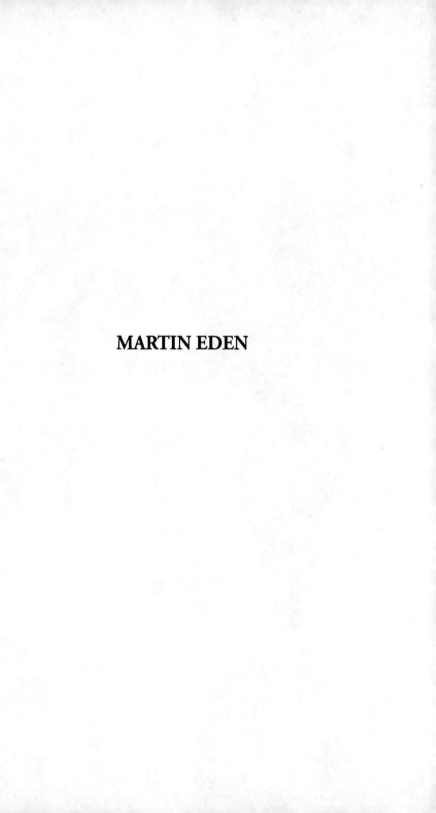

MARTIN EDEN

CHAPTER I

The one opened the door with a latch-key and went in, followed by a young fellow who awkwardly removed his cap. He wore rough clothes that smacked of the sea, and he was manifestly out of place in the spacious hall in which he found himself. He did not know what to do with his cap, and was stuffing it into his coat pocket when the other took it from him. The act was done quietly and naturally, and the awkward young fellow appreciated it. "He understands," was his thought. "He'll see me through all right."

He walked at the other's heels with a swing to his shoulders, and his legs spread unwittingly, as if the level floors were tilting up and sinking down to the heave and lunge of the sea. The wide rooms seemed too narrow for his rolling gait, and to himself he was in terror lest his broad shoulders should collide with the doorways or sweep the bric-a-brac from the low mantel. He recoiled from side to side between the various objects and multiplied the hazards that in reality lodged only in his mind. Between a grand piano and a centre-table piled high with books was space for a half a dozen to walk abreast, yet he essayed it with trepidation. His heavy arms hung loosely at his sides. He did not know what to do with those arms and hands, and when, to his excited vision, one arm seemed liable to brush against the books on the table, he lurched away like a frightened horse, barely missing the piano stool. He watched the easy walk of the other in front of him, and for the first time realized that his walk was different from that of other men. He experienced a momentary pang of shame that he should walk so uncouthly. The sweat burst through the skin of his forehead in tiny beads, and he paused and mopped his bronzed face with his handkerchief.

"Hold on, Arthur, my boy," he said, attempting to mask his anxiety with facetious utterance. "This is too much all at once for yours truly. Give me a chance to get my nerve. You know I didn't want to come, an' I guess your fam'ly ain't hankerin' to see me neither."

"That's all right," was the reassuring answer. "You mustn't be frightened at us. We're just homely people—Hello, there's a letter for me."

He stepped back to the table, tore open the envelope, and began to read, giving the stranger an opportunity to recover himself. And the stranger understood and appreciated. His was the gift of sympathy, understanding; and beneath his alarmed exterior that sympathetic process went on. He mopped his forehead dry and glanced about him with a controlled face, though in the eyes there was an expression such as wild animals betray when they fear the trap. He was surrounded by the unknown, apprehensive of what might happen, ignorant of what he should do, aware that he walked and bore himself awkwardly, fearful that every attribute and power of him was similarly afflicted. He was keenly sensitive, hopelessly self-conscious, and the amused glance that the other stole privily at him over the top of the letter burned into him like a dagger-thrust. He saw the glance, but he gave no sign, for among the things he had learned was discipline. Also, that dagger-thrust went to his pride. He cursed himself for having come, and at the same time resolved that, happen what would, having come, he would carry it through. The lines of his face hardened, and into his eyes came a fighting light. He looked about more unconcernedly, sharply observant, every detail of the pretty interior registering itself on his brain. His eyes were wide apart; nothing in their field of vision escaped; and as they drank in the beauty before them the fighting light died out and a warm glow took its place. He was responsive to beauty, and here was cause to respond.

An oil painting caught and held him. A heavy surf thundered and burst over an outjutting rock; lowering storm-clouds covered the sky; and, outside the line of surf, a pilot-schooner, close-hauled, heeled over till every detail of her deck was visible, was surging along against a stormy sunset sky. There was beauty, and it drew him irresistibly. He forgot his awkward walk and came closer to the painting, very close. The beauty faded out of the canvas. His face expressed his bepuzzlement. He stared at what seemed a careless daub of paint, then stepped away. Immediately all the beauty flashed back into the canvas. "A trick picture," was his thought, as he dismissed it, though in the midst of the multitudinous impressions he was receiving he found time to feel a prod of indignation that so much beauty should be sacrificed to make a trick. He did not know painting. He had been brought up on chromos and lithographs that were always definite and sharp, near or far. He had seen oil paintings, it was true, in the show windows of shops, but the glass of the windows had prevented his eager eyes from approaching too near.

He glanced around at his friend reading the letter and saw the books on the table. Into his eyes leaped a wistfulness and a yearning as promptly as the yearning leaps into the eyes of a starving man at sight of food. An impulsive stride, with one lurch to right and left of the shoulders, brought him to the table, where he began affectionately handling the books. He glanced at the titles and the authors' names, read fragments of text, caressing the volumes with his eyes and hands, and, once, recognized a book he had read. For the rest, they were strange books and strange authors. He chanced upon a volume of Swinburne and began reading steadily, forgetful of where he was, his face glowing. Twice he closed the book on his forefinger to look at the name of the author. Swinburne! he would remember that name. That fellow had eyes, and he had certainly seen color and flashing light. But who was Swinburne? Was he dead a hundred years or so, like most of the poets? Or was he alive still, and writing? He turned to the title-page . . . yes, he had written other books; well, he would go to the free library the first thing in the morning and try to get hold of some of Swinburne's stuff. He went back to the text and lost himself. He did not notice that a young woman had entered the room. The first he knew was when he heard Arthur's voice saying:-

"Ruth, this is Mr. Eden."

The book was closed on his forefinger, and before he turned he was thrilling to the first new impression, which was not of the girl, but of her brother's words. Under that muscled body of his he was a mass of quivering sensibilities. At the slightest impact of the outside world upon his consciousness, his thoughts, sympathies, and emotions leapt and played like lambent flame. He was extraordinarily receptive and responsive, while his imagination, pitched high, was ever at work establishing relations of likeness and difference. "Mr. Eden," was what he had thrilled to—he who had been called "Eden," or "Martin Eden," or just "Martin," all his life. And "Mister!" It was certainly going some, was his internal comment. His mind seemed to turn, on the instant, into a vast camera obscura, and he saw arrayed around his consciousness endless pictures from his life, of stoke-holes and forecastles, camps and beaches, jails and boozing-kens, fever-hospitals and slum streets, wherein the thread of association was the fashion in which he had been addressed in those various situations.

And then he turned and saw the girl. The phantasmagoria of his brain vanished at sight of her. She was a pale, ethereal creature, with wide, spiritual blue eyes and a wealth of golden hair. He did not know how she was dressed, except that the dress was as wonderful as she. He likened her to a pale gold flower upon a slender stem. No, she was a spirit, a divinity, a goddess; such sublimated beauty was not of the earth. Or perhaps the books were right, and there were many such as she in the upper walks of life. She might well be sung by that chap, Swinburne. Perhaps he had had somebody like her in mind when he painted that girl, Iseult, in the book there on the table. All this plethora of sight, and feeling, and thought occurred on the instant. There was no pause of the realities wherein he moved. He saw her hand coming out to his, and she looked him straight in the eyes as she shook hands, frankly, like a man. The women he had known did not shake hands that way. For that matter, most of them did not shake hands at all. A flood of associations, visions of various ways he had made the acquaintance of women, rushed into his mind and threatened to swamp it. But he shook them aside and looked at her. Never had he seen such a woman. The women he had known! Immediately, beside her, on either hand, ranged the women he had known. For an eternal second he stood in the midst of a portrait gallery, wherein she occupied the central place, while about her were limned many women, all to be weighed and measured by a fleeting glance, herself the unit of weight and measure. He saw the weak and sickly faces of the girls of the factories, and the simpering, boisterous girls from the south of Market. There were women of the cattle camps, and swarthy cigarette-smoking women of Old Mexico. These, in turn, were crowded out by Japanese women, doll-like, stepping mincingly on wooden clogs; by Eurasians, delicate featured, stamped with degeneracy; by full-bodied South-Sea-Island women, flower-crowned and brown-skinned. All these were blotted out by a grotesque and terrible nightmare brood—frowsy, shuffling creatures from the pavements of Whitechapel, gin-bloated hags of the stews, and all the vast hell's following of harpies, vile-mouthed and filthy, that under the guise of monstrous female form prey upon sailors, the scrapings of the ports, the scum and slime of the human pit.

"Won't you sit down, Mr. Eden?" the girl was saying. "I have been looking forward to meeting you ever since Arthur told us. It was brave of you—"

He waved his hand deprecatingly and muttered that it was nothing at all, what he had done, and that any fellow would have done it. She noticed that the hand he waved was covered with fresh abrasions, in the process of healing, and a glance at the other loose-hanging hand showed it to be in the same condition. Also, with quick, critical eye, she noted a scar on his cheek, another that peeped out from under the hair of the forehead, and a third that ran down and disappeared under the starched collar. She repressed a smile at sight of the red line that marked the chafe of the collar against the bronzed neck. He was evidently unused to stiff collars. Likewise her feminine eye took in the clothes he wore, the cheap and unaesthetic cut, the wrinkling of the coat across the shoulders, and the series of wrinkles in the sleeves that advertised bulging biceps muscles.

While he waved his hand and muttered that he had done nothing at all, he was obeying her behest by trying to get into a chair. He found time to admire the ease with which she sat down, then lurched toward a chair facing her, overwhelmed with consciousness of the awkward figure he was cutting. This was a new experience for him. All his life, up to then, he had been unaware of being either graceful or awkward. Such thoughts of self had never entered his mind. He sat down gingerly on the edge of the chair, greatly worried by his hands. They were in the way wherever he put them. Arthur was leaving the room, and Martin Eden followed his exit with longing eyes. He felt lost, alone there in the room with that pale spirit of a woman. There was no bar-keeper upon whom to call for drinks, no small boy to send around the corner for a can of beer and by means of that social fluid start the amenities of friendship flowing.

"You have such a scar on your neck, Mr. Eden," the girl was saying. "How did it happen? I am sure it must have been some adventure."

"A Mexican with a knife, miss," he answered, moistening his parched lips and clearing his throat. "It was just a fight. After I got the knife away, he tried to bite off my nose."

Baldly as he had stated it, in his eyes was a rich vision of that hot, starry night at Salina Cruz, the white strip of beach, the lights of the sugar steamers in the harbor, the voices of the drunken sailors in the distance, the jostling stevedores, the flaming passion in the Mexican's face, the glint of the beast-eyes in the starlight, the sting of the steel in his neck, and the rush of blood, the crowd and the cries, the two bodies, his and the Mexican's, locked together, rolling over and over and tearing up the sand, and from away off somewhere the mellow tinkling of a guitar. Such was the picture, and he thrilled to the memory of it, wondering if the man could paint it who had painted the pilot-schooner on the wall. The white beach, the stars, and the lights of the sugar steamers would look great, he thought, and midway on the sand the dark group of figures that surrounded the fighters. The knife occupied a place in the picture, he decided, and would show well, with a sort of gleam, in the light of the stars. But of all this no hint had crept into his speech. "He tried to bite off my nose," he concluded.

"Oh," the girl said, in a faint, far voice, and he noticed the shock in her sensitive face.

He felt a shock himself, and a blush of embarrassment shone faintly on his sunburned cheeks, though to him it burned as hotly as when his cheeks had been exposed to the open furnace-door in the fire-room. Such sordid things as stabbing affrays were evidently not fit subjects for conversation with a lady. People in the books, in her walk of life, did not talk about such things—perhaps they did not know about them, either.

There was a brief pause in the conversation they were trying to get started. Then she asked tentatively about the scar on his cheek. Even as she asked, he realized that she was making an effort to talk his talk, and he resolved to get away from it and talk hers.

"It was just an accident," he said, putting his hand to his cheek. "One night, in a calm, with a heavy sea running, the main-boom-lift carried away,

440

an' next the tackle. The lift was wire, an' it was threshin' around like a snake. The whole watch was tryin' to grab it, an' I rushed in an' got swatted."

"Oh," she said, this time with an accent of comprehension, though secretly his speech had been so much Greek to her and she was wondering what a *lift* was and what *swatted* meant.

"This man Swineburne," he began, attempting to put his plan into execution and pronouncing the *i* long.

"Who?"

"Swineburne," he repeated, with the same mispronunciation. "The poet."

"Swinburne," she corrected.

"Yes, that's the chap," he stammered, his cheeks hot again. "How long since he died?"

"Why, I haven't heard that he was dead." She looked at him curiously. "Where did you make his acquaintance?"

"I never clapped eyes on him," was the reply. "But I read some of his poetry out of that book there on the table just before you come in. How do you like his poetry?"

And thereat she began to talk quickly and easily upon the subject he had suggested. He felt better, and settled back slightly from the edge of the chair, holding tightly to its arms with his hands, as if it might get away from him and buck him to the floor. He had succeeded in making her talk her talk, and while she rattled on, he strove to follow her, marvelling at all the knowledge that was stowed away in that pretty head of hers, and drinking in the pale beauty of her face. Follow her he did, though bothered by unfamiliar words that fell glibly from her lips and by critical phrases and thought-processes that were foreign to his mind, but that nevertheless stimulated his mind and set it tingling. Here was intellectual life, he thought, and here was beauty, warm and wonderful as he had never dreamed it could be. He forgot himself and stared at her with hungry eyes. Here was something to

441

live for, to win to, to fight for—ay, and die for. The books were true. There were such women in the world. She was one of them. She lent wings to his imagination, and great, luminous canvases spread themselves before him whereon loomed vague, gigantic figures of love and romance, and of heroic deeds for woman's sake—for a pale woman, a flower of gold. And through the swaying, palpitant vision, as through a fairy mirage, he stared at the real woman, sitting there and talking of literature and art. He listened as well, but he stared, unconscious of the fixity of his gaze or of the fact that all that was essentially masculine in his nature was shining in his eyes. But she, who knew little of the world of men, being a woman, was keenly aware of his burning eyes. She had never had men look at her in such fashion, and it embarrassed her. She stumbled and halted in her utterance. The thread of argument slipped from her. He frightened her, and at the same time it was strangely pleasant to be so looked upon. Her training warned her of peril and of wrong, subtle, mysterious, luring; while her instincts rang clarion-voiced through her being, impelling her to hurdle caste and place and gain to this traveller from another world, to this uncouth young fellow with lacerated hands and a line of raw red caused by the unaccustomed linen at his throat, who, all too evidently, was soiled and tainted by ungracious existence. She was clean, and her cleanness revolted; but she was woman, and she was just beginning to learn the paradox of woman.

"As I was saying—what was I saying?" She broke off abruptly and laughed merrily at her predicament.

"You was saying that this man Swinburne failed bein' a great poet because—an' that was as far as you got, miss," he prompted, while to himself he seemed suddenly hungry, and delicious little thrills crawled up and down his spine at the sound of her laughter. Like silver, he thought to himself, like tinkling silver bells; and on the instant, and for an instant, he was transported to a far land, where under pink cherry blossoms, he smoked a cigarette and listened to the bells of the peaked pagoda calling straw-sandalled devotees to worship.

"Yes, thank you," she said. "Swinburne fails, when all is said, because he is, well, indelicate. There are many of his poems that should never be read.

Every line of the really great poets is filled with beautiful truth, and calls to all that is high and noble in the human. Not a line of the great poets can be spared without impoverishing the world by that much."

"I thought it was great," he said hesitatingly, "the little I read. I had no idea he was such a—a scoundrel. I guess that crops out in his other books."

"There are many lines that could be spared from the book you were reading," she said, her voice primly firm and dogmatic.

"I must 'a' missed 'em," he announced. "What I read was the real goods. It was all lighted up an' shining, an' it shun right into me an' lighted me up inside, like the sun or a searchlight. That's the way it landed on me, but I guess I ain't up much on poetry, miss."

He broke off lamely. He was confused, painfully conscious of his inarticulateness. He had felt the bigness and glow of life in what he had read, but his speech was inadequate. He could not express what he felt, and to himself he likened himself to a sailor, in a strange ship, on a dark night, groping about in the unfamiliar running rigging. Well, he decided, it was up to him to get acquainted in this new world. He had never seen anything that he couldn't get the hang of when he wanted to and it was about time for him to want to learn to talk the things that were inside of him so that she could understand. *She* was bulking large on his horizon.

"Now Longfellow—" she was saying.

"Yes, I've read 'm," he broke in impulsively, spurred on to exhibit and make the most of his little store of book knowledge, desirous of showing her that he was not wholly a stupid clod. "'The Psalm of Life,' 'Excelsior,' an' . . . I guess that's all."

She nodded her head and smiled, and he felt, somehow, that her smile was tolerant, pitifully tolerant. He was a fool to attempt to make a pretence that way. That Longfellow chap most likely had written countless books of poetry.

"Excuse me, miss, for buttin' in that way. I guess the real facts is that I don't know nothin' much about such things. It ain't in my class. But I'm goin' to make it in my class."

It sounded like a threat. His voice was determined, his eyes were flashing, the lines of his face had grown harsh. And to her it seemed that the angle of his jaw had changed; its pitch had become unpleasantly aggressive. At the same time a wave of intense virility seemed to surge out from him and impinge upon her.

"I think you could make it in—in your class," she finished with a laugh. "You are very strong."

Her gaze rested for a moment on the muscular neck, heavy corded, almost bull-like, bronzed by the sun, spilling over with rugged health and strength. And though he sat there, blushing and humble, again she felt drawn to him. She was surprised by a wanton thought that rushed into her mind. It seemed to her that if she could lay her two hands upon that neck that all its strength and vigor would flow out to her. She was shocked by this thought. It seemed to reveal to her an undreamed depravity in her nature. Besides, strength to her was a gross and brutish thing. Her ideal of masculine beauty had always been slender gracefulness. Yet the thought still persisted. It bewildered her that she should desire to place her hands on that sunburned neck. In truth, she was far from robust, and the need of her body and mind was for strength. But she did not know it. She knew only that no man had ever affected her before as this one had, who shocked her from moment to moment with his awful grammar.

"Yes, I ain't no invalid," he said. "When it comes down to hard-pan, I can digest scrap-iron. But just now I've got dyspepsia. Most of what you was sayin' I can't digest. Never trained that way, you see. I like books and poetry, and what time I've had I've read 'em, but I've never thought about 'em the way you have. That's why I can't talk about 'em. I'm like a navigator adrift on a strange sea without chart or compass. Now I want to get my bearin's. Mebbe you can put me right. How did you learn all this you've ben talkin'?"

"By going to school, I fancy, and by studying," she answered.

"I went to school when I was a kid," he began to object.

"Yes; but I mean high school, and lectures, and the university."

"You've gone to the university?" he demanded in frank amazement. He felt that she had become remoter from him by at least a million miles.

"I'm going there now. I'm taking special courses in English."

He did not know what "English" meant, but he made a mental note of that item of ignorance and passed on.

"How long would I have to study before I could go to the university?" he asked.

She beamed encouragement upon his desire for knowledge, and said: "That depends upon how much studying you have already done. You have never attended high school? Of course not. But did you finish grammar school?"

"I had two years to run, when I left," he answered. "But I was always honorably promoted at school."

The next moment, angry with himself for the boast, he had gripped the arms of the chair so savagely that every finger-end was stinging. At the same moment he became aware that a woman was entering the room. He saw the girl leave her chair and trip swiftly across the floor to the newcomer. They kissed each other, and, with arms around each other's waists, they advanced toward him. That must be her mother, he thought. She was a tall, blond woman, slender, and stately, and beautiful. Her gown was what he might expect in such a house. His eyes delighted in the graceful lines of it. She and her dress together reminded him of women on the stage. Then he remembered seeing similar grand ladies and gowns entering the London theatres while he stood and watched and the policemen shoved him back into the drizzle beyond the awning. Next his mind leaped to the Grand Hotel at Yokohama, where, too, from the sidewalk, he had seen grand ladies. Then the city and the harbor of Yokohama, in a thousand pictures, began flashing before his eyes. But he swiftly dismissed the kaleidoscope of memory, oppressed by the urgent need of the present. He knew that he must stand up to be introduced, and he struggled painfully to his feet, where he stood with trousers bagging at the knees, his arms loose-hanging and ludicrous, his face set hard for the impending ordeal.

CHAPTER II

The process of getting into the dining room was a nightmare to him. Between halts and stumbles, jerks and lurches, locomotion had at times seemed impossible. But at last he had made it, and was seated alongside of Her. The array of knives and forks frightened him. They bristled with unknown perils, and he gazed at them, fascinated, till their dazzle became a background across which moved a succession of forecastle pictures, wherein he and his mates sat eating salt beef with sheath-knives and fingers, or scooping thick pea-soup out of pannikins by means of battered iron spoons. The stench of bad beef was in his nostrils, while in his ears, to the accompaniment of creaking timbers and groaning bulkheads, echoed the loud mouth-noises of the eaters. He watched them eating, and decided that they ate like pigs. Well, he would be careful here. He would make no noise. He would keep his mind upon it all the time.

He glanced around the table. Opposite him was Arthur, and Arthur's brother, Norman. They were her brothers, he reminded himself, and his heart warmed toward them. How they loved each other, the members of this family! There flashed into his mind the picture of her mother, of the kiss of greeting, and of the pair of them walking toward him with arms entwined. Not in his world were such displays of affection between parents and children made. It was a revelation of the heights of existence that were attained in the world above. It was the finest thing yet that he had seen in this small glimpse of that world. He was moved deeply by appreciation of it, and his heart was melting with sympathetic tenderness. He had starved for love all his life. His nature craved love. It was an organic demand of his being. Yet he had gone without, and hardened himself in the process. He had not known that he needed love. Nor did he know it now. He merely saw it in operation, and thrilled to it, and thought it fine, and high, and splendid.

He was glad that Mr. Morse was not there. It was difficult enough getting acquainted with her, and her mother, and her brother, Norman.

Arthur he already knew somewhat. The father would have been too much for him, he felt sure. It seemed to him that he had never worked so hard in his life. The severest toil was child's play compared with this. Tiny nodules of moisture stood out on his forehead, and his shirt was wet with sweat from the exertion of doing so many unaccustomed things at once. He had to eat as he had never eaten before, to handle strange tools, to glance surreptitiously about and learn how to accomplish each new thing, to receive the flood of impressions that was pouring in upon him and being mentally annotated and classified; to be conscious of a yearning for her that perturbed him in the form of a dull, aching restlessness; to feel the prod of desire to win to the walk in life whereon she trod, and to have his mind ever and again straying off in speculation and vague plans of how to reach to her. Also, when his secret glance went across to Norman opposite him, or to any one else, to ascertain just what knife or fork was to be used in any particular occasion, that person's features were seized upon by his mind, which automatically strove to appraise them and to divine what they were—all in relation to her. Then he had to talk, to hear what was said to him and what was said back and forth, and to answer, when it was necessary, with a tongue prone to looseness of speech that required a constant curb. And to add confusion to confusion, there was the servant, an unceasing menace, that appeared noiselessly at his shoulder, a dire Sphinx that propounded puzzles and conundrums demanding instantaneous solution. He was oppressed throughout the meal by the thought of finger-bowls. Irrelevantly, insistently, scores of times, he wondered when they would come on and what they looked like. He had heard of such things, and now, sooner or later, somewhere in the next few minutes, he would see them, sit at table with exalted beings who used them—ay, and he would use them himself. And most important of all, far down and yet always at the surface of his thought, was the problem of how he should comport himself toward these persons. What should his attitude be? He wrestled continually and anxiously with the problem. There were cowardly suggestions that he should make believe, assume a part; and there were still more cowardly suggestions that warned him he would fail in such course, that his nature was not fitted to live up to it, and that he would make a fool of himself.

It was during the first part of the dinner, struggling to decide upon his attitude, that he was very quiet. He did not know that his quietness was giving the lie to Arthur's words of the day before, when that brother of hers had announced that he was going to bring a wild man home to dinner and for them not to be alarmed, because they would find him an interesting wild man. Martin Eden could not have found it in him, just then, to believe that her brother could be guilty of such treachery—especially when he had been the means of getting this particular brother out of an unpleasant row. So he sat at table, perturbed by his own unfitness and at the same time charmed by all that went on about him. For the first time he realized that eating was something more than a utilitarian function. He was unaware of what he ate. It was merely food. He was feasting his love of beauty at this table where eating was an aesthetic function. It was an intellectual function, too. His mind was stirred. He heard words spoken that were meaningless to him, and other words that he had seen only in books and that no man or woman he had known was of large enough mental caliber to pronounce. When he heard such words dropping carelessly from the lips of the members of this marvellous family, her family, he thrilled with delight. The romance, and beauty, and high vigor of the books were coming true. He was in that rare and blissful state wherein a man sees his dreams stalk out from the crannies of fantasy and become fact.

Never had he been at such an altitude of living, and he kept himself in the background, listening, observing, and pleasuring, replying in reticent monosyllables, saying, "Yes, miss," and "No, miss," to her, and "Yes, ma'am," and "No, ma'am," to her mother. He curbed the impulse, arising out of his sea-training, to say "Yes, sir," and "No, sir," to her brothers. He felt that it would be inappropriate and a confession of inferiority on his part—which would never do if he was to win to her. Also, it was a dictate of his pride. "By God!" he cried to himself, once; "I'm just as good as them, and if they do know lots that I don't, I could learn 'm a few myself, all the same!" And the next moment, when she or her mother addressed him as "Mr. Eden," his aggressive pride was forgotten, and he was glowing and warm with delight. He was a civilized man, that was what he was, shoulder to shoulder, at dinner, with people he had read about in books. He was in the books himself, adventuring through the printed pages of bound volumes.

But while he belied Arthur's description, and appeared a gentle lamb rather than a wild man, he was racking his brains for a course of action. He was no gentle lamb, and the part of second fiddle would never do for the high-pitched dominance of his nature. He talked only when he had to, and then his speech was like his walk to the table, filled with jerks and halts as he groped in his polyglot vocabulary for words, debating over words he knew were fit but which he feared he could not pronounce, rejecting other words he knew would not be understood or would be raw and harsh. But all the time he was oppressed by the consciousness that this carefulness of diction was making a booby of him, preventing him from expressing what he had in him. Also, his love of freedom chafed against the restriction in much the same way his neck chafed against the starched fetter of a collar. Besides, he was confident that he could not keep it up. He was by nature powerful of thought and sensibility, and the creative spirit was restive and urgent. He was swiftly mastered by the concept or sensation in him that struggled in birth-throes to receive expression and form, and then he forgot himself and where he was, and the old words—the tools of speech he knew—slipped out.

Once, he declined something from the servant who interrupted and pestered at his shoulder, and he said, shortly and emphatically, "Pew!"

On the instant those at the table were keyed up and expectant, the servant was smugly pleased, and he was wallowing in mortification. But he recovered himself quickly.

"It's the Kanaka for 'finish,'" he explained, "and it just come out naturally. It's spelt p-a-u."

He caught her curious and speculative eyes fixed on his hands, and, being in explanatory mood, he said:-

"I just come down the Coast on one of the Pacific mail steamers. She was behind time, an' around the Puget Sound ports we worked like niggers, storing cargo-mixed freight, if you know what that means. That's how the skin got knocked off."

"Oh, it wasn't that," she hastened to explain, in turn. "Your hands seemed too small for your body."

450

His cheeks were hot. He took it as an exposure of another of his deficiencies.

"Yes," he said depreciatingly. "They ain't big enough to stand the strain. I can hit like a mule with my arms and shoulders. They are too strong, an' when I smash a man on the jaw the hands get smashed, too."

He was not happy at what he had said. He was filled with disgust at himself. He had loosed the guard upon his tongue and talked about things that were not nice.

"It was brave of you to help Arthur the way you did—and you a stranger," she said tactfully, aware of his discomfiture though not of the reason for it.

He, in turn, realized what she had done, and in the consequent warm surge of gratefulness that overwhelmed him forgot his loose-worded tongue.

"It wasn't nothin' at all," he said. "Any guy 'ud do it for another. That bunch of hoodlums was lookin' for trouble, an' Arthur wasn't botherin' 'em none. They butted in on 'm, an' then I butted in on them an' poked a few. That's where some of the skin off my hands went, along with some of the teeth of the gang. I wouldn't 'a' missed it for anything. When I seen—"

He paused, open-mouthed, on the verge of the pit of his own depravity and utter worthlessness to breathe the same air she did. And while Arthur took up the tale, for the twentieth time, of his adventure with the drunken hoodlums on the ferry-boat and of how Martin Eden had rushed in and rescued him, that individual, with frowning brows, meditated upon the fool he had made of himself, and wrestled more determinedly with the problem of how he should conduct himself toward these people. He certainly had not succeeded so far. He wasn't of their tribe, and he couldn't talk their lingo, was the way he put it to himself. He couldn't fake being their kind. The masquerade would fail, and besides, masquerade was foreign to his nature. There was no room in him for sham or artifice. Whatever happened, he must be real. He couldn't talk their talk just yet, though in time he would. Upon that he was resolved. But in the meantime, talk he must, and it must be his own talk, toned down, of course, so as to be comprehensible to them and so

451

as not to shook them too much. And furthermore, he wouldn't claim, not even by tacit acceptance, to be familiar with anything that was unfamiliar. In pursuance of this decision, when the two brothers, talking university shop, had used "trig" several times, Martin Eden demanded:-

"What is *trig*?"

"Trignometry," Norman said; "a higher form of math."

"And what is math?" was the next question, which, somehow, brought the laugh on Norman.

"Mathematics, arithmetic," was the answer.

Martin Eden nodded. He had caught a glimpse of the apparently illimitable vistas of knowledge. What he saw took on tangibility. His abnormal power of vision made abstractions take on concrete form. In the alchemy of his brain, trigonometry and mathematics and the whole field of knowledge which they betokened were transmuted into so much landscape. The vistas he saw were vistas of green foliage and forest glades, all softly luminous or shot through with flashing lights. In the distance, detail was veiled and blurred by a purple haze, but behind this purple haze, he knew, was the glamour of the unknown, the lure of romance. It was like wine to him. Here was adventure, something to do with head and hand, a world to conquer—and straightway from the back of his consciousness rushed the thought, *conquering, to win to her, that lily-pale spirit sitting beside him.*

The glimmering vision was rent asunder and dissipated by Arthur, who, all evening, had been trying to draw his wild man out. Martin Eden remembered his decision. For the first time he became himself, consciously and deliberately at first, but soon lost in the joy of creating in making life as he knew it appear before his listeners' eyes. He had been a member of the crew of the smuggling schooner *Halcyon* when she was captured by a revenue cutter. He saw with wide eyes, and he could tell what he saw. He brought the pulsing sea before them, and the men and the ships upon the sea. He communicated his power of vision, till they saw with his eyes what he had seen. He selected from the vast mass of detail with an artist's touch, drawing pictures of life that glowed and burned with light and color, injecting movement so that his listeners surged along with him on the flood of rough eloquence, enthusiasm, and power. At times he shocked them with the vividness of the narrative and his terms of speech, but beauty always followed fast upon the heels of violence, and tragedy was relieved by humor, by interpretations of the strange twists and quirks of sailors' minds.

And while he talked, the girl looked at him with startled eyes. His fire warmed her. She wondered if she had been cold all her days. She wanted to lean toward this burning, blazing man that was like a volcano spouting forth strength, robustness, and health. She felt that she must lean toward him, and resisted by an effort. Then, too, there was the counter impulse to shrink away from him. She was repelled by those lacerated hands, grimed by toil so that the very dirt of life was ingrained in the flesh itself, by that red chafe of the collar and those bulging muscles. His roughness frightened her; each roughness of speech was an insult to her ear, each rough phase of his life an insult to her soul. And ever and again would come the draw of him, till she thought he must be evil to have such power over her. All that was most firmly established in her mind was rocking. His romance and adventure were battering at the conventions. Before his facile perils and ready laugh, life was no longer an affair of serious effort and restraint, but a toy, to be played with and turned topsy-turvy, carelessly to be lived and pleasured in, and carelessly to be flung aside. "Therefore, play!" was the cry that rang through her. "Lean toward him, if so you will, and place your two hands upon his neck!" She wanted to cry out at the recklessness of the thought, and in vain she appraised her own cleanness and culture and balanced all that she was against what he was not. She glanced about her and saw the others gazing at him with rapt attention; and she would have despaired had not she seen horror in her mother's eyes—fascinated horror, it was true, but none the less horror. This man from outer darkness was evil. Her mother saw it, and her mother was right. She would trust her mother's judgment in this as she had always trusted it in all things. The fire of him was no longer warm, and the fear of him was no longer poignant.

Later, at the piano, she played for him, and at him, aggressively, with the vague intent of emphasizing the impassableness of the gulf that separated them. Her music was a club that she swung brutally upon his head; and though it stunned him and crushed him down, it incited him. He gazed upon her in awe. In his mind, as in her own, the gulf widened; but faster than it widened, towered his ambition to win across it. But he was too complicated a plexus of sensibilities to sit staring at a gulf a whole evening, especially when there was music. He was remarkably susceptible to music. It was like strong drink, firing him to audacities of feeling,—a drug that laid hold of his imagination and went cloud-soaring through the sky. It banished sordid fact, flooded his mind with beauty, loosed romance and to its heels added wings. He did not understand the music she played. It was different from the dance-hall piano-banging and blatant brass bands he had heard. But he had caught hints of such music from the books, and he accepted her playing largely on faith, patiently waiting, at first, for the lifting measures of pronounced and simple rhythm, puzzled because those measures were not long continued. Just as he caught the swing of them and started, his imagination attuned in flight, always they vanished away in a chaotic scramble of sounds that was meaningless to him, and that dropped his imagination, an inert weight, back to earth.

Once, it entered his mind that there was a deliberate rebuff in all this. He caught her spirit of antagonism and strove to divine the message that her hands pronounced upon the keys. Then he dismissed the thought as unworthy and impossible, and yielded himself more freely to the music. The old delightful condition began to be induced. His feet were no longer clay, and his flesh became spirit; before his eyes and behind his eyes shone a great glory; and then the scene before him vanished and he was away, rocking over the world that was to him a very dear world. The known and the unknown were commingled in the dream-pageant that thronged his vision. He entered strange ports of sun-washed lands, and trod market-places among barbaric peoples that no man had ever seen. The scent of the spice islands was in his nostrils as he had known it on warm, breathless nights at sea, or he beat up against the southeast trades through long tropic days, sinking palm-tufted coral islets in the turquoise sea behind and lifting palm-tufted coral islets in the turquoise sea ahead. Swift as thought the pictures came and went. One instant he was astride a broncho and flying through the fairy-colored Painted

Desert country; the next instant he was gazing down through shimmering heat into the whited sepulchre of Death Valley, or pulling an oar on a freezing ocean where great ice islands towered and glistened in the sun. He lay on a coral beach where the cocoanuts grew down to the mellow-sounding surf. The hulk of an ancient wreck burned with blue fires, in the light of which danced the *hula* dancers to the barbaric love-calls of the singers, who chanted to tinkling *ukuleles* and rumbling tom-toms. It was a sensuous, tropic night. In the background a volcano crater was silhouetted against the stars. Overhead drifted a pale crescent moon, and the Southern Cross burned low in the sky.

He was a harp; all life that he had known and that was his consciousness was the strings; and the flood of music was a wind that poured against those strings and set them vibrating with memories and dreams. He did not merely feel. Sensation invested itself in form and color and radiance, and what his imagination dared, it objectified in some sublimated and magic way. Past, present, and future mingled; and he went on oscillating across the broad, warm world, through high adventure and noble deeds to Her—ay, and with her, winning her, his arm about her, and carrying her on in flight through the empery of his mind.

And she, glancing at him across her shoulder, saw something of all this in his face. It was a transfigured face, with great shining eyes that gazed beyond the veil of sound and saw behind it the leap and pulse of life and the gigantic phantoms of the spirit. She was startled. The raw, stumbling lout was gone. The ill-fitting clothes, battered hands, and sunburned face remained; but these seemed the prison-bars through which she saw a great soul looking forth, inarticulate and dumb because of those feeble lips that would not give it speech. Only for a flashing moment did she see this, then she saw the lout returned, and she laughed at the whim of her fancy. But the impression of that fleeting glimpse lingered, and when the time came for him to beat a stumbling retreat and go, she lent him the volume of Swinburne, and another of Browning—she was studying Browning in one of her English courses. He seemed such a boy, as he stood blushing and stammering his thanks, that a wave of pity, maternal in its prompting, welled up in her. She did not remember the lout, nor the imprisoned soul, nor the man who had stared at her in all masculineness and delighted and frightened her. She saw before her only a boy, who was shaking her hand with a hand so calloused that it felt like a nutmeg-grater and rasped her skin, and who was saying jerkily:-

"The greatest time of my life. You see, I ain't used to things. . . " He looked about him helplessly. "To people and houses like this. It's all new to me, and I like it."

"I hope you'll call again," she said, as he was saying good night to her brothers.

He pulled on his cap, lurched desperately through the doorway, and was gone.

"Well, what do you think of him?" Arthur demanded.

"He is most interesting, a whiff of ozone," she answered. "How old is he?"

"Twenty—almost twenty-one. I asked him this afternoon. I didn't think he was that young."

And I am three years older, was the thought in her mind as she kissed her brothers goodnight.

CHAPTER III

As Martin Eden went down the steps, his hand dropped into his coat pocket. It came out with a brown rice paper and a pinch of Mexican tobacco, which were deftly rolled together into a cigarette. He drew the first whiff of smoke deep into his lungs and expelled it in a long and lingering exhalation. "By God!" he said aloud, in a voice of awe and wonder. "By God!" he repeated. And yet again he murmured, "By God!" Then his hand went to his collar, which he ripped out of the shirt and stuffed into his pocket. A cold drizzle was falling, but he bared his head to it and unbuttoned his vest, swinging along in splendid unconcern. He was only dimly aware that it was raining. He was in an ecstasy, dreaming dreams and reconstructing the scenes just past.

He had met the woman at last—the woman that he had thought little about, not being given to thinking about women, but whom he had expected, in a remote way, he would sometime meet. He had sat next to her at table. He had felt her hand in his, he had looked into her eyes and caught a vision of a beautiful spirit;—but no more beautiful than the eyes through which it shone, nor than the flesh that gave it expression and form. He did not think of her flesh as flesh,—which was new to him; for of the women he had known that was the only way he thought. Her flesh was somehow different. He did not conceive of her body as a body, subject to the ills and frailties of bodies. Her body was more than the garb of her spirit. It was an emanation of her spirit, a pure and gracious crystallization of her divine essence. This feeling of the divine startled him. It shocked him from his dreams to sober thought. No word, no clew, no hint, of the divine had ever reached him before. He had never believed in the divine. He had always been irreligious, scoffing good-naturedly at the sky-pilots and their immortality of the soul. There was no life beyond, he had contended; it was here and now, then darkness everlasting. But what he had seen in her eyes was soul—immortal soul that could never die. No man he had known, nor any woman, had given him the message of immortality. But she had. She had whispered it to him the first moment she looked at him. Her face shimmered before his eyes as he walked along,—pale and serious, sweet and sensitive, smiling with pity and tenderness as only a spirit could smile, and pure as he had never dreamed purity could be. Her purity smote him like a blow. It startled him. He had known good and bad; but purity, as an attribute of existence, had never entered his mind. And now, in her, he conceived purity to be the superlative of goodness and of cleanness, the sum of which constituted eternal life.

And promptly urged his ambition to grasp at eternal life. He was not fit to carry water for her—he knew that; it was a miracle of luck and a fantastic stroke that had enabled him to see her and be with her and talk with her that night. It was accidental. There was no merit in it. He did not deserve such fortune. His mood was essentially religious. He was humble and meek, filled with self-disparagement and abasement. In such frame of mind sinners come to the penitent form. He was convicted of sin. But as the meek and lowly at the penitent form catch splendid glimpses of their future lordly existence, so did he catch similar glimpses of the state he would gain to by possessing her. But this possession of her was dim and nebulous and totally different from possession as he had known it. Ambition soared on mad wings, and he saw himself climbing the heights with her, sharing thoughts with her, pleasuring in beautiful and noble things with her. It was a soul-possession he dreamed, refined beyond any grossness, a free comradeship of spirit that he could not put into definite thought. He did not think it. For that matter, he did not think at all. Sensation usurped reason, and he was quivering and palpitant with emotions he had never known, drifting deliciously on a sea of sensibility where feeling itself was exalted and spiritualized and carried beyond the summits of life.

He staggered along like a drunken man, murmuring fervently aloud: "By God! By God!"

A policeman on a street corner eyed him suspiciously, then noted his sailor roll.

"Where did you get it?" the policeman demanded.

Martin Eden came back to earth. His was a fluid organism, swiftly adjustable, capable of flowing into and filling all sorts of nooks and crannies.

With the policeman's hail he was immediately his ordinary self, grasping the situation clearly.

"It's a beaut, ain't it?" he laughed back. "I didn't know I was talkin' out loud."

"You'll be singing next," was the policeman's diagnosis.

"No, I won't. Gimme a match an' I'll catch the next car home."

He lighted his cigarette, said good night, and went on. "Now wouldn't that rattle you?" he ejaculated under his breath. "That copper thought I was drunk." He smiled to himself and meditated. "I guess I was," he added; "but I didn't think a woman's face'd do it."

He caught a Telegraph Avenue car that was going to Berkeley. It was crowded with youths and young men who were singing songs and ever and again barking out college yells. He studied them curiously. They were university boys. They went to the same university that she did, were in her class socially, could know her, could see her every day if they wanted to. He wondered that they did not want to, that they had been out having a good time instead of being with her that evening, talking with her, sitting around her in a worshipful and adoring circle. His thoughts wandered on. He noticed one with narrow-slitted eyes and a loose-lipped mouth. That fellow was vicious, he decided. On shipboard he would be a sneak, a whiner, a tattler. He, Martin Eden, was a better man than that fellow. The thought cheered him. It seemed to draw him nearer to Her. He began comparing himself with the students. He grew conscious of the muscled mechanism of his body and felt confident that he was physically their master. But their heads were filled with knowledge that enabled them to talk her talk,—the thought depressed him. But what was a brain for? he demanded passionately. What they had done, he could do. They had been studying about life from the books while he had been busy living life. His brain was just as full of knowledge as theirs, though it was a different kind of knowledge. How many of them could tie a lanyard knot, or take a wheel or a lookout? His life spread out before him in a series of pictures of danger and daring, hardship and toil. He remembered his failures and scrapes in the process of learning. He was that much to the good, anyway. Later on they would have to begin living life and going through the mill as he had gone. Very well. While they were busy with that, he could be learning the other side of life from the books.

As the car crossed the zone of scattered dwellings that separated Oakland from Berkeley, he kept a lookout for a familiar, two-story building along the front of which ran the proud sign, HIGGINBOTHAM'S CASH STORE. Martin Eden got off at this corner. He stared up for a moment at the sign. It carried a message to him beyond its mere wording. A personality of smallness and egotism and petty underhandedness seemed to emanate from the letters themselves. Bernard Higginbotham had married his sister, and he knew him well. He let himself in with a latch-key and climbed the stairs to the second floor. Here lived his brother-in-law. The grocery was below. There was a smell of stale vegetables in the air. As he groped his way across the hall he stumbled over a toy-cart, left there by one of his numerous nephews and nieces, and brought up against a door with a resounding bang. "The pincher," was his thought; "too miserly to burn two cents' worth of gas and save his boarders' necks."

He fumbled for the knob and entered a lighted room, where sat his sister and Bernard Higginbotham. She was patching a pair of his trousers, while his lean body was distributed over two chairs, his feet dangling in dilapidated carpet-slippers over the edge of the second chair. He glanced across the top of the paper he was reading, showing a pair of dark, insincere, sharp-staring eyes. Martin Eden never looked at him without experiencing a sense of repulsion. What his sister had seen in the man was beyond him. The other affected him as so much vermin, and always aroused in him an impulse to crush him under his foot. "Some day I'll beat the face off of him," was the way he often consoled himself for enduring the man's existence. The eyes, weasel-like and cruel, were looking at him complainingly.

"Well," Martin demanded. "Out with it."

"I had that door painted only last week," Mr. Higginbotham half whined, half bullied; "and you know what union wages are. You should be more careful."

Martin had intended to reply, but he was struck by the hopelessness of it. He gazed across the monstrous sordidness of soul to a chromo on the wall. It surprised him. He had always liked it, but it seemed that now he was seeing it for the first time. It was cheap, that was what it was, like everything else in this house. His mind went back to the house he had just left, and he saw, first, the paintings, and next, Her, looking at him with melting sweetness as she shook his hand at leaving. He forgot where he was and Bernard Higginbotham's existence, till that gentleman demanded:-

"Seen a ghost?"

Martin came back and looked at the beady eyes, sneering, truculent, cowardly, and there leaped into his vision, as on a screen, the same eyes when their owner was making a sale in the store below—subservient eyes, smug, and oily, and flattering.

"Yes," Martin answered. "I seen a ghost. Good night. Good night, Gertrude."

He started to leave the room, tripping over a loose seam in the slatternly carpet.

"Don't bang the door," Mr. Higginbotham cautioned him.

He felt the blood crawl in his veins, but controlled himself and closed the door softly behind him.

Mr. Higginbotham looked at his wife exultantly.

"He's ben drinkin'," he proclaimed in a hoarse whisper. "I told you he would."

She nodded her head resignedly.

"His eyes was pretty shiny," she confessed; "and he didn't have no collar, though he went away with one. But mebbe he didn't have more'n a couple of glasses."

"He couldn't stand up straight," asserted her husband. "I watched him. He couldn't walk across the floor without stumblin'. You heard 'm yourself almost fall down in the hall."

"I think it was over Alice's cart," she said. "He couldn't see it in the dark."

Mr. Higginbotham's voice and wrath began to rise. All day he effaced himself in the store, reserving for the evening, with his family, the privilege of being himself.

"I tell you that precious brother of yours was drunk."

His voice was cold, sharp, and final, his lips stamping the enunciation of each word like the die of a machine. His wife sighed and remained silent. She was a large, stout woman, always dressed slatternly and always tired from the burdens of her flesh, her work, and her husband.

"He's got it in him, I tell you, from his father," Mr. Higginbotham went on accusingly. "An' he'll croak in the gutter the same way. You know that."

She nodded, sighed, and went on stitching. They were agreed that Martin had come home drunk. They did not have it in their souls to know beauty, or they would have known that those shining eyes and that glowing face betokened youth's first vision of love.

"Settin' a fine example to the children," Mr. Higginbotham snorted, suddenly, in the silence for which his wife was responsible and which he resented. Sometimes he almost wished she would oppose him more. "If he does it again, he's got to get out. Understand! I won't put up with his shinanigan—debotchin' innocent children with his boozing." Mr. Higginbotham liked the word, which was a new one in his vocabulary, recently gleaned from a newspaper column. "That's what it is, debotchin'—there ain't no other name for it."

Still his wife sighed, shook her head sorrowfully, and stitched on. Mr. Higginbotham resumed the newspaper.

"Has he paid last week's board?" he shot across the top of the newspaper.

She nodded, then added, "He still has some money."

"When is he goin' to sea again?"

"When his pay-day's spent, I guess," she answered. "He was over to San Francisco yesterday looking for a ship. But he's got money, yet, an' he's particular about the kind of ship he signs for."

"It's not for a deck-swab like him to put on airs," Mr. Higginbotham snorted. "Particular! Him!"

"He said something about a schooner that's gettin' ready to go off to some outlandish place to look for buried treasure, that he'd sail on her if his money held out."

"If he only wanted to steady down, I'd give him a job drivin' the wagon," her husband said, but with no trace of benevolence in his voice. "Tom's quit."

His wife looked alarm and interrogation.

"Quit to-night. Is goin' to work for Carruthers. They paid 'm more'n I could afford."

"I told you you'd lose 'm," she cried out. "He was worth more'n you was giving him."

"Now look here, old woman," Higginbotham bullied, "for the thousandth time I've told you to keep your nose out of the business. I won't tell you again."

"I don't care," she sniffled. "Tom was a good boy." Her husband glared at her. This was unqualified defiance.

"If that brother of yours was worth his salt, he could take the wagon," he snorted.

"He pays his board, just the same," was the retort. "An' he's my brother, an' so long as he don't owe you money you've got no right to be jumping on him all the time. I've got some feelings, if I have been married to you for seven years."

"Did you tell 'm you'd charge him for gas if he goes on readin' in bed?" he demanded.

Mrs. Higginbotham made no reply. Her revolt faded away, her spirit wilting down into her tired flesh. Her husband was triumphant. He had her. His eyes snapped vindictively, while his ears joyed in the sniffles she emitted. He extracted great happiness from squelching her, and she squelched easily these days, though it had been different in the first years of their married life, before the brood of children and his incessant nagging had sapped her energy.

"Well, you tell 'm to-morrow, that's all," he said. "An' I just want to tell you, before I forget it, that you'd better send for Marian to-morrow to take care of the children. With Tom quit, I'll have to be out on the wagon, an' you can make up your mind to it to be down below waitin' on the counter."

"But to-morrow's wash day," she objected weakly.

"Get up early, then, an' do it first. I won't start out till ten o'clock."

He crinkled the paper viciously and resumed his reading.

CHAPTER IV

Martin Eden, with blood still crawling from contact with his brother-in-law, felt his way along the unlighted back hall and entered his room, a tiny cubbyhole with space for a bed, a wash-stand, and one chair. Mr. Higginbotham was too thrifty to keep a servant when his wife could do the work. Besides, the servant's room enabled them to take in two boarders instead of one. Martin placed the Swinburne and Browning on the chair, took off his coat, and sat down on the bed. A screeching of asthmatic springs greeted the weight of his body, but he did not notice them. He started to take off his shoes, but fell to staring at the white plaster wall opposite him, broken by long streaks of dirty brown where rain had leaked through the roof. On this befouled background visions began to flow and burn. He forgot his shoes and stared long, till his lips began to move and he murmured, "Ruth."

"Ruth." He had not thought a simple sound could be so beautiful. It delighted his ear, and he grew intoxicated with the repetition of it. "Ruth." It was a talisman, a magic word to conjure with. Each time he murmured it, her face shimmered before him, suffusing the foul wall with a golden radiance. This radiance did not stop at the wall. It extended on into infinity, and through its golden depths his soul went questing after hers. The best that was in him was out in splendid flood. The very thought of her ennobled and purified him, made him better, and made him want to be better. This was new to him. He had never known women who had made him better. They had always had the counter effect of making him beastly. He did not know that many of them had done their best, bad as it was. Never having been conscious of himself, he did not know that he had that in his being that drew love from women and which had been the cause of their reaching out for his youth. Though they had often bothered him, he had never bothered about them; and he would never have dreamed that there were women who had been better because of him. Always in sublime carelessness had he lived, till now, and now it seemed to him that they had always reached out and dragged at him with vile hands. This was not just to them, nor to himself.

But he, who for the first time was becoming conscious of himself, was in no condition to judge, and he burned with shame as he stared at the vision of his infamy.

He got up abruptly and tried to see himself in the dirty looking-glass over the wash-stand. He passed a towel over it and looked again, long and carefully. It was the first time he had ever really seen himself. His eyes were made for seeing, but up to that moment they had been filled with the ever changing panorama of the world, at which he had been too busy gazing, ever to gaze at himself. He saw the head and face of a young fellow of twenty, but, being unused to such appraisement, he did not know how to value it. Above a square-domed forehead he saw a mop of brown hair, nut-brown, with a wave to it and hints of curls that were a delight to any woman, making hands tingle to stroke it and fingers tingle to pass caresses through it. But he passed it by as without merit, in Her eyes, and dwelt long and thoughtfully on the high, square forehead,—striving to penetrate it and learn the quality of its content. What kind of a brain lay behind there? was his insistent interrogation. What was it capable of? How far would it take him? Would it take him to her?

He wondered if there was soul in those steel-gray eyes that were often quite blue of color and that were strong with the briny airs of the sun-washed deep. He wondered, also, how his eyes looked to her. He tried to imagine himself she, gazing into those eyes of his, but failed in the jugglery. He could successfully put himself inside other men's minds, but they had to be men whose ways of life he knew. He did not know her way of life. She was wonder and mystery, and how could he guess one thought of hers? Well, they were honest eyes, he concluded, and in them was neither smallness nor meanness. The brown sunburn of his face surprised him. He had not dreamed he was so black. He rolled up his shirt-sleeve and compared the white underside if the arm with his face. Yes, he was a white man, after all. But the arms were sunburned, too. He twisted his arm, rolled the biceps over with his other hand, and gazed underneath where he was least touched by the sun. It was very white. He laughed at his bronzed face in the glass at the thought that it was once as white as the underside of his arm; nor did he dream that in the world there were few pale spirits of women who could boast fairer or smoother skins than he—fairer than where he had escaped the ravages of the sun.

His might have been a cherub's mouth, had not the full, sensuous lips a trick, under stress, of drawing firmly across the teeth. At times, so tightly did they draw, the mouth became stern and harsh, even ascetic. They were the lips of a fighter and of a lover. They could taste the sweetness of life with relish, and they could put the sweetness aside and command life. The chin and jaw, strong and just hinting of square aggressiveness, helped the lips to command life. Strength balanced sensuousness and had upon it a tonic effect, compelling him to love beauty that was healthy and making him vibrate to sensations that were wholesome. And between the lips were teeth that had never known nor needed the dentist's care. They were white and strong and regular, he decided, as he looked at them. But as he looked, he began to be troubled. Somewhere, stored away in the recesses of his mind and vaguely remembered, was the impression that there were people who washed their teeth every day. They were the people from up above—people in her class. She must wash her teeth every day, too. What would she think if she learned that he had never washed his teeth in all the days of his life? He resolved to get a tooth-brush and form the habit. He would begin at once, to-morrow. It was not by mere achievement that he could hope to win to her. He must make a personal reform in all things, even to tooth-washing and neck-gear, though a starched collar affected him as a renunciation of freedom.

He held up his hand, rubbing the ball of the thumb over the calloused palm and gazing at the dirt that was ingrained in the flesh itself and which no brush could scrub away. How different was her palm! He thrilled deliciously at the remembrance. Like a rose-petal, he thought; cool and soft as a snowflake. He had never thought that a mere woman's hand could be so sweetly soft. He caught himself imagining the wonder of a caress from such a hand, and flushed guiltily. It was too gross a thought for her. In ways it seemed to impugn her high spirituality. She was a pale, slender spirit, exalted far beyond the flesh; but nevertheless the softness of her palm persisted in his thoughts. He was used to the harsh callousness of factory girls and working women. Well he knew why their hands were rough; but this hand of hers .

. . It was soft because she had never used it to work with. The gulf yawned between her and him at the awesome thought of a person who did not have to work for a living. He suddenly saw the aristocracy of the people who did not labor. It towered before him on the wall, a figure in brass, arrogant and powerful. He had worked himself; his first memories seemed connected with work, and all his family had worked. There was Gertrude. When her hands were not hard from the endless housework, they were swollen and red like boiled beef, what of the washing. And there was his sister Marian. She had worked in the cannery the preceding summer, and her slim, pretty hands were all scarred with the tomato-knives. Besides, the tips of two of her fingers had been left in the cutting machine at the paper-box factory the preceding winter. He remembered the hard palms of his mother as she lay in her coffin. And his father had worked to the last fading gasp; the horned growth on his hands must have been half an inch thick when he died. But Her hands were soft, and her mother's hands, and her brothers'. This last came to him as a surprise; it was tremendously indicative of the highness of their caste, of the enormous distance that stretched between her and him.

He sat back on the bed with a bitter laugh, and finished taking off his shoes. He was a fool; he had been made drunken by a woman's face and by a woman's soft, white hands. And then, suddenly, before his eyes, on the foul plaster-wall appeared a vision. He stood in front of a gloomy tenement house. It was night-time, in the East End of London, and before him stood Margey, a little factory girl of fifteen. He had seen her home after the bean-feast. She lived in that gloomy tenement, a place not fit for swine. His hand was going out to hers as he said good night. She had put her lips up to be kissed, but he wasn't going to kiss her. Somehow he was afraid of her. And then her hand closed on his and pressed feverishly. He felt her calluses grind and grate on his, and a great wave of pity welled over him. He saw her yearning, hungry eyes, and her ill-fed female form which had been rushed from childhood into a frightened and ferocious maturity; then he put his arms about her in large tolerance and stooped and kissed her on the lips. Her glad little cry rang in his ears, and he felt her clinging to him like a cat. Poor little starveling! He continued to stare at the vision of what had happened in the long ago. His flesh was crawling as it had crawled that night when she clung to him, and his heart was warm with pity. It was a gray scene, greasy gray, and the rain drizzled greasily on the pavement stones. And then a radiant glory shone on the wall, and up through the other vision, displacing it, glimmered Her pale face under its crown of golden hair, remote and inaccessible as a star.

He took the Browning and the Swinburne from the chair and kissed them. Just the same, she told me to call again, he thought. He took another look at himself in the glass, and said aloud, with great solemnity:-

"Martin Eden, the first thing to-morrow you go to the free library an' read up on etiquette. Understand!"

He turned off the gas, and the springs shrieked under his body.

"But you've got to quit cussin', Martin, old boy; you've got to quit cussin'," he said aloud.

Then he dozed off to sleep and to dream dreams that for madness and audacity rivalled those of poppy-eaters.

CHAPTER V

He awoke next morning from rosy scenes of dream to a steamy atmosphere that smelled of soapsuds and dirty clothes, and that was vibrant with the jar and jangle of tormented life. As he came out of his room he heard the slosh of water, a sharp exclamation, and a resounding smack as his sister visited her irritation upon one of her numerous progeny. The squall of the child went through him like a knife. He was aware that the whole thing, the very air he breathed, was repulsive and mean. How different, he thought, from the atmosphere of beauty and repose of the house wherein Ruth dwelt. There it was all spiritual. Here it was all material, and meanly material.

"Come here, Alfred," he called to the crying child, at the same time thrusting his hand into his trousers pocket, where he carried his money loose in the same large way that he lived life in general. He put a quarter in the youngster's hand and held him in his arms a moment, soothing his sobs. "Now run along and get some candy, and don't forget to give some to your brothers and sisters. Be sure and get the kind that lasts longest."

His sister lifted a flushed face from the wash-tub and looked at him.

"A nickel'd ha' ben enough," she said. "It's just like you, no idea of the value of money. The child'll eat himself sick."

"That's all right, sis," he answered jovially. "My money'll take care of itself. If you weren't so busy, I'd kiss you good morning."

He wanted to be affectionate to this sister, who was good, and who, in her way, he knew, loved him. But, somehow, she grew less herself as the years went by, and more and more baffling. It was the hard work, the many children, and the nagging of her husband, he decided, that had changed her. It came to him, in a flash of fancy, that her nature seemed taking on the attributes of stale vegetables, smelly soapsuds, and of the greasy dimes, nickels, and quarters she took in over the counter of the store.

"Go along an' get your breakfast," she said roughly, though secretly pleased. Of all her wandering brood of brothers he had always been her favorite. "I declare I *will* kiss you," she said, with a sudden stir at her heart.

With thumb and forefinger she swept the dripping suds first from one arm and then from the other. He put his arms round her massive waist and kissed her wet steamy lips. The tears welled into her eyes—not so much from strength of feeling as from the weakness of chronic overwork. She shoved him away from her, but not before he caught a glimpse of her moist eyes.

"You'll find breakfast in the oven," she said hurriedly. "Jim ought to be up now. I had to get up early for the washing. Now get along with you and get out of the house early. It won't be nice to-day, what of Tom quittin' an' nobody but Bernard to drive the wagon."

Martin went into the kitchen with a sinking heart, the image of her red face and slatternly form eating its way like acid into his brain. She might love him if she only had some time, he concluded. But she was worked to death. Bernard Higginbotham was a brute to work her so hard. But he could not help but feel, on the other hand, that there had not been anything beautiful in that kiss. It was true, it was an unusual kiss. For years she had kissed him only when he returned from voyages or departed on voyages. But this kiss had tasted soapsuds, and the lips, he had noticed, were flabby. There had been no quick, vigorous lip-pressure such as should accompany any kiss. Hers was the kiss of a tired woman who had been tired so long that she had forgotten how to kiss. He remembered her as a girl, before her marriage, when she would dance with the best, all night, after a hard day's work at the laundry, and think nothing of leaving the dance to go to another day's hard work. And then he thought of Ruth and the cool sweetness that must reside in her lips as it resided in all about her. Her kiss would be like her hand-shake or the way she looked at one, firm and frank. In imagination he dared to think of her lips on his, and so vividly did he imagine that he went dizzy at the thought and seemed to rift through clouds of rose-petals, filling his brain with their perfume.

In the kitchen he found Jim, the other boarder, eating mush very languidly, with a sick, far-away look in his eyes. Jim was a plumber's apprentice whose weak chin and hedonistic temperament, coupled with a certain nervous stupidity, promised to take him nowhere in the race for bread and butter.

"Why don't you eat?" he demanded, as Martin dipped dolefully into the cold, half-cooked oatmeal mush. "Was you drunk again last night?"

Martin shook his head. He was oppressed by the utter squalidness of it all. Ruth Morse seemed farther removed than ever.

"I was," Jim went on with a boastful, nervous giggle. "I was loaded right to the neck. Oh, she was a daisy. Billy brought me home."

Martin nodded that he heard,—it was a habit of nature with him to pay heed to whoever talked to him,—and poured a cup of lukewarm coffee.

"Goin' to the Lotus Club dance to-night?" Jim demanded. "They're goin' to have beer, an' if that Temescal bunch comes, there'll be a rough-house. I don't care, though. I'm takin' my lady friend just the same. Cripes, but I've got a taste in my mouth!"

He made a wry face and attempted to wash the taste away with coffee.

"D'ye know Julia?"

Martin shook his head.

"She's my lady friend," Jim explained, "and she's a peach. I'd introduce you to her, only you'd win her. I don't see what the girls see in you, honest I don't; but the way you win them away from the fellers is sickenin'."

"I never got any away from you," Martin answered uninterestedly. The breakfast had to be got through somehow.

"Yes, you did, too," the other asserted warmly. "There was Maggie."

"Never had anything to do with her. Never danced with her except that one night."

"Yes, an' that's just what did it," Jim cried out. "You just danced with her an' looked at her, an' it was all off. Of course you didn't mean nothin'

472

by it, but it settled me for keeps. Wouldn't look at me again. Always askin' about you. She'd have made fast dates enough with you if you'd wanted to."

"But I didn't want to."

"Wasn't necessary. I was left at the pole." Jim looked at him admiringly. "How d'ye do it, anyway, Mart?"

"By not carin' about 'em," was the answer.

"You mean makin' b'lieve you don't care about them?" Jim queried eagerly.

Martin considered for a moment, then answered, "Perhaps that will do, but with me I guess it's different. I never have cared—much. If you can put it on, it's all right, most likely."

"You should 'a' ben up at Riley's barn last night," Jim announced inconsequently. "A lot of the fellers put on the gloves. There was a peach from West Oakland. They called 'm 'The Rat.' Slick as silk. No one could touch 'm. We was all wishin' you was there. Where was you anyway?"

"Down in Oakland," Martin replied.

"To the show?"

Martin shoved his plate away and got up.

"Comin' to the dance to-night?" the other called after him.

"No, I think not," he answered.

He went downstairs and out into the street, breathing great breaths of air. He had been suffocating in that atmosphere, while the apprentice's chatter had driven him frantic. There had been times when it was all he could do to refrain from reaching over and mopping Jim's face in the mush-plate. The more he had chattered, the more remote had Ruth seemed to him. How could he, herding with such cattle, ever become worthy of her? He was appalled at the problem confronting him, weighted down by the incubus of his working-class station. Everything reached out to hold him down—his sister, his sister's house and family, Jim the apprentice, everybody he knew, every tie of life. Existence did not taste good in his mouth. Up to then he had accepted existence, as he had lived it with all about him, as a good thing. He had never questioned it, except when he read books; but then, they were only books, fairy stories of a fairer and impossible world. But now he had seen that world, possible and real, with a flower of a woman called Ruth in the midmost centre of it; and thenceforth he must know bitter tastes, and longings sharp as pain, and hopelessness that tantalized because it fed on hope.

He had debated between the Berkeley Free Library and the Oakland Free Library, and decided upon the latter because Ruth lived in Oakland. Who could tell?—a library was a most likely place for her, and he might see her there. He did not know the way of libraries, and he wandered through endless rows of fiction, till the delicate-featured French-looking girl who seemed in charge, told him that the reference department was upstairs. He did not know enough to ask the man at the desk, and began his adventures in the philosophy alcove. He had heard of book philosophy, but had not imagined there had been so much written about it. The high, bulging shelves of heavy tomes humbled him and at the same time stimulated him. Here was work for the vigor of his brain. He found books on trigonometry in the mathematics section, and ran the pages, and stared at the meaningless formulas and figures. He could read English, but he saw there an alien speech. Norman and Arthur knew that speech. He had heard them talking it. And they were her brothers. He left the alcove in despair. From every side the books seemed to press upon him and crush him.

He had never dreamed that the fund of human knowledge bulked so big. He was frightened. How could his brain ever master it all? Later, he remembered that there were other men, many men, who had mastered it; and he breathed a great oath, passionately, under his breath, swearing that his brain could do what theirs had done.

And so he wandered on, alternating between depression and elation as he stared at the shelves packed with wisdom. In one miscellaneous section he came upon a "Norrie's Epitome." He turned the pages reverently. In a way, it spoke a kindred speech. Both he and it were of the sea. Then he found a "Bowditch" and books by Lecky and Marshall. There it was; he would teach himself navigation. He would quit drinking, work up, and become a captain. Ruth seemed very near to him in that moment. As a captain, he could marry her (if she would have him). And if she wouldn't, well—he would live a good life among men, because of Her, and he would quit drinking anyway. Then he remembered the underwriters and the owners, the two masters a captain must serve, either of which could and would break him and whose interests were diametrically opposed. He cast his eyes about the room and closed the lids down on a vision of ten thousand books. No; no more of the sea for him. There was power in all that wealth of books, and if he would do great things, he must do them on the land. Besides, captains were not allowed to take their wives to sea with them.

Noon came, and afternoon. He forgot to eat, and sought on for the books on etiquette; for, in addition to career, his mind was vexed by a simple and very concrete problem: *When you meet a young lady and she asks you to call, how soon can you call?* was the way he worded it to himself. But when he found the right shelf, he sought vainly for the answer. He was appalled at the vast edifice of etiquette, and lost himself in the mazes of visiting-card conduct between persons in polite society. He abandoned his search. He had not found what he wanted, though he had found that it would take all of a man's time to be polite, and that he would have to live a preliminary life in which to learn how to be polite.

"Did you find what you wanted?" the man at the desk asked him as he was leaving.

"Yes, sir," he answered. "You have a fine library here."

The man nodded. "We should be glad to see you here often. Are you a sailor?"

"Yes, sir," he answered. "And I'll come again."

Now, how did he know that? he asked himself as he went down the stairs.

And for the first block along the street he walked very stiff and straight and awkwardly, until he forgot himself in his thoughts, whereupon his rolling gait gracefully returned to him.

CHAPTER VI

A terrible restlessness that was akin to hunger afflicted Martin Eden. He was famished for a sight of the girl whose slender hands had gripped his life with a giant's grasp. He could not steel himself to call upon her. He was afraid that he might call too soon, and so be guilty of an awful breach of that awful thing called etiquette. He spent long hours in the Oakland and Berkeley libraries, and made out application blanks for membership for himself, his sisters Gertrude and Marian, and Jim, the latter's consent being obtained at the expense of several glasses of beer. With four cards permitting him to draw books, he burned the gas late in the servant's room, and was charged fifty cents a week for it by Mr. Higginbotham.

The many books he read but served to whet his unrest. Every page of every book was a peep-hole into the realm of knowledge. His hunger fed upon what he read, and increased. Also, he did not know where to begin, and continually suffered from lack of preparation. The commonest references, that he could see plainly every reader was expected to know, he did not know. And the same was true of the poetry he read which maddened him with delight. He read more of Swinburne than was contained in the volume Ruth had lent him; and "Dolores" he understood thoroughly. But surely Ruth did not understand it, he concluded. How could she, living the refined life she did? Then he chanced upon Kipling's poems, and was swept away by the lilt and swing and glamour with which familiar things had been invested. He was amazed at the man's sympathy with life and at his incisive psychology. Psychology was a new word in Martin's vocabulary. He had bought a dictionary, which deed had decreased his supply of money and brought nearer the day on which he must sail in search of more. Also, it incensed Mr. Higginbotham, who would have preferred the money taking the form of board.

He dared not go near Ruth's neighborhood in the daytime, but night found him lurking like a thief around the Morse home, stealing glimpses at the windows and loving the very walls that sheltered her. Several times he barely escaped being caught by her brothers, and once he trailed Mr. Morse down town and studied his face in the lighted streets, longing all the while for some quick danger of death to threaten so that he might spring in and save her father. On another night, his vigil was rewarded by a glimpse of Ruth through a second-story window. He saw only her head and shoulders, and her arms raised as she fixed her hair before a mirror. It was only for a moment, but it was a long moment to him, during which his blood turned to wine and sang through his veins. Then she pulled down the shade. But it was her room—he had learned that; and thereafter he strayed there often, hiding under a dark tree on the opposite side of the street and smoking countless cigarettes. One afternoon he saw her mother coming out of a bank, and received another proof of the enormous distance that separated Ruth from him. She was of the class that dealt with banks. He had never been inside a bank in his life, and he had an idea that such institutions were frequented only by the very rich and the very powerful.

In one way, he had undergone a moral *revolution*. Her cleanness and purity had reacted upon him, and he felt in his being a crying need to be clean. He must be that if he were ever to be worthy of breathing the same air with her. He washed his teeth, and scrubbed his hands with a kitchen scrub-brush till he saw a nail-brush in a drug-store window and divined its use. While purchasing it, the clerk glanced at his nails, suggested a nail-file, and so he became possessed of an additional toilet-tool. He ran across a book in the library on the care of the body, and promptly developed a penchant for a cold-water bath every morning, much to the amazement of Jim, and to the bewilderment of Mr. Higginbotham, who was not in sympathy with such high-fangled notions and who seriously debated whether or not he should charge Martin extra for the water. Another stride was in the direction of creased trousers. Now that Martin was aroused in such matters, he swiftly noted the difference between the baggy knees of the trousers worn by the working class and the straight line from knee to foot of those worn by the men above the working class. Also, he learned the reason why, and invaded his sister's kitchen in search of irons and ironing-board. He had misadventures at first, hopelessly burning one pair and buying another, which expenditure again brought nearer the day on which he must put to sea.

But the reform went deeper than mere outward appearance. He still smoked, but he drank no more. Up to that time, drinking had seemed to him the proper thing for men to do, and he had prided himself on his strong head which enabled him to drink most men under the table. Whenever he encountered a chance shipmate, and there were many in San Francisco, he treated them and was treated in turn, as of old, but he ordered for himself root beer or ginger ale and good-naturedly endured their chaffing. And as they waxed maudlin he studied them, watching the beast rise and master them and thanking God that he was no longer as they. They had their limitations to forget, and when they were drunk, their dim, stupid spirits were even as gods, and each ruled in his heaven of intoxicated desire. With Martin the need for strong drink had vanished. He was drunken in new and more profound ways—with Ruth, who had fired him with love and with a glimpse of higher and eternal life; with books, that had set a myriad maggots of desire gnawing in his brain; and with the sense of personal cleanliness he was achieving, that gave him even more superb health than what he had enjoyed and that made his whole body sing with physical well-being.

One night he went to the theatre, on the blind chance that he might see her there, and from the second balcony he did see her. He saw her come down the aisle, with Arthur and a strange young man with a football mop of hair and eyeglasses, the sight of whom spurred him to instant apprehension and jealousy. He saw her take her seat in the orchestra circle, and little else than her did he see that night—a pair of slender white shoulders and a mass of pale gold hair, dim with distance. But there were others who saw, and now and again, glancing at those about him, he noted two young girls who looked back from the row in front, a dozen seats along, and who smiled at him with bold eyes. He had always been easy-going. It was not in his nature to give rebuff. In the old days he would have smiled back, and gone further and encouraged smiling. But now it was different. He did smile back, then looked away, and looked no more deliberately. But several times, forgetting the existence of the two girls, his eyes caught their smiles. He could not re-thumb himself in a day, nor could he violate the intrinsic kindliness of his nature; so, at such moments, he smiled at the girls in warm human friendliness. It was nothing new to him. He knew they were reaching out their woman's hands to him.

But it was different now. Far down there in the orchestra circle was the one woman in all the world, so different, so terrifically different, from these two girls of his class, that he could feel for them only pity and sorrow. He had it in his heart to wish that they could possess, in some small measure, her goodness and glory. And not for the world could he hurt them because of their outreaching. He was not flattered by it; he even felt a slight shame at his lowliness that permitted it. He knew, did he belong in Ruth's class, that there would be no overtures from these girls; and with each glance of theirs he felt the fingers of his own class clutching at him to hold him down.

He left his seat before the curtain went down on the last act, intent on seeing Her as she passed out. There were always numbers of men who stood on the sidewalk outside, and he could pull his cap down over his eyes and screen himself behind some one's shoulder so that she should not see him. He emerged from the theatre with the first of the crowd; but scarcely had he taken his position on the edge of the sidewalk when the two girls appeared. They were looking for him, he knew; and for the moment he could have cursed that in him which drew women. Their casual edging across the sidewalk to the curb, as they drew near, apprised him of discovery. They slowed down, and were in the thick of the crown as they came up with him. One of them brushed against him and apparently for the first time noticed him. She was a slender, dark girl, with black, defiant eyes. But they smiled at him, and he smiled back.

"Hello," he said.

It was automatic; he had said it so often before under similar circumstances of first meetings. Besides, he could do no less. There was that large tolerance and sympathy in his nature that would permit him to do no less. The black-eyed girl smiled gratification and greeting, and showed signs of stopping, while her companion, arm linked in arm, giggled and likewise showed signs of halting. He thought quickly. It would never do for Her to come out and see him talking there with them. Quite naturally, as a matter of course, he swung in along-side the dark-eyed one and walked with her. There was no awkwardness on his part, no numb tongue. He was at home here, and he held his own royally in the badinage, bristling with slang and sharpness, that was always the preliminary to getting acquainted in these swift-moving affairs. At the corner where the main stream of people flowed onward, he started to edge out into the cross street. But the girl with the black eyes caught his arm, following him and dragging her companion after her, as she cried:

"Hold on, Bill! What's yer rush? You're not goin' to shake us so sudden as all that?"

He halted with a laugh, and turned, facing them. Across their shoulders he could see the moving throng passing under the street lamps. Where he stood it was not so light, and, unseen, he would be able to see Her as she passed by. She would certainly pass by, for that way led home.

"What's her name?" he asked of the giggling girl, nodding at the dark-eyed one.

"You ask her," was the convulsed response.

"Well, what is it?" he demanded, turning squarely on the girl in question.

"You ain't told me yours, yet," she retorted.

"You never asked it," he smiled. "Besides, you guessed the first rattle. It's Bill, all right, all right."

"Aw, go 'long with you." She looked him in the eyes, her own sharply passionate and inviting. "What is it, honest?"

Again she looked. All the centuries of woman since sex began were eloquent in her eyes. And he measured her in a careless way, and knew, bold now, that she would begin to retreat, coyly and delicately, as he pursued, ever ready to reverse the game should he turn fainthearted. And, too, he was human, and could feel the draw of her, while his ego could not but appreciate the flattery of her kindness. Oh, he knew it all, and knew them well, from A to Z. Good, as goodness might be measured in their particular class, hard-working for meagre wages and scorning the sale of self for easier ways, nervously desirous for some small pinch of happiness in the desert of existence, and facing a future that was a gamble between the ugliness

481

of unending toil and the black pit of more terrible wretchedness, the way whereto being briefer though better paid.

"Bill," he answered, nodding his head. "Sure, Pete, Bill an' no other."

"No joshin'?" she queried.

"It ain't Bill at all," the other broke in.

"How do you know?" he demanded. "You never laid eyes on me before."

"No need to, to know you're lyin'," was the retort.

"Straight, Bill, what is it?" the first girl asked.

"Bill'll do," he confessed.

She reached out to his arm and shook him playfully. "I knew you was lyin', but you look good to me just the same."

He captured the hand that invited, and felt on the palm familiar markings and distortions.

"When'd you chuck the cannery?" he asked.

"How'd yeh know?" and, "My, ain't cheh a mind-reader!" the girls chorussed.

And while he exchanged the stupidities of stupid minds with them, before his inner sight towered the book-shelves of the library, filled with the wisdom of the ages. He smiled bitterly at the incongruity of it, and was assailed by doubts. But between inner vision and outward pleasantry he found time to watch the theatre crowd streaming by. And then he saw Her, under the lights, between her brother and the strange young man with glasses, and his heart seemed to stand still. He had waited long for this moment. He had time to note the light, fluffy something that hid her queenly head, the tasteful lines of her wrapped figure, the gracefulness of her carriage and of the hand that caught up her skirts; and then she was gone and he was left staring at the two girls of the cannery, at their tawdry attempts at prettiness of dress, their tragic efforts to be clean and trim, the cheap cloth, the cheap ribbons, and the cheap rings on the fingers. He felt a tug at his arm, and heard a voice saying:-

"Wake up, Bill! What's the matter with you?"

"What was you sayin'?" he asked.

"Oh, nothin'," the dark girl answered, with a toss of her head. "I was only remarkin'—"

"What?"

"Well, I was whisperin' it'd be a good idea if you could dig up a gentleman friend—for her" (indicating her companion), "and then, we could go off an' have ice-cream soda somewhere, or coffee, or anything."

He was afflicted by a sudden spiritual nausea. The transition from Ruth to this had been too abrupt. Ranged side by side with the bold, defiant eyes of the girl before him, he saw Ruth's clear, luminous eyes, like a saint's, gazing at him out of unplumbed depths of purity. And, somehow, he felt within him a stir of power. He was better than this. Life meant more to him than it meant to these two girls whose thoughts did not go beyond ice-cream and a gentleman friend. He remembered that he had led always a secret life in his thoughts. These thoughts he had tried to share, but never had he found a woman capable of understanding—nor a man. He had tried, at times, but had only puzzled his listeners. And as his thoughts had been beyond them, so, he argued now, he must be beyond them. He felt power move in him, and clenched his fists. If life meant more to him, then it was for him to demand more from life, but he could not demand it from such companionship as this. Those bold black eyes had nothing to offer. He knew the thoughts behind them—of ice-cream and of something else. But those saint's eyes alongside—they offered all he knew and more than he could guess. They offered books and painting, beauty and repose, and all the fine elegance of higher existence. Behind those black eyes he knew every thought process. It was like clockwork. He could watch every wheel go around. Their bid was low pleasure, narrow as the grave, that palled, and the grave was at the end of it. But the bid of the saint's eyes was mystery, and wonder unthinkable, and eternal life. He had caught glimpses of the soul in them, and glimpses of his own soul, too.

"There's only one thing wrong with the programme," he said aloud. "I've got a date already."

The girl's eyes blazed her disappointment.

"To sit up with a sick friend, I suppose?" she sneered.

"No, a real, honest date with—" he faltered, "with a girl."

"You're not stringin' me?" she asked earnestly.

He looked her in the eyes and answered: "It's straight, all right. But why can't we meet some other time? You ain't told me your name yet. An' where d'ye live?"

"Lizzie," she replied, softening toward him, her hand pressing his arm, while her body leaned against his. "Lizzie Connolly. And I live at Fifth an' Market."

He talked on a few minutes before saying good night. He did not go home immediately; and under the tree where he kept his vigils he looked up at a window and murmured: "That date was with you, Ruth. I kept it for you."

CHAPTER VII

A week of heavy reading had passed since the evening he first met Ruth Morse, and still he dared not call. Time and again he nerved himself up to call, but under the doubts that assailed him his determination died away. He did not know the proper time to call, nor was there any one to tell him, and he was afraid of committing himself to an irretrievable blunder. Having shaken himself free from his old companions and old ways of life, and having no new companions, nothing remained for him but to read, and the long hours he devoted to it would have ruined a dozen pairs of ordinary eyes. But his eyes were strong, and they were backed by a body superbly strong. Furthermore, his mind was fallow. It had lain fallow all his life so far as the abstract thought of the books was concerned, and it was ripe for the sowing. It had never been jaded by study, and it bit hold of the knowledge in the books with sharp teeth that would not let go.

It seemed to him, by the end of the week, that he had lived centuries, so far behind were the old life and outlook. But he was baffled by lack of preparation. He attempted to read books that required years of preliminary specialization. One day he would read a book of antiquated philosophy, and the next day one that was ultra-modern, so that his head would be whirling with the conflict and contradiction of ideas. It was the same with the economists. On the one shelf at the library he found Karl Marx, Ricardo, Adam Smith, and Mill, and the abstruse formulas of the one gave no clew that the ideas of another were obsolete. He was bewildered, and yet he wanted to know. He had become interested, in a day, in economics, industry, and politics. Passing through the City Hall Park, he had noticed a group of men, in the centre of which were half a dozen, with flushed faces and raised voices, earnestly carrying on a discussion. He joined the listeners, and heard a new, alien tongue in the mouths of the philosophers of the people. One was a tramp, another was a labor agitator, a third was a law-school student, and the remainder was composed of wordy workingmen. For the first time he heard of socialism, anarchism, and single tax, and learned that there were warring social philosophies. He heard hundreds of technical words that were new to him, belonging to fields of thought that his meagre reading had never touched upon. Because of this he could not follow the arguments closely, and he could only guess at and surmise the ideas wrapped up in such strange expressions. Then there was a black-eyed restaurant waiter who was a theosophist, a union baker who was an agnostic, an old man who baffled all of them with the strange philosophy that *what is is right,* and another old man who discoursed interminably about the cosmos and the father-atom and the mother-atom.

Martin Eden's head was in a state of addlement when he went away after several hours, and he hurried to the library to look up the definitions of a dozen unusual words. And when he left the library, he carried under his arm four volumes: Madam Blavatsky's "Secret Doctrine," "Progress and Poverty," "The Quintessence of Socialism," and, "Warfare of Religion and Science." Unfortunately, he began on the "Secret Doctrine." Every line bristled with many-syllabled words he did not understand. He sat up in bed, and the dictionary was in front of him more often than the book. He looked up so many new words that when they recurred, he had forgotten their meaning and had to look them up again. He devised the plan of writing the definitions in a note-book, and filled page after page with them. And still he could not understand. He read until three in the morning, and his brain was in a turmoil, but not one essential thought in the text had he grasped. He looked up, and it seemed that the room was lifting, heeling, and plunging like a ship upon the sea. Then he hurled the "Secret Doctrine" and many curses across the room, turned off the gas, and composed himself to sleep. Nor did he have much better luck with the other three books. It was not that his brain was weak or incapable; it could think these thoughts were it not for lack of training in thinking and lack of the thought-tools with which to think. He guessed this, and for a while entertained the idea of reading nothing but the dictionary until he had mastered every word in it.

Poetry, however, was his solace, and he read much of it, finding his greatest joy in the simpler poets, who were more understandable. He loved beauty, and there he found beauty. Poetry, like music, stirred him profoundly, and, though he did not know it, he was preparing his mind for the heavier work that was to come. The pages of his mind were blank, and, without effort, much he read and liked, stanza by stanza, was impressed upon those pages, so that he was soon able to extract great joy from chanting aloud or under his breath the music and the beauty of the printed words he had read. Then he stumbled upon Gayley's "Classic Myths" and Bulfinch's "Age of Fable," side by side on a library shelf. It was illumination, a great light in the darkness of his ignorance, and he read poetry more avidly than ever.

The man at the desk in the library had seen Martin there so often that he had become quite cordial, always greeting him with a smile and a nod when he entered. It was because of this that Martin did a daring thing. Drawing out some books at the desk, and while the man was stamping the cards, Martin blurted out:-

"Say, there's something I'd like to ask you."

The man smiled and paid attention.

"When you meet a young lady an' she asks you to call, how soon can you call?"

Martin felt his shirt press and cling to his shoulders, what of the sweat of the effort.

"Why I'd say any time," the man answered.

"Yes, but this is different," Martin objected. "She—I—well, you see, it's this way: maybe she won't be there. She goes to the university."

"Then call again."

"What I said ain't what I meant," Martin confessed falteringly, while he made up his mind to throw himself wholly upon the other's mercy. "I'm just a rough sort of a fellow, an' I ain't never seen anything of society. This girl is all that I ain't, an' I ain't anything that she is. You don't think I'm playin' the fool, do you?" he demanded abruptly.

"No, no; not at all, I assure you," the other protested. "Your request is not exactly in the scope of the reference department, but I shall be only too pleased to assist you."

Martin looked at him admiringly.

"If I could tear it off that way, I'd be all right," he said.

"I beg pardon?"

"I mean if I could talk easy that way, an' polite, an' all the rest."

"Oh," said the other, with comprehension.

"What is the best time to call? The afternoon?—not too close to meal-time? Or the evening? Or Sunday?"

"I'll tell you," the librarian said with a brightening face. "You call her up on the telephone and find out."

"I'll do it," he said, picking up his books and starting away.

He turned back and asked:-

"When you're speakin' to a young lady—say, for instance, Miss Lizzie Smith—do you say 'Miss Lizzie'? or 'Miss Smith'?"

"Say 'Miss Smith,'" the librarian stated authoritatively. "Say 'Miss Smith' always—until you come to know her better."

So it was that Martin Eden solved the problem.

"Come down any time; I'll be at home all afternoon," was Ruth's reply over the telephone to his stammered request as to when he could return the borrowed books.

She met him at the door herself, and her woman's eyes took in immediately the creased trousers and the certain slight but indefinable change in him for the better. Also, she was struck by his face. It was almost violent, this health of his, and it seemed to rush out of him and at her in waves of force. She felt the urge again of the desire to lean toward him for warmth, and marvelled again at the effect his presence produced upon her. And he, in turn, knew again the swimming sensation of bliss when he felt the contact of her hand in greeting. The difference between them lay in that she was cool and self-possessed while his face flushed to the roots of the hair. He stumbled with his old awkwardness after her, and his shoulders swung and lurched perilously.

Once they were seated in the living-room, he began to get on easily— more easily by far than he had expected. She made it easy for him; and the gracious spirit with which she did it made him love her more madly than ever. They talked first of the borrowed books, of the Swinburne he was devoted to, and of the Browning he did not understand; and she led the conversation on from subject to subject, while she pondered the problem of how she could be of help to him. She had thought of this often since their first meeting. She wanted to help him. He made a call upon her pity and tenderness that no one had ever made before, and the pity was not so much derogatory of him as maternal in her. Her pity could not be of the common sort, when the man who drew it was so much man as to shock her with maidenly fears and set her mind and pulse thrilling with strange thoughts and feelings. The old fascination of his neck was there, and there was sweetness in the thought of laying her hands upon it. It seemed still a wanton impulse, but she had grown more used to it. She did not dream that in such guise new-born love would epitomize itself. Nor did she dream that the feeling he excited in her was love. She thought she was merely interested in him as an unusual type possessing various potential excellencies, and she even felt philanthropic about it.

She did not know she desired him; but with him it was different. He knew that he loved her, and he desired her as he had never before desired anything in his life. He had loved poetry for beauty's sake; but since he met her the gates to the vast field of love-poetry had been opened wide. She had given him understanding even more than Bulfinch and Gayley. There was a line that a week before he would not have favored with a second thought— "God's own mad lover dying on a kiss"; but now it was ever insistent in his mind. He marvelled at the wonder of it and the truth; and as he gazed upon her he knew that he could die gladly upon a kiss. He felt himself God's own mad lover, and no accolade of knighthood could have given him greater pride. And at last he knew the meaning of life and why he had been born.

As he gazed at her and listened, his thoughts grew daring. He reviewed all the wild delight of the pressure of her hand in his at the door, and longed for it again. His gaze wandered often toward her lips, and he yearned for them hungrily. But there was nothing gross or earthly about this yearning. It gave him exquisite delight to watch every movement and play of those lips as they enunciated the words she spoke; yet they were not ordinary lips such as all men and women had. Their substance was not mere human clay. They were lips of pure spirit, and his desire for them seemed absolutely different from the desire that had led him to other women's lips. He could kiss her lips, rest his own physical lips upon them, but it would be with the lofty and awful fervor with which one would kiss the robe of God. He was not conscious of this transvaluation of values that had taken place in him, and was unaware that the light that shone in his eyes when he looked at her was quite the same light that shines in all men's eyes when the desire of love is upon them. He did not dream how ardent and masculine his gaze was, nor that the warm flame of it was affecting the alchemy of her spirit. Her penetrative virginity exalted and disguised his own emotions, elevating his thoughts to a star-cool chastity, and he would have been startled to learn that there was that shining out of his eyes, like warm waves, that flowed through her and kindled a kindred warmth. She was subtly perturbed by it, and more than once, though she knew not why, it disrupted her train of thought with its delicious intrusion and compelled her to grope for the remainder of ideas partly uttered. Speech was always easy with her, and these interruptions would have puzzled her had she not decided that it was because he was a remarkable type. She was very sensitive to impressions, and it was not strange, after all, that this aura of a traveller from another world should so affect her.

The problem in the background of her consciousness was how to help him, and she turned the conversation in that direction; but it was Martin who came to the point first.

"I wonder if I can get some advice from you," he began, and received an acquiescence of willingness that made his heart bound. "You remember the other time I was here I said I couldn't talk about books an' things because I didn't know how? Well, I've ben doin' a lot of thinkin' ever since. I've ben to the library a whole lot, but most of the books I've tackled have ben over my head. Mebbe I'd better begin at the beginnin'. I ain't never had no advantages. I've worked pretty hard ever since I was a kid, an' since I've ben to the library, lookin' with new eyes at books—an' lookin' at new books, too—I've just about concluded that I ain't ben reading the right kind. You know the books you find in cattle-camps an' fo'c's'ls ain't the same you've got in this house, for instance. Well, that's the sort of readin' matter I've ben accustomed to. And yet—an' I ain't just makin' a brag of it—I've ben different from the people I've herded with. Not that I'm any better than the sailors an' cow-punchers I travelled with,—I was cow-punchin' for a short time, you know,—but I always liked books, read everything I could lay hands on, an'—well, I guess I think differently from most of 'em.

"Now, to come to what I'm drivin' at. I was never inside a house like this. When I come a week ago, an' saw all this, an' you, an' your mother, an' brothers, an' everything—well, I liked it. I'd heard about such things an' read about such things in some of the books, an' when I looked around at your house, why, the books come true. But the thing I'm after is I liked it. I wanted it. I want it now. I want to breathe air like you get in this house—air that is filled with books, and pictures, and beautiful things, where people talk in low voices an' are clean, an' their thoughts are clean. The air I always breathed was mixed up with grub an' house-rent an' scrappin' an booze an' that's all they talked about, too. Why, when you was crossin' the room to kiss your mother, I thought it was the most beautiful thing I ever seen. I've seen a whole lot of life, an' somehow I've seen a whole lot more of it than most of them that was with me. I like to see, an' I want to see more, an' I want to see it different.

"But I ain't got to the point yet. Here it is. I want to make my way to the kind of life you have in this house. There's more in life than booze, an' hard work, an' knockin' about. Now, how am I goin' to get it? Where do I take hold an' begin? I'm willin' to work my passage, you know, an' I can make most men sick when it comes to hard work. Once I get started, I'll

491

work night an' day. Mebbe you think it's funny, me askin' you about all this. I know you're the last person in the world I ought to ask, but I don't know anybody else I could ask—unless it's Arthur. Mebbe I ought to ask him. If I was—"

His voice died away. His firmly planned intention had come to a halt on the verge of the horrible probability that he should have asked Arthur and that he had made a fool of himself. Ruth did not speak immediately. She was too absorbed in striving to reconcile the stumbling, uncouth speech and its simplicity of thought with what she saw in his face. She had never looked in eyes that expressed greater power. Here was a man who could do anything, was the message she read there, and it accorded ill with the weakness of his spoken thought. And for that matter so complex and quick was her own mind that she did not have a just appreciation of simplicity. And yet she had caught an impression of power in the very groping of this mind. It had seemed to her like a giant writhing and straining at the bonds that held him down. Her face was all sympathy when she did speak.

"What you need, you realize yourself, and it is education. You should go back and finish grammar school, and then go through to high school and university."

"But that takes money," he interrupted.

"Oh!" she cried. "I had not thought of that. But then you have relatives, somebody who could assist you?"

He shook his head.

"My father and mother are dead. I've two sisters, one married, an' the other'll get married soon, I suppose. Then I've a string of brothers,—I'm the youngest,—but they never helped nobody. They've just knocked around over the world, lookin' out for number one. The oldest died in India. Two are in South Africa now, an' another's on a whaling voyage, an' one's travellin' with a circus—he does trapeze work. An' I guess I'm just like them. I've taken care of myself since I was eleven—that's when my mother died. I've got to study by myself, I guess, an' what I want to know is where to begin."

"I should say the first thing of all would be to get a grammar. Your grammar is—" She had intended saying "awful," but she amended it to "is not particularly good."

He flushed and sweated.

"I know I must talk a lot of slang an' words you don't understand. But then they're the only words I know—how to speak. I've got other words in my mind, picked 'em up from books, but I can't pronounce 'em, so I don't use 'em."

"It isn't what you say, so much as how you say it. You don't mind my being frank, do you? I don't want to hurt you."

"No, no," he cried, while he secretly blessed her for her kindness. "Fire away. I've got to know, an' I'd sooner know from you than anybody else."

"Well, then, you say, 'You was'; it should be, 'You were.' You say 'I seen' for 'I saw.' You use the double negative—"

"What's the double negative?" he demanded; then added humbly, "You see, I don't even understand your explanations."

"I'm afraid I didn't explain that," she smiled. "A double negative is—let me see—well, you say, 'never helped nobody.' 'Never' is a negative. 'Nobody' is another negative. It is a rule that two negatives make a positive. 'Never helped nobody' means that, not helping nobody, they must have helped somebody."

"That's pretty clear," he said. "I never thought of it before. But it don't mean they *must* have helped somebody, does it? Seems to me that 'never helped nobody' just naturally fails to say whether or not they helped somebody. I never thought of it before, and I'll never say it again."

She was pleased and surprised with the quickness and surety of his mind. As soon as he had got the clew he not only understood but corrected her error.

"You'll find it all in the grammar," she went on. "There's something else I noticed in your speech. You say 'don't' when you shouldn't. 'Don't' is a contraction and stands for two words. Do you know them?"

He thought a moment, then answered, "'Do not.'"

She nodded her head, and said, "And you use 'don't' when you mean 'does not.'"

He was puzzled over this, and did not get it so quickly.

"Give me an illustration," he asked.

"Well—" She puckered her brows and pursed up her mouth as she thought, while he looked on and decided that her expression was most adorable. "'It don't do to be hasty.' Change 'don't' to 'do not,' and it reads, 'It do not do to be hasty,' which is perfectly absurd."

He turned it over in his mind and considered.

"Doesn't it jar on your ear?" she suggested.

"Can't say that it does," he replied judicially.

"Why didn't you say, 'Can't say that it do'?" she queried.

"That sounds wrong," he said slowly. "As for the other I can't make up my mind. I guess my ear ain't had the trainin' yours has."

"There is no such word as 'ain't,'" she said, prettily emphatic.

Martin flushed again.

"And you say 'ben' for 'been,'" she continued; "'come' for 'came'; and the way you chop your endings is something dreadful."

"How do you mean?" He leaned forward, feeling that he ought to get down on his knees before so marvellous a mind. "How do I chop?"

"You don't complete the endings. 'A-n-d' spells 'and.' You pronounce it 'an'.' 'I-n-g' spells 'ing.' Sometimes you pronounce it 'ing' and sometimes you leave off the 'g.' And then you slur by dropping initial letters and diphthongs.

'T-h-e-m' spells 'them.' You pronounce it—oh, well, it is not necessary to go over all of them. What you need is the grammar. I'll get one and show you how to begin."

As she arose, there shot through his mind something that he had read in the etiquette books, and he stood up awkwardly, worrying as to whether he was doing the right thing, and fearing that she might take it as a sign that he was about to go.

"By the way, Mr. Eden," she called back, as she was leaving the room. "What is *booze*? You used it several times, you know."

"Oh, booze," he laughed. "It's slang. It means whiskey an' beer—anything that will make you drunk."

"And another thing," she laughed back. "Don't use 'you' when you are impersonal. 'You' is very personal, and your use of it just now was not precisely what you meant."

"I don't just see that."

"Why, you said just now, to me, 'whiskey and beer—anything that will make you drunk'—make me drunk, don't you see?"

"Well, it would, wouldn't it?"

"Yes, of course," she smiled. "But it would be nicer not to bring me into it. Substitute 'one' for 'you' and see how much better it sounds."

When she returned with the grammar, she drew a chair near his—he wondered if he should have helped her with the chair—and sat down beside him. She turned the pages of the grammar, and their heads were inclined toward each other. He could hardly follow her outlining of the work he must do, so amazed was he by her delightful propinquity. But when she began to lay down the importance of conjugation, he forgot all about her. He had never heard of conjugation, and was fascinated by the glimpse he was catching into the tie-ribs of language. He leaned closer to the page, and her hair touched his cheek. He had fainted but once in his life, and he thought he was going to faint again. He could scarcely breathe, and his heart was pounding the blood up into his throat and suffocating him. Never had she seemed so accessible as now. For the moment the great gulf that separated them was bridged. But there was no diminution in the loftiness of his feeling for her. She had not descended to him. It was he who had been caught up into the clouds and carried to her. His reverence for her, in that moment, was of same order as religious awe and fervor. It seemed to him that he had intruded upon the holy of holies, and slowly and carefully he moved his head aside from the contact which thrilled him like an electric shock and of which she had not been aware.

CHAPTER VIII

Several weeks went by, during which Martin Eden studied his grammar, reviewed the books on etiquette, and read voraciously the books that caught his fancy. Of his own class he saw nothing. The girls of the Lotus Club wondered what had become of him and worried Jim with questions, and some of the fellows who put on the glove at Riley's were glad that Martin came no more. He made another discovery of treasure-trove in the library. As the grammar had shown him the tie-ribs of language, so that book showed him the tie-ribs of poetry, and he began to learn metre and construction and form, beneath the beauty he loved finding the why and wherefore of that beauty. Another modern book he found treated poetry as a representative art, treated it exhaustively, with copious illustrations from the best in literature. Never had he read fiction with so keen zest as he studied these books. And his fresh mind, untaxed for twenty years and impelled by maturity of desire, gripped hold of what he read with a virility unusual to the student mind.

When he looked back now from his vantage-ground, the old world he had known, the world of land and sea and ships, of sailor-men and harpy-women, seemed a very small world; and yet it blended in with this new world and expanded. His mind made for unity, and he was surprised when at first he began to see points of contact between the two worlds. And he was ennobled, as well, by the loftiness of thought and beauty he found in the books. This led him to believe more firmly than ever that up above him, in society like Ruth and her family, all men and women thought these thoughts and lived them. Down below where he lived was the ignoble, and he wanted to purge himself of the ignoble that had soiled all his days, and to rise to that sublimated realm where dwelt the upper classes. All his childhood and youth had been troubled by a vague unrest; he had never known what he wanted, but he had wanted something that he had hunted vainly for until he met Ruth. And now his unrest had become sharp and painful, and he knew at last, clearly and definitely, that it was beauty, and intellect, and love that he must have.

During those several weeks he saw Ruth half a dozen times, and each time was an added inspiration. She helped him with his English, corrected his pronunciation, and started him on arithmetic. But their intercourse was not all devoted to elementary study. He had seen too much of life, and his mind was too matured, to be wholly content with fractions, cube root, parsing, and analysis; and there were times when their conversation turned on other themes—the last poetry he had read, the latest poet she had studied. And when she read aloud to him her favorite passages, he ascended to the topmost heaven of delight. Never, in all the women he had heard speak, had he heard a voice like hers. The least sound of it was a stimulus to his love, and he thrilled and throbbed with every word she uttered. It was the quality of it, the repose, and the musical modulation—the soft, rich, indefinable product of culture and a gentle soul. As he listened to her, there rang in the ears of his memory the harsh cries of barbarian women and of hags, and, in lesser degrees of harshness, the strident voices of working women and of the girls of his own class. Then the chemistry of vision would begin to work, and they would troop in review across his mind, each, by contrast, multiplying Ruth's glories. Then, too, his bliss was heightened by the knowledge that her mind was comprehending what she read and was quivering with appreciation of the beauty of the written thought. She read to him much from "The Princess," and often he saw her eyes swimming with tears, so finely was her aesthetic nature strung. At such moments her own emotions elevated him till he was as a god, and, as he gazed at her and listened, he seemed gazing on the face of life and reading its deepest secrets. And then, becoming aware of the heights of exquisite sensibility he attained, he decided that this was love and that love was the greatest thing in the world. And in review would pass along the corridors of memory all previous thrills and burnings he had known,—the drunkenness of wine, the caresses of women, the rough play and give and take of physical contests,—and they seemed trivial and mean compared with this sublime ardor he now enjoyed.

The situation was obscured to Ruth. She had never had any experiences of the heart. Her only experiences in such matters were of the books, where the facts of ordinary day were translated by fancy into a fairy realm of unreality; and she little knew that this rough sailor was creeping into her heart and storing there pent forces that would some day burst forth and surge through her in waves of fire. She did not know the actual fire of love. Her knowledge of love was purely theoretical, and she conceived of it as lambent flame, gentle as the fall of dew or the ripple of quiet water, and cool as the velvet-dark of summer nights. Her idea of love was more that of placid affection, serving the loved one softly in an atmosphere, flower-scented and dim-lighted, of ethereal calm. She did not dream of the volcanic convulsions of love, its scorching heat and sterile wastes of parched ashes. She knew neither her own potencies, nor the potencies of the world; and the deeps of life were to her seas of illusion. The conjugal affection of her father and mother constituted her ideal of love-affinity, and she looked forward some day to emerging, without shock or friction, into that same quiet sweetness of existence with a loved one.

So it was that she looked upon Martin Eden as a novelty, a strange individual, and she identified with novelty and strangeness the effects he produced upon her. It was only natural. In similar ways she had experienced unusual feelings when she looked at wild animals in the menagerie, or when she witnessed a storm of wind, or shuddered at the bright-ribbed lightning. There was something cosmic in such things, and there was something cosmic in him. He came to her breathing of large airs and great spaces. The blaze of tropic suns was in his face, and in his swelling, resilient muscles was the primordial vigor of life. He was marred and scarred by that mysterious world of rough men and rougher deeds, the outposts of which began beyond her horizon. He was untamed, wild, and in secret ways her vanity was touched by the fact that he came so mildly to her hand. Likewise she was stirred by the common impulse to tame the wild thing. It was an unconscious impulse, and farthest from her thoughts that her desire was to re-thumb the clay of him into a likeness of her father's image, which image she believed to be the finest in the world. Nor was there any way, out of her inexperience, for her to know that the cosmic feel she caught of him was that most cosmic of things, love, which with equal power drew men and women together across the world, compelled stags to kill each other in the rutting season, and drove even the elements irresistibly to unite.

His swift development was a source of surprise and interest. She detected unguessed finenesses in him that seemed to bud, day by day, like flowers

499

in congenial soil. She read Browning aloud to him, and was often puzzled by the strange interpretations he gave to mooted passages. It was beyond her to realize that, out of his experience of men and women and life, his interpretations were far more frequently correct than hers. His conceptions seemed naive to her, though she was often fired by his daring flights of comprehension, whose orbit-path was so wide among the stars that she could not follow and could only sit and thrill to the impact of unguessed power. Then she played to him—no longer at him—and probed him with music that sank to depths beyond her plumb-line. His nature opened to music as a flower to the sun, and the transition was quick from his working-class rag-time and jingles to her classical display pieces that she knew nearly by heart. Yet he betrayed a democratic fondness for Wagner, and the "Tannhäuser" overture, when she had given him the clew to it, claimed him as nothing else she played. In an immediate way it personified his life. All his past was the *Venusburg motif,* while her he identified somehow with the *Pilgrim's Chorus motif;* and from the exalted state this elevated him to, he swept onward and upward into that vast shadow-realm of spirit-groping, where good and evil war eternally.

Sometimes he questioned, and induced in her mind temporary doubts as to the correctness of her own definitions and conceptions of music. But her singing he did not question. It was too wholly her, and he sat always amazed at the divine melody of her pure soprano voice. And he could not help but contrast it with the weak pipings and shrill quaverings of factory girls, ill-nourished and untrained, and with the raucous shriekings from gin-cracked throats of the women of the seaport towns. She enjoyed singing and playing to him. In truth, it was the first time she had ever had a human soul to play with, and the plastic clay of him was a delight to mould; for she thought she was moulding it, and her intentions were good. Besides, it was pleasant to be with him. He did not repel her. That first repulsion had been really a fear of her undiscovered self, and the fear had gone to sleep. Though she did not know it, she had a feeling in him of proprietary right. Also, he had a tonic effect upon her. She was studying hard at the university, and it seemed to strengthen her to emerge from the dusty books and have the fresh sea-breeze of his personality blow upon her. Strength! Strength was what she needed, and he gave it to her in generous measure. To come into the same room with him, or to meet him at the door, was to take heart of life. And when he had gone, she would return to her books with a keener zest and fresh store of energy.

She knew her Browning, but it had never sunk into her that it was an awkward thing to play with souls. As her interest in Martin increased, the remodelling of his life became a passion with her.

"There is Mr. Butler," she said one afternoon, when grammar and arithmetic and poetry had been put aside.

"He had comparatively no advantages at first. His father had been a bank cashier, but he lingered for years, dying of consumption in Arizona, so that when he was dead, Mr. Butler, Charles Butler he was called, found himself alone in the world. His father had come from Australia, you know, and so he had no relatives in California. He went to work in a printing-office,—I have heard him tell of it many times,—and he got three dollars a week, at first. His income to-day is at least thirty thousand a year. How did he do it? He was honest, and faithful, and industrious, and economical. He denied himself the enjoyments that most boys indulge in. He made it a point to save so much every week, no matter what he had to do without in order to save it. Of course, he was soon earning more than three dollars a week, and as his wages increased he saved more and more.

"He worked in the daytime, and at night he went to night school. He had his eyes fixed always on the future. Later on he went to night high school. When he was only seventeen, he was earning excellent wages at setting type, but he was ambitious. He wanted a career, not a livelihood, and he was content to make immediate sacrifices for his ultimate again. He decided upon the law, and he entered father's office as an office boy—think of that!— and got only four dollars a week. But he had learned how to be economical, and out of that four dollars he went on saving money."

She paused for breath, and to note how Martin was receiving it. His face was lighted up with interest in the youthful struggles of Mr. Butler; but there was a frown upon his face as well.

"I'd say they was pretty hard lines for a young fellow," he remarked. "Four dollars a week! How could he live on it? You can bet he didn't have any frills. Why, I pay five dollars a week for board now, an' there's nothin' excitin' about it, you can lay to that. He must have lived like a dog. The food he ate—"

"He cooked for himself," she interrupted, "on a little kerosene stove."

"The food he ate must have been worse than what a sailor gets on the worst-feedin' deep-water ships, than which there ain't much that can be possibly worse."

"But think of him now!" she cried enthusiastically. "Think of what his income affords him. His early denials are paid for a thousand-fold."

Martin looked at her sharply.

"There's one thing I'll bet you," he said, "and it is that Mr. Butler is nothin' gay-hearted now in his fat days. He fed himself like that for years an' years, on a boy's stomach, an' I bet his stomach's none too good now for it."

Her eyes dropped before his searching gaze.

"I'll bet he's got dyspepsia right now!" Martin challenged.

"Yes, he has," she confessed; "but—"

"An' I bet," Martin dashed on, "that he's solemn an' serious as an old owl, an' doesn't care a rap for a good time, for all his thirty thousand a year. An' I'll bet he's not particularly joyful at seein' others have a good time. Ain't I right?"

She nodded her head in agreement, and hastened to explain:-

"But he is not that type of man. By nature he is sober and serious. He always was that."

"You can bet he was," Martin proclaimed. "Three dollars a week, an' four dollars a week, an' a young boy cookin' for himself on an oil-burner an' layin' up money, workin' all day an' studyin' all night, just workin' an' never playin', never havin' a good time, an' never learnin' how to have a good time—of course his thirty thousand came along too late."

His sympathetic imagination was flashing upon his inner sight all the thousands of details of the boy's existence and of his narrow spiritual development into a thirty-thousand-dollar-a-year man. With the swiftness and wide-reaching of multitudinous thought Charles Butler's whole life was telescoped upon his vision.

"Do you know," he added, "I feel sorry for Mr. Butler. He was too young to know better, but he robbed himself of life for the sake of thirty thousand a year that's clean wasted upon him. Why, thirty thousand, lump sum, wouldn't buy for him right now what ten cents he was layin' up would have bought him, when he was a kid, in the way of candy an' peanuts or a seat in nigger heaven."

It was just such uniqueness of points of view that startled Ruth. Not only were they new to her, and contrary to her own beliefs, but she always felt in them germs of truth that threatened to unseat or modify her own convictions. Had she been fourteen instead of twenty-four, she might have been changed by them; but she was twenty-four, conservative by nature and upbringing, and already crystallized into the cranny of life where she had been born and formed. It was true, his bizarre judgments troubled her in the moments they were uttered, but she ascribed them to his novelty of type and strangeness of living, and they were soon forgotten. Nevertheless, while she disapproved of them, the strength of their utterance, and the flashing of eyes and earnestness of face that accompanied them, always thrilled her and drew her toward him. She would never have guessed that this man who had come from beyond her horizon, was, in such moments, flashing on beyond her horizon with wider and deeper concepts. Her own limits were the limits of her horizon; but limited minds can recognize limitations only in others. And so she felt that her outlook was very wide indeed, and that where his conflicted with hers marked his limitations; and she dreamed of helping him to see as she saw, of widening his horizon until it was identified with hers.

"But I have not finished my story," she said. "He worked, so father says, as no other office boy he ever had. Mr. Butler was always eager to work.

He never was late, and he was usually at the office a few minutes before his regular time. And yet he saved his time. Every spare moment was devoted to study. He studied book-keeping and type-writing, and he paid for lessons in shorthand by dictating at night to a court reporter who needed practice. He quickly became a clerk, and he made himself invaluable. Father appreciated him and saw that he was bound to rise. It was on father's suggestion that he went to law college. He became a lawyer, and hardly was he back in the office when father took him in as junior partner. He is a great man. He refused the United States Senate several times, and father says he could become a justice of the Supreme Court any time a vacancy occurs, if he wants to. Such a life is an inspiration to all of us. It shows us that a man with will may rise superior to his environment."

"He is a great man," Martin said sincerely.

But it seemed to him there was something in the recital that jarred upon his sense of beauty and life. He could not find an adequate motive in Mr. Butler's life of pinching and privation. Had he done it for love of a woman, or for attainment of beauty, Martin would have understood. God's own mad lover should do anything for the kiss, but not for thirty thousand dollars a year. He was dissatisfied with Mr. Butler's career. There was something paltry about it, after all. Thirty thousand a year was all right, but dyspepsia and inability to be humanly happy robbed such princely income of all its value.

Much of this he strove to express to Ruth, and shocked her and made it clear that more remodelling was necessary. Hers was that common insularity of mind that makes human creatures believe that their color, creed, and politics are best and right and that other human creatures scattered over the world are less fortunately placed than they. It was the same insularity of mind that made the ancient Jew thank God he was not born a woman, and sent the modern missionary god-substituting to the ends of the earth; and it made Ruth desire to shape this man from other crannies of life into the likeness of the men who lived in her particular cranny of life.

504

CHAPTER IX

Back from sea Martin Eden came, homing for California with a lover's desire. His store of money exhausted, he had shipped before the mast on the treasure-hunting schooner; and the Solomon Islands, after eight months of failure to find treasure, had witnessed the breaking up of the expedition. The men had been paid off in Australia, and Martin had immediately shipped on a deep-water vessel for San Francisco. Not alone had those eight months earned him enough money to stay on land for many weeks, but they had enabled him to do a great deal of studying and reading.

His was the student's mind, and behind his ability to learn was the indomitability of his nature and his love for Ruth. The grammar he had taken along he went through again and again until his unjaded brain had mastered it. He noticed the bad grammar used by his shipmates, and made a point of mentally correcting and reconstructing their crudities of speech. To his great joy he discovered that his ear was becoming sensitive and that he was developing grammatical nerves. A double negative jarred him like a discord, and often, from lack of practice, it was from his own lips that the jar came. His tongue refused to learn new tricks in a day.

After he had been through the grammar repeatedly, he took up the dictionary and added twenty words a day to his vocabulary. He found that this was no light task, and at wheel or lookout he steadily went over and over his lengthening list of pronunciations and definitions, while he invariably memorized himself to sleep. "Never did anything," "if I were," and "those things," were phrases, with many variations, that he repeated under his breath in order to accustom his tongue to the language spoken by Ruth. "And" and "ing," with the "d" and "g" pronounced emphatically, he went over thousands of times; and to his surprise he noticed that he was beginning to speak cleaner and more correct English than the officers themselves and the gentleman-adventurers in the cabin who had financed the expedition.

The captain was a fishy-eyed Norwegian who somehow had fallen into possession of a complete Shakespeare, which he never read, and Martin had washed his clothes for him and in return been permitted access to the precious volumes. For a time, so steeped was he in the plays and in the many favorite passages that impressed themselves almost without effort on his brain, that all the world seemed to shape itself into forms of Elizabethan tragedy or comedy and his very thoughts were in blank verse. It trained his ear and gave him a fine appreciation for noble English; withal it introduced into his mind much that was archaic and obsolete.

The eight months had been well spent, and, in addition to what he had learned of right speaking and high thinking, he had learned much of himself. Along with his humbleness because he knew so little, there arose a conviction of power. He felt a sharp gradation between himself and his shipmates, and was wise enough to realize that the difference lay in potentiality rather than achievement. What he could do,—they could do; but within him he felt a confused ferment working that told him there was more in him than he had done. He was tortured by the exquisite beauty of the world, and wished that Ruth were there to share it with him. He decided that he would describe to her many of the bits of South Sea beauty. The creative spirit in him flamed up at the thought and urged that he recreate this beauty for a wider audience than Ruth. And then, in splendor and glory, came the great idea. He would write. He would be one of the eyes through which the world saw, one of the ears through which it heard, one of the hearts through which it felt. He would write—everything—poetry and prose, fiction and description, and plays like Shakespeare. There was career and the way to win to Ruth. The men of literature were the world's giants, and he conceived them to be far finer than the Mr. Butlers who earned thirty thousand a year and could be Supreme Court justices if they wanted to.

Once the idea had germinated, it mastered him, and the return voyage to San Francisco was like a dream. He was drunken with unguessed power and felt that he could do anything. In the midst of the great and lonely sea he gained perspective. Clearly, and for the first lime, he saw Ruth and her world. It was all visualized in his mind as a concrete thing which he could take up in his two hands and turn around and about and examine. There was much that was dim and nebulous in that world, but he saw it as a whole and not in detail, and he saw, also, the way to master it. To write! The thought was fire in him. He would begin as soon as he got back. The first thing he would do would be to describe the voyage of the treasure-hunters. He would sell it to some San Francisco newspaper. He would not tell Ruth anything about it, and she would be surprised and pleased when she saw his name in print. While he wrote, he could go on studying. There were twenty-four hours in each day. He was invincible. He knew how to work, and the citadels would go down before him. He would not have to go to sea again—as a sailor; and for the instant he caught a vision of a steam yacht. There were other writers who possessed steam yachts. Of course, he cautioned himself, it would be slow succeeding at first, and for a time he would be content to earn enough money by his writing to enable him to go on studying. And then, after some time,—a very indeterminate time,—when he had learned and prepared himself, he would write the great things and his name would be on all men's lips. But greater than that, infinitely greater and greatest of all, he would have proved himself worthy of Ruth. Fame was all very well, but it was for Ruth that his splendid dream arose. He was not a fame-monger, but merely one of God's mad lovers.

Arrived in Oakland, with his snug pay-day in his pocket, he took up his old room at Bernard Higginbotham's and set to work. He did not even let Ruth know he was back. He would go and see her when he finished the article on the treasure-hunters. It was not so difficult to abstain from seeing her, because of the violent heat of creative fever that burned in him. Besides, the very article he was writing would bring her nearer to him. He did not know how long an article he should write, but he counted the words in a double-page article in the Sunday supplement of the *San Francisco Examiner*, and guided himself by that. Three days, at white heat, completed his narrative; but when he had copied it carefully, in a large scrawl that was easy to read, he learned from a rhetoric he picked up in the library that there were such things as paragraphs and quotation marks. He had never thought of such things before; and he promptly set to work writing the article over, referring continually to the pages of the rhetoric and learning more in a day about composition than the average schoolboy in a year. When he had copied the article a second time and rolled it up carefully, he read in a newspaper an item on hints to beginners, and discovered the iron law that manuscripts should never be rolled and that they should be written on one side of the paper. He had violated the law on both counts. Also, he learned from the item that first-class papers paid a minimum of ten dollars a column. So, while he copied the manuscript a third time, he consoled himself by multiplying ten columns by ten dollars. The product was always the same, one hundred dollars, and he decided that that was better than seafaring. If it hadn't been for his blunders, he would have finished the article in three days. One hundred dollars in three days! It would have taken him three months and longer on the sea to earn a similar amount. A man was a fool to go to sea when he could write, he concluded, though the money in itself meant nothing to him. Its value was in the liberty it would get him, the presentable garments it would buy him, all of which would bring him nearer, swiftly nearer, to the slender, pale girl who had turned his life back upon itself and given him inspiration.

He mailed the manuscript in a flat envelope, and addressed it to the editor of the *San Francisco Examiner*. He had an idea that anything accepted by a paper was published immediately, and as he had sent the manuscript in on Friday he expected it to come out on the following Sunday. He conceived that it would be fine to let that event apprise Ruth of his return. Then, Sunday afternoon, he would call and see her. In the meantime he was occupied by another idea, which he prided himself upon as being a particularly sane, careful, and modest idea. He would write an adventure story for boys and sell it to *The Youth's Companion*. He went to the free reading-room and looked through the files of *The Youth's Companion*. Serial stories, he found, were usually published in that weekly in five instalments of about three thousand words each. He discovered several serials that ran to seven instalments, and decided to write one of that length.

He had been on a whaling voyage in the Arctic, once—a voyage that was to have been for three years and which had terminated in shipwreck at the end of six months. While his imagination was fanciful, even fantastic at times, he had a basic love of reality that compelled him to write about the things he knew. He knew whaling, and out of the real materials of his knowledge he proceeded to manufacture the fictitious adventures of the two boys he intended to use as joint heroes. It was easy work, he decided on Saturday evening. He had completed on that day the first instalment of three thousand words—much to the amusement of Jim, and to the open derision of Mr. Higginbotham, who sneered throughout meal-time at the "litery" person they had discovered in the family.

Martin contented himself by picturing his brother-in-law's surprise on Sunday morning when he opened his *Examiner* and saw the article on the treasure-hunters. Early that morning he was out himself to the front door, nervously racing through the many-sheeted newspaper. He went through it a second time, very carefully, then folded it up and left it where he had found it. He was glad he had not told any one about his article. On second thought he concluded that he had been wrong about the speed with which things found their way into newspaper columns. Besides, there had not been any news value in his article, and most likely the editor would write to him about it first.

After breakfast he went on with his serial. The words flowed from his pen, though he broke off from the writing frequently to look up definitions in the dictionary or to refer to the rhetoric. He often read or re-read a chapter at a time, during such pauses; and he consoled himself that while he was not writing the great things he felt to be in him, he was learning composition, at any rate, and training himself to shape up and express his thoughts. He toiled on till dark, when he went out to the reading-room and explored magazines and weeklies until the place closed at ten o'clock. This was his programme for a week. Each day he did three thousand words, and each evening he puzzled his way through the magazines, taking note of the stories, articles, and poems that editors saw fit to publish. One thing was certain: What these multitudinous writers did he could do, and only give him time and he would do what they could not do. He was cheered to read in *Book News*, in a paragraph on the payment of magazine writers, not that Rudyard Kipling received a dollar per word, but that the minimum rate paid by first-class magazines was two cents a word. *The Youth's Companion* was certainly first class, and at that rate the three thousand words he had written that day would bring him sixty dollars—two months' wages on the sea!

On Friday night he finished the serial, twenty-one thousand words long. At two cents a word, he calculated, that would bring him four hundred and twenty dollars. Not a bad week's work. It was more money than he had ever possessed at one time. He did not know how he could spend it all. He had tapped a gold mine. Where this came from he could always get more. He planned to buy some more clothes, to subscribe to many magazines, and to buy dozens of reference books that at present he was compelled to go to the library to consult. And still there was a large portion of the four hundred and twenty dollars unspent. This worried him until the thought came to him of hiring a servant for Gertrude and of buying a bicycle for Marion.

He mailed the bulky manuscript to *The Youth's Companion*, and on Saturday afternoon, after having planned an article on pearl-diving, he went to see Ruth. He had telephoned, and she went herself to greet him at the door. The old familiar blaze of health rushed out from him and struck her like a blow. It seemed to enter into her body and course through her veins in a liquid glow, and to set her quivering with its imparted strength. He flushed warmly as he took her hand and looked into her blue eyes, but the fresh bronze of eight months of sun hid the flush, though it did not protect the neck from the gnawing chafe of the stiff collar. She noted the red line of it with amusement which quickly vanished as she glanced at his clothes. They really fitted him,—it was his first made-to-order suit,—and he seemed slimmer and better modelled. In addition, his cloth cap had been replaced by a soft hat, which she commanded him to put on and then complimented him on his appearance. She did not remember when she had felt so happy. This change in him was her handiwork, and she was proud of it and fired with ambition further to help him.

But the most radical change of all, and the one that pleased her most, was the change in his speech. Not only did he speak more correctly, but he spoke more easily, and there were many new words in his vocabulary. When he grew excited or enthusiastic, however, he dropped back into the old slurring and the dropping of final consonants. Also, there was an awkward hesitancy, at times, as he essayed the new words he had learned. On the other hand, along with his ease of expression, he displayed a lightness and facetiousness of thought that delighted her. It was his old spirit of humor and badinage that had made him a favorite in his own class, but which he had hitherto been unable to use in her presence through lack of words and training. He was just beginning to orientate himself and to feel that he was not wholly an intruder. But he was very tentative, fastidiously so, letting Ruth set the pace of sprightliness and fancy, keeping up with her but never daring to go beyond her.

He told her of what he had been doing, and of his plan to write for a livelihood and of going on with his studies. But he was disappointed at her lack of approval. She did not think much of his plan.

"You see," she said frankly, "writing must be a trade, like anything else. Not that I know anything about it, of course. I only bring common judgment to bear. You couldn't hope to be a blacksmith without spending three years at learning the trade—or is it five years! Now writers are so much better paid than blacksmiths that there must be ever so many more men who would like to write, who—try to write."

"But then, may not I be peculiarly constituted to write?" he queried, secretly exulting at the language he had used, his swift imagination throwing the whole scene and atmosphere upon a vast screen along with a thousand other scenes from his life—scenes that were rough and raw, gross and bestial.

The whole composite vision was achieved with the speed of light, producing no pause in the conversation, nor interrupting his calm train of thought. On the screen of his imagination he saw himself and this sweet and beautiful girl, facing each other and conversing in good English, in a room of books and paintings and tone and culture, and all illuminated by a bright light of steadfast brilliance; while ranged about and fading away to the remote edges of the screen were antithetical scenes, each scene a picture, and he the onlooker, free to look at will upon what he wished. He saw these other scenes through drifting vapors and swirls of sullen fog dissolving before shafts of red and garish light. He saw cowboys at the bar, drinking fierce whiskey, the air filled with obscenity and ribald language, and he saw himself with them drinking and cursing with the wildest, or sitting at table with them, under smoking kerosene lamps, while the chips clicked and clattered and the cards were dealt around. He saw himself, stripped to the waist, with naked fists, fighting his great fight with Liverpool Red in the forecastle of the *Susquehanna*; and he saw the bloody deck of the *John Rogers*, that gray morning of attempted mutiny, the mate kicking in death-throes on the main-hatch, the revolver in the old man's hand spitting fire and smoke, the men with passion-wrenched faces, of brutes screaming vile blasphemies and falling about him—and then he returned to the central scene, calm and clean in the steadfast light, where Ruth sat and talked with him amid books and paintings; and he saw the grand piano upon which she would later play to him; and he heard the echoes of his own selected and correct words, "But then, may I not be peculiarly constituted to write?"

"But no matter how peculiarly constituted a man may be for blacksmithing," she was laughing, "I never heard of one becoming a blacksmith without first serving his apprenticeship."

"What would you advise?" he asked. "And don't forget that I feel in me this capacity to write—I can't explain it; I just know that it is in me."

"You must get a thorough education," was the answer, "whether or not you ultimately become a writer. This education is indispensable for whatever career you select, and it must not be slipshod or sketchy. You should go to high school."

"Yes—" he began; but she interrupted with an afterthought:-

"Of course, you could go on with your writing, too."

"I would have to," he said grimly.

"Why?" She looked at him, prettily puzzled, for she did not quite like the persistence with which he clung to his notion.

"Because, without writing there wouldn't be any high school. I must live and buy books and clothes, you know."

"I'd forgotten that," she laughed. "Why weren't you born with an income?"

512

"I'd rather have good health and imagination," he answered. "I can make good on the income, but the other things have to be made good for—" He almost said "you," then amended his sentence to, "have to be made good for one."

"Don't say 'make good,'" she cried, sweetly petulant. "It's slang, and it's horrid."

He flushed, and stammered, "That's right, and I only wish you'd correct me every time."

"I—I'd like to," she said haltingly. "You have so much in you that is good that I want to see you perfect."

He was clay in her hands immediately, as passionately desirous of being moulded by her as she was desirous of shaping him into the image of her ideal of man. And when she pointed out the opportuneness of the time, that the entrance examinations to high school began on the following Monday, he promptly volunteered that he would take them.

Then she played and sang to him, while he gazed with hungry yearning at her, drinking in her loveliness and marvelling that there should not be a hundred suitors listening there and longing for her as he listened and longed.

CHAPTER X

He stopped to dinner that evening, and, much to Ruth's satisfaction, made a favorable impression on her father. They talked about the sea as a career, a subject which Martin had at his finger-ends, and Mr. Morse remarked afterward that he seemed a very clear-headed young man. In his avoidance of slang and his search after right words, Martin was compelled to talk slowly, which enabled him to find the best thoughts that were in him. He was more at ease than that first night at dinner, nearly a year before, and his shyness and modesty even commended him to Mrs. Morse, who was pleased at his manifest improvement.

"He is the first man that ever drew passing notice from Ruth," she told her husband. "She has been so singularly backward where men are concerned that I have been worried greatly."

Mr. Morse looked at his wife curiously.

"You mean to use this young sailor to wake her up?" he questioned.

"I mean that she is not to die an old maid if I can help it," was the answer. "If this young Eden can arouse her interest in mankind in general, it will be a good thing."

"A very good thing," he commented. "But suppose,—and we must suppose, sometimes, my dear,—suppose he arouses her interest too particularly in him?"

"Impossible," Mrs. Morse laughed. "She is three years older than he, and, besides, it is impossible. Nothing will ever come of it. Trust that to me."

And so Martin's rôle was arranged for him, while he, led on by Arthur and Norman, was meditating an extravagance. They were going out for a ride into the hills Sunday morning on their wheels, which did not interest Martin until he learned that Ruth, too, rode a wheel and was going along. He did not ride, nor own a wheel, but if Ruth rode, it was up to him to begin, was his decision; and when he said good night, he stopped in at a cyclery on his way home and spent forty dollars for a wheel. It was more than a month's hard-earned wages, and it reduced his stock of money amazingly; but when he added the hundred dollars he was to receive from the *Examiner* to the four hundred and twenty dollars that was the least *The Youth's Companion* could pay him, he felt that he had reduced the perplexity the unwonted amount of money had caused him. Nor did he mind, in the course of learning to ride the wheel home, the fact that he ruined his suit of clothes. He caught the tailor by telephone that night from Mr. Higginbotham's store and ordered another suit. Then he carried the wheel up the narrow stairway that clung like a fire-escape to the rear wall of the building, and when he had moved his bed out from the wall, found there was just space enough in the small room for himself and the wheel.

Sunday he had intended to devote to studying for the high school examination, but the pearl-diving article lured him away, and he spent the day in the white-hot fever of re-creating the beauty and romance that burned in him. The fact that the *Examiner* of that morning had failed to publish his treasure-hunting article did not dash his spirits. He was at too great a height for that, and having been deaf to a twice-repeated summons, he went without the heavy Sunday dinner with which Mr. Higginbotham invariably graced his table. To Mr. Higginbotham such a dinner was advertisement of his worldly achievement and prosperity, and he honored it by delivering platitudinous sermonettes upon American institutions and the opportunity said institutions gave to any hard-working man to rise—the rise, in his case, which he pointed out unfailingly, being from a grocer's clerk to the ownership of Higginbotham's Cash Store.

Martin Eden looked with a sigh at his unfinished "Pearl-diving" on Monday morning, and took the car down to Oakland to the high school. And when, days later, he applied for the results of his examinations, he learned that he had failed in everything save grammar.

"Your grammar is excellent," Professor Hilton informed him, staring at him through heavy spectacles; "but you know nothing, positively nothing, in the other branches, and your United States history is abominable—there is no other word for it, abominable. I should advise you—"

Professor Hilton paused and glared at him, unsympathetic and unimaginative as one of his own test-tubes. He was professor of physics in the high school, possessor of a large family, a meagre salary, and a select fund of parrot-learned knowledge.

"Yes, sir," Martin said humbly, wishing somehow that the man at the desk in the library was in Professor Hilton's place just then.

"And I should advise you to go back to the grammar school for at least two years. Good day."

Martin was not deeply affected by his failure, though he was surprised at Ruth's shocked expression when he told her Professor Hilton's advice. Her disappointment was so evident that he was sorry he had failed, but chiefly so for her sake.

"You see I was right," she said. "You know far more than any of the students entering high school, and yet you can't pass the examinations. It is because what education you have is fragmentary, sketchy. You need the discipline of study, such as only skilled teachers can give you. You must be thoroughly grounded. Professor Hilton is right, and if I were you, I'd go to night school. A year and a half of it might enable you to catch up that additional six months. Besides, that would leave you your days in which to write, or, if you could not make your living by your pen, you would have your days in which to work in some position."

But if my days are taken up with work and my nights with school, when am I going to see you?—was Martin's first thought, though he refrained from uttering it. Instead, he said:-

"It seems so babyish for me to be going to night school. But I wouldn't mind that if I thought it would pay. But I don't think it will pay. I can do the work quicker than they can teach me. It would be a loss of time—" he thought of her and his desire to have her—"and I can't afford the time. I haven't the time to spare, in fact."

"There is so much that is necessary." She looked at him gently, and he was a brute to oppose her. "Physics and chemistry—you can't do them without laboratory study; and you'll find algebra and geometry almost hopeless without instruction. You need the skilled teachers, the specialists in the art of imparting knowledge."

He was silent for a minute, casting about for the least vainglorious way in which to express himself.

"Please don't think I'm bragging," he began. "I don't intend it that way at all. But I have a feeling that I am what I may call a natural student. I can study by myself. I take to it kindly, like a duck to water. You see yourself what I did with grammar. And I've learned much of other things— you would never dream how much. And I'm only getting started. Wait till I get—" He hesitated and assured himself of the pronunciation before he said "momentum. I'm getting my first real feel of things now. I'm beginning to size up the situation—"

"Please don't say 'size up,'" she interrupted.

"To get a line on things," he hastily amended.

"That doesn't mean anything in correct English," she objected.

He floundered for a fresh start.

"What I'm driving at is that I'm beginning to get the lay of the land."

Out of pity she forebore, and he went on.

"Knowledge seems to me like a chart-room. Whenever I go into the library, I am impressed that way. The part played by teachers is to teach the student the contents of the chart-room in a systematic way. The teachers are guides to the chart-room, that's all. It's not something that they have in their own heads. They don't make it up, don't create it. It's all in the chart-room and they know their way about in it, and it's their business to show the place to strangers who might else get lost. Now I don't get lost easily. I have the bump of location. I usually know where I'm at—What's wrong now?"

"Don't say 'where I'm at.'"

"That's right," he said gratefully, "where I am. But where am I at—I mean, where am I? Oh, yes, in the chart-room. Well, some people—"

"Persons," she corrected.

"Some persons need guides, most persons do; but I think I can get along without them. I've spent a lot of time in the chart-room now, and I'm on the edge of knowing my way about, what charts I want to refer to, what coasts I want to explore. And from the way I line it up, I'll explore a whole lot more quickly by myself. The speed of a fleet, you know, is the speed of the slowest ship, and the speed of the teachers is affected the same way. They can't go any faster than the ruck of their scholars, and I can set a faster pace for myself than they set for a whole schoolroom."

"'He travels the fastest who travels alone,'" she quoted at him.

But I'd travel faster with you just the same, was what he wanted to blurt out, as he caught a vision of a world without end of sunlit spaces and starry voids through which he drifted with her, his arm around her, her pale gold hair blowing about his face. In the same instant he was aware of the pitiful inadequacy of speech. God! If he could so frame words that she could see what he then saw! And he felt the stir in him, like a throe of yearning pain, of the desire to paint these visions that flashed unsummoned on the mirror of his mind. Ah, that was it! He caught at the hem of the secret. It was the very thing that the great writers and master-poets did. That was why they were giants. They knew how to express what they thought, and felt, and saw. Dogs asleep in the sun often whined and barked, but they were unable to tell what they saw that made them whine and bark. He had often wondered what it was. And that was all he was, a dog asleep in the sun. He saw noble and beautiful visions, but he could only whine and bark at Ruth. But he would cease sleeping in the sun. He would stand up, with open eyes, and he would struggle and toil and learn until, with eyes unblinded and tongue untied, he could share with her his visioned wealth. Other men had discovered the trick of expression, of making words obedient servitors, and of making combinations of words mean more than the sum of their separate meanings. He was stirred profoundly by the passing glimpse at the secret, and he was again caught up in the vision of sunlit spaces and starry voids—until it came to him that it was very quiet, and he saw Ruth regarding him with an amused expression and a smile in her eyes.

"I have had a great visioning," he said, and at the sound of his words in his own ears his heart gave a leap. Where had those words come from? They had adequately expressed the pause his vision had put in the conversation. It was a miracle. Never had he so loftily framed a lofty thought. But never had he attempted to frame lofty thoughts in words. That was it. That explained it. He had never tried. But Swinburne had, and Tennyson, and Kipling, and all the other poets. His mind flashed on to his "Pearl-diving." He had never dared the big things, the spirit of the beauty that was a fire in him. That article would be a different thing when he was done with it. He was appalled by the vastness of the beauty that rightfully belonged in it, and again his mind flashed and dared, and he demanded of himself why he could not chant that beauty in noble verse as the great poets did. And there was all the mysterious delight and spiritual wonder of his love for Ruth. Why could he not chant that, too, as the poets did? They had sung of love. So would he. By God!—

And in his frightened ears he heard his exclamation echoing. Carried away, he had breathed it aloud. The blood surged into his face, wave upon wave, mastering the bronze of it till the blush of shame flaunted itself from collar-rim to the roots of his hair.

"I—I—beg your pardon," he stammered. "I was thinking."

"It sounded as if you were praying," she said bravely, but she felt herself inside to be withering and shrinking. It was the first time she had heard an oath from the lips of a man she knew, and she was shocked, not merely as a matter of principle and training, but shocked in spirit by this rough blast of life in the garden of her sheltered maidenhood.

But she forgave, and with surprise at the ease of her forgiveness. Somehow it was not so difficult to forgive him anything. He had not had a chance to be as other men, and he was trying so hard, and succeeding, too. It never entered her head that there could be any other reason for her being kindly disposed toward him. She was tenderly disposed toward him, but she did not know it. She had no way of knowing it. The placid poise of twenty-four years without a single love affair did not fit her with a keen perception of her own feelings, and she who had never warmed to actual love was unaware that she was warming now.

CHAPTER XI

Martin went back to his pearl-diving article, which would have been finished sooner if it had not been broken in upon so frequently by his attempts to write poetry. His poems were love poems, inspired by Ruth, but they were never completed. Not in a day could he learn to chant in noble verse. Rhyme and metre and structure were serious enough in themselves, but there was, over and beyond them, an intangible and evasive something that he caught in all great poetry, but which he could not catch and imprison in his own. It was the elusive spirit of poetry itself that he sensed and sought after but could not capture. It seemed a glow to him, a warm and trailing vapor, ever beyond his reaching, though sometimes he was rewarded by catching at shreds of it and weaving them into phrases that echoed in his brain with haunting notes or drifted across his vision in misty wafture of unseen beauty. It was baffling. He ached with desire to express and could but gibber prosaically as everybody gibbered. He read his fragments aloud. The metre marched along on perfect feet, and the rhyme pounded a longer and equally faultless rhythm, but the glow and high exaltation that he felt within were lacking. He could not understand, and time and again, in despair, defeated and depressed, he returned to his article. Prose was certainly an easier medium.

Following the "Pearl-diving," he wrote an article on the sea as a career, another on turtle-catching, and a third on the northeast trades. Then he tried, as an experiment, a short story, and before he broke his stride he had finished six short stories and despatched them to various magazines. He wrote prolifically, intensely, from morning till night, and late at night, except when he broke off to go to the reading-room, draw books from the library, or to call on Ruth. He was profoundly happy. Life was pitched high. He was in a fever that never broke. The joy of creation that is supposed to belong to the gods was his. All the life about him—the odors of stale vegetables and soapsuds, the slatternly form of his sister, and the jeering face of Mr. Higginbotham— was a dream. The real world was in his mind, and the stories he wrote were so many pieces of reality out of his mind.

The days were too short. There was so much he wanted to study. He cut his sleep down to five hours and found that he could get along upon it. He tried four hours and a half, and regretfully came back to five. He could joyfully have spent all his waking hours upon any one of his pursuits. It was with regret that he ceased from writing to study, that he ceased from study to go to the library, that he tore himself away from that chart-room of knowledge or from the magazines in the reading-room that were filled with the secrets of writers who succeeded in selling their wares. It was like severing heart strings, when he was with Ruth, to stand up and go; and he scorched through the dark streets so as to get home to his books at the least possible expense of time. And hardest of all was it to shut up the algebra or physics, put note-book and pencil aside, and close his tired eyes in sleep. He hated the thought of ceasing to live, even for so short a time, and his sole consolation was that the alarm clock was set five hours ahead. He would lose only five hours anyway, and then the jangling bell would jerk him out of unconsciousness and he would have before him another glorious day of nineteen hours.

In the meantime the weeks were passing, his money was ebbing low, and there was no money coming in. A month after he had mailed it, the adventure serial for boys was returned to him by *The Youth's Companion*. The rejection slip was so tactfully worded that he felt kindly toward the editor. But he did not feel so kindly toward the editor of the *San Francisco Examiner*. After waiting two whole weeks, Martin had written to him. A week later he wrote again. At the end of the month, he went over to San Francisco and personally called upon the editor. But he did not meet that exalted personage, thanks to a Cerberus of an office boy, of tender years and red hair, who guarded the portals. At the end of the fifth week the manuscript came back to him, by mail, without comment. There was no rejection slip, no explanation, nothing. In the same way his other articles were tied up with the other leading San Francisco papers. When he recovered them, he sent them to the magazines in the East, from which they were returned more promptly, accompanied always by the printed rejection slips.

The short stories were returned in similar fashion. He read them over and over, and liked them so much that he could not puzzle out the cause of their rejection, until, one day, he read in a newspaper that manuscripts should always be typewritten. That explained it. Of course editors were so busy that they could not afford the time and strain of reading handwriting. Martin rented a typewriter and spent a day mastering the machine. Each day he typed what he composed, and he typed his earlier manuscripts as fast as they were returned him. He was surprised when the typed ones began to come back. His jaw seemed to become squarer, his chin more aggressive, and he bundled the manuscripts off to new editors.

The thought came to him that he was not a good judge of his own work. He tried it out on Gertrude. He read his stories aloud to her. Her eyes glistened, and she looked at him proudly as she said:-

"Ain't it grand, you writin' those sort of things."

"Yes, yes," he demanded impatiently. "But the story—how did you like it?"

"Just grand," was the reply. "Just grand, an' thrilling, too. I was all worked up."

He could see that her mind was not clear. The perplexity was strong in her good-natured face. So he waited.

"But, say, Mart," after a long pause, "how did it end? Did that young man who spoke so highfalutin' get her?"

And, after he had explained the end, which he thought he had made artistically obvious, she would say:-

"That's what I wanted to know. Why didn't you write that way in the story?"

One thing he learned, after he had read her a number of stories, namely, that she liked happy endings.

"That story was perfectly grand," she announced, straightening up from the wash-tub with a tired sigh and wiping the sweat from her forehead with a red, steamy hand; "but it makes me sad. I want to cry. There is too many sad things in the world anyway. It makes me happy to think about happy things. Now if he'd married her, and—You don't mind, Mart?" she queried apprehensively. "I just happen to feel that way, because I'm tired, I guess. But the story was grand just the same, perfectly grand. Where are you goin' to sell it?"

"That's a horse of another color," he laughed.

"But if you *did* sell it, what do you think you'd get for it?"

"Oh, a hundred dollars. That would be the least, the way prices go."

"My! I do hope you'll sell it!"

"Easy money, eh?" Then he added proudly: "I wrote it in two days. That's fifty dollars a day."

He longed to read his stories to Ruth, but did not dare. He would wait till some were published, he decided, then she would understand what he had been working for. In the meantime he toiled on. Never had the spirit of adventure lured him more strongly than on this amazing exploration of the realm of mind. He bought the text-books on physics and chemistry, and, along with his algebra, worked out problems and demonstrations. He took the laboratory proofs on faith, and his intense power of vision enabled him to see the reactions of chemicals more understandingly than the average student saw them in the laboratory. Martin wandered on through the heavy pages, overwhelmed by the clews he was getting to the nature of things. He had accepted the world as the world, but now he was comprehending the organization of it, the play and interplay of force and matter. Spontaneous explanations of old matters were continually arising in his mind. Levers and purchases fascinated him, and his mind roved backward to hand-spikes and blocks and tackles at sea. The theory of navigation, which enabled the ships to travel unerringly their courses over the pathless ocean, was made clear to him. The mysteries of storm, and rain, and tide were revealed, and the reason for the existence of trade-winds made him wonder whether he had written his article on the northeast trade too soon. At any rate he knew he could write it better now. One afternoon he went out with Arthur to the

University of California, and, with bated breath and a feeling of religious awe, went through the laboratories, saw demonstrations, and listened to a physics professor lecturing to his classes.

But he did not neglect his writing. A stream of short stories flowed from his pen, and he branched out into the easier forms of verse—the kind he saw printed in the magazines—though he lost his head and wasted two weeks on a tragedy in blank verse, the swift rejection of which, by half a dozen magazines, dumfounded him. Then he discovered Henley and wrote a series of sea-poems on the model of "Hospital Sketches." They were simple poems, of light and color, and romance and adventure. "Sea Lyrics," he called them, and he judged them to be the best work he had yet done. There were thirty, and he completed them in a month, doing one a day after having done his regular day's work on fiction, which day's work was the equivalent to a week's work of the average successful writer. The toil meant nothing to him. It was not toil. He was finding speech, and all the beauty and wonder that had been pent for years behind his inarticulate lips was now pouring forth in a wild and virile flood.

He showed the "Sea Lyrics" to no one, not even to the editors. He had become distrustful of editors. But it was not distrust that prevented him from submitting the "Lyrics." They were so beautiful to him that he was impelled to save them to share with Ruth in some glorious, far-off time when he would dare to read to her what he had written. Against that time he kept them with him, reading them aloud, going over them until he knew them by heart.

He lived every moment of his waking hours, and he lived in his sleep, his subjective mind rioting through his five hours of surcease and combining the thoughts and events of the day into grotesque and impossible marvels. In reality, he never rested, and a weaker body or a less firmly poised brain would have been prostrated in a general break-down. His late afternoon calls on Ruth were rarer now, for June was approaching, when she would take her degree and finish with the university. Bachelor of Arts!—when he thought of her degree, it seemed she fled beyond him faster than he could pursue.

One afternoon a week she gave to him, and arriving late, he usually stayed for dinner and for music afterward. Those were his red-letter days. The atmosphere of the house, in such contrast with that in which he lived, and the mere nearness to her, sent him forth each time with a firmer grip on his resolve to climb the heights. In spite of the beauty in him, and the aching desire to create, it was for her that he struggled. He was a lover first and always. All other things he subordinated to love.

Greater than his adventure in the world of thought was his love-adventure. The world itself was not so amazing because of the atoms and molecules that composed it according to the propulsions of irresistible force; what made it amazing was the fact that Ruth lived in it. She was the most amazing thing he had ever known, or dreamed, or guessed.

But he was oppressed always by her remoteness. She was so far from him, and he did not know how to approach her. He had been a success with girls and women in his own class; but he had never loved any of them, while he did love her, and besides, she was not merely of another class. His very love elevated her above all classes. She was a being apart, so far apart that he did not know how to draw near to her as a lover should draw near. It was true, as he acquired knowledge and language, that he was drawing nearer, talking her speech, discovering ideas and delights in common; but this did not satisfy his lover's yearning. His lover's imagination had made her holy, too holy, too spiritualized, to have any kinship with him in the flesh. It was his own love that thrust her from him and made her seem impossible for him. Love itself denied him the one thing that it desired.

And then, one day, without warning, the gulf between them was bridged for a moment, and thereafter, though the gulf remained, it was ever narrower. They had been eating cherries—great, luscious, black cherries with a juice of the color of dark wine. And later, as she read aloud to him from "The Princess," he chanced to notice the stain of the cherries on her lips. For the moment her divinity was shattered. She was clay, after all, mere clay, subject to the common law of clay as his clay was subject, or anybody's clay. Her lips were flesh like his, and cherries dyed them as cherries dyed his. And if so with her lips, then was it so with all of her. She was woman, all woman, just like any woman. It came upon him abruptly. It was a revelation that stunned him. It was as if he had seen the sun fall out of the sky, or had seen worshipped purity polluted.

Then he realized the significance of it, and his heart began pounding and challenging him to play the lover with this woman who was not a spirit from other worlds but a mere woman with lips a cherry could stain. He trembled at the audacity of his thought; but all his soul was singing, and reason, in a triumphant paean, assured him he was right. Something of this change in him must have reached her, for she paused from her reading, looked up at him, and smiled. His eyes dropped from her blue eyes to her lips, and the sight of the stain maddened him. His arms all but flashed out to her and around her, in the way of his old careless life. She seemed to lean toward him, to wait, and all his will fought to hold him back.

"You were not following a word," she pouted.

Then she laughed at him, delighting in his confusion, and as he looked into her frank eyes and knew that she had divined nothing of what he felt, he became abashed. He had indeed in thought dared too far. Of all the women he had known there was no woman who would not have guessed—save her. And she had not guessed. There was the difference. She was different. He was appalled by his own grossness, awed by her clear innocence, and he gazed again at her across the gulf. The bridge had broken down.

But still the incident had brought him nearer. The memory of it persisted, and in the moments when he was most cast down, he dwelt upon it eagerly. The gulf was never again so wide. He had accomplished a distance vastly greater than a bachelorship of arts, or a dozen bachelorships. She was pure, it was true, as he had never dreamed of purity; but cherries stained her lips. She was subject to the laws of the universe just as inexorably as he was. She had to eat to live, and when she got her feet wet, she caught cold. But that was not the point. If she could feel hunger and thirst, and heat and cold, then could she feel love—and love for a man. Well, he was a man. And why could he not be the man? "It's up to me to make good," he would murmur fervently. "I will be *the* man. I will make myself the man. I will make good."

CHAPTER XII

Early one evening, struggling with a sonnet that twisted all awry the beauty and thought that trailed in glow and vapor through his brain, Martin was called to the telephone.

"It's a lady's voice, a fine lady's," Mr. Higginbotham, who had called him, jeered.

Martin went to the telephone in the corner of the room, and felt a wave of warmth rush through him as he heard Ruth's voice. In his battle with the sonnet he had forgotten her existence, and at the sound of her voice his love for her smote him like a sudden blow. And such a voice!—delicate and sweet, like a strain of music heard far off and faint, or, better, like a bell of silver, a perfect tone, crystal-pure. No mere woman had a voice like that. There was something celestial about it, and it came from other worlds. He could scarcely hear what it said, so ravished was he, though he controlled his face, for he knew that Mr. Higginbotham's ferret eyes were fixed upon him.

It was not much that Ruth wanted to say—merely that Norman had been going to take her to a lecture that night, but that he had a headache, and she was so disappointed, and she had the tickets, and that if he had no other engagement, would he be good enough to take her?

Would he! He fought to suppress the eagerness in his voice. It was amazing. He had always seen her in her own house. And he had never dared to ask her to go anywhere with him. Quite irrelevantly, still at the telephone and talking with her, he felt an overpowering desire to die for her, and visions of heroic sacrifice shaped and dissolved in his whirling brain. He loved her so much, so terribly, so hopelessly. In that moment of mad happiness that she should go out with him, go to a lecture with him—with him, Martin Eden—she soared so far above him that there seemed nothing else for him to do than die for her. It was the only fit way in which he could express the tremendous and lofty emotion he felt for her. It was the sublime abnegation of true love that comes to all lovers, and it came to him there, at the telephone, in a whirlwind of fire and glory; and to die for her, he felt, was to have lived and loved well. And he was only twenty-one, and he had never been in love before.

His hand trembled as he hung up the receiver, and he was weak from the organ which had stirred him. His eyes were shining like an angel's, and his face was transfigured, purged of all earthly dross, and pure and holy.

"Makin' dates outside, eh?" his brother-in-law sneered. "You know what that means. You'll be in the police court yet."

But Martin could not come down from the height. Not even the bestiality of the allusion could bring him back to earth. Anger and hurt were beneath him. He had seen a great vision and was as a god, and he could feel only profound and awful pity for this maggot of a man. He did not look at him, and though his eyes passed over him, he did not see him; and as in a dream he passed out of the room to dress. It was not until he had reached his own room and was tying his necktie that he became aware of a sound that lingered unpleasantly in his ears. On investigating this sound he identified it as the final snort of Bernard Higginbotham, which somehow had not penetrated to his brain before.

As Ruth's front door closed behind them and he came down the steps with her, he found himself greatly perturbed. It was not unalloyed bliss, taking her to the lecture. He did not know what he ought to do. He had seen, on the streets, with persons of her class, that the women took the men's arms. But then, again, he had seen them when they didn't; and he wondered if it was only in the evening that arms were taken, or only between husbands and wives and relatives.

Just before he reached the sidewalk, he remembered Minnie. Minnie had always been a stickler. She had called him down the second time she walked out with him, because he had gone along on the inside, and she had laid the law down to him that a gentleman always walked on the outside—when he was with a lady. And Minnie had made a practice of kicking his heels, whenever they crossed from one side of the street to the other, to remind him to get over on the outside. He wondered where she had got that item of etiquette, and whether it had filtered down from above and was all right.

It wouldn't do any harm to try it, he decided, by the time they had reached the sidewalk; and he swung behind Ruth and took up his station on the outside. Then the other problem presented itself. Should he offer her his arm? He had never offered anybody his arm in his life. The girls he had known never took the fellows' arms. For the first several times they walked freely, side by side, and after that it was arms around the waists, and heads against the fellows' shoulders where the streets were unlighted. But this was different. She wasn't that kind of a girl. He must do something.

He crooked the arm next to her—crooked it very slightly and with secret tentativeness, not invitingly, but just casually, as though he was accustomed to walk that way. And then the wonderful thing happened. He felt her hand upon his arm. Delicious thrills ran through him at the contact, and for a few sweet moments it seemed that he had left the solid earth and was flying with her through the air. But he was soon back again, perturbed by a new complication. They were crossing the street. This would put him on the inside. He should be on the outside. Should he therefore drop her arm and change over? And if he did so, would he have to repeat the manoeuvre the next time? And the next? There was something wrong about it, and he resolved not to caper about and play the fool. Yet he was not satisfied with his conclusion, and when he found himself on the inside, he talked quickly and earnestly, making a show of being carried away by what he was saying, so that, in case he was wrong in not changing sides, his enthusiasm would seem the cause for his carelessness.

As they crossed Broadway, he came face to face with a new problem. In the blaze of the electric lights, he saw Lizzie Connolly and her giggly friend. Only for an instant he hesitated, then his hand went up and his hat came off. He could not be disloyal to his kind, and it was to more than Lizzie Connolly that his hat was lifted. She nodded and looked at him boldly, not with soft and gentle eyes like Ruth's, but with eyes that were handsome and hard, and that swept on past him to Ruth and itemized her face and dress and station. And he was aware that Ruth looked, too, with quick eyes that were timid and mild as a dove's, but which saw, in a look that was a flutter on and past, the working-class girl in her cheap finery and under the strange hat that all working-class girls were wearing just then.

"What a pretty girl!" Ruth said a moment later.

Martin could have blessed her, though he said:-

"I don't know. I guess it's all a matter of personal taste, but she doesn't strike me as being particularly pretty."

"Why, there isn't one woman in ten thousand with features as regular as hers. They are splendid. Her face is as clear-cut as a cameo. And her eyes are beautiful."

"Do you think so?" Martin queried absently, for to him there was only one beautiful woman in the world, and she was beside him, her hand upon his arm.

"Do I think so? If that girl had proper opportunity to dress, Mr. Eden, and if she were taught how to carry herself, you would be fairly dazzled by her, and so would all men."

"She would have to be taught how to speak," he commented, "or else most of the men wouldn't understand her. I'm sure you couldn't understand a quarter of what she said if she just spoke naturally."

"Nonsense! You are as bad as Arthur when you try to make your point."

"You forget how I talked when you first met me. I have learned a new language since then. Before that time I talked as that girl talks. Now I can manage to make myself understood sufficiently in your language to explain that you do not know that other girl's language. And do you know why she carries herself the way she does? I think about such things now, though I never used to think about them, and I am beginning to understand—much."

"But why does she?"

"She has worked long hours for years at machines. When one's body is young, it is very pliable, and hard work will mould it like putty according to the nature of the work. I can tell at a glance the trades of many workingmen I meet on the street. Look at me. Why am I rolling all about the shop? Because of the years I put in on the sea. If I'd put in the same years cow-punching, with my body young and pliable, I wouldn't be rolling now, but I'd be bow-legged. And so with that girl. You noticed that her eyes were what I might call hard. She has never been sheltered. She has had to take care of herself, and a young girl can't take care of herself and keep her eyes soft and gentle like—like yours, for example."

"I think you are right," Ruth said in a low voice. "And it is too bad. She is such a pretty girl."

He looked at her and saw her eyes luminous with pity. And then he remembered that he loved her and was lost in amazement at his fortune that permitted him to love her and to take her on his arm to a lecture.

Who are you, Martin Eden? he demanded of himself in the looking-glass, that night when he got back to his room. He gazed at himself long and curiously. Who are you? What are you? Where do you belong? You belong by rights to girls like Lizzie Connolly. You belong with the legions of toil, with all that is low, and vulgar, and unbeautiful. You belong with the oxen and the drudges, in dirty surroundings among smells and stenches. There are the stale vegetables now. Those potatoes are rotting. Smell them, damn you, smell them. And yet you dare to open the books, to listen to beautiful music, to learn to love beautiful paintings, to speak good English, to think thoughts that none of your own kind thinks, to tear yourself away from the oxen and the Lizzie Connollys and to love a pale spirit of a woman who is a million miles beyond you and who lives in the stars! Who are you? and what are you? damn you! And are you going to make good?

He shook his fist at himself in the glass, and sat down on the edge of the bed to dream for a space with wide eyes. Then he got out note-book and algebra and lost himself in quadratic equations, while the hours slipped by, and the stars dimmed, and the gray of dawn flooded against his window.

CHAPTER XIII

It was the knot of wordy socialists and working-class philosophers that held forth in the City Hall Park on warm afternoons that was responsible for the great discovery. Once or twice in the month, while riding through the park on his way to the library, Martin dismounted from his wheel and listened to the arguments, and each time he tore himself away reluctantly. The tone of discussion was much lower than at Mr. Morse's table. The men were not grave and dignified. They lost their tempers easily and called one another names, while oaths and obscene allusions were frequent on their lips. Once or twice he had seen them come to blows. And yet, he knew not why, there seemed something vital about the stuff of these men's thoughts. Their logomachy was far more stimulating to his intellect than the reserved and quiet dogmatism of Mr. Morse. These men, who slaughtered English, gesticulated like lunatics, and fought one another's ideas with primitive anger, seemed somehow to be more alive than Mr. Morse and his crony, Mr. Butler.

Martin had heard Herbert Spencer quoted several times in the park, but one afternoon a disciple of Spencer's appeared, a seedy tramp with a dirty coat buttoned tightly at the throat to conceal the absence of a shirt. Battle royal was waged, amid the smoking of many cigarettes and the expectoration of much tobacco-juice, wherein the tramp successfully held his own, even when a socialist workman sneered, "There is no god but the Unknowable, and Herbert Spencer is his prophet." Martin was puzzled as to what the discussion was about, but when he rode on to the library he carried with him a new-born interest in Herbert Spencer, and because of the frequency with which the tramp had mentioned "First Principles," Martin drew out that volume.

So the great discovery began. Once before he had tried Spencer, and choosing the "Principles of Psychology" to begin with, he had failed as abjectly as he had failed with Madam Blavatsky. There had been no understanding the book, and he had returned it unread. But this night, after algebra and physics, and an attempt at a sonnet, he got into bed and opened "First Principles." Morning found him still reading. It was impossible for him to sleep. Nor did he write that day. He lay on the bed till his body grew tired, when he tried the hard floor, reading on his back, the book held in the air above him, or changing from side to side. He slept that night, and did his writing next morning, and then the book tempted him and he fell, reading all afternoon, oblivious to everything and oblivious to the fact that that was the afternoon Ruth gave to him. His first consciousness of the immediate world about him was when Bernard Higginbotham jerked open the door and demanded to know if he thought they were running a restaurant.

Martin Eden had been mastered by curiosity all his days. He wanted to know, and it was this desire that had sent him adventuring over the world. But he was now learning from Spencer that he never had known, and that he never could have known had he continued his sailing and wandering forever. He had merely skimmed over the surface of things, observing detached phenomena, accumulating fragments of facts, making superficial little generalizations—and all and everything quite unrelated in a capricious and disorderly world of whim and chance. The mechanism of the flight of birds he had watched and reasoned about with understanding; but it had never entered his head to try to explain the process whereby birds, as organic flying mechanisms, had been developed. He had never dreamed there was such a process. That birds should have come to be, was unguessed. They always had been. They just happened.

And as it was with birds, so had it been with everything. His ignorant and unprepared attempts at philosophy had been fruitless. The medieval metaphysics of Kant had given him the key to nothing, and had served the sole purpose of making him doubt his own intellectual powers. In similar manner his attempt to study evolution had been confined to a hopelessly technical volume by Romanes. He had understood nothing, and the only idea he had gathered was that evolution was a dry-as-dust theory, of a lot of little men possessed of huge and unintelligible vocabularies. And now he learned that evolution was no mere theory but an accepted process of development; that scientists no longer disagreed about it, their only differences being over the method of evolution.

And here was the man Spencer, organizing all knowledge for him, reducing everything to unity, elaborating ultimate realities, and presenting to his startled gaze a universe so concrete of realization that it was like the model of a ship such as sailors make and put into glass bottles. There was no caprice, no chance. All was law. It was in obedience to law that the bird flew, and it was in obedience to the same law that fermenting slime had writhed and squirmed and put out legs and wings and become a bird.

Martin had ascended from pitch to pitch of intellectual living, and here he was at a higher pitch than ever. All the hidden things were laying their secrets bare. He was drunken with comprehension. At night, asleep, he lived with the gods in colossal nightmare; and awake, in the day, he went around like a somnambulist, with absent stare, gazing upon the world he had just discovered. At table he failed to hear the conversation about petty and ignoble things, his eager mind seeking out and following cause and effect in everything before him. In the meat on the platter he saw the shining sun and traced its energy back through all its transformations to its source a hundred million miles away, or traced its energy ahead to the moving muscles in his arms that enabled him to cut the meat, and to the brain wherewith he willed the muscles to move to cut the meat, until, with inward gaze, he saw the same sun shining in his brain. He was entranced by illumination, and did not hear the "Bughouse," whispered by Jim, nor see the anxiety on his sister's face, nor notice the rotary motion of Bernard Higginbotham's finger, whereby he imparted the suggestion of wheels revolving in his brother-in-law's head.

What, in a way, most profoundly impressed Martin, was the correlation of knowledge—of all knowledge. He had been curious to know things, and whatever he acquired he had filed away in separate memory compartments in his brain. Thus, on the subject of sailing he had an immense store. On the subject of woman he had a fairly large store. But these two subjects had been unrelated. Between the two memory compartments there had been no connection. That, in the fabric of knowledge, there should be any connection whatever between a woman with hysterics and a schooner carrying a weather-helm or heaving to in a gale, would have struck him as ridiculous and impossible. But Herbert Spencer had shown him not only that it was not ridiculous, but that it was impossible for there to be no connection. All things were related to all other things from the farthermost star in the wastes of space to the myriads of atoms in the grain of sand under one's foot. This new concept was a perpetual amazement to Martin, and he found himself engaged continually in tracing the relationship between all things under the sun and on the other side of the sun. He drew up lists of the most incongruous things and was unhappy until he succeeded in establishing kinship between them all—kinship between love, poetry, earthquake, fire, rattlesnakes, rainbows, precious gems, monstrosities, sunsets, the roaring of lions, illuminating gas, cannibalism, beauty, murder, lovers, fulcrums, and tobacco. Thus, he unified the universe and held it up and looked at it, or wandered through its byways and alleys and jungles, not as a terrified traveller in the thick of mysteries seeking an unknown goal, but observing and charting and becoming familiar with all there was to know. And the more he knew, the more passionately he admired the universe, and life, and his own life in the midst of it all.

"You fool!" he cried at his image in the looking-glass. "You wanted to write, and you tried to write, and you had nothing in you to write about. What did you have in you?—some childish notions, a few half-baked sentiments, a lot of undigested beauty, a great black mass of ignorance, a heart filled to bursting with love, and an ambition as big as your love and as futile as your ignorance. And you wanted to write! Why, you're just on the edge of beginning to get something in you to write about. You wanted to create beauty, but how could you when you knew nothing about the nature of beauty? You wanted to write about life when you knew nothing of the essential characteristics of life. You wanted to write about the world and the scheme of existence when the world was a Chinese puzzle to you and all that you could have written would have been about what you did not know of the scheme of existence. But cheer up, Martin, my boy. You'll write yet. You know a little, a very little, and you're on the right road now to know more. Some day, if you're lucky, you may come pretty close to knowing all that may be known. Then you will write."

He brought his great discovery to Ruth, sharing with her all his joy and wonder in it. But she did not seem to be so enthusiastic over it. She tacitly accepted it and, in a way, seemed aware of it from her own studies. It did not stir her deeply, as it did him, and he would have been surprised had he not reasoned it out that it was not new and fresh to her as it was to him. Arthur and Norman, he found, believed in evolution and had read Spencer, though it did not seem to have made any vital impression upon them, while the young fellow with the glasses and the mop of hair, Will Olney, sneered disagreeably at Spencer and repeated the epigram, "There is no god but the Unknowable, and Herbert Spencer is his prophet."

But Martin forgave him the sneer, for he had begun to discover that Olney was not in love with Ruth. Later, he was dumfounded to learn from various little happenings not only that Olney did not care for Ruth, but that he had a positive dislike for her. Martin could not understand this. It was a bit of phenomena that he could not correlate with all the rest of the phenomena in the universe. But nevertheless he felt sorry for the young fellow because of the great lack in his nature that prevented him from a proper appreciation of Ruth's fineness and beauty. They rode out into the hills several Sundays on their wheels, and Martin had ample opportunity to observe the armed truce that existed between Ruth and Olney. The latter chummed with Norman, throwing Arthur and Martin into company with Ruth, for which Martin was duly grateful.

Those Sundays were great days for Martin, greatest because he was with Ruth, and great, also, because they were putting him more on a par with the young men of her class. In spite of their long years of disciplined education, he was finding himself their intellectual equal, and the hours spent with them in conversation was so much practice for him in the use of the grammar he had studied so hard. He had abandoned the etiquette books, falling back upon observation to show him the right things to do. Except when carried away by his enthusiasm, he was always on guard, keenly watchful of their actions and learning their little courtesies and refinements of conduct.

The fact that Spencer was very little read was for some time a source of surprise to Martin. "Herbert Spencer," said the man at the desk in the library, "oh, yes, a great mind." But the man did not seem to know anything of the content of that great mind. One evening, at dinner, when Mr. Butler was there, Martin turned the conversation upon Spencer. Mr. Morse bitterly arraigned the English philosopher's agnosticism, but confessed that he had not read "First Principles"; while Mr. Butler stated that he had no patience with Spencer, had never read a line of him, and had managed to get along quite well without him. Doubts arose in Martin's mind, and had he been less strongly individual he would have accepted the general opinion and given Herbert Spencer up. As it was, he found Spencer's explanation of things convincing; and, as he phrased it to himself, to give up Spencer would be equivalent to a navigator throwing the compass and chronometer overboard. So Martin went on into a thorough study of evolution, mastering more and more the subject himself, and being convinced by the corroborative testimony of a thousand independent writers. The more he studied, the more vistas he caught of fields of knowledge yet unexplored, and the regret that days were only twenty-four hours long became a chronic complaint with him.

One day, because the days were so short, he decided to give up algebra and geometry. Trigonometry he had not even attempted. Then he cut chemistry from his study-list, retaining only physics.

"I am not a specialist," he said, in defence, to Ruth. "Nor am I going to try to be a specialist. There are too many special fields for any one man, in a whole lifetime, to master a tithe of them. I must pursue general knowledge. When I need the work of specialists, I shall refer to their books."

"But that is not like having the knowledge yourself," she protested.

"But it is unnecessary to have it. We profit from the work of the specialists. That's what they are for. When I came in, I noticed the chimney-sweeps at work. They're specialists, and when they get done, you will enjoy clean chimneys without knowing anything about the construction of chimneys."

"That's far-fetched, I am afraid."

She looked at him curiously, and he felt a reproach in her gaze and manner. But he was convinced of the rightness of his position.

"All thinkers on general subjects, the greatest minds in the world, in fact, rely on the specialists. Herbert Spencer did that. He generalized upon the findings of thousands of investigators. He would have had to live a thousand lives in order to do it all himself. And so with Darwin. He took advantage of all that had been learned by the florists and cattle-breeders."

"You're right, Martin," Olney said. "You know what you're after, and Ruth doesn't. She doesn't know what she is after for herself even."

"—Oh, yes," Olney rushed on, heading off her objection, "I know you call it general culture. But it doesn't matter what you study if you want general culture. You can study French, or you can study German, or cut them both out and study Esperanto, you'll get the culture tone just the same. You can study Greek or Latin, too, for the same purpose, though it will never be any use to you. It will be culture, though. Why, Ruth studied Saxon, became clever in it,—that was two years ago,—and all that she remembers of it now is 'Whan that sweet Aprile with his schowers soote'—isn't that the way it goes?"

"But it's given you the culture tone just the same," he laughed, again heading her off. "I know. We were in the same classes."

"But you speak of culture as if it should be a means to something," Ruth cried out. Her eyes were flashing, and in her cheeks were two spots of color. "Culture is the end in itself."

"But that is not what Martin wants."

"How do you know?"

"What do you want, Martin?" Olney demanded, turning squarely upon him.

Martin felt very uncomfortable, and looked entreaty at Ruth.

"Yes, what do you want?" Ruth asked. "That will settle it."

"Yes, of course, I want culture," Martin faltered. "I love beauty, and culture will give me a finer and keener appreciation of beauty."

She nodded her head and looked triumph.

"Rot, and you know it," was Olney's comment. "Martin's after career, not culture. It just happens that culture, in his case, is incidental to career. If he wanted to be a chemist, culture would be unnecessary. Martin wants to write, but he's afraid to say so because it will put you in the wrong."

"And why does Martin want to write?" he went on. "Because he isn't rolling in wealth. Why do you fill your head with Saxon and general culture? Because you don't have to make your way in the world. Your father sees to that. He buys your clothes for you, and all the rest. What rotten good is our education, yours and mine and Arthur's and Norman's? We're soaked in general culture, and if our daddies went broke to-day, we'd be falling down to-morrow on teachers' examinations. The best job you could get, Ruth, would be a country school or music teacher in a girls' boarding-school."

"And pray what would you do?" she asked.

"Not a blessed thing. I could earn a dollar and a half a day, common labor, and I might get in as instructor in Hanley's cramming joint—I say might, mind you, and I might be chucked out at the end of the week for sheer inability."

Martin followed the discussion closely, and while he was convinced that Olney was right, he resented the rather cavalier treatment he accorded Ruth. A new conception of love formed in his mind as he listened. Reason had nothing to do with love. It mattered not whether the woman he loved reasoned correctly or incorrectly. Love was above reason. If it just happened that she did not fully appreciate his necessity for a career, that did not make her a bit less lovable. She was all lovable, and what she thought had nothing to do with her lovableness.

"What's that?" he replied to a question from Olney that broke in upon his train of thought.

"I was saying that I hoped you wouldn't be fool enough to tackle Latin."

"But Latin is more than culture," Ruth broke in. "It is equipment."

"Well, are you going to tackle it?" Olney persisted.

Martin was sore beset. He could see that Ruth was hanging eagerly upon his answer.

"I am afraid I won't have time," he said finally. "I'd like to, but I won't have time."

"You see, Martin's not seeking culture," Olney exulted. "He's trying to get somewhere, to do something."

"Oh, but it's mental training. It's mind discipline. It's what makes disciplined minds." Ruth looked expectantly at Martin, as if waiting for him to change his judgment. "You know, the foot-ball players have to train before the big game. And that is what Latin does for the thinker. It trains."

"Rot and bosh! That's what they told us when we were kids. But there is one thing they didn't tell us then. They let us find it out for ourselves afterwards." Olney paused for effect, then added, "And what they didn't tell us was that every gentleman should have studied Latin, but that no gentleman should know Latin."

"Now that's unfair," Ruth cried. "I knew you were turning the conversation just in order to get off something."

"It's clever all right," was the retort, "but it's fair, too. The only men who know their Latin are the apothecaries, the lawyers, and the Latin professors. And if Martin wants to be one of them, I miss my guess. But what's all that got to do with Herbert Spencer anyway? Martin's just discovered Spencer, and he's wild over him. Why? Because Spencer is taking him somewhere. Spencer couldn't take me anywhere, nor you. We haven't got anywhere to go. You'll get married some day, and I'll have nothing to do but keep track of the lawyers and business agents who will take care of the money my father's going to leave me."

Onley got up to go, but turned at the door and delivered a parting shot.

"You leave Martin alone, Ruth. He knows what's best for himself. Look at what he's done already. He makes me sick sometimes, sick and ashamed of myself. He knows more now about the world, and life, and man's place, and

540

all the rest, than Arthur, or Norman, or I, or you, too, for that matter, and in spite of all our Latin, and French, and Saxon, and culture."

"But Ruth is my teacher," Martin answered chivalrously. "She is responsible for what little I have learned."

"Rats!" Olney looked at Ruth, and his expression was malicious. "I suppose you'll be telling me next that you read Spencer on her recommendation—only you didn't. And she doesn't know anything more about Darwin and evolution than I do about King Solomon's mines. What's that jawbreaker definition about something or other, of Spencer's, that you sprang on us the other day—that indefinite, incoherent homogeneity thing? Spring it on her, and see if she understands a word of it. That isn't culture, you see. Well, tra la, and if you tackle Latin, Martin, I won't have any respect for you."

And all the while, interested in the discussion, Martin had been aware of an irk in it as well. It was about studies and lessons, dealing with the rudiments of knowledge, and the schoolboyish tone of it conflicted with the big things that were stirring in him—with the grip upon life that was even then crooking his fingers like eagle's talons, with the cosmic thrills that made him ache, and with the inchoate consciousness of mastery of it all. He likened himself to a poet, wrecked on the shores of a strange land, filled with power of beauty, stumbling and stammering and vainly trying to sing in the rough, barbaric tongue of his brethren in the new land. And so with him. He was alive, painfully alive, to the great universal things, and yet he was compelled to potter and grope among schoolboy topics and debate whether or not he should study Latin.

"What in hell has Latin to do with it?" he demanded before his mirror that night. "I wish dead people would stay dead. Why should I and the beauty in me be ruled by the dead? Beauty is alive and everlasting. Languages come and go. They are the dust of the dead."

And his next thought was that he had been phrasing his ideas very well, and he went to bed wondering why he could not talk in similar fashion when he was with Ruth. He was only a schoolboy, with a schoolboy's tongue, when he was in her presence.

"Give me time," he said aloud. "Only give me time."

Time! Time! Time! was his unending plaint.

CHAPTER XIV

It was not because of Olney, but in spite of Ruth, and his love for Ruth, that he finally decided not to take up Latin. His money meant time. There was so much that was more important than Latin, so many studies that clamored with imperious voices. And he must write. He must earn money. He had had no acceptances. Twoscore of manuscripts were travelling the endless round of the magazines. How did the others do it? He spent long hours in the free reading-room, going over what others had written, studying their work eagerly and critically, comparing it with his own, and wondering, wondering, about the secret trick they had discovered which enabled them to sell their work.

He was amazed at the immense amount of printed stuff that was dead. No light, no life, no color, was shot through it. There was no breath of life in it, and yet it sold, at two cents a word, twenty dollars a thousand—the newspaper clipping had said so. He was puzzled by countless short stories, written lightly and cleverly he confessed, but without vitality or reality. Life was so strange and wonderful, filled with an immensity of problems, of dreams, and of heroic toils, and yet these stories dealt only with the commonplaces of life. He felt the stress and strain of life, its fevers and sweats and wild insurgences—surely this was the stuff to write about! He wanted to glorify the leaders of forlorn hopes, the mad lovers, the giants that fought under stress and strain, amid terror and tragedy, making life crackle with the strength of their endeavor. And yet the magazine short stories seemed intent on glorifying the Mr. Butlers, the sordid dollar-chasers, and the commonplace little love affairs of commonplace little men and women. Was it because the editors of the magazines were commonplace? he demanded. Or were they afraid of life, these writers and editors and readers?

But his chief trouble was that he did not know any editors or writers. And not merely did he not know any writers, but he did not know anybody who had ever attempted to write. There was nobody to tell him, to hint to him, to give him the least word of advice. He began to doubt that editors were real men. They seemed cogs in a machine. That was what it was, a machine. He poured his soul into stories, articles, and poems, and intrusted them to the machine. He folded them just so, put the proper stamps inside the long envelope along with the manuscript, sealed the envelope, put more stamps outside, and dropped it into the mail-box. It travelled across the continent, and after a certain lapse of time the postman returned him the manuscript in another long envelope, on the outside of which were the stamps he had enclosed. There was no human editor at the other end, but a mere cunning arrangement of cogs that changed the manuscript from one envelope to another and stuck on the stamps. It was like the slot machines wherein one dropped pennies, and, with a metallic whirl of machinery had delivered to him a stick of chewing-gum or a tablet of chocolate. It depended upon which slot one dropped the penny in, whether he got chocolate or gum. And so with the editorial machine. One slot brought checks and the other brought rejection slips. So far he had found only the latter slot.

It was the rejection slips that completed the horrible machinelikeness of the process. These slips were printed in stereotyped forms and he had received hundreds of them—as many as a dozen or more on each of his earlier manuscripts. If he had received one line, one personal line, along with one rejection of all his rejections, he would have been cheered. But not one editor had given that proof of existence. And he could conclude only that there were no warm human men at the other end, only mere cogs, well oiled and running beautifully in the machine.

He was a good fighter, whole-souled and stubborn, and he would have been content to continue feeding the machine for years; but he was bleeding to death, and not years but weeks would determine the fight. Each week his board bill brought him nearer destruction, while the postage on forty manuscripts bled him almost as severely. He no longer bought books, and he economized in petty ways and sought to delay the inevitable end; though he did not know how to economize, and brought the end nearer by a week when he gave his sister Marian five dollars for a dress.

He struggled in the dark, without advice, without encouragement, and in the teeth of discouragement. Even Gertrude was beginning to look

544

askance. At first she had tolerated with sisterly fondness what she conceived to be his foolishness; but now, out of sisterly solicitude, she grew anxious. To her it seemed that his foolishness was becoming a madness. Martin knew this and suffered more keenly from it than from the open and nagging contempt of Bernard Higginbotham. Martin had faith in himself, but he was alone in this faith. Not even Ruth had faith. She had wanted him to devote himself to study, and, though she had not openly disapproved of his writing, she had never approved.

He had never offered to show her his work. A fastidious delicacy had prevented him. Besides, she had been studying heavily at the university, and he felt averse to robbing her of her time. But when she had taken her degree, she asked him herself to let her see something of what he had been doing. Martin was elated and diffident. Here was a judge. She was a bachelor of arts. She had studied literature under skilled instructors. Perhaps the editors were capable judges, too. But she would be different from them. She would not hand him a stereotyped rejection slip, nor would she inform him that lack of preference for his work did not necessarily imply lack of merit in his work. She would talk, a warm human being, in her quick, bright way, and, most important of all, she would catch glimpses of the real Martin Eden. In his work she would discern what his heart and soul were like, and she would come to understand something, a little something, of the stuff of his dreams and the strength of his power.

Martin gathered together a number of carbon copies of his short stories, hesitated a moment, then added his "Sea Lyrics." They mounted their wheels on a late June afternoon and rode for the hills. It was the second time he had been out with her alone, and as they rode along through the balmy warmth, just chilled by she sea-breeze to refreshing coolness, he was profoundly impressed by the fact that it was a very beautiful and well-ordered world and that it was good to be alive and to love. They left their wheels by the roadside and climbed to the brown top of an open knoll where the sunburnt grass breathed a harvest breath of dry sweetness and content.

"Its work is done," Martin said, as they seated themselves, she upon his coat, and he sprawling close to the warm earth. He sniffed the sweetness of the tawny grass, which entered his brain and set his thoughts whirling on from the particular to the universal. "It has achieved its reason for existence," he went on, patting the dry grass affectionately. "It quickened with ambition under the dreary downpour of last winter, fought the violent early spring, flowered, and lured the insects and the bees, scattered its seeds, squared itself with its duty and the world, and—"

"Why do you always look at things with such dreadfully practical eyes?" she interrupted.

"Because I've been studying evolution, I guess. It's only recently that I got my eyesight, if the truth were told."

"But it seems to me you lose sight of beauty by being so practical, that you destroy beauty like the boys who catch butterflies and rub the down off their beautiful wings."

He shook his head.

"Beauty has significance, but I never knew its significance before. I just accepted beauty as something meaningless, as something that was just beautiful without rhyme or reason. I did not know anything about beauty. But now I know, or, rather, am just beginning to know. This grass is more beautiful to me now that I know why it is grass, and all the hidden chemistry of sun and rain and earth that makes it become grass. Why, there is romance in the life-history of any grass, yes, and adventure, too. The very thought of it stirs me. When I think of the play of force and matter, and all the tremendous struggle of it, I feel as if I could write an epic on the grass.

"How well you talk," she said absently, and he noted that she was looking at him in a searching way.

He was all confusion and embarrassment on the instant, the blood flushing red on his neck and brow.

"I hope I am learning to talk," he stammered. "There seems to be so much in me I want to say. But it is all so big. I can't find ways to say what is really in me. Sometimes it seems to me that all the world, all life, everything, had taken up residence inside of me and was clamoring for me to be the spokesman. I feel—oh, I can't describe it—I feel the bigness of it, but when I speak, I babble like a little child. It is a great task to transmute feeling and sensation into speech, written or spoken, that will, in turn, in him who reads or listens, transmute itself back into the selfsame feeling and sensation. It is a lordly task. See, I bury my face in the grass, and the breath I draw in through my nostrils sets me quivering with a thousand thoughts and fancies. It is a breath of the universe I have breathed. I know song and laughter, and success and pain, and struggle and death; and I see visions that arise in my brain somehow out of the scent of the grass, and I would like to tell them to you, to the world. But how can I? My tongue is tied. I have tried, by the spoken word, just now, to describe to you the effect on me of the scent of the grass. But I have not succeeded. I have no more than hinted in awkward speech. My words seem gibberish to me. And yet I am stifled with desire to tell. Oh!—" he threw up his hands with a despairing gesture—"it is impossible! It is not understandable! It is incommunicable!"

"But you do talk well," she insisted. "Just think how you have improved in the short time I have known you. Mr. Butler is a noted public speaker. He is always asked by the State Committee to go out on stump during campaign. Yet you talked just as well as he the other night at dinner. Only he was more controlled. You get too excited; but you will get over that with practice. Why, you would make a good public speaker. You can go far—if you want to. You are masterly. You can lead men, I am sure, and there is no reason why you should not succeed at anything you set your hand to, just as you have succeeded with grammar. You would make a good lawyer. You should shine in politics. There is nothing to prevent you from making as great a success as Mr. Butler has made. And minus the dyspepsia," she added with a smile.

They talked on; she, in her gently persistent way, returning always to the need of thorough grounding in education and to the advantages of Latin as part of the foundation for any career. She drew her ideal of the successful man, and it was largely in her father's image, with a few unmistakable lines and touches of color from the image of Mr. Butler. He listened eagerly, with receptive ears, lying on his back and looking up and joying in each

547

movement of her lips as she talked. But his brain was not receptive. There was nothing alluring in the pictures she drew, and he was aware of a dull pain of disappointment and of a sharper ache of love for her. In all she said there was no mention of his writing, and the manuscripts he had brought to read lay neglected on the ground.

At last, in a pause, he glanced at the sun, measured its height above the horizon, and suggested his manuscripts by picking them up.

"I had forgotten," she said quickly. "And I am so anxious to hear."

He read to her a story, one that he flattered himself was among his very best. He called it "The Wine of Life," and the wine of it, that had stolen into his brain when he wrote it, stole into his brain now as he read it. There was a certain magic in the original conception, and he had adorned it with more magic of phrase and touch. All the old fire and passion with which he had written it were reborn in him, and he was swayed and swept away so that he was blind and deaf to the faults of it. But it was not so with Ruth. Her trained ear detected the weaknesses and exaggerations, the overemphasis of the tyro, and she was instantly aware each time the sentence-rhythm tripped and faltered. She scarcely noted the rhythm otherwise, except when it became too pompous, at which moments she was disagreeably impressed with its amateurishness. That was her final judgment on the story as a whole— amateurish, though she did not tell him so. Instead, when he had done, she pointed out the minor flaws and said that she liked the story.

But he was disappointed. Her criticism was just. He acknowledged that, but he had a feeling that he was not sharing his work with her for the purpose of schoolroom correction. The details did not matter. They could take care of themselves. He could mend them, he could learn to mend them. Out of life he had captured something big and attempted to imprison it in the story. It was the big thing out of life he had read to her, not sentence-structure and semicolons. He wanted her to feel with him this big thing that was his, that he had seen with his own eyes, grappled with his own brain, and placed there on the page with his own hands in printed words. Well, he had failed, was his secret decision. Perhaps the editors were right. He had felt the big thing, but he had failed to transmute it. He concealed his disappointment, and joined so easily with her in her criticism that she did not realize that deep down in him was running a strong undercurrent of disagreement.

"This next thing I've called 'The Pot'," he said, unfolding the manuscript. "It has been refused by four or five magazines now, but still I think it is good. In fact, I don't know what to think of it, except that I've caught something there. Maybe it won't affect you as it does me. It's a short thing—only two thousand words."

"How dreadful!" she cried, when he had finished. "It is horrible, unutterably horrible!"

He noted her pale face, her eyes wide and tense, and her clenched hands, with secret satisfaction. He had succeeded. He had communicated the stuff of fancy and feeling from out of his brain. It had struck home. No matter whether she liked it or not, it had gripped her and mastered her, made her sit there and listen and forget details.

"It is life," he said, "and life is not always beautiful. And yet, perhaps because I am strangely made, I find something beautiful there. It seems to me that the beauty is tenfold enhanced because it is there—"

"But why couldn't the poor woman—" she broke in disconnectedly. Then she left the revolt of her thought unexpressed to cry out: "Oh! It is degrading! It is not nice! It is *nasty*!"

For the moment it seemed to him that his heart stood still. Nasty! He had never dreamed it. He had not meant it. The whole sketch stood before him in letters of fire, and in such blaze of illumination he sought vainly for nastiness. Then his heart began to beat again. He was not guilty.

"Why didn't you select a nice subject?" she was saying. "*We know there are nasty things in the world*, but that is no reason—"

She talked on in her indignant strain, but he was not following her. He was smiling to himself as he looked up into her virginal face, so innocent, so penetratingly innocent, that its purity seemed always to enter into him, driving out of him all dross and bathing him in some ethereal effulgence that was as cool and soft and velvety as starshine. We know there are nasty things in the world! He cuddled to him the notion of her knowing, and chuckled over it as a love joke. The next moment, in a flashing vision of multitudinous detail, he sighted the whole sea of life's nastiness that he had known and voyaged over and through, and he forgave her for not understanding the story. It was through no fault of hers that she could not understand. He thanked God that she had been born and sheltered to such innocence. But he knew life, its foulness as well as its fairness, its greatness in spite of the slime that infested it, and by God he was going to have his say on it to the world. Saints in heaven—how could they be anything but fair and pure? No praise to them. But saints in slime—ah, that was the everlasting wonder! That was what made life worth while. To see moral grandeur rising out of cesspools of iniquity; to rise himself and first glimpse beauty, faint and far, through mud-dripping eyes; to see out of weakness, and frailty, and viciousness, and all abysmal brutishness, arising strength, and truth, and high spiritual endowment—

He caught a stray sequence of sentences she was uttering.

"The tone of it all is low. And there is so much that is high. Take 'In Memoriam.'"

He was impelled to suggest "Locksley Hall," and would have done so, had not his vision gripped him again and left him staring at her, the female of his kind, who, out of the primordial ferment, creeping and crawling up the vast ladder of life for a thousand thousand centuries, had emerged on the topmost rung, having become one Ruth, pure, and fair, and divine, and with power to make him know love, and to aspire toward purity, and to desire to taste divinity—him, Martin Eden, who, too, had come up in some amazing fashion from out of the ruck and the mire and the countless mistakes and abortions of unending creation. There was the romance, and the wonder, and the glory. There was the stuff to write, if he could only find speech. Saints in heaven!—They were only saints and could not help themselves. But he was a man.

"You have strength," he could hear her saying, "but it is untutored strength."

"Like a bull in a china shop," he suggested, and won a smile.

"And you must develop discrimination. You must consult taste, and fineness, and tone."

"I dare too much," he muttered.

She smiled approbation, and settled herself to listen to another story.

"I don't know what you'll make of this," he said apologetically. "It's a funny thing. I'm afraid I got beyond my depth in it, but my intentions were good. Don't bother about the little features of it. Just see if you catch the feel of the big thing in it. It is big, and it is true, though the chance is large that I have failed to make it intelligible."

He read, and as he read he watched her. At last he had reached her, he thought. She sat without movement, her eyes steadfast upon him, scarcely breathing, caught up and out of herself, he thought, by the witchery of the thing he had created. He had entitled the story "Adventure," and it was the apotheosis of adventure—not of the adventure of the storybooks, but of real adventure, the savage taskmaster, awful of punishment and awful of reward, faithless and whimsical, demanding terrible patience and heartbreaking days and nights of toil, offering the blazing sunlight glory or dark death at the end of thirst and famine or of the long drag and monstrous delirium of rotting fever, through blood and sweat and stinging insects leading up by long chains of petty and ignoble contacts to royal culminations and lordly achievements.

It was this, all of it, and more, that he had put into his story, and it was this, he believed, that warmed her as she sat and listened. Her eyes were wide, color was in her pale cheeks, and before he finished it seemed to him that she was almost panting. Truly, she was warmed; but she was warmed, not by the story, but by him. She did not think much of the story; it was Martin's intensity of power, the old excess of strength that seemed to pour from his body and on and over her. The paradox of it was that it was the story itself that was freighted with his power, that was the channel, for the time being, through which his strength poured out to her. She was aware only of the strength, and not of the medium, and when she seemed most carried away by what he had written, in reality she had been carried away by something quite foreign to it—by a thought, terrible and perilous, that had formed itself unsummoned in her brain. She had caught herself wondering what marriage was like, and the becoming conscious of the waywardness and ardor of the thought had terrified her. It was unmaidenly. It was not like her. She had never been tormented by womanhood, and she had lived in a dreamland of Tennysonian poesy, dense even to the full significance of that delicate master's delicate allusions to the grossnesses that intrude upon the relations of queens and knights. She had been asleep, always, and now life was thundering imperatively at all her doors. Mentally she was in a panic to shoot the bolts and drop the bars into place, while wanton instincts urged her to throw wide her portals and bid the deliciously strange visitor to enter in.

Martin waited with satisfaction for her verdict. He had no doubt of what it would be, and he was astounded when he heard her say:

"It is beautiful."

"It is beautiful," she repeated, with emphasis, after a pause.

Of course it was beautiful; but there was something more than mere beauty in it, something more stingingly splendid which had made beauty its handmaiden. He sprawled silently on the ground, watching the grisly form of a great doubt rising before him. He had failed. He was inarticulate. He had seen one of the greatest things in the world, and he had not expressed it.

"What did you think of the—" He hesitated, abashed at his first attempt to use a strange word. "Of the *motif*?" he asked.

"It was confused," she answered. "That is my only criticism in the large way. I followed the story, but there seemed so much else. It is too wordy. You clog the action by introducing so much extraneous material."

"That was the major *motif*," he hurriedly explained, "the big underrunning *motif*, the cosmic and universal thing. I tried to make it keep time with the story itself, which was only superficial after all. I was on the right scent, but

552

I guess I did it badly. I did not succeed in suggesting what I was driving at. But I'll learn in time."

She did not follow him. She was a bachelor of arts, but he had gone beyond her limitations. This she did not comprehend, attributing her incomprehension to his incoherence.

"You were too voluble," she said. "But it was beautiful, in places."

He heard her voice as from far off, for he was debating whether he would read her the "Sea Lyrics." He lay in dull despair, while she watched him searchingly, pondering again upon unsummoned and wayward thoughts of marriage.

"You want to be famous?" she asked abruptly.

"Yes, a little bit," he confessed. "That is part of the adventure. It is not the being famous, but the process of becoming so, that counts. And after all, to be famous would be, for me, only a means to something else. I want to be famous very much, for that matter, and for that reason."

"For your sake," he wanted to add, and might have added had she proved enthusiastic over what he had read to her.

But she was too busy in her mind, carving out a career for him that would at least be possible, to ask what the ultimate something was which he had hinted at. There was no career for him in literature. Of that she was convinced. He had proved it to-day, with his amateurish and sophomoric productions. He could talk well, but he was incapable of expressing himself in a literary way. She compared Tennyson, and Browning, and her favorite prose masters with him, and to his hopeless discredit. Yet she did not tell him her whole mind. Her strange interest in him led her to temporize. His desire to write was, after all, a little weakness which he would grow out of in time. Then he would devote himself to the more serious affairs of life. And he would succeed, too. She knew that. He was so strong that he could not fail—if only he would drop writing.

"I wish you would show me all you write, Mr. Eden," she said.

He flushed with pleasure. She was interested, that much was sure. And at least she had not given him a rejection slip. She had called certain portions of his work beautiful, and that was the first encouragement he had ever received from any one.

"I will," he said passionately. "And I promise you, Miss Morse, that I will make good. I have come far, I know that; and I have far to go, and I will cover it if I have to do it on my hands and knees." He held up a bunch of manuscript. "Here are the 'Sea Lyrics.' When you get home, I'll turn them over to you to read at your leisure. And you must be sure to tell me just what you think of them. What I need, you know, above all things, is criticism. And do, please, be frank with me."

"I will be perfectly frank," she promised, with an uneasy conviction that she had not been frank with him and with a doubt if she could be quite frank with him the next time.

CHAPTER XV

"The first battle, fought and finished," Martin said to the looking-glass ten days later. "But there will be a second battle, and a third battle, and battles to the end of time, unless—"

He had not finished the sentence, but looked about the mean little room and let his eyes dwell sadly upon a heap of returned manuscripts, still in their long envelopes, which lay in a corner on the floor. He had no stamps with which to continue them on their travels, and for a week they had been piling up. More of them would come in on the morrow, and on the next day, and the next, till they were all in. And he would be unable to start them out again. He was a month's rent behind on the typewriter, which he could not pay, having barely enough for the week's board which was due and for the employment office fees.

He sat down and regarded the table thoughtfully. There were ink stains upon it, and he suddenly discovered that he was fond of it.

"Dear old table," he said, "I've spent some happy hours with you, and you've been a pretty good friend when all is said and done. You never turned me down, never passed me out a reward-of-unmerit rejection slip, never complained about working overtime."

He dropped his arms upon the table and buried his face in them. His throat was aching, and he wanted to cry. It reminded him of his first fight, when he was six years old, when he punched away with the tears running down his cheeks while the other boy, two years his elder, had beaten and pounded him into exhaustion. He saw the ring of boys, howling like barbarians as he went down at last, writhing in the throes of nausea, the blood streaming from his nose and the tears from his bruised eyes.

"Poor little shaver," he murmured. "And you're just as badly licked now. You're beaten to a pulp. You're down and out."

But the vision of that first fight still lingered under his eyelids, and as he watched he saw it dissolve and reshape into the series of fights which had followed. Six months later Cheese-Face (that was the boy) had whipped him again. But he had blacked Cheese-Face's eye that time. That was going some. He saw them all, fight after fight, himself always whipped and Cheese-Face exulting over him. But he had never run away. He felt strengthened by the memory of that. He had always stayed and taken his medicine. Cheese-Face had been a little fiend at fighting, and had never once shown mercy to him. But he had stayed! He had stayed with it!

Next, he saw a narrow alley, between ramshackle frame buildings. The end of the alley was blocked by a one-story brick building, out of which issued the rhythmic thunder of the presses, running off the first edition of the *Enquirer*. He was eleven, and Cheese-Face was thirteen, and they both carried the *Enquirer*. That was why they were there, waiting for their papers. And, of course, Cheese-Face had picked on him again, and there was another fight that was indeterminate, because at quarter to four the door of the press-room was thrown open and the gang of boys crowded in to fold their papers.

"I'll lick you to-morrow," he heard Cheese-Face promise; and he heard his own voice, piping and trembling with unshed tears, agreeing to be there on the morrow.

And he had come there the next day, hurrying from school to be there first, and beating Cheese-Face by two minutes. The other boys said he was all right, and gave him advice, pointing out his faults as a scrapper and promising him victory if he carried out their instructions. The same boys gave Cheese-Face advice, too. How they had enjoyed the fight! He paused in his recollections long enough to envy them the spectacle he and Cheese-Face had put up. Then the fight was on, and it went on, without rounds, for thirty minutes, until the press-room door was opened.

He watched the youthful apparition of himself, day after day, hurrying from school to the *Enquirer* alley. He could not walk very fast. He was stiff and lame from the incessant fighting. His forearms were black and blue from wrist to elbow, what of the countless blows he had warded off, and here and there the tortured flesh was beginning to fester. His head and arms and shoulders ached, the small of his back ached,—he ached all over, and his brain was heavy and dazed. He did not play at school. Nor did he study. Even to sit still all day at his desk, as he did, was a torment. It seemed centuries since he had begun the round of daily fights, and time stretched away into a nightmare and infinite future of daily fights. Why couldn't Cheese-Face be licked? he often thought; that would put him, Martin, out of his misery. It never entered his head to cease fighting, to allow Cheese-Face to whip him.

And so he dragged himself to the *Enquirer* alley, sick in body and soul, but learning the long patience, to confront his eternal enemy, Cheese-Face, who was just as sick as he, and just a bit willing to quit if it were not for the gang of newsboys that looked on and made pride painful and necessary. One afternoon, after twenty minutes of desperate efforts to annihilate each other according to set rules that did not permit kicking, striking below the belt, nor hitting when one was down, Cheese-Face, panting for breath and reeling, offered to call it quits. And Martin, head on arms, thrilled at the picture he caught of himself, at that moment in the afternoon of long ago, when he reeled and panted and choked with the blood that ran into his mouth and down his throat from his cut lips; when he tottered toward Cheese-Face, spitting out a mouthful of blood so that he could speak, crying out that he would never quit, though Cheese-Face could give in if he wanted to. And Cheese-Face did not give in, and the fight went on.

The next day and the next, days without end, witnessed the afternoon fight. When he put up his arms, each day, to begin, they pained exquisitely, and the first few blows, struck and received, racked his soul; after that things grew numb, and he fought on blindly, seeing as in a dream, dancing and wavering, the large features and burning, animal-like eyes of Cheese-Face. He concentrated upon that face; all else about him was a whirling void. There was nothing else in the world but that face, and he would never know rest, blessed rest, until he had beaten that face into a pulp with his bleeding knuckles, or until the bleeding knuckles that somehow belonged to that face had beaten him into a pulp. And then, one way or the other, he would have rest. But to quit,—for him, Martin, to quit,—that was impossible!

Came the day when he dragged himself into the *Enquirer* alley, and there was no Cheese-Face. Nor did Cheese-Face come. The boys congratulated him, and told him that he had licked Cheese-Face. But Martin was not satisfied. He had not licked Cheese-Face, nor had Cheese-Face licked him. The problem had not been solved. It was not until afterward that they learned that Cheese-Face's father had died suddenly that very day.

Martin skipped on through the years to the night in the nigger heaven at the Auditorium. He was seventeen and just back from sea. A row started. Somebody was bullying somebody, and Martin interfered, to be confronted by Cheese-Face's blazing eyes.

"I'll fix you after de show," his ancient enemy hissed.

Martin nodded. The nigger-heaven bouncer was making his way toward the disturbance.

"I'll meet you outside, after the last act," Martin whispered, the while his face showed undivided interest in the buck-and-wing dancing on the stage.

The bouncer glared and went away.

"Got a gang?" he asked Cheese-Face, at the end of the act.

"Sure."

"Then I got to get one," Martin announced.

Between the acts he mustered his following—three fellows he knew from the nail works, a railroad fireman, and half a dozen of the Boo Gang, along with as many more from the dread Eighteen-and-Market Gang.

When the theatre let out, the two gangs strung along inconspicuously on opposite sides of the street. When they came to a quiet corner, they united and held a council of war.

"Eighth Street Bridge is the place," said a red-headed fellow belonging to Cheese-Face's Gang. "You kin fight in the middle, under the electric light, an' whichever way the bulls come in we kin sneak the other way."

"That's agreeable to me," Martin said, after consulting with the leaders of his own gang.

558

The Eighth Street Bridge, crossing an arm of San Antonio Estuary, was the length of three city blocks. In the middle of the bridge, and at each end, were electric lights. No policeman could pass those end-lights unseen. It was the safe place for the battle that revived itself under Martin's eyelids. He saw the two gangs, aggressive and sullen, rigidly keeping apart from each other and backing their respective champions; and he saw himself and Cheese-Face stripping. A short distance away lookouts were set, their task being to watch the lighted ends of the bridge. A member of the Boo Gang held Martin's coat, and shirt, and cap, ready to race with them into safety in case the police interfered. Martin watched himself go into the centre, facing Cheese-Face, and he heard himself say, as he held up his hand warningly:-

"They ain't no hand-shakin' in this. Understand? They ain't nothin' but scrap. No throwin' up the sponge. This is a grudge-fight an' it's to a finish. Understand? Somebody's goin' to get licked."

Cheese-Face wanted to demur,—Martin could see that,—but Cheese-Face's old perilous pride was touched before the two gangs.

"Aw, come on," he replied. "Wot's the good of chewin' de rag about it? I'm wit' cheh to de finish."

Then they fell upon each other, like young bulls, in all the glory of youth, with naked fists, with hatred, with desire to hurt, to maim, to destroy. All the painful, thousand years' gains of man in his upward climb through creation were lost. Only the electric light remained, a milestone on the path of the great human adventure. Martin and Cheese-Face were two savages, of the stone age, of the squatting place and the tree refuge. They sank lower and lower into the muddy abyss, back into the dregs of the raw beginnings of life, striving blindly and chemically, as atoms strive, as the star-dust of the heavens strives, colliding, recoiling, and colliding again and eternally again.

"God! We are animals! Brute-beasts!" Martin muttered aloud, as he watched the progress of the fight. It was to him, with his splendid power of vision, like gazing into a kinetoscope. He was both onlooker and participant. His long months of culture and refinement shuddered at the sight; then the present was blotted out of his consciousness and the ghosts of the past possessed him, and he was Martin Eden, just returned from sea and fighting Cheese-Face on the Eighth Street Bridge. He suffered and toiled and sweated and bled, and exulted when his naked knuckles smashed home.

They were twin whirlwinds of hatred, revolving about each other monstrously. The time passed, and the two hostile gangs became very quiet. They had never witnessed such intensity of ferocity, and they were awed by it. The two fighters were greater brutes than they. The first splendid velvet edge of youth and condition wore off, and they fought more cautiously and deliberately. There had been no advantage gained either way. "It's anybody's fight," Martin heard some one saying. Then he followed up a feint, right and left, was fiercely countered, and felt his cheek laid open to the bone. No bare knuckle had done that. He heard mutters of amazement at the ghastly damage wrought, and was drenched with his own blood. But he gave no sign. He became immensely wary, for he was wise with knowledge of the low cunning and foul vileness of his kind. He watched and waited, until he feigned a wild rush, which he stopped midway, for he had seen the glint of metal.

"Hold up yer hand!" he screamed. "Them's brass knuckles, an' you hit me with 'em!"

Both gangs surged forward, growling and snarling. In a second there would be a free-for-all fight, and he would be robbed of his vengeance. He was beside himself.

"You guys keep out!" he screamed hoarsely. "Understand? Say, d'ye understand?"

They shrank away from him. They were brutes, but he was the arch-brute, a thing of terror that towered over them and dominated them.

"This is my scrap, an' they ain't goin' to be no buttin' in. Gimme them knuckles."

Cheese-Face, sobered and a bit frightened, surrendered the foul weapon.

"You passed 'em to him, you red-head sneakin' in behind the push there," Martin went on, as he tossed the knuckles into the water. "I seen you, an' I was wonderin' what you was up to. If you try anything like that again, I'll beat cheh to death. Understand?"

They fought on, through exhaustion and beyond, to exhaustion immeasurable and inconceivable, until the crowd of brutes, its blood-lust sated, terrified by what it saw, begged them impartially to cease. And Cheese-Face, ready to drop and die, or to stay on his legs and die, a grisly monster out of whose features all likeness to Cheese-Face had been beaten, wavered and hesitated; but Martin sprang in and smashed him again and again.

Next, after a seeming century or so, with Cheese-Face weakening fast, in a mix-up of blows there was a loud snap, and Martin's right arm dropped to his side. It was a broken bone. Everybody heard it and knew; and Cheese-Face knew, rushing like a tiger in the other's extremity and raining blow on blow. Martin's gang surged forward to interfere. Dazed by the rapid succession of blows, Martin warned them back with vile and earnest curses sobbed out and groaned in ultimate desolation and despair.

He punched on, with his left hand only, and as he punched, doggedly, only half-conscious, as from a remote distance he heard murmurs of fear in the gangs, and one who said with shaking voice: "This ain't a scrap, fellows. It's murder, an' we ought to stop it."

But no one stopped it, and he was glad, punching on wearily and endlessly with his one arm, battering away at a bloody something before him that was not a face but a horror, an oscillating, hideous, gibbering, nameless thing that persisted before his wavering vision and would not go away. And he punched on and on, slower and slower, as the last shreds of vitality oozed from him, through centuries and aeons and enormous lapses of time, until, in a dim way, he became aware that the nameless thing was sinking, slowly sinking down to the rough board-planking of the bridge. And the next moment he was standing over it, staggering and swaying on shaky legs, clutching at the air for support, and saying in a voice he did not recognize:-

"D'ye want any more? Say, d'ye want any more?"

He was still saying it, over and over,—demanding, entreating, threatening, to know if it wanted any more,—when he felt the fellows of his gang laying hands on him, patting him on the back and trying to put his coat on him. And then came a sudden rush of blackness and oblivion.

The tin alarm-clock on the table ticked on, but Martin Eden, his face buried on his arms, did not hear it. He heard nothing. He did not think. So absolutely had he relived life that he had fainted just as he fainted years before on the Eighth Street Bridge. For a full minute the blackness and the blankness endured. Then, like one from the dead, he sprang upright, eyes flaming, sweat pouring down his face, shouting:-

"I licked you, Cheese-Face! It took me eleven years, but I licked you!"

His knees were trembling under him, he felt faint, and he staggered back to the bed, sinking down and sitting on the edge of it. He was still in the clutch of the past. He looked about the room, perplexed, alarmed, wondering where he was, until he caught sight of the pile of manuscripts in the corner. Then the wheels of memory slipped ahead through four years of time, and he was aware of the present, of the books he had opened and the universe he had won from their pages, of his dreams and ambitions, and of his love for a pale wraith of a girl, sensitive and sheltered and ethereal, who would die of horror did she witness but one moment of what he had just lived through—one moment of all the muck of life through which he had waded.

He arose to his feet and confronted himself in the looking-glass.

"And so you arise from the mud, Martin Eden," he said solemnly. "And you cleanse your eyes in a great brightness, and thrust your shoulders among the stars, doing what all life has done, letting the 'ape and tiger die' and wresting highest heritage from all powers that be."

He looked more closely at himself and laughed.

"A bit of hysteria and melodrama, eh?" he queried. "Well, never mind. You licked Cheese-Face, and you'll lick the editors if it takes twice eleven years to do it in. You can't stop here. You've got to go on. It's to a finish, you know."

CHAPTER XVI

The alarm-clock went off, jerking Martin out of sleep with a suddenness that would have given headache to one with less splendid constitution. Though he slept soundly, he awoke instantly, like a cat, and he awoke eagerly, glad that the five hours of unconsciousness were gone. He hated the oblivion of sleep. There was too much to do, too much of life to live. He grudged every moment of life sleep robbed him of, and before the clock had ceased its clattering he was head and ears in the washbasin and thrilling to the cold bite of the water.

But he did not follow his regular programme. There was no unfinished story waiting his hand, no new story demanding articulation. He had studied late, and it was nearly time for breakfast. He tried to read a chapter in Fiske, but his brain was restless and he closed the book. To-day witnessed the beginning of the new battle, wherein for some time there would be no writing. He was aware of a sadness akin to that with which one leaves home and family. He looked at the manuscripts in the corner. That was it. He was going away from them, his pitiful, dishonored children that were welcome nowhere. He went over and began to rummage among them, reading snatches here and there, his favorite portions. "The Pot" he honored with reading aloud, as he did "Adventure." "Joy," his latest-born, completed the day before and tossed into the corner for lack of stamps, won his keenest approbation.

"I can't understand," he murmured. "Or maybe it's the editors who can't understand. There's nothing wrong with that. They publish worse every month. Everything they publish is worse—nearly everything, anyway."

After breakfast he put the type-writer in its case and carried it down into Oakland.

"I owe a month on it," he told the clerk in the store. "But you tell the manager I'm going to work and that I'll be in in a month or so and straighten up."

He crossed on the ferry to San Francisco and made his way to an employment office. "Any kind of work, no trade," he told the agent; and was interrupted by a new-comer, dressed rather foppishly, as some workingmen dress who have instincts for finer things. The agent shook his head despondently.

"Nothin' doin' eh?" said the other. "Well, I got to get somebody to-day."

He turned and stared at Martin, and Martin, staring back, noted the puffed and discolored face, handsome and weak, and knew that he had been making a night of it.

"Lookin' for a job?" the other queried. "What can you do?"

"Hard labor, sailorizing, run a type-writer, no shorthand, can sit on a horse, willing to do anything and tackle anything," was the answer.

The other nodded.

"Sounds good to me. My name's Dawson, Joe Dawson, an' I'm tryin' to scare up a laundryman."

"Too much for me." Martin caught an amusing glimpse of himself ironing fluffy white things that women wear. But he had taken a liking to the other, and he added: "I might do the plain washing. I learned that much at sea." Joe Dawson thought visibly for a moment.

"Look here, let's get together an' frame it up. Willin' to listen?"

Martin nodded.

"This is a small laundry, up country, belongs to Shelly Hot Springs,—hotel, you know. Two men do the work, boss and assistant. I'm the boss. You don't work for me, but you work under me. Think you'd be willin' to learn?"

Martin paused to think. The prospect was alluring. A few months of it, and he would have time to himself for study. He could work hard and study hard.

"Good grub an' a room to yourself," Joe said.

That settled it. A room to himself where he could burn the midnight oil unmolested.

"But work like hell," the other added.

Martin caressed his swelling shoulder-muscles significantly. "That came from hard work."

"Then let's get to it." Joe held his hand to his head for a moment. "Gee, but it's a stem-winder. Can hardly see. I went down the line last night—everything—everything. Here's the frame-up. The wages for two is a hundred and board. I've ben drawin' down sixty, the second man forty. But he knew the biz. You're green. If I break you in, I'll be doing plenty of your work at first. Suppose you begin at thirty, an' work up to the forty. I'll play fair. Just as soon as you can do your share you get the forty."

"I'll go you," Martin announced, stretching out his hand, which the other shook. "Any advance?—for rail-road ticket and extras?"

"I blew it in," was Joe's sad answer, with another reach at his aching head. "All I got is a return ticket."

"And I'm broke—when I pay my board."

"Jump it," Joe advised.

"Can't. Owe it to my sister."

Joe whistled a long, perplexed whistle, and racked his brains to little purpose.

"I've got the price of the drinks," he said desperately. "Come on, an' mebbe we'll cook up something."

Martin declined.

"Water-wagon?"

This time Martin nodded, and Joe lamented, "Wish I was."

"But I somehow just can't," he said in extenuation. "After I've ben workin' like hell all week I just got to booze up. If I didn't, I'd cut my throat or burn up the premises. But I'm glad you're on the wagon. Stay with it."

Martin knew of the enormous gulf between him and this man—the gulf the books had made; but he found no difficulty in crossing back over that gulf. He had lived all his life in the working-class world, and the *camaraderie* of labor was second nature with him. He solved the difficulty of transportation that was too much for the other's aching head. He would send his trunk up to Shelly Hot Springs on Joe's ticket. As for himself, there was his wheel. It was seventy miles, and he could ride it on Sunday and be ready for work Monday morning. In the meantime he would go home and pack up. There was no one to say good-by to. Ruth and her whole family were spending the long summer in the Sierras, at Lake Tahoe.

He arrived at Shelly Hot Springs, tired and dusty, on Sunday night. Joe greeted him exuberantly. With a wet towel bound about his aching brow, he had been at work all day.

"Part of last week's washin' mounted up, me bein' away to get you," he explained. "Your box arrived all right. It's in your room. But it's a hell of a thing to call a trunk. An' what's in it? Gold bricks?"

Joe sat on the bed while Martin unpacked. The box was a packing-case for breakfast food, and Mr. Higginbotham had charged him half a dollar for it. Two rope handles, nailed on by Martin, had technically transformed it into a trunk eligible for the baggage-car. Joe watched, with bulging eyes, a few shirts and several changes of underclothes come out of the box, followed by books, and more books.

"Books clean to the bottom?" he asked.

Martin nodded, and went on arranging the books on a kitchen table which served in the room in place of a wash-stand.

"Gee!" Joe exploded, then waited in silence for the deduction to arise in his brain. At last it came.

566

"Say, you don't care for the girls—much?" he queried.

"No," was the answer. "I used to chase a lot before I tackled the books. But since then there's no time."

"And there won't be any time here. All you can do is work an' sleep."

Martin thought of his five hours' sleep a night, and smiled. The room was situated over the laundry and was in the same building with the engine that pumped water, made electricity, and ran the laundry machinery. The engineer, who occupied the adjoining room, dropped in to meet the new hand and helped Martin rig up an electric bulb, on an extension wire, so that it travelled along a stretched cord from over the table to the bed.

The next morning, at quarter-past six, Martin was routed out for a quarter-to-seven breakfast. There happened to be a bath-tub for the servants in the laundry building, and he electrified Joe by taking a cold bath.

"Gee, but you're a hummer!" Joe announced, as they sat down to breakfast in a corner of the hotel kitchen.

With them was the engineer, the gardener, and the assistant gardener, and two or three men from the stable. They ate hurriedly and gloomily, with but little conversation, and as Martin ate and listened he realized how far he had travelled from their status. Their small mental caliber was depressing to him, and he was anxious to get away from them. So he bolted his breakfast, a sickly, sloppy affair, as rapidly as they, and heaved a sigh of relief when he passed out through the kitchen door.

It was a perfectly appointed, small steam laundry, wherein the most modern machinery did everything that was possible for machinery to do. Martin, after a few instructions, sorted the great heaps of soiled clothes, while Joe started the masher and made up fresh supplies of soft-soap, compounded of biting chemicals that compelled him to swathe his mouth and nostrils and eyes in bath-towels till he resembled a mummy. Finished the sorting, Martin lent a hand in wringing the clothes. This was done by dumping them into a spinning receptacle that went at a rate of a few thousand *revolutions* a minute, tearing the water from the clothes by centrifugal force. Then Martin began to alternate between the dryer and the wringer, between times "shaking out" socks and stockings. By the afternoon, one feeding and one, stacking up, they were running socks and stockings through the mangle while the irons were heating. Then it was hot irons and underclothes till six o'clock, at which time Joe shook his head dubiously.

"Way behind," he said. "Got to work after supper." And after supper they worked until ten o'clock, under the blazing electric lights, until the last piece of under-clothing was ironed and folded away in the distributing room. It was a hot California night, and though the windows were thrown wide, the room, with its red-hot ironing-stove, was a furnace. Martin and Joe, down to undershirts, bare armed, sweated and panted for air.

"Like trimming cargo in the tropics," Martin said, when they went upstairs.

"You'll do," Joe answered. "You take hold like a good fellow. If you keep up the pace, you'll be on thirty dollars only one month. The second month you'll be gettin' your forty. But don't tell me you never ironed before. I know better."

"Never ironed a rag in my life, honestly, until to-day," Martin protested.

He was surprised at his weariness when he got into his room, forgetful of the fact that he had been on his feet and working without let up for fourteen hours. He set the alarm clock at six, and measured back five hours to one o'clock. He could read until then. Slipping off his shoes, to ease his swollen feet, he sat down at the table with his books. He opened Fiske, where he had left off to read. But he found trouble and began to read it through a second time. Then he awoke, in pain from his stiffened muscles and chilled by the mountain wind that had begun to blow in through the window. He looked at the clock. It marked two. He had been asleep four hours. He pulled off his clothes and crawled into bed, where he was asleep the moment after his head touched the pillow.

Tuesday was a day of similar unremitting toil. The speed with which Joe worked won Martin's admiration. Joe was a dozen of demons for work.

He was keyed up to concert pitch, and there was never a moment in the long day when he was not fighting for moments. He concentrated himself upon his work and upon how to save time, pointing out to Martin where he did in five motions what could be done in three, or in three motions what could be done in two. "Elimination of waste motion," Martin phrased it as he watched and patterned after. He was a good workman himself, quick and deft, and it had always been a point of pride with him that no man should do any of his work for him or outwork him. As a result, he concentrated with a similar singleness of purpose, greedily snapping up the hints and suggestions thrown out by his working mate. He "rubbed out" collars and cuffs, rubbing the starch out from between the double thicknesses of linen so that there would be no blisters when it came to the ironing, and doing it at a pace that elicited Joe's praise.

There was never an interval when something was not at hand to be done. Joe waited for nothing, waited on nothing, and went on the jump from task to task. They starched two hundred white shirts, with a single gathering movement seizing a shirt so that the wristbands, neckband, yoke, and bosom protruded beyond the circling right hand. At the same moment the left hand held up the body of the shirt so that it would not enter the starch, and at the moment the right hand dipped into the starch—starch so hot that, in order to wring it out, their hands had to thrust, and thrust continually, into a bucket of cold water. And that night they worked till half-past ten, dipping "fancy starch"—all the frilled and airy, delicate wear of ladies.

"Me for the tropics and no clothes," Martin laughed.

"And me out of a job," Joe answered seriously. "I don't know nothin' but laundrying."

"And you know it well."

"I ought to. Began in the Contra Costa in Oakland when I was eleven, shakin' out for the mangle. That was eighteen years ago, an' I've never done a tap of anything else. But this job is the fiercest I ever had. Ought to be one more man on it at least. We work to-morrow night. Always run the mangle Wednesday nights—collars an' cuffs."

Martin set his alarm, drew up to the table, and opened Fiske. He did not finish the first paragraph. The lines blurred and ran together and his head nodded. He walked up and down, batting his head savagely with his fists, but he could not conquer the numbness of sleep. He propped the book before him, and propped his eyelids with his fingers, and fell asleep with his eyes wide open. Then he surrendered, and, scarcely conscious of what he did, got off his clothes and into bed. He slept seven hours of heavy, animal-like sleep, and awoke by the alarm, feeling that he had not had enough.

"Doin' much readin'?" Joe asked.

Martin shook his head.

"Never mind. We got to run the mangle to-night, but Thursday we'll knock off at six. That'll give you a chance."

Martin washed woollens that day, by hand, in a large barrel, with strong soft-soap, by means of a hub from a wagon wheel, mounted on a plunger-pole that was attached to a spring-pole overhead.

"My invention," Joe said proudly. "Beats a washboard an' your knuckles, and, besides, it saves at least fifteen minutes in the week, an' fifteen minutes ain't to be sneezed at in this shebang."

Running the collars and cuffs through the mangle was also Joe's idea. That night, while they toiled on under the electric lights, he explained it.

"Something no laundry ever does, except this one. An' I got to do it if I'm goin' to get done Saturday afternoon at three o'clock. But I know how, an' that's the difference. Got to have right heat, right pressure, and run 'em through three times. Look at that!" He held a cuff aloft. "Couldn't do it better by hand or on a tiler."

Thursday, Joe was in a rage. A bundle of extra "fancy starch" had come in.

"I'm goin' to quit," he announced. "I won't stand for it. I'm goin' to quit it cold. What's the good of me workin' like a slave all week, a-savin' minutes, an' them a-comin' an' ringin' in fancy-starch extras on me? This is a free country, an' I'm to tell that fat Dutchman what I think of him. An' I won't tell 'm in French. Plain United States is good enough for me. Him a-ringin' in fancy starch extras!"

"We got to work to-night," he said the next moment, reversing his judgment and surrendering to fate.

And Martin did no reading that night. He had seen no daily paper all week, and, strangely to him, felt no desire to see one. He was not interested in the news. He was too tired and jaded to be interested in anything, though he planned to leave Saturday afternoon, if they finished at three, and ride on his wheel to Oakland. It was seventy miles, and the same distance back on Sunday afternoon would leave him anything but rested for the second week's work. It would have been easier to go on the train, but the round trip was two dollars and a half, and he was intent on saving money.

CHAPTER XVII

Martin learned to do many things. In the course of the first week, in one afternoon, he and Joe accounted for the two hundred white shirts. Joe ran the tiler, a machine wherein a hot iron was hooked on a steel string which furnished the pressure. By this means he ironed the yoke, wristbands, and neckband, setting the latter at right angles to the shirt, and put the glossy finish on the bosom. As fast as he finished them, he flung the shirts on a rack between him and Martin, who caught them up and "backed" them. This task consisted of ironing all the unstarched portions of the shirts.

It was exhausting work, carried on, hour after hour, at top speed. Out on the broad verandas of the hotel, men and women, in cool white, sipped iced drinks and kept their circulation down. But in the laundry the air was sizzling. The huge stove roared red hot and white hot, while the irons, moving over the damp cloth, sent up clouds of steam. The heat of these irons was different from that used by housewives. An iron that stood the ordinary test of a wet finger was too cold for Joe and Martin, and such test was useless. They went wholly by holding the irons close to their cheeks, gauging the heat by some secret mental process that Martin admired but could not understand. When the fresh irons proved too hot, they hooked them on iron rods and dipped them into cold water. This again required a precise and subtle judgment. A fraction of a second too long in the water and the fine and silken edge of the proper heat was lost, and Martin found time to marvel at the accuracy he developed—an automatic accuracy, founded upon criteria that were machine-like and unerring.

But there was little time in which to marvel. All Martin's consciousness was concentrated in the work. Ceaselessly active, head and hand, an intelligent machine, all that constituted him a man was devoted to furnishing that intelligence. There was no room in his brain for the universe and its mighty problems. All the broad and spacious corridors of his mind were closed and hermetically sealed. The echoing chamber of his soul was a narrow room, a conning tower, whence were directed his arm and shoulder muscles, his ten nimble fingers, and the swift-moving iron along its steaming path in broad, sweeping strokes, just so many strokes and no more, just so far with each stroke and not a fraction of an inch farther, rushing along interminable sleeves, sides, backs, and tails, and tossing the finished shirts, without rumpling, upon the receiving frame. And even as his hurrying soul tossed, it was reaching for another shirt. This went on, hour after hour, while outside all the world swooned under the overhead California sun. But there was no swooning in that superheated room. The cool guests on the verandas needed clean linen.

The sweat poured from Martin. He drank enormous quantities of water, but so great was the heat of the day and of his exertions, that the water sluiced through the interstices of his flesh and out at all his pores. Always, at sea, except at rare intervals, the work he performed had given him ample opportunity to commune with himself. The master of the ship had been lord of Martin's time; but here the manager of the hotel was lord of Martin's thoughts as well. He had no thoughts save for the nerve-racking, body-destroying toil. Outside of that it was impossible to think. He did not know that he loved Ruth. She did not even exist, for his driven soul had no time to remember her. It was only when he crawled to bed at night, or to breakfast in the morning, that she asserted herself to him in fleeting memories.

"This is hell, ain't it?" Joe remarked once.

Martin nodded, but felt a rasp of irritation. The statement had been obvious and unnecessary. They did not talk while they worked. Conversation threw them out of their stride, as it did this time, compelling Martin to miss a stroke of his iron and to make two extra motions before he caught his stride again.

On Friday morning the washer ran. Twice a week they had to put through hotel linen,—the sheets, pillow-slips, spreads, table-cloths, and napkins. This finished, they buckled down to "fancy starch." It was slow work, fastidious and delicate, and Martin did not learn it so readily. Besides, he could not take chances. Mistakes were disastrous.

"See that," Joe said, holding up a filmy corset-cover that he could have crumpled from view in one hand. "Scorch that an' it's twenty dollars out of your wages."

So Martin did not scorch that, and eased down on his muscular tension, though nervous tension rose higher than ever, and he listened sympathetically to the other's blasphemies as he toiled and suffered over the beautiful things that women wear when they do not have to do their own laundrying. "Fancy starch" was Martin's nightmare, and it was Joe's, too. It was "fancy starch" that robbed them of their hard-won minutes. They toiled at it all day. At seven in the evening they broke off to run the hotel linen through the mangle. At ten o'clock, while the hotel guests slept, the two laundrymen sweated on at "fancy starch" till midnight, till one, till two. At half-past two they knocked off.

Saturday morning it was "fancy starch," and odds and ends, and at three in the afternoon the week's work was done.

"You ain't a-goin' to ride them seventy miles into Oakland on top of this?" Joe demanded, as they sat on the stairs and took a triumphant smoke.

"Got to," was the answer.

"What are you goin' for?—a girl?"

"No; to save two and a half on the railroad ticket. I want to renew some books at the library."

"Why don't you send 'em down an' up by express? That'll cost only a quarter each way."

Martin considered it.

"An' take a rest to-morrow," the other urged. "You need it. I know I do. I'm plumb tuckered out."

He looked it. Indomitable, never resting, fighting for seconds and minutes all week, circumventing delays and crushing down obstacles, a fount of resistless energy, a high-driven human motor, a demon for work, now that

574

he had accomplished the week's task he was in a state of collapse. He was worn and haggard, and his handsome face drooped in lean exhaustion. He pulled his cigarette spiritlessly, and his voice was peculiarly dead and monotonous. All the snap and fire had gone out of him. His triumph seemed a sorry one.

"An' next week we got to do it all over again," he said sadly. "An' what's the good of it all, hey? Sometimes I wish I was a hobo. They don't work, an' they get their livin'. Gee! I wish I had a glass of beer; but I can't get up the gumption to go down to the village an' get it. You'll stay over, an' send your books dawn by express, or else you're a damn fool."

"But what can I do here all day Sunday?" Martin asked.

"Rest. You don't know how tired you are. Why, I'm that tired Sunday I can't even read the papers. I was sick once—typhoid. In the hospital two months an' a half. Didn't do a tap of work all that time. It was beautiful."

"It was beautiful," he repeated dreamily, a minute later.

Martin took a bath, after which he found that the head laundryman had disappeared. Most likely he had gone for a glass of beer Martin decided, but the half-mile walk down to the village to find out seemed a long journey to him. He lay on his bed with his shoes off, trying to make up his mind. He did not reach out for a book. He was too tired to feel sleepy, and he lay, scarcely thinking, in a semi-stupor of weariness, until it was time for supper. Joe did not appear for that function, and when Martin heard the gardener remark that most likely he was ripping the slats off the bar, Martin understood. He went to bed immediately afterward, and in the morning decided that he was greatly rested. Joe being still absent, Martin procured a Sunday paper and lay down in a shady nook under the trees. The morning passed, he knew not how. He did not sleep, nobody disturbed him, and he did not finish the paper. He came back to it in the afternoon, after dinner, and fell asleep over it.

So passed Sunday, and Monday morning he was hard at work, sorting clothes, while Joe, a towel bound tightly around his head, with groans and blasphemies, was running the washer and mixing soft-soap.

575

"I simply can't help it," he explained. "I got to drink when Saturday night comes around."

Another week passed, a great battle that continued under the electric lights each night and that culminated on Saturday afternoon at three o'clock, when Joe tasted his moment of wilted triumph and then drifted down to the village to forget. Martin's Sunday was the same as before. He slept in the shade of the trees, toiled aimlessly through the newspaper, and spent long hours lying on his back, doing nothing, thinking nothing. He was too dazed to think, though he was aware that he did not like himself. He was self-repelled, as though he had undergone some degradation or was intrinsically foul. All that was god-like in him was blotted out. The spur of ambition was blunted; he had no vitality with which to feel the prod of it. He was dead. His soul seemed dead. He was a beast, a work-beast. He saw no beauty in the sunshine sifting down through the green leaves, nor did the azure vault of the sky whisper as of old and hint of cosmic vastness and secrets trembling to disclosure. Life was intolerably dull and stupid, and its taste was bad in his mouth. A black screen was drawn across his mirror of inner vision, and fancy lay in a darkened sick-room where entered no ray of light. He envied Joe, down in the village, rampant, tearing the slats off the bar, his brain gnawing with maggots, exulting in maudlin ways over maudlin things, fantastically and gloriously drunk and forgetful of Monday morning and the week of deadening toil to come.

A third week went by, and Martin loathed himself, and loathed life. He was oppressed by a sense of failure. There was reason for the editors refusing his stuff. He could see that clearly now, and laugh at himself and the dreams he had dreamed. Ruth returned his "Sea Lyrics" by mail. He read her letter apathetically. She did her best to say how much she liked them and that they were beautiful. But she could not lie, and she could not disguise the truth from herself. She knew they were failures, and he read her disapproval in every perfunctory and unenthusiastic line of her letter. And she was right. He was firmly convinced of it as he read the poems over. Beauty and wonder had departed from him, and as he read the poems he caught himself puzzling as to what he had had in mind when he wrote them. His audacities of phrase struck him as grotesque, his felicities of expression were monstrosities, and everything was absurd, unreal, and impossible. He would have burned the "Sea Lyrics" on the spot, had his will been strong enough to set them aflame. There was the engine-room, but the exertion of carrying them to the furnace was not worth while. All his exertion was used in washing other persons' clothes. He did not have any left for private affairs.

He resolved that when Sunday came he would pull himself together and answer Ruth's letter. But Saturday afternoon, after work was finished and he had taken a bath, the desire to forget overpowered him. "I guess I'll go down and see how Joe's getting on," was the way he put it to himself; and in the same moment he knew that he lied. But he did not have the energy to consider the lie. If he had had the energy, he would have refused to consider the lie, because he wanted to forget. He started for the village slowly and casually, increasing his pace in spite of himself as he neared the saloon.

"I thought you was on the water-wagon," was Joe's greeting.

Martin did not deign to offer excuses, but called for whiskey, filling his own glass brimming before he passed the bottle.

"Don't take all night about it," he said roughly.

The other was dawdling with the bottle, and Martin refused to wait for him, tossing the glass off in a gulp and refilling it.

"Now, I can wait for you," he said grimly; "but hurry up."

Joe hurried, and they drank together.

"The work did it, eh?" Joe queried.

Martin refused to discuss the matter.

"It's fair hell, I know," the other went on, "but I kind of hate to see you come off the wagon, Mart. Well, here's how!"

Martin drank on silently, biting out his orders and invitations and awing the barkeeper, an effeminate country youngster with watery blue eyes and hair parted in the middle.

"It's something scandalous the way they work us poor devils," Joe was remarking. "If I didn't bowl up, I'd break loose an' burn down the shebang. My bowlin' up is all that saves 'em, I can tell you that."

But Martin made no answer. A few more drinks, and in his brain he felt the maggots of intoxication beginning to crawl. Ah, it was living, the first breath of life he had breathed in three weeks. His dreams came back to him. Fancy came out of the darkened room and lured him on, a thing of flaming brightness. His mirror of vision was silver-clear, a flashing, dazzling palimpsest of imagery. Wonder and beauty walked with him, hand in hand, and all power was his. He tried to tell it to Joe, but Joe had visions of his own, infallible schemes whereby he would escape the slavery of laundry-work and become himself the owner of a great steam laundry.

"I tell yeh, Mart, they won't be no kids workin' in my laundry—not on yer life. An' they won't be no workin' a livin' soul after six P.M. You hear me talk! They'll be machinery enough an' hands enough to do it all in decent workin' hours, an' Mart, s'help me, I'll make yeh superintendent of the shebang—the whole of it, all of it. Now here's the scheme. I get on the water-wagon an' save my money for two years—save an' then—"

But Martin turned away, leaving him to tell it to the barkeeper, until that worthy was called away to furnish drinks to two farmers who, coming in, accepted Martin's invitation. Martin dispensed royal largess, inviting everybody up, farm-hands, a stableman, and the gardener's assistant from the hotel, the barkeeper, and the furtive hobo who slid in like a shadow and like a shadow hovered at the end of the bar.

CHAPTER XVIII

Monday morning, Joe groaned over the first truck load of clothes to the washer.

"I say," he began.

"Don't talk to me," Martin snarled.

"I'm sorry, Joe," he said at noon, when they knocked off for dinner.

Tears came into the other's eyes.

"That's all right, old man," he said. "We're in hell, an' we can't help ourselves. An', you know, I kind of like you a whole lot. That's what made it—hurt. I cottoned to you from the first."

Martin shook his hand.

"Let's quit," Joe suggested. "Let's chuck it, an' go hoboin'. I ain't never tried it, but it must be dead easy. An' nothin' to do. Just think of it, nothin' to do. I was sick once, typhoid, in the hospital, an' it was beautiful. I wish I'd get sick again."

The week dragged on. The hotel was full, and extra "fancy starch" poured in upon them. They performed prodigies of valor. They fought late each night under the electric lights, bolted their meals, and even got in a half hour's work before breakfast. Martin no longer took his cold baths. Every moment was drive, drive, drive, and Joe was the masterful shepherd of moments, herding them carefully, never losing one, counting them over like a miser counting gold, working on in a frenzy, toil-mad, a feverish machine, aided ably by that other machine that thought of itself as once having been one Martin Eden, a man.

But it was only at rare moments that Martin was able to think. The house of thought was closed, its windows boarded up, and he was its shadowy caretaker. He was a shadow. Joe was right. They were both shadows, and this was the unending limbo of toil. Or was it a dream? Sometimes, in the steaming, sizzling heat, as he swung the heavy irons back and forth over the white garments, it came to him that it was a dream. In a short while, or maybe after a thousand years or so, he would awake, in his little room with the ink-stained table, and take up his writing where he had left off the day before. Or maybe that was a dream, too, and the awakening would be the changing of the watches, when he would drop down out of his bunk in the lurching forecastle and go up on deck, under the tropic stars, and take the wheel and feel the cool tradewind blowing through his flesh.

Came Saturday and its hollow victory at three o'clock.

"Guess I'll go down an' get a glass of beer," Joe said, in the queer, monotonous tones that marked his week-end collapse.

Martin seemed suddenly to wake up. He opened the kit bag and oiled his wheel, putting graphite on the chain and adjusting the bearings. Joe was halfway down to the saloon when Martin passed by, bending low over the handle-bars, his legs driving the ninety-six gear with rhythmic strength, his face set for seventy miles of road and grade and dust. He slept in Oakland that night, and on Sunday covered the seventy miles back. And on Monday morning, weary, he began the new week's work, but he had kept sober.

A fifth week passed, and a sixth, during which he lived and toiled as a machine, with just a spark of something more in him, just a glimmering bit of soul, that compelled him, at each week-end, to scorch off the hundred and forty miles. But this was not rest. It was super-machinelike, and it helped to crush out the glimmering bit of soul that was all that was left him from former life. At the end of the seventh week, without intending it, too weak to resist, he drifted down to the village with Joe and drowned life and found life until Monday morning.

Again, at the week-ends, he ground out the one hundred and forty miles, obliterating the numbness of too great exertion by the numbness of still greater exertion. At the end of three months he went down a third time to the village with Joe. He forgot, and lived again, and, living, he saw, in clear illumination, the beast he was making of himself—not by the drink, but by the work. The drink was an effect, not a cause. It followed inevitably upon the work, as the night follows upon the day. Not by becoming a toil-beast could he win to the heights, was the message the whiskey whispered to him, and he nodded approbation. The whiskey was wise. It told secrets on itself.

He called for paper and pencil, and for drinks all around, and while they drank his very good health, he clung to the bar and scribbled.

"A telegram, Joe," he said. "Read it."

Joe read it with a drunken, quizzical leer. But what he read seemed to sober him. He looked at the other reproachfully, tears oozing into his eyes and down his cheeks.

"You ain't goin' back on me, Mart?" he queried hopelessly.

Martin nodded, and called one of the loungers to him to take the message to the telegraph office.

"Hold on," Joe muttered thickly. "Lemme think."

He held on to the bar, his legs wobbling under him, Martin's arm around him and supporting him, while he thought.

"Make that two laundrymen," he said abruptly. "Here, lemme fix it."

"What are you quitting for?" Martin demanded.

"Same reason as you."

"But I'm going to sea. You can't do that."

"Nope," was the answer, "but I can hobo all right, all right."

Martin looked at him searchingly for a moment, then cried:-

"By God, I think you're right! Better a hobo than a beast of toil. Why, man, you'll live. And that's more than you ever did before."

"I was in hospital, once," Joe corrected. "It was beautiful. Typhoid—did I tell you?"

While Martin changed the telegram to "two laundrymen," Joe went on:-

"I never wanted to drink when I was in hospital. Funny, ain't it? But when I've ben workin' like a slave all week, I just got to bowl up. Ever noticed that cooks drink like hell?—an' bakers, too? It's the work. They've sure got to. Here, lemme pay half of that telegram."

"I'll shake you for it," Martin offered.

"Come on, everybody drink," Joe called, as they rattled the dice and rolled them out on the damp bar.

Monday morning Joe was wild with anticipation. He did not mind his aching head, nor did he take interest in his work. Whole herds of moments stole away and were lost while their careless shepherd gazed out of the window at the sunshine and the trees.

"Just look at it!" he cried. "An' it's all mine! It's free. I can lie down under them trees an' sleep for a thousan' years if I want to. Aw, come on, Mart, let's chuck it. What's the good of waitin' another moment. That's the land of nothin' to do out there, an' I got a ticket for it—an' it ain't no return ticket, b'gosh!"

A few minutes later, filling the truck with soiled clothes for the washer, Joe spied the hotel manager's shirt. He knew its mark, and with a sudden glorious consciousness of freedom he threw it on the floor and stamped on it.

"I wish you was in it, you pig-headed Dutchman!" he shouted. "In it, an' right there where I've got you! Take that! an' that! an' that! damn you! Hold me back, somebody! Hold me back!"

Martin laughed and held him to his work. On Tuesday night the new laundrymen arrived, and the rest of the week was spent breaking them into the routine. Joe sat around and explained his system, but he did no more work.

"Not a tap," he announced. "Not a tap. They can fire me if they want to, but if they do, I'll quit. No more work in mine, thank you kindly. Me for the freight cars an' the shade under the trees. Go to it, you slaves! That's right. Slave an' sweat! Slave an' sweat! An' when you're dead, you'll rot the same as me, an' what's it matter how you live?—eh? Tell me that—what's it matter in the long run?"

On Saturday they drew their pay and came to the parting of the ways.

"They ain't no use in me askin' you to change your mind an' hit the road with me?" Joe asked hopelessly:

Martin shook his head. He was standing by his wheel, ready to start. They shook hands, and Joe held on to his for a moment, as he said:-

"I'm goin' to see you again, Mart, before you an' me die. That's straight dope. I feel it in my bones. Good-by, Mart, an' be good. I like you like hell, you know."

He stood, a forlorn figure, in the middle of the road, watching until Martin turned a bend and was gone from sight.

"He's a good Indian, that boy," he muttered. "A good Indian."

Then he plodded down the road himself, to the water tank, where half a dozen empties lay on a side-track waiting for the up freight.

CHAPTER XIX

Ruth and her family were home again, and Martin, returned to Oakland, saw much of her. Having gained her degree, she was doing no more studying; and he, having worked all vitality out of his mind and body, was doing no writing. This gave them time for each other that they had never had before, and their intimacy ripened fast.

At first, Martin had done nothing but rest. He had slept a great deal, and spent long hours musing and thinking and doing nothing. He was like one recovering from some terrible bout of hardship. The first signs of reawakening came when he discovered more than languid interest in the daily paper. Then he began to read again—light novels, and poetry; and after several days more he was head over heels in his long-neglected Fiske. His splendid body and health made new vitality, and he possessed all the resiliency and rebound of youth.

Ruth showed her disappointment plainly when he announced that he was going to sea for another voyage as soon as he was well rested.

"Why do you want to do that?" she asked.

"Money," was the answer. "I'll have to lay in a supply for my next attack on the editors. Money is the sinews of war, in my case—money and patience."

"But if all you wanted was money, why didn't you stay in the laundry?"

"Because the laundry was making a beast of me. Too much work of that sort drives to drink."

She stared at him with horror in her eyes.

"Do you mean—?" she quavered.

It would have been easy for him to get out of it; but his natural impulse was for frankness, and he remembered his old resolve to be frank, no matter what happened.

"Yes," he answered. "Just that. Several times."

She shivered and drew away from him.

"No man that I have ever known did that—ever did that."

"Then they never worked in the laundry at Shelly Hot Springs," he laughed bitterly. "Toil is a good thing. It is necessary for human health, so all the preachers say, and Heaven knows I've never been afraid of it. But there is such a thing as too much of a good thing, and the laundry up there is one of them. And that's why I'm going to sea one more voyage. It will be my last, I think, for when I come back, I shall break into the magazines. I am certain of it."

She was silent, unsympathetic, and he watched her moodily, realizing how impossible it was for her to understand what he had been through.

"Some day I shall write it up—'The Degradation of Toil' or the 'Psychology of Drink in the Working-class,' or something like that for a title."

Never, since the first meeting, had they seemed so far apart as that day. His confession, told in frankness, with the spirit of revolt behind, had repelled her. But she was more shocked by the repulsion itself than by the cause of it. It pointed out to her how near she had drawn to him, and once accepted, it paved the way for greater intimacy. Pity, too, was aroused, and innocent, idealistic thoughts of reform. She would save this raw young man who had come so far. She would save him from the curse of his early environment, and she would save him from himself in spite of himself. And all this affected her as a very noble state of consciousness; nor did she dream that behind it and underlying it were the jealousy and desire of love.

They rode on their wheels much in the delightful fall weather, and out in the hills they read poetry aloud, now one and now the other, noble, uplifting poetry that turned one's thoughts to higher things. Renunciation, sacrifice, patience, industry, and high endeavor were the principles she thus indirectly preached—such abstractions being objectified in her mind by her father, and Mr. Butler, and by Andrew Carnegie, who, from a poor immigrant boy had arisen to be the book-giver of the world. All of which was appreciated and enjoyed by Martin. He followed her mental processes more clearly now, and her soul was no longer the sealed wonder it had been. He was on terms of intellectual equality with her. But the points of disagreement did not affect his love. His love was more ardent than ever, for he loved her for what she was, and even her physical frailty was an added charm in his eyes. He read of sickly Elizabeth Barrett, who for years had not placed her feet upon the ground, until that day of flame when she eloped with Browning and stood upright, upon the earth, under the open sky; and what Browning had done for her, Martin decided he could do for Ruth. But first, she must love him. The rest would be easy. He would give her strength and health. And he caught glimpses of their life, in the years to come, wherein, against a background of work and comfort and general well-being, he saw himself and Ruth reading and discussing poetry, she propped amid a multitude of cushions on the ground while she read aloud to him. This was the key to the life they would live. And always he saw that particular picture. Sometimes it was she who leaned against him while he read, one arm about her, her head upon his shoulder. Sometimes they pored together over the printed pages of beauty. Then, too, she loved nature, and with generous imagination he changed the scene of their reading—sometimes they read in closed-in valleys with precipitous walls, or in high mountain meadows, and, again, down by the gray sand-dunes with a wreath of billows at their feet, or afar on some volcanic tropic isle where waterfalls descended and became mist, reaching the sea in vapor veils that swayed and shivered to every vagrant wisp of wind. But always, in the foreground, lords of beauty and eternally reading and sharing, lay he and Ruth, and always in the background that was beyond the background of nature, dim and hazy, were work and success and money earned that made them free of the world and all its treasures.

"I should recommend my little girl to be careful," her mother warned her one day.

"I know what you mean. But it is impossible. He is not—"

Ruth was blushing, but it was the blush of maidenhood called upon for the first time to discuss the sacred things of life with a mother held equally sacred.

586

"Your kind." Her mother finished the sentence for her.

Ruth nodded.

"I did not want to say it, but he is not. He is rough, brutal, strong—too strong. He has not—"

She hesitated and could not go on. It was a new experience, talking over such matters with her mother. And again her mother completed her thought for her.

"He has not lived a clean life, is what you wanted to say."

Again Ruth nodded, and again a blush mantled her face.

"It is just that," she said. "It has not been his fault, but he has played much with—"

"With pitch?"

"Yes, with pitch. And he frightens me. Sometimes I am positively in terror of him, when he talks in that free and easy way of the things he has done—as if they did not matter. They do matter, don't they?"

They sat with their arms twined around each other, and in the pause her mother patted her hand and waited for her to go on.

"But I am interested in him dreadfully," she continued. "In a way he is my protégé. Then, too, he is my first boy friend—but not exactly friend; rather protégé and friend combined. Sometimes, too, when he frightens me, it seems that he is a bulldog I have taken for a plaything, like some of the 'frat' girls, and he is tugging hard, and showing his teeth, and threatening to break loose."

Again her mother waited.

"He interests me, I suppose, like the bulldog. And there is much good in him, too; but there is much in him that I would not like in—in the other way. You see, I have been thinking. He swears, he smokes, he drinks, he has fought with his fists (he has told me so, and he likes it; he says so). He is all that a man should not be—a man I would want for my—" her voice sank very low—"husband. Then he is too strong. My prince must be tall, and slender, and dark—a graceful, bewitching prince. No, there is no danger of my failing in love with Martin Eden. It would be the worst fate that could befall me."

"But it is not that that I spoke about," her mother equivocated. "Have you thought about him? He is so ineligible in every way, you know, and suppose he should come to love you?"

"But he does—already," she cried.

"It was to be expected," Mrs. Morse said gently. "How could it be otherwise with any one who knew you?"

"Olney hates me!" she exclaimed passionately. "And I hate Olney. I feel always like a cat when he is around. I feel that I must be nasty to him, and even when I don't happen to feel that way, why, he's nasty to me, anyway. But I am happy with Martin Eden. No one ever loved me before—no man, I mean, in that way. And it is sweet to be loved—that way. You know what I mean, mother dear. It is sweet to feel that you are really and truly a woman." She buried her face in her mother's lap, sobbing. "You think I am dreadful, I know, but I am honest, and I tell you just how I feel."

Mrs. Morse was strangely sad and happy. Her child-daughter, who was a bachelor of arts, was gone; but in her place was a woman-daughter. The experiment had succeeded. The strange void in Ruth's nature had been filled, and filled without danger or penalty. This rough sailor-fellow had been the instrument, and, though Ruth did not love him, he had made her conscious of her womanhood.

"His hand trembles," Ruth was confessing, her face, for shame's sake, still buried. "It is most amusing and ridiculous, but I feel sorry for him, too. And when his hands are too trembly, and his eyes too shiny, why, I lecture him about his life and the wrong way he is going about it to mend it. But he worships me, I know. His eyes and his hands do not lie. And it makes me feel grown-up, the thought of it, the very thought of it; and I feel that I am possessed of something that is by rights my own—that makes me like the other girls—and—and young women. And, then, too, I knew that I was not like them before, and I knew that it worried you. You thought you did not let me know that dear worry of yours, but I did, and I wanted to—'to make good,' as Martin Eden says."

It was a holy hour for mother and daughter, and their eyes were wet as they talked on in the twilight, Ruth all white innocence and frankness, her mother sympathetic, receptive, yet calmly explaining and guiding.

"He is four years younger than you," she said. "He has no place in the world. He has neither position nor salary. He is impractical. Loving you, he should, in the name of common sense, be doing something that would give him the right to marry, instead of paltering around with those stories of his and with childish dreams. Martin Eden, I am afraid, will never grow up. He does not take to responsibility and a man's work in the world like your father did, or like all our friends, Mr. Butler for one. Martin Eden, I am afraid, will never be a money-earner. And this world is so ordered that money is necessary to happiness—oh, no, not these swollen fortunes, but enough of money to permit of common comfort and decency. He—he has never spoken?"

"He has not breathed a word. He has not attempted to; but if he did, I would not let him, because, you see, I do not love him."

"I am glad of that. I should not care to see my daughter, my one daughter, who is so clean and pure, love a man like him. There are noble men in the world who are clean and true and manly. Wait for them. You will find one some day, and you will love him and be loved by him, and you will be happy with him as your father and I have been happy with each other. And there is one thing you must always carry in mind—"

"Yes, mother."

Mrs. Morse's voice was low and sweet as she said, "And that is the children."

"I—have thought about them," Ruth confessed, remembering the wanton thoughts that had vexed her in the past, her face again red with maiden shame that she should be telling such things.

"And it is that, the children, that makes Mr. Eden impossible," Mrs. Morse went on incisively. "Their heritage must be clean, and he is, I am afraid, not clean. Your father has told me of sailors' lives, and—and you understand."

Ruth pressed her mother's hand in assent, feeling that she really did understand, though her conception was of something vague, remote, and terrible that was beyond the scope of imagination.

"You know I do nothing without telling you," she began. "—Only, sometimes you must ask me, like this time. I wanted to tell you, but I did not know how. It is false modesty, I know it is that, but you can make it easy for me. Sometimes, like this time, you must ask me, you must give me a chance."

"Why, mother, you are a woman, too!" she cried exultantly, as they stood up, catching her mother's hands and standing erect, facing her in the twilight, conscious of a strangely sweet equality between them. "I should never have thought of you in that way if we had not had this talk. I had to learn that I was a woman to know that you were one, too."

"We are women together," her mother said, drawing her to her and kissing her. "We are women together," she repeated, as they went out of the room, their arms around each other's waists, their hearts swelling with a new sense of companionship.

"Our little girl has become a woman," Mrs. Morse said proudly to her husband an hour later.

"That means," he said, after a long look at his wife, "that means she is in love."

"No, but that she is loved," was the smiling rejoinder. "The experiment has succeeded. She is awakened at last."

"Then we'll have to get rid of him." Mr. Morse spoke briskly, in matter-of-fact, businesslike tones.

But his wife shook her head. "It will not be necessary. Ruth says he is going to sea in a few days. When he comes back, she will not be here. We will send her to Aunt Clara's. And, besides, a year in the East, with the change in climate, people, ideas, and everything, is just the thing she needs."

CHAPTER XX

The desire to write was stirring in Martin once more. Stories and poems were springing into spontaneous creation in his brain, and he made notes of them against the future time when he would give them expression. But he did not write. This was his little vacation; he had resolved to devote it to rest and love, and in both matters he prospered. He was soon spilling over with vitality, and each day he saw Ruth, at the moment of meeting, she experienced the old shock of his strength and health.

"Be careful," her mother warned her once again. "I am afraid you are seeing too much of Martin Eden."

But Ruth laughed from security. She was sure of herself, and in a few days he would be off to sea. Then, by the time he returned, she would be away on her visit East. There was a magic, however, in the strength and health of Martin. He, too, had been told of her contemplated Eastern trip, and he felt the need for haste. Yet he did not know how to make love to a girl like Ruth. Then, too, he was handicapped by the possession of a great fund of experience with girls and women who had been absolutely different from her. They had known about love and life and flirtation, while she knew nothing about such things. Her prodigious innocence appalled him, freezing on his lips all ardors of speech, and convincing him, in spite of himself, of his own unworthiness. Also he was handicapped in another way. He had himself never been in love before. He had liked women in that turgid past of his, and been fascinated by some of them, but he had not known what it was to love them. He had whistled in a masterful, careless way, and they had come to him. They had been diversions, incidents, part of the game men play, but a small part at most. And now, and for the first time, he was a suppliant, tender and timid and doubting. He did not know the way of love, nor its speech, while he was frightened at his loved one's clear innocence.

In the course of getting acquainted with a varied world, whirling on through the ever changing phases of it, he had learned a rule of conduct which was to the effect that when one played a strange game, he should let the other fellow play first. This had stood him in good stead a thousand times and trained him as an observer as well. He knew how to watch the thing that was strange, and to wait for a weakness, for a place of entrance, to divulge itself. It was like sparring for an opening in fist-fighting. And when such an opening came, he knew by long experience to play for it and to play hard.

So he waited with Ruth and watched, desiring to speak his love but not daring. He was afraid of shocking her, and he was not sure of himself. Had he but known it, he was following the right course with her. Love came into the world before articulate speech, and in its own early youth it had learned ways and means that it had never forgotten. It was in this old, primitive way that Martin wooed Ruth. He did not know he was doing it at first, though later he divined it. The touch of his hand on hers was vastly more potent than any word he could utter, the impact of his strength on her imagination was more alluring than the printed poems and spoken passions of a thousand generations of lovers. Whatever his tongue could express would have appealed, in part, to her judgment; but the touch of hand, the fleeting contact, made its way directly to her instinct. Her judgment was as young as she, but her instincts were as old as the race and older. They had been young when love was young, and they were wiser than convention and opinion and all the new-born things. So her judgment did not act. There was no call upon it, and she did not realize the strength of the appeal Martin made from moment to moment to her love-nature. That he loved her, on the other hand, was as clear as day, and she consciously delighted in beholding his love-manifestations—the glowing eyes with their tender lights, the trembling hands, and the never failing swarthy flush that flooded darkly under his sunburn. She even went farther, in a timid way inciting him, but doing it so delicately that he never suspected, and doing it half-consciously, so that she scarcely suspected herself. She thrilled with these proofs of her power that proclaimed her a woman, and she took an Eve-like delight in tormenting him and playing upon him.

Tongue-tied by inexperience and by excess of ardor, wooing unwittingly and awkwardly, Martin continued his approach by contact. The touch of his hand was pleasant to her, and something deliciously more than pleasant. Martin did not know it, but he did know that it was not distasteful to her. Not that they touched hands often, save at meeting and parting; but that in handling the bicycles, in strapping on the books of verse they carried into the hills, and in conning the pages of books side by side, there were opportunities for hand to stray against hand. And there were opportunities, too, for her hair to brush his cheek, and for shoulder to touch shoulder, as they leaned together over the beauty of the books. She smiled to herself at vagrant impulses which arose from nowhere and suggested that she rumple his hair; while he desired greatly, when they tired of reading, to rest his head in her lap and dream with closed eyes about the future that was to be theirs. On Sunday picnics at Shellmound Park and Schuetzen Park, in the past, he had rested his head on many laps, and, usually, he had slept soundly and selfishly while the girls shaded his face from the sun and looked down and loved him and wondered at his lordly carelessness of their love. To rest his head in a girl's lap had been the easiest thing in the world until now, and now he found Ruth's lap inaccessible and impossible. Yet it was right here, in his reticence, that the strength of his wooing lay. It was because of this reticence that he never alarmed her. Herself fastidious and timid, she never awakened to the perilous trend of their intercourse. Subtly and unaware she grew toward him and closer to him, while he, sensing the growing closeness, longed to dare but was afraid.

Once he dared, one afternoon, when he found her in the darkened living room with a blinding headache.

"Nothing can do it any good," she had answered his inquiries. "And besides, I don't take headache powders. Doctor Hall won't permit me."

"I can cure it, I think, and without drugs," was Martin's answer. "I am not sure, of course, but I'd like to try. It's simply massage. I learned the trick first from the Japanese. They are a race of masseurs, you know. Then I learned it all over again with variations from the Hawaiians. They call it *lomi-lomi*. It can accomplish most of the things drugs accomplish and a few things that drugs can't."

594

Scarcely had his hands touched her head when she sighed deeply.

"That is so good," she said.

She spoke once again, half an hour later, when she asked, "Aren't you tired?"

The question was perfunctory, and she knew what the answer would be. Then she lost herself in drowsy contemplation of the soothing balm of his strength: Life poured from the ends of his fingers, driving the pain before it, or so it seemed to her, until with the easement of pain, she fell asleep and he stole away.

She called him up by telephone that evening to thank him.

"I slept until dinner," she said. "You cured me completely, Mr. Eden, and I don't know how to thank you."

He was warm, and bungling of speech, and very happy, as he replied to her, and there was dancing in his mind, throughout the telephone conversation, the memory of Browning and of sickly Elizabeth Barrett. What had been done could be done again, and he, Martin Eden, could do it and would do it for Ruth Morse. He went back to his room and to the volume of Spencer's "Sociology" lying open on the bed. But he could not read. Love tormented him and overrode his will, so that, despite all determination, he found himself at the little ink-stained table. The sonnet he composed that night was the first of a love-cycle of fifty sonnets which was completed within two months. He had the "Love-sonnets from the Portuguese" in mind as he wrote, and he wrote under the best conditions for great work, at a climacteric of living, in the throes of his own sweet love-madness.

The many hours he was not with Ruth he devoted to the "Love-cycle," to reading at home, or to the public reading-rooms, where he got more closely in touch with the magazines of the day and the nature of their policy and content. The hours he spent with Ruth were maddening alike in promise and in inconclusiveness. It was a week after he cured her headache that a moonlight sail on Lake Merritt was proposed by Norman and seconded by Arthur and Olney. Martin was the only one capable of handling a boat, and he was pressed into service. Ruth sat near him in the stern, while the three young fellows lounged amidships, deep in a wordy wrangle over "frat" affairs.

The moon had not yet risen, and Ruth, gazing into the starry vault of the sky and exchanging no speech with Martin, experienced a sudden feeling of loneliness. She glanced at him. A puff of wind was heeling the boat over till the deck was awash, and he, one hand on tiller and the other on main-sheet, was luffing slightly, at the same time peering ahead to make out the near-lying north shore. He was unaware of her gaze, and she watched him intently, speculating fancifully about the strange warp of soul that led him, a young man with signal powers, to fritter away his time on the writing of stories and poems foredoomed to mediocrity and failure.

Her eyes wandered along the strong throat, dimly seen in the starlight, and over the firm-poised head, and the old desire to lay her hands upon his neck came back to her. The strength she abhorred attracted her. Her feeling of loneliness became more pronounced, and she felt tired. Her position on the heeling boat irked her, and she remembered the headache he had cured and the soothing rest that resided in him. He was sitting beside her, quite beside her, and the boat seemed to tilt her toward him. Then arose in her the impulse to lean against him, to rest herself against his strength—a vague, half-formed impulse, which, even as she considered it, mastered her and made her lean toward him. Or was it the heeling of the boat? She did not know. She never knew. She knew only that she was leaning against him and that the easement and soothing rest were very good. Perhaps it had been the boat's fault, but she made no effort to retrieve it. She leaned lightly against his shoulder, but she leaned, and she continued to lean when he shifted his position to make it more comfortable for her.

It was a madness, but she refused to consider the madness. She was no longer herself but a woman, with a woman's clinging need; and though she leaned ever so lightly, the need seemed satisfied. She was no longer tired. Martin did not speak. Had he, the spell would have been broken. But his reticence of love prolonged it. He was dazed and dizzy. He could not understand what was happening. It was too wonderful to be anything but a delirium. He conquered a mad desire to let go sheet and tiller and to clasp her in his arms. His intuition told him it was the wrong thing to do, and he was glad that sheet and tiller kept his hands occupied and fended off temptation. But he luffed the boat less delicately, spilling the wind shamelessly from the sail so as to prolong the tack to the north shore. The shore would compel him to go about, and the contact would be broken. He sailed with skill, stopping way on the boat without exciting the notice of the wranglers, and mentally forgiving his hardest voyages in that they had made this marvellous night possible, giving him mastery over sea and boat and wind so that he could sail with her beside him, her dear weight against him on his shoulder.

When the first light of the rising moon touched the sail, illuminating the boat with pearly radiance, Ruth moved away from him. And, even as she moved, she felt him move away. The impulse to avoid detection was mutual. The episode was tacitly and secretly intimate. She sat apart from him with burning cheeks, while the full force of it came home to her. She had been guilty of something she would not have her brothers see, nor Olney see. Why had she done it? She had never done anything like it in her life, and yet she had been moonlight-sailing with young men before. She had never desired to do anything like it. She was overcome with shame and with the mystery of her own burgeoning womanhood. She stole a glance at Martin, who was busy putting the boat about on the other tack, and she could have hated him for having made her do an immodest and shameful thing. And he, of all men! Perhaps her mother was right, and she was seeing too much of him. It would never happen again, she resolved, and she would see less of him in the future. She entertained a wild idea of explaining to him the first time they were alone together, of lying to him, of mentioning casually the attack of faintness that had overpowered her just before the moon came up. Then she remembered how they had drawn mutually away before the revealing moon, and she knew he would know it for a lie.

In the days that swiftly followed she was no longer herself but a strange, puzzling creature, wilful over judgment and scornful of self-analysis, refusing to peer into the future or to think about herself and whither she was drifting. She was in a fever of tingling mystery, alternately frightened and charmed, and in constant bewilderment. She had one idea firmly fixed, however, which insured her security. She would not let Martin speak his love. As long as she did this, all would be well. In a few days he would be off to sea. And even if he did speak, all would be well. It could not be otherwise, for she did not love him. Of course, it would be a painful half hour for him, and an embarrassing half hour for her, because it would be her first proposal. She thrilled deliciously at the thought. She was really a woman, with a man ripe to ask for her in marriage. It was a lure to all that was fundamental in her sex. The fabric of her life, of all that constituted her, quivered and grew tremulous. The thought fluttered in her mind like a flame-attracted moth. She went so far as to imagine Martin proposing, herself putting the words into his mouth; and she rehearsed her refusal, tempering it with kindness and exhorting him to true and noble manhood. And especially he must stop smoking cigarettes. She would make a point of that. But no, she must not let him speak at all. She could stop him, and she had told her mother that she would. All flushed and burning, she regretfully dismissed the conjured situation. Her first proposal would have to be deferred to a more propitious time and a more eligible suitor.

CHAPTER XXI

Came a beautiful fall day, warm and languid, palpitant with the hush of the changing season, a California Indian summer day, with hazy sun and wandering wisps of breeze that did not stir the slumber of the air. Filmy purple mists, that were not vapors but fabrics woven of color, hid in the recesses of the hills. San Francisco lay like a blur of smoke upon her heights. The intervening bay was a dull sheen of molten metal, whereon sailing craft lay motionless or drifted with the lazy tide. Far Tamalpais, barely seen in the silver haze, bulked hugely by the Golden Gate, the latter a pale gold pathway under the westering sun. Beyond, the Pacific, dim and vast, was raising on its sky-line tumbled cloud-masses that swept landward, giving warning of the first blustering breath of winter.

The erasure of summer was at hand. Yet summer lingered, fading and fainting among her hills, deepening the purple of her valleys, spinning a shroud of haze from waning powers and sated raptures, dying with the calm content of having lived and lived well. And among the hills, on their favorite knoll, Martin and Ruth sat side by side, their heads bent over the same pages, he reading aloud from the love-sonnets of the woman who had loved Browning as it is given to few men to be loved.

But the reading languished. The spell of passing beauty all about them was too strong. The golden year was dying as it had lived, a beautiful and unrepentant voluptuary, and reminiscent rapture and content freighted heavily the air. It entered into them, dreamy and languorous, weakening the fibres of resolution, suffusing the face of morality, or of judgment, with haze and purple mist. Martin felt tender and melting, and from time to time warm glows passed over him. His head was very near to hers, and when wandering phantoms of breeze stirred her hair so that it touched his face, the printed pages swam before his eyes.

"I don't believe you know a word of what you are reading," she said once when he had lost his place.

He looked at her with burning eyes, and was on the verge of becoming awkward, when a retort came to his lips.

"I don't believe you know either. What was the last sonnet about?"

"I don't know," she laughed frankly. "I've already forgotten. Don't let us read any more. The day is too beautiful."

"It will be our last in the hills for some time," he announced gravely. "There's a storm gathering out there on the sea-rim."

The book slipped from his hands to the ground, and they sat idly and silently, gazing out over the dreamy bay with eyes that dreamed and did not see. Ruth glanced sidewise at his neck. She did not lean toward him. She was drawn by some force outside of herself and stronger than gravitation, strong as destiny. It was only an inch to lean, and it was accomplished without volition on her part. Her shoulder touched his as lightly as a butterfly touches a flower, and just as lightly was the counter-pressure. She felt his shoulder press hers, and a tremor run through him. Then was the time for her to draw back. But she had become an automaton. Her actions had passed beyond the control of her will—she never thought of control or will in the delicious madness that was upon her. His arm began to steal behind her and around her. She waited its slow progress in a torment of delight. She waited, she knew not for what, panting, with dry, burning lips, a leaping pulse, and a fever of expectancy in all her blood. The girdling arm lifted higher and drew her toward him, drew her slowly and caressingly. She could wait no longer. With a tired sigh, and with an impulsive movement all her own, unpremeditated, spasmodic, she rested her head upon his breast. His head bent over swiftly, and, as his lips approached, hers flew to meet them.

This must be love, she thought, in the one rational moment that was vouchsafed her. If it was not love, it was too shameful. It could be nothing else than love. She loved the man whose arms were around her and whose lips were pressed to hers. She pressed more, tightly to him, with a snuggling movement of her body. And a moment later, tearing herself half out of his embrace, suddenly and exultantly she reached up and placed both hands upon Martin Eden's sunburnt neck. So exquisite was the pang of love and

600

desire fulfilled that she uttered a low moan, relaxed her hands, and lay half-swooning in his arms.

Not a word had been spoken, and not a word was spoken for a long time. Twice he bent and kissed her, and each time her lips met his shyly and her body made its happy, nestling movement. She clung to him, unable to release herself, and he sat, half supporting her in his arms, as he gazed with unseeing eyes at the blur of the great city across the bay. For once there were no visions in his brain. Only colors and lights and glows pulsed there, warm as the day and warm as his love. He bent over her. She was speaking.

"When did you love me?" she whispered.

"From the first, the very first, the first moment I laid eye on you. I was mad for love of you then, and in all the time that has passed since then I have only grown the madder. I am maddest, now, dear. I am almost a lunatic, my head is so turned with joy."

"I am glad I am a woman, Martin—dear," she said, after a long sigh.

He crushed her in his arms again and again, and then asked:-

"And you? When did you first know?"

"Oh, I knew it all the time, almost, from the first."

"And I have been as blind as a bat!" he cried, a ring of vexation in his voice. "I never dreamed it until just how, when I—when I kissed you."

"I didn't mean that." She drew herself partly away and looked at him. "I meant I knew you loved almost from the first."

"And you?" he demanded.

"It came to me suddenly." She was speaking very slowly, her eyes warm and fluttery and melting, a soft flush on her cheeks that did not go away. "I never knew until just now when—you put your arms around me. And I never expected to marry you, Martin, not until just now. How did you make me love you?"

"I don't know," he laughed, "unless just by loving you, for I loved you hard enough to melt the heart of a stone, much less the heart of the living, breathing woman you are."

"This is so different from what I thought love would be," she announced irrelevantly.

"What did you think it would be like?"

"I didn't think it would be like this." She was looking into his eyes at the moment, but her own dropped as she continued, "You see, I didn't know what this was like."

He offered to draw her toward him again, but it was no more than a tentative muscular movement of the girdling arm, for he feared that he might be greedy. Then he felt her body yielding, and once again she was close in his arms and lips were pressed on lips.

"What will my people say?" she queried, with sudden apprehension, in one of the pauses.

"I don't know. We can find out very easily any time we are so minded."

"But if mamma objects? I am sure I am afraid to tell her."

"Let me tell her," he volunteered valiantly. "I think your mother does not like me, but I can win her around. A fellow who can win you can win anything. And if we don't—"

"Yes?"

"Why, we'll have each other. But there's no danger not winning your mother to our marriage. She loves you too well."

"I should not like to break her heart," Ruth said pensively.

He felt like assuring her that mothers' hearts were not so easily broken, but instead he said, "And love is the greatest thing in the world."

"Do you know, Martin, you sometimes frighten me. I am frightened now, when I think of you and of what you have been. You must be very,

very good to me. Remember, after all, that I am only a child. I never loved before."

"Nor I. We are both children together. And we are fortunate above most, for we have found our first love in each other."

"But that is impossible!" she cried, withdrawing herself from his arms with a swift, passionate movement. "Impossible for you. You have been a sailor, and sailors, I have heard, are—are—"

Her voice faltered and died away.

"Are addicted to having a wife in every port?" he suggested. "Is that what you mean?"

"Yes," she answered in a low voice.

"But that is not love." He spoke authoritatively. "I have been in many ports, but I never knew a passing touch of love until I saw you that first night. Do you know, when I said good night and went away, I was almost arrested."

"Arrested?"

"Yes. The policeman thought I was drunk; and I was, too—with love for you."

"But you said we were children, and I said it was impossible, for you, and we have strayed away from the point."

"I said that I never loved anybody but you," he replied. "You are my first, my very first."

"And yet you have been a sailor," she objected.

"But that doesn't prevent me from loving you the first."

"And there have been women—other women—oh!"

And to Martin Eden's supreme surprise, she burst into a storm of tears that took more kisses than one and many caresses to drive away. And all the while there was running through his head Kipling's line: "*And the Colonel's lady and Judy O'Grady are sisters under their skins."* It was true, he decided; though the novels he had read had led him to believe otherwise. His idea, for which the novels were responsible, had been that only formal proposals obtained in the upper classes. It was all right enough, down whence he had come, for youths and maidens to win each other by contact; but for the exalted personages up above on the heights to make love in similar fashion had seemed unthinkable. Yet the novels were wrong. Here was a proof of it. The same pressures and caresses, unaccompanied by speech, that were efficacious with the girls of the working-class, were equally efficacious with the girls above the working-class. They were all of the same flesh, after all, sisters under their skins; and he might have known as much himself had he remembered his Spencer. As he held Ruth in his arms and soothed her, he took great consolation in the thought that the Colonel's lady and Judy O'Grady were pretty much alike under their skins. It brought Ruth closer to him, made her possible. Her dear flesh was as anybody's flesh, as his flesh. There was no bar to their marriage. Class difference was the only difference, and class was extrinsic. It could be shaken off. A slave, he had read, had risen to the Roman purple. That being so, then he could rise to Ruth. Under her purity, and saintliness, and culture, and ethereal beauty of soul, she was, in things fundamentally human, just like Lizzie Connolly and all Lizzie Connollys. All that was possible of them was possible of her. She could love, and hate, maybe have hysterics; and she could certainly be jealous, as she was jealous now, uttering her last sobs in his arms.

"Besides, I am older than you," she remarked suddenly, opening her eyes and looking up at him, "three years older."

"Hush, you are only a child, and I am forty years older than you, in experience," was his answer.

In truth, they were children together, so far as love was concerned, and they were as naive and immature in the expression of their love as a pair of children, and this despite the fact that she was crammed with a university education and that his head was full of scientific philosophy and the hard facts of life.

They sat on through the passing glory of the day, talking as lovers are prone to talk, marvelling at the wonder of love and at destiny that had flung them so strangely together, and dogmatically believing that they loved to a degree never attained by lovers before. And they returned insistently, again and again, to a rehearsal of their first impressions of each other and to hopeless attempts to analyze just precisely what they felt for each other and how much there was of it.

The cloud-masses on the western horizon received the descending sun, and the circle of the sky turned to rose, while the zenith glowed with the same warm color. The rosy light was all about them, flooding over them, as she sang, "Good-by, Sweet Day." She sang softly, leaning in the cradle of his arm, her hands in his, their hearts in each other's hands.

CHAPTER XXII

Mrs. Morse did not require a mother's intuition to read the advertisement in Ruth's face when she returned home. The flush that would not leave the cheeks told the simple story, and more eloquently did the eyes, large and bright, reflecting an unmistakable inward glory.

"What has happened?" Mrs. Morse asked, having bided her time till Ruth had gone to bed.

"You know?" Ruth queried, with trembling lips.

For reply, her mother's arm went around her, and a hand was softly caressing her hair.

"He did not speak," she blurted out. "I did not intend that it should happen, and I would never have let him speak—only he didn't speak."

"But if he did not speak, then nothing could have happened, could it?"

"But it did, just the same."

"In the name of goodness, child, what are you babbling about?" Mrs. Morse was bewildered. "I don't think I know what happened, after all. What did happen?"

Ruth looked at her mother in surprise.

"I thought you knew. Why, we're engaged, Martin and I."

Mrs. Morse laughed with incredulous vexation.

"No, he didn't speak," Ruth explained. "He just loved me, that was all. I was as surprised as you are. He didn't say a word. He just put his arm around me. And—and I was not myself. And he kissed me, and I kissed him. I couldn't help it. I just had to. And then I knew I loved him."

She paused, waiting with expectancy the benediction of her mother's kiss, but Mrs. Morse was coldly silent.

"It is a dreadful accident, I know," Ruth recommenced with a sinking voice. "And I don't know how you will ever forgive me. But I couldn't help it. I did not dream that I loved him until that moment. And you must tell father for me."

"Would it not be better not to tell your father? Let me see Martin Eden, and talk with him, and explain. He will understand and release you."

"No! no!" Ruth cried, starting up. "I do not want to be released. I love him, and love is very sweet. I am going to marry him—of course, if you will let me."

"We have other plans for you, Ruth, dear, your father and I—oh, no, no; no man picked out for you, or anything like that. Our plans go no farther than your marrying some man in your own station in life, a good and honorable gentleman, whom you will select yourself, when you love him."

"But I love Martin already," was the plaintive protest.

"We would not influence your choice in any way; but you are our daughter, and we could not bear to see you make a marriage such as this. He has nothing but roughness and coarseness to offer you in exchange for all that is refined and delicate in you. He is no match for you in any way. He could not support you. We have no foolish ideas about wealth, but comfort is another matter, and our daughter should at least marry a man who can give her that—and not a penniless adventurer, a sailor, a cowboy, a smuggler, and Heaven knows what else, who, in addition to everything, is hare-brained and irresponsible."

Ruth was silent. Every word she recognized as true.

"He wastes his time over his writing, trying to accomplish what geniuses and rare men with college educations sometimes accomplish. A man thinking of marriage should be preparing for marriage. But not he. As I have said, and I know you agree with me, he is irresponsible. And why should he not be? It is the way of sailors. He has never learned to be economical or temperate. The spendthrift years have marked him. It is not his fault, of course, but that does not alter his nature. And have you thought of the years of licentiousness he inevitably has lived? Have you thought of that, daughter? You know what marriage means."

Ruth shuddered and clung close to her mother.

"I have thought." Ruth waited a long time for the thought to frame itself. "And it is terrible. It sickens me to think of it. I told you it was a dreadful accident, my loving him; but I can't help myself. Could you help loving father? Then it is the same with me. There is something in me, in him—I never knew it was there until to-day—but it is there, and it makes me love him. I never thought to love him, but, you see, I do," she concluded, a certain faint triumph in her voice.

They talked long, and to little purpose, in conclusion agreeing to wait an indeterminate time without doing anything.

The same conclusion was reached, a little later that night, between Mrs. Morse and her husband, after she had made due confession of the miscarriage of her plans.

"It could hardly have come otherwise," was Mr. Morse's judgment. "This sailor-fellow has been the only man she was in touch with. Sooner or later she was going to awaken anyway; and she did awaken, and lo! here was this sailor-fellow, the only accessible man at the moment, and of course she promptly loved him, or thought she did, which amounts to the same thing."

Mrs. Morse took it upon herself to work slowly and indirectly upon Ruth, rather than to combat her. There would be plenty of time for this, for Martin was not in position to marry.

"Let her see all she wants of him," was Mr. Morse's advice. "The more she knows him, the less she'll love him, I wager. And give her plenty of contrast. Make a point of having young people at the house. Young women and young men, all sorts of young men, clever men, men who have done something or who are doing things, men of her own class, gentlemen. She can gauge him by them. They will show him up for what he is. And after all, he is a mere boy of twenty-one. Ruth is no more than a child. It is calf love with the pair of them, and they will grow out of it."

So the matter rested. Within the family it was accepted that Ruth and Martin were engaged, but no announcement was made. The family did not think it would ever be necessary. Also, it was tacitly understood that it was to be a long engagement. They did not ask Martin to go to work, nor to cease writing. They did not intend to encourage him to mend himself. And he aided and abetted them in their unfriendly designs, for going to work was farthest from his thoughts.

"I wonder if you'll like what I have done!" he said to Ruth several days later. "I've decided that boarding with my sister is too expensive, and I am going to board myself. I've rented a little room out in North Oakland, retired neighborhood and all the rest, you know, and I've bought an oil-burner on which to cook."

Ruth was overjoyed. The oil-burner especially pleased her.

"That was the way Mr. Butler began his start," she said.

Martin frowned inwardly at the citation of that worthy gentleman, and went on: "I put stamps on all my manuscripts and started them off to the editors again. Then to-day I moved in, and to-morrow I start to work."

"A position!" she cried, betraying the gladness of her surprise in all her body, nestling closer to him, pressing his hand, smiling. "And you never told me! What is it?"

He shook his head.

"I meant that I was going to work at my writing." Her face fell, and he went on hastily. "Don't misjudge me. I am not going in this time with any iridescent ideas. It is to be a cold, prosaic, matter-of-fact business proposition. It is better than going to sea again, and I shall earn more money than any position in Oakland can bring an unskilled man."

"You see, this vacation I have taken has given me perspective. I haven't been working the life out of my body, and I haven't been writing, at least not for publication. All I've done has been to love you and to think. I've read some, too, but it has been part of my thinking, and I have read principally magazines. I have generalized about myself, and the world, my place in it, and my chance to win to a place that will be fit for you. Also, I've been reading Spencer's 'Philosophy of Style,' and found out a lot of what was the matter with me—or my writing, rather; and for that matter with most of the writing that is published every month in the magazines."

"But the upshot of it all—of my thinking and reading and loving—is that I am going to move to Grub Street. I shall leave masterpieces alone and do hack-work—jokes, paragraphs, feature articles, humorous verse, and society verse—all the rot for which there seems so much demand. Then there are the newspaper syndicates, and the newspaper short-story syndicates, and the syndicates for the Sunday supplements. I can go ahead and hammer out the stuff they want, and earn the equivalent of a good salary by it. There are free-lances, you know, who earn as much as four or five hundred a month. I don't care to become as they; but I'll earn a good living, and have plenty of time to myself, which I wouldn't have in any position."

"Then, I'll have my spare time for study and for real work. In between the grind I'll try my hand at masterpieces, and I'll study and prepare myself for the writing of masterpieces. Why, I am amazed at the distance I have come already. When I first tried to write, I had nothing to write about except a few paltry experiences which I neither understood nor appreciated. But I had no thoughts. I really didn't. I didn't even have the words with which to think. My experiences were so many meaningless pictures. But as I began to add to my knowledge, and to my vocabulary, I saw something more in my experiences than mere pictures. I retained the pictures and I found their interpretation. That was when I began to do good work, when I wrote 'Adventure,' 'Joy,' 'The Pot,' 'The Wine of Life,' 'The Jostling Street,' the 'Love-cycle,' and the 'Sea Lyrics.' I shall write more like them, and better; but I shall do it in my spare time. My feet are on the solid earth, now. Hack-work and income first, masterpieces afterward. Just to show you, I wrote half a dozen jokes last night for the comic weeklies; and just as I was going to bed, the thought struck me to try my hand at a triolet—a humorous one; and inside an hour I had written four. They ought to be worth a dollar apiece. Four dollars right there for a few afterthoughts on the way to bed."

"Of course it's all valueless, just so much dull and sordid plodding; but it is no more dull and sordid than keeping books at sixty dollars a month, adding up endless columns of meaningless figures until one dies. And furthermore, the hack-work keeps me in touch with things literary and gives me time to try bigger things."

"But what good are these bigger-things, these masterpieces?" Ruth demanded. "You can't sell them."

"Oh, yes, I can," he began; but she interrupted.

"All those you named, and which you say yourself are good—you have not sold any of them. We can't get married on masterpieces that won't sell."

"Then we'll get married on triolets that will sell," he asserted stoutly, putting his arm around her and drawing a very unresponsive sweetheart toward him.

"Listen to this," he went on in attempted gayety. "It's not art, but it's a dollar.

> *"He came in*
>
> *When I was out,*
>
> *To borrow some tin*
>
> *Was why he came in,*
>
> *And he went without;*
>
> *So I was in*
>
> *And he was out."*

The merry lilt with which he had invested the jingle was at variance with the dejection that came into his face as he finished. He had drawn no smile from Ruth. She was looking at him in an earnest and troubled way.

"It may be a dollar," she said, "but it is a jester's dollar, the fee of a clown. Don't you see, Martin, the whole thing is lowering. I want the man I love and honor to be something finer and higher than a perpetrator of jokes and doggerel."

"You want him to be like—say Mr. Butler?" he suggested.

"I know you don't like Mr. Butler," she began.

"Mr. Butler's all right," he interrupted. "It's only his indigestion I find fault with. But to save me I can't see any difference between writing jokes or comic verse and running a type-writer, taking dictation, or keeping sets of books. It is all a means to an end. Your theory is for me to begin with keeping books in order to become a successful lawyer or man of business. Mine is to begin with hack-work and develop into an able author."

"There is a difference," she insisted.

"What is it?"

"Why, your good work, what you yourself call good, you can't sell. You have tried, you know that,—but the editors won't buy it."

"Give me time, dear," he pleaded. "The hack-work is only makeshift, and I don't take it seriously. Give me two years. I shall succeed in that time, and the editors will be glad to buy my good work. I know what I am saying; I have faith in myself. I know what I have in me; I know what literature is, now; I know the average rot that is poured out by a lot of little men; and I know that at the end of two years I shall be on the highroad to success. As for business, I shall never succeed at it. I am not in sympathy with it. It strikes me as dull, and stupid, and mercenary, and tricky. Anyway I am not adapted for it. I'd never get beyond a clerkship, and how could you and I be happy on the paltry earnings of a clerk? I want the best of everything in the world for you, and the only time when I won't want it will be when there is something better. And I'm going to get it, going to get all of it. The income of a successful author makes Mr. Butler look cheap. A 'best-seller' will earn anywhere between fifty and a hundred thousand dollars—sometimes more and sometimes less; but, as a rule, pretty close to those figures."

She remained silent; her disappointment was apparent.

"Well?" he asked.

"I had hoped and planned otherwise. I had thought, and I still think, that the best thing for you would be to study shorthand—you already know type-writing—and go into father's office. You have a good mind, and I am confident you would succeed as a lawyer."

CHAPTER XXIII

That Ruth had little faith in his power as a writer, did not alter her nor diminish her in Martin's eyes. In the breathing spell of the vacation he had taken, he had spent many hours in self-analysis, and thereby learned much of himself. He had discovered that he loved beauty more than fame, and that what desire he had for fame was largely for Ruth's sake. It was for this reason that his desire for fame was strong. He wanted to be great in the world's eyes; "to make good," as he expressed it, in order that the woman he loved should be proud of him and deem him worthy.

As for himself, he loved beauty passionately, and the joy of serving her was to him sufficient wage. And more than beauty he loved Ruth. He considered love the finest thing in the world. It was love that had worked the *revolution* in him, changing him from an uncouth sailor to a student and an artist; therefore, to him, the finest and greatest of the three, greater than learning and artistry, was love. Already he had discovered that his brain went beyond Ruth's, just as it went beyond the brains of her brothers, or the brain of her father. In spite of every advantage of university training, and in the face of her bachelorship of arts, his power of intellect overshadowed hers, and his year or so of self-study and equipment gave him a mastery of the affairs of the world and art and life that she could never hope to possess.

All this he realized, but it did not affect his love for her, nor her love for him. Love was too fine and noble, and he was too loyal a lover for him to besmirch love with criticism. What did love have to do with Ruth's divergent views on art, right conduct, the French *Revolution*, or equal suffrage? They were mental processes, but love was beyond reason; it was superrational. He could not belittle love. He worshipped it. Love lay on the mountain-tops beyond the valley-land of reason. It was a sublimates condition of existence, the topmost peak of living, and it came rarely. Thanks to the school of scientific philosophers he favored, he knew the biological significance of love; but by a refined process of the same scientific reasoning he reached the conclusion that the human organism achieved its highest purpose in love, that love must not be questioned, but must be accepted as the highest guerdon of life. Thus, he considered the lover blessed over all creatures, and it was a delight to him to think of "God's own mad lover," rising above the things of earth, above wealth and judgment, public opinion and applause, rising above life itself and "dying on a kiss."

Much of this Martin had already reasoned out, and some of it he reasoned out later. In the meantime he worked, taking no recreation except when he went to see Ruth, and living like a Spartan. He paid two dollars and a half a month rent for the small room he got from his Portuguese landlady, Maria Silva, a virago and a widow, hard working and harsher tempered, rearing her large brood of children somehow, and drowning her sorrow and fatigue at irregular intervals in a gallon of the thin, sour wine that she bought from the corner grocery and saloon for fifteen cents. From detesting her and her foul tongue at first, Martin grew to admire her as he observed the brave fight she made. There were but four rooms in the little house—three, when Martin's was subtracted. One of these, the parlor, gay with an ingrain carpet and dolorous with a funeral card and a death-picture of one of her numerous departed babes, was kept strictly for company. The blinds were always down, and her barefooted tribe was never permitted to enter the sacred precinct save on state occasions. She cooked, and all ate, in the kitchen, where she likewise washed, starched, and ironed clothes on all days of the week except Sunday; for her income came largely from taking in washing from her more prosperous neighbors. Remained the bedroom, small as the one occupied by Martin, into which she and her seven little ones crowded and slept. It was an everlasting miracle to Martin how it was accomplished, and from her side of the thin partition he heard nightly every detail of the going to bed, the squalls and squabbles, the soft chattering, and the sleepy, twittering noises as of birds. Another source of income to Maria were her cows, two of them, which she milked night and morning and which gained a surreptitious livelihood from vacant lots and the grass that grew on either side the public side walks, attended always by one or more of her ragged boys, whose watchful guardianship consisted chiefly in keeping their eyes out for the poundmen.

In his own small room Martin lived, slept, studied, wrote, and kept house. Before the one window, looking out on the tiny front porch, was the kitchen table that served as desk, library, and type-writing stand. The bed, against the rear wall, occupied two-thirds of the total space of the room. The table was flanked on one side by a gaudy bureau, manufactured for profit and not for service, the thin veneer of which was shed day by day. This bureau stood in the corner, and in the opposite corner, on the table's other flank, was the kitchen—the oil-stove on a dry-goods box, inside of which were dishes and cooking utensils, a shelf on the wall for provisions, and a bucket of water on the floor. Martin had to carry his water from the kitchen sink, there being no tap in his room. On days when there was much steam to his cooking, the harvest of veneer from the bureau was unusually generous. Over the bed, hoisted by a tackle to the ceiling, was his bicycle. At first he had tried to keep it in the basement; but the tribe of Silva, loosening the bearings and puncturing the tires, had driven him out. Next he attempted the tiny front porch, until a howling southeaster drenched the wheel a night-long. Then he had retreated with it to his room and slung it aloft.

A small closet contained his clothes and the books he had accumulated and for which there was no room on the table or under the table. Hand in hand with reading, he had developed the habit of making notes, and so copiously did he make them that there would have been no existence for him in the confined quarters had he not rigged several clothes-lines across the room on which the notes were hung. Even so, he was crowded until navigating the room was a difficult task. He could not open the door without first closing the closet door, and *vice versa*. It was impossible for him anywhere to traverse the room in a straight line. To go from the door to the head of the bed was a zigzag course that he was never quite able to accomplish in the dark without collisions. Having settled the difficulty of the conflicting doors, he had to steer sharply to the right to avoid the kitchen. Next, he sheered to the left, to escape the foot of the bed; but this sheer, if too generous, brought him against the corner of the table. With a sudden twitch and lurch, he terminated the sheer and bore off to the right along a sort of canal, one bank of which was the bed, the other the table. When the one chair in the room was at its usual place before the table, the canal was unnavigable. When the chair was not in use, it reposed on top of the bed, though sometimes he sat on the chair when cooking, reading a book while the water boiled, and even becoming skilful enough to manage a paragraph or two while steak was frying. Also, so small was the little corner that constituted the kitchen, he was able, sitting down, to reach anything he needed. In fact, it was expedient to cook sitting down; standing up, he was too often in his own way.

In conjunction with a perfect stomach that could digest anything, he possessed knowledge of the various foods that were at the same time nutritious and cheap. Pea-soup was a common article in his diet, as well as potatoes and beans, the latter large and brown and cooked in Mexican style. Rice, cooked as American housewives never cook it and can never learn to cook it, appeared on Martin's table at least once a day. Dried fruits were less expensive than fresh, and he had usually a pot of them, cooked and ready at hand, for they took the place of butter on his bread. Occasionally he graced his table with a piece of round-steak, or with a soup-bone. Coffee, without cream or milk, he had twice a day, in the evening substituting tea; but both coffee and tea were excellently cooked.

There was need for him to be economical. His vacation had consumed nearly all he had earned in the laundry, and he was so far from his market that weeks must elapse before he could hope for the first returns from his hack-work. Except at such times as he saw Ruth, or dropped in to see his sister Gertrude, he lived a recluse, in each day accomplishing at least three days' labor of ordinary men. He slept a scant five hours, and only one with a constitution of iron could have held himself down, as Martin did, day after day, to nineteen consecutive hours of toil. He never lost a moment. On the looking-glass were lists of definitions and pronunciations; when shaving, or dressing, or combing his hair, he conned these lists over. Similar lists were on the wall over the oil-stove, and they were similarly conned while he was engaged in cooking or in washing the dishes. New lists continually displaced the old ones. Every strange or partly familiar word encountered in his reading was immediately jotted down, and later, when a sufficient number had been accumulated, were typed and pinned to the wall or looking-glass. He even carried them in his pockets, and reviewed them at odd moments on the street, or while waiting in butcher shop or grocery to be served.

He went farther in the matter. Reading the works of men who had arrived, he noted every result achieved by them, and worked out the tricks by which they had been achieved—the tricks of narrative, of exposition, of style, the points of view, the contrasts, the epigrams; and of all these he made lists for study. He did not ape. He sought principles. He drew up lists of effective and fetching mannerisms, till out of many such, culled from many writers, he was able to induce the general principle of mannerism, and, thus equipped, to cast about for new and original ones of his own, and to weigh and measure and appraise them properly. In similar manner he collected lists of strong phrases, the phrases of living language, phrases that bit like acid and scorched like flame, or that glowed and were mellow and luscious in the midst of the arid desert of common speech. He sought always for the principle that lay behind and beneath. He wanted to know how the thing was done; after that he could do it for himself. He was not content with the fair face of beauty. He dissected beauty in his crowded little bedroom laboratory, where cooking smells alternated with the outer bedlam of the Silva tribe; and, having dissected and learned the anatomy of beauty, he was nearer being able to create beauty itself.

He was so made that he could work only with understanding. He could not work blindly, in the dark, ignorant of what he was producing and trusting to chance and the star of his genius that the effect produced should be right and fine. He had no patience with chance effects. He wanted to know why and how. His was deliberate creative genius, and, before he began a story or poem, the thing itself was already alive in his brain, with the end in sight and the means of realizing that end in his conscious possession. Otherwise the effort was doomed to failure. On the other hand, he appreciated the chance effects in words and phrases that came lightly and easily into his brain, and that later stood all tests of beauty and power and developed tremendous and incommunicable connotations. Before such he bowed down and marvelled, knowing that they were beyond the deliberate creation of any man. And no matter how much he dissected beauty in search of the principles that underlie beauty and make beauty possible, he was aware, always, of the innermost mystery of beauty to which he did not penetrate and to which no man had ever penetrated. He knew full well, from his Spencer, that man can never attain ultimate knowledge of anything, and that the mystery of beauty was no less than that of life—nay, more that the fibres of beauty and life were intertwisted, and that he himself was but a bit of the same nonunderstandable fabric, twisted of sunshine and star-dust and wonder.

In fact, it was when filled with these thoughts that he wrote his essay entitled "Star-dust," in which he had his fling, not at the principles of criticism, but at the principal critics. It was brilliant, deep, philosophical, and deliciously touched with laughter. Also it was promptly rejected by the magazines as often as it was submitted. But having cleared his mind of it, he went serenely on his way. It was a habit he developed, of incubating and maturing his thought upon a subject, and of then rushing into the type-writer with it. That it did not see print was a matter of small moment with him. The writing of it was the culminating act of a long mental process, the drawing together of scattered threads of thought and the final generalizing upon all the data with which his mind was burdened. To write such an article was the conscious effort by which he freed his mind and made it ready for fresh material and problems. It was in a way akin to that common habit of men and women troubled by real or fancied grievances, who periodically and volubly break their long-suffering silence and "have their say" till the last word is said.

CHAPTER XXIV

The weeks passed. Martin ran out of money, and publishers' checks were far away as ever. All his important manuscripts had come back and been started out again, and his hack-work fared no better. His little kitchen was no longer graced with a variety of foods. Caught in the pinch with a part sack of rice and a few pounds of dried apricots, rice and apricots was his menu three times a day for five days hand-running. Then he startled to realize on his credit. The Portuguese grocer, to whom he had hitherto paid cash, called a halt when Martin's bill reached the magnificent total of three dollars and eighty-five cents.

"For you see," said the grocer, "you no catcha da work, I losa da mon'."

And Martin could reply nothing. There was no way of explaining. It was not true business principle to allow credit to a strong-bodied young fellow of the working-class who was too lazy to work.

"You catcha da job, I let you have mora da grub," the grocer assured Martin. "No job, no grub. Thata da business." And then, to show that it was purely business foresight and not prejudice, "Hava da drink on da house— good friends justa da same."

So Martin drank, in his easy way, to show that he was good friends with the house, and then went supperless to bed.

The fruit store, where Martin had bought his vegetables, was run by an American whose business principles were so weak that he let Martin run a bill of five dollars before stopping his credit. The baker stopped at two dollars, and the butcher at four dollars. Martin added his debts and found that he was possessed of a total credit in all the world of fourteen dollars and eighty-five cents. He was up with his type-writer rent, but he estimated that he could get two months' credit on that, which would be eight dollars. When that occurred, he would have exhausted all possible credit.

The last purchase from the fruit store had been a sack of potatoes, and for a week he had potatoes, and nothing but potatoes, three times a day. An occasional dinner at Ruth's helped to keep strength in his body, though he found it tantalizing enough to refuse further helping when his appetite was raging at sight of so much food spread before it. Now and again, though afflicted with secret shame, he dropped in at his sister's at meal-time and ate as much as he dared—more than he dared at the Morse table.

Day by day he worked on, and day by day the postman delivered to him rejected manuscripts. He had no money for stamps, so the manuscripts accumulated in a heap under the table. Came a day when for forty hours he had not tasted food. He could not hope for a meal at Ruth's, for she was away to San Rafael on a two weeks' visit; and for very shame's sake he could not go to his sister's. To cap misfortune, the postman, in his afternoon round, brought him five returned manuscripts. Then it was that Martin wore his overcoat down into Oakland, and came back without it, but with five dollars tinkling in his pocket. He paid a dollar each on account to the four tradesmen, and in his kitchen fried steak and onions, made coffee, and stewed a large pot of prunes. And having dined, he sat down at his table-desk and completed before midnight an essay which he entitled "The Dignity of Usury." Having typed it out, he flung it under the table, for there had been nothing left from the five dollars with which to buy stamps.

Later on he pawned his watch, and still later his wheel, reducing the amount available for food by putting stamps on all his manuscripts and sending them out. He was disappointed with his hack-work. Nobody cared to buy. He compared it with what he found in the newspapers, weeklies, and cheap magazines, and decided that his was better, far better, than the average; yet it would not sell. Then he discovered that most of the newspapers printed a great deal of what was called "plate" stuff, and he got the address of the association that furnished it. His own work that he sent in was returned, along with a stereotyped slip informing him that the staff supplied all the copy that was needed.

In one of the great juvenile periodicals he noted whole columns of incident and anecdote. Here was a chance. His paragraphs were returned, and though he tried repeatedly he never succeeded in placing one. Later on, when it no longer mattered, he learned that the associate editors and sub-editors augmented their salaries by supplying those paragraphs themselves. The comic weeklies returned his jokes and humorous verse, and the light society verse he wrote for the large magazines found no abiding-place. Then there was the newspaper storiette. He knew that he could write better ones than were published. Managing to obtain the addresses of two newspaper syndicates, he deluged them with storiettes. When he had written twenty and failed to place one of them, he ceased. And yet, from day to day, he read storiettes in the dailies and weeklies, scores and scores of storiettes, not one of which would compare with his. In his despondency, he concluded that he had no judgment whatever, that he was hypnotized by what he wrote, and that he was a self-deluded pretender.

The inhuman editorial machine ran smoothly as ever. He folded the stamps in with his manuscript, dropped it into the letter-box, and from three weeks to a month afterward the postman came up the steps and handed him the manuscript. Surely there were no live, warm editors at the other end. It was all wheels and cogs and oil-cups—a clever mechanism operated by automatons. He reached stages of despair wherein he doubted if editors existed at all. He had never received a sign of the existence of one, and from absence of judgment in rejecting all he wrote it seemed plausible that editors were myths, manufactured and maintained by office boys, typesetters, and pressmen.

The hours he spent with Ruth were the only happy ones he had, and they were not all happy. He was afflicted always with a gnawing restlessness, more tantalizing than in the old days before he possessed her love; for now that he did possess her love, the possession of her was far away as ever. He had asked for two years; time was flying, and he was achieving nothing. Again, he was always conscious of the fact that she did not approve what he was doing. She did not say so directly. Yet indirectly she let him understand it as clearly and definitely as she could have spoken it. It was not resentment with her, but disapproval; though less sweet-natured women might have resented where she was no more than disappointed. Her disappointment lay in that this man she had taken to mould, refused to be moulded. To a certain extent she had found his clay plastic, then it had developed stubbornness, declining to be shaped in the image of her father or of Mr. Butler.

What was great and strong in him, she missed, or, worse yet, misunderstood. This man, whose clay was so plastic that he could live in any number of pigeonholes of human existence, she thought wilful and most obstinate because she could not shape him to live in her pigeonhole, which was the only one she knew. She could not follow the flights of his mind, and when his brain got beyond her, she deemed him erratic. Nobody else's brain ever got beyond her. She could always follow her father and mother, her brothers and Olney; wherefore, when she could not follow Martin, she believed the fault lay with him. It was the old tragedy of insularity trying to serve as mentor to the universal.

"You worship at the shrine of the established," he told her once, in a discussion they had over Praps and Vanderwater. "I grant that as authorities to quote they are most excellent—the two foremost literary critics in the United States. Every school teacher in the land looks up to Vanderwater as the Dean of American criticism. Yet I read his stuff, and it seems to me the perfection of the felicitous expression of the inane. Why, he is no more than a ponderous bromide, thanks to Gelett Burgess. And Praps is no better. His 'Hemlock Mosses,' for instance is beautifully written. Not a comma is out of place; and the tone—ah!—is lofty, so lofty. He is the best-paid critic in the United States. Though, Heaven forbid! he's not a critic at all. They do criticism better in England.

"But the point is, they sound the popular note, and they sound it so beautifully and morally and contentedly. Their reviews remind me of a British Sunday. They are the popular mouthpieces. They back up your professors of English, and your professors of English back them up. And there isn't an original idea in any of their skulls. They know only the established,—in fact, they are the established. They are weak minded, and the established impresses itself upon them as easily as the name of the brewery is impressed on a beer bottle. And their function is to catch all the young fellows attending the university, to drive out of their minds any glimmering originality that may chance to be there, and to put upon them the stamp of the established."

"I think I am nearer the truth," she replied, "when I stand by the established, than you are, raging around like an iconoclastic South Sea Islander."

"It was the missionary who did the image breaking," he laughed. "And unfortunately, all the missionaries are off among the heathen, so there are none left at home to break those old images, Mr. Vanderwater and Mr. Praps."

"And the college professors, as well," she added.

He shook his head emphatically. "No; the science professors should live. They're really great. But it would be a good deed to break the heads of nine-tenths of the English professors—little, microscopic-minded parrots!"

Which was rather severe on the professors, but which to Ruth was blasphemy. She could not help but measure the professors, neat, scholarly, in fitting clothes, speaking in well-modulated voices, breathing of culture and refinement, with this almost indescribable young fellow whom somehow she loved, whose clothes never would fit him, whose heavy muscles told of damning toil, who grew excited when he talked, substituting abuse for calm statement and passionate utterance for cool self-possession. They at least earned good salaries and were—yes, she compelled herself to face it—were gentlemen; while he could not earn a penny, and he was not as they.

She did not weigh Martin's words nor judge his argument by them. Her conclusion that his argument was wrong was reached—unconsciously, it is true—by a comparison of externals. They, the professors, were right in their literary judgments because they were successes. Martin's literary judgments were wrong because he could not sell his wares. To use his own phrase, they made good, and he did not make good. And besides, it did not seem reasonable that he should be right—he who had stood, so short a time before, in that same living room, blushing and awkward, acknowledging his introduction, looking fearfully about him at the bric-a-brac his swinging shoulders threatened to break, asking how long since Swinburne died, and boastfully announcing that he had read "Excelsior" and the "Psalm of Life."

Unwittingly, Ruth herself proved his point that she worshipped the established. Martin followed the processes of her thoughts, but forbore to go farther. He did not love her for what she thought of Praps and Vanderwater and English professors, and he was coming to realize, with increasing conviction, that he possessed brain-areas and stretches of knowledge which she could never comprehend nor know existed.

In music she thought him unreasonable, and in the matter of opera not only unreasonable but wilfully perverse.

"How did you like it?" she asked him one night, on the way home from the opera.

It was a night when he had taken her at the expense of a month's rigid economizing on food. After vainly waiting for him to speak about it, herself still tremulous and stirred by what she had just seen and heard, she had asked the question.

"I liked the overture," was his answer. "It was splendid."

"Yes, but the opera itself?"

"That was splendid too; that is, the orchestra was, though I'd have enjoyed it more if those jumping-jacks had kept quiet or gone off the stage."

Ruth was aghast.

"You don't mean Tetralani or Barillo?" she queried.

"All of them—the whole kit and crew."

"But they are great artists," she protested.

"They spoiled the music just the same, with their antics and unrealities."

"But don't you like Barillo's voice?" Ruth asked. "He is next to Caruso, they say."

"Of course I liked him, and I liked Tetralani even better. Her voice is exquisite—or at least I think so."

"But, but—" Ruth stammered. "I don't know what you mean, then. You admire their voices, yet say they spoiled the music."

"Precisely that. I'd give anything to hear them in concert, and I'd give even a bit more not to hear them when the orchestra is playing. I'm afraid I am a hopeless realist. Great singers are not great actors. To hear Barillo sing a love passage with the voice of an angel, and to hear Tetralani reply like another angel, and to hear it all accompanied by a perfect orgy of glowing and colorful music—is ravishing, most ravishing. I do not admit it. I assert it. But the whole effect is spoiled when I look at them—at Tetralani, five feet ten in her stocking feet and weighing a hundred and ninety pounds, and at Barillo, a scant five feet four, greasy-featured, with the chest of a squat, undersized blacksmith, and at the pair of them, attitudinizing, clasping their breasts, flinging their arms in the air like demented creatures in an asylum; and when I am expected to accept all this as the faithful illusion of a love-scene between a slender and beautiful princess and a handsome, romantic, young prince—why, I can't accept it, that's all. It's rot; it's absurd; it's unreal. That's what's the matter with it. It's not real. Don't tell me that anybody in this world ever made love that way. Why, if I'd made love to you in such fashion, you'd have boxed my ears."

"But you misunderstand," Ruth protested. "Every form of art has its limitations." (She was busy recalling a lecture she had heard at the university on the conventions of the arts.) "In painting there are only two dimensions to the canvas, yet you accept the illusion of three dimensions which the art of a painter enables him to throw into the canvas. In writing, again, the author must be omnipotent. You accept as perfectly legitimate the author's account of the secret thoughts of the heroine, and yet all the time you know that the heroine was alone when thinking these thoughts, and that neither the author nor any one else was capable of hearing them. And so with the stage, with sculpture, with opera, with every art form. Certain irreconcilable things must be accepted."

"Yes, I understood that," Martin answered. "All the arts have their conventions." (Ruth was surprised at his use of the word. It was as if he had studied at the university himself, instead of being ill-equipped from browsing at haphazard through the books in the library.) "But even the conventions must be real. Trees, painted on flat cardboard and stuck up on each side of the stage, we accept as a forest. It is a real enough convention. But, on the other hand, we would not accept a sea scene as a forest. We can't do it. It violates our senses. Nor would you, or, rather, should you, accept the ravings and writhings and agonized contortions of those two lunatics to-night as a convincing portrayal of love."

"But you don't hold yourself superior to all the judges of music?" she protested.

"No, no, not for a moment. I merely maintain my right as an individual. I have just been telling you what I think, in order to explain why the elephantine gambols of Madame Tetralani spoil the orchestra for me. The world's judges of music may all be right. But I am I, and I won't subordinate my taste to the unanimous judgment of mankind. If I don't like a thing, I don't like it, that's all; and there is no reason under the sun why I should ape a liking for it just because the majority of my fellow-creatures like it, or make believe they like it. I can't follow the fashions in the things I like or dislike."

"But music, you know, is a matter of training," Ruth argued; "and opera is even more a matter of training. May it not be—"

"That I am not trained in opera?" he dashed in.

She nodded.

"The very thing," he agreed. "And I consider I am fortunate in not having been caught when I was young. If I had, I could have wept sentimental tears to-night, and the clownish antics of that precious pair would have but enhanced the beauty of their voices and the beauty of the accompanying orchestra. You are right. It's mostly a matter of training. And I am too old, now. I must have the real or nothing. An illusion that won't convince is a palpable lie, and that's what grand opera is to me when little Barillo throws a fit, clutches mighty Tetralani in his arms (also in a fit), and tells her how passionately he adores her."

Again Ruth measured his thoughts by comparison of externals and in accordance with her belief in the established. Who was he that he should be right and all the cultured world wrong? His words and thoughts made no impression upon her. She was too firmly intrenched in the established to have any sympathy with revolutionary ideas. She had always been used to music, and she had enjoyed opera ever since she was a child, and all her world had enjoyed it, too. Then by what right did Martin Eden emerge, as he had so recently emerged, from his rag-time and working-class songs, and pass judgment on the world's music? She was vexed with him, and as she walked beside him she had a vague feeling of outrage. At the best, in her most charitable frame of mind, she considered the statement of his views to be a caprice, an erratic and uncalled-for prank. But when he took her in his arms at the door and kissed her good night in tender lover-fashion, she forgot everything in the outrush of her own love to him. And later, on a sleepless pillow, she puzzled, as she had often puzzled of late, as to how it was that she loved so strange a man, and loved him despite the disapproval of her people.

And next day Martin Eden cast hack-work aside, and at white heat hammered out an essay to which he gave the title, "The Philosophy of Illusion." A stamp started it on its travels, but it was destined to receive many stamps and to be started on many travels in the months that followed.

CHAPTER XXV

Maria Silva was poor, and all the ways of poverty were clear to her. Poverty, to Ruth, was a word signifying a not-nice condition of existence. That was her total knowledge on the subject. She knew Martin was poor, and his condition she associated in her mind with the boyhood of Abraham Lincoln, of Mr. Butler, and of other men who had become successes. Also, while aware that poverty was anything but delectable, she had a comfortable middle-class feeling that poverty was salutary, that it was a sharp spur that urged on to success all men who were not degraded and hopeless drudges. So that her knowledge that Martin was so poor that he had pawned his watch and overcoat did not disturb her. She even considered it the hopeful side of the situation, believing that sooner or later it would arouse him and compel him to abandon his writing.

Ruth never read hunger in Martin's face, which had grown lean and had enlarged the slight hollows in the cheeks. In fact, she marked the change in his face with satisfaction. It seemed to refine him, to remove from him much of the dross of flesh and the too animal-like vigor that lured her while she detested it. Sometimes, when with her, she noted an unusual brightness in his eyes, and she admired it, for it made him appear more the poet and the scholar—the things he would have liked to be and which she would have liked him to be. But Maria Silva read a different tale in the hollow cheeks and the burning eyes, and she noted the changes in them from day to day, by them following the ebb and flow of his fortunes. She saw him leave the house with his overcoat and return without it, though the day was chill and raw, and promptly she saw his cheeks fill out slightly and the fire of hunger leave his eyes. In the same way she had seen his wheel and watch go, and after each event she had seen his vigor bloom again.

Likewise she watched his toils, and knew the measure of the midnight oil he burned. Work! She knew that he outdid her, though his work was of a different order. And she was surprised to behold that the less food he had, the harder he worked. On occasion, in a casual sort of way, when she thought hunger pinched hardest, she would send him in a loaf of new baking, awkwardly covering the act with banter to the effect that it was better than he could bake. And again, she would send one of her toddlers in to him with a great pitcher of hot soup, debating inwardly the while whether she was justified in taking it from the mouths of her own flesh and blood. Nor was Martin ungrateful, knowing as he did the lives of the poor, and that if ever in the world there was charity, this was it.

On a day when she had filled her brood with what was left in the house, Maria invested her last fifteen cents in a gallon of cheap wine. Martin, coming into her kitchen to fetch water, was invited to sit down and drink. He drank her very-good health, and in return she drank his. Then she drank to prosperity in his undertakings, and he drank to the hope that James Grant would show up and pay her for his washing. James Grant was a journeymen carpenter who did not always pay his bills and who owed Maria three dollars.

Both Maria and Martin drank the sour new wine on empty stomachs, and it went swiftly to their heads. Utterly differentiated creatures that they were, they were lonely in their misery, and though the misery was tacitly ignored, it was the bond that drew them together. Maria was amazed to learn that he had been in the Azores, where she had lived until she was eleven. She was doubly amazed that he had been in the Hawaiian Islands, whither she had migrated from the Azores with her people. But her amazement passed all bounds when he told her he had been on Maui, the particular island whereon she had attained womanhood and married. Kahului, where she had first met her husband,—he, Martin, had been there twice! Yes, she remembered the sugar steamers, and he had been on them—well, well, it was a small world. And Wailuku! That place, too! Did he know the head-luna of the plantation? Yes, and had had a couple of drinks with him.

And so they reminiscenced and drowned their hunger in the raw, sour wine. To Martin the future did not seem so dim. Success trembled just before him. He was on the verge of clasping it. Then he studied the deep-lined face of the toil-worn woman before him, remembered her soups and loaves of new baking, and felt spring up in him the warmest gratitude and philanthropy.

"Maria," he exclaimed suddenly. "What would you like to have?"

She looked at him, bepuzzled.

"What would you like to have now, right now, if you could get it?"

"Shoe alla da roun' for da childs—seven pairs da shoe."

"You shall have them," he announced, while she nodded her head gravely. "But I mean a big wish, something big that you want."

Her eyes sparkled good-naturedly. He was choosing to make fun with her, Maria, with whom few made fun these days.

"Think hard," he cautioned, just as she was opening her mouth to speak.

"Alla right," she answered. "I thinka da hard. I lika da house, dis house—all mine, no paya da rent, seven dollar da month."

"You shall have it," he granted, "and in a short time. Now wish the great wish. Make believe I am God, and I say to you anything you want you can have. Then you wish that thing, and I listen."

Maria considered solemnly for a space.

"You no 'fraid?" she asked warningly.

"No, no," he laughed, "I'm not afraid. Go ahead."

"Most verra big," she warned again.

"All right. Fire away."

"Well, den—" She drew a big breath like a child, as she voiced to the uttermost all she cared to demand of life. "I lika da have one milka ranch—good milka ranch. Plenty cow, plenty land, plenty grass. I lika da have near San Le-an; my sister liva dere. I sella da milk in Oakland. I maka da plentee mon. Joe an' Nick no runna da cow. Dey go-a to school. Bimeby maka da good engineer, worka da railroad. Yes, I lika da milka ranch."

She paused and regarded Martin with twinkling eyes.

"You shall have it," he answered promptly.

She nodded her head and touched her lips courteously to the wine-glass and to the giver of the gift she knew would never be given. His heart was right, and in her own heart she appreciated his intention as much as if the gift had gone with it.

"No, Maria," he went on; "Nick and Joe won't have to peddle milk, and all the kids can go to school and wear shoes the whole year round. It will be a first-class milk ranch—everything complete. There will be a house to live in and a stable for the horses, and cow-barns, of course. There will be chickens, pigs, vegetables, fruit trees, and everything like that; and there will be enough cows to pay for a hired man or two. Then you won't have anything to do but take care of the children. For that matter, if you find a good man, you can marry and take it easy while he runs the ranch."

And from such largess, dispensed from his future, Martin turned and took his one good suit of clothes to the pawnshop. His plight was desperate for him to do this, for it cut him off from Ruth. He had no second-best suit that was presentable, and though he could go to the butcher and the baker, and even on occasion to his sister's, it was beyond all daring to dream of entering the Morse home so disreputably apparelled.

He toiled on, miserable and well-nigh hopeless. It began to appear to him that the second battle was lost and that he would have to go to work. In doing this he would satisfy everybody—the grocer, his sister, Ruth, and even Maria, to whom he owed a month's room rent. He was two months behind with his type-writer, and the agency was clamoring for payment or for the return of the machine. In desperation, all but ready to surrender, to make a truce with fate until he could get a fresh start, he took the civil service examinations for the Railway Mail. To his surprise, he passed first. The job was assured, though when the call would come to enter upon his duties nobody knew.

It was at this time, at the lowest ebb, that the smooth-running editorial machine broke down. A cog must have slipped or an oil-cup run dry, for the postman brought him one morning a short, thin envelope. Martin glanced at the upper left-hand corner and read the name and address of the *Transcontinental Monthly*. His heart gave a great leap, and he suddenly felt faint, the sinking feeling accompanied by a strange trembling of the knees. He staggered into his room and sat down on the bed, the envelope still unopened, and in that moment came understanding to him how people suddenly fall dead upon receipt of extraordinarily good news.

Of course this was good news. There was no manuscript in that thin envelope, therefore it was an acceptance. He knew the story in the hands of the *Transcontinental*. It was "The Ring of Bells," one of his horror stories, and it was an even five thousand words. And, since first-class magazines always paid on acceptance, there was a check inside. Two cents a word—twenty dollars a thousand; the check must be a hundred dollars. One hundred dollars! As he tore the envelope open, every item of all his debts surged in his brain—$3.85 to the grocer; butcher $4.00 flat; baker, $2.00; fruit store, $5.00; total, $14.85. Then there was room rent, $2.50; another month in advance, $2.50; two months' type-writer, $8.00; a month in advance, $4.00; total, $31.85. And finally to be added, his pledges, plus interest, with the pawnbroker—watch, $5.50; overcoat, $5.50; wheel, $7.75; suit of clothes, $5.50 (60 % interest, but what did it matter?)—grand total, $56.10. He saw, as if visible in the air before him, in illuminated figures, the whole sum, and the subtraction that followed and that gave a remainder of $43.90. When he had squared every debt, redeemed every pledge, he would still have jingling in his pockets a princely $43.90. And on top of that he would have a month's rent paid in advance on the type-writer and on the room.

By this time he had drawn the single sheet of type-written letter out and spread it open. There was no check. He peered into the envelope, held it to the light, but could not trust his eyes, and in trembling haste tore the envelope apart. There was no check. He read the letter, skimming it line by line, dashing through the editor's praise of his story to the meat of the letter, the statement why the check had not been sent. He found no such statement, but he did find that which made him suddenly wilt. The letter slid from his hand. His eyes went lack-lustre, and he lay back on the pillow, pulling the blanket about him and up to his chin.

Five dollars for "The Ring of Bells"—five dollars for five thousand words! Instead of two cents a word, ten words for a cent! And the editor had praised it, too. And he would receive the check when the story was published. Then it was all poppycock, two cents a word for minimum rate and payment upon acceptance. It was a lie, and it had led him astray. He would never have attempted to write had he known that. He would have gone to work—to work for Ruth. He went back to the day he first attempted to write, and was appalled at the enormous waste of time—and all for ten words for a cent. And the other high rewards of writers, that he had read about, must be lies, too. His second-hand ideas of authorship were wrong, for here was the proof of it.

The *Transcontinental* sold for twenty-five cents, and its dignified and artistic cover proclaimed it as among the first-class magazines. It was a staid, respectable magazine, and it had been published continuously since long before he was born. Why, on the outside cover were printed every month the words of one of the world's great writers, words proclaiming the inspired mission of the *Transcontinental* by a star of literature whose first coruscations had appeared inside those self-same covers. And the high and lofty, heaven-inspired *Transcontinental* paid five dollars for five thousand words! The great writer had recently died in a foreign land—in dire poverty, Martin remembered, which was not to be wondered at, considering the magnificent pay authors receive.

Well, he had taken the bait, the newspaper lies about writers and their pay, and he had wasted two years over it. But he would disgorge the bait now. Not another line would he ever write. He would do what Ruth wanted him to do, what everybody wanted him to do—get a job. The thought of going to work reminded him of Joe—Joe, tramping through the land of nothing-to-do. Martin heaved a great sigh of envy. The reaction of nineteen hours a day for many days was strong upon him. But then, Joe was not in love, had none of the responsibilities of love, and he could afford to loaf through the land of nothing-to-do. He, Martin, had something to work for, and go to work he would. He would start out early next morning to hunt a job. And he would let Ruth know, too, that he had mended his ways and was willing to go into her father's office.

Five dollars for five thousand words, ten words for a cent, the market price for art. The disappointment of it, the lie of it, the infamy of it, were uppermost in his thoughts; and under his closed eyelids, in fiery figures, burned the "$3.85" he owed the grocer. He shivered, and was aware of an aching in his bones. The small of his back ached especially. His head ached, the top of it ached, the back of it ached, the brains inside of it ached and seemed to be swelling, while the ache over his brows was intolerable. And beneath the brows, planted under his lids, was the merciless "$3.85." He opened his eyes to escape it, but the white light of the room seemed to sear the balls and forced him to close his eyes, when the "$3.85" confronted him again.

Five dollars for five thousand words, ten words for a cent—that particular thought took up its residence in his brain, and he could no more escape it than he could the "$3.85" under his eyelids. A change seemed to come over the latter, and he watched curiously, till "$2.00" burned in its stead. Ah, he thought, that was the baker. The next sum that appeared was "$2.50." It puzzled him, and he pondered it as if life and death hung on the solution. He owed somebody two dollars and a half, that was certain, but who was it? To find it was the task set him by an imperious and malignant universe, and he wandered through the endless corridors of his mind, opening all manner of lumber rooms and chambers stored with odds and ends of memories and knowledge as he vainly sought the answer. After several centuries it came to him, easily, without effort, that it was Maria. With a great relief he turned his soul to the screen of torment under his lids. He had solved the problem; now he could rest. But no, the "$2.50" faded away, and in its place burned "$8.00." Who was that? He must go the dreary round of his mind again and find out.

How long he was gone on this quest he did not know, but after what seemed an enormous lapse of time, he was called back to himself by a knock at the door, and by Maria's asking if he was sick. He replied in a muffled voice he did not recognize, saying that he was merely taking a nap. He was surprised when he noted the darkness of night in the room. He had received the letter at two in the afternoon, and he realized that he was sick.

Then the "$8.00" began to smoulder under his lids again, and he returned himself to servitude. But he grew cunning. There was no need for him to wander through his mind. He had been a fool. He pulled a lever and made his mind revolve about him, a monstrous wheel of fortune, a merry-go-round of memory, a revolving sphere of wisdom. Faster and faster it revolved, until its vortex sucked him in and he was flung whirling through black chaos.

Quite naturally he found himself at a mangle, feeding starched cuffs. But as he fed he noticed figures printed in the cuffs. It was a new way of marking linen, he thought, until, looking closer, he saw "$3.85" on one of the cuffs. Then it came to him that it was the grocer's bill, and that these were his bills flying around on the drum of the mangle. A crafty idea came to him. He would throw the bills on the floor and so escape paying them. No sooner thought than done, and he crumpled the cuffs spitefully as he flung them upon an unusually dirty floor. Ever the heap grew, and though each bill was duplicated a thousand times, he found only one for two dollars and a half, which was what he owed Maria. That meant that Maria would not press for payment, and he resolved generously that it would be the only one he would pay; so he began searching through the cast-out heap for hers. He sought it desperately, for ages, and was still searching when the manager of the hotel entered, the fat Dutchman. His face blazed with wrath, and he shouted in stentorian tones that echoed down the universe, "I shall deduct the cost of those cuffs from your wages!" The pile of cuffs grew into a mountain, and Martin knew that he was doomed to toil for a thousand years to pay for them. Well, there was nothing left to do but kill the manager and burn down the laundry. But the big Dutchman frustrated him, seizing him by the nape of the neck and dancing him up and down. He danced him over the ironing tables, the stove, and the mangles, and out into the wash-room and over the wringer and washer. Martin was danced until his teeth rattled and his head ached, and he marvelled that the Dutchman was so strong.

And then he found himself before the mangle, this time receiving the cuffs an editor of a magazine was feeding from the other side. Each cuff was a check, and Martin went over them anxiously, in a fever of expectation, but they were all blanks. He stood there and received the blanks for a million years or so, never letting one go by for fear it might be filled out. At last he found it. With trembling fingers he held it to the light. It was for five dollars. "Ha! Ha!" laughed the editor across the mangle. "Well, then, I shall kill you," Martin said. He went out into the wash-room to get the axe, and found Joe starching manuscripts. He tried to make him desist, then swung the axe for him. But the weapon remained poised in mid-air, for Martin found himself back in the ironing room in the midst of a snow-storm. No, it was not snow that was falling, but checks of large denomination, the smallest not less than a thousand dollars. He began to collect them and sort them out, in packages of a hundred, tying each package securely with twine.

He looked up from his task and saw Joe standing before him juggling flat-irons, starched shirts, and manuscripts. Now and again he reached out and added a bundle of checks to the flying miscellany that soared through the roof and out of sight in a tremendous circle. Martin struck at him, but he seized the axe and added it to the flying circle. Then he plucked Martin and added him. Martin went up through the roof, clutching at manuscripts, so that by the time he came down he had a large armful. But no sooner down than up again, and a second and a third time and countless times he flew around the circle. From far off he could hear a childish treble singing: "Waltz me around again, Willie, around, around, around."

He recovered the axe in the midst of the Milky Way of checks, starched shirts, and manuscripts, and prepared, when he came down, to kill Joe. But he did not come down. Instead, at two in the morning, Maria, having heard his groans through the thin partition, came into his room, to put hot flat-irons against his body and damp cloths upon his aching eyes.

CHAPTER XXVI

Martin Eden did not go out to hunt for a job in the morning. It was late afternoon before he came out of his delirium and gazed with aching eyes about the room. Mary, one of the tribe of Silva, eight years old, keeping watch, raised a screech at sight of his returning consciousness. Maria hurried into the room from the kitchen. She put her work-calloused hand upon his hot forehead and felt his pulse.

"You lika da eat?" she asked.

He shook his head. Eating was farthest from his desire, and he wondered that he should ever have been hungry in his life.

"I'm sick, Maria," he said weakly. "What is it? Do you know?"

"Grip," she answered. "Two or three days you alla da right. Better you no eat now. Bimeby plenty can eat, to-morrow can eat maybe."

Martin was not used to sickness, and when Maria and her little girl left him, he essayed to get up and dress. By a supreme exertion of will, with rearing brain and eyes that ached so that he could not keep them open, he managed to get out of bed, only to be left stranded by his senses upon the table. Half an hour later he managed to regain the bed, where he was content to lie with closed eyes and analyze his various pains and weaknesses. Maria came in several times to change the cold cloths on his forehead. Otherwise she left him in peace, too wise to vex him with chatter. This moved him to gratitude, and he murmured to himself, "Maria, you getta da milka ranch, all righta, all right."

Then he remembered his long-buried past of yesterday.

It seemed a life-time since he had received that letter from the *Transcontinental*, a life-time since it was all over and done with and a new page turned. He had shot his bolt, and shot it hard, and now he was down on his back. If he hadn't starved himself, he wouldn't have been caught by La

Grippe. He had been run down, and he had not had the strength to throw off the germ of disease which had invaded his system. This was what resulted.

"What does it profit a man to write a whole library and lose his own life?" he demanded aloud. "This is no place for me. No more literature in mine. Me for the counting-house and ledger, the monthly salary, and the little home with Ruth."

Two days later, having eaten an egg and two slices of toast and drunk a cup of tea, he asked for his mail, but found his eyes still hurt too much to permit him to read.

"You read for me, Maria," he said. "Never mind the big, long letters. Throw them under the table. Read me the small letters."

"No can," was the answer. "Teresa, she go to school, she can."

So Teresa Silva, aged nine, opened his letters and read them to him. He listened absently to a long dun from the type-writer people, his mind busy with ways and means of finding a job. Suddenly he was shocked back to himself.

"'We offer you forty dollars for all serial rights in your story,'" Teresa slowly spelled out, "'provided you allow us to make the alterations suggested.'"

"What magazine is that?" Martin shouted. "Here, give it to me!"

He could see to read, now, and he was unaware of the pain of the action. It was the *White Mouse* that was offering him forty dollars, and the story was "The Whirlpool," another of his early horror stories. He read the letter through again and again. The editor told him plainly that he had not handled the idea properly, but that it was the idea they were buying because it was original. If they could cut the story down one-third, they would take it and send him forty dollars on receipt of his answer.

He called for pen and ink, and told the editor he could cut the story down three-thirds if he wanted to, and to send the forty dollars right along.

The letter despatched to the letter-box by Teresa, Martin lay back and thought. It wasn't a lie, after all. The *White Mouse* paid on acceptance. There were three thousand words in "The Whirlpool." Cut down a third, there would be two thousand. At forty dollars that would be two cents a word. Pay on acceptance and two cents a word—the newspapers had told the truth. And he had thought the *White Mouse* a third-rater! It was evident that he did not know the magazines. He had deemed the *Transcontinental* a first-rater, and it paid a cent for ten words. He had classed the *White Mouse* as of no account, and it paid twenty times as much as the *Transcontinental* and also had paid on acceptance.

Well, there was one thing certain: when he got well, he would not go out looking for a job. There were more stories in his head as good as "The Whirlpool," and at forty dollars apiece he could earn far more than in any job or position. Just when he thought the battle lost, it was won. He had proved for his career. The way was clear. Beginning with the *White Mouse* he would add magazine after magazine to his growing list of patrons. Hackwork could be put aside. For that matter, it had been wasted time, for it had not brought him a dollar. He would devote himself to work, good work, and he would pour out the best that was in him. He wished Ruth was there to share in his joy, and when he went over the letters left lying on his bed, he found one from her. It was sweetly reproachful, wondering what had kept him away for so dreadful a length of time. He reread the letter adoringly, dwelling over her handwriting, loving each stroke of her pen, and in the end kissing her signature.

And when he answered, he told her recklessly that he had not been to see her because his best clothes were in pawn. He told her that he had been sick, but was once more nearly well, and that inside ten days or two weeks (as soon as a letter could travel to New York City and return) he would redeem his clothes and be with her.

But Ruth did not care to wait ten days or two weeks. Besides, her lover was sick. The next afternoon, accompanied by Arthur, she arrived in the Morse carriage, to the unqualified delight of the Silva tribe and of all the urchins on the street, and to the consternation of Maria. She boxed the ears of the Silvas who crowded about the visitors on the tiny front porch, and in more than usual atrocious English tried to apologize for her appearance.

Sleeves rolled up from soap-flecked arms and a wet gunny-sack around her waist told of the task at which she had been caught. So flustered was she by two such grand young people asking for her lodger, that she forgot to invite them to sit down in the little parlor. To enter Martin's room, they passed through the kitchen, warm and moist and steamy from the big washing in progress. Maria, in her excitement, jammed the bedroom and bedroom-closet doors together, and for five minutes, through the partly open door, clouds of steam, smelling of soap-suds and dirt, poured into the sick chamber.

Ruth succeeded in veering right and left and right again, and in running the narrow passage between table and bed to Martin's side; but Arthur veered too wide and fetched up with clatter and bang of pots and pans in the corner where Martin did his cooking. Arthur did not linger long. Ruth occupied the only chair, and having done his duty, he went outside and stood by the gate, the centre of seven marvelling Silvas, who watched him as they would have watched a curiosity in a side-show. All about the carriage were gathered the children from a dozen blocks, waiting and eager for some tragic and terrible dénouement. Carriages were seen on their street only for weddings and funerals. Here was neither marriage nor death: therefore, it was something transcending experience and well worth waiting for.

Martin had been wild to see Ruth. His was essentially a love-nature, and he possessed more than the average man's need for sympathy. He was starving for sympathy, which, with him, meant intelligent understanding; and he had yet to learn that Ruth's sympathy was largely sentimental and tactful, and that it proceeded from gentleness of nature rather than from understanding of the objects of her sympathy. So it was while Martin held her hand and gladly talked, that her love for him prompted her to press his hand in return, and that her eyes were moist and luminous at sight of his helplessness and of the marks suffering had stamped upon his face.

But while he told her of his two acceptances, of his despair when he received the one from the *Transcontinental*, and of the corresponding delight with which he received the one from the *White Mouse*, she did not follow him. She heard the words he uttered and understood their literal import, but she was not with him in his despair and his delight. She could not get out of herself. She was not interested in selling stories to magazines. What was important to her was matrimony. She was not aware of it, however, any more than she was aware that her desire that Martin take a position was the instinctive and preparative impulse of motherhood. She would have blushed had she been told as much in plain, set terms, and next, she might have grown indignant and asserted that her sole interest lay in the man she loved and her desire for him to make the best of himself. So, while Martin poured out his heart to her, elated with the first success his chosen work in the world had received, she paid heed to his bare words only, gazing now and again about the room, shocked by what she saw.

For the first time Ruth gazed upon the sordid face of poverty. Starving lovers had always seemed romantic to her,—but she had had no idea how starving lovers lived. She had never dreamed it could be like this. Ever her gaze shifted from the room to him and back again. The steamy smell of dirty clothes, which had entered with her from the kitchen, was sickening. Martin must be soaked with it, Ruth concluded, if that awful woman washed frequently. Such was the contagiousness of degradation. When she looked at Martin, she seemed to see the smirch left upon him by his surroundings. She had never seen him unshaven, and the three days' growth of beard on his face was repulsive to her. Not alone did it give him the same dark and murky aspect of the Silva house, inside and out, but it seemed to emphasize that animal-like strength of his which she detested. And here he was, being confirmed in his madness by the two acceptances he took such pride in telling her about. A little longer and he would have surrendered and gone to work. Now he would continue on in this horrible house, writing and starving for a few more months.

"What is that smell?" she asked suddenly.

"Some of Maria's washing smells, I imagine," was the answer. "I am growing quite accustomed to them."

"No, no; not that. It is something else. A stale, sickish smell."

Martin sampled the air before replying.

"I can't smell anything else, except stale tobacco smoke," he announced.

"That's it. It is terrible. Why do you smoke so much, Martin?"

"I don't know, except that I smoke more than usual when I am lonely. And then, too, it's such a long-standing habit. I learned when I was only a youngster."

"It is not a nice habit, you know," she reproved. "It smells to heaven."

"That's the fault of the tobacco. I can afford only the cheapest. But wait until I get that forty-dollar check. I'll use a brand that is not offensive even to the angels. But that wasn't so bad, was it, two acceptances in three days? That forty-five dollars will pay about all my debts."

"For two years' work?" she queried.

"No, for less than a week's work. Please pass me that book over on the far corner of the table, the account book with the gray cover." He opened it and began turning over the pages rapidly. "Yes, I was right. Four days for 'The Ring of Bells,' two days for 'The Whirlpool.' That's forty-five dollars for a week's work, one hundred and eighty dollars a month. That beats any salary I can command. And, besides, I'm just beginning. A thousand dollars a month is not too much to buy for you all I want you to have. A salary of five hundred a month would be too small. That forty-five dollars is just a starter. Wait till I get my stride. Then watch my smoke."

Ruth misunderstood his slang, and reverted to cigarettes.

"You smoke more than enough as it is, and the brand of tobacco will make no difference. It is the smoking itself that is not nice, no matter what the brand may be. You are a chimney, a living volcano, a perambulating smoke-stack, and you are a perfect disgrace, Martin dear, you know you are."

She leaned toward him, entreaty in her eyes, and as he looked at her delicate face and into her pure, limpid eyes, as of old he was struck with his own unworthiness.

"I wish you wouldn't smoke any more," she whispered. "Please, for—my sake."

"All right, I won't," he cried. "I'll do anything you ask, dear love, anything; you know that."

A great temptation assailed her. In an insistent way she had caught glimpses of the large, easy-going side of his nature, and she felt sure, if she asked him to cease attempting to write, that he would grant her wish. In the swift instant that elapsed, the words trembled on her lips. But she did not utter them. She was not quite brave enough; she did not quite dare. Instead, she leaned toward him to meet him, and in his arms murmured:-

"You know, it is really not for my sake, Martin, but for your own. I am sure smoking hurts you; and besides, it is not good to be a slave to anything, to a drug least of all."

"I shall always be your slave," he smiled.

"In which case, I shall begin issuing my commands."

She looked at him mischievously, though deep down she was already regretting that she had not preferred her largest request.

"I live but to obey, your majesty."

"Well, then, my first commandment is, Thou shalt not omit to shave every day. Look how you have scratched my cheek."

And so it ended in caresses and love-laughter. But she had made one point, and she could not expect to make more than one at a time. She felt a woman's pride in that she had made him stop smoking. Another time she would persuade him to take a position, for had he not said he would do anything she asked?

She left his side to explore the room, examining the clothes-lines of notes overhead, learning the mystery of the tackle used for suspending his wheel under the ceiling, and being saddened by the heap of manuscripts under the table which represented to her just so much wasted time. The oil-stove won her admiration, but on investigating the food shelves she found them empty.

"Why, you haven't anything to eat, you poor dear," she said with tender compassion. "You must be starving."

644

"I store my food in Maria's safe and in her pantry," he lied. "It keeps better there. No danger of my starving. Look at that."

She had come back to his side, and she saw him double his arm at the elbow, the biceps crawling under his shirt-sleeve and swelling into a knot of muscle, heavy and hard. The sight repelled her. Sentimentally, she disliked it. But her pulse, her blood, every fibre of her, loved it and yearned for it, and, in the old, inexplicable way, she leaned toward him, not away from him. And in the moment that followed, when he crushed her in his arms, the brain of her, concerned with the superficial aspects of life, was in revolt; while the heart of her, the woman of her, concerned with life itself, exulted triumphantly. It was in moments like this that she felt to the uttermost the greatness of her love for Martin, for it was almost a swoon of delight to her to feel his strong arms about her, holding her tightly, hurting her with the grip of their fervor. At such moments she found justification for her treason to her standards, for her violation of her own high ideals, and, most of all, for her tacit disobedience to her mother and father. They did not want her to marry this man. It shocked them that she should love him. It shocked her, too, sometimes, when she was apart from him, a cool and reasoning creature. With him, she loved him—in truth, at times a vexed and worried love; but love it was, a love that was stronger than she.

"This La Grippe is nothing," he was saying. "It hurts a bit, and gives one a nasty headache, but it doesn't compare with break-bone fever."

"Have you had that, too?" she queried absently, intent on the heaven-sent justification she was finding in his arms.

And so, with absent queries, she led him on, till suddenly his words startled her.

He had had the fever in a secret colony of thirty lepers on one of the Hawaiian Islands.

"But why did you go there?" she demanded.

Such royal carelessness of body seemed criminal.

645

"Because I didn't know," he answered. "I never dreamed of lepers. When I deserted the schooner and landed on the beach, I headed inland for some place of hiding. For three days I lived off guavas, *ohia*-apples, and bananas, all of which grew wild in the jungle. On the fourth day I found the trail—a mere foot-trail. It led inland, and it led up. It was the way I wanted to go, and it showed signs of recent travel. At one place it ran along the crest of a ridge that was no more than a knife-edge. The trail wasn't three feet wide on the crest, and on either side the ridge fell away in precipices hundreds of feet deep. One man, with plenty of ammunition, could have held it against a hundred thousand.

"It was the only way in to the hiding-place. Three hours after I found the trail I was there, in a little mountain valley, a pocket in the midst of lava peaks. The whole place was terraced for taro-patches, fruit trees grew there, and there were eight or ten grass huts. But as soon as I saw the inhabitants I knew what I'd struck. One sight of them was enough."

"What did you do?" Ruth demanded breathlessly, listening, like any Desdemona, appalled and fascinated.

"Nothing for me to do. Their leader was a kind old fellow, pretty far gone, but he ruled like a king. He had discovered the little valley and founded the settlement—all of which was against the law. But he had guns, plenty of ammunition, and those Kanakas, trained to the shooting of wild cattle and wild pig, were dead shots. No, there wasn't any running away for Martin Eden. He stayed—for three months."

"But how did you escape?"

"I'd have been there yet, if it hadn't been for a girl there, a half-Chinese, quarter-white, and quarter-Hawaiian. She was a beauty, poor thing, and well educated. Her mother, in Honolulu, was worth a million or so. Well, this girl got me away at last. Her mother financed the settlement, you see, so the girl wasn't afraid of being punished for letting me go. But she made me swear, first, never to reveal the hiding-place; and I never have. This is the first time I have even mentioned it. The girl had just the first signs of leprosy. The fingers of her right hand were slightly twisted, and there was a small spot on her arm. That was all. I guess she is dead, now."

646

"But weren't you frightened? And weren't you glad to get away without catching that dreadful disease?"

"Well," he confessed, "I was a bit shivery at first; but I got used to it. I used to feel sorry for that poor girl, though. That made me forget to be afraid. She was such a beauty, in spirit as well as in appearance, and she was only slightly touched; yet she was doomed to lie there, living the life of a primitive savage and rotting slowly away. Leprosy is far more terrible than you can imagine it."

"Poor thing," Ruth murmured softly. "It's a wonder she let you get away."

"How do you mean?" Martin asked unwittingly.

"Because she must have loved you," Ruth said, still softly. "Candidly, now, didn't she?"

Martin's sunburn had been bleached by his work in the laundry and by the indoor life he was living, while the hunger and the sickness had made his face even pale; and across this pallor flowed the slow wave of a blush. He was opening his mouth to speak, but Ruth shut him off.

"Never mind, don't answer; it's not necessary," she laughed.

But it seemed to him there was something metallic in her laughter, and that the light in her eyes was cold. On the spur of the moment it reminded him of a gale he had once experienced in the North Pacific. And for the moment the apparition of the gale rose before his eyes—a gale at night, with a clear sky and under a full moon, the huge seas glinting coldly in the moonlight. Next, he saw the girl in the leper refuge and remembered it was for love of him that she had let him go.

"She was noble," he said simply. "She gave me life."

That was all of the incident, but he heard Ruth muffle a dry sob in her throat, and noticed that she turned her face away to gaze out of the window. When she turned it back to him, it was composed, and there was no hint of the gale in her eyes.

"I'm such a silly," she said plaintively. "But I can't help it. I do so love you, Martin, I do, I do. I shall grow more catholic in time, but at present I can't help being jealous of those ghosts of the past, and you know your past is full of ghosts."

"It must be," she silenced his protest. "It could not be otherwise. And there's poor Arthur motioning me to come. He's tired waiting. And now good-by, dear."

"There's some kind of a mixture, put up by the druggists, that helps men to stop the use of tobacco," she called back from the door, "and I am going to send you some."

The door closed, but opened again.

"I do, I do," she whispered to him; and this time she was really gone.

Maria, with worshipful eyes that none the less were keen to note the texture of Ruth's garments and the cut of them (a cut unknown that produced an effect mysteriously beautiful), saw her to the carriage. The crowd of disappointed urchins stared till the carriage disappeared from view, then transferred their stare to Maria, who had abruptly become the most important person on the street. But it was one of her progeny who blasted Maria's reputation by announcing that the grand visitors had been for her lodger. After that Maria dropped back into her old obscurity and Martin began to notice the respectful manner in which he was regarded by the small fry of the neighborhood. As for Maria, Martin rose in her estimation a full hundred per cent, and had the Portuguese grocer witnessed that afternoon carriage-call he would have allowed Martin an additional three-dollars-and-eighty-five-cents' worth of credit.

CHAPTER XXVII

The sun of Martin's good fortune rose. The day after Ruth's visit, he received a check for three dollars from a New York scandal weekly in payment for three of his triolets. Two days later a newspaper published in Chicago accepted his "Treasure Hunters," promising to pay ten dollars for it on publication. The price was small, but it was the first article he had written, his very first attempt to express his thought on the printed page. To cap everything, the adventure serial for boys, his second attempt, was accepted before the end of the week by a juvenile monthly calling itself *Youth and Age*. It was true the serial was twenty-one thousand words, and they offered to pay him sixteen dollars on publication, which was something like seventy-five cents a thousand words; but it was equally true that it was the second thing he had attempted to write and that he was himself thoroughly aware of its clumsy worthlessness.

But even his earliest efforts were not marked with the clumsiness of mediocrity. What characterized them was the clumsiness of too great strength—the clumsiness which the tyro betrays when he crushes butterflies with battering rams and hammers out vignettes with a war-club. So it was that Martin was glad to sell his early efforts for songs. He knew them for what they were, and it had not taken him long to acquire this knowledge. What he pinned his faith to was his later work. He had striven to be something more than a mere writer of magazine fiction. He had sought to equip himself with the tools of artistry. On the other hand, he had not sacrificed strength. His conscious aim had been to increase his strength by avoiding excess of strength. Nor had he departed from his love of reality. His work was realism, though he had endeavored to fuse with it the fancies and beauties of imagination. What he sought was an impassioned realism, shot through with human aspiration and faith. What he wanted was life as it was, with all its spirit-groping and soul-reaching left in.

He had discovered, in the course of his reading, two schools of fiction. One treated of man as a god, ignoring his earthly origin; the other treated of man as a clod, ignoring his heaven-sent dreams and divine possibilities. Both the god and the clod schools erred, in Martin's estimation, and erred through too great singleness of sight and purpose. There was a compromise that approximated the truth, though it flattered not the school of god, while it challenged the brute-savageness of the school of clod. It was his story, "Adventure," which had dragged with Ruth, that Martin believed had achieved his ideal of the true in fiction; and it was in an essay, "God and Clod," that he had expressed his views on the whole general subject.

But "Adventure," and all that he deemed his best work, still went begging among the editors. His early work counted for nothing in his eyes except for the money it brought, and his horror stories, two of which he had sold, he did not consider high work nor his best work. To him they were frankly imaginative and fantastic, though invested with all the glamour of the real, wherein lay their power. This investiture of the grotesque and impossible with reality, he looked upon as a trick—a skilful trick at best. Great literature could not reside in such a field. Their artistry was high, but he denied the worthwhileness of artistry when divorced from humanness. The trick had been to fling over the face of his artistry a mask of humanness, and this he had done in the half-dozen or so stories of the horror brand he had written before he emerged upon the high peaks of "Adventure," "Joy," "The Pot," and "The Wine of Life."

The three dollars he received for the triolets he used to eke out a precarious existence against the arrival of the *White Mouse* check. He cashed the first check with the suspicious Portuguese grocer, paying a dollar on account and dividing the remaining two dollars between the baker and the fruit store. Martin was not yet rich enough to afford meat, and he was on slim allowance when the *White Mouse* check arrived. He was divided on the cashing of it. He had never been in a bank in his life, much less been in one on business, and he had a naive and childlike desire to walk into one of the big banks down in Oakland and fling down his indorsed check for forty dollars. On the other hand, practical common sense ruled that he should cash it with his grocer and thereby make an impression that would later result in an increase of credit. Reluctantly Martin yielded to the claims of the grocer, paying his bill with him in full, and receiving in change a pocketful of jingling coin. Also, he paid the other tradesmen in full, redeemed his suit and his bicycle, paid one month's rent on the type-writer, and paid Maria the overdue month for his room and a month in advance. This left him in his pocket, for emergencies, a balance of nearly three dollars.

In itself, this small sum seemed a fortune. Immediately on recovering his clothes he had gone to see Ruth, and on the way he could not refrain from jingling the little handful of silver in his pocket. He had been so long without money that, like a rescued starving man who cannot let the unconsumed food out of his sight, Martin could not keep his hand off the silver. He was not mean, nor avaricious, but the money meant more than so many dollars and cents. It stood for success, and the eagles stamped upon the coins were to him so many winged victories.

It came to him insensibly that it was a very good world. It certainly appeared more beautiful to him. For weeks it had been a very dull and sombre world; but now, with nearly all debts paid, three dollars jingling in his pocket, and in his mind the consciousness of success, the sun shone bright and warm, and even a rain-squall that soaked unprepared pedestrians seemed a merry happening to him. When he starved, his thoughts had dwelt often upon the thousands he knew were starving the world over; but now that he was feasted full, the fact of the thousands starving was no longer pregnant in his brain. He forgot about them, and, being in love, remembered the countless lovers in the world. Without deliberately thinking about it, *motifs* for love-lyrics began to agitate his brain. Swept away by the creative impulse, he got off the electric car, without vexation, two blocks beyond his crossing.

He found a number of persons in the Morse home. Ruth's two girl-cousins were visiting her from San Rafael, and Mrs. Morse, under pretext of entertaining them, was pursuing her plan of surrounding Ruth with young people. The campaign had begun during Martin's enforced absence, and was already in full swing. She was making a point of having at the house men who were doing things. Thus, in addition to the cousins Dorothy and

Florence, Martin encountered two university professors, one of Latin, the other of English; a young army officer just back from the Philippines, one-time school-mate of Ruth's; a young fellow named Melville, private secretary to Joseph Perkins, head of the San Francisco Trust Company; and finally of the men, a live bank cashier, Charles Hapgood, a youngish man of thirty-five, graduate of Stanford University, member of the Nile Club and the Unity Club, and a conservative speaker for the Republican Party during campaigns—in short, a rising young man in every way. Among the women was one who painted portraits, another who was a professional musician, and still another who possessed the degree of Doctor of Sociology and who was locally famous for her social settlement work in the slums of San Francisco. But the women did not count for much in Mrs. Morse's plan. At the best, they were necessary accessories. The men who did things must be drawn to the house somehow.

"Don't get excited when you talk," Ruth admonished Martin, before the ordeal of introduction began.

He bore himself a bit stiffly at first, oppressed by a sense of his own awkwardness, especially of his shoulders, which were up to their old trick of threatening destruction to furniture and ornaments. Also, he was rendered self-conscious by the company. He had never before been in contact with such exalted beings nor with so many of them. Melville, the bank cashier, fascinated him, and he resolved to investigate him at the first opportunity. For underneath Martin's awe lurked his assertive ego, and he felt the urge to measure himself with these men and women and to find out what they had learned from the books and life which he had not learned.

Ruth's eyes roved to him frequently to see how he was getting on, and she was surprised and gladdened by the ease with which he got acquainted with her cousins. He certainly did not grow excited, while being seated removed from him the worry of his shoulders. Ruth knew them for clever girls, superficially brilliant, and she could scarcely understand their praise of Martin later that night at going to bed. But he, on the other hand, a wit in his own class, a gay quizzer and laughter-maker at dances and Sunday picnics, had found the making of fun and the breaking of good-natured lances simple enough in this environment. And on this evening success stood at his back, patting him on the shoulder and telling him that he was making good, so that he could afford to laugh and make laughter and remain unabashed.

Later, Ruth's anxiety found justification. Martin and Professor Caldwell had got together in a conspicuous corner, and though Martin no longer wove the air with his hands, to Ruth's critical eye he permitted his own eyes to flash and glitter too frequently, talked too rapidly and warmly, grew too intense, and allowed his aroused blood to redden his cheeks too much. He lacked decorum and control, and was in decided contrast to the young professor of English with whom he talked.

But Martin was not concerned with appearances! He had been swift to note the other's trained mind and to appreciate his command of knowledge. Furthermore, Professor Caldwell did not realize Martin's concept of the average English professor. Martin wanted him to talk shop, and, though he seemed averse at first, succeeded in making him do it. For Martin did not see why a man should not talk shop.

"It's absurd and unfair," he had told Ruth weeks before, "this objection to talking shop. For what reason under the sun do men and women come together if not for the exchange of the best that is in them? And the best that is in them is what they are interested in, the thing by which they make their living, the thing they've specialized on and sat up days and nights over, and even dreamed about. Imagine Mr. Butler living up to social etiquette and enunciating his views on Paul Verlaine or the German drama or the novels of D'Annunzio. We'd be bored to death. I, for one, if I must listen to Mr. Butler, prefer to hear him talk about his law. It's the best that is in him, and life is so short that I want the best of every man and woman I meet."

"But," Ruth had objected, "there are the topics of general interest to all."

"There, you mistake," he had rushed on. "All persons in society, all cliques in society—or, rather, nearly all persons and cliques—ape their betters. Now, who are the best betters? The idlers, the wealthy idlers. They do not know, as a rule, the things known by the persons who are doing something in the world. To listen to conversation about such things would mean to be bored, wherefore the idlers decree that such things are shop and must not be talked about. Likewise they decree the things that are not shop and which may be talked about, and those things are the latest operas, latest novels, cards, billiards, cocktails, automobiles, horse shows, trout fishing, tuna-fishing, big-game shooting, yacht sailing, and so forth—and mark you, these are the things the idlers know. In all truth, they constitute the shop-talk of the idlers. And the funniest part of it is that many of the clever people, and all the would-be clever people, allow the idlers so to impose upon them. As for me, I want the best a man's got in him, call it shop vulgarity or anything you please."

And Ruth had not understood. This attack of his on the established had seemed to her just so much wilfulness of opinion.

So Martin contaminated Professor Caldwell with his own earnestness, challenging him to speak his mind. As Ruth paused beside them she heard Martin saying:-

"You surely don't pronounce such heresies in the University of California?"

Professor Caldwell shrugged his shoulders. "The honest taxpayer and the politician, you know. Sacramento gives us our appropriations and therefore we kowtow to Sacramento, and to the Board of Regents, and to the party press, or to the press of both parties."

"Yes, that's clear; but how about you?" Martin urged. "You must be a fish out of the water."

"Few like me, I imagine, in the university pond. Sometimes I am fairly sure I am out of water, and that I should belong in Paris, in Grub Street, in a hermit's cave, or in some sadly wild Bohemian crowd, drinking claret,—dago-red they call it in San Francisco,—dining in cheap restaurants in the Latin Quarter, and expressing vociferously radical views upon all creation. Really, I am frequently almost sure that I was cut out to be a radical. But then, there are so many questions on which I am not sure. I grow timid when I am face to face with my human frailty, which ever prevents me from grasping all the factors in any problem—human, vital problems, you know."

And as he talked on, Martin became aware that to his own lips had come the "Song of the Trade Wind":-

"I am strongest at noon,

But under the moon

I stiffen the bunt of the sail."

He was almost humming the words, and it dawned upon him that the other reminded him of the trade wind, of the Northeast Trade, steady, and cool, and strong. He was equable, he was to be relied upon, and withal there was a certain bafflement about him. Martin had the feeling that he never spoke his full mind, just as he had often had the feeling that the trades never blew their strongest but always held reserves of strength that were never used. Martin's trick of visioning was active as ever. His brain was a most accessible storehouse of remembered fact and fancy, and its contents seemed ever ordered and spread for his inspection. Whatever occurred in the instant present, Martin's mind immediately presented associated antithesis or similitude which ordinarily expressed themselves to him in vision. It was sheerly automatic, and his visioning was an unfailing accompaniment to the living present. Just as Ruth's face, in a momentary jealousy had called before his eyes a forgotten moonlight gale, and as Professor Caldwell made him see again the Northeast Trade herding the white billows across the purple sea, so, from moment to moment, not disconcerting but rather identifying and classifying, new memory-visions rose before him, or spread under his eyelids, or were thrown upon the screen of his consciousness. These visions came out of the actions and sensations of the past, out of things and events and books of yesterday and last week—a countless host of apparitions that, waking or sleeping, forever thronged his mind.

So it was, as he listened to Professor Caldwell's easy flow of speech—the conversation of a clever, cultured man—that Martin kept seeing himself down all his past. He saw himself when he had been quite the hoodlum, wearing a "stiff-rim" Stetson hat and a square-cut, double-breasted coat, with a certain swagger to the shoulders and possessing the ideal of being as tough as the police permitted. He did not disguise it to himself, nor attempt to palliate it. At one time in his life he had been just a common hoodlum, the leader of a gang that worried the police and terrorized honest, working-class householders. But his ideals had changed. He glanced about him at the well-bred, well-dressed men and women, and breathed into his lungs the atmosphere of culture and refinement, and at the same moment the ghost of his early youth, in stiff-rim and square-cut, with swagger and toughness, stalked across the room. This figure, of the corner hoodlum, he saw merge into himself, sitting and talking with an actual university professor.

For, after all, he had never found his permanent abiding place. He had fitted in wherever he found himself, been a favorite always and everywhere by virtue of holding his own at work and at play and by his willingness and ability to fight for his rights and command respect. But he had never taken root. He had fitted in sufficiently to satisfy his fellows but not to satisfy himself. He had been perturbed always by a feeling of unrest, had heard always the call of something from beyond, and had wandered on through life seeking it until he found books and art and love. And here he was, in the midst of all this, the only one of all the comrades he had adventured with who could have made themselves eligible for the inside of the Morse home.

But such thoughts and visions did not prevent him from following Professor Caldwell closely. And as he followed, comprehendingly and critically, he noted the unbroken field of the other's knowledge. As for himself, from moment to moment the conversation showed him gaps and open stretches, whole subjects with which he was unfamiliar. Nevertheless, thanks to his Spencer, he saw that he possessed the outlines of the field of knowledge. It was a matter only of time, when he would fill in the outline. Then watch out, he thought—'ware shoal, everybody! He felt like sitting at the feet of the professor, worshipful and absorbent; but, as he listened, he began to discern a weakness in the other's judgments—a weakness so stray and elusive that he might not have caught it had it not been ever present. And when he did catch it, he leapt to equality at once.

Ruth came up to them a second time, just as Martin began to speak.

"I'll tell you where you are wrong, or, rather, what weakens your judgments," he said. "You lack biology. It has no place in your scheme of things.—Oh, I mean the real interpretative biology, from the ground up, from the laboratory and the test-tube and the vitalized inorganic right on up to the widest aesthetic and sociological generalizations."

Ruth was appalled. She had sat two lecture courses under Professor Caldwell and looked up to him as the living repository of all knowledge.

"I scarcely follow you," he said dubiously.

Martin was not so sure but what he had followed him.

"Then I'll try to explain," he said. "I remember reading in Egyptian history something to the effect that understanding could not be had of Egyptian art without first studying the land question."

"Quite right," the professor nodded.

"And it seems to me," Martin continued, "that knowledge of the land question, in turn, of all questions, for that matter, cannot be had without previous knowledge of the stuff and the constitution of life. How can we understand laws and institutions, religions and customs, without understanding, not merely the nature of the creatures that made them, but the nature of the stuff out of which the creatures are made? Is literature less human than the architecture and sculpture of Egypt? Is there one thing in the known universe that is not subject to the law of evolution?—Oh, I know there is an elaborate evolution of the various arts laid down, but it seems to me to be too mechanical. The human himself is left out. The evolution of the tool, of the harp, of music and song and dance, are all beautifully elaborated; but how about the evolution of the human himself, the development of the basic and intrinsic parts that were in him before he made his first tool or gibbered his first chant? It is that which you do not consider, and which I call biology. It is biology in its largest aspects.

"I know I express myself incoherently, but I've tried to hammer out the idea. It came to me as you were talking, so I was not primed and ready to deliver it. You spoke yourself of the human frailty that prevented one from taking all the factors into consideration. And you, in turn,—or so it seems to me,—leave out the biological factor, the very stuff out of which has been spun the fabric of all the arts, the warp and the woof of all human actions and achievements."

To Ruth's amazement, Martin was not immediately crushed, and that the professor replied in the way he did struck her as forbearance for Martin's youth. Professor Caldwell sat for a full minute, silent and fingering his watch chain.

"Do you know," he said at last, "I've had that same criticism passed on me once before—by a very great man, a scientist and evolutionist, Joseph Le Conte. But he is dead, and I thought to remain undetected; and now you come along and expose me. Seriously, though—and this is confession—I think there is something in your contention—a great deal, in fact. I am too classical, not enough up-to-date in the interpretative branches of science, and I can only plead the disadvantages of my education and a temperamental slothfulness that prevents me from doing the work. I wonder if you'll believe that I've never been inside a physics or chemistry laboratory? It is true, nevertheless. Le Conte was right, and so are you, Mr. Eden, at least to an extent—how much I do not know."

Ruth drew Martin away with her on a pretext; when she had got him aside, whispering:-

"You shouldn't have monopolized Professor Caldwell that way. There may be others who want to talk with him."

"My mistake," Martin admitted contritely. "But I'd got him stirred up, and he was so interesting that I did not think. Do you know, he is the brightest, the most intellectual, man I have ever talked with. And I'll tell you something else. I once thought that everybody who went to universities, or who sat in the high places in society, was just as brilliant and intelligent as he."

"He's an exception," she answered.

"I should say so. Whom do you want me to talk to now?—Oh, say, bring me up against that cashier-fellow."

Martin talked for fifteen minutes with him, nor could Ruth have wished better behavior on her lover's part. Not once did his eyes flash nor his cheeks flush, while the calmness and poise with which he talked surprised her. But in Martin's estimation the whole tribe of bank cashiers fell a few hundred per cent, and for the rest of the evening he labored under the impression that bank cashiers and talkers of platitudes were synonymous phrases. The army officer he found good-natured and simple, a healthy, wholesome young fellow, content to occupy the place in life into which birth and luck had flung him. On learning that he had completed two years in the university, Martin was puzzled to know where he had stored it away. Nevertheless Martin liked him better than the platitudinous bank cashier.

"I really don't object to platitudes," he told Ruth later; "but what worries me into nervousness is the pompous, smugly complacent, superior certitude with which they are uttered and the time taken to do it. Why, I could give that man the whole history of the Reformation in the time he took to tell me that the Union-Labor Party had fused with the Democrats. Do you know, he skins his words as a professional poker-player skins the cards that are dealt out to him. Some day I'll show you what I mean."

"I'm sorry you don't like him," was her reply. "He's a favorite of Mr. Butler's. Mr. Butler says he is safe and honest—calls him the Rock, Peter, and says that upon him any banking institution can well be built."

"I don't doubt it—from the little I saw of him and the less I heard from him; but I don't think so much of banks as I did. You don't mind my speaking my mind this way, dear?"

"No, no; it is most interesting."

"Yes," Martin went on heartily, "I'm no more than a barbarian getting my first impressions of civilization. Such impressions must be entertainingly novel to the civilized person."

"What did you think of my cousins?" Ruth queried.

"I liked them better than the other women. There's plenty of fun in them along with paucity of pretense."

"Then you did like the other women?"

He shook his head.

"That social-settlement woman is no more than a sociological poll-parrot. I swear, if you winnowed her out between the stars, like Tomlinson, there would be found in her not one original thought. As for the portrait-painter, she was a positive bore. She'd make a good wife for the cashier. And the musician woman! I don't care how nimble her fingers are, how perfect her technique, how wonderful her expression—the fact is, she knows nothing about music."

"She plays beautifully," Ruth protested.

"Yes, she's undoubtedly gymnastic in the externals of music, but the intrinsic spirit of music is unguessed by her. I asked her what music meant to her—you know I'm always curious to know that particular thing; and she did not know what it meant to her, except that she adored it, that it was the greatest of the arts, and that it meant more than life to her."

"You were making them talk shop," Ruth charged him.

"I confess it. And if they were failures on shop, imagine my sufferings if they had discoursed on other subjects. Why, I used to think that up here, where all the advantages of culture were enjoyed—" He paused for a moment, and watched the youthful shade of himself, in stiff-rim and square-cut, enter the door and swagger across the room. "As I was saying, up here I thought all men and women were brilliant and radiant. But now, from what little I've seen of them, they strike me as a pack of ninnies, most of them, and ninety percent of the remainder as bores. Now there's Professor Caldwell—he's different. He's a man, every inch of him and every atom of his gray matter."

Ruth's face brightened.

"Tell me about him," she urged. "Not what is large and brilliant—I know those qualities; but whatever you feel is adverse. I am most curious to know."

660

"Perhaps I'll get myself in a pickle." Martin debated humorously for a moment. "Suppose you tell me first. Or maybe you find in him nothing less than the best."

"I attended two lecture courses under him, and I have known him for two years; that is why I am anxious for your first impression."

"Bad impression, you mean? Well, here goes. He is all the fine things you think about him, I guess. At least, he is the finest specimen of intellectual man I have met; but he is a man with a secret shame."

"Oh, no, no!" he hastened to cry. "Nothing paltry nor vulgar. What I mean is that he strikes me as a man who has gone to the bottom of things, and is so afraid of what he saw that he makes believe to himself that he never saw it. Perhaps that's not the clearest way to express it. Here's another way. A man who has found the path to the hidden temple but has not followed it; who has, perhaps, caught glimpses of the temple and striven afterward to convince himself that it was only a mirage of foliage. Yet another way. A man who could have done things but who placed no value on the doing, and who, all the time, in his innermost heart, is regretting that he has not done them; who has secretly laughed at the rewards for doing, and yet, still more secretly, has yearned for the rewards and for the joy of doing."

"I don't read him that way," she said. "And for that matter, I don't see just what you mean."

"It is only a vague feeling on my part," Martin temporized. "I have no reason for it. It is only a feeling, and most likely it is wrong. You certainly should know him better than I."

From the evening at Ruth's Martin brought away with him strange confusions and conflicting feelings. He was disappointed in his goal, in the persons he had climbed to be with. On the other hand, he was encouraged with his success. The climb had been easier than he expected. He was superior to the climb, and (he did not, with false modesty, hide it from himself) he was superior to the beings among whom he had climbed—with the exception, of course, of Professor Caldwell. About life and the books he knew more than they, and he wondered into what nooks and crannies they had cast aside their educations. He did not know that he was himself possessed of unusual brain vigor; nor did he know that the persons who were given to probing the depths and to thinking ultimate thoughts were not to be found in the drawing rooms of the world's Morses; nor did he dream that such persons were as lonely eagles sailing solitary in the azure sky far above the earth and its swarming freight of gregarious life.

CHAPTER XXVIII

But success had lost Martin's address, and her messengers no longer came to his door. For twenty-five days, working Sundays and holidays, he toiled on "The Shame of the Sun," a long essay of some thirty thousand words. It was a deliberate attack on the mysticism of the Maeterlinck school—an attack from the citadel of positive science upon the wonder-dreamers, but an attack nevertheless that retained much of beauty and wonder of the sort compatible with ascertained fact. It was a little later that he followed up the attack with two short essays, "The Wonder-Dreamers" and "The Yardstick of the Ego." And on essays, long and short, he began to pay the travelling expenses from magazine to magazine.

During the twenty-five days spent on "The Shame of the Sun," he sold hack-work to the extent of six dollars and fifty cents. A joke had brought in fifty cents, and a second one, sold to a high-grade comic weekly, had fetched a dollar. Then two humorous poems had earned two dollars and three dollars respectively. As a result, having exhausted his credit with the tradesmen (though he had increased his credit with the grocer to five dollars), his wheel and suit of clothes went back to the pawnbroker. The type-writer people were again clamoring for money, insistently pointing out that according to the agreement rent was to be paid strictly in advance.

Encouraged by his several small sales, Martin went back to hack-work. Perhaps there was a living in it, after all. Stored away under his table were the twenty storiettes which had been rejected by the newspaper short-story syndicate. He read them over in order to find out how not to write newspaper storiettes, and so doing, reasoned out the perfect formula. He found that the newspaper storiette should never be tragic, should never end unhappily, and should never contain beauty of language, subtlety of thought, nor real delicacy of sentiment. Sentiment it must contain, plenty of it, pure and noble, of the sort that in his own early youth had brought his applause from "nigger heaven"—the "For-God-my-country-and-the-Czar" and "I-may-be-poor-but-I-am-honest" brand of sentiment.

Having learned such precautions, Martin consulted "The Duchess" for tone, and proceeded to mix according to formula. The formula consists of three parts: (1) a pair of lovers are jarred apart; (2) by some deed or event they are reunited; (3) marriage bells. The third part was an unvarying quantity, but the first and second parts could be varied an infinite number of times. Thus, the pair of lovers could be jarred apart by misunderstood motives, by accident of fate, by jealous rivals, by irate parents, by crafty guardians, by scheming relatives, and so forth and so forth; they could be reunited by a brave deed of the man lover, by a similar deed of the woman lover, by change of heart in one lover or the other, by forced confession of crafty guardian, scheming relative, or jealous rival, by voluntary confession of same, by discovery of some unguessed secret, by lover storming girl's heart, by lover making long and noble self-sacrifice, and so on, endlessly. It was very fetching to make the girl propose in the course of being reunited, and Martin discovered, bit by bit, other decidedly piquant and fetching ruses. But marriage bells at the end was the one thing he could take no liberties with; though the heavens rolled up as a scroll and the stars fell, the wedding bells must go on ringing just the same. In quantity, the formula prescribed twelve hundred words minimum dose, fifteen hundred words maximum dose.

Before he got very far along in the art of the storiette, Martin worked out half a dozen stock forms, which he always consulted when constructing storiettes. These forms were like the cunning tables used by mathematicians, which may be entered from top, bottom, right, and left, which entrances consist of scores of lines and dozens of columns, and from which may be drawn, without reasoning or thinking, thousands of different conclusions, all unchallengably precise and true. Thus, in the course of half an hour with his forms, Martin could frame up a dozen or so storiettes, which he put aside and filled in at his convenience. He found that he could fill one in, after a day of serious work, in the hour before going to bed. As he later confessed to Ruth, he could almost do it in his sleep. The real work was in constructing the frames, and that was merely mechanical.

He had no doubt whatever of the efficacy of his formula, and for once he knew the editorial mind when he said positively to himself that the first two he sent off would bring checks. And checks they brought, for four dollars each, at the end of twelve days.

In the meantime he was making fresh and alarming discoveries concerning the magazines. Though the *Transcontinental* had published "The Ring of Bells," no check was forthcoming. Martin needed it, and he wrote for it. An evasive answer and a request for more of his work was all he received. He had gone hungry two days waiting for the reply, and it was then that he put his wheel back in pawn. He wrote regularly, twice a week, to the *Transcontinental* for his five dollars, though it was only semi-occasionally that he elicited a reply. He did not know that the *Transcontinental* had been staggering along precariously for years, that it was a fourth-rater, or tenth-rater, without standing, with a crazy circulation that partly rested on petty bullying and partly on patriotic appealing, and with advertisements that were scarcely more than charitable donations. Nor did he know that the *Transcontinental* was the sole livelihood of the editor and the business manager, and that they could wring their livelihood out of it only by moving to escape paying rent and by never paying any bill they could evade. Nor could he have guessed that the particular five dollars that belonged to him had been appropriated by the business manager for the painting of his house in Alameda, which painting he performed himself, on week-day afternoons, because he could not afford to pay union wages and because the first scab he had employed had had a ladder jerked out from under him and been sent to the hospital with a broken collar-bone.

The ten dollars for which Martin had sold "Treasure Hunters" to the Chicago newspaper did not come to hand. The article had been published, as he had ascertained at the file in the Central Reading-room, but no word could he get from the editor. His letters were ignored. To satisfy himself that they had been received, he registered several of them. It was nothing less than robbery, he concluded—a cold-blooded steal; while he starved, he was pilfered of his merchandise, of his goods, the sale of which was the sole way of getting bread to eat.

Youth and Age was a weekly, and it had published two-thirds of his twenty-one-thousand-word serial when it went out of business. With it went all hopes of getting his sixteen dollars.

To cap the situation, "The Pot," which he looked upon as one of the best things he had written, was lost to him. In despair, casting about frantically among the magazines, he had sent it to *The Billow*, a society weekly in San Francisco. His chief reason for submitting it to that publication was that, having only to travel across the bay from Oakland, a quick decision could be reached. Two weeks later he was overjoyed to see, in the latest number on the news-stand, his story printed in full, illustrated, and in the place of honor. He went home with leaping pulse, wondering how much they would pay him for one of the best things he had done. Also, the celerity with which it had been accepted and published was a pleasant thought to him. That the editor had not informed him of the acceptance made the surprise more complete. After waiting a week, two weeks, and half a week longer, desperation conquered diffidence, and he wrote to the editor of *The Billow*, suggesting that possibly through some negligence of the business manager his little account had been overlooked.

Even if it isn't more than five dollars, Martin thought to himself, it will buy enough beans and pea-soup to enable me to write half a dozen like it, and possibly as good.

Back came a cool letter from the editor that at least elicited Martin's admiration.

"We thank you," it ran, "for your excellent contribution. All of us in the office enjoyed it immensely, and, as you see, it was given the place of honor and immediate publication. We earnestly hope that you liked the illustrations.

"On rereading your letter it seems to us that you are laboring under the misapprehension that we pay for unsolicited manuscripts. This is not our custom, and of course yours was unsolicited. We assumed, naturally, when we received your story, that you understood the situation. We can only deeply regret this unfortunate misunderstanding, and assure you of our unfailing regard. Again, thanking you for your kind contribution, and hoping to receive more from you in the near future, we remain, etc."

There was also a postscript to the effect that though *The Billow* carried no free-list, it took great pleasure in sending him a complimentary subscription for the ensuing year.

After that experience, Martin typed at the top of the first sheet of all his manuscripts: "Submitted at your usual rate."

Some day, he consoled himself, they will be submitted at *my* usual rate.

He discovered in himself, at this period, a passion for perfection, under the sway of which he rewrote and polished "The Jostling Street," "The Wine of Life," "Joy," the "Sea Lyrics," and others of his earlier work. As of old, nineteen hours of labor a day was all too little to suit him. He wrote prodigiously, and he read prodigiously, forgetting in his toil the pangs caused by giving up his tobacco. Ruth's promised cure for the habit, flamboyantly labelled, he stowed away in the most inaccessible corner of his bureau. Especially during his stretches of famine he suffered from lack of the weed; but no matter how often he mastered the craving, it remained with him as strong as ever. He regarded it as the biggest thing he had ever achieved. Ruth's point of view was that he was doing no more than was right. She brought him the anti-tobacco remedy, purchased out of her glove money, and in a few days forgot all about it.

His machine-made storiettes, though he hated them and derided them, were successful. By means of them he redeemed all his pledges, paid most of his bills, and bought a new set of tires for his wheel. The storiettes at least kept the pot a-boiling and gave him time for ambitious work; while the one thing that upheld him was the forty dollars he had received from The *White Mouse*. He anchored his faith to that, and was confident that the really first-class magazines would pay an unknown writer at least an equal rate, if not a better one. But the thing was, how to get into the first-class magazines. His best stories, essays, and poems went begging among them, and yet, each month, he read reams of dull, prosy, inartistic stuff between all their various covers. If only one editor, he sometimes thought, would descend from his high seat of pride to write me one cheering line! No matter if my work is unusual, no matter if it is unfit, for prudential reasons, for their pages, surely there must be some sparks in it, somewhere, a few, to warm them to some sort of appreciation. And thereupon he would get out one or another of his manuscripts, such as "Adventure," and read it over and over in a vain attempt to vindicate the editorial silence.

As the sweet California spring came on, his period of plenty came to an end. For several weeks he had been worried by a strange silence on the part of the newspaper storiette syndicate. Then, one day, came back to him through the mail ten of his immaculate machine-made storiettes. They were accompanied by a brief letter to the effect that the syndicate was overstocked, and that some months would elapse before it would be in the market again for manuscripts. Martin had even been extravagant on the strength of those ten storiettes. Toward the last the syndicate had been paying him five dollars each for them and accepting every one he sent. So he had looked upon the ten as good as sold, and he had lived accordingly, on a basis of fifty dollars in the bank. So it was that he entered abruptly upon a lean period, wherein he continued selling his earlier efforts to publications that would not pay and submitting his later work to magazines that would not buy. Also, he resumed his trips to the pawn-broker down in Oakland. A few jokes and snatches of humorous verse, sold to the New York weeklies, made existence barely possible for him. It was at this time that he wrote letters of inquiry to the several great monthly and quarterly reviews, and learned in reply that they rarely considered unsolicited articles, and that most of their contents were written upon order by well-known specialists who were authorities in their various fields.

CHAPTER XXIX

It was a hard summer for Martin. Manuscript readers and editors were away on vacation, and publications that ordinarily returned a decision in three weeks now retained his manuscript for three months or more. The consolation he drew from it was that a saving in postage was effected by the deadlock. Only the robber-publications seemed to remain actively in business, and to them Martin disposed of all his early efforts, such as "Pearl-diving," "The Sea as a Career," "Turtle-catching," and "The Northeast Trades." For these manuscripts he never received a penny. It is true, after six months' correspondence, he effected a compromise, whereby he received a safety razor for "Turtle-catching," and that *The Acropolis*, having agreed to give him five dollars cash and five yearly subscriptions: for "The Northeast Trades," fulfilled the second part of the agreement.

For a sonnet on Stevenson he managed to wring two dollars out of a Boston editor who was running a magazine with a Matthew Arnold taste and a penny-dreadful purse. "The Peri and the Pearl," a clever skit of a poem of two hundred lines, just finished, white hot from his brain, won the heart of the editor of a San Francisco magazine published in the interest of a great railroad. When the editor wrote, offering him payment in transportation, Martin wrote back to inquire if the transportation was transferable. It was not, and so, being prevented from peddling it, he asked for the return of the poem. Back it came, with the editor's regrets, and Martin sent it to San Francisco again, this time to The *Hornet*, a pretentious monthly that had been fanned into a constellation of the first magnitude by the brilliant journalist who founded it. But *The Hornet's* light had begun to dim long before Martin was born. The editor promised Martin fifteen dollars for the poem, but, when it was published, seemed to forget about it. Several of his letters being ignored, Martin indicted an angry one which drew a reply. It was written by a new editor, who coolly informed Martin that he declined to be held responsible for the old editor's mistakes, and that he did not think much of "The Peri and the Pearl" anyway.

But *The Globe*, a Chicago magazine, gave Martin the most cruel treatment of all. He had refrained from offering his "Sea Lyrics" for publication, until driven to it by starvation. After having been rejected by a dozen magazines, they had come to rest in *The Globe* office. There were thirty poems in the collection, and he was to receive a dollar apiece for them. The first month four were published, and he promptly received a cheek for four dollars; but when he looked over the magazine, he was appalled at the slaughter. In some cases the titles had been altered: "Finis," for instance, being changed to "The Finish," and "The Song of the Outer Reef" to "The Song of the Coral Reef." In one case, an absolutely different title, a misappropriate title, was substituted. In place of his own, "Medusa Lights," the editor had printed, "The Backward Track." But the slaughter in the body of the poems was terrifying. Martin groaned and sweated and thrust his hands through his hair. Phrases, lines, and stanzas were cut out, interchanged, or juggled about in the most incomprehensible manner. Sometimes lines and stanzas not his own were substituted for his. He could not believe that a sane editor could be guilty of such maltreatment, and his favorite hypothesis was that his poems must have been doctored by the office boy or the stenographer. Martin wrote immediately, begging the editor to cease publishing the lyrics and to return them to him.

He wrote again and again, begging, entreating, threatening, but his letters were ignored. Month by month the slaughter went on till the thirty poems were published, and month by month he received a check for those which had appeared in the current number.

Despite these various misadventures, the memory of the *White Mouse* forty-dollar check sustained him, though he was driven more and more to hack-work. He discovered a bread-and-butter field in the agricultural weeklies and trade journals, though among the religious weeklies he found he could easily starve. At his lowest ebb, when his black suit was in pawn, he made a ten-strike—or so it seemed to him—in a prize contest arranged by the County Committee of the Republican Party. There were three branches of the contest, and he entered them all, laughing at himself bitterly the while in that he was driven to such straits to live. His poem won the first prize of ten dollars, his campaign song the second prize of five dollars, his essay on the principles of the Republican Party the first prize of twenty-five dollars. Which was very gratifying to him until he tried to collect. Something had gone wrong in the County Committee, and, though a rich banker and a state senator were members of it, the money was not forthcoming. While this affair was hanging fire, he proved that he understood the principles of the Democratic Party by winning the first prize for his essay in a similar contest. And, moreover, he received the money, twenty-five dollars. But the forty dollars won in the first contest he never received.

Driven to shifts in order to see Ruth, and deciding that the long walk from north Oakland to her house and back again consumed too much time, he kept his black suit in pawn in place of his bicycle. The latter gave him exercise, saved him hours of time for work, and enabled him to see Ruth just the same. A pair of knee duck trousers and an old sweater made him a presentable wheel costume, so that he could go with Ruth on afternoon rides. Besides, he no longer had opportunity to see much of her in her own home, where Mrs. Morse was thoroughly prosecuting her campaign of entertainment. The exalted beings he met there, and to whom he had looked up but a short time before, now bored him. They were no longer exalted. He was nervous and irritable, what of his hard times, disappointments, and close application to work, and the conversation of such people was maddening. He was not unduly egotistic. He measured the narrowness of their minds by the minds of the thinkers in the books he read. At Ruth's home he never met a large mind, with the exception of Professor Caldwell, and Caldwell he had met there only once. As for the rest, they were numskulls, ninnies, superficial, dogmatic, and ignorant. It was their ignorance that astounded him. What was the matter with them? What had they done with their educations? They had had access to the same books he had. How did it happen that they had drawn nothing from them?

He knew that the great minds, the deep and rational thinkers, existed. He had his proofs from the books, the books that had educated him beyond the Morse standard. And he knew that higher intellects than those of the Morse circle were to be found in the world. He read English society

671

novels, wherein he caught glimpses of men and women talking politics and philosophy. And he read of salons in great cities, even in the United States, where art and intellect congregated. Foolishly, in the past, he had conceived that all well-groomed persons above the working class were persons with power of intellect and vigor of beauty. Culture and collars had gone together, to him, and he had been deceived into believing that college educations and mastery were the same things.

Well, he would fight his way on and up higher. And he would take Ruth with him. Her he dearly loved, and he was confident that she would shine anywhere. As it was clear to him that he had been handicapped by his early environment, so now he perceived that she was similarly handicapped. She had not had a chance to expand. The books on her father's shelves, the paintings on the walls, the music on the piano—all was just so much meretricious display. To real literature, real painting, real music, the Morses and their kind, were dead. And bigger than such things was life, of which they were densely, hopelessly ignorant. In spite of their Unitarian proclivities and their masks of conservative broadmindedness, they were two generations behind interpretative science: their mental processes were mediaeval, while their thinking on the ultimate data of existence and of the universe struck him as the same metaphysical method that was as young as the youngest race, as old as the cave-man, and older—the same that moved the first Pleistocene ape-man to fear the dark; that moved the first hasty Hebrew savage to incarnate Eve from Adam's rib; that moved Descartes to build an idealistic system of the universe out of the projections of his own puny ego; and that moved the famous British ecclesiastic to denounce evolution in satire so scathing as to win immediate applause and leave his name a notorious scrawl on the page of history.

So Martin thought, and he thought further, till it dawned upon him that the difference between these lawyers, officers, business men, and bank cashiers he had met and the members of the working class he had known was on a par with the difference in the food they ate, clothes they wore, neighborhoods in which they lived. Certainly, in all of them was lacking something more which he found in himself and in the books. The Morses had shown him the best their social position could produce, and he was not impressed by it. A pauper himself, a slave to the money-lender, he knew himself the superior of those he met at the Morses'; and, when his one decent suit of clothes was out of pawn, he moved among them a lord of life, quivering with a sense of outrage akin to what a prince would suffer if condemned to live with goat-herds.

"You hate and fear the socialists," he remarked to Mr. Morse, one evening at dinner; "but why? You know neither them nor their doctrines."

The conversation had been swung in that direction by Mrs. Morse, who had been invidiously singing the praises of Mr. Hapgood. The cashier was Martin's black beast, and his temper was a trifle short where the talker of platitudes was concerned.

"Yes," he had said, "Charley Hapgood is what they call a rising young man—somebody told me as much. And it is true. He'll make the Governor's Chair before he dies, and, who knows? maybe the United States Senate."

"What makes you think so?" Mrs. Morse had inquired.

"I've heard him make a campaign speech. It was so cleverly stupid and unoriginal, and also so convincing, that the leaders cannot help but regard him as safe and sure, while his platitudes are so much like the platitudes of the average voter that—oh, well, you know you flatter any man by dressing up his own thoughts for him and presenting them to him."

"I actually think you are jealous of Mr. Hapgood," Ruth had chimed in.

"Heaven forbid!"

The look of horror on Martin's face stirred Mrs. Morse to belligerence.

"You surely don't mean to say that Mr. Hapgood is stupid?" she demanded icily.

"No more than the average Republican," was the retort, "or average Democrat, either. They are all stupid when they are not crafty, and very few of them are crafty. The only wise Republicans are the millionnaires and their conscious henchmen. They know which side their bread is buttered on, and they know why."

"I am a Republican," Mr. Morse put in lightly. "Pray, how do you classify me?"

"Oh, you are an unconscious henchman."

"Henchman?"

"Why, yes. You do corporation work. You have no working-class nor criminal practice. You don't depend upon wife-beaters and pickpockets for your income. You get your livelihood from the masters of society, and whoever feeds a man is that man's master. Yes, you are a henchman. You are interested in advancing the interests of the aggregations of capital you serve."

Mr. Morse's face was a trifle red.

"I confess, sir," he said, "that you talk like a scoundrelly socialist."

Then it was that Martin made his remark:

"You hate and fear the socialists; but why? You know neither them nor their doctrines."

"Your doctrine certainly sounds like socialism," Mr. Morse replied, while Ruth gazed anxiously from one to the other, and Mrs. Morse beamed happily at the opportunity afforded of rousing her liege lord's antagonism.

"Because I say Republicans are stupid, and hold that liberty, equality, and fraternity are exploded bubbles, does not make me a socialist," Martin said with a smile. "Because I question Jefferson and the unscientific Frenchmen who informed his mind, does not make me a socialist. Believe me, Mr. Morse, you are far nearer socialism than I who am its avowed enemy."

"Now you please to be facetious," was all the other could say.

"Not at all. I speak in all seriousness. You still believe in equality, and yet you do the work of the corporations, and the corporations, from day to day, are busily engaged in burying equality. And you call me a socialist because I deny equality, because I affirm just what you live up to. The Republicans are foes to equality, though most of them fight the battle against equality with the very word itself the slogan on their lips. In the name of equality they destroy equality. That was why I called them stupid. As for myself, I am an individualist. I believe the race is to the swift, the battle to the strong. Such is the lesson I have learned from biology, or at least think I have learned. As I said, I am an individualist, and individualism is the hereditary and eternal foe of socialism."

"But you frequent socialist meetings," Mr. Morse challenged.

"Certainly, just as spies frequent hostile camps. How else are you to learn about the enemy? Besides, I enjoy myself at their meetings. They are good fighters, and, right or wrong, they have read the books. Any one of them knows far more about sociology and all the other ologies than the average captain of industry. Yes, I have been to half a dozen of their meetings, but that doesn't make me a socialist any more than hearing Charley Hapgood orate made me a Republican."

"I can't help it," Mr. Morse said feebly, "but I still believe you incline that way."

Bless me, Martin thought to himself, he doesn't know what I was talking about. He hasn't understood a word of it. What did he do with his education, anyway?

Thus, in his development, Martin found himself face to face with economic morality, or the morality of class; and soon it became to him a grisly monster. Personally, he was an intellectual moralist, and more offending to him than platitudinous pomposity was the morality of those about him, which was a curious hotchpotch of the economic, the metaphysical, the sentimental, and the imitative.

A sample of this curious messy mixture he encountered nearer home. His sister Marian had been keeping company with an industrious young mechanic, of German extraction, who, after thoroughly learning the trade, had set up for himself in a bicycle-repair shop. Also, having got the agency for

675

a low-grade make of wheel, he was prosperous. Marian had called on Martin in his room a short time before to announce her engagement, during which visit she had playfully inspected Martin's palm and told his fortune. On her next visit she brought Hermann von Schmidt along with her. Martin did the honors and congratulated both of them in language so easy and graceful as to affect disagreeably the peasant-mind of his sister's lover. This bad impression was further heightened by Martin's reading aloud the half-dozen stanzas of verse with which he had commemorated Marian's previous visit. It was a bit of society verse, airy and delicate, which he had named "The Palmist." He was surprised, when he finished reading it, to note no enjoyment in his sister's face. Instead, her eyes were fixed anxiously upon her betrothed, and Martin, following her gaze, saw spread on that worthy's asymmetrical features nothing but black and sullen disapproval. The incident passed over, they made an early departure, and Martin forgot all about it, though for the moment he had been puzzled that any woman, even of the working class, should not have been flattered and delighted by having poetry written about her.

Several evenings later Marian again visited him, this time alone. Nor did she waste time in coming to the point, upbraiding him sorrowfully for what he had done.

"Why, Marian," he chided, "you talk as though you were ashamed of your relatives, or of your brother at any rate."

"And I am, too," she blurted out.

Martin was bewildered by the tears of mortification he saw in her eyes. The mood, whatever it was, was genuine.

"But, Marian, why should your Hermann be jealous of my writing poetry about my own sister?"

"He ain't jealous," she sobbed. "He says it was indecent, ob—obscene."

Martin emitted a long, low whistle of incredulity, then proceeded to resurrect and read a carbon copy of "The Palmist."

"I can't see it," he said finally, proffering the manuscript to her. "Read it yourself and show me whatever strikes you as obscene—that was the word, wasn't it?"

"He says so, and he ought to know," was the answer, with a wave aside of the manuscript, accompanied by a look of loathing. "And he says you've got to tear it up. He says he won't have no wife of his with such things written about her which anybody can read. He says it's a disgrace, an' he won't stand for it."

"Now, look here, Marian, this is nothing but nonsense," Martin began; then abruptly changed his mind.

He saw before him an unhappy girl, knew the futility of attempting to convince her husband or her, and, though the whole situation was absurd and preposterous, he resolved to surrender.

"All right," he announced, tearing the manuscript into half a dozen pieces and throwing it into the waste-basket.

He contented himself with the knowledge that even then the original type-written manuscript was reposing in the office of a New York magazine. Marian and her husband would never know, and neither himself nor they nor the world would lose if the pretty, harmless poem ever were published.

Marian, starting to reach into the waste-basket, refrained.

"Can I?" she pleaded.

He nodded his head, regarding her thoughtfully as she gathered the torn pieces of manuscript and tucked them into the pocket of her jacket—ocular evidence of the success of her mission. She reminded him of Lizzie Connolly, though there was less of fire and gorgeous flaunting life in her than in that other girl of the working class whom he had seen twice. But they were on a par, the pair of them, in dress and carriage, and he smiled with inward amusement at the caprice of his fancy which suggested the appearance of either of them in Mrs. Morse's drawing-room. The amusement faded, and he was aware of a great loneliness. This sister of his and the Morse drawing-room were milestones of the road he had travelled. And he had left them behind. He glanced affectionately about him at his few books. They were all the comrades left to him.

"Hello, what's that?" he demanded in startled surprise.

Marian repeated her question.

"Why don't I go to work?" He broke into a laugh that was only half-hearted. "That Hermann of yours has been talking to you."

She shook her head.

"Don't lie," he commanded, and the nod of her head affirmed his charge.

"Well, you tell that Hermann of yours to mind his own business; that when I write poetry about the girl he's keeping company with it's his business, but that outside of that he's got no say so. Understand?

"So you don't think I'll succeed as a writer, eh?" he went on. "You think I'm no good?—that I've fallen down and am a disgrace to the family?"

"I think it would be much better if you got a job," she said firmly, and he saw she was sincere. "Hermann says—"

"Damn Hermann!" he broke out good-naturedly. "What I want to know is when you're going to get married. Also, you find out from your Hermann if he will deign to permit you to accept a wedding present from me."

He mused over the incident after she had gone, and once or twice broke out into laughter that was bitter as he saw his sister and her betrothed, all the members of his own class and the members of Ruth's class, directing their narrow little lives by narrow little formulas—herd-creatures, flocking together and patterning their lives by one another's opinions, failing of being individuals and of really living life because of the childlike formulas by which they were enslaved. He summoned them before him in apparitional procession: Bernard Higginbotham arm in arm with Mr. Butler, Hermann von Schmidt cheek by jowl with Charley Hapgood, and one by one and in

678

pairs he judged them and dismissed them—judged them by the standards of intellect and morality he had learned from the books. Vainly he asked: Where are the great souls, the great men and women? He found them not among the careless, gross, and stupid intelligences that answered the call of vision to his narrow room. He felt a loathing for them such as Circe must have felt for her swine. When he had dismissed the last one and thought himself alone, a late-comer entered, unexpected and unsummoned. Martin watched him and saw the stiff-rim, the square-cut, double-breasted coat and the swaggering shoulders, of the youthful hoodlum who had once been he.

"You were like all the rest, young fellow," Martin sneered. "Your morality and your knowledge were just the same as theirs. You did not think and act for yourself. Your opinions, like your clothes, were ready made; your acts were shaped by popular approval. You were cock of your gang because others acclaimed you the real thing. You fought and ruled the gang, not because you liked to,—you know you really despised it,—but because the other fellows patted you on the shoulder. You licked Cheese-Face because you wouldn't give in, and you wouldn't give in partly because you were an abysmal brute and for the rest because you believed what every one about you believed, that the measure of manhood was the carnivorous ferocity displayed in injuring and marring fellow-creatures' anatomies. Why, you whelp, you even won other fellows' girls away from them, not because you wanted the girls, but because in the marrow of those about you, those who set your moral pace, was the instinct of the wild stallion and the bull-seal. Well, the years have passed, and what do you think about it now?"

As if in reply, the vision underwent a swift metamorphosis. The stiff-rim and the square-cut vanished, being replaced by milder garments; the toughness went out of the face, the hardness out of the eyes; and, the face, chastened and refined, was irradiated from an inner life of communion with beauty and knowledge. The apparition was very like his present self, and, as he regarded it, he noted the student-lamp by which it was illuminated, and the book over which it pored. He glanced at the title and read, "The Science of AEsthetics." Next, he entered into the apparition, trimmed the student-lamp, and himself went on reading "The Science of AEsthetics."

CHAPTER XXX

On a beautiful fall day, a day of similar Indian summer to that which had seen their love declared the year before, Martin read his "Love-cycle" to Ruth. It was in the afternoon, and, as before, they had ridden out to their favorite knoll in the hills. Now and again she had interrupted his reading with exclamations of pleasure, and now, as he laid the last sheet of manuscript with its fellows, he waited her judgment.

She delayed to speak, and at last she spoke haltingly, hesitating to frame in words the harshness of her thought.

"I think they are beautiful, very beautiful," she said; "but you can't sell them, can you? You see what I mean," she said, almost pleaded. "This writing of yours is not practical. Something is the matter—maybe it is with the market—that prevents you from earning a living by it. And please, dear, don't misunderstand me. I am flattered, and made proud, and all that—I could not be a true woman were it otherwise—that you should write these poems to me. But they do not make our marriage possible. Don't you see, Martin? Don't think me mercenary. It is love, the thought of our future, with which I am burdened. A whole year has gone by since we learned we loved each other, and our wedding day is no nearer. Don't think me immodest in thus talking about our wedding, for really I have my heart, all that I am, at stake. Why don't you try to get work on a newspaper, if you are so bound up in your writing? Why not become a reporter?—for a while, at least?"

"It would spoil my style," was his answer, in a low, monotonous voice. "You have no idea how I've worked for style."

"But those storiettes," she argued. "You called them hack-work. You wrote many of them. Didn't they spoil your style?"

"No, the cases are different. The storiettes were ground out, jaded, at the end of a long day of application to style. But a reporter's work is all hack from morning till night, is the one paramount thing of life. And it is a whirlwind life, the life of the moment, with neither past nor future, and certainly without thought of any style but reportorial style, and that certainly is not literature. To become a reporter now, just as my style is taking form, crystallizing, would be to commit literary suicide. As it is, every storiette, every word of every storiette, was a violation of myself, of my self-respect, of my respect for beauty. I tell you it was sickening. I was guilty of sin. And I was secretly glad when the markets failed, even if my clothes did go into pawn. But the joy of writing the 'Love-cycle'! The creative joy in its noblest form! That was compensation for everything."

Martin did not know that Ruth was unsympathetic concerning the creative joy. She used the phrase—it was on her lips he had first heard it. She had read about it, studied about it, in the university in the course of earning her Bachelorship of Arts; but she was not original, not creative, and all manifestations of culture on her part were but harpings of the harpings of others.

"May not the editor have been right in his revision of your 'Sea Lyrics'?" she questioned. "Remember, an editor must have proved qualifications or else he would not be an editor."

"That's in line with the persistence of the established," he rejoined, his heat against the editor-folk getting the better of him. "What is, is not only right, but is the best possible. The existence of anything is sufficient vindication of its fitness to exist—to exist, mark you, as the average person unconsciously believes, not merely in present conditions, but in all conditions. It is their ignorance, of course, that makes them believe such rot—their ignorance, which is nothing more nor less than the henidical mental process described by Weininger. They think they think, and such thinkless creatures are the arbiters of the lives of the few who really think."

He paused, overcome by the consciousness that he had been talking over Ruth's head.

"I'm sure I don't know who this Weininger is," she retorted. "And you are so dreadfully general that I fail to follow you. What I was speaking of was the qualification of editors—"

"And I'll tell you," he interrupted. "The chief qualification of ninety-nine per cent of all editors is failure. They have failed as writers. Don't think they prefer the drudgery of the desk and the slavery to their circulation and to the business manager to the joy of writing. They have tried to write, and they have failed. And right there is the cursed paradox of it. Every portal to success in literature is guarded by those watch-dogs, the failures in literature. The editors, sub-editors, associate editors, most of them, and the manuscript-readers for the magazines and book-publishers, most of them, nearly all of them, are men who wanted to write and who have failed. And yet they, of all creatures under the sun the most unfit, are the very creatures who decide what shall and what shall not find its way into print—they, who have proved themselves not original, who have demonstrated that they lack the divine fire, sit in judgment upon originality and genius. And after them come the reviewers, just so many more failures. Don't tell me that they have not dreamed the dream and attempted to write poetry or fiction; for they have, and they have failed. Why, the average review is more nauseating than cod-liver oil. But you know my opinion on the reviewers and the alleged critics. There are great critics, but they are as rare as comets. If I fail as a writer, I shall have proved for the career of editorship. There's bread and butter and jam, at any rate."

Ruth's mind was quick, and her disapproval of her lover's views was buttressed by the contradiction she found in his contention.

"But, Martin, if that be so, if all the doors are closed as you have shown so conclusively, how is it possible that any of the great writers ever arrived?"

"They arrived by achieving the impossible," he answered. "They did such blazing, glorious work as to burn to ashes those that opposed them. They arrived by course of miracle, by winning a thousand-to-one wager against them. They arrived because they were Carlyle's battle-scarred giants who will not be kept down. And that is what I must do; I must achieve the impossible."

"But if you fail? You must consider me as well, Martin."

"If I fail?" He regarded her for a moment as though the thought she had uttered was unthinkable. Then intelligence illumined his eyes. "If I fail, I shall become an editor, and you will be an editor's wife."

She frowned at his facetiousness—a pretty, adorable frown that made him put his arm around her and kiss it away.

"There, that's enough," she urged, by an effort of will withdrawing herself from the fascination of his strength. "I have talked with father and mother. I never before asserted myself so against them. I demanded to be heard. I was very undutiful. They are against you, you know; but I assured them over and over of my abiding love for you, and at last father agreed that if you wanted to, you could begin right away in his office. And then, of his own accord, he said he would pay you enough at the start so that we could get married and have a little cottage somewhere. Which I think was very fine of him—don't you?"

Martin, with the dull pain of despair at his heart, mechanically reaching for the tobacco and paper (which he no longer carried) to roll a cigarette, muttered something inarticulate, and Ruth went on.

"Frankly, though, and don't let it hurt you—I tell you, to show you precisely how you stand with him—he doesn't like your radical views, and he thinks you are lazy. Of course I know you are not. I know you work hard."

How hard, even she did not know, was the thought in Martin's mind.

"Well, then," he said, "how about my views? Do you think they are so radical?"

He held her eyes and waited the answer.

"I think them, well, very disconcerting," she replied.

The question was answered for him, and so oppressed was he by the grayness of life that he forgot the tentative proposition she had made for him to go to work. And she, having gone as far as she dared, was willing to wait the answer till she should bring the question up again.

She had not long to wait. Martin had a question of his own to propound to her. He wanted to ascertain the measure of her faith in him, and within the week each was answered. Martin precipitated it by reading to her his "The Shame of the Sun."

"Why don't you become a reporter?" she asked when he had finished. "You love writing so, and I am sure you would succeed. You could rise in journalism and make a name for yourself. There are a number of great special correspondents. Their salaries are large, and their field is the world. They are sent everywhere, to the heart of Africa, like Stanley, or to interview the Pope, or to explore unknown Thibet."

"Then you don't like my essay?" he rejoined. "You believe that I have some show in journalism but none in literature?"

"No, no; I do like it. It reads well. But I am afraid it's over the heads of your readers. At least it is over mine. It sounds beautiful, but I don't understand it. Your scientific slang is beyond me. You are an extremist, you know, dear, and what may be intelligible to you may not be intelligible to the rest of us."

"I imagine it's the philosophic slang that bothers you," was all he could say.

He was flaming from the fresh reading of the ripest thought he had expressed, and her verdict stunned him.

"No matter how poorly it is done," he persisted, "don't you see anything in it?—in the thought of it, I mean?"

She shook her head.

"No, it is so different from anything I have read. I read Maeterlinck and understand him—"

"His mysticism, you understand that?" Martin flashed out.

"Yes, but this of yours, which is supposed to be an attack upon him, I don't understand. Of course, if originality counts—"

He stopped her with an impatient gesture that was not followed by speech. He became suddenly aware that she was speaking and that she had been speaking for some time.

"After all, your writing has been a toy to you," she was saying. "Surely you have played with it long enough. It is time to take up life seriously—our life, Martin. Hitherto you have lived solely your own."

"You want me to go to work?" he asked.

"Yes. Father has offered—"

"I understand all that," he broke in; "but what I want to know is whether or not you have lost faith in me?"

She pressed his hand mutely, her eyes dim.

"In your writing, dear," she admitted in a half-whisper.

"You've read lots of my stuff," he went on brutally. "What do you think of it? Is it utterly hopeless? How does it compare with other men's work?"

"But they sell theirs, and you—don't."

"That doesn't answer my question. Do you think that literature is not at all my vocation?"

"Then I will answer." She steeled herself to do it. "I don't think you were made to write. Forgive me, dear. You compel me to say it; and you know I know more about literature than you do."

"Yes, you are a Bachelor of Arts," he said meditatively; "and you ought to know."

"But there is more to be said," he continued, after a pause painful to both. "I know what I have in me. No one knows that so well as I. I know I shall succeed. I will not be kept down. I am afire with what I have to say in verse, and fiction, and essay. I do not ask you to have faith in that, though. I do not ask you to have faith in me, nor my writing. What I do ask of you is to love me and have faith in love."

"A year ago I believed for two years. One of those years is yet to run. And I do believe, upon my honor and my soul, that before that year is run I shall have succeeded. You remember what you told me long ago, that I must serve my apprenticeship to writing. Well, I have served it. I have crammed it and telescoped it. With you at the end awaiting me, I have never shirked. Do you know, I have forgotten what it is to fall peacefully asleep. A few million years ago I knew what it was to sleep my fill and to awake naturally from very glut of sleep. I am awakened always now by an alarm clock. If I fall asleep early or late, I set the alarm accordingly; and this, and the putting out of the lamp, are my last conscious actions."

"When I begin to feel drowsy, I change the heavy book I am reading for a lighter one. And when I doze over that, I beat my head with my knuckles in order to drive sleep away. Somewhere I read of a man who was afraid to sleep. Kipling wrote the story. This man arranged a spur so that when unconsciousness came, his naked body pressed against the iron teeth. Well, I've done the same. I look at the time, and I resolve that not until midnight, or not until one o'clock, or two o'clock, or three o'clock, shall the spur be removed. And so it rowels me awake until the appointed time. That spur has been my bed-mate for months. I have grown so desperate that five and a half hours of sleep is an extravagance. I sleep four hours now. I am starved for sleep. There are times when I am light-headed from want of sleep, times when death, with its rest and sleep, is a positive lure to me, times when I am haunted by Longfellow's lines:

> "'The sea is still and deep;
>
> All things within its bosom sleep;
>
> A single step and all is o'er,
>
> A plunge, a bubble, and no more.'

"Of course, this is sheer nonsense. It comes from nervousness, from an overwrought mind. But the point is: Why have I done this? For you. To shorten my apprenticeship. To compel Success to hasten. And my apprenticeship is now served. I know my equipment. I swear that I learn more each month than the average college man learns in a year. I know it, I tell you. But were my need for you to understand not so desperate I should not tell you. It is not boasting. I measure the results by the books. Your brothers, to-day, are ignorant barbarians compared with me and the knowledge I have wrung from the books in the hours they were sleeping. Long ago I wanted to be famous. I care very little for fame now. What I want is you; I am more hungry for you than for food, or clothing, or recognition. I have a dream of laying my head on your breast and sleeping an aeon or so, and the dream will come true ere another year is gone."

His power beat against her, wave upon wave; and in the moment his will opposed hers most she felt herself most strongly drawn toward him. The strength that had always poured out from him to her was now flowering in his impassioned voice, his flashing eyes, and the vigor of life and intellect surging in him. And in that moment, and for the moment, she was aware of a rift that showed in her certitude—a rift through which she caught sight of the real Martin Eden, splendid and invincible; and as animal-trainers have their moments of doubt, so she, for the instant, seemed to doubt her power to tame this wild spirit of a man.

"And another thing," he swept on. "You love me. But why do you love me? The thing in me that compels me to write is the very thing that draws your love. You love me because I am somehow different from the men you have known and might have loved. I was not made for the desk and counting-house, for petty business squabbling, and legal jangling. Make me do such things, make me like those other men, doing the work they do, breathing the air they breathe, developing the point of view they have developed, and you have destroyed the difference, destroyed me, destroyed the thing you love. My desire to write is the most vital thing in me. Had I been a mere clod, neither would I have desired to write, nor would you have desired me for a husband."

"But you forget," she interrupted, the quick surface of her mind glimpsing a parallel. "There have been eccentric inventors, starving their families while they sought such chimeras as perpetual motion. Doubtless their wives loved them, and suffered with them and for them, not because of but in spite of their infatuation for perpetual motion."

"True," was the reply. "But there have been inventors who were not eccentric and who starved while they sought to invent practical things; and sometimes, it is recorded, they succeeded. Certainly I do not seek any impossibilities—"

"You have called it 'achieving the impossible,'" she interpolated.

"I spoke figuratively. I seek to do what men have done before me—to write and to live by my writing."

Her silence spurred him on.

"To you, then, my goal is as much a chimera as perpetual motion?" he demanded.

He read her answer in the pressure of her hand on his—the pitying mother-hand for the hurt child. And to her, just then, he was the hurt child, the infatuated man striving to achieve the impossible.

Toward the close of their talk she warned him again of the antagonism of her father and mother.

"But you love me?" he asked.

"I do! I do!" she cried.

"And I love you, not them, and nothing they do can hurt me." Triumph sounded in his voice. "For I have faith in your love, not fear of their enmity. All things may go astray in this world, but not love. Love cannot go wrong unless it be a weakling that faints and stumbles by the way."

CHAPTER XXXI

Martin had encountered his sister Gertrude by chance on Broadway—as it proved, a most propitious yet disconcerting chance. Waiting on the corner for a car, she had seen him first, and noted the eager, hungry lines of his face and the desperate, worried look of his eyes. In truth, he was desperate and worried. He had just come from a fruitless interview with the pawnbroker, from whom he had tried to wring an additional loan on his wheel. The muddy fall weather having come on, Martin had pledged his wheel some time since and retained his black suit.

"There's the black suit," the pawnbroker, who knew his every asset, had answered. "You needn't tell me you've gone and pledged it with that Jew, Lipka. Because if you have—"

The man had looked the threat, and Martin hastened to cry:-

"No, no; I've got it. But I want to wear it on a matter of business."

"All right," the mollified usurer had replied. "And I want it on a matter of business before I can let you have any more money. You don't think I'm in it for my health?"

"But it's a forty-dollar wheel, in good condition," Martin had argued. "And you've only let me have seven dollars on it. No, not even seven. Six and a quarter; you took the interest in advance."

"If you want some more, bring the suit," had been the reply that sent Martin out of the stuffy little den, so desperate at heart as to reflect it in his face and touch his sister to pity.

Scarcely had they met when the Telegraph Avenue car came along and stopped to take on a crowd of afternoon shoppers. Mrs. Higginbotham divined from the grip on her arm as he helped her on, that he was not going to follow her. She turned on the step and looked down upon him. His haggard face smote her to the heart again.

"Ain't you comin'?" she asked

The next moment she had descended to his side.

"I'm walking—exercise, you know," he explained.

"Then I'll go along for a few blocks," she announced. "Mebbe it'll do me good. I ain't ben feelin' any too spry these last few days."

Martin glanced at her and verified her statement in her general slovenly appearance, in the unhealthy fat, in the drooping shoulders, the tired face with the sagging lines, and in the heavy fall of her feet, without elasticity—a very caricature of the walk that belongs to a free and happy body.

"You'd better stop here," he said, though she had already come to a halt at the first corner, "and take the next car."

"My goodness!—if I ain't all tired a'ready!" she panted. "But I'm just as able to walk as you in them soles. They're that thin they'll bu'st long before you git out to North Oakland."

"I've a better pair at home," was the answer.

"Come out to dinner to-morrow," she invited irrelevantly. "Mr. Higginbotham won't be there. He's goin' to San Leandro on business."

Martin shook his head, but he had failed to keep back the wolfish, hungry look that leapt into his eyes at the suggestion of dinner.

"You haven't a penny, Mart, and that's why you're walkin'. Exercise!" She tried to sniff contemptuously, but succeeded in producing only a sniffle. "Here, lemme see."

And, fumbling in her satchel, she pressed a five-dollar piece into his hand. "I guess I forgot your last birthday, Mart," she mumbled lamely.

Martin's hand instinctively closed on the piece of gold. In the same instant he knew he ought not to accept, and found himself struggling in the throes of indecision. That bit of gold meant food, life, and light in his body and brain, power to go on writing, and—who was to say?—maybe to write

690

something that would bring in many pieces of gold. Clear on his vision burned the manuscripts of two essays he had just completed. He saw them under the table on top of the heap of returned manuscripts for which he had no stamps, and he saw their titles, just as he had typed them—"The High Priests of Mystery," and "The Cradle of Beauty." He had never submitted them anywhere. They were as good as anything he had done in that line. If only he had stamps for them! Then the certitude of his ultimate success rose up in him, an able ally of hunger, and with a quick movement he slipped the coin into his pocket.

"I'll pay you back, Gertrude, a hundred times over," he gulped out, his throat painfully contracted and in his eyes a swift hint of moisture.

"Mark my words!" he cried with abrupt positiveness. "Before the year is out I'll put an even hundred of those little yellow-boys into your hand. I don't ask you to believe me. All you have to do is wait and see."

Nor did she believe. Her incredulity made her uncomfortable, and failing of other expedient, she said:-

"I know you're hungry, Mart. It's sticking out all over you. Come in to meals any time. I'll send one of the children to tell you when Mr. Higginbotham ain't to be there. An' Mart—"

He waited, though he knew in his secret heart what she was about to say, so visible was her thought process to him.

"Don't you think it's about time you got a job?"

"You don't think I'll win out?" he asked.

She shook her head.

"Nobody has faith in me, Gertrude, except myself." His voice was passionately rebellious. "I've done good work already, plenty of it, and sooner or later it will sell."

"How do you know it is good?"

"Because—" He faltered as the whole vast field of literature and the history of literature stirred in his brain and pointed the futility of his attempting to convey to her the reasons for his faith. "Well, because it's better than ninety-nine per cent of what is published in the magazines."

"I wish't you'd listen to reason," she answered feebly, but with unwavering belief in the correctness of her diagnosis of what was ailing him. "I wish't you'd listen to reason," she repeated, "an' come to dinner to-morrow."

After Martin had helped her on the car, he hurried to the post-office and invested three of the five dollars in stamps; and when, later in the day, on the way to the Morse home, he stopped in at the post-office to weigh a large number of long, bulky envelopes, he affixed to them all the stamps save three of the two-cent denomination.

It proved a momentous night for Martin, for after dinner he met Russ Brissenden. How he chanced to come there, whose friend he was or what acquaintance brought him, Martin did not know. Nor had he the curiosity to inquire about him of Ruth. In short, Brissenden struck Martin as anaemic and feather-brained, and was promptly dismissed from his mind. An hour later he decided that Brissenden was a boor as well, what of the way he prowled about from one room to another, staring at the pictures or poking his nose into books and magazines he picked up from the table or drew from the shelves. Though a stranger in the house he finally isolated himself in the midst of the company, huddling into a capacious Morris chair and reading steadily from a thin volume he had drawn from his pocket. As he read, he abstractedly ran his fingers, with a caressing movement, through his hair. Martin noticed him no more that evening, except once when he observed him chaffing with great apparent success with several of the young women.

It chanced that when Martin was leaving, he overtook Brissenden already half down the walk to the street.

"Hello, is that you?" Martin said.

The other replied with an ungracious grunt, but swung alongside. Martin made no further attempt at conversation, and for several blocks unbroken silence lay upon them.

"Pompous old ass!"

The suddenness and the virulence of the exclamation startled Martin. He felt amused, and at the same time was aware of a growing dislike for the other.

"What do you go to such a place for?" was abruptly flung at him after another block of silence.

"Why do you?" Martin countered.

"Bless me, I don't know," came back. "At least this is my first indiscretion. There are twenty-four hours in each day, and I must spend them somehow. Come and have a drink."

"All right," Martin answered.

The next moment he was nonplussed by the readiness of his acceptance. At home was several hours' hack-work waiting for him before he went to bed, and after he went to bed there was a volume of Weismann waiting for him, to say nothing of Herbert Spencer's Autobiography, which was as replete for him with romance as any thrilling novel. Why should he waste any time with this man he did not like? was his thought. And yet, it was not so much the man nor the drink as was it what was associated with the drink—the bright lights, the mirrors and dazzling array of glasses, the warm and glowing faces and the resonant hum of the voices of men. That was it, it was the voices of men, optimistic men, men who breathed success and spent their money for drinks like men. He was lonely, that was what was the matter with him; that was why he had snapped at the invitation as a bonita strikes at a white rag on a hook. Not since with Joe, at Shelly Hot Springs, with the one exception of the wine he took with the Portuguese grocer, had Martin had a drink at a public bar. Mental exhaustion did not produce a craving for liquor such as physical exhaustion did, and he had felt no need for it. But just now he felt desire for the drink, or, rather, for the atmosphere wherein drinks were dispensed and disposed of. Such a place was the Grotto, where Brissenden and he lounged in capacious leather chairs and drank Scotch and soda.

They talked. They talked about many things, and now Brissenden and now Martin took turn in ordering Scotch and soda. Martin, who was extremely strong-headed, marvelled at the other's capacity for liquor, and ever and anon broke off to marvel at the other's conversation. He was not long in assuming that Brissenden knew everything, and in deciding that here was the second intellectual man he had met. But he noted that Brissenden had what Professor Caldwell lacked—namely, fire, the flashing insight and perception, the flaming uncontrol of genius. Living language flowed from him. His thin lips, like the dies of a machine, stamped out phrases that cut and stung; or again, pursing caressingly about the inchoate sound they articulated, the thin lips shaped soft and velvety things, mellow phrases of glow and glory, of haunting beauty, reverberant of the mystery and inscrutableness of life; and yet again the thin lips were like a bugle, from which rang the crash and tumult of cosmic strife, phrases that sounded clear as silver, that were luminous as starry spaces, that epitomized the final word of science and yet said something more—the poet's word, the transcendental truth, elusive and without words which could express, and which none the less found expression in the subtle and all but ungraspable connotations of common words. He, by some wonder of vision, saw beyond the farthest outpost of empiricism, where was no language for narration, and yet, by some golden miracle of speech, investing known words with unknown significances, he conveyed to Martin's consciousness messages that were incommunicable to ordinary souls.

Martin forgot his first impression of dislike. Here was the best the books had to offer coming true. Here was an intelligence, a living man for him to look up to. "I am down in the dirt at your feet," Martin repeated to himself again and again.

"You've studied biology," he said aloud, in significant allusion.

To his surprise Brissenden shook his head.

"But you are stating truths that are substantiated only by biology," Martin insisted, and was rewarded by a blank stare. "Your conclusions are in line with the books which you must have read."

"I am glad to hear it," was the answer. "That my smattering of knowledge should enable me to short-cut my way to truth is most reassuring. As for myself, I never bother to find out if I am right or not. It is all valueless anyway. Man can never know the ultimate verities."

"You are a disciple of Spencer!" Martin cried triumphantly.

"I haven't read him since adolescence, and all I read then was his 'Education.'"

"I wish I could gather knowledge as carelessly," Martin broke out half an hour later. He had been closely analyzing Brissenden's mental equipment. "You are a sheer dogmatist, and that's what makes it so marvellous. You state dogmatically the latest facts which science has been able to establish only by *à posteriori* reasoning. You jump at correct conclusions. You certainly short-cut with a vengeance. You feel your way with the speed of light, by some hyperrational process, to truth."

"Yes, that was what used to bother Father Joseph, and Brother Dutton," Brissenden replied. "Oh, no," he added; "I am not anything. It was a lucky trick of fate that sent me to a Catholic college for my education. Where did you pick up what you know?"

And while Martin told him, he was busy studying Brissenden, ranging from a long, lean, aristocratic face and drooping shoulders to the overcoat on a neighboring chair, its pockets sagged and bulged by the freightage of many books. Brissenden's face and long, slender hands were browned by the sun—excessively browned, Martin thought. This sunburn bothered Martin. It was patent that Brissenden was no outdoor man. Then how had he been ravaged by the sun? Something morbid and significant attached to that sunburn, was Martin's thought as he returned to a study of the face, narrow, with high cheek-bones and cavernous hollows, and graced with as delicate and fine an aquiline nose as Martin had ever seen. There was nothing remarkable about the size of the eyes. They were neither large nor small, while their color was a nondescript brown; but in them smouldered a fire, or, rather, lurked an expression dual and strangely contradictory. Defiant, indomitable, even harsh to excess, they at the same time aroused pity. Martin found himself pitying him he knew not why, though he was soon to learn.

"Oh, I'm a lunger," Brissenden announced, offhand, a little later, having already stated that he came from Arizona. "I've been down there a couple of years living on the climate."

"Aren't you afraid to venture it up in this climate?"

"Afraid?"

There was no special emphasis of his repetition of Martin's word. But Martin saw in that ascetic face the advertisement that there was nothing of which it was afraid. The eyes had narrowed till they were eagle-like, and Martin almost caught his breath as he noted the eagle beak with its dilated nostrils, defiant, assertive, aggressive. Magnificent, was what he commented to himself, his blood thrilling at the sight. Aloud, he quoted:-

> "*Under the bludgeoning of Chance*
> *My head is bloody but unbowed.*"

"You like Henley," Brissenden said, his expression changing swiftly to large graciousness and tenderness. "Of course, I couldn't have expected anything else of you. Ah, Henley! A brave soul. He stands out among contemporary rhymesters—magazine rhymesters—as a gladiator stands out in the midst of a band of eunuchs."

"You don't like the magazines," Martin softly impeached.

"Do you?" was snarled back at him so savagely as to startle him.

"I—I write, or, rather, try to write, for the magazines," Martin faltered.

"That's better," was the mollified rejoinder. "You try to write, but you don't succeed. I respect and admire your failure. I know what you write. I can see it with half an eye, and there's one ingredient in it that shuts it out of the magazines. It's guts, and magazines have no use for that particular commodity. What they want is wish-wash and slush, and God knows they get it, but not from you."

"I'm not above hack-work," Martin contended.

"On the contrary—" Brissenden paused and ran an insolent eye over Martin's objective poverty, passing from the well-worn tie and the saw-edged collar to the shiny sleeves of the coat and on to the slight fray of one cuff, winding up and dwelling upon Martin's sunken cheeks. "On the contrary, hack-work is above you, so far above you that you can never hope to rise to it. Why, man, I could insult you by asking you to have something to eat."

Martin felt the heat in his face of the involuntary blood, and Brissenden laughed triumphantly.

"A full man is not insulted by such an invitation," he concluded.

"You are a devil," Martin cried irritably.

"Anyway, I didn't ask you."

"You didn't dare."

"Oh, I don't know about that. I invite you now."

Brissenden half rose from his chair as he spoke, as if with the intention of departing to the restaurant forthwith.

Martin's fists were tight-clenched, and his blood was drumming in his temples.

"Bosco! He eats 'em alive! Eats 'em alive!" Brissenden exclaimed, imitating the *spieler* of a locally famous snake-eater.

"I could certainly eat you alive," Martin said, in turn running insolent eyes over the other's disease-ravaged frame.

"Only I'm not worthy of it?"

"On the contrary," Martin considered, "because the incident is not worthy." He broke into a laugh, hearty and wholesome. "I confess you made a fool of me, Brissenden. That I am hungry and you are aware of it are only ordinary phenomena, and there's no disgrace. You see, I laugh at the conventional little moralities of the herd; then you drift by, say a sharp, true word, and immediately I am the slave of the same little moralities."

"You were insulted," Brissenden affirmed.

"I certainly was, a moment ago. The prejudice of early youth, you know. I learned such things then, and they cheapen what I have since learned. They are the skeletons in my particular closet."

"But you've got the door shut on them now?"

"I certainly have."

"Sure?"

"Sure."

"Then let's go and get something to eat."

"I'll go you," Martin answered, attempting to pay for the current Scotch and soda with the last change from his two dollars and seeing the waiter bullied by Brissenden into putting that change back on the table.

Martin pocketed it with a grimace, and felt for a moment the kindly weight of Brissenden's hand upon his shoulder.

CHAPTER XXXII

Promptly, the next afternoon, Maria was excited by Martin's second visitor. But she did not lose her head this time, for she seated Brissenden in her parlor's grandeur of respectability.

"Hope you don't mind my coming?" Brissenden began.

"No, no, not at all," Martin answered, shaking hands and waving him to the solitary chair, himself taking to the bed. "But how did you know where I lived?"

"Called up the Morses. Miss Morse answered the 'phone. And here I am." He tugged at his coat pocket and flung a thin volume on the table. "There's a book, by a poet. Read it and keep it." And then, in reply to Martin's protest: "What have I to do with books? I had another hemorrhage this morning. Got any whiskey? No, of course not. Wait a minute."

He was off and away. Martin watched his long figure go down the outside steps, and, on turning to close the gate, noted with a pang the shoulders, which had once been broad, drawn in now over, the collapsed ruin of the chest. Martin got two tumblers, and fell to reading the book of verse, Henry Vaughn Marlow's latest collection.

"No Scotch," Brissenden announced on his return. "The beggar sells nothing but American whiskey. But here's a quart of it."

"I'll send one of the youngsters for lemons, and we'll make a toddy," Martin offered.

"I wonder what a book like that will earn Marlow?" he went on, holding up the volume in question.

"Possibly fifty dollars," came the answer. "Though he's lucky if he pulls even on it, or if he can inveigle a publisher to risk bringing it out."

"Then one can't make a living out of poetry?"

Martin's tone and face alike showed his dejection.

"Certainly not. What fool expects to? Out of rhyming, yes. There's Bruce, and Virginia Spring, and Sedgwick. They do very nicely. But poetry—do you know how Vaughn Marlow makes his living?—teaching in a boys' cramming-joint down in Pennsylvania, and of all private little hells such a billet is the limit. I wouldn't trade places with him if he had fifty years of life before him. And yet his work stands out from the ruck of the contemporary versifiers as a balas ruby among carrots. And the reviews he gets! Damn them, all of them, the crass manikins!"

"Too much is written by the men who can't write about the men who do write," Martin concurred. "Why, I was appalled at the quantities of rubbish written about Stevenson and his work."

"Ghouls and harpies!" Brissenden snapped out with clicking teeth. "Yes, I know the spawn—complacently pecking at him for his Father Damien letter, analyzing him, weighing him—"

"Measuring him by the yardstick of their own miserable egos," Martin broke in.

"Yes, that's it, a good phrase,—mouthing and besliming the True, and Beautiful, and Good, and finally patting him on the back and saying, 'Good dog, Fido.' Faugh! 'The little chattering daws of men,' Richard Realf called them the night he died."

"Pecking at star-dust," Martin took up the strain warmly; "at the meteoric flight of the master-men. I once wrote a squib on them—the critics, or the reviewers, rather."

"Let's see it," Brissenden begged eagerly.

So Martin unearthed a carbon copy of "Star-dust," and during the reading of it Brissenden chuckled, rubbed his hands, and forgot to sip his toddy.

"Strikes me you're a bit of star-dust yourself, flung into a world of cowled gnomes who cannot see," was his comment at the end of it. "Of course it was snapped up by the first magazine?"

700

Martin ran over the pages of his manuscript book. "It has been refused by twenty-seven of them."

Brissenden essayed a long and hearty laugh, but broke down in a fit of coughing.

"Say, you needn't tell me you haven't tackled poetry," he gasped. "Let me see some of it."

"Don't read it now," Martin pleaded. "I want to talk with you. I'll make up a bundle and you can take it home."

Brissenden departed with the "Love-cycle," and "The Peri and the Pearl," returning next day to greet Martin with:-

"I want more."

Not only did he assure Martin that he was a poet, but Martin learned that Brissenden also was one. He was swept off his feet by the other's work, and astounded that no attempt had been made to publish it.

"A plague on all their houses!" was Brissenden's answer to Martin's volunteering to market his work for him. "Love Beauty for its own sake," was his counsel, "and leave the magazines alone. Back to your ships and your sea—that's my advice to you, Martin Eden. What do you want in these sick and rotten cities of men? You are cutting your throat every day you waste in them trying to prostitute beauty to the needs of magazinedom. What was it you quoted me the other day?—Oh, yes, 'Man, the latest of the ephemera.' Well, what do you, the latest of the ephemera, want with fame? If you got it, it would be poison to you. You are too simple, too elemental, and too rational, by my faith, to prosper on such pap. I hope you never do sell a line to the magazines. Beauty is the only master to serve. Serve her and damn the multitude! Success! What in hell's success if it isn't right there in your Stevenson sonnet, which outranks Henley's 'Apparition,' in that 'Love-cycle,' in those sea-poems?

"It is not in what you succeed in doing that you get your joy, but in the doing of it. You can't tell me. I know it. You know it. Beauty hurts you. It is an everlasting pain in you, a wound that does not heal, a knife of flame. Why should you palter with magazines? Let beauty be your end. Why should you mint beauty into gold? Anyway, you can't; so there's no use in my getting excited over it. You can read the magazines for a thousand years and you won't find the value of one line of Keats. Leave fame and coin alone, sign away on a ship to-morrow, and go back to your sea."

"Not for fame, but for love," Martin laughed. "Love seems to have no place in your Cosmos; in mine, Beauty is the handmaiden of Love."

Brissenden looked at him pityingly and admiringly. "You are so young, Martin boy, so young. You will flutter high, but your wings are of the finest gauze, dusted with the fairest pigments. Do not scorch them. But of course you have scorched them already. It required some glorified petticoat to account for that 'Love-cycle,' and that's the shame of it."

"It glorifies love as well as the petticoat," Martin laughed.

"The philosophy of madness," was the retort. "So have I assured myself when wandering in hasheesh dreams. But beware. These bourgeois cities will kill you. Look at that den of traitors where I met you. Dry rot is no name for it. One can't keep his sanity in such an atmosphere. It's degrading. There's not one of them who is not degrading, man and woman, all of them animated stomachs guided by the high intellectual and artistic impulses of clams—"

He broke off suddenly and regarded Martin. Then, with a flash of divination, he saw the situation. The expression on his face turned to wondering horror.

"And you wrote that tremendous 'Love-cycle' to her—that pale, shrivelled, female thing!"

The next instant Martin's right hand had shot to a throttling clutch on his throat, and he was being shaken till his teeth rattled. But Martin, looking into his eyes, saw no fear there,—naught but a curious and mocking devil. Martin remembered himself, and flung Brissenden, by the neck, sidelong upon the bed, at the same moment releasing his hold.

702

Brissenden panted and gasped painfully for a moment, then began to chuckle.

"You had made me eternally your debtor had you shaken out the flame," he said.

"My nerves are on a hair-trigger these days," Martin apologized. "Hope I didn't hurt you. Here, let me mix a fresh toddy."

"Ah, you young Greek!" Brissenden went on. "I wonder if you take just pride in that body of yours. You are devilish strong. You are a young panther, a lion cub. Well, well, it is you who must pay for that strength."

"What do you mean?" Martin asked curiously, passing aim a glass. "Here, down this and be good."

"Because—" Brissenden sipped his toddy and smiled appreciation of it. "Because of the women. They will worry you until you die, as they have already worried you, or else I was born yesterday. Now there's no use in your choking me; I'm going to have my say. This is undoubtedly your calf love; but for Beauty's sake show better taste next time. What under heaven do you want with a daughter of the bourgeoisie? Leave them alone. Pick out some great, wanton flame of a woman, who laughs at life and jeers at death and loves one while she may. There are such women, and they will love you just as readily as any pusillanimous product of bourgeois sheltered life."

"Pusillanimous?" Martin protested.

"Just so, pusillanimous; prattling out little moralities that have been prattled into them, and afraid to live life. They will love you, Martin, but they will love their little moralities more. What you want is the magnificent abandon of life, the great free souls, the blazing butterflies and not the little gray moths. Oh, you will grow tired of them, too, of all the female things, if you are unlucky enough to live. But you won't live. You won't go back to your ships and sea; therefore, you'll hang around these pest-holes of cities until your bones are rotten, and then you'll die."

"You can lecture me, but you can't make me talk back," Martin said. "After all, you have but the wisdom of your temperament, and the wisdom of my temperament is just as unimpeachable as yours."

They disagreed about love, and the magazines, and many things, but they liked each other, and on Martin's part it was no less than a profound liking. Day after day they were together, if for no more than the hour Brissenden spent in Martin's stuffy room. Brissenden never arrived without his quart of whiskey, and when they dined together down-town, he drank Scotch and soda throughout the meal. He invariably paid the way for both, and it was through him that Martin learned the refinements of food, drank his first champagne, and made acquaintance with Rhenish wines.

But Brissenden was always an enigma. With the face of an ascetic, he was, in all the failing blood of him, a frank voluptuary. He was unafraid to die, bitter and cynical of all the ways of living; and yet, dying, he loved life, to the last atom of it. He was possessed by a madness to live, to thrill, "to squirm my little space in the cosmic dust whence I came," as he phrased it once himself. He had tampered with drugs and done many strange things in quest of new thrills, new sensations. As he told Martin, he had once gone three days without water, had done so voluntarily, in order to experience the exquisite delight of such a thirst assuaged. Who or what he was, Martin never learned. He was a man without a past, whose future was the imminent grave and whose present was a bitter fever of living.

CHAPTER XXXIII

Martin was steadily losing his battle. Economize as he would, the earnings from hack-work did not balance expenses. Thanksgiving found him with his black suit in pawn and unable to accept the Morses' invitation to dinner. Ruth was not made happy by his reason for not coming, and the corresponding effect on him was one of desperation. He told her that he would come, after all; that he would go over to San Francisco, to the *Transcontinental* office, collect the five dollars due him, and with it redeem his suit of clothes.

In the morning he borrowed ten cents from Maria. He would have borrowed it, by preference, from Brissenden, but that erratic individual had disappeared. Two weeks had passed since Martin had seen him, and he vainly cudgelled his brains for some cause of offence. The ten cents carried Martin across the ferry to San Francisco, and as he walked up Market Street he speculated upon his predicament in case he failed to collect the money. There would then be no way for him to return to Oakland, and he knew no one in San Francisco from whom to borrow another ten cents.

The door to the *Transcontinental* office was ajar, and Martin, in the act of opening it, was brought to a sudden pause by a loud voice from within, which exclaimed:- "But that is not the question, Mr. Ford." (Ford, Martin knew, from his correspondence, to be the editor's name.) "The question is, are you prepared to pay?—cash, and cash down, I mean? I am not interested in the prospects of the *Transcontinental* and what you expect to make it next year. What I want is to be paid for what I do. And I tell you, right now, the Christmas *Transcontinental* don't go to press till I have the money in my hand. Good day. When you get the money, come and see me."

The door jerked open, and the man flung past Martin, with an angry countenance and went down the corridor, muttering curses and clenching his fists. Martin decided not to enter immediately, and lingered in the hallways for a quarter of an hour. Then he shoved the door open and walked in. It was a new experience, the first time he had been inside an editorial office. Cards evidently were not necessary in that office, for the boy carried word to an inner room that there was a man who wanted to see Mr. Ford. Returning, the boy beckoned him from halfway across the room and led him to the private office, the editorial sanctum. Martin's first impression was of the disorder and cluttered confusion of the room. Next he noticed a bewhiskered, youthful-looking man, sitting at a roll-top desk, who regarded him curiously. Martin marvelled at the calm repose of his face. It was evident that the squabble with the printer had not affected his equanimity.

"I—I am Martin Eden," Martin began the conversation. ("And I want my five dollars," was what he would have liked to say.)

But this was his first editor, and under the circumstances he did not desire to scare him too abruptly. To his surprise, Mr. Ford leaped into the air with a "You don't say so!" and the next moment, with both hands, was shaking Martin's hand effusively.

"Can't say how glad I am to see you, Mr. Eden. Often wondered what you were like."

Here he held Martin off at arm's length and ran his beaming eyes over Martin's second-best suit, which was also his worst suit, and which was ragged and past repair, though the trousers showed the careful crease he had put in with Maria's flat-irons.

"I confess, though, I conceived you to be a much older man than you are. Your story, you know, showed such breadth, and vigor, such maturity and depth of thought. A masterpiece, that story—I knew it when I had read the first half-dozen lines. Let me tell you how I first read it. But no; first let me introduce you to the staff."

Still talking, Mr. Ford led him into the general office, where he introduced him to the associate editor, Mr. White, a slender, frail little man whose hand seemed strangely cold, as if he were suffering from a chill, and whose whiskers were sparse and silky.

"And Mr. Ends, Mr. Eden. Mr. Ends is our business manager, you know."

Martin found himself shaking hands with a cranky-eyed, bald-headed man, whose face looked youthful enough from what little could be seen of it, for most of it was covered by a snow-white beard, carefully trimmed—by his wife, who did it on Sundays, at which times she also shaved the back of his neck.

The three men surrounded Martin, all talking admiringly and at once, until it seemed to him that they were talking against time for a wager.

"We often wondered why you didn't call," Mr. White was saying.

"I didn't have the carfare, and I live across the Bay," Martin answered bluntly, with the idea of showing them his imperative need for the money.

Surely, he thought to himself, my glad rags in themselves are eloquent advertisement of my need. Time and again, whenever opportunity offered, he hinted about the purpose of his business. But his admirers' ears were deaf. They sang his praises, told him what they had thought of his story at first sight, what they subsequently thought, what their wives and families thought; but not one hint did they breathe of intention to pay him for it.

"Did I tell you how I first read your story?" Mr. Ford said. "Of course I didn't. I was coming west from New York, and when the train stopped at Ogden, the train-boy on the new run brought aboard the current number of the *Transcontinental*."

My God! Martin thought; you can travel in a Pullman while I starve for the paltry five dollars you owe me. A wave of anger rushed over him. The wrong done him by the *Transcontinental* loomed colossal, for strong upon him were all the dreary months of vain yearning, of hunger and privation, and his present hunger awoke and gnawed at him, reminding him that he had eaten nothing since the day before, and little enough then. For the moment he saw red. These creatures were not even robbers. They were sneak-thieves. By lies and broken promises they had tricked him out of his story. Well, he would show them. And a great resolve surged into his will to the effect that he would not leave the office until he got his money. He remembered, if he did not get it, that there was no way for him to go back to Oakland. He controlled himself with an effort, but not before the wolfish expression of his face had awed and perturbed them.

They became more voluble than ever. Mr. Ford started anew to tell how he had first read "The Ring of Bells," and Mr. Ends at the same time was striving to repeat his niece's appreciation of "The Ring of Bells," said niece being a school-teacher in Alameda.

"I'll tell you what I came for," Martin said finally. "To be paid for that story all of you like so well. Five dollars, I believe, is what you promised me would be paid on publication."

Mr. Ford, with an expression on his mobile features of mediate and happy acquiescence, started to reach for his pocket, then turned suddenly to Mr. Ends, and said that he had left his money home. That Mr. Ends resented this, was patent; and Martin saw the twitch of his arm as if to protect his trousers pocket. Martin knew that the money was there.

"I am sorry," said Mr. Ends, "but I paid the printer not an hour ago, and he took my ready change. It was careless of me to be so short; but the bill was not yet due, and the printer's request, as a favor, to make an immediate advance, was quite unexpected."

Both men looked expectantly at Mr. White, but that gentleman laughed and shrugged his shoulders. His conscience was clean at any rate. He had come into the *Transcontinental* to learn magazine-literature, instead of which he had principally learned finance. The *Transcontinental* owed him four months' salary, and he knew that the printer must be appeased before the associate editor.

"It's rather absurd, Mr. Eden, to have caught us in this shape," Mr. Ford preambled airily. "All carelessness, I assure you. But I'll tell you what we'll do. We'll mail you a check the first thing in the morning. You have Mr. Eden's address, haven't you, Mr. Ends?"

Yes, Mr. Ends had the address, and the check would be mailed the first thing in the morning. Martin's knowledge of banks and checks was hazy, but he could see no reason why they should not give him the check on this day just as well as on the next.

"Then it is understood, Mr. Eden, that we'll mail you the check to-morrow?" Mr. Ford said.

"I need the money to-day," Martin answered stolidly.

"The unfortunate circumstances—if you had chanced here any other day," Mr. Ford began suavely, only to be interrupted by Mr. Ends, whose cranky eyes justified themselves in his shortness of temper.

"Mr. Ford has already explained the situation," he said with asperity. "And so have I. The check will be mailed—"

"I also have explained," Martin broke in, "and I have explained that I want the money to-day."

He had felt his pulse quicken a trifle at the business manager's brusqueness, and upon him he kept an alert eye, for it was in that gentleman's trousers pocket that he divined the *Transcontinental's* ready cash was reposing.

"It is too bad—" Mr. Ford began.

But at that moment, with an impatient movement, Mr. Ends turned as if about to leave the room. At the same instant Martin sprang for him, clutching him by the throat with one hand in such fashion that Mr. Ends' snow-white beard, still maintaining its immaculate trimness, pointed ceilingward at an angle of forty-five degrees. To the horror of Mr. White and Mr. Ford, they saw their business manager shaken like an Astrakhan rug.

"Dig up, you venerable discourager of rising young talent!" Martin exhorted. "Dig up, or I'll shake it out of you, even if it's all in nickels." Then, to the two affrighted onlookers: "Keep away! If you interfere, somebody's liable to get hurt."

Mr. Ends was choking, and it was not until the grip on his throat was eased that he was able to signify his acquiescence in the digging-up programme. All together, after repeated digs, its trousers pocket yielded four dollars and fifteen cents.

"Inside out with it," Martin commanded.

An additional ten cents fell out. Martin counted the result of his raid a second time to make sure.

"You next!" he shouted at Mr. Ford. "I want seventy-five cents more."

Mr. Ford did not wait, but ransacked his pockets, with the result of sixty cents.

"Sure that is all?" Martin demanded menacingly, possessing himself of it. "What have you got in your vest pockets?"

In token of his good faith, Mr. Ford turned two of his pockets inside out. A strip of cardboard fell to the floor from one of them. He recovered it and was in the act of returning it, when Martin cried:-

"What's that?—A ferry ticket? Here, give it to me. It's worth ten cents. I'll credit you with it. I've now got four dollars and ninety-five cents, including the ticket. Five cents is still due me."

He looked fiercely at Mr. White, and found that fragile creature in the act of handing him a nickel.

"Thank you," Martin said, addressing them collectively. "I wish you a good day."

"Robber!" Mr. Ends snarled after him.

"Sneak-thief!" Martin retorted, slamming the door as he passed out.

Martin was elated—so elated that when he recollected that The Hornet owed him fifteen dollars for "The Peri and the Pearl," he decided forthwith to go and collect it. But The Hornet was run by a set of clean-shaven, strapping young men, frank buccaneers who robbed everything and everybody, not excepting one another. After some breakage of the office furniture, the editor (an ex-college athlete), ably assisted by the business manager, an advertising agent, and the porter, succeeded in removing Martin from the office and in accelerating, by initial impulse, his descent of the first flight of stairs.

"Come again, Mr. Eden; glad to see you any time," they laughed down at him from the landing above.

Martin grinned as he picked himself up.

"Phew!" he murmured back. "The *Transcontinental* crowd were nanny-goats, but you fellows are a lot of prize-fighters."

More laughter greeted this.

"I must say, Mr. Eden," the editor of The Hornet called down, "that for a poet you can go some yourself. Where did you learn that right cross—if I may ask?"

"Where you learned that half-Nelson," Martin answered. "Anyway, you're going to have a black eye."

"I hope your neck doesn't stiffen up," the editor wished solicitously: "What do you say we all go out and have a drink on it—not the neck, of course, but the little rough-house?"

"I'll go you if I lose," Martin accepted.

And robbers and robbed drank together, amicably agreeing that the battle was to the strong, and that the fifteen dollars for "The Peri and the Pearl" belonged by right to *The Hornet's* editorial staff.

CHAPTER XXXIV

Arthur remained at the gate while Ruth climbed Maria's front steps. She heard the rapid click of the type-writer, and when Martin let her in, found him on the last page of a manuscript. She had come to make certain whether or not he would be at their table for Thanksgiving dinner; but before she could broach the subject Martin plunged into the one with which he was full.

"Here, let me read you this," he cried, separating the carbon copies and running the pages of manuscript into shape. "It's my latest, and different from anything I've done. It is so altogether different that I am almost afraid of it, and yet I've a sneaking idea it is good. You be judge. It's an Hawaiian story. I've called it 'Wiki-wiki.'"

His face was bright with the creative glow, though she shivered in the cold room and had been struck by the coldness of his hands at greeting. She listened closely while he read, and though he from time to time had seen only disapprobation in her face, at the close he asked:-

"Frankly, what do you think of it?"

"I—I don't know," she, answered. "Will it—do you think it will sell?"

"I'm afraid not," was the confession. "It's too strong for the magazines. But it's true, on my word it's true."

"But why do you persist in writing such things when you know they won't sell?" she went on inexorably. "The reason for your writing is to make a living, isn't it?"

"Yes, that's right; but the miserable story got away with me. I couldn't help writing it. It demanded to be written."

"But that character, that Wiki-Wiki, why do you make him talk so roughly? Surely it will offend your readers, and surely that is why the editors are justified in refusing your work."

"Because the real Wiki-Wiki would have talked that way."

"But it is not good taste."

"It is life," he replied bluntly. "It is real. It is true. And I must write life as I see it."

She made no answer, and for an awkward moment they sat silent. It was because he loved her that he did not quite understand her, and she could not understand him because he was so large that he bulked beyond her horizon.

"Well, I've collected from the *Transcontinental*," he said in an effort to shift the conversation to a more comfortable subject. The picture of the bewhiskered trio, as he had last seen them, mulcted of four dollars and ninety cents and a ferry ticket, made him chuckle.

"Then you'll come!" she cried joyously. "That was what I came to find out."

"Come?" he muttered absently. "Where?"

"Why, to dinner to-morrow. You know you said you'd recover your suit if you got that money."

"I forgot all about it," he said humbly. "You see, this morning the poundman got Maria's two cows and the baby calf, and—well, it happened that Maria didn't have any money, and so I had to recover her cows for her. That's where the *Transcontinental* fiver went—'The Ring of Bells' went into the poundman's pocket."

"Then you won't come?"

He looked down at his clothing.

"I can't."

Tears of disappointment and reproach glistened in her blue eyes, but she said nothing.

"Next Thanksgiving you'll have dinner with me in Delmonico's," he said cheerily; "or in London, or Paris, or anywhere you wish. I know it."

"I saw in the paper a few days ago," she announced abruptly, "that there had been several local appointments to the Railway Mail. You passed first, didn't you?"

He was compelled to admit that the call had come for him, but that he had declined it. "I was so sure—I am so sure—of myself," he concluded. "A year from now I'll be earning more than a dozen men in the Railway Mail. You wait and see."

"Oh," was all she said, when he finished. She stood up, pulling at her gloves. "I must go, Martin. Arthur is waiting for me."

He took her in his arms and kissed her, but she proved a passive sweetheart. There was no tenseness in her body, her arms did not go around him, and her lips met his without their wonted pressure.

She was angry with him, he concluded, as he returned from the gate. But why? It was unfortunate that the poundman had gobbled Maria's cows. But it was only a stroke of fate. Nobody could be blamed for it. Nor did it enter his head that he could have done aught otherwise than what he had done. Well, yes, he was to blame a little, was his next thought, for having refused the call to the Railway Mail. And she had not liked "Wiki-Wiki."

He turned at the head of the steps to meet the letter-carrier on his afternoon round. The ever recurrent fever of expectancy assailed Martin as he took the bundle of long envelopes. One was not long. It was short and thin, and outside was printed the address of *The New York Outview*. He paused in the act of tearing the envelope open. It could not be an acceptance. He had no manuscripts with that publication. Perhaps—his heart almost stood still at the—wild thought—perhaps they were ordering an article from him; but the next instant he dismissed the surmise as hopelessly impossible.

It was a short, formal letter, signed by the office editor, merely informing him that an anonymous letter which they had received was enclosed, and that he could rest assured the *Outview's* staff never under any circumstances gave consideration to anonymous correspondence.

The enclosed letter Martin found to be crudely printed by hand. It was a hotchpotch of illiterate abuse of Martin, and of assertion that the "so-called Martin Eden" who was selling stories to magazines was no writer at all, and that in reality he was stealing stories from old magazines, typing them, and sending them out as his own. The envelope was postmarked "San Leandro." Martin did not require a second thought to discover the author. Higginbotham's grammar, Higginbotham's colloquialisms, Higginbotham's mental quirks and processes, were apparent throughout. Martin saw in every line, not the fine Italian hand, but the coarse grocer's fist, of his brother-in-law.

But why? he vainly questioned. What injury had he done Bernard Higginbotham? The thing was so unreasonable, so wanton. There was no explaining it. In the course of the week a dozen similar letters were forwarded to Martin by the editors of various Eastern magazines. The editors were behaving handsomely, Martin concluded. He was wholly unknown to them, yet some of them had even been sympathetic. It was evident that they detested anonymity. He saw that the malicious attempt to hurt him had failed. In fact, if anything came of it, it was bound to be good, for at least his name had been called to the attention of a number of editors. Sometime, perhaps, reading a submitted manuscript of his, they might remember him as the fellow about whom they had received an anonymous letter. And who was to say that such a remembrance might not sway the balance of their judgment just a trifle in his favor?

It was about this time that Martin took a great slump in Maria's estimation. He found her in the kitchen one morning groaning with pain, tears of weakness running down her cheeks, vainly endeavoring to put through a large ironing. He promptly diagnosed her affliction as La Grippe, dosed her with hot whiskey (the remnants in the bottles for which Brissenden was responsible), and ordered her to bed. But Maria was refractory. The ironing had to be done, she protested, and delivered that night, or else there would be no food on the morrow for the seven small and hungry Silvas.

To her astonishment (and it was something that she never ceased from relating to her dying day), she saw Martin Eden seize an iron from the stove and throw a fancy shirt-waist on the ironing-board. It was Kate Flanagan's best Sunday waist, than whom there was no more exacting and fastidiously dressed woman in Maria's world. Also, Miss Flanagan had sent special instruction that said waist must be delivered by that night. As every one knew, she was keeping company with John Collins, the blacksmith, and, as Maria knew privily, Miss Flanagan and Mr. Collins were going next day to Golden Gate Park. Vain was Maria's attempt to rescue the garment. Martin guided her tottering footsteps to a chair, from where she watched him with bulging eyes. In a quarter of the time it would have taken her she saw the shirt-waist safely ironed, and ironed as well as she could have done it, as Martin made her grant.

"I could work faster," he explained, "if your irons were only hotter."

To her, the irons he swung were much hotter than she ever dared to use.

"Your sprinkling is all wrong," he complained next. "Here, let me teach you how to sprinkle. Pressure is what's wanted. Sprinkle under pressure if you want to iron fast."

He procured a packing-case from the woodpile in the cellar, fitted a cover to it, and raided the scrap-iron the Silva tribe was collecting for the junkman. With fresh-sprinkled garments in the box, covered with the board and pressed by the iron, the device was complete and in operation.

"Now you watch me, Maria," he said, stripping off to his undershirt and gripping an iron that was what he called "really hot."

"An' when he feenish da iron' he washa da wools," as she described it afterward. "He say, 'Maria, you are da greata fool. I showa you how to washa da wools,' an' he shows me, too. Ten minutes he maka da machine—one barrel, one wheel-hub, two poles, justa like dat."

Martin had learned the contrivance from Joe at the Shelly Hot Springs. The old wheel-hub, fixed on the end of the upright pole, constituted the plunger. Making this, in turn, fast to the spring-pole attached to the kitchen rafters, so that the hub played upon the woollens in the barrel, he was able, with one hand, thoroughly to pound them.

716

"No more Maria washa da wools," her story always ended. "I maka da kids worka da pole an' da hub an' da barrel. Him da smarta man, Mister Eden."

Nevertheless, by his masterly operation and improvement of her kitchen-laundry he fell an immense distance in her regard. The glamour of romance with which her imagination had invested him faded away in the cold light of fact that he was an ex-laundryman. All his books, and his grand friends who visited him in carriages or with countless bottles of whiskey, went for naught. He was, after all, a mere workingman, a member of her own class and caste. He was more human and approachable, but, he was no longer mystery.

Martin's alienation from his family continued. Following upon Mr. Higginbotham's unprovoked attack, Mr. Hermann von Schmidt showed his hand. The fortunate sale of several storiettes, some humorous verse, and a few jokes gave Martin a temporary splurge of prosperity. Not only did he partially pay up his bills, but he had sufficient balance left to redeem his black suit and wheel. The latter, by virtue of a twisted crank-hanger, required repairing, and, as a matter of friendliness with his future brother-in-law, he sent it to Von Schmidt's shop.

The afternoon of the same day Martin was pleased by the wheel being delivered by a small boy. Von Schmidt was also inclined to be friendly, was Martin's conclusion from this unusual favor. Repaired wheels usually had to be called for. But when he examined the wheel, he discovered no repairs had been made. A little later in the day he telephoned his sister's betrothed, and learned that that person didn't want anything to do with him in "any shape, manner, or form."

"Hermann von Schmidt," Martin answered cheerfully, "I've a good mind to come over and punch that Dutch nose of yours."

"You come to my shop," came the reply, "an' I'll send for the police. An' I'll put you through, too. Oh, I know you, but you can't make no rough-house with me. I don't want nothin' to do with the likes of you. You're a loafer, that's what, an' I ain't asleep. You ain't goin' to do no spongin' off me just because I'm marryin' your sister. Why don't you go to work an' earn an honest livin', eh? Answer me that."

Martin's philosophy asserted itself, dissipating his anger, and he hung up the receiver with a long whistle of incredulous amusement. But after the amusement came the reaction, and he was oppressed by his loneliness. Nobody understood him, nobody seemed to have any use for him, except Brissenden, and Brissenden had disappeared, God alone knew where.

Twilight was falling as Martin left the fruit store and turned homeward, his marketing on his arm. At the corner an electric car had stopped, and at sight of a lean, familiar figure alighting, his heart leapt with joy. It was Brissenden, and in the fleeting glimpse, ere the car started up, Martin noted the overcoat pockets, one bulging with books, the other bulging with a quart bottle of whiskey.

CHAPTER XXXV

Brissenden gave no explanation of his long absence, nor did Martin pry into it. He was content to see his friend's cadaverous face opposite him through the steam rising from a tumbler of toddy.

"I, too, have not been idle," Brissenden proclaimed, after hearing Martin's account of the work he had accomplished.

He pulled a manuscript from his inside coat pocket and passed it to Martin, who looked at the title and glanced up curiously.

"Yes, that's it," Brissenden laughed. "Pretty good title, eh? 'Ephemera'— it is the one word. And you're responsible for it, what of your *man*, who is always the erected, the vitalized inorganic, the latest of the ephemera, the creature of temperature strutting his little space on the thermometer. It got into my head and I had to write it to get rid of it. Tell me what you think of it."

Martin's face, flushed at first, paled as he read on. It was perfect art. Form triumphed over substance, if triumph it could be called where the last conceivable atom of substance had found expression in so perfect construction as to make Martin's head swim with delight, to put passionate tears into his eyes, and to send chills creeping up and down his back. It was a long poem of six or seven hundred lines, and it was a fantastic, amazing, unearthly thing. It was terrific, impossible; and yet there it was, scrawled in black ink across the sheets of paper. It dealt with man and his soul-gropings in their ultimate terms, plumbing the abysses of space for the testimony of remotest suns and rainbow spectrums. It was a mad orgy of imagination, wassailing in the skull of a dying man who half sobbed under his breath and was quick with the wild flutter of fading heart-beats. The poem swung in majestic rhythm to the cool tumult of interstellar conflict, to the onset of starry hosts, to the impact of cold suns and the flaming up of nebulae in the darkened void; and through it all, unceasing and faint, like a silver shuttle, ran the frail, piping voice of man, a querulous chirp amid the screaming of planets and the crash of systems.

"There is nothing like it in literature," Martin said, when at last he was able to speak. "It's wonderful!—wonderful! It has gone to my head. I am drunken with it. That great, infinitesimal question—I can't shake it out of my thoughts. That questing, eternal, ever recurring, thin little wailing voice of man is still ringing in my ears. It is like the dead-march of a gnat amid the trumpeting of elephants and the roaring of lions. It is insatiable with microscopic desire. I now I'm making a fool of myself, but the thing has obsessed me. You are—I don't know what you are—you are wonderful, that's all. But how do you do it? How do you do it?"

Martin paused from his rhapsody, only to break out afresh.

"I shall never write again. I am a dauber in clay. You have shown me the work of the real artificer-artisan. Genius! This is something more than genius. It transcends genius. It is truth gone mad. It is true, man, every line of it. I wonder if you realize that, you dogmatist. Science cannot give you the lie. It is the truth of the sneer, stamped out from the black iron of the Cosmos and interwoven with mighty rhythms of sound into a fabric of splendor and beauty. And now I won't say another word. I am overwhelmed, crushed. Yes, I will, too. Let me market it for you."

Brissenden grinned. "There's not a magazine in Christendom that would dare to publish it—you know that."

"I know nothing of the sort. I know there's not a magazine in Christendom that wouldn't jump at it. They don't get things like that every day. That's no mere poem of the year. It's the poem of the century."

"I'd like to take you up on the proposition."

"Now don't get cynical," Martin exhorted. "The magazine editors are not wholly fatuous. I know that. And I'll close with you on the bet. I'll wager anything you want that 'Ephemera' is accepted either on the first or second offering."

"There's just one thing that prevents me from taking you." Brissenden waited a moment. "The thing is big—the biggest I've ever done. I know that. It's my swan song. I am almighty proud of it. I worship it. It's better than

720

whiskey. It is what I dreamed of—the great and perfect thing—when I was a simple young man, with sweet illusions and clean ideals. And I've got it, now, in my last grasp, and I'll not have it pawed over and soiled by a lot of swine. No, I won't take the bet. It's mine. I made it, and I've shared it with you."

"But think of the rest of the world," Martin protested. "The function of beauty is joy-making."

"It's my beauty."

"Don't be selfish."

"I'm not selfish." Brissenden grinned soberly in the way he had when pleased by the thing his thin lips were about to shape. "I'm as unselfish as a famished hog."

In vain Martin strove to shake him from his decision. Martin told him that his hatred of the magazines was rabid, fanatical, and that his conduct was a thousand times more despicable than that of the youth who burned the temple of Diana at Ephesus. Under the storm of denunciation Brissenden complacently sipped his toddy and affirmed that everything the other said was quite true, with the exception of the magazine editors. His hatred of them knew no bounds, and he excelled Martin in denunciation when he turned upon them.

"I wish you'd type it for me," he said. "You know how a thousand times better than any stenographer. And now I want to give you some advice." He drew a bulky manuscript from his outside coat pocket. "Here's your 'Shame of the Sun.' I've read it not once, but twice and three times—the highest compliment I can pay you. After what you've said about 'Ephemera' I must be silent. But this I will say: when 'The Shame of the Sun' is published, it will make a hit. It will start a controversy that will be worth thousands to you just in advertising."

Martin laughed. "I suppose your next advice will be to submit it to the magazines."

"By all means no—that is, if you want to see it in print. Offer it to the first-class houses. Some publisher's reader may be mad enough or drunk enough to report favorably on it. You've read the books. The meat of them has been transmuted in the alembic of Martin Eden's mind and poured into 'The Shame of the Sun,' and one day Martin Eden will be famous, and not the least of his fame will rest upon that work. So you must get a publisher for it—the sooner the better."

Brissenden went home late that night; and just as he mounted the first step of the car, he swung suddenly back on Martin and thrust into his hand a small, tightly crumpled wad of paper.

"Here, take this," he said. "I was out to the races to-day, and I had the right dope."

The bell clanged and the car pulled out, leaving Martin wondering as to the nature of the crinkly, greasy wad he clutched in his hand. Back in his room he unrolled it and found a hundred-dollar bill.

He did not scruple to use it. He knew his friend had always plenty of money, and he knew also, with profound certitude, that his success would enable him to repay it. In the morning he paid every bill, gave Maria three months' advance on the room, and redeemed every pledge at the pawnshop. Next he bought Marian's wedding present, and simpler presents, suitable to Christmas, for Ruth and Gertrude. And finally, on the balance remaining to him, he herded the whole Silva tribe down into Oakland. He was a winter late in redeeming his promise, but redeemed it was, for the last, least Silva got a pair of shoes, as well as Maria herself. Also, there were horns, and dolls, and toys of various sorts, and parcels and bundles of candies and nuts that filled the arms of all the Silvas to overflowing.

It was with this extraordinary procession trooping at his and Maria's heels into a confectioner's in quest if the biggest candy-cane ever made, that he encountered Ruth and her mother. Mrs. Morse was shocked. Even Ruth was hurt, for she had some regard for appearances, and her lover, cheek by jowl with Maria, at the head of that army of Portuguese ragamuffins, was not a pretty sight. But it was not that which hurt so much as what she took to be his lack of pride and self-respect. Further, and keenest of all, she read into the incident the impossibility of his living down his working-class origin.

There was stigma enough in the fact of it, but shamelessly to flaunt it in the face of the world—her world—was going too far. Though her engagement to Martin had been kept secret, their long intimacy had not been unproductive of gossip; and in the shop, glancing covertly at her lover and his following, had been several of her acquaintances. She lacked the easy largeness of Martin and could not rise superior to her environment. She had been hurt to the quick, and her sensitive nature was quivering with the shame of it. So it was, when Martin arrived later in the day, that he kept her present in his breast-pocket, deferring the giving of it to a more propitious occasion. Ruth in tears—passionate, angry tears—was a revelation to him. The spectacle of her suffering convinced him that he had been a brute, yet in the soul of him he could not see how nor why. It never entered his head to be ashamed of those he knew, and to take the Silvas out to a Christmas treat could in no way, so it seemed to him, show lack of consideration for Ruth. On the other hand, he did see Ruth's point of view, after she had explained it; and he looked upon it as a feminine weakness, such as afflicted all women and the best of women.

CHAPTER XXXVI

"Come on,—I'll show you the real dirt," Brissenden said to him, one evening in January.

They had dined together in San Francisco, and were at the Ferry Building, returning to Oakland, when the whim came to him to show Martin the "real dirt." He turned and fled across the water-front, a meagre shadow in a flapping overcoat, with Martin straining to keep up with him. At a wholesale liquor store he bought two gallon-demijohns of old port, and with one in each hand boarded a Mission Street car, Martin at his heels burdened with several quart-bottles of whiskey.

If Ruth could see me now, was his thought, while he wondered as to what constituted the real dirt.

"Maybe nobody will be there," Brissenden said, when they dismounted and plunged off to the right into the heart of the working-class ghetto, south of Market Street. "In which case you'll miss what you've been looking for so long."

"And what the deuce is that?" Martin asked.

"Men, intelligent men, and not the gibbering nonentities I found you consorting with in that trader's den. You read the books and you found yourself all alone. Well, I'm going to show you to-night some other men who've read the books, so that you won't be lonely any more."

"Not that I bother my head about their everlasting discussions," he said at the end of a block. "I'm not interested in book philosophy. But you'll find these fellows intelligences and not bourgeois swine. But watch out, they'll talk an arm off of you on any subject under the sun."

"Hope Norton's there," he panted a little later, resisting Martin's effort to relieve him of the two demijohns. "Norton's an idealist—a Harvard man. Prodigious memory. Idealism led him to philosophic anarchy, and his family threw him off. Father's a railroad president and many times millionnaire, but the son's starving in 'Frisco, editing an anarchist sheet for twenty-five a month."

Martin was little acquainted in San Francisco, and not at all south of Market; so he had no idea of where he was being led.

"Go ahead," he said; "tell me about them beforehand. What do they do for a living? How do they happen to be here?"

"Hope Hamilton's there." Brissenden paused and rested his hands. "Strawn-Hamilton's his name—hyphenated, you know—comes of old Southern stock. He's a tramp—laziest man I ever knew, though he's clerking, or trying to, in a socialist coöperative store for six dollars a week. But he's a confirmed hobo. Tramped into town. I've seen him sit all day on a bench and never a bite pass his lips, and in the evening, when I invited him to dinner—restaurant two blocks away—have him say, 'Too much trouble, old man. Buy me a package of cigarettes instead.' He was a Spencerian like you till Kreis turned him to materialistic monism. I'll start him on monism if I can. Norton's another monist—only he affirms naught but spirit. He can give Kreis and Hamilton all they want, too."

"Who is Kreis?" Martin asked.

"His rooms we're going to. One time professor—fired from university—usual story. A mind like a steel trap. Makes his living any old way. I know he's been a street fakir when he was down. Unscrupulous. Rob a corpse of a shroud—anything. Difference between him—and the bourgeoisie is that he robs without illusion. He'll talk Nietzsche, or Schopenhauer, or Kant, or anything, but the only thing in this world, not excepting Mary, that he really cares for, is his monism. Haeckel is his little tin god. The only way to insult him is to take a slap at Haeckel."

"Here's the hang-out." Brissenden rested his demijohn at the upstairs entrance, preliminary to the climb. It was the usual two-story corner building, with a saloon and grocery underneath. "The gang lives here—got the whole upstairs to themselves. But Kreis is the only one who has two rooms. Come on."

No lights burned in the upper hall, but Brissenden threaded the utter blackness like a familiar ghost. He stopped to speak to Martin.

"There's one fellow—Stevens—a theosophist. Makes a pretty tangle when he gets going. Just now he's dish-washer in a restaurant. Likes a good cigar. I've seen him eat in a ten-cent hash-house and pay fifty cents for the cigar he smoked afterward. I've got a couple in my pocket for him, if he shows up."

"And there's another fellow—Parry—an Australian, a statistician and a sporting encyclopaedia. Ask him the grain output of Paraguay for 1903, or the English importation of sheetings into China for 1890, or at what weight Jimmy Britt fought Battling Nelson, or who was welter-weight champion of the United States in '68, and you'll get the correct answer with the automatic celerity of a slot-machine. And there's Andy, a stone-mason, has ideas on everything, a good chess-player; and another fellow, Harry, a baker, red hot socialist and strong union man. By the way, you remember Cooks' and Waiters' strike—Hamilton was the chap who organized that union and precipitated the strike—planned it all out in advance, right here in Kreis's rooms. Did it just for the fun of it, but was too lazy to stay by the union. Yet he could have risen high if he wanted to. There's no end to the possibilities in that man—if he weren't so insuperably lazy."

Brissenden advanced through the darkness till a thread of light marked the threshold of a door. A knock and an answer opened it, and Martin found himself shaking hands with Kreis, a handsome brunette man, with dazzling white teeth, a drooping black mustache, and large, flashing black eyes. Mary, a matronly young blonde, was washing dishes in the little back room that served for kitchen and dining room. The front room served as bedchamber and living room. Overhead was the week's washing, hanging in festoons so low that Martin did not see at first the two men talking in a corner. They hailed Brissenden and his demijohns with acclamation, and, on being introduced, Martin learned they were Andy and Parry. He joined them and listened attentively to the description of a prize-fight Parry had seen the night before; while Brissenden, in his glory, plunged into the manufacture of a toddy and the serving of wine and whiskey-and-sodas. At his command, "Bring in the clan," Andy departed to go the round of the rooms for the lodgers.

"We're lucky that most of them are here," Brissenden whispered to Martin. "There's Norton and Hamilton; come on and meet them. Stevens isn't around, I hear. I'm going to get them started on monism if I can. Wait till they get a few jolts in them and they'll warm up."

At first the conversation was desultory. Nevertheless Martin could not fail to appreciate the keen play of their minds. They were men with opinions, though the opinions often clashed, and, though they were witty and clever, they were not superficial. He swiftly saw, no matter upon what they talked, that each man applied the correlation of knowledge and had also a deep-seated and unified conception of society and the Cosmos. Nobody manufactured their opinions for them; they were all rebels of one variety or another, and their lips were strangers to platitudes. Never had Martin, at the Morses', heard so amazing a range of topics discussed. There seemed no limit save time to the things they were alive to. The talk wandered from Mrs. Humphry Ward's new book to Shaw's latest play, through the future of the drama to reminiscences of Mansfield. They appreciated or sneered at the morning editorials, jumped from labor conditions in New Zealand to Henry James and Brander Matthews, passed on to the German designs in the Far East and the economic aspect of the Yellow Peril, wrangled over the German elections and Bebel's last speech, and settled down to local politics, the latest plans and scandals in the union labor party administration, and the wires that were pulled to bring about the Coast Seamen's strike. Martin was struck by the inside knowledge they possessed. They knew what was never printed in the newspapers—the wires and strings and the hidden hands that made the puppets dance. To Martin's surprise, the girl, Mary, joined in the conversation, displaying an intelligence he had never encountered in the few women he had met. They talked together on Swinburne and Rossetti, after which she led him beyond his depth into the by-paths of French literature. His revenge came when she defended Maeterlinck and he brought into action the carefully-thought-out thesis of "The Shame of the Sun."

Several other men had dropped in, and the air was thick with tobacco smoke, when Brissenden waved the red flag.

"Here's fresh meat for your axe, Kreis," he said; "a rose-white youth with the ardor of a lover for Herbert Spencer. Make a Haeckelite of him—if you can."

Kreis seemed to wake up and flash like some metallic, magnetic thing, while Norton looked at Martin sympathetically, with a sweet, girlish smile, as much as to say that he would be amply protected.

Kreis began directly on Martin, but step by step Norton interfered, until he and Kreis were off and away in a personal battle. Martin listened and fain would have rubbed his eyes. It was impossible that this should be, much less in the labor ghetto south of Market. The books were alive in these men. They talked with fire and enthusiasm, the intellectual stimulant stirring them as he had seen drink and anger stir other men. What he heard was no longer the philosophy of the dry, printed word, written by half-mythical demigods like Kant and Spencer. It was living philosophy, with warm, red blood, incarnated in these two men till its very features worked with excitement. Now and again other men joined in, and all followed the discussion with cigarettes going out in their hands and with alert, intent faces.

Idealism had never attracted Martin, but the exposition it now received at the hands of Norton was a revelation. The logical plausibility of it, that made an appeal to his intellect, seemed missed by Kreis and Hamilton, who sneered at Norton as a metaphysician, and who, in turn, sneered back at them as metaphysicians. *Phenomenon* and *noumenon* were bandied back and forth. They charged him with attempting to explain consciousness by itself. He charged them with word-jugglery, with reasoning from words to theory instead of from facts to theory. At this they were aghast. It was the cardinal tenet of their mode of reasoning to start with facts and to give names to the facts.

When Norton wandered into the intricacies of Kant, Kreis reminded him that all good little German philosophies when they died went to Oxford. A little later Norton reminded them of Hamilton's Law of Parsimony, the application of which they immediately claimed for every reasoning process of theirs. And Martin hugged his knees and exulted in it all. But Norton was no

Spencerian, and he, too, strove for Martin's philosophic soul, talking as much at him as to his two opponents.

"You know Berkeley has never been answered," he said, looking directly at Martin. "Herbert Spencer came the nearest, which was not very near. Even the stanchest of Spencer's followers will not go farther. I was reading an essay of Saleeby's the other day, and the best Saleeby could say was that Herbert Spencer *nearly* succeeded in answering Berkeley."

"You know what Hume said?" Hamilton asked. Norton nodded, but Hamilton gave it for the benefit of the rest. "He said that Berkeley's arguments admit of no answer and produce no conviction."

"In his, Hume's, mind," was the reply. "And Hume's mind was the same as yours, with this difference: he was wise enough to admit there was no answering Berkeley."

Norton was sensitive and excitable, though he never lost his head, while Kreis and Hamilton were like a pair of cold-blooded savages, seeking out tender places to prod and poke. As the evening grew late, Norton, smarting under the repeated charges of being a metaphysician, clutching his chair to keep from jumping to his feet, his gray eyes snapping and his girlish face grown harsh and sure, made a grand attack upon their position.

"All right, you Haeckelites, I may reason like a medicine man, but, pray, how do you reason? You have nothing to stand on, you unscientific dogmatists with your positive science which you are always lugging about into places it has no right to be. Long before the school of materialistic monism arose, the ground was removed so that there could be no foundation. Locke was the man, John Locke. Two hundred years ago—more than that, even in his 'Essay concerning the Human Understanding,' he proved the non-existence of innate ideas. The best of it is that that is precisely what you claim. To-night, again and again, you have asserted the non-existence of innate ideas.

"And what does that mean? It means that you can never know ultimate reality. Your brains are empty when you are born. Appearances, or phenomena, are all the content your minds can receive from your five senses.

Then noumena, which are not in your minds when you are born, have no way of getting in—"

"I deny—" Kreis started to interrupt.

"You wait till I'm done," Norton shouted. "You can know only that much of the play and interplay of force and matter as impinges in one way or another on our senses. You see, I am willing to admit, for the sake of the argument, that matter exists; and what I am about to do is to efface you by your own argument. I can't do it any other way, for you are both congenitally unable to understand a philosophic abstraction."

"And now, what do you know of matter, according to your own positive science? You know it only by its phenomena, its appearances. You are aware only of its changes, or of such changes in it as cause changes in your consciousness. Positive science deals only with phenomena, yet you are foolish enough to strive to be ontologists and to deal with noumena. Yet, by the very definition of positive science, science is concerned only with appearances. As somebody has said, phenomenal knowledge cannot transcend phenomena."

"You cannot answer Berkeley, even if you have annihilated Kant, and yet, perforce, you assume that Berkeley is wrong when you affirm that science proves the non-existence of God, or, as much to the point, the existence of matter.—You know I granted the reality of matter only in order to make myself intelligible to your understanding. Be positive scientists, if you please; but ontology has no place in positive science, so leave it alone. Spencer is right in his agnosticism, but if Spencer—"

But it was time to catch the last ferry-boat for Oakland, and Brissenden and Martin slipped out, leaving Norton still talking and Kreis and Hamilton waiting to pounce on him like a pair of hounds as soon as he finished.

"You have given me a glimpse of fairyland," Martin said on the ferry-boat. "It makes life worth while to meet people like that. My mind is all worked up. I never appreciated idealism before. Yet I can't accept it. I know that I shall always be a realist. I am so made, I guess. But I'd like to have made a reply to Kreis and Hamilton, and I think I'd have had a word or two for Norton. I didn't see that Spencer was damaged any. I'm as excited as a child on its first visit to the circus. I see I must read up some more. I'm going to get hold of Saleeby. I still think Spencer is unassailable, and next time I'm going to take a hand myself."

But Brissenden, breathing painfully, had dropped off to sleep, his chin buried in a scarf and resting on his sunken chest, his body wrapped in the long overcoat and shaking to the vibration of the propellers.

CHAPTER XXXVII

The first thing Martin did next morning was to go counter both to Brissenden's advice and command. "The Shame of the Sun" he wrapped and mailed to *The Acropolis*. He believed he could find magazine publication for it, and he felt that recognition by the magazines would commend him to the book-publishing houses. "Ephemera" he likewise wrapped and mailed to a magazine. Despite Brissenden's prejudice against the magazines, which was a pronounced mania with him, Martin decided that the great poem should see print. He did not intend, however, to publish it without the other's permission. His plan was to get it accepted by one of the high magazines, and, thus armed, again to wrestle with Brissenden for consent.

Martin began, that morning, a story which he had sketched out a number of weeks before and which ever since had been worrying him with its insistent clamor to be created. Apparently it was to be a rattling sea story, a tale of twentieth-century adventure and romance, handling real characters, in a real world, under real conditions. But beneath the swing and go of the story was to be something else—something that the superficial reader would never discern and which, on the other hand, would not diminish in any way the interest and enjoyment for such a reader. It was this, and not the mere story, that impelled Martin to write it. For that matter, it was always the great, universal *motif* that suggested plots to him. After having found such a *motif*, he cast about for the particular persons and particular location in time and space wherewith and wherein to utter the universal thing. "Overdue" was the title he had decided for it, and its length he believed would not be more than sixty thousand words—a bagatelle for him with his splendid vigor of production. On this first day he took hold of it with conscious delight in the mastery of his tools. He no longer worried for fear that the sharp, cutting edges should slip and mar his work. The long months of intense application and study had brought their reward. He could now devote himself with sure hand to the larger phases of the thing he shaped; and as he worked, hour after hour, he felt, as never before, the sure and cosmic grasp with which he held life and the affairs of life. "Overdue" would tell a story that would be true of its particular characters and its particular events; but it would tell, too, he was confident, great vital things that would be true of all time, and all sea, and all life—thanks to Herbert Spencer, he thought, leaning back for a moment from the table. Ay, thanks to Herbert Spencer and to the master-key of life, evolution, which Spencer had placed in his hands.

He was conscious that it was great stuff he was writing. "It will go! It will go!" was the refrain that kept, sounding in his ears. Of course it would go. At last he was turning out the thing at which the magazines would jump. The whole story worked out before him in lightning flashes. He broke off from it long enough to write a paragraph in his note-book. This would be the last paragraph in "Overdue"; but so thoroughly was the whole book already composed in his brain that he could write, weeks before he had arrived at the end, the end itself. He compared the tale, as yet unwritten, with the tales of the sea-writers, and he felt it to be immeasurably superior. "There's only one man who could touch it," he murmured aloud, "and that's Conrad. And it ought to make even him sit up and shake hands with me, and say, 'Well done, Martin, my boy.'"

He toiled on all day, recollecting, at the last moment, that he was to have dinner at the Morses'. Thanks to Brissenden, his black suit was out of pawn and he was again eligible for dinner parties. Down town he stopped off long enough to run into the library and search for Saleeby's books. He drew out "The Cycle of Life," and on the car turned to the essay Norton had mentioned on Spencer. As Martin read, he grew angry. His face flushed, his jaw set, and unconsciously his hand clenched, unclenched, and clenched again as if he were taking fresh grips upon some hateful thing out of which he was squeezing the life. When he left the car, he strode along the sidewalk as a wrathful man will stride, and he rang the Morse bell with such viciousness that it roused him to consciousness of his condition, so that he entered in good nature, smiling with amusement at himself. No sooner, however, was he inside than a great depression descended upon him. He fell from the height where he had been up-borne all day on the wings of inspiration. "Bourgeois," "trader's den"—Brissenden's epithets repeated themselves in his mind. But what of that? he demanded angrily. He was marrying Ruth, not her family.

It seemed to him that he had never seen Ruth more beautiful, more spiritual and ethereal and at the same time more healthy. There was color in her cheeks, and her eyes drew him again and again—the eyes in which he had first read immortality. He had forgotten immortality of late, and the trend of his scientific reading had been away from it; but here, in Ruth's eyes, he read an argument without words that transcended all worded arguments. He saw that in her eyes before which all discussion fled away, for he saw love there. And in his own eyes was love; and love was unanswerable. Such was his passionate doctrine.

The half hour he had with her, before they went in to dinner, left him supremely happy and supremely satisfied with life. Nevertheless, at table, the inevitable reaction and exhaustion consequent upon the hard day seized hold of him. He was aware that his eyes were tired and that he was irritable. He remembered it was at this table, at which he now sneered and was so often bored, that he had first eaten with civilized beings in what he had imagined was an atmosphere of high culture and refinement. He caught a glimpse of that pathetic figure of him, so long ago, a self-conscious savage, sprouting sweat at every pore in an agony of apprehension, puzzled by the bewildering minutiae of eating-implements, tortured by the ogre of a servant, striving at a leap to live at such dizzy social altitude, and deciding in the end to be frankly himself, pretending no knowledge and no polish he did not possess.

He glanced at Ruth for reassurance, much in the same manner that a passenger, with sudden panic thought of possible shipwreck, will strive to locate the life preservers. Well, that much had come out of it—love and Ruth. All the rest had failed to stand the test of the books. But Ruth and love had stood the test; for them he found a biological sanction. Love was the most exalted expression of life. Nature had been busy designing him, as she had been busy with all normal men, for the purpose of loving. She had spent ten thousand centuries—ay, a hundred thousand and a million centuries—upon the task, and he was the best she could do. She had made love the strongest thing in him, increased its power a myriad per cent with her gift of imagination, and sent him forth into the ephemera to thrill and melt and mate. His hand sought Ruth's hand beside him hidden by the table, and a warm pressure was given and received. She looked at him a swift instant, and her eyes were radiant and melting. So were his in the thrill that pervaded him; nor did he realize how much that was radiant and melting in her eyes had been aroused by what she had seen in his.

Across the table from him, cater-cornered, at Mr. Morse's right, sat Judge Blount, a local superior court judge. Martin had met him a number of times and had failed to like him. He and Ruth's father were discussing labor union politics, the local situation, and socialism, and Mr. Morse was endeavoring to twit Martin on the latter topic. At last Judge Blount looked across the table with benignant and fatherly pity. Martin smiled to himself.

"You'll grow out of it, young man," he said soothingly. "Time is the best cure for such youthful distempers." He turned to Mr. Morse. "I do not believe discussion is good in such cases. It makes the patient obstinate."

"That is true," the other assented gravely. "But it is well to warn the patient occasionally of his condition."

Martin laughed merrily, but it was with an effort. The day had been too long, the day's effort too intense, and he was deep in the throes of the reaction.

"Undoubtedly you are both excellent doctors," he said; "but if you care a whit for the opinion of the patient, let him tell you that you are poor diagnosticians. In fact, you are both suffering from the disease you think you find in me. As for me, I am immune. The socialist philosophy that riots half-baked in your veins has passed me by."

"Clever, clever," murmured the judge. "An excellent ruse in controversy, to reverse positions."

"Out of your mouth." Martin's eyes were sparkling, but he kept control of himself. "You see, Judge, I've heard your campaign speeches. By some henidical process—henidical, by the way is a favorite word of mine which nobody understands—by some henidical process you persuade yourself that you believe in the competitive system and the survival of the strong, and at the same time you indorse with might and main all sorts of measures to shear the strength from the strong."

"My young man—"

"Remember, I've heard your campaign speeches," Martin warned. "It's on record, your position on interstate commerce regulation, on regulation of the railway trust and Standard Oil, on the conservation of the forests, on a thousand and one restrictive measures that are nothing else than socialistic."

"Do you mean to tell me that you do not believe in regulating these various outrageous exercises of power?"

"That's not the point. I mean to tell you that you are a poor diagnostician. I mean to tell you that I am not suffering from the microbe of socialism. I mean to tell you that it is you who are suffering from the emasculating ravages of that same microbe. As for me, I am an inveterate opponent of socialism just as I am an inveterate opponent of your own mongrel democracy that is nothing else than pseudo-socialism masquerading under a garb of words that will not stand the test of the dictionary."

"I am a reactionary—so complete a reactionary that my position is incomprehensible to you who live in a veiled lie of social organization and whose sight is not keen enough to pierce the veil. You make believe that you believe in the survival of the strong and the rule of the strong. I believe. That is the difference. When I was a trifle younger,—a few months younger,—I believed the same thing. You see, the ideas of you and yours had impressed me. But merchants and traders are cowardly rulers at best; they grunt and grub all their days in the trough of money-getting, and I have swung back to aristocracy, if you please. I am the only individualist in this room. I look to the state for nothing. I look only to the strong man, the man on horseback, to save the state from its own rotten futility."

"Nietzsche was right. I won't take the time to tell you who Nietzsche was, but he was right. The world belongs to the strong—to the strong who are noble as well and who do not wallow in the swine-trough of trade and exchange. The world belongs to the true nobleman, to the great blond beasts, to the noncompromisers, to the 'yes-sayers.' And they will eat you up, you socialists—who are afraid of socialism and who think yourselves individualists. Your slave-morality of the meek and lowly will never save you.—Oh, it's all

Greek, I know, and I won't bother you any more with it. But remember one thing. There aren't half a dozen individualists in Oakland, but Martin Eden is one of them."

He signified that he was done with the discussion, and turned to Ruth.

"I'm wrought up to-day," he said in an undertone. "All I want to do is to love, not talk."

He ignored Mr. Morse, who said:-

"I am unconvinced. All socialists are Jesuits. That is the way to tell them."

"We'll make a good Republican out of you yet," said Judge Blount.

"The man on horseback will arrive before that time," Martin retorted with good humor, and returned to Ruth.

But Mr. Morse was not content. He did not like the laziness and the disinclination for sober, legitimate work of this prospective son-in-law of his, for whose ideas he had no respect and of whose nature he had no understanding. So he turned the conversation to Herbert Spencer. Judge Blount ably seconded him, and Martin, whose ears had pricked at the first mention of the philosopher's name, listened to the judge enunciate a grave and complacent diatribe against Spencer. From time to time Mr. Morse glanced at Martin, as much as to say, "There, my boy, you see."

"Chattering daws," Martin muttered under his breath, and went on talking with Ruth and Arthur.

But the long day and the "real dirt" of the night before were telling upon him; and, besides, still in his burnt mind was what had made him angry when he read it on the car.

"What is the matter?" Ruth asked suddenly alarmed by the effort he was making to contain himself.

"There is no god but the Unknowable, and Herbert Spencer is its prophet," Judge Blount was saying at that moment.

Martin turned upon him.

"A cheap judgment," he remarked quietly. "I heard it first in the City Hall Park, on the lips of a workingman who ought to have known better. I have heard it often since, and each time the clap-trap of it nauseates me. You ought to be ashamed of yourself. To hear that great and noble man's name upon your lips is like finding a dew-drop in a cesspool. You are disgusting."

It was like a thunderbolt. Judge Blount glared at him with apoplectic countenance, and silence reigned. Mr. Morse was secretly pleased. He could see that his daughter was shocked. It was what he wanted to do—to bring out the innate ruffianism of this man he did not like.

Ruth's hand sought Martin's beseechingly under the table, but his blood was up. He was inflamed by the intellectual pretence and fraud of those who sat in the high places. A Superior Court Judge! It was only several years before that he had looked up from the mire at such glorious entities and deemed them gods.

Judge Blount recovered himself and attempted to go on, addressing himself to Martin with an assumption of politeness that the latter understood was for the benefit of the ladies. Even this added to his anger. Was there no honesty in the world?

"You can't discuss Spencer with me," he cried. "You do not know any more about Spencer than do his own countrymen. But it is no fault of yours, I grant. It is just a phase of the contemptible ignorance of the times. I ran across a sample of it on my way here this evening. I was reading an essay by Saleeby on Spencer. You should read it. It is accessible to all men. You can buy it in any book-store or draw it from the public library. You would feel ashamed of your paucity of abuse and ignorance of that noble man compared with what Saleeby has collected on the subject. It is a record of shame that would shame your shame."

"'The philosopher of the half-educated,' he was called by an academic Philosopher who was not worthy to pollute the atmosphere he breathed. I don't think you have read ten pages of Spencer, but there have been critics, assumably more intelligent than you, who have read no more than you of Spencer, who publicly challenged his followers to adduce one single idea from all his writings—from Herbert Spencer's writings, the man who has impressed the stamp of his genius over the whole field of scientific research and modern thought; the father of psychology; the man who revolutionized pedagogy, so that to-day the child of the French peasant is taught the three R's according to principles laid down by him. And the little gnats of men sting his memory when they get their very bread and butter from the technical application of his ideas. What little of worth resides in their brains is largely due to him. It is certain that had he never lived, most of what is correct in their parrot-learned knowledge would be absent."

"And yet a man like Principal Fairbanks of Oxford—a man who sits in an even higher place than you, Judge Blount—has said that Spencer will be dismissed by posterity as a poet and dreamer rather than a thinker. Yappers and blatherskites, the whole brood of them! '"First Principles" is not wholly destitute of a certain literary power,' said one of them. And others of them have said that he was an industrious plodder rather than an original thinker. Yappers and blatherskites! Yappers and blatherskites!"

Martin ceased abruptly, in a dead silence. Everybody in Ruth's family looked up to Judge Blount as a man of power and achievement, and they were horrified at Martin's outbreak. The remainder of the dinner passed like a funeral, the judge and Mr. Morse confining their talk to each other, and the rest of the conversation being extremely desultory. Then afterward, when Ruth and Martin were alone, there was a scene.

"You are unbearable," she wept.

But his anger still smouldered, and he kept muttering, "The beasts! The beasts!"

When she averred he had insulted the judge, he retorted:-

"By telling the truth about him?"

"I don't care whether it was true or not," she insisted. "There are certain bounds of decency, and you had no license to insult anybody."

"Then where did Judge Blount get the license to assault truth?" Martin demanded. "Surely to assault truth is a more serious misdemeanor than to insult a pygmy personality such as the judge's. He did worse than that. He blackened the name of a great, noble man who is dead. Oh, the beasts! The beasts!"

His complex anger flamed afresh, and Ruth was in terror of him. Never had she seen him so angry, and it was all mystified and unreasonable to her comprehension. And yet, through her very terror ran the fibres of fascination that had drawn and that still drew her to him—that had compelled her to lean towards him, and, in that mad, culminating moment, lay her hands upon his neck. She was hurt and outraged by what had taken place, and yet she lay in his arms and quivered while he went on muttering, "The beasts! The beasts!" And she still lay there when he said: "I'll not bother your table again, dear. They do not like me, and it is wrong of me to thrust my objectionable presence upon them. Besides, they are just as objectionable to me. Faugh! They are sickening. And to think of it, I dreamed in my innocence that the persons who sat in the high places, who lived in fine houses and had educations and bank accounts, were worth while!"

CHAPTER XXXVIII

"Come on, let's go down to the local."

So spoke Brissenden, faint from a hemorrhage of half an hour before—the second hemorrhage in three days. The perennial whiskey glass was in his hands, and he drained it with shaking fingers.

"What do I want with socialism?" Martin demanded.

"Outsiders are allowed five-minute speeches," the sick man urged. "Get up and spout. Tell them why you don't want socialism. Tell them what you think about them and their ghetto ethics. Slam Nietzsche into them and get walloped for your pains. Make a scrap of it. It will do them good. Discussion is what they want, and what you want, too. You see, I'd like to see you a socialist before I'm gone. It will give you a sanction for your existence. It is the one thing that will save you in the time of disappointment that is coming to you."

"I never can puzzle out why you, of all men, are a socialist," Martin pondered. "You detest the crowd so. Surely there is nothing in the canaille to recommend it to your aesthetic soul." He pointed an accusing finger at the whiskey glass which the other was refilling. "Socialism doesn't seem to save you."

"I'm very sick," was the answer. "With you it is different. You have health and much to live for, and you must be handcuffed to life somehow. As for me, you wonder why I am a socialist. I'll tell you. It is because Socialism is inevitable; because the present rotten and irrational system cannot endure; because the day is past for your man on horseback. The slaves won't stand for it. They are too many, and willy-nilly they'll drag down the would-be equestrian before ever he gets astride. You can't get away from them, and you'll have to swallow the whole slave-morality. It's not a nice mess, I'll allow. But it's been a-brewing and swallow it you must. You are antediluvian anyway, with your Nietzsche ideas. The past is past, and the man who says history repeats itself is a liar. Of course I don't like the crowd, but what's a poor chap to do? We can't have the man on horseback, and anything is preferable to the timid swine that now rule. But come on, anyway. I'm loaded to the guards now, and if I sit here any longer, I'll get drunk. And you know the doctor says—damn the doctor! I'll fool him yet."

It was Sunday night, and they found the small hall packed by the Oakland socialists, chiefly members of the working class. The speaker, a clever Jew, won Martin's admiration at the same time that he aroused his antagonism. The man's stooped and narrow shoulders and weazened chest proclaimed him the true child of the crowded ghetto, and strong on Martin was the age-long struggle of the feeble, wretched slaves against the lordly handful of men who had ruled over them and would rule over them to the end of time. To Martin this withered wisp of a creature was a symbol. He was the figure that stood forth representative of the whole miserable mass of weaklings and inefficients who perished according to biological law on the ragged confines of life. They were the unfit. In spite of their cunning philosophy and of their antlike proclivities for coöperation, Nature rejected them for the exceptional man. Out of the plentiful spawn of life she flung from her prolific hand she selected only the best. It was by the same method that men, aping her, bred race-horses and cucumbers. Doubtless, a creator of a Cosmos could have devised a better method; but creatures of this particular Cosmos must put up with this particular method. Of course, they could squirm as they perished, as the socialists squirmed, as the speaker on the platform and the perspiring crowd were squirming even now as they counselled together for some new device with which to minimize the penalties of living and outwit the Cosmos.

So Martin thought, and so he spoke when Brissenden urged him to give them hell. He obeyed the mandate, walking up to the platform, as was the custom, and addressing the chairman. He began in a low voice, haltingly, forming into order the ideas which had surged in his brain while the Jew was speaking. In such meetings five minutes was the time allotted to each speaker; but when Martin's five minutes were up, he was in full stride, his attack upon their doctrines but half completed. He had caught their interest, and the audience urged the chairman by acclamation to extend Martin's time.

They appreciated him as a foeman worthy of their intellect, and they listened intently, following every word. He spoke with fire and conviction, mincing no words in his attack upon the slaves and their morality and tactics and frankly alluding to his hearers as the slaves in question. He quoted Spencer and Malthus, and enunciated the biological law of development.

"And so," he concluded, in a swift résumé, "no state composed of the slave-types can endure. The old law of development still holds. In the struggle for existence, as I have shown, the strong and the progeny of the strong tend to survive, while the weak and the progeny of the weak are crushed and tend to perish. The result is that the strong and the progeny of the strong survive, and, so long as the struggle obtains, the strength of each generation increases. That is development. But you slaves—it is too bad to be slaves, I grant—but you slaves dream of a society where the law of development will be annulled, where no weaklings and inefficients will perish, where every inefficient will have as much as he wants to eat as many times a day as he desires, and where all will marry and have progeny—the weak as well as the strong. What will be the result? No longer will the strength and life-value of each generation increase. On the contrary, it will diminish. There is the Nemesis of your slave philosophy. Your society of slaves—of, by, and for, slaves—must inevitably weaken and go to pieces as the life which composes it weakens and goes to pieces.

"Remember, I am enunciating biology and not sentimental ethics. No state of slaves can stand—"

"How about the United States?" a man yelled from the audience.

"And how about it?" Martin retorted. "The thirteen colonies threw off their rulers and formed the Republic so-called. The slaves were their own masters. There were no more masters of the sword. But you couldn't get along without masters of some sort, and there arose a new set of masters—not the great, virile, noble men, but the shrewd and spidery traders and money-lenders. And they enslaved you over again—but not frankly, as the true, noble men would do with weight of their own right arms, but secretly, by spidery machinations and by wheedling and cajolery and lies. They have purchased your slave judges, they have debauched your slave legislatures, and they have forced to worse horrors than chattel slavery your slave boys and girls. Two million of your children are toiling to-day in this trader-oligarchy of the United States. Ten millions of you slaves are not properly sheltered nor properly fed."

"But to return. I have shown that no society of slaves can endure, because, in its very nature, such society must annul the law of development. No sooner can a slave society be organized than deterioration sets in. It is easy for you to talk of annulling the law of development, but where is the new law of development that will maintain your strength? Formulate it. Is it already formulated? Then state it."

Martin took his seat amidst an uproar of voices. A score of men were on their feet clamoring for recognition from the chair. And one by one, encouraged by vociferous applause, speaking with fire and enthusiasm and excited gestures, they replied to the attack. It was a wild night—but it was wild intellectually, a battle of ideas. Some strayed from the point, but most of the speakers replied directly to Martin. They shook him with lines of thought that were new to him; and gave him insights, not into new biological laws, but into new applications of the old laws. They were too earnest to be always polite, and more than once the chairman rapped and pounded for order.

It chanced that a cub reporter sat in the audience, detailed there on a day dull of news and impressed by the urgent need of journalism for sensation. He was not a bright cub reporter. He was merely facile and glib. He was too dense to follow the discussion. In fact, he had a comfortable feeling that he was vastly superior to these wordy maniacs of the working class. Also, he had a great respect for those who sat in the high places and dictated the policies of nations and newspapers. Further, he had an ideal, namely, of achieving that excellence of the perfect reporter who is able to make something—even a great deal—out of nothing.

He did not know what all the talk was about. It was not necessary. Words like *revolution* gave him his cue. Like a paleontologist, able to reconstruct an entire skeleton from one fossil bone, he was able to reconstruct a whole speech from the one word *revolution*. He did it that night, and he did it well; and since Martin had made the biggest stir, he put it all into his mouth and made him the arch-anarch of the show, transforming his reactionary individualism into the most lurid, red-shirt socialist utterance. The cub reporter was an artist, and it was a large brush with which he laid on the local color—wild-eyed long-haired men, neurasthenic and degenerate types of men, voices shaken with passion, clenched fists raised on high, and all projected against a background of oaths, yells, and the throaty rumbling of angry men.

CHAPTER XXXIX

Over the coffee, in his little room, Martin read next morning's paper. It was a novel experience to find himself head-lined, on the first page at that; and he was surprised to learn that he was the most notorious leader of the Oakland socialists. He ran over the violent speech the cub reporter had constructed for him, and, though at first he was angered by the fabrication, in the end he tossed the paper aside with a laugh.

"Either the man was drunk or criminally malicious," he said that afternoon, from his perch on the bed, when Brissenden had arrived and dropped limply into the one chair.

"But what do you care?" Brissenden asked. "Surely you don't desire the approval of the bourgeois swine that read the newspapers?"

Martin thought for a while, then said:-

"No, I really don't care for their approval, not a whit. On the other hand, it's very likely to make my relations with Ruth's family a trifle awkward. Her father always contended I was a socialist, and this miserable stuff will clinch his belief. Not that I care for his opinion—but what's the odds? I want to read you what I've been doing to-day. It's 'Overdue,' of course, and I'm just about halfway through."

He was reading aloud when Maria thrust open the door and ushered in a young man in a natty suit who glanced briskly about him, noting the oil-burner and the kitchen in the corner before his gaze wandered on to Martin.

"Sit down," Brissenden said.

Martin made room for the young man on the bed and waited for him to broach his business.

"I heard you speak last night, Mr. Eden, and I've come to interview you," he began.

Brissenden burst out in a hearty laugh.

"A brother socialist?" the reporter asked, with a quick glance at Brissenden that appraised the color-value of that cadaverous and dying man.

"And he wrote that report," Martin said softly. "Why, he is only a boy!"

"Why don't you poke him?" Brissenden asked. "I'd give a thousand dollars to have my lungs back for five minutes."

The cub reporter was a trifle perplexed by this talking over him and around him and at him. But he had been commended for his brilliant description of the socialist meeting and had further been detailed to get a personal interview with Martin Eden, the leader of the organized menace to society.

"You do not object to having your picture taken, Mr. Eden?" he said. "I've a staff photographer outside, you see, and he says it will be better to take you right away before the sun gets lower. Then we can have the interview afterward."

"A photographer," Brissenden said meditatively. "Poke him, Martin! Poke him!"

"I guess I'm getting old," was the answer. "I know I ought, but I really haven't the heart. It doesn't seem to matter."

"For his mother's sake," Brissenden urged.

"It's worth considering," Martin replied; "but it doesn't seem worth while enough to rouse sufficient energy in me. You see, it does take energy to give a fellow a poking. Besides, what does it matter?"

"That's right—that's the way to take it," the cub announced airily, though he had already begun to glance anxiously at the door.

"But it wasn't true, not a word of what he wrote," Martin went on, confining his attention to Brissenden.

"It was just in a general way a description, you understand," the cub ventured, "and besides, it's good advertising. That's what counts. It was a favor to you."

"It's good advertising, Martin, old boy," Brissenden repeated solemnly.

"And it was a favor to me—think of that!" was Martin's contribution.

"Let me see—where were you born, Mr. Eden?" the cub asked, assuming an air of expectant attention.

"He doesn't take notes," said Brissenden. "He remembers it all."

"That is sufficient for me." The cub was trying not to look worried. "No decent reporter needs to bother with notes."

"That was sufficient—for last night." But Brissenden was not a disciple of quietism, and he changed his attitude abruptly. "Martin, if you don't poke him, I'll do it myself, if I fall dead on the floor the next moment."

"How will a spanking do?" Martin asked.

Brissenden considered judicially, and nodded his head.

The next instant Martin was seated on the edge of the bed with the cub face downward across his knees.

"Now don't bite," Martin warned, "or else I'll have to punch your face. It would be a pity, for it is such a pretty face."

His uplifted hand descended, and thereafter rose and fell in a swift and steady rhythm. The cub struggled and cursed and squirmed, but did not offer to bite. Brissenden looked on gravely, though once he grew excited and gripped the whiskey bottle, pleading, "Here, just let me swat him once."

"Sorry my hand played out," Martin said, when at last he desisted. "It is quite numb."

He uprighted the cub and perched him on the bed.

"I'll have you arrested for this," he snarled, tears of boyish indignation running down his flushed cheeks. "I'll make you sweat for this. You'll see."

"The pretty thing," Martin remarked. "He doesn't realize that he has entered upon the downward path. It is not honest, it is not square, it is not manly, to tell lies about one's fellow-creatures the way he has done, and he doesn't know it."

"He has to come to us to be told," Brissenden filled in a pause.

"Yes, to me whom he has maligned and injured. My grocery will undoubtedly refuse me credit now. The worst of it is that the poor boy will keep on this way until he deteriorates into a first-class newspaper man and also a first-class scoundrel."

"But there is yet time," quoth Brissenden. "Who knows but what you may prove the humble instrument to save him. Why didn't you let me swat him just once? I'd like to have had a hand in it."

"I'll have you arrested, the pair of you, you b-b-big brutes," sobbed the erring soul.

"No, his mouth is too pretty and too weak." Martin shook his head lugubriously. "I'm afraid I've numbed my hand in vain. The young man cannot reform. He will become eventually a very great and successful newspaper man. He has no conscience. That alone will make him great."

With that the cub passed out the door in trepidation to the last for fear that Brissenden would hit him in the back with the bottle he still clutched.

In the next morning's paper Martin learned a great deal more about himself that was new to him. "We are the sworn enemies of society," he found himself quoted as saying in a column interview. "No, we are not anarchists but socialists." When the reporter pointed out to him that there seemed little difference between the two schools, Martin had shrugged his shoulders in silent affirmation. His face was described as bilaterally asymmetrical, and various other signs of degeneration were described. Especially notable were his thuglike hands and the fiery gleams in his blood-shot eyes.

He learned, also, that he spoke nightly to the workmen in the City Hall Park, and that among the anarchists and agitators that there inflamed the minds of the people he drew the largest audiences and made the most revolutionary speeches. The cub painted a high-light picture of his poor little room, its oil-stove and the one chair, and of the death's-head tramp who kept him company and who looked as if he had just emerged from twenty years of solitary confinement in some fortress dungeon.

The cub had been industrious. He had scurried around and nosed out Martin's family history, and procured a photograph of Higginbotham's Cash Store with Bernard Higginbotham himself standing out in front. That gentleman was depicted as an intelligent, dignified businessman who had no patience with his brother-in-law's socialistic views, and no patience with the brother-in-law, either, whom he was quoted as characterizing as a lazy good-for-nothing who wouldn't take a job when it was offered to him and who would go to jail yet. Hermann Von Schmidt, Marian's husband, had likewise been interviewed. He had called Martin the black sheep of the family and repudiated him. "He tried to sponge off of me, but I put a stop to that good and quick," Von Schmidt had said to the reporter. "He knows better than to come bumming around here. A man who won't work is no good, take that from me."

This time Martin was genuinely angry. Brissenden looked upon the affair as a good joke, but he could not console Martin, who knew that it would be no easy task to explain to Ruth. As for her father, he knew that he must be overjoyed with what had happened and that he would make the most of it to break off the engagement. How much he would make of it he was soon to realize. The afternoon mail brought a letter from Ruth. Martin opened it with a premonition of disaster, and read it standing at the open door when he had received it from the postman. As he read, mechanically his hand sought his pocket for the tobacco and brown paper of his old cigarette days. He was not aware that the pocket was empty or that he had even reached for the materials with which to roll a cigarette.

It was not a passionate letter. There were no touches of anger in it. But all the way through, from the first sentence to the last, was sounded the note of hurt and disappointment. She had expected better of him. She had thought he had got over his youthful wildness, that her love for him had been sufficiently worth while to enable him to live seriously and decently. And now her father and mother had taken a firm stand and commanded that the engagement be broken. That they were justified in this she could not but admit. Their relation could never be a happy one. It had been unfortunate from the first. But one regret she voiced in the whole letter, and it was a bitter one to Martin. "If only you had settled down to some position and attempted to make something of yourself," she wrote. "But it was not to be. Your past life had been too wild and irregular. I can understand that you are not to be blamed. You could act only according to your nature and your early training. So I do not blame you, Martin. Please remember that. It was simply a mistake. As father and mother have contended, we were not made for each other, and we should both be happy because it was discovered not too late." . . "There is no use trying to see me," she said toward the last. "It would be an unhappy meeting for both of us, as well as for my mother. I feel, as it is, that I have caused her great pain and worry. I shall have to do much living to atone for it."

He read it through to the end, carefully, a second time, then sat down and replied. He outlined the remarks he had uttered at the socialist meeting, pointing out that they were in all ways the converse of what the newspaper had put in his mouth. Toward the end of the letter he was God's own lover pleading passionately for love. "Please answer," he said, "and in your answer you have to tell me but one thing. Do you love me? That is all—the answer to that one question."

But no answer came the next day, nor the next. "Overdue" lay untouched upon the table, and each day the heap of returned manuscripts under the table grew larger. For the first time Martin's glorious sleep was interrupted by insomnia, and he tossed through long, restless nights. Three times he called at the Morse home, but was turned away by the servant who answered the bell. Brissenden lay sick in his hotel, too feeble to stir out, and, though Martin was with him often, he did not worry him with his troubles.

For Martin's troubles were many. The aftermath of the cub reporter's deed was even wider than Martin had anticipated. The Portuguese grocer refused him further credit, while the greengrocer, who was an American and proud of it, had called him a traitor to his country and refused further dealings with him—carrying his patriotism to such a degree that he cancelled Martin's account and forbade him ever to attempt to pay it. The talk in the neighborhood reflected the same feeling, and indignation against Martin ran high. No one would have anything to do with a socialist traitor. Poor Maria was dubious and frightened, but she remained loyal. The children of the neighborhood recovered from the awe of the grand carriage which once had visited Martin, and from safe distances they called him "hobo" and "bum." The Silva tribe, however, stanchly defended him, fighting more than one pitched battle for his honor, and black eyes and bloody noses became quite the order of the day and added to Maria's perplexities and troubles.

Once, Martin met Gertrude on the street, down in Oakland, and learned what he knew could not be otherwise—that Bernard Higginbotham was furious with him for having dragged the family into public disgrace, and that he had forbidden him the house.

"Why don't you go away, Martin?" Gertrude had begged. "Go away and get a job somewhere and steady down. Afterwards, when this all blows over, you can come back."

Martin shook his head, but gave no explanations. How could he explain? He was appalled at the awful intellectual chasm that yawned between him and his people. He could never cross it and explain to them his position,—the Nietzschean position, in regard to socialism. There were not words enough in the English language, nor in any language, to make his attitude and conduct intelligible to them. Their highest concept of right conduct, in his case, was to get a job. That was their first word and their last. It constituted their whole lexicon of ideas. Get a job! Go to work! Poor, stupid slaves, he thought, while his sister talked. Small wonder the world belonged to the strong. The slaves were obsessed by their own slavery. A job was to them a golden fetich before which they fell down and worshipped.

He shook his head again, when Gertrude offered him money, though he knew that within the day he would have to make a trip to the pawnbroker.

"Don't come near Bernard now," she admonished him. "After a few months, when he is cooled down, if you want to, you can get the job of drivin' delivery-wagon for him. Any time you want me, just send for me an' I'll come. Don't forget."

She went away weeping audibly, and he felt a pang of sorrow shoot through him at sight of her heavy body and uncouth gait. As he watched her go, the Nietzschean edifice seemed to shake and totter. The slave-class in the abstract was all very well, but it was not wholly satisfactory when it was brought home to his own family. And yet, if there was ever a slave trampled by the strong, that slave was his sister Gertrude. He grinned savagely at the paradox. A fine Nietzsche-man he was, to allow his intellectual concepts to be shaken by the first sentiment or emotion that strayed along—ay, to be shaken by the slave-morality itself, for that was what his pity for his sister really was. The true noble men were above pity and compassion. Pity and compassion had been generated in the subterranean barracoons of the slaves and were no more than the agony and sweat of the crowded miserables and weaklings.

CHAPTER XL

"Overdue" still continued to lie forgotten on the table. Every manuscript that he had had out now lay under the table. Only one manuscript he kept going, and that was Brissenden's "Ephemera." His bicycle and black suit were again in pawn, and the type-writer people were once more worrying about the rent. But such things no longer bothered him. He was seeking a new orientation, and until that was found his life must stand still.

After several weeks, what he had been waiting for happened. He met Ruth on the street. It was true, she was accompanied by her brother, Norman, and it was true that they tried to ignore him and that Norman attempted to wave him aside.

"If you interfere with my sister, I'll call an officer," Norman threatened. "She does not wish to speak with you, and your insistence is insult."

"If you persist, you'll have to call that officer, and then you'll get your name in the papers," Martin answered grimly. "And now, get out of my way and get the officer if you want to. I'm going to talk with Ruth."

"I want to have it from your own lips," he said to her.

She was pale and trembling, but she held up and looked inquiringly.

"The question I asked in my letter," he prompted.

Norman made an impatient movement, but Martin checked him with a swift look.

She shook her head.

"Is all this of your own free will?" he demanded.

"It is." She spoke in a low, firm voice and with deliberation. "It is of my own free will. You have disgraced me so that I am ashamed to meet my friends. They are all talking about me, I know. That is all I can tell you. You have made me very unhappy, and I never wish to see you again."

"Friends! Gossip! Newspaper misreports! Surely such things are not stronger than love! I can only believe that you never loved me."

A blush drove the pallor from her face.

"After what has passed?" she said faintly. "Martin, you do not know what you are saying. I am not common."

"You see, she doesn't want to have anything to do with you," Norman blurted out, starting on with her.

Martin stood aside and let them pass, fumbling unconsciously in his coat pocket for the tobacco and brown papers that were not there.

It was a long walk to North Oakland, but it was not until he went up the steps and entered his room that he knew he had walked it. He found himself sitting on the edge of the bed and staring about him like an awakened somnambulist. He noticed "Overdue" lying on the table and drew up his chair and reached for his pen. There was in his nature a logical compulsion toward completeness. Here was something undone. It had been deferred against the completion of something else. Now that something else had been finished, and he would apply himself to this task until it was finished. What he would do next he did not know. All that he did know was that a climacteric in his life had been attained. A period had been reached, and he was rounding it off in workman-like fashion. He was not curious about the future. He would soon enough find out what it held in store for him. Whatever it was, it did not matter. Nothing seemed to matter.

For five days he toiled on at "Overdue," going nowhere, seeing nobody, and eating meagrely. On the morning of the sixth day the postman brought him a thin letter from the editor of *The Parthenon*. A glance told him that "Ephemera" was accepted. "We have submitted the poem to Mr. Cartwright Bruce," the editor went on to say, "and he has reported so favorably upon it that we cannot let it go. As an earnest of our pleasure in publishing the poem, let me tell you that we have set it for the August number, our July number being already made up. Kindly extend our pleasure and our thanks to Mr. Brissenden. Please send by return mail his photograph and biographical data.

If our honorarium is unsatisfactory, kindly telegraph us at once and state what you consider a fair price."

Since the honorarium they had offered was three hundred and fifty dollars, Martin thought it not worth while to telegraph. Then, too, there was Brissenden's consent to be gained. Well, he had been right, after all. Here was one magazine editor who knew real poetry when he saw it. And the price was splendid, even though it was for the poem of a century. As for Cartwright Bruce, Martin knew that he was the one critic for whose opinions Brissenden had any respect.

Martin rode down town on an electric car, and as he watched the houses and cross-streets slipping by he was aware of a regret that he was not more elated over his friend's success and over his own signal victory. The one critic in the United States had pronounced favorably on the poem, while his own contention that good stuff could find its way into the magazines had proved correct. But enthusiasm had lost its spring in him, and he found that he was more anxious to see Brissenden than he was to carry the good news. The acceptance of *The Parthenon* had recalled to him that during his five days' devotion to "Overdue" he had not heard from Brissenden nor even thought about him. For the first time Martin realized the daze he had been in, and he felt shame for having forgotten his friend. But even the shame did not burn very sharply. He was numb to emotions of any sort save the artistic ones concerned in the writing of "Overdue." So far as other affairs were concerned, he had been in a trance. For that matter, he was still in a trance. All this life through which the electric car whirred seemed remote and unreal, and he would have experienced little interest and less shock if the great stone steeple of the church he passed had suddenly crumbled to mortar-dust upon his head.

At the hotel he hurried up to Brissenden's room, and hurried down again. The room was empty. All luggage was gone.

"Did Mr. Brissenden leave any address?" he asked the clerk, who looked at him curiously for a moment.

"Haven't you heard?" he asked.

Martin shook his head.

"Why, the papers were full of it. He was found dead in bed. Suicide. Shot himself through the head."

"Is he buried yet?" Martin seemed to hear his voice, like some one else's voice, from a long way off, asking the question.

"No. The body was shipped East after the inquest. Lawyers engaged by his people saw to the arrangements."

"They were quick about it, I must say," Martin commented.

"Oh, I don't know. It happened five days ago."

"Five days ago?"

"Yes, five days ago."

"Oh," Martin said as he turned and went out.

At the corner he stepped into the Western Union and sent a telegram to *The Parthenon*, advising them to proceed with the publication of the poem. He had in his pocket but five cents with which to pay his carfare home, so he sent the message collect.

Once in his room, he resumed his writing. The days and nights came and went, and he sat at his table and wrote on. He went nowhere, save to the pawnbroker, took no exercise, and ate methodically when he was hungry and had something to cook, and just as methodically went without when he had nothing to cook. Composed as the story was, in advance, chapter by chapter, he nevertheless saw and developed an opening that increased the power of it, though it necessitated twenty thousand additional words. It was not that there was any vital need that the thing should be well done, but that his artistic canons compelled him to do it well. He worked on in the daze, strangely detached from the world around him, feeling like a familiar ghost among these literary trappings of his former life. He remembered that some one had said that a ghost was the spirit of a man who was dead and who did not have sense enough to know it; and he paused for the moment to wonder if he were really dead and unaware of it.

Came the day when "Overdue" was finished. The agent of the type-writer firm had come for the machine, and he sat on the bed while Martin, on the one chair, typed the last pages of the final chapter. "Finis," he wrote, in capitals, at the end, and to him it was indeed finis. He watched the type-writer carried out the door with a feeling of relief, then went over and lay down on the bed. He was faint from hunger. Food had not passed his lips in thirty-six hours, but he did not think about it. He lay on his back, with closed eyes, and did not think at all, while the daze or stupor slowly welled up, saturating his consciousness. Half in delirium, he began muttering aloud the lines of an anonymous poem Brissenden had been fond of quoting to him. Maria, listening anxiously outside his door, was perturbed by his monotonous utterance. The words in themselves were not significant to her, but the fact that he was saying them was. "I have done," was the burden of the poem.

> "'I have done—
>
> Put by the lute.
>
> Song and singing soon are over
>
> As the airy shades that hover
>
> In among the purple clover.
>
> I have done—
>
> Put by the lute.
>
> Once I sang as early thrushes
>
> Sing among the dewy bushes;
>
> Now I'm mute.
>
> I am like a weary linnet,
>
> For my throat has no song in it;

I have had my singing minute.

I have done.

Put by the lute.'"

Maria could stand it no longer, and hurried away to the stove, where she filled a quart-bowl with soup, putting into it the lion's share of chopped meat and vegetables which her ladle scraped from the bottom of the pot. Martin roused himself and sat up and began to eat, between spoonfuls reassuring Maria that he had not been talking in his sleep and that he did not have any fever.

After she left him he sat drearily, with drooping shoulders, on the edge of the bed, gazing about him with lack-lustre eyes that saw nothing until the torn wrapper of a magazine, which had come in the morning's mail and which lay unopened, shot a gleam of light into his darkened brain. It is *The Parthenon*, he thought, the August Parthenon, and it must contain "Ephemera." If only Brissenden were here to see!

He was turning the pages of the magazine, when suddenly he stopped. "Ephemera" had been featured, with gorgeous head-piece and Beardsley-like margin decorations. On one side of the head-piece was Brissenden's photograph, on the other side was the photograph of Sir John Value, the British Ambassador. A preliminary editorial note quoted Sir John Value as saying that there were no poets in America, and the publication of "Ephemera" was *The Parthenon*'s. "There, take that, Sir John Value!" Cartwright Bruce was described as the greatest critic in America, and he was quoted as saying that "Ephemera" was the greatest poem ever written in America. And finally, the editor's foreword ended with: "We have not yet made up our minds entirely as to the merits of 'Ephemera'; perhaps we shall never be able to do so. But we have read it often, wondering at the words and their arrangement, wondering where Mr. Brissenden got them, and how he could fasten them together." Then followed the poem.

"Pretty good thing you died, Briss, old man," Martin murmured, letting the magazine slip between his knees to the floor.

The cheapness and vulgarity of it was nauseating, and Martin noted apathetically that he was not nauseated very much. He wished he could get angry, but did not have energy enough to try. He was too numb. His blood was too congealed to accelerate to the swift tidal flow of indignation. After all, what did it matter? It was on a par with all the rest that Brissenden had condemned in bourgeois society.

"Poor Briss," Martin communed; "he would never have forgiven me."

Rousing himself with an effort, he possessed himself of a box which had once contained type-writer paper. Going through its contents, he drew forth eleven poems which his friend had written. These he tore lengthwise and crosswise and dropped into the waste basket. He did it languidly, and, when he had finished, sat on the edge of the bed staring blankly before him.

How long he sat there he did not know, until, suddenly, across his sightless vision he saw form a long horizontal line of white. It was curious. But as he watched it grow in definiteness he saw that it was a coral reef smoking in the white Pacific surges. Next, in the line of breakers he made out a small canoe, an outrigger canoe. In the stern he saw a young bronzed god in scarlet hip-cloth dipping a flashing paddle. He recognized him. He was Moti, the youngest son of Tati, the chief, and this was Tahiti, and beyond that smoking reef lay the sweet land of Papara and the chief's grass house by the river's mouth. It was the end of the day, and Moti was coming home from the fishing. He was waiting for the rush of a big breaker whereon to jump the reef. Then he saw himself, sitting forward in the canoe as he had often sat in the past, dipping a paddle that waited Moti's word to dig in like mad when the turquoise wall of the great breaker rose behind them. Next, he was no longer an onlooker but was himself in the canoe, Moti was crying out, they were both thrusting hard with their paddles, racing on the steep face of the flying turquoise. Under the bow the water was hissing as from a steam jet, the air was filled with driven spray, there was a rush and rumble and long-echoing roar, and the canoe floated on the placid water of the lagoon. Moti laughed and shook the salt water from his eyes, and together they paddled in to the pounded-coral beach where Tati's grass walls through the cocoanut-palms showed golden in the setting sun.

760

The picture faded, and before his eyes stretched the disorder of his squalid room. He strove in vain to see Tahiti again. He knew there was singing among the trees and that the maidens were dancing in the moonlight, but he could not see them. He could see only the littered writing-table, the empty space where the type-writer had stood, and the unwashed window-pane. He closed his eyes with a groan, and slept.

CHAPTER XLI

He slept heavily all night, and did not stir until aroused by the postman on his morning round. Martin felt tired and passive, and went through his letters aimlessly. One thin envelope, from a robber magazine, contained for twenty-two dollars. He had been dunning for it for a year and a half. He noted its amount apathetically. The old-time thrill at receiving a publisher's check was gone. Unlike his earlier checks, this one was not pregnant with promise of great things to come. To him it was a check for twenty-two dollars, that was all, and it would buy him something to eat.

Another check was in the same mail, sent from a New York weekly in payment for some humorous verse which had been accepted months before. It was for ten dollars. An idea came to him, which he calmly considered. He did not know what he was going to do, and he felt in no hurry to do anything. In the meantime he must live. Also he owed numerous debts. Would it not be a paying investment to put stamps on the huge pile of manuscripts under the table and start them on their travels again? One or two of them might be accepted. That would help him to live. He decided on the investment, and, after he had cashed the checks at the bank down in Oakland, he bought ten dollars' worth of postage stamps. The thought of going home to cook breakfast in his stuffy little room was repulsive to him. For the first time he refused to consider his debts. He knew that in his room he could manufacture a substantial breakfast at a cost of from fifteen to twenty cents. But, instead, he went into the Forum Café and ordered a breakfast that cost two dollars. He tipped the waiter a quarter, and spent fifty cents for a package of Egyptian cigarettes. It was the first time he had smoked since Ruth had asked him to stop. But he could see now no reason why he should not, and besides, he wanted to smoke. And what did the money matter? For five cents he could have bought a package of Durham and brown papers and rolled forty cigarettes—but what of it? Money had no meaning to him now except what it would immediately buy. He was chartless and rudderless, and he had no port to make, while drifting involved the least living, and it was living that hurt.

The days slipped along, and he slept eight hours regularly every night. Though now, while waiting for more checks, he ate in the Japanese restaurants where meals were served for ten cents, his wasted body filled out, as did the hollows in his cheeks. He no longer abused himself with short sleep, overwork, and overstudy. He wrote nothing, and the books were closed. He walked much, out in the hills, and loafed long hours in the quiet parks. He had no friends nor acquaintances, nor did he make any. He had no inclination. He was waiting for some impulse, from he knew not where, to put his stopped life into motion again. In the meantime his life remained run down, planless, and empty and idle.

Once he made a trip to San Francisco to look up the "real dirt." But at the last moment, as he stepped into the upstairs entrance, he recoiled and turned and fled through the swarming ghetto. He was frightened at the thought of hearing philosophy discussed, and he fled furtively, for fear that some one of the "real dirt" might chance along and recognize him.

Sometimes he glanced over the magazines and newspapers to see how "Ephemera" was being maltreated. It had made a hit. But what a hit! Everybody had read it, and everybody was discussing whether or not it was really poetry. The local papers had taken it up, and daily there appeared columns of learned criticisms, facetious editorials, and serious letters from subscribers. Helen Della Delmar (proclaimed with a flourish of trumpets and rolling of tomtoms to be the greatest woman poet in the United States) denied Brissenden a seat beside her on Pegasus and wrote voluminous letters to the public, proving that he was no poet.

The Parthenon came out in its next number patting itself on the back for the stir it had made, sneering at Sir John Value, and exploiting Brissenden's death with ruthless commercialism. A newspaper with a sworn circulation of half a million published an original and spontaneous poem by Helen Della Delmar, in which she gibed and sneered at Brissenden. Also, she was guilty of a second poem, in which she parodied him.

Martin had many times to be glad that Brissenden was dead. He had hated the crowd so, and here all that was finest and most sacred of him had been thrown to the crowd. Daily the vivisection of Beauty went on. Every nincompoop in the land rushed into free print, floating their wizened little egos into the public eye on the surge of Brissenden's greatness. Quoth one paper: "We have received a letter from a gentleman who wrote a poem just like it, only better, some time ago." Another paper, in deadly seriousness, reproving Helen Della Delmar for her parody, said: "But unquestionably Miss Delmar wrote it in a moment of badinage and not quite with the respect that one great poet should show to another and perhaps to the greatest. However, whether Miss Delmar be jealous or not of the man who invented 'Ephemera,' it is certain that she, like thousands of others, is fascinated by his work, and that the day may come when she will try to write lines like his."

Ministers began to preach sermons against "Ephemera," and one, who too stoutly stood for much of its content, was expelled for heresy. The great poem contributed to the gayety of the world. The comic verse-writers and the cartoonists took hold of it with screaming laughter, and in the personal columns of society weeklies jokes were perpetrated on it to the effect that Charley Frensham told Archie Jennings, in confidence, that five lines of "Ephemera" would drive a man to beat a cripple, and that ten lines would send him to the bottom of the river.

Martin did not laugh; nor did he grit his teeth in anger. The effect produced upon him was one of great sadness. In the crash of his whole world, with love on the pinnacle, the crash of magazinedom and the dear public was a small crash indeed. Brissenden had been wholly right in his judgment of the magazines, and he, Martin, had spent arduous and futile years in order to find it out for himself. The magazines were all Brissenden had said they were and more. Well, he was done, he solaced himself. He had hitched his wagon to a star and been landed in a pestiferous marsh. The visions of Tahiti—clean, sweet Tahiti—were coming to him more frequently. And there were the low Paumotus, and the high Marquesas; he saw himself often, now, on board trading schooners or frail little cutters, slipping out at dawn through the reef at Papeete and beginning the long beat through the pearl-atolls to Nukahiva and the Bay of Taiohae, where Tamari, he knew, would kill a pig in honor of his coming, and where Tamari's flower-garlanded daughters would seize his hands and with song and laughter garland him with flowers. The South Seas were calling, and he knew that sooner or later he would answer the call.

In the meantime he drifted, resting and recuperating after the long traverse he had made through the realm of knowledge. When *The Parthenon* check of three hundred and fifty dollars was forwarded to him, he turned it over to the local lawyer who had attended to Brissenden's affairs for his family. Martin took a receipt for the check, and at the same time gave a note for the hundred dollars Brissenden had let him have.

The time was not long when Martin ceased patronizing the Japanese restaurants. At the very moment when he had abandoned the fight, the tide turned. But it had turned too late. Without a thrill he opened a thick envelope from *The Millennium*, scanned the face of a check that represented three hundred dollars, and noted that it was the payment on acceptance for "Adventure." Every debt he owed in the world, including the pawnshop, with its usurious interest, amounted to less than a hundred dollars. And when he had paid everything, and lifted the hundred-dollar note with Brissenden's lawyer, he still had over a hundred dollars in pocket. He ordered a suit of clothes from the tailor and ate his meals in the best cafés in town. He still slept in his little room at Maria's, but the sight of his new clothes caused the neighborhood children to cease from calling him "hobo" and "tramp" from the roofs of woodsheds and over back fences.

"Wiki-Wiki," his Hawaiian short story, was bought by *Warren's Monthly* for two hundred and fifty dollars. *The Northern Review* took his essay, "The Cradle of Beauty," and *Mackintosh's Magazine* took "The Palmist"—the poem he had written to Marian. The editors and readers were back from their summer vacations, and manuscripts were being handled quickly. But Martin could not puzzle out what strange whim animated them to this general acceptance of the things they had persistently rejected for two years. Nothing of his had been published. He was not known anywhere outside of Oakland, and in Oakland, with the few who thought they knew him, he was notorious as a red-shirt and a socialist. So there was no explaining this sudden acceptability of his wares. It was sheer jugglery of fate.

After it had been refused by a number of magazines, he had taken Brissenden's rejected advice and started, "The Shame of the Sun" on the round of publishers. After several refusals, Singletree, Darnley & Co. accepted it, promising fall publication. When Martin asked for an advance on royalties, they wrote that such was not their custom, that books of that nature rarely paid for themselves, and that they doubted if his book would sell a thousand copies. Martin figured what the book would earn him on such a sale. Retailed at a dollar, on a royalty of fifteen per cent, it would bring him one hundred and fifty dollars. He decided that if he had it to do over again he would confine himself to fiction. "Adventure," one-fourth as long, had brought him twice as much from *The Millennium*. That newspaper paragraph he had read so long ago had been true, after all. The first-class magazines did not pay on acceptance, and they paid well. Not two cents a word, but four cents a word, had *The Millennium* paid him. And, furthermore, they bought good stuff, too, for were they not buying his? This last thought he accompanied with a grin.

He wrote to Singletree, Darnley & Co., offering to sell out his rights in "The Shame of the Sun" for a hundred dollars, but they did not care to take the risk. In the meantime he was not in need of money, for several of his later stories had been accepted and paid for. He actually opened a bank account, where, without a debt in the world, he had several hundred dollars to his credit. "Overdue," after having been declined by a number of magazines, came to rest at the Meredith-Lowell Company. Martin remembered the five dollars Gertrude had given him, and his resolve to return it to her a hundred times over; so he wrote for an advance on royalties of five hundred dollars. To his surprise a check for that amount, accompanied by a contract, came by return mail. He cashed the check into five-dollar gold pieces and telephoned Gertrude that he wanted to see her.

She arrived at the house panting and short of breath from the haste she had made. Apprehensive of trouble, she had stuffed the few dollars she possessed into her hand-satchel; and so sure was she that disaster had overtaken her brother, that she stumbled forward, sobbing, into his arms, at the same time thrusting the satchel mutely at him.

"I'd have come myself," he said. "But I didn't want a row with Mr. Higginbotham, and that is what would have surely happened."

"He'll be all right after a time," she assured him, while she wondered what the trouble was that Martin was in. "But you'd best get a job first an' steady down. Bernard does like to see a man at honest work. That stuff in the newspapers broke 'm all up. I never saw 'm so mad before."

"I'm not going to get a job," Martin said with a smile. "And you can tell him so from me. I don't need a job, and there's the proof of it."

He emptied the hundred gold pieces into her lap in a glinting, tinkling stream.

"You remember that fiver you gave me the time I didn't have carfare? Well, there it is, with ninety-nine brothers of different ages but all of the same size."

If Gertrude had been frightened when she arrived, she was now in a panic of fear. Her fear was such that it was certitude. She was not suspicious. She was convinced. She looked at Martin in horror, and her heavy limbs shrank under the golden stream as though it were burning her.

"It's yours," he laughed.

She burst into tears, and began to moan, "My poor boy, my poor boy!"

He was puzzled for a moment. Then he divined the cause of her agitation and handed her the Meredith-Lowell letter which had accompanied the check. She stumbled through it, pausing now and again to wipe her eyes, and when she had finished, said:-

"An' does it mean that you come by the money honestly?"

"More honestly than if I'd won it in a lottery. I earned it."

Slowly faith came back to her, and she reread the letter carefully. It took him long to explain to her the nature of the transaction which had put the money into his possession, and longer still to get her to understand that the money was really hers and that he did not need it.

"I'll put it in the bank for you," she said finally.

"You'll do nothing of the sort. It's yours, to do with as you please, and if you won't take it, I'll give it to Maria. She'll know what to do with it. I'd suggest, though, that you hire a servant and take a good long rest."

"I'm goin' to tell Bernard all about it," she announced, when she was leaving.

Martin winced, then grinned.

"Yes, do," he said. "And then, maybe, he'll invite me to dinner again."

"Yes, he will—I'm sure he will!" she exclaimed fervently, as she drew him to her and kissed and hugged him.

CHAPTER XLII

One day Martin became aware that he was lonely. He was healthy and strong, and had nothing to do. The cessation from writing and studying, the death of Brissenden, and the estrangement from Ruth had made a big hole in his life; and his life refused to be pinned down to good living in cafés and the smoking of Egyptian cigarettes. It was true the South Seas were calling to him, but he had a feeling that the game was not yet played out in the United States. Two books were soon to be published, and he had more books that might find publication. Money could be made out of them, and he would wait and take a sackful of it into the South Seas. He knew a valley and a bay in the Marquesas that he could buy for a thousand Chili dollars. The valley ran from the horseshoe, land-locked bay to the tops of the dizzy, cloud-capped peaks and contained perhaps ten thousand acres. It was filled with tropical fruits, wild chickens, and wild pigs, with an occasional herd of wild cattle, while high up among the peaks were herds of wild goats harried by packs of wild dogs. The whole place was wild. Not a human lived in it. And he could buy it and the bay for a thousand Chili dollars.

The bay, as he remembered it, was magnificent, with water deep enough to accommodate the largest vessel afloat, and so safe that the South Pacific Directory recommended it to the best careening place for ships for hundreds of miles around. He would buy a schooner—one of those yacht-like, coppered crafts that sailed like witches—and go trading copra and pearling among the islands. He would make the valley and the bay his headquarters. He would build a patriarchal grass house like Tati's, and have it and the valley and the schooner filled with dark-skinned servitors. He would entertain there the factor of Taiohae, captains of wandering traders, and all the best of the South Pacific riffraff. He would keep open house and entertain like a prince. And he would forget the books he had opened and the world that had proved an illusion.

To do all this he must wait in California to fill the sack with money. Already it was beginning to flow in. If one of the books made a strike, it might enable him to sell the whole heap of manuscripts. Also he could collect the stories and the poems into books, and make sure of the valley and the bay and the schooner. He would never write again. Upon that he was resolved. But in the meantime, awaiting the publication of the books, he must do something more than live dazed and stupid in the sort of uncaring trance into which he had fallen.

He noted, one Sunday morning, that the Bricklayers' Picnic took place that day at Shell Mound Park, and to Shell Mound Park he went. He had been to the working-class picnics too often in his earlier life not to know what they were like, and as he entered the park he experienced a recrudescence of all the old sensations. After all, they were his kind, these working people. He had been born among them, he had lived among them, and though he had strayed for a time, it was well to come back among them.

"If it ain't Mart!" he heard some one say, and the next moment a hearty hand was on his shoulder. "Where you ben all the time? Off to sea? Come on an' have a drink."

It was the old crowd in which he found himself—the old crowd, with here and there a gap, and here and there a new face. The fellows were not bricklayers, but, as in the old days, they attended all Sunday picnics for the dancing, and the fighting, and the fun. Martin drank with them, and began to feel really human once more. He was a fool to have ever left them, he thought; and he was very certain that his sum of happiness would have been greater had he remained with them and let alone the books and the people who sat in the high places. Yet the beer seemed not so good as of yore. It didn't taste as it used to taste. Brissenden had spoiled him for steam beer, he concluded, and wondered if, after all, the books had spoiled him for companionship with these friends of his youth. He resolved that he would not be so spoiled, and he went on to the dancing pavilion. Jimmy, the plumber, he met there, in the company of a tall, blond girl who promptly forsook him for Martin.

"Gee, it's like old times," Jimmy explained to the gang that gave him the laugh as Martin and the blonde whirled away in a waltz. "An' I don't give a rap. I'm too damned glad to see 'm back. Watch 'm waltz, eh? It's like silk. Who'd blame any girl?"

But Martin restored the blonde to Jimmy, and the three of them, with half a dozen friends, watched the revolving couples and laughed and joked with one another. Everybody was glad to see Martin back. No book of his been published; he carried no fictitious value in their eyes. They liked him for himself. He felt like a prince returned from excile, and his lonely heart burgeoned in the geniality in which it bathed. He made a mad day of it, and was at his best. Also, he had money in his pockets, and, as in the old days when he returned from sea with a pay-day, he made the money fly.

Once, on the dancing-floor, he saw Lizzie Connolly go by in the arms of a young workingman; and, later, when he made the round of the pavilion, he came upon her sitting by a refreshment table. Surprise and greetings over, he led her away into the grounds, where they could talk without shouting down the music. From the instant he spoke to her, she was his. He knew it. She showed it in the proud humility of her eyes, in every caressing movement of her proudly carried body, and in the way she hung upon his speech. She was not the young girl as he had known her. She was a woman, now, and Martin noted that her wild, defiant beauty had improved, losing none of its wildness, while the defiance and the fire seemed more in control. "A beauty, a perfect beauty," he murmured admiringly under his breath. And he knew she was his, that all he had to do was to say "Come," and she would go with him over the world wherever he led.

Even as the thought flashed through his brain he received a heavy blow on the side of his head that nearly knocked him down. It was a man's fist, directed by a man so angry and in such haste that the fist had missed the jaw for which it was aimed. Martin turned as he staggered, and saw the fist coming at him in a wild swing. Quite as a matter of course he ducked, and the fist flew harmlessly past, pivoting the man who had driven it. Martin hooked with his left, landing on the pivoting man with the weight of his body behind the blow. The man went to the ground sidewise, leaped to his feet, and made a mad rush. Martin saw his passion-distorted face and wondered what could be the cause of the fellow's anger. But while he wondered, he shot in a straight left, the weight of his body behind the blow. The man went over backward and fell in a crumpled heap. Jimmy and others of the gang were running toward them.

771

Martin was thrilling all over. This was the old days with a vengeance, with their dancing, and their fighting, and their fun. While he kept a wary eye on his antagonist, he glanced at Lizzie. Usually the girls screamed when the fellows got to scrapping, but she had not screamed. She was looking on with bated breath, leaning slightly forward, so keen was her interest, one hand pressed to her breast, her cheek flushed, and in her eyes a great and amazed admiration.

The man had gained his feet and was struggling to escape the restraining arms that were laid on him.

"She was waitin' for me to come back!" he was proclaiming to all and sundry. "She was waitin' for me to come back, an' then that fresh guy comes buttin' in. Let go o' me, I tell yeh. I'm goin' to fix 'm."

"What's eatin' yer?" Jimmy was demanding, as he helped hold the young fellow back. "That guy's Mart Eden. He's nifty with his mits, lemme tell you that, an' he'll eat you alive if you monkey with 'm."

"He can't steal her on me that way," the other interjected.

"He licked the Flyin' Dutchman, an' you know *him*," Jimmy went on expostulating. "An' he did it in five rounds. You couldn't last a minute against him. See?"

This information seemed to have a mollifying effect, and the irate young man favored Martin with a measuring stare.

"He don't look it," he sneered; but the sneer was without passion.

"That's what the Flyin' Dutchman thought," Jimmy assured him. "Come on, now, let's get outa this. There's lots of other girls. Come on."

The young fellow allowed himself to be led away toward the pavilion, and the gang followed after him.

"Who is he?" Martin asked Lizzie. "And what's it all about, anyway?"

Already the zest of combat, which of old had been so keen and lasting, had died down, and he discovered that he was self-analytical, too much so to live, single heart and single hand, so primitive an existence.

Lizzie tossed her head.

"Oh, he's nobody," she said. "He's just ben keepin' company with me."

"I had to, you see," she explained after a pause. "I was gettin' pretty lonesome. But I never forgot." Her voice sank lower, and she looked straight before her. "I'd throw 'm down for you any time."

Martin looking at her averted face, knowing that all he had to do was to reach out his hand and pluck her, fell to pondering whether, after all, there was any real worth in refined, grammatical English, and, so, forgot to reply to her.

"You put it all over him," she said tentatively, with a laugh.

"He's a husky young fellow, though," he admitted generously. "If they hadn't taken him away, he might have given me my hands full."

"Who was that lady friend I seen you with that night?" she asked abruptly.

"Oh, just a lady friend," was his answer.

"It was a long time ago," she murmured contemplatively. "It seems like a thousand years."

But Martin went no further into the matter. He led the conversation off into other channels. They had lunch in the restaurant, where he ordered wine and expensive delicacies and afterward he danced with her and with no one but her, till she was tired. He was a good dancer, and she whirled around and around with him in a heaven of delight, her head against his shoulder, wishing that it could last forever. Later in the afternoon they strayed off among the trees, where, in the good old fashion, she sat down while he sprawled on his back, his head in her lap. He lay and dozed, while she fondled his hair, looked down on his closed eyes, and loved him without reserve. Looking up suddenly, he read the tender advertisement in her face. Her eyes fluttered down, then they opened and looked into his with soft defiance.

"I've kept straight all these years," she said, her voice so low that it was almost a whisper.

In his heart Martin knew that it was the miraculous truth. And at his heart pleaded a great temptation. It was in his power to make her happy. Denied happiness himself, why should he deny happiness to her? He could marry her and take her down with him to dwell in the grass-walled castle in the Marquesas. The desire to do it was strong, but stronger still was the imperative command of his nature not to do it. In spite of himself he was still faithful to Love. The old days of license and easy living were gone. He could not bring them back, nor could he go back to them. He was changed—how changed he had not realized until now.

"I am not a marrying man, Lizzie," he said lightly.

The hand caressing his hair paused perceptibly, then went on with the same gentle stroke. He noticed her face harden, but it was with the hardness of resolution, for still the soft color was in her cheeks and she was all glowing and melting.

"I did not mean that—" she began, then faltered. "Or anyway I don't care."

"I don't care," she repeated. "I'm proud to be your friend. I'd do anything for you. I'm made that way, I guess."

Martin sat up. He took her hand in his. He did it deliberately, with warmth but without passion; and such warmth chilled her.

"Don't let's talk about it," she said.

"You are a great and noble woman," he said. "And it is I who should be proud to know you. And I am, I am. You are a ray of light to me in a very dark world, and I've got to be straight with you, just as straight as you have been."

"I don't care whether you're straight with me or not. You could do anything with me. You could throw me in the dirt an' walk on me. An' you're the only man in the world that can," she added with a defiant flash. "I ain't taken care of myself ever since I was a kid for nothin'."

"And it's just because of that that I'm not going to," he said gently. "You are so big and generous that you challenge me to equal generousness. I'm not marrying, and I'm not—well, loving without marrying, though I've done my share of that in the past. I'm sorry I came here to-day and met you. But it can't be helped now, and I never expected it would turn out this way."

"But look here, Lizzie. I can't begin to tell you how much I like you. I do more than like you. I admire and respect you. You are magnificent, and you are magnificently good. But what's the use of words? Yet there's something I'd like to do. You've had a hard life; let me make it easy for you." (A joyous light welled into her eyes, then faded out again.) "I'm pretty sure of getting hold of some money soon—lots of it."

In that moment he abandoned the idea of the valley and the bay, the grass-walled castle and the trim, white schooner. After all, what did it matter? He could go away, as he had done so often, before the mast, on any ship bound anywhere.

"I'd like to turn it over to you. There must be something you want—to go to school or business college. You might like to study and be a stenographer. I could fix it for you. Or maybe your father and mother are living—I could set them up in a grocery store or something. Anything you want, just name it, and I can fix it for you."

She made no reply, but sat, gazing straight before her, dry-eyed and motionless, but with an ache in the throat which Martin divined so strongly that it made his own throat ache. He regretted that he had spoken. It seemed so tawdry what he had offered her—mere money—compared with what she offered him. He offered her an extraneous thing with which he could part without a pang, while she offered him herself, along with disgrace and shame, and sin, and all her hopes of heaven.

"Don't let's talk about it," she said with a catch in her voice that she changed to a cough. She stood up. "Come on, let's go home. I'm all tired out."

The day was done, and the merrymakers had nearly all departed. But as Martin and Lizzie emerged from the trees they found the gang waiting for them. Martin knew immediately the meaning of it. Trouble was brewing. The gang was his body-guard. They passed out through the gates of the park with, straggling in the rear, a second gang, the friends that Lizzie's young man had collected to avenge the loss of his lady. Several constables and special police officers, anticipating trouble, trailed along to prevent it, and herded the two gangs separately aboard the train for San Francisco. Martin told Jimmy that he would get off at Sixteenth Street Station and catch the electric car into Oakland. Lizzie was very quiet and without interest in what was impending. The train pulled in to Sixteenth Street Station, and the waiting electric car could be seen, the conductor of which was impatiently clanging the gong.

"There she is," Jimmy counselled. "Make a run for it, an' we'll hold 'em back. Now you go! Hit her up!"

The hostile gang was temporarily disconcerted by the manoeuvre, then it dashed from the train in pursuit. The staid and sober Oakland folk who sat upon the car scarcely noted the young fellow and the girl who ran for it and found a seat in front on the outside. They did not connect the couple with Jimmy, who sprang on the steps, crying to the motorman:-

"Slam on the juice, old man, and beat it outa here!"

The next moment Jimmy whirled about, and the passengers saw him land his fist on the face of a running man who was trying to board the car. But fists were landing on faces the whole length of the car. Thus, Jimmy and his gang, strung out on the long, lower steps, met the attacking gang. The car started with a great clanging of its gong, and, as Jimmy's gang drove off the last assailants, they, too, jumped off to finish the job. The car dashed on, leaving the flurry of combat far behind, and its dumfounded passengers never dreamed that the quiet young man and the pretty working-girl sitting in the corner on the outside seat had been the cause of the row.

Martin had enjoyed the fight, with a recrudescence of the old fighting thrills. But they quickly died away, and he was oppressed by a great sadness. He felt very old—centuries older than those careless, care-free young companions of his others days. He had travelled far, too far to go back. Their mode of life, which had once been his, was now distasteful to him. He was disappointed in it all. He had developed into an alien. As the steam beer had tasted raw, so their companionship seemed raw to him. He was too far removed. Too many thousands of opened books yawned between them and him. He had exiled himself. He had travelled in the vast realm of intellect until he could no longer return home. On the other hand, he was human, and his gregarious need for companionship remained unsatisfied. He had found no new home. As the gang could not understand him, as his own family could not understand him, as the bourgeoisie could not understand him, so this girl beside him, whom he honored high, could not understand him nor the honor he paid her. His sadness was not untouched with bitterness as he thought it over.

"Make it up with him," he advised Lizzie, at parting, as they stood in front of the workingman's shack in which she lived, near Sixth and Market. He referred to the young fellow whose place he had usurped that day.

"I can't—now," she said.

"Oh, go on," he said jovially. "All you have to do is whistle and he'll come running."

"I didn't mean that," she said simply.

And he knew what she had meant.

She leaned toward him as he was about to say good night. But she leaned not imperatively, not seductively, but wistfully and humbly. He was touched to the heart. His large tolerance rose up in him. He put his arms around her, and kissed her, and knew that upon his own lips rested as true a kiss as man ever received.

"My God!" she sobbed. "I could die for you. I could die for you."

She tore herself from him suddenly and ran up the steps. He felt a quick moisture in his eyes.

"Martin Eden," he communed. "You're not a brute, and you're a damn poor Nietzscheman. You'd marry her if you could and fill her quivering heart full with happiness. But you can't, you can't. And it's a damn shame."

"'A poor old tramp explains his poor old ulcers,'" he muttered, remembering his Henly. "'Life is, I think, a blunder and a shame.' It is—a blunder and a shame."

CHAPTER XLIII

"The Shame of the Sun" was published in October. As Martin cut the cords of the express package and the half-dozen complimentary copies from the publishers spilled out on the table, a heavy sadness fell upon him. He thought of the wild delight that would have been his had this happened a few short months before, and he contrasted that delight that should have been with his present uncaring coldness. His book, his first book, and his pulse had not gone up a fraction of a beat, and he was only sad. It meant little to him now. The most it meant was that it might bring some money, and little enough did he care for money.

He carried a copy out into the kitchen and presented it to Maria.

"I did it," he explained, in order to clear up her bewilderment. "I wrote it in the room there, and I guess some few quarts of your vegetable soup went into the making of it. Keep it. It's yours. Just to remember me by, you know."

He was not bragging, not showing off. His sole motive was to make her happy, to make her proud of him, to justify her long faith in him. She put the book in the front room on top of the family Bible. A sacred thing was this book her lodger had made, a fetich of friendship. It softened the blow of his having been a laundryman, and though she could not understand a line of it, she knew that every line of it was great. She was a simple, practical, hard-working woman, but she possessed faith in large endowment.

Just as emotionlessly as he had received "The Shame of the Sun" did he read the reviews of it that came in weekly from the clipping bureau. The book was making a hit, that was evident. It meant more gold in the money sack. He could fix up Lizzie, redeem all his promises, and still have enough left to build his grass-walled castle.

Singletree, Darnley & Co. had cautiously brought out an edition of fifteen hundred copies, but the first reviews had started a second edition of twice the size through the presses; and ere this was delivered a third edition of five thousand had been ordered. A London firm made arrangements by cable for an English edition, and hot-footed upon this came the news of French, German, and Scandinavian translations in progress. The attack upon the Maeterlinck school could not have been made at a more opportune moment. A fierce controversy was precipitated. Saleeby and Haeckel indorsed and defended "The Shame of the Sun," for once finding themselves on the same side of a question. Crookes and Wallace ranged up on the opposing side, while Sir Oliver Lodge attempted to formulate a compromise that would jibe with his particular cosmic theories. Maeterlinck's followers rallied around the standard of mysticism. Chesterton set the whole world laughing with a series of alleged non-partisan essays on the subject, and the whole affair, controversy and controversialists, was well-nigh swept into the pit by a thundering broadside from George Bernard Shaw. Needless to say the arena was crowded with hosts of lesser lights, and the dust and sweat and din became terrific.

"It is a most marvellous happening," Singletree, Darnley & Co. wrote Martin, "a critical philosophic essay selling like a novel. You could not have chosen your subject better, and all contributory factors have been unwarrantedly propitious. We need scarcely to assure you that we are making hay while the sun shines. Over forty thousand copies have already been sold in the United States and Canada, and a new edition of twenty thousand is on the presses. We are overworked, trying to supply the demand. Nevertheless we have helped to create that demand. We have already spent five thousand dollars in advertising. The book is bound to be a record-breaker."

"Please find herewith a contract in duplicate for your next book which we have taken the liberty of forwarding to you. You will please note that we have increased your royalties to twenty per cent, which is about as high as a conservative publishing house dares go. If our offer is agreeable to you, please fill in the proper blank space with the title of your book. We make no stipulations concerning its nature. Any book on any subject. If you have one already written, so much the better. Now is the time to strike. The iron could not be hotter."

"On receipt of signed contract we shall be pleased to make you an advance on royalties of five thousand dollars. You see, we have faith in you, and we are going in on this thing big. We should like, also, to discuss with you the drawing up of a contract for a term of years, say ten, during which we shall have the exclusive right of publishing in book-form all that you produce. But more of this anon."

Martin laid down the letter and worked a problem in mental arithmetic, finding the product of fifteen cents times sixty thousand to be nine thousand dollars. He signed the new contract, inserting "The Smoke of Joy" in the blank space, and mailed it back to the publishers along with the twenty storiettes he had written in the days before he discovered the formula for the newspaper storiette. And promptly as the United States mail could deliver and return, came Singletree, Darnley & Co.'s check for five thousand dollars.

"I want you to come down town with me, Maria, this afternoon about two o'clock," Martin said, the morning the check arrived. "Or, better, meet me at Fourteenth and Broadway at two o'clock. I'll be looking out for you."

At the appointed time she was there; but *shoes* was the only clew to the mystery her mind had been capable of evolving, and she suffered a distinct shock of disappointment when Martin walked her right by a shoe-store and dived into a real estate office. What happened thereupon resided forever after in her memory as a dream. Fine gentlemen smiled at her benevolently as they talked with Martin and one another; a type-writer clicked; signatures were affixed to an imposing document; her own landlord was there, too, and affixed his signature; and when all was over and she was outside on the sidewalk, her landlord spoke to her, saying, "Well, Maria, you won't have to pay me no seven dollars and a half this month."

Maria was too stunned for speech.

"Or next month, or the next, or the next," her landlord said.

She thanked him incoherently, as if for a favor. And it was not until she had returned home to North Oakland and conferred with her own kind, and had the Portuguese grocer investigate, that she really knew that she was the owner of the little house in which she had lived and for which she had paid rent so long.

"Why don't you trade with me no more?" the Portuguese grocer asked Martin that evening, stepping out to hail him when he got off the car; and Martin explained that he wasn't doing his own cooking any more, and then went in and had a drink of wine on the house. He noted it was the best wine the grocer had in stock.

"Maria," Martin announced that night, "I'm going to leave you. And you're going to leave here yourself soon. Then you can rent the house and be a landlord yourself. You've a brother in San Leandro or Haywards, and he's in the milk business. I want you to send all your washing back unwashed—understand?—unwashed, and to go out to San Leandro to-morrow, or Haywards, or wherever it is, and see that brother of yours. Tell him to come to see me. I'll be stopping at the Metropole down in Oakland. He'll know a good milk-ranch when he sees one."

And so it was that Maria became a landlord and the sole owner of a dairy, with two hired men to do the work for her and a bank account that steadily increased despite the fact that her whole brood wore shoes and went to school. Few persons ever meet the fairy princes they dream about; but Maria, who worked hard and whose head was hard, never dreaming about fairy princes, entertained hers in the guise of an ex-laundryman.

In the meantime the world had begun to ask: "Who is this Martin Eden?" He had declined to give any biographical data to his publishers, but the newspapers were not to be denied. Oakland was his own town, and the reporters nosed out scores of individuals who could supply information. All that he was and was not, all that he had done and most of what he had not done, was spread out for the delectation of the public, accompanied by snapshots and photographs—the latter procured from the local photographer who had once taken Martin's picture and who promptly copyrighted it and put it on the market. At first, so great was his disgust with the magazines and all bourgeois society, Martin fought against publicity; but in the end, because it was easier than not to, he surrendered. He found that he could not refuse himself to the special writers who travelled long distances to see him. Then again, each day was so many hours long, and, since he no longer was occupied with writing and studying, those hours had to be occupied somehow; so he yielded to what was to him a whim, permitted interviews, gave his opinions on literature and philosophy, and even accepted invitations of the bourgeoisie. He had settled down into a strange and comfortable state of mind. He no longer cared. He forgave everybody, even the cub reporter who had painted him red and to whom he now granted a full page with specially posed photographs.

He saw Lizzie occasionally, and it was patent that she regretted the greatness that had come to him. It widened the space between them. Perhaps it was with the hope of narrowing it that she yielded to his persuasions to go to night school and business college and to have herself gowned by a wonderful dressmaker who charged outrageous prices. She improved visibly from day to day, until Martin wondered if he was doing right, for he knew that all her compliance and endeavor was for his sake. She was trying to make herself of worth in his eyes—of the sort of worth he seemed to value. Yet he gave her no hope, treating her in brotherly fashion and rarely seeing her.

"Overdue" was rushed upon the market by the Meredith-Lowell Company in the height of his popularity, and being fiction, in point of sales it made even a bigger strike than "The Shame of the Sun." Week after week his was the credit of the unprecedented performance of having two books at the head of the list of best-sellers. Not only did the story take with the fiction-readers, but those who read "The Shame of the Sun" with avidity were likewise attracted to the sea-story by the cosmic grasp of mastery with which he had handled it. First he had attacked the literature of mysticism, and had done it exceeding well; and, next, he had successfully supplied the very literature he had exposited, thus proving himself to be that rare genius, a critic and a creator in one.

Money poured in on him, fame poured in on him; he flashed, comet-like, through the world of literature, and he was more amused than interested by the stir he was making. One thing was puzzling him, a little thing that would have puzzled the world had it known. But the world would have puzzled over his bepuzzlement rather than over the little thing that to him loomed gigantic. Judge Blount invited him to dinner. That was the little thing, or the beginning of the little thing, that was soon to become the big thing. He had insulted Judge Blount, treated him abominably, and Judge Blount, meeting him on the street, invited him to dinner. Martin bethought himself of the numerous occasions on which he had met Judge Blount at the Morses' and when Judge Blount had not invited him to dinner. Why had he not invited him to dinner then? he asked himself. He had not changed. He was the same Martin Eden. What made the difference? The fact that the stuff he had written had appeared inside the covers of books? But it was work performed. It was not something he had done since. It was achievement accomplished at the very time Judge Blount was sharing this general view and sneering at his Spencer and his intellect. Therefore it was not for any real value, but for a purely fictitious value that Judge Blount invited him to dinner.

Martin grinned and accepted the invitation, marvelling the while at his complacence. And at the dinner, where, with their womankind, were half a dozen of those that sat in high places, and where Martin found himself quite the lion, Judge Blount, warmly seconded by Judge Hanwell, urged privately that Martin should permit his name to be put up for the Styx—the ultra-select club to which belonged, not the mere men of wealth, but the men of attainment. And Martin declined, and was more puzzled than ever.

He was kept busy disposing of his heap of manuscripts. He was overwhelmed by requests from editors. It had been discovered that he was a stylist, with meat under his style. *The Northern Review*, after publishing "The Cradle of Beauty," had written him for half a dozen similar essays, which would have been supplied out of the heap, had not *Burton's Magazine*, in a speculative mood, offered him five hundred dollars each for five essays. He wrote back that he would supply the demand, but at a thousand dollars an essay. He remembered that all these manuscripts had been refused by the very magazines that were now clamoring for them. And their refusals had been cold-blooded, automatic, stereotyped. They had made him sweat, and now he intended to make them sweat. *Burton's Magazine* paid his price for five essays, and the remaining four, at the same rate, were snapped up by *Mackintosh's Monthly*, *The Northern Review* being too poor to stand the pace. Thus went out to the world "The High Priests of Mystery," "The Wonder-

Dreamers," "The Yardstick of the Ego," "Philosophy of Illusion," "God and Clod," "Art and Biology," "Critics and Test-tubes," "Star-dust," and "The Dignity of Usury,"—to raise storms and rumblings and mutterings that were many a day in dying down.

Editors wrote to him telling him to name his own terms, which he did, but it was always for work performed. He refused resolutely to pledge himself to any new thing. The thought of again setting pen to paper maddened him. He had seen Brissenden torn to pieces by the crowd, and despite the fact that him the crowd acclaimed, he could not get over the shock nor gather any respect for the crowd. His very popularity seemed a disgrace and a treason to Brissenden. It made him wince, but he made up his mind to go on and fill the money-bag.

He received letters from editors like the following: "About a year ago we were unfortunate enough to refuse your collection of love-poems. We were greatly impressed by them at the time, but certain arrangements already entered into prevented our taking them. If you still have them, and if you will be kind enough to forward them, we shall be glad to publish the entire collection on your own terms. We are also prepared to make a most advantageous offer for bringing them out in book-form."

Martin recollected his blank-verse tragedy, and sent it instead. He read it over before mailing, and was particularly impressed by its sophomoric amateurishness and general worthlessness. But he sent it; and it was published, to the everlasting regret of the editor. The public was indignant and incredulous. It was too far a cry from Martin Eden's high standard to that serious bosh. It was asserted that he had never written it, that the magazine had faked it very clumsily, or that Martin Eden was emulating the elder Dumas and at the height of success was hiring his writing done for him. But when he explained that the tragedy was an early effort of his literary childhood, and that the magazine had refused to be happy unless it got it, a great laugh went up at the magazine's expense and a change in the editorship followed. The tragedy was never brought out in book-form, though Martin pocketed the advance royalties that had been paid.

Coleman's Weekly sent Martin a lengthy telegram, costing nearly three hundred dollars, offering him a thousand dollars an article for twenty articles. He was to travel over the United States, with all expenses paid, and select whatever topics interested him. The body of the telegram was devoted to hypothetical topics in order to show him the freedom of range that was to be his. The only restriction placed upon him was that he must confine himself to the United States. Martin sent his inability to accept and his regrets by wire "collect."

"Wiki-Wiki," published in *Warren's Monthly*, was an instantaneous success. It was brought out forward in a wide-margined, beautifully decorated volume that struck the holiday trade and sold like wildfire. The critics were unanimous in the belief that it would take its place with those two classics by two great writers, "The Bottle Imp" and "The Magic Skin."

The public, however, received the "Smoke of Joy" collection rather dubiously and coldly. The audacity and unconventionality of the storiettes was a shock to bourgeois morality and prejudice; but when Paris went mad over the immediate translation that was made, the American and English reading public followed suit and bought so many copies that Martin compelled the conservative house of Singletree, Darnley & Co. to pay a flat royalty of twenty-five per cent for a third book, and thirty per cent flat for a fourth. These two volumes comprised all the short stories he had written and which had received, or were receiving, serial publication. "The Ring of Bells" and his horror stories constituted one collection; the other collection was composed of "Adventure," "The Pot," "The Wine of Life," "The Whirlpool," "The Jostling Street," and four other stories. The Lowell-Meredith Company captured the collection of all his essays, and the Maxmillian Company got his "Sea Lyrics" and the "Love-cycle," the latter receiving serial publication in the *Ladies' Home Companion* after the payment of an extortionate price.

Martin heaved a sigh of relief when he had disposed of the last manuscript. The grass-walled castle and the white, coppered schooner were very near to him. Well, at any rate he had discovered Brissenden's contention that nothing of merit found its way into the magazines. His own success demonstrated that Brissenden had been wrong.

786

And yet, somehow, he had a feeling that Brissenden had been right, after all. "The Shame of the Sun" had been the cause of his success more than the stuff he had written. That stuff had been merely incidental. It had been rejected right and left by the magazines. The publication of "The Shame of the Sun" had started a controversy and precipitated the landslide in his favor. Had there been no "Shame of the Sun" there would have been no landslide, and had there been no miracle in the go of "The Shame of the Sun" there would have been no landslide. Singletree, Darnley & Co. attested that miracle. They had brought out a first edition of fifteen hundred copies and been dubious of selling it. They were experienced publishers and no one had been more astounded than they at the success which had followed. To them it had been in truth a miracle. They never got over it, and every letter they wrote him reflected their reverent awe of that first mysterious happening. They did not attempt to explain it. There was no explaining it. It had happened. In the face of all experience to the contrary, it had happened.

So it was, reasoning thus, that Martin questioned the validity of his popularity. It was the bourgeoisie that bought his books and poured its gold into his money-sack, and from what little he knew of the bourgeoisie it was not clear to him how it could possibly appreciate or comprehend what he had written. His intrinsic beauty and power meant nothing to the hundreds of thousands who were acclaiming him and buying his books. He was the fad of the hour, the adventurer who had stormed Parnassus while the gods nodded. The hundreds of thousands read him and acclaimed him with the same brute non-understanding with which they had flung themselves on Brissenden's "Ephemera" and torn it to pieces—a wolf-rabble that fawned on him instead of fanging him. Fawn or fang, it was all a matter of chance. One thing he knew with absolute certitude: "Ephemera" was infinitely greater than anything he had done. It was infinitely greater than anything he had in him. It was a poem of centuries. Then the tribute the mob paid him was a sorry tribute indeed, for that same mob had wallowed "Ephemera" into the mire. He sighed heavily and with satisfaction. He was glad the last manuscript was sold and that he would soon be done with it all.

CHAPTER XLIV

Mr. Morse met Martin in the office of the Hotel Metropole. Whether he had happened there just casually, intent on other affairs, or whether he had come there for the direct purpose of inviting him to dinner, Martin never could quite make up his mind, though he inclined toward the second hypothesis. At any rate, invited to dinner he was by Mr. Morse—Ruth's father, who had forbidden him the house and broken off the engagement.

Martin was not angry. He was not even on his dignity. He tolerated Mr. Morse, wondering the while how it felt to eat such humble pie. He did not decline the invitation. Instead, he put it off with vagueness and indefiniteness and inquired after the family, particularly after Mrs. Morse and Ruth. He spoke her name without hesitancy, naturally, though secretly surprised that he had had no inward quiver, no old, familiar increase of pulse and warm surge of blood.

He had many invitations to dinner, some of which he accepted. Persons got themselves introduced to him in order to invite him to dinner. And he went on puzzling over the little thing that was becoming a great thing. Bernard Higginbotham invited him to dinner. He puzzled the harder. He remembered the days of his desperate starvation when no one invited him to dinner. That was the time he needed dinners, and went weak and faint for lack of them and lost weight from sheer famine. That was the paradox of it. When he wanted dinners, no one gave them to him, and now that he could buy a hundred thousand dinners and was losing his appetite, dinners were thrust upon him right and left. But why? There was no justice in it, no merit on his part. He was no different. All the work he had done was even at that time *work performed*. Mr. and Mrs. Morse had condemned him for an idler and a shirk and through Ruth had urged that he take a clerk's position in an office. Furthermore, they had been aware of his work performed. Manuscript after manuscript of his had been turned over to them by Ruth. They had read them. It was the very same work that had put his name in all the papers, and, it was his name being in all the papers that led them to invite him.

One thing was certain: the Morses had not cared to have him for himself or for his work. Therefore they could not want him now for himself or for his work, but for the fame that was his, because he was somebody amongst men, and—why not?—because he had a hundred thousand dollars or so. That was the way bourgeois society valued a man, and who was he to expect it otherwise? But he was proud. He disdained such valuation. He desired to be valued for himself, or for his work, which, after all, was an expression of himself. That was the way Lizzie valued him. The work, with her, did not even count. She valued him, himself. That was the way Jimmy, the plumber, and all the old gang valued him. That had been proved often enough in the days when he ran with them; it had been proved that Sunday at Shell Mound Park. His work could go hang. What they liked, and were willing to scrap for, was just Mart Eden, one of the bunch and a pretty good guy.

Then there was Ruth. She had liked him for himself, that was indisputable. And yet, much as she had liked him she had liked the bourgeois standard of valuation more. She had opposed his writing, and principally, it seemed to him, because it did not earn money. That had been her criticism of his "Love-cycle." She, too, had urged him to get a job. It was true, she refined it to "position," but it meant the same thing, and in his own mind the old nomenclature stuck. He had read her all that he wrote—poems, stories, essays—"Wiki-Wiki," "The Shame of the Sun," everything. And she had always and consistently urged him to get a job, to go to work—good God!—as if he hadn't been working, robbing sleep, exhausting life, in order to be worthy of her.

So the little thing grew bigger. He was healthy and normal, ate regularly, slept long hours, and yet the growing little thing was becoming an obsession. Work performed. The phrase haunted his brain. He sat opposite Bernard Higginbotham at a heavy Sunday dinner over Higginbotham's Cash Store, and it was all he could do to restrain himself from shouting out:-

"It was work performed! And now you feed me, when then you let me starve, forbade me your house, and damned me because I wouldn't get a job. And the work was already done, all done. And now, when I speak, you check the thought unuttered on your lips and hang on my lips and pay respectful attention to whatever I choose to say. I tell you your party is rotten and filled with grafters, and instead of flying into a rage you hum and haw and admit there is a great deal in what I say. And why? Because I'm famous; because I've a lot of money. Not because I'm Martin Eden, a pretty good fellow and not particularly a fool. I could tell you the moon is made of green cheese and you would subscribe to the notion, at least you would not repudiate it, because I've got dollars, mountains of them. And it was all done long ago; it was work performed, I tell you, when you spat upon me as the dirt under your feet."

But Martin did not shout out. The thought gnawed in his brain, an unceasing torment, while he smiled and succeeded in being tolerant. As he grew silent, Bernard Higginbotham got the reins and did the talking. He was a success himself, and proud of it. He was self-made. No one had helped him. He owed no man. He was fulfilling his duty as a citizen and bringing up a large family. And there was Higginbotham's Cash Store, that monument of his own industry and ability. He loved Higginbotham's Cash Store as some men loved their wives. He opened up his heart to Martin, showed with what keenness and with what enormous planning he had made the store. And he had plans for it, ambitious plans. The neighborhood was growing up fast. The store was really too small. If he had more room, he would be able to put in a score of labor-saving and money-saving improvements. And he would do it yet. He was straining every effort for the day when he could buy the adjoining lot and put up another two-story frame building. The upstairs he could rent, and the whole ground-floor of both buildings would be Higginbotham's Cash Store. His eyes glistened when he spoke of the new sign that would stretch clear across both buildings.

Martin forgot to listen. The refrain of "Work performed," in his own brain, was drowning the other's clatter. The refrain maddened him, and he tried to escape from it.

"How much did you say it would cost?" he asked suddenly.

His brother-in-law paused in the middle of an expatiation on the business opportunities of the neighborhood. He hadn't said how much it would cost. But he knew. He had figured it out a score of times.

"At the way lumber is now," he said, "four thousand could do it."

"Including the sign?"

"I didn't count on that. It'd just have to come, onc't the buildin' was there."

"And the ground?"

"Three thousand more."

He leaned forward, licking his lips, nervously spreading and closing his fingers, while he watched Martin write a check. When it was passed over to him, he glanced at the amount-seven thousand dollars.

"I—I can't afford to pay more than six per cent," he said huskily.

Martin wanted to laugh, but, instead, demanded:-

"How much would that be?"

"Lemme see. Six per cent—six times seven—four hundred an' twenty."

"That would be thirty-five dollars a month, wouldn't it?"

Higginbotham nodded.

"Then, if you've no objection, we'll arrange it this way." Martin glanced at Gertrude. "You can have the principal to keep for yourself, if you'll use the thirty-five dollars a month for cooking and washing and scrubbing. The seven thousand is yours if you'll guarantee that Gertrude does no more drudgery. Is it a go?"

Mr. Higginbotham swallowed hard. That his wife should do no more housework was an affront to his thrifty soul. The magnificent present was the coating of a pill, a bitter pill. That his wife should not work! It gagged him.

"All right, then," Martin said. "I'll pay the thirty-five a month, and—"

He reached across the table for the check. But Bernard Higginbotham got his hand on it first, crying:

"I accept! I accept!"

When Martin got on the electric car, he was very sick and tired. He looked up at the assertive sign.

"The swine," he groaned. "The swine, the swine."

When *Mackintosh's Magazine* published "The Palmist," featuring it with decorations by Berthier and with two pictures by Wenn, Hermann von Schmidt forgot that he had called the verses obscene. He announced that his wife had inspired the poem, saw to it that the news reached the ears of a reporter, and submitted to an interview by a staff writer who was accompanied by a staff photographer and a staff artist. The result was a full page in a Sunday supplement, filled with photographs and idealized drawings of Marian, with many intimate details of Martin Eden and his family, and with the full text of "The Palmist" in large type, and republished by special permission of *Mackintosh's Magazine*. It caused quite a stir in the neighborhood, and good housewives were proud to have the acquaintance of the great writer's sister, while those who had not made haste to cultivate it. Hermann von Schmidt chuckled in his little repair shop and decided to order a new lathe. "Better than advertising," he told Marian, "and it costs nothing."

"We'd better have him to dinner," she suggested.

And to dinner Martin came, making himself agreeable with the fat wholesale butcher and his fatter wife—important folk, they, likely to be of use to a rising young man like Hermann Von Schmidt. No less a bait, however, had been required to draw them to his house than his great brother-in-law. Another man at table who had swallowed the same bait was the superintendent of the Pacific Coast agencies for the Asa Bicycle Company. Him Von Schmidt desired to please and propitiate because from him could be obtained the Oakland agency for the bicycle. So Hermann von Schmidt found it a goodly asset to have Martin for a brother-in-law, but in his heart of hearts he couldn't understand where it all came in. In the silent watches of the night, while his wife slept, he had floundered through Martin's books and poems, and decided that the world was a fool to buy them.

And in his heart of hearts Martin understood the situation only too well, as he leaned back and gloated at Von Schmidt's head, in fancy punching it well-nigh off of him, sending blow after blow home just right—the chuckle-headed Dutchman! One thing he did like about him, however. Poor as he was, and determined to rise as he was, he nevertheless hired one servant to take the heavy work off of Marian's hands. Martin talked with the superintendent of the Asa agencies, and after dinner he drew him aside with Hermann, whom he backed financially for the best bicycle store with fittings in Oakland. He went further, and in a private talk with Hermann told him to keep his eyes open for an automobile agency and garage, for there was no reason that he should not be able to run both establishments successfully.

With tears in her eyes and her arms around his neck, Marian, at parting, told Martin how much she loved him and always had loved him. It was true, there was a perceptible halt midway in her assertion, which she glossed over with more tears and kisses and incoherent stammerings, and which Martin inferred to be her appeal for forgiveness for the time she had lacked faith in him and insisted on his getting a job.

"He can't never keep his money, that's sure," Hermann von Schmidt confided to his wife. "He got mad when I spoke of interest, an' he said damn the principal and if I mentioned it again, he'd punch my Dutch head off. That's what he said—my Dutch head. But he's all right, even if he ain't no business man. He's given me my chance, an' he's all right."

Invitations to dinner poured in on Martin; and the more they poured, the more he puzzled. He sat, the guest of honor, at an Arden Club banquet, with men of note whom he had heard about and read about all his life; and they told him how, when they had read "The Ring of Bells" in the *Transcontinental,* and "The Peri and the Pearl" in The Hornet, they had immediately picked him for a winner. My God! and I was hungry and in rags, he thought to himself. Why didn't you give me a dinner then? Then was the time. It was work performed. If you are feeding me now for work performed, why did you not feed me then when I needed it? Not one word in "The Ring of Bells," nor in "The Peri and the Pearl" has been changed. No; you're not feeding me now for work performed. You are feeding me because everybody else is feeding me and because it is an honor to feed me. You are feeding me now because you are herd animals; because you are part of the mob; because the one blind, automatic thought in the mob-mind just now is to feed me. And where does Martin Eden and the work Martin Eden performed come in in all this? he asked himself plaintively, then arose to respond cleverly and wittily to a clever and witty toast.

So it went. Wherever he happened to be—at the Press Club, at the Redwood Club, at pink teas and literary gatherings—always were remembered "The Ring of Bells" and "The Peri and the Pearl" when they were first published. And always was Martin's maddening and unuttered demand: Why didn't you feed me then? It was work performed. "The Ring of Bells" and "The Peri and the Pearl" are not changed one iota. They were just as artistic, just as worth while, then as now. But you are not feeding me for their sake, nor for the sake of anything else I have written. You're feeding me because it is the style of feeding just now, because the whole mob is crazy with the idea of feeding Martin Eden.

And often, at such times, he would abruptly see slouch in among the company a young hoodlum in square-cut coat and under a stiff-rim Stetson hat. It happened to him at the Gallina Society in Oakland one afternoon. As he rose from his chair and stepped forward across the platform, he saw stalk through the wide door at the rear of the great room the young hoodlum with the square-cut coat and stiff-rim hat. Five hundred fashionably gowned women turned their heads, so intent and steadfast was Martin's gaze, to see what he was seeing. But they saw only the empty centre aisle. He saw the young tough lurching down that aisle and wondered if he would remove the stiff-rim which never yet had he seen him without. Straight down the aisle he came, and up the platform. Martin could have wept over that youthful shade of himself, when he thought of all that lay before him. Across the platform he swaggered, right up to Martin, and into the foreground of Martin's consciousness disappeared. The five hundred women applauded softly with gloved hands, seeking to encourage the bashful great man who was their guest. And Martin shook the vision from his brain, smiled, and began to speak.

794

The Superintendent of Schools, good old man, stopped Martin on the street and remembered him, recalling seances in his office when Martin was expelled from school for fighting.

"I read your 'Ring of Bells' in one of the magazines quite a time ago," he said. "It was as good as Poe. Splendid, I said at the time, splendid!"

Yes, and twice in the months that followed you passed me on the street and did not know me, Martin almost said aloud. Each time I was hungry and heading for the pawnbroker. Yet it was work performed. You did not know me then. Why do you know me now?

"I was remarking to my wife only the other day," the other was saying, "wouldn't it be a good idea to have you out to dinner some time? And she quite agreed with me. Yes, she quite agreed with me."

"Dinner?" Martin said so sharply that it was almost a snarl.

"Why, yes, yes, dinner, you know—just pot luck with us, with your old superintendent, you rascal," he uttered nervously, poking Martin in an attempt at jocular fellowship.

Martin went down the street in a daze. He stopped at the corner and looked about him vacantly.

"Well, I'll be damned!" he murmured at last. "The old fellow was afraid of me."

CHAPTER XLV

Kreis came to Martin one day—Kreis, of the "real dirt"; and Martin turned to him with relief, to receive the glowing details of a scheme sufficiently wild-catty to interest him as a fictionist rather than an investor. Kreis paused long enough in the midst of his exposition to tell him that in most of his "Shame of the Sun" he had been a chump.

"But I didn't come here to spout philosophy," Kreis went on. "What I want to know is whether or not you will put a thousand dollars in on this deal?"

"No, I'm not chump enough for that, at any rate," Martin answered. "But I'll tell you what I will do. You gave me the greatest night of my life. You gave me what money cannot buy. Now I've got money, and it means nothing to me. I'd like to turn over to you a thousand dollars of what I don't value for what you gave me that night and which was beyond price. You need the money. I've got more than I need. You want it. You came for it. There's no use scheming it out of me. Take it."

Kreis betrayed no surprise. He folded the check away in his pocket.

"At that rate I'd like the contract of providing you with many such nights," he said.

"Too late." Martin shook his head. "That night was the one night for me. I was in paradise. It's commonplace with you, I know. But it wasn't to me. I shall never live at such a pitch again. I'm done with philosophy. I want never to hear another word of it."

"The first dollar I ever made in my life out of my philosophy," Kreis remarked, as he paused in the doorway. "And then the market broke."

Mrs. Morse drove by Martin on the street one day, and smiled and nodded. He smiled back and lifted his hat. The episode did not affect him. A month before it might have disgusted him, or made him curious and set him to speculating about her state of consciousness at that moment. But now it was not provocative of a second thought. He forgot about it the next moment. He forgot about it as he would have forgotten the Central Bank Building or the City Hall after having walked past them. Yet his mind was preternaturally active. His thoughts went ever around and around in a circle. The centre of that circle was "work performed"; it ate at his brain like a deathless maggot. He awoke to it in the morning. It tormented his dreams at night. Every affair of life around him that penetrated through his senses immediately related itself to "work performed." He drove along the path of relentless logic to the conclusion that he was nobody, nothing. Mart Eden, the hoodlum, and Mart Eden, the sailor, had been real, had been he; but Martin Eden! the famous writer, did not exist. Martin Eden, the famous writer, was a vapor that had arisen in the mob-mind and by the mob-mind had been thrust into the corporeal being of Mart Eden, the hoodlum and sailor. But it couldn't fool him. He was not that sun-myth that the mob was worshipping and sacrificing dinners to. He knew better.

He read the magazines about himself, and pored over portraits of himself published therein until he was unable to associate his identity with those portraits. He was the fellow who had lived and thrilled and loved; who had been easy-going and tolerant of the frailties of life; who had served in the forecastle, wandered in strange lands, and led his gang in the old fighting days. He was the fellow who had been stunned at first by the thousands of books in the free library, and who had afterward learned his way among them and mastered them; he was the fellow who had burned the midnight oil and bedded with a spur and written books himself. But the one thing he was not was that colossal appetite that all the mob was bent upon feeding.

There were things, however, in the magazines that amused him. All the magazines were claiming him. *Warren's Monthly* advertised to its subscribers that it was always on the quest after new writers, and that, among others, it had introduced Martin Eden to the reading public. The *White Mouse* claimed him; so did *The Northern Review* and *Mackintosh's Magazine*, until silenced by *The Globe*, which pointed triumphantly to its files where the mangled "Sea Lyrics" lay buried. Youth and Age, which had come to life again after having escaped paying its bills, put in a prior claim, which nobody but farmers' children ever read. The *Transcontinental* made a dignified and convincing statement of how it first discovered Martin Eden, which was warmly disputed by The Hornet, with the exhibit of "The Peri and the Pearl." The modest claim of Singletree, Darnley & Co. was lost in the din. Besides, that publishing firm did not own a magazine wherewith to make its claim less modest.

The newspapers calculated Martin's royalties. In some way the magnificent offers certain magazines had made him leaked out, and Oakland ministers called upon him in a friendly way, while professional begging letters began to clutter his mail. But worse than all this were the women. His photographs were published broadcast, and special writers exploited his strong, bronzed face, his scars, his heavy shoulders, his clear, quiet eyes, and the slight hollows in his cheeks like an ascetic's. At this last he remembered his wild youth and smiled. Often, among the women he met, he would see now one, now another, looking at him, appraising him, selecting him. He laughed to himself. He remembered Brissenden's warning and laughed again. The women would never destroy him, that much was certain. He had gone past that stage.

Once, walking with Lizzie toward night school, she caught a glance directed toward him by a well-gowned, handsome woman of the bourgeoisie. The glance was a trifle too long, a shade too considerate. Lizzie knew it for what it was, and her body tensed angrily. Martin noticed, noticed the cause of it, told her how used he was becoming to it and that he did not care anyway.

"You ought to care," she answered with blazing eyes. "You're sick. That's what's the matter."

"Never healthier in my life. I weigh five pounds more than I ever did."

"It ain't your body. It's your head. Something's wrong with your think-machine. Even I can see that, an' I ain't nobody."

He walked on beside her, reflecting.

"I'd give anything to see you get over it," she broke out impulsively. "You ought to care when women look at you that way, a man like you. It's not natural. It's all right enough for sissy-boys. But you ain't made that way. So help me, I'd be willing an' glad if the right woman came along an' made you care."

When he left Lizzie at night school, he returned to the Metropole.

Once in his rooms, he dropped into a Morris chair and sat staring straight before him. He did not doze. Nor did he think. His mind was a blank, save for the intervals when unsummoned memory pictures took form and color and radiance just under his eyelids. He saw these pictures, but he was scarcely conscious of them—no more so than if they had been dreams. Yet he was not asleep. Once, he roused himself and glanced at his watch. It was just eight o'clock. He had nothing to do, and it was too early for bed. Then his mind went blank again, and the pictures began to form and vanish under his eyelids. There was nothing distinctive about the pictures. They were always masses of leaves and shrub-like branches shot through with hot sunshine.

A knock at the door aroused him. He was not asleep, and his mind immediately connected the knock with a telegram, or letter, or perhaps one of the servants bringing back clean clothes from the laundry. He was thinking about Joe and wondering where he was, as he said, "Come in."

He was still thinking about Joe, and did not turn toward the door. He heard it close softly. There was a long silence. He forgot that there had been a knock at the door, and was still staring blankly before him when he heard a woman's sob. It was involuntary, spasmodic, checked, and stifled—he noted that as he turned about. The next instant he was on his feet.

"Ruth!" he said, amazed and bewildered.

Her face was white and strained. She stood just inside the door, one hand against it for support, the other pressed to her side. She extended both hands toward him piteously, and started forward to meet him. As he caught her hands and led her to the Morris chair he noticed how cold they were. He drew up another chair and sat down on the broad arm of it. He was too confused to speak. In his own mind his affair with Ruth was closed and sealed. He felt much in the same way that he would have felt had the Shelly Hot Springs Laundry suddenly invaded the Hotel Metropole with a whole week's washing ready for him to pitch into. Several times he was about to speak, and each time he hesitated.

"No one knows I am here," Ruth said in a faint voice, with an appealing smile.

"What did you say?"

He was surprised at the sound of his own voice.

She repeated her words.

"Oh," he said, then wondered what more he could possibly say.

"I saw you come in, and I waited a few minutes."

"Oh," he said again.

He had never been so tongue-tied in his life. Positively he did not have an idea in his head. He felt stupid and awkward, but for the life of him he could think of nothing to say. It would have been easier had the intrusion been the Shelly Hot Springs laundry. He could have rolled up his sleeves and gone to work.

"And then you came in," he said finally.

She nodded, with a slightly arch expression, and loosened the scarf at her throat.

"I saw you first from across the street when you were with that girl."

"Oh, yes," he said simply. "I took her down to night school."

"Well, aren't you glad to see me?" she said at the end of another silence.

"Yes, yes." He spoke hastily. "But wasn't it rash of you to come here?"

"I slipped in. Nobody knows I am here. I wanted to see you. I came to tell you I have been very foolish. I came because I could no longer stay away, because my heart compelled me to come, because—because I wanted to come."

She came forward, out of her chair and over to him. She rested her hand on his shoulder a moment, breathing quickly, and then slipped into his arms. And in his large, easy way, desirous of not inflicting hurt, knowing that to repulse this proffer of herself was to inflict the most grievous hurt a woman could receive, he folded his arms around her and held her close. But there was no warmth in the embrace, no caress in the contact. She had come into his arms, and he held her, that was all. She nestled against him, and then, with a change of position, her hands crept up and rested upon his neck. But his flesh was not fire beneath those hands, and he felt awkward and uncomfortable.

"What makes you tremble so?" he asked. "Is it a chill? Shall I light the grate?"

He made a movement to disengage himself, but she clung more closely to him, shivering violently.

"It is merely nervousness," she said with chattering teeth. "I'll control myself in a minute. There, I am better already."

Slowly her shivering died away. He continued to hold her, but he was no longer puzzled. He knew now for what she had come.

"My mother wanted me to marry Charley Hapgood," she announced.

"Charley Hapgood, that fellow who speaks always in platitudes?" Martin groaned. Then he added, "And now, I suppose, your mother wants you to marry me."

He did not put it in the form of a question. He stated it as a certitude, and before his eyes began to dance the rows of figures of his royalties.

"She will not object, I know that much," Ruth said.

"She considers me quite eligible?"

Ruth nodded.

"And yet I am not a bit more eligible now than I was when she broke our engagement," he meditated. "I haven't changed any. I'm the same Martin

Eden, though for that matter I'm a bit worse—I smoke now. Don't you smell my breath?"

In reply she pressed her open fingers against his lips, placed them graciously and playfully, and in expectancy of the kiss that of old had always been a consequence. But there was no caressing answer of Martin's lips. He waited until the fingers were removed and then went on.

"I am not changed. I haven't got a job. I'm not looking for a job. Furthermore, I am not going to look for a job. And I still believe that Herbert Spencer is a great and noble man and that Judge Blount is an unmitigated ass. I had dinner with him the other night, so I ought to know."

"But you didn't accept father's invitation," she chided.

"So you know about that? Who sent him? Your mother?"

She remained silent.

"Then she did send him. I thought so. And now I suppose she has sent you."

"No one knows that I am here," she protested. "Do you think my mother would permit this?"

"She'd permit you to marry me, that's certain."

She gave a sharp cry. "Oh, Martin, don't be cruel. You have not kissed me once. You are as unresponsive as a stone. And think what I have dared to do." She looked about her with a shiver, though half the look was curiosity. "Just think of where I am."

"*I could die for you! I could die for you!*"—Lizzie's words were ringing in his ears.

"Why didn't you dare it before?" he asked harshly. "When I hadn't a job? When I was starving? When I was just as I am now, as a man, as an artist, the same Martin Eden? That's the question I've been propounding to myself for many a day—not concerning you merely, but concerning everybody. You see I have not changed, though my sudden apparent appreciation in value compels me constantly to reassure myself on that point. I've got the same flesh on my bones, the same ten fingers and toes. I am the same. I have not developed any new strength nor virtue. My brain is the same old brain. I haven't made even one new generalization on literature or philosophy. I am personally of the same value that I was when nobody wanted me. And what is puzzling me is why they want me now. Surely they don't want me for myself, for myself is the same old self they did not want. Then they must want me for something else, for something that is outside of me, for something that is not I! Shall I tell you what that something is? It is for the recognition I have received. That recognition is not I. It resides in the minds of others. Then again for the money I have earned and am earning. But that money is not I. It resides in banks and in the pockets of Tom, Dick, and Harry. And is it for that, for the recognition and the money, that you now want me?"

"You are breaking my heart," she sobbed. "You know I love you, that I am here because I love you."

"I am afraid you don't see my point," he said gently. "What I mean is: if you love me, how does it happen that you love me now so much more than you did when your love was weak enough to deny me?"

"Forget and forgive," she cried passionately. "I loved you all the time, remember that, and I am here, now, in your arms."

"I'm afraid I am a shrewd merchant, peering into the scales, trying to weigh your love and find out what manner of thing it is."

She withdrew herself from his arms, sat upright, and looked at him long and searchingly. She was about to speak, then faltered and changed her mind.

"You see, it appears this way to me," he went on. "When I was all that I am now, nobody out of my own class seemed to care for me. When my books were all written, no one who had read the manuscripts seemed to care for them. In point of fact, because of the stuff I had written they seemed to care even less for me. In writing the stuff it seemed that I had committed acts that were, to say the least, derogatory. 'Get a job,' everybody said."

She made a movement of dissent.

"Yes, yes," he said; "except in your case you told me to get a position. The homely word *job*, like much that I have written, offends you. It is brutal. But I assure you it was no less brutal to me when everybody I knew recommended it to me as they would recommend right conduct to an immoral creature. But to return. The publication of what I had written, and the public notice I received, wrought a change in the fibre of your love. Martin Eden, with his work all performed, you would not marry. Your love for him was not strong enough to enable you to marry him. But your love is now strong enough, and I cannot avoid the conclusion that its strength arises from the publication and the public notice. In your case I do not mention royalties, though I am certain that they apply to the change wrought in your mother and father. Of course, all this is not flattering to me. But worst of all, it makes me question love, sacred love. Is love so gross a thing that it must feed upon publication and public notice? It would seem so. I have sat and thought upon it till my head went around."

"Poor, dear head." She reached up a hand and passed the fingers soothingly through his hair. "Let it go around no more. Let us begin anew, now. I loved you all the time. I know that I was weak in yielding to my mother's will. I should not have done so. Yet I have heard you speak so often with broad charity of the fallibility and frailty of humankind. Extend that charity to me. I acted mistakenly. Forgive me."

"Oh, I do forgive," he said impatiently. "It is easy to forgive where there is really nothing to forgive. Nothing that you have done requires forgiveness. One acts according to one's lights, and more than that one cannot do. As well might I ask you to forgive me for my not getting a job."

"I meant well," she protested. "You know that I could not have loved you and not meant well."

"True; but you would have destroyed me out of your well-meaning."

"Yes, yes," he shut off her attempted objection. "You would have destroyed my writing and my career. Realism is imperative to my nature, and the bourgeois spirit hates realism. The bourgeoisie is cowardly. It is afraid of life. And all your effort was to make me afraid of life. You would have formalized me. You would have compressed me into a two-by-four pigeonhole of life, where all life's values are unreal, and false, and vulgar." He felt her stir protestingly. "Vulgarity—a hearty vulgarity, I'll admit—is the basis of bourgeois refinement and culture. As I say, you wanted to formalize me, to make me over into one of your own class, with your class-ideals, class-values, and class-prejudices." He shook his head sadly. "And you do not understand, even now, what I am saying. My words do not mean to you what I endeavor to make them mean. What I say is so much fantasy to you. Yet to me it is vital reality. At the best you are a trifle puzzled and amused that this raw boy, crawling up out of the mire of the abyss, should pass judgment upon your class and call it vulgar."

She leaned her head wearily against his shoulder, and her body shivered with recurrent nervousness. He waited for a time for her to speak, and then went on.

"And now you want to renew our love. You want us to be married. You want me. And yet, listen—if my books had not been noticed, I'd nevertheless have been just what I am now. And you would have stayed away. It is all those damned books—"

"Don't swear," she interrupted.

Her reproof startled him. He broke into a harsh laugh.

"That's it," he said, "at a high moment, when what seems your life's happiness is at stake, you are afraid of life in the same old way—afraid of life and a healthy oath."

She was stung by his words into realization of the puerility of her act, and yet she felt that he had magnified it unduly and was consequently resentful. They sat in silence for a long time, she thinking desperately and he pondering upon his love which had departed. He knew, now, that he had not really loved her. It was an idealized Ruth he had loved, an ethereal creature of his own creating, the bright and luminous spirit of his love-poems. The real bourgeois Ruth, with all the bourgeois failings and with the hopeless cramp of the bourgeois *psychology* in her mind, he had never loved.

She suddenly began to speak.

"I know that much you have said is so. I have been afraid of life. I did not love you well enough. I have learned to love better. I love you for what you are, for what you were, for the ways even by which you have become. I love you for the ways wherein you differ from what you call my class, for your beliefs which I do not understand but which I know I can come to understand. I shall devote myself to understanding them. And even your smoking and your swearing—they are part of you and I will love you for them, too. I can still learn. In the last ten minutes I have learned much. That I have dared to come here is a token of what I have already learned. Oh, Martin!—"

She was sobbing and nestling close against him.

For the first time his arms folded her gently and with sympathy, and she acknowledged it with a happy movement and a brightening face.

"It is too late," he said. He remembered Lizzie's words. "I am a sick man—oh, not my body. It is my soul, my brain. I seem to have lost all values. I care for nothing. If you had been this way a few months ago, it would have been different. It is too late, now."

"It is not too late," she cried. "I will show you. I will prove to you that my love has grown, that it is greater to me than my class and all that is dearest to me. All that is dearest to the bourgeoisie I will flout. I am no longer afraid of life. I will leave my father and mother, and let my name become a by-word with my friends. I will come to you here and now, in free love if you will, and I will be proud and glad to be with you. If I have been a traitor to love, I will now, for love's sake, be a traitor to all that made that earlier treason."

She stood before him, with shining eyes.

"I am waiting, Martin," she whispered, "waiting for you to accept me. Look at me."

It was splendid, he thought, looking at her. She had redeemed herself for all that she had lacked, rising up at last, true woman, superior to the iron rule of bourgeois convention. It was splendid, magnificent, desperate. And yet, what was the matter with him? He was not thrilled nor stirred by what she had done. It was splendid and magnificent only intellectually. In what should have been a moment of fire, he coldly appraised her. His heart was untouched. He was unaware of any desire for her. Again he remembered Lizzie's words.

"I am sick, very sick," he said with a despairing gesture. "How sick I did not know till now. Something has gone out of me. I have always been unafraid of life, but I never dreamed of being sated with life. Life has so filled me that I am empty of any desire for anything. If there were room, I should want you, now. You see how sick I am."

He leaned his head back and closed his eyes; and like a child, crying, that forgets its grief in watching the sunlight percolate through the tear-dimmed films over the pupils, so Martin forgot his sickness, the presence of Ruth, everything, in watching the masses of vegetation, shot through hotly with sunshine that took form and blazed against this background of his eyelids. It was not restful, that green foliage. The sunlight was too raw and glaring. It hurt him to look at it, and yet he looked, he knew not why.

He was brought back to himself by the rattle of the door-knob. Ruth was at the door.

"How shall I get out?" she questioned tearfully. "I am afraid."

"Oh, forgive me," he cried, springing to his feet. "I'm not myself, you know. I forgot you were here." He put his hand to his head. "You see, I'm not just right. I'll take you home. We can go out by the servants' entrance. No one will see us. Pull down that veil and everything will be all right."

She clung to his arm through the dim-lighted passages and down the narrow stairs.

"I am safe now," she said, when they emerged on the sidewalk, at the same time starting to take her hand from his arm.

"No, no, I'll see you home," he answered.

"No, please don't," she objected. "It is unnecessary."

Again she started to remove her hand. He felt a momentary curiosity. Now that she was out of danger she was afraid. She was in almost a panic to be quit of him. He could see no reason for it and attributed it to her nervousness. So he restrained her withdrawing hand and started to walk on with her. Halfway down the block, he saw a man in a long overcoat shrink back into a doorway. He shot a glance in as he passed by, and, despite the high turned-up collar, he was certain that he recognized Ruth's brother, Norman.

During the walk Ruth and Martin held little conversation. She was stunned. He was apathetic. Once, he mentioned that he was going away, back to the South Seas, and, once, she asked him to forgive her having come to him. And that was all. The parting at her door was conventional. They shook hands, said good night, and he lifted his hat. The door swung shut, and he lighted a cigarette and turned back for his hotel. When he came to the doorway into which he had seen Norman shrink, he stopped and looked in in a speculative humor.

"She lied," he said aloud. "She made believe to me that she had dared greatly, and all the while she knew the brother that brought her was waiting to take her back." He burst into laughter. "Oh, these bourgeois! When I was broke, I was not fit to be seen with his sister. When I have a bank account, he brings her to me."

As he swung on his heel to go on, a tramp, going in the same direction, begged him over his shoulder.

"Say, *mister*, can you give me a quarter to get a bed?" were the words.

But it was the voice that made Martin turn around. The next instant he had Joe by the hand.

"D'ye remember that time we parted at the Hot Springs?" the other was saying. "I said then we'd meet again. I felt it in my bones. An' here we are."

"You're looking good," Martin said admiringly, "and you've put on weight."

"I sure have." Joe's face was beaming. "I never knew what it was to live till I hit hoboin'. I'm thirty pounds heavier an' feel tiptop all the time. Why, I was worked to skin an' bone in them old days. Hoboin' sure agrees with me."

"But you're looking for a bed just the same," Martin chided, "and it's a cold night."

"Huh? Lookin' for a bed?" Joe shot a hand into his hip pocket and brought it out filled with small change. "That beats hard graft," he exulted. "You just looked good; that's why I battered you."

Martin laughed and gave in.

"You've several full-sized drunks right there," he insinuated.

Joe slid the money back into his pocket.

"Not in mine," he announced. "No gettin' oryide for me, though there ain't nothin' to stop me except I don't want to. I've ben drunk once since I seen you last, an' then it was unexpected, bein' on an empty stomach. When I work like a beast, I drink like a beast. When I live like a man, I drink like a man—a jolt now an' again when I feel like it, an' that's all."

Martin arranged to meet him next day, and went on to the hotel. He paused in the office to look up steamer sailings. The *Mariposa* sailed for Tahiti in five days.

"Telephone over to-morrow and reserve a stateroom for me," he told the clerk. "No deck-stateroom, but down below, on the weather-side,—the port-side, remember that, the port-side. You'd better write it down."

Once in his room he got into bed and slipped off to sleep as gently as a child. The occurrences of the evening had made no impression on him. His mind was dead to impressions. The glow of warmth with which he met Joe had been most fleeting. The succeeding minute he had been bothered by the ex-laundryman's presence and by the compulsion of conversation. That in five more days he sailed for his loved South Seas meant nothing to him. So he closed his eyes and slept normally and comfortably for eight uninterrupted hours. He was not restless. He did not change his position, nor did he dream. Sleep had become to him oblivion, and each day that he awoke, he awoke with regret. Life worried and bored him, and time was a vexation.

CHAPTER XLVI

"Say, Joe," was his greeting to his old-time working-mate next morning, "there's a Frenchman out on Twenty-eighth Street. He's made a pot of money, and he's going back to France. It's a dandy, well-appointed, small steam laundry. There's a start for you if you want to settle down. Here, take this; buy some clothes with it and be at this man's office by ten o'clock. He looked up the laundry for me, and he'll take you out and show you around. If you like it, and think it is worth the price—twelve thousand—let me know and it is yours. Now run along. I'm busy. I'll see you later."

"Now look here, Mart," the other said slowly, with kindling anger, "I come here this mornin' to see you. Savve? I didn't come here to get no laundry. I come a here for a talk for old friends' sake, and you shove a laundry at me. I tell you, what you can do. You can take that laundry an' go to hell."

He was out of the room when Martin caught him and whirled him around.

"Now look here, Joe," he said; "if you act that way, I'll punch your head. An for old friends' sake I'll punch it hard. Savve?—you will, will you?"

Joe had clinched and attempted to throw him, and he was twisting and writhing out of the advantage of the other's hold. They reeled about the room, locked in each other's arms, and came down with a crash across the splintered wreckage of a wicker chair. Joe was underneath, with arms spread out and held and with Martin's knee on his chest. He was panting and gasping for breath when Martin released him.

"Now we'll talk a moment," Martin said. "You can't get fresh with me. I want that laundry business finished first of all. Then you can come back and we'll talk for old sake's sake. I told you I was busy. Look at that."

A servant had just come in with the morning mail, a great mass of letters and magazines.

"How can I wade through that and talk with you? You go and fix up that laundry, and then we'll get together."

"All right," Joe admitted reluctantly. "I thought you was turnin' me down, but I guess I was mistaken. But you can't lick me, Mart, in a stand-up fight. I've got the reach on you."

"We'll put on the gloves sometime and see," Martin said with a smile.

"Sure; as soon as I get that laundry going." Joe extended his arm. "You see that reach? It'll make you go a few."

Martin heaved a sigh of relief when the door closed behind the laundryman. He was becoming anti-social. Daily he found it a severer strain to be decent with people. Their presence perturbed him, and the effort of conversation irritated him. They made him restless, and no sooner was he in contact with them than he was casting about for excuses to get rid of them.

He did not proceed to attack his mail, and for a half hour he lolled in his chair, doing nothing, while no more than vague, half-formed thoughts occasionally filtered through his intelligence, or rather, at wide intervals, themselves constituted the flickering of his intelligence.

He roused himself and began glancing through his mail. There were a dozen requests for autographs—he knew them at sight; there were professional begging letters; and there were letters from cranks, ranging from the man with a working model of perpetual motion, and the man who demonstrated that the surface of the earth was the inside of a hollow sphere, to the man seeking financial aid to purchase the Peninsula of Lower California for the purpose of communist colonization. There were letters from women seeking to know him, and over one such he smiled, for enclosed was her receipt for pew-rent, sent as evidence of her good faith and as proof of her respectability.

Editors and publishers contributed to the daily heap of letters, the former on their knees for his manuscripts, the latter on their knees for his books—his poor disdained manuscripts that had kept all he possessed in pawn for so many dreary months in order to fund them in postage. There were unexpected checks for English serial rights and for advance payments on foreign translations. His English agent announced the sale of German translation rights in three of his books, and informed him that Swedish editions, from which he could expect nothing because Sweden was not a party to the Berne Convention, were already on the market. Then there was a nominal request for his permission for a Russian translation, that country being likewise outside the Berne Convention.

He turned to the huge bundle of clippings which had come in from his press bureau, and read about himself and his vogue, which had become a furore. All his creative output had been flung to the public in one magnificent sweep. That seemed to account for it. He had taken the public off its feet, the way Kipling had, that time when he lay near to death and all the mob, animated by a mob-mind thought, began suddenly to read him. Martin remembered how that same world-mob, having read him and acclaimed him and not understood him in the least, had, abruptly, a few months later, flung itself upon him and torn him to pieces. Martin grinned at the thought. Who was he that he should not be similarly treated in a few more months? Well, he would fool the mob. He would be away, in the South Seas, building his grass house, trading for pearls and copra, jumping reefs in frail outriggers, catching sharks and bonitas, hunting wild goats among the cliffs of the valley that lay next to the valley of Taiohae.

In the moment of that thought the desperateness of his situation dawned upon him. He saw, cleared eyed, that he was in the Valley of the Shadow. All the life that was in him was fading, fainting, making toward death.

He realized how much he slept, and how much he desired to sleep. Of old, he had hated sleep. It had robbed him of precious moments of living. Four hours of sleep in the twenty-four had meant being robbed of four hours of life. How he had grudged sleep! Now it was life he grudged. Life was not good; its taste in his mouth was without tang, and bitter. This was his peril. Life that did not yearn toward life was in fair way toward ceasing. Some remote instinct for preservation stirred in him, and he knew he must get away. He glanced about the room, and the thought of packing was burdensome. Perhaps it would be better to leave that to the last. In the meantime he might be getting an outfit.

He put on his hat and went out, stopping in at a gun-store, where he spent the remainder of the morning buying automatic rifles, ammunition, and fishing tackle. Fashions changed in trading, and he knew he would have to wait till he reached Tahiti before ordering his trade-goods. They could come up from Australia, anyway. This solution was a source of pleasure. He had avoided doing something, and the doing of anything just now was unpleasant. He went back to the hotel gladly, with a feeling of satisfaction in that the comfortable Morris chair was waiting for him; and he groaned inwardly, on entering his room, at sight of Joe in the Morris chair.

Joe was delighted with the laundry. Everything was settled, and he would enter into possession next day. Martin lay on the bed, with closed eyes, while the other talked on. Martin's thoughts were far away—so far away that he was rarely aware that he was thinking. It was only by an effort that he occasionally responded. And yet this was Joe, whom he had always liked. But Joe was too keen with life. The boisterous impact of it on Martin's jaded mind was a hurt. It was an aching probe to his tired sensitiveness. When Joe reminded him that sometime in the future they were going to put on the gloves together, he could almost have screamed.

"Remember, Joe, you're to run the laundry according to those old rules you used to lay down at Shelly Hot Springs," he said. "No overworking. No working at night. And no children at the mangles. No children anywhere. And a fair wage."

Joe nodded and pulled out a note-book.

"Look at here. I was workin' out them rules before breakfast this A.M. What d'ye think of them?"

He read them aloud, and Martin approved, worrying at the same time as to when Joe would take himself off.

It was late afternoon when he awoke. Slowly the fact of life came back to him. He glanced about the room. Joe had evidently stolen away after he had dozed off. That was considerate of Joe, he thought. Then he closed his eyes and slept again.

In the days that followed Joe was too busy organizing and taking hold of the laundry to bother him much; and it was not until the day before sailing that the newspapers made the announcement that he had taken passage on the *Mariposa*. Once, when the instinct of preservation fluttered, he went to a doctor and underwent a searching physical examination. Nothing could be found the matter with him. His heart and lungs were pronounced magnificent. Every organ, so far as the doctor could know, was normal and was working normally.

"There is nothing the matter with you, Mr. Eden," he said, "positively nothing the matter with you. You are in the pink of condition. Candidly, I envy you your health. It is superb. Look at that chest. There, and in your stomach, lies the secret of your remarkable constitution. Physically, you are a man in a thousand—in ten thousand. Barring accidents, you should live to be a hundred."

And Martin knew that Lizzie's diagnosis had been correct. Physically he was all right. It was his "think-machine" that had gone wrong, and there was no cure for that except to get away to the South Seas. The trouble was that now, on the verge of departure, he had no desire to go. The South Seas charmed him no more than did bourgeois civilization. There was no zest in the thought of departure, while the act of departure appalled him as a weariness of the flesh. He would have felt better if he were already on board and gone.

The last day was a sore trial. Having read of his sailing in the morning papers, Bernard Higginbotham, Gertrude, and all the family came to say good-by, as did Hermann von Schmidt and Marian. Then there was business to be transacted, bills to be paid, and everlasting reporters to be endured. He said good-by to Lizzie Connolly, abruptly, at the entrance to night school, and hurried away. At the hotel he found Joe, too busy all day with the laundry to have come to him earlier. It was the last straw, but Martin gripped the arms of his chair and talked and listened for half an hour.

"You know, Joe," he said, "that you are not tied down to that laundry. There are no strings on it. You can sell it any time and blow the money. Any time you get sick of it and want to hit the road, just pull out. Do what will make you the happiest."

Joe shook his head.

"No more road in mine, thank you kindly. Hoboin's all right, exceptin' for one thing—the girls. I can't help it, but I'm a ladies' man. I can't get along without 'em, and you've got to get along without 'em when you're hoboin'. The times I've passed by houses where dances an' parties was goin' on, an' heard the women laugh, an' saw their white dresses and smiling faces through the windows—Gee! I tell you them moments was plain hell. I like dancin' an' picnics, an' walking in the moonlight, an' all the rest too well. Me for the laundry, and a good front, with big iron dollars clinkin' in my jeans. I seen a girl already, just yesterday, and, d'ye know, I'm feelin' already I'd just as soon marry her as not. I've ben whistlin' all day at the thought of it. She's a beaut, with the kindest eyes and softest voice you ever heard. Me for her, you can stack on that. Say, why don't you get married with all this money to burn? You could get the finest girl in the land."

Martin shook his head with a smile, but in his secret heart he was wondering why any man wanted to marry. It seemed an amazing and incomprehensible thing.

From the deck of the *Mariposa*, at the sailing hour, he saw Lizzie Connolly hiding in the skirts of the crowd on the wharf. Take her with you, came the thought. It is easy to be kind. She will be supremely happy. It was almost a temptation one moment, and the succeeding moment it became a terror. He was in a panic at the thought of it. His tired soul cried out in protest. He turned away from the rail with a groan, muttering, "Man, you are too sick, you are too sick."

He fled to his stateroom, where he lurked until the steamer was clear of the dock. In the dining saloon, at luncheon, he found himself in the place of honor, at the captain's right; and he was not long in discovering that he was the great man on board. But no more unsatisfactory great man ever sailed on a ship. He spent the afternoon in a deck-chair, with closed eyes, dozing brokenly most of the time, and in the evening went early to bed.

After the second day, recovered from seasickness, the full passenger list was in evidence, and the more he saw of the passengers the more he disliked them. Yet he knew that he did them injustice. They were good and kindly people, he forced himself to acknowledge, and in the moment of acknowledgment he qualified—good and kindly like all the bourgeoisie, with all the psychological cramp and intellectual futility of their kind, they bored him when they talked with him, their little superficial minds were so filled with emptiness; while the boisterous high spirits and the excessive energy of the younger people shocked him. They were never quiet, ceaselessly playing deck-quoits, tossing rings, promenading, or rushing to the rail with loud cries to watch the leaping porpoises and the first schools of flying fish.

He slept much. After breakfast he sought his deck-chair with a magazine he never finished. The printed pages tired him. He puzzled that men found so much to write about, and, puzzling, dozed in his chair. When the gong awoke him for luncheon, he was irritated that he must awaken. There was no satisfaction in being awake.

Once, he tried to arouse himself from his lethargy, and went forward into the forecastle with the sailors. But the breed of sailors seemed to have changed since the days he had lived in the forecastle. He could find no kinship with these stolid-faced, ox-minded bestial creatures. He was in despair. Up above nobody had wanted Martin Eden for his own sake, and he could not go back to those of his own class who had wanted him in the past. He did not want them. He could not stand them any more than he could stand the stupid first-cabin passengers and the riotous young people.

Life was to him like strong, white light that hurts the tired eyes of a sick person. During every conscious moment life blazed in a raw glare around him and upon him. It hurt. It hurt intolerably. It was the first time in his life that Martin had travelled first class. On ships at sea he had always been in the forecastle, the steerage, or in the black depths of the coal-hold, passing coal. In those days, climbing up the iron ladders out the pit of stifling heat, he had often caught glimpses of the passengers, in cool white, doing nothing but enjoy themselves, under awnings spread to keep the sun and wind away from them, with subservient stewards taking care of their every want and whim, and it had seemed to him that the realm in which they moved and had their being was nothing else than paradise. Well, here he was, the great man on board, in the midmost centre of it, sitting at the captain's right hand, and yet vainly harking back to forecastle and stoke-hole in quest of the Paradise he had lost. He had found no new one, and now he could not find the old one.

He strove to stir himself and find something to interest him. He ventured the petty officers' mess, and was glad to get away. He talked with a quartermaster off duty, an intelligent man who promptly prodded him with the socialist propaganda and forced into his hands a bunch of leaflets and pamphlets. He listened to the man expounding the slave-morality, and as he listened, he thought languidly of his own Nietzsche philosophy. But what was it worth, after all? He remembered one of Nietzsche's mad utterances wherein that madman had doubted truth. And who was to say? Perhaps Nietzsche had been right. Perhaps there was no truth in anything, no truth in truth—no such thing as truth. But his mind wearied quickly, and he was content to go back to his chair and doze.

Miserable as he was on the steamer, a new misery came upon him. What when the steamer reached Tahiti? He would have to go ashore. He would have to order his trade-goods, to find a passage on a schooner to the Marquesas, to do a thousand and one things that were awful to contemplate. Whenever he steeled himself deliberately to think, he could see the desperate peril in which he stood. In all truth, he was in the Valley of the Shadow, and his danger lay in that he was not afraid. If he were only afraid, he would make toward life. Being unafraid, he was drifting deeper into the shadow. He found no delight in the old familiar things of life. The *Mariposa* was now in the northeast trades, and this wine of wind, surging against him, irritated him. He had his chair moved to escape the embrace of this lusty comrade of old days and nights.

The day the *Mariposa* entered the doldrums, Martin was more miserable than ever. He could no longer sleep. He was soaked with sleep, and perforce he must now stay awake and endure the white glare of life. He moved about restlessly. The air was sticky and humid, and the rain-squalls were unrefreshing. He ached with life. He walked around the deck until that hurt too much, then sat in his chair until he was compelled to walk again. He forced himself at last to finish the magazine, and from the steamer library he culled several volumes of poetry. But they could not hold him, and once more he took to walking.

He stayed late on deck, after dinner, but that did not help him, for when he went below, he could not sleep. This surcease from life had failed him. It was too much. He turned on the electric light and tried to read. One of the volumes was a Swinburne. He lay in bed, glancing through its pages, until suddenly he became aware that he was reading with interest. He finished the stanza, attempted to read on, then came back to it. He rested the book face downward on his breast and fell to thinking. That was it. The very thing. Strange that it had never come to him before. That was the meaning of it all; he had been drifting that way all the time, and now Swinburne showed him that it was the happy way out. He wanted rest, and here was rest awaiting him. He glanced at the open port-hole. Yes, it was large enough. For the first time in weeks he felt happy. At last he had discovered the cure of his ill. He picked up the book and read the stanza slowly aloud:-

"*From too much love of living,*

From hope and fear set free,

We thank with brief thanksgiving

Whatever gods may be

That no life lives forever;

That dead men rise up never;

That even the weariest river

Winds somewhere safe to sea."

He looked again at the open port. Swinburne had furnished the key. Life was ill, or, rather, it had become ill—an unbearable thing. "That dead men rise up never!" That line stirred him with a profound feeling of gratitude. It was the one beneficent thing in the universe. When life became an aching weariness, death was ready to soothe away to everlasting sleep. But what was he waiting for? It was time to go.

He arose and thrust his head out the port-hole, looking down into the milky wash. The *Mariposa* was deeply loaded, and, hanging by his hands, his feet would be in the water. He could slip in noiselessly. No one would hear. A smother of spray dashed up, wetting his face. It tasted salt on his lips, and the taste was good. He wondered if he ought to write a swan-song, but laughed the thought away. There was no time. He was too impatient to be gone.

Turning off the light in his room so that it might not betray him, he went out the port-hole feet first. His shoulders stuck, and he forced himself back so as to try it with one arm down by his side. A roll of the steamer aided him, and he was through, hanging by his hands. When his feet touched the sea, he let go. He was in a milky froth of water. The side of the *Mariposa* rushed past him like a dark wall, broken here and there by lighted ports. She was certainly making time. Almost before he knew it, he was astern, swimming gently on the foam-crackling surface.

A bonita struck at his white body, and he laughed aloud. It had taken a piece out, and the sting of it reminded him of why he was there. In the work to do he had forgotten the purpose of it. The lights of the *Mariposa* were growing dim in the distance, and there he was, swimming confidently, as though it were his intention to make for the nearest land a thousand miles or so away.

It was the automatic instinct to live. He ceased swimming, but the moment he felt the water rising above his mouth the hands struck out sharply with a lifting movement. The will to live, was his thought, and the thought was accompanied by a sneer. Well, he had will,—ay, will strong enough that with one last exertion it could destroy itself and cease to be.

He changed his position to a vertical one. He glanced up at the quiet stars, at the same time emptying his lungs of air. With swift, vigorous propulsion of hands and feet, he lifted his shoulders and half his chest out of water. This was to gain impetus for the descent. Then he let himself go and sank without movement, a white statue, into the sea. He breathed in the water deeply, deliberately, after the manner of a man taking an anaesthetic. When he strangled, quite involuntarily his arms and legs clawed the water and drove him up to the surface and into the clear sight of the stars.

The will to live, he thought disdainfully, vainly endeavoring not to breathe the air into his bursting lungs. Well, he would have to try a new way. He filled his lungs with air, filled them full. This supply would take him far down. He turned over and went down head first, swimming with all his strength and all his will. Deeper and deeper he went. His eyes were open, and he watched the ghostly, phosphorescent trails of the darting bonita. As he swam, he hoped that they would not strike at him, for it might snap the tension of his will. But they did not strike, and he found time to be grateful for this last kindness of life.

Down, down, he swam till his arms and leg grew tired and hardly moved. He knew that he was deep. The pressure on his ear-drums was a pain, and there was a buzzing in his head. His endurance was faltering, but he compelled his arms and legs to drive him deeper until his will snapped and the air drove from his lungs in a great explosive rush. The bubbles rubbed and bounded like tiny balloons against his cheeks and eyes as they took their upward flight. Then came pain and strangulation. This hurt was not death, was the thought that oscillated through his reeling consciousness. Death did not hurt. It was life, the pangs of life, this awful, suffocating feeling; it was the last blow life could deal him.

His wilful hands and feet began to beat and churn about, spasmodically and feebly. But he had fooled them and the will to live that made them beat and churn. He was too deep down. They could never bring him to the surface. He seemed floating languidly in a sea of dreamy vision. Colors and radiances surrounded him and bathed him and pervaded him. What was that? It seemed a lighthouse; but it was inside his brain—a flashing, bright white light. It flashed swifter and swifter. There was a long rumble of sound, and it seemed to him that he was falling down a vast and interminable stairway. And somewhere at the bottom he fell into darkness. That much he knew. He had fallen into darkness. And at the instant he knew, he ceased to know.

About Author

John Griffith London (born **John Griffith Chaney**; January 12, 1876 – November 22, 1916) was an American novelist, journalist, and social activist. A pioneer in the world of commercial magazine fiction, he was one of the first writers to become a worldwide celebrity and earn a large fortune from writing. He was also an innovator in the genre that would later become known as science fiction.

His most famous works include The Call of the Wild and White Fang, both set in the Klondike Gold Rush, as well as the short stories "To Build a Fire", "An Odyssey of the North", and "Love of Life". He also wrote about the South Pacific in stories such as "The Pearls of Parlay", and "The Heathen".

London was part of the radical literary group "The Crowd" in San Francisco and a passionate advocate of unionization, workers' rights, socialism, and eugenics. He wrote several works dealing with these topics, such as his dystopian novel The Iron Heel, his non-fiction exposé The People of the Abyss, The War of the Classes, and Before Adam.

Family

Jack London's mother, Flora Wellman, was the fifth and youngest child of Pennsylvania Canal builder Marshall Wellman and his first wife, Eleanor Garrett Jones. Marshall Wellman was descended from Thomas Wellman, an early Puritan settler in the Massachusetts Bay Colony. Flora left Ohio and moved to the Pacific coast when her father remarried after her mother died. In San Francisco, Flora worked as a music teacher and spiritualist, claiming to channel the spirit of a Sauk chief, Black Hawk.

Biographer Clarice Stasz and others believe London's father was astrologer William Chaney. Flora Wellman was living with Chaney in San Francisco when she became pregnant. Whether Wellman and Chaney were legally married is unknown. Stasz notes that in his memoirs, Chaney refers to London's mother Flora Wellman as having been his "wife"; he also cites an advertisement in which Flora called herself "Florence Wellman Chaney".

According to Flora Wellman's account, as recorded in the San Francisco Chronicle of June 4, 1875, Chaney demanded that she have an abortion. When she refused, he disclaimed responsibility for the child. In desperation, she shot herself. She was not seriously wounded, but she was temporarily deranged. After giving birth, Flora turned the baby over for care to Virginia Prentiss, an African-American woman and former slave. She was a major maternal figure throughout London's life. Late in 1876, Flora Wellman married John London, a partially disabled Civil War veteran, and brought her baby John, later known as Jack, to live with the newly married couple. The family moved around the San Francisco Bay Area before settling in Oakland, where London completed public grade school.

In 1897, when he was 21 and a student at the University of California, Berkeley, London searched for and read the newspaper accounts of his mother's suicide attempt and the name of his biological father. He wrote to William Chaney, then living in Chicago. Chaney responded that he could not be London's father because he was impotent; he casually asserted that London's mother had relations with other men and averred that she had slandered him when she said he insisted on an abortion. Chaney concluded by saying that he was more to be pitied than London. London was devastated by his father's letter; in the months following, he quit school at Berkeley and went to the Klondike during the gold rush boom.

Early life

London was born near Third and Brannan Streets in San Francisco. The house burned down in the fire after the 1906 San Francisco earthquake; the California Historical Society placed a plaque at the site in 1953. Although the family was working class, it was not as impoverished as London's later accounts claimed. London was largely self-educated.

In 1885, London found and read Ouida's long Victorian novel Signa. He credited this as the seed of his literary success. In 1886, he went to the Oakland Public Library and found a sympathetic librarian, Ina Coolbrith, who encouraged his learning. (She later became California's first poet laureate and an important figure in the San Francisco literary community).

In 1889, London began working 12 to 18 hours a day at Hickmott's Cannery. Seeking a way out, he borrowed money from his foster mother Virginia Prentiss, bought the sloop Razzle-Dazzle from an oyster pirate named French Frank, and became an oyster pirate himself. In his memoir, John Barleycorn, he claims also to have stolen French Frank's mistress Mamie. After a few months, his sloop became damaged beyond repair. London hired on as a member of the California Fish Patrol.

In 1893, he signed on to the sealing schooner Sophie Sutherland, bound for the coast of Japan. When he returned, the country was in the grip of the panic of '93 and Oakland was swept by labor unrest. After grueling jobs in a jute mill and a street-railway power plant, London joined Coxey's Army and began his career as a tramp. In 1894, he spent 30 days for vagrancy in the Erie County Penitentiary at Buffalo, New York. In The Road, he wrote:

> Man-handling was merely one of the very minor unprintable horrors of the Erie County Pen. I say 'unprintable'; and in justice I must also say undescribable. They were unthinkable to me until I saw them, and I was no spring chicken in the ways of the world and the awful abysses of human degradation. It would take a deep plummet to reach bottom in the Erie County Pen, and I do but skim lightly and facetiously the surface of things as I there saw them.

> — Jack London, The Road

After many experiences as a hobo and a sailor, he returned to Oakland and attended Oakland High School. He contributed a number of articles to the high school's magazine, The Aegis. His first published work was "Typhoon off the Coast of Japan", an account of his sailing experiences.

As a schoolboy, London often studied at Heinold's First and Last Chance Saloon, a port-side bar in Oakland. At 17, he confessed to the bar's owner, John Heinold, his desire to attend university and pursue a career as a writer. Heinold lent London tuition money to attend college.

London desperately wanted to attend the University of California, located in Berkeley. In 1896, after a summer of intense studying to pass certification exams, he was admitted. Financial circumstances forced him to leave in 1897 and he never graduated. No evidence has surfaced that he ever wrote for student publications while studying at Berkeley.

While at Berkeley, London continued to study and spend time at Heinold's saloon, where he was introduced to the sailors and adventurers who would influence his writing. In his autobiographical novel, John Barleycorn, London mentioned the pub's likeness seventeen times. Heinold's was the place where London met Alexander McLean, a captain known for his cruelty at sea. London based his protagonist Wolf Larsen, in the novel The Sea-Wolf, on McLean.

Heinold's First and Last Chance Saloon is now unofficially named Jack London's Rendezvous in his honor.

Gold rush and first success

On July 12, 1897, London (age 21) and his sister's husband Captain Shepard sailed to join the Klondike Gold Rush. This was the setting for some of his first successful stories. London's time in the harsh Klondike, however, was detrimental to his health. Like so many other men who were malnourished in the goldfields, London developed scurvy. His gums became swollen, leading to the loss of his four front teeth. A constant gnawing pain affected his hip and leg muscles, and his face was stricken with marks that always reminded him of the struggles he faced in the Klondike. Father William Judge, "The Saint of Dawson", had a facility in Dawson that provided shelter, food and any available medicine to London and others. His struggles there inspired London's short story, "To Build a Fire" (1902, revised in 1908), which many critics assess as his best.

His landlords in Dawson were mining engineers Marshall Latham Bond and Louis Whitford Bond, educated at Yale and Stanford, respectively. The brothers' father, Judge Hiram Bond, was a wealthy mining investor. The Bonds, especially Hiram, were active Republicans. Marshall Bond's diary mentions friendly sparring with London on political issues as a camp pastime.

London left Oakland with a social conscience and socialist leanings; he returned to become an activist for socialism. He concluded that his only hope of escaping the work "trap" was to get an education and "sell his brains". He saw his writing as a business, his ticket out of poverty, and, he hoped, a means of beating the wealthy at their own game. On returning to California in 1898, London began working to get published, a struggle described in his novel, Martin Eden (serialized in 1908, published in 1909). His first published story since high school was "To the Man On Trail", which has frequently been collected in anthologies. When The Overland Monthly offered him only five dollars for it—and was slow paying—London came close to abandoning his writing career. In his words, "literally and literarily I was saved" when The Black Cat accepted his story "A Thousand Deaths", and paid him $40—the "first money I ever received for a story".

London began his writing career just as new printing technologies enabled lower-cost production of magazines. This resulted in a boom in popular magazines aimed at a wide public audience and a strong market for short fiction. In 1900, he made $2,500 in writing, about $77,000 in today's currency. Among the works he sold to magazines was a short story known as either "Diable" (1902) or "Bâtard" (1904), two editions of the same basic story; London received $141.25 for this story on May 27, 1902. In the text, a cruel French Canadian brutalizes his dog, and the dog retaliates and kills the man. London told some of his critics that man's actions are the main cause of the behavior of their animals, and he would show this in another story, The Call of the Wild.

In early 1903, London sold The Call of the Wild to The Saturday Evening Post for $750, and the book rights to Macmillan for $2,000. Macmillan's promotional campaign propelled it to swift success.

While living at his rented villa on Lake Merritt in Oakland, California, London met poet George Sterling; in time they became best friends. In 1902, Sterling helped London find a home closer to his own in nearby Piedmont. In his letters London addressed Sterling as "Greek", owing to Sterling's aquiline nose and classical profile, and he signed them as "Wolf". London was later to depict Sterling as Russ Brissenden in his autobiographical novel Martin Eden (1910) and as Mark Hall in The Valley of the Moon (1913).

In later life London indulged his wide-ranging interests by accumulating a personal library of 15,000 volumes. He referred to his books as "the tools of my trade".

First marriage (1900–04)

London married Elizabeth "Bessie" Maddern on April 7, 1900, the same day The Son of the Wolf was published. Bess had been part of his circle of friends for a number of years. She was related to stage actresses Minnie Maddern Fiske and Emily Stevens. Stasz says, "Both acknowledged publicly that they were not marrying out of love, but from friendship and a belief that they would produce sturdy children." Kingman says, "they were comfortable together... Jack had made it clear to Bessie that he did not love her, but that he liked her enough to make a successful marriage."

London met Bessie through his friend at Oakland High School, Fred Jacobs; she was Fred's fiancée. Bessie, who tutored at Anderson's University Academy in Alameda California, tutored Jack in preparation for his entrance exams for the University of California at Berkeley in 1896. Jacobs was killed aboard the USAT Scandia in 1897, but Jack and Bessie continued their friendship, which included taking photos and developing the film together. This was the beginning of Jack's passion for photography.

During the marriage, London continued his friendship with Anna Strunsky, co-authoring The Kempton-Wace Letters, an epistolary novel contrasting two philosophies of love. Anna, writing "Dane Kempton's" letters, arguing for a romantic view of marriage, while London, writing "Herbert Wace's" letters, argued for a scientific view, based on Darwinism and eugenics. In the novel, his fictional character contrasted two women he had known.

London's pet name for Bess was "Mother-Girl" and Bess's for London was "Daddy-Boy". Their first child, Joan, was born on January 15, 1901, and their second, Bessie (later called Becky), on October 20, 1902. Both children were born in Piedmont, California. Here London wrote one of his most celebrated works, The Call of the Wild.

While London had pride in his children, the marriage was strained. Kingman says that by 1903 the couple were close to separation as they were "extremely incompatible". "Jack was still so kind and gentle with Bessie that when Cloudsley Johns was a house guest in February 1903 he didn't suspect a breakup of their marriage."

London reportedly complained to friends Joseph Noel and George Sterling:

> [Bessie] is devoted to purity. When I tell her morality is only evidence of low blood pressure, she hates me. She'd sell me and the children out for her damned purity. It's terrible. Every time I come back after being away from home for a night she won't let me be in the same room with her if she can help it.

Stasz writes that these were "code words for fear that was consorting with prostitutes and might bring home venereal disease."

On July 24, 1903, London told Bessie he was leaving and moved out. During 1904, London and Bess negotiated the terms of a divorce, and the decree was granted on November 11, 1904.

War correspondent (1904)

London accepted an assignment of the San Francisco Examiner to cover the Russo-Japanese War in early 1904, arriving in Yokohama on January 25, 1904. He was arrested by Japanese authorities in Shimonoseki, but released through the intervention of American ambassador Lloyd Griscom. After travelling to Korea, he was again arrested by Japanese authorities for straying too close to the border with Manchuria without official permission, and was sent back to Seoul. Released again, London was permitted to travel with the Imperial Japanese Army to the border, and to observe the Battle of the Yalu.

London asked William Randolph Hearst, the owner of the San Francisco Examiner, to be allowed to transfer to the Imperial Russian Army, where he felt that restrictions on his reporting and his movements would be less severe. However, before this could be arranged, he was arrested for a third time in four months, this time for assaulting his Japanese assistants, whom he accused of stealing the fodder for his horse. Released through the personal intervention of President Theodore Roosevelt, London departed the front in June 1904.

Bohemian Club

On August 18, 1904, London went with his close friend, the poet George Sterling, to "Summer High Jinks" at the Bohemian Grove. London was elected to honorary membership in the Bohemian Club and took part in many activities. Other noted members of the Bohemian Club during this time included Ambrose Bierce, Gelett Burgess, Allan Dunn, John Muir, Frank Norris, and Herman George Scheffauer.

Beginning in December 1914, London worked on The Acorn Planter, A California Forest Play, to be performed as one of the annual Grove Plays, but it was never selected. It was described as too difficult to set to music. London published The Acorn Planter in 1916.

Second marriage

After divorcing Maddern, London married Charmian Kittredge in 1905. London had been introduced to Kittredge in 1900 by her aunt Netta Eames, who was an editor at Overland Monthly magazine in San Francisco. The two met prior to his first marriage but became lovers years later after Jack and Bessie London visited Wake Robin, Netta Eames' Sonoma County resort, in 1903. London was injured when he fell from a buggy, and Netta arranged for Charmian to care for him. The two developed a friendship, as Charmian, Netta, her husband Roscoe, and London were politically aligned with socialist causes. At some point the relationship became romantic, and Jack divorced his wife to marry Charmian, who was five years his senior.

Biographer Russ Kingman called Charmian "Jack's soul-mate, always at his side, and a perfect match." Their time together included numerous trips, including a 1907 cruise on the yacht Snark to Hawaii and Australia. Many of London's stories are based on his visits to Hawaii, the last one for 10 months beginning in December 1915.

The couple also visited Goldfield, Nevada, in 1907, where they were guests of the Bond brothers, London's Dawson City landlords. The Bond brothers were working in Nevada as mining engineers.

London had contrasted the concepts of the "Mother Girl" and the "Mate Woman" in The Kempton-Wace Letters. His pet name for Bess had been "Mother-Girl;" his pet name for Charmian was "Mate-Woman."Charmian's aunt and foster mother, a disciple of Victoria Woodhull, had raised her without prudishness.Every biographer alludes to Charmian's uninhibited sexuality.

Joseph Noel calls the events from 1903 to 1905 "a domestic drama that would have intrigued the pen of an Ibsen.... London's had comedy relief in it and a sort of easy-going romance." In broad outline, London was restless in his first marriage, sought extramarital sexual affairs, and found, in Charmian Kittredge, not only a sexually active and adventurous partner, but his future life-companion. They attempted to have children; one child died at birth, and another pregnancy ended in a miscarriage.

In 1906, London published in Collier's magazine his eye-witness report of the San Francisco earthquake.

Beauty Ranch (1905–16)

In 1905, London purchased a 1,000 acres (4.0 km2) ranch in Glen Ellen, Sonoma County, California, on the eastern slope of Sonoma Mountain.He wrote: "Next to my wife, the ranch is the dearest thing in the world to me." He desperately wanted the ranch to become a successful business enterprise. Writing, always a commercial enterprise with London, now became even more a means to an end: "I write for no other purpose than to add to the beauty that now belongs to me. I write a book for no other reason than to add three or four hundred acres to my magnificent estate."

Stasz writes that London "had taken fully to heart the vision, expressed in his agrarian fiction, of the land as the closest earthly version of Eden ... he educated himself through the study of agricultural manuals and scientific tomes. He conceived of a system of ranching that today would be praised for its ecological wisdom." He was proud to own the first concrete silo in California, a circular piggery that he designed. He hoped to adapt the wisdom of Asian sustainable agriculture to the United States. He hired both Italian and Chinese stonemasons, whose distinctly different styles are obvious.

The ranch was an economic failure. Sympathetic observers such as Stasz treat his projects as potentially feasible, and ascribe their failure to bad luck or to being ahead of their time. Unsympathetic historians such as Kevin Starr suggest that he was a bad manager, distracted by other concerns and impaired by his alcoholism. Starr notes that London was absent from his ranch about six months a year between 1910 and 1916 and says, "He liked the show of managerial power, but not grinding attention to detail .... London's workers laughed at his efforts to play big-time rancher the operation a rich man's hobby."

London spent $80,000 ($2,280,000 in current value) to build a 15,000-square-foot (1,400 m2) stone mansion called Wolf House on the property. Just as the mansion was nearing completion, two weeks before the Londons planned to move in, it was destroyed by fire.

London's last visit to Hawaii, beginning in December 1915, lasted eight months. He met with Duke Kahanamoku, Prince Jonah Kūhiō Kalaniana'ole, Queen Lili'uokalani and many others, before returning to his ranch in July 1916. He was suffering from kidney failure, but he continued to work.

The ranch (abutting stone remnants of Wolf House) is now a National Historic Landmark and is protected in Jack London State Historic Park.

Animal activism

London witnessed animal cruelty in the training of circus animals, and his subsequent novels Jerry of the Islands and Michael, Brother of Jerry included a foreword entreating the public to become more informed about this practice. In 1918, the Massachusetts Society for the Prevention of Cruelty to Animals and the American Humane Education Society teamed up to create the Jack London Club, which sought to inform the public about cruelty to circus animals and encourage them to protest this establishment. Support from Club members led to a temporary cessation of trained animal acts at Ringling-Barnum and Bailey in 1925.

Death

London died November 22, 1916, in a sleeping porch in a cottage on his ranch. London had been a robust man but had suffered several serious illnesses, including scurvy in the Klondike. Additionally, during travels on the Snark, he and Charmian picked up unspecified tropical infections, and diseases, including yaws. At the time of his death, he suffered from dysentery, late-stage alcoholism, and uremia; he was in extreme pain and taking morphine.

London's ashes were buried on his property not far from the Wolf House. London's funeral took place on November 26, 1916, attended only by close friends, relatives, and workers of the property. In accordance with his wishes, he was cremated and buried next to some pioneer children, under a rock that belonged to the Wolf House. After Charmian's death in 1955, she was also cremated and then buried with her husband in the same spot that her husband chose. The grave is marked by a mossy boulder. The buildings and property were later preserved as Jack London State Historic Park, in Glen Ellen, California.

Suicide debate

Because he was using morphine, many older sources describe London's death as a suicide, and some still do. This conjecture appears to be a rumor, or speculation based on incidents in his fiction writings. His death certificate gives the cause as uremia, following acute renal colic.

The biographer Stasz writes, "Following London's death, for a number of reasons, a biographical myth developed in which he has been portrayed as an alcoholic womanizer who committed suicide. Recent scholarship based upon firsthand documents challenges this caricature." Most biographers, including Russ Kingman, now agree he died of uremia aggravated by an accidental morphine overdose.

London's fiction featured several suicides. In his autobiographical memoir John Barleycorn, he claims, as a youth, to have drunkenly stumbled overboard into the San Francisco Bay, "some maundering fancy of going out with the tide suddenly obsessed me". He said he drifted and nearly succeeded in drowning before sobering up and being rescued by fishermen. In the dénouement of The Little Lady of the Big House, the heroine, confronted by the pain of a mortal gunshot wound, undergoes a physician-assisted suicide by morphine. Also, in Martin Eden, the principal protagonist, who shares certain characteristics with London, drowns himself.

Plagiarism accusations

London was vulnerable to accusations of plagiarism, both because he was such a conspicuous, prolific, and successful writer and because of his methods of working. He wrote in a letter to Elwyn Hoffman, "expression, you see—with me—is far easier than invention." He purchased plots and novels from the young Sinclair Lewis and used incidents from newspaper clippings as writing material.

In July 1901, two pieces of fiction appeared within the same month: London's "Moon-Face", in the San Francisco Argonaut, and Frank Norris' "The Passing of Cock-eye Blacklock", in Century Magazine. Newspapers showed the similarities between the stories, which London said were "quite different in manner of treatment, patently the same in foundation and motive." London explained both writers based their stories on the same newspaper account. A year later, it was discovered that Charles Forrest McLean had published a fictional story also based on the same incident.

Egerton Ryerson Young claimed The Call of the Wild (1903) was taken from Young's book My Dogs in the Northland (1902). London acknowledged using it as a source and claimed to have written a letter to Young thanking him.

In 1906, the New York World published "deadly parallel" columns showing eighteen passages from London's short story "Love of Life" side by side with similar passages from a nonfiction article by Augustus Biddle and J. K. Macdonald, titled "Lost in the Land of the Midnight Sun". London noted the World did not accuse him of "plagiarism", but only of "identity of time and situation", to which he defiantly "pled guilty".

The most serious charge of plagiarism was based on London's "The Bishop's Vision", Chapter 7 of his novel The Iron Heel (1908). The chapter is nearly identical to an ironic essay that Frank Harris published in 1901, titled "The Bishop of London and Public Morality". Harris was incensed and suggested he should receive 1/60th of the royalties from The Iron Heel, the disputed material constituting about that fraction of the whole novel. London insisted he had clipped a reprint of the article, which had appeared in an American newspaper, and believed it to be a genuine speech delivered by the Bishop of London.

Views

Atheism

London was an atheist. He is quoted as saying, "I believe that when I am dead, I am dead. I believe that with my death I am just as much obliterated as the last mosquito you and I squashed."

Socialism

London wrote from a socialist viewpoint, which is evident in his novel The Iron Heel. Neither a theorist nor an intellectual socialist, London's socialism grew out of his life experience. As London explained in his essay, "How I Became a Socialist", his views were influenced by his experience with people at the bottom of the social pit. His optimism and individualism faded, and he vowed never to do more hard physical work than necessary. He wrote that his individualism was hammered out of him, and he was politically reborn. He often closed his letters "Yours for the Revolution."

London joined the Socialist Labor Party in April 1896. In the same year, the San Francisco Chronicle published a story about the twenty-year-old London's giving nightly speeches in Oakland's City Hall Park, an activity he was arrested for a year later. In 1901, he left the Socialist Labor Party and joined the new Socialist Party of America. He ran unsuccessfully as the high-profile Socialist candidate for mayor of Oakland in 1901 (receiving 245 votes) and 1905 (improving to 981 votes), toured the country lecturing on socialism in 1906, and published two collections of essays about socialism: The War of the Classes (1905) and Revolution, and other Essays (1906).

Stasz notes that "London regarded the Wobblies as a welcome addition to the Socialist cause, although he never joined them in going so far as to recommend sabotage." Stasz mentions a personal meeting between London and Big Bill Haywood in 1912.

In his late (1913) book The Cruise of the Snark, London writes about appeals to him for membership of the Snark's crew from office workers and other "toilers" who longed for escape from the cities, and of being cheated by workmen.

In his Glen Ellen ranch years, London felt some ambivalence toward socialism and complained about the "inefficient Italian labourers" in his employ. In 1916, he resigned from the Glen Ellen chapter of the Socialist Party, but stated emphatically he did so "because of its lack of fire and fight, and its loss of emphasis on the class struggle." In an unflattering portrait of London's ranch days, California cultural historian Kevin Starr refers to this period as "post-socialist" and says "... by 1911 ... London was more bored by the class struggle than he cared to admit."

Race

London shared common concerns among many European Americans in California about Asian immigration, described as "the yellow peril"; he used the latter term as the title of a 1904 essay. This theme was also the subject of a story he wrote in 1910 called "The Unparalleled Invasion". Presented as an historical essay set in the future, the story narrates events between 1976 and 1987, in which China, with an ever-increasing population, is taking over and colonizing its neighbors with the intention of taking over the entire Earth. The western nations respond with biological warfare and bombard China with dozens of the most infectious diseases. On his fears about China, he admits, "it must be taken into consideration that the above postulate is itself a product of Western race-egotism, urged by our belief in our own righteousness and fostered by a faith in ourselves which may be as erroneous as are most fond race fancies."

836

By contrast, many of London's short stories are notable for their empathetic portrayal of Mexican ("The Mexican"), Asian ("The Chinago"), and Hawaiian ("Koolau the Leper") characters. London's war correspondence from the Russo-Japanese War, as well as his unfinished novel Cherry, show he admired much about Japanese customs and capabilities. London's writings have been popular among the Japanese, who believe he portrayed them positively.

In "Koolau the Leper", London describes Koolau, who is a Hawaiian leper—and thus a very different sort of "superman" than Martin Eden—and who fights off an entire cavalry troop to elude capture, as "indomitable spiritually—a ... magnificent rebel". This character is based on Hawaiian leper Kaluaikoolau, who in 1893 revolted and resisted capture from forces of the Provisional Government of Hawaii in the Kalalau Valley.

An amateur boxer and avid boxing fan, London reported on the 1910 Johnson–Jeffries fight, in which the black boxer Jack Johnson vanquished Jim Jeffries, known as the "Great White Hope". In 1908, London had reported on an earlier fight of Johnson's, contrasting the black boxer's coolness and intellectual style, with the apelike appearance and fighting style of his Canadian opponent, Tommy Burns:

> [What won] on Saturday was bigness, coolness, quickness, cleverness, and vast physical superiority ... Because a white man wishes a white man to win, this should not prevent him from giving absolute credit to the best man, even when that best man was black. All hail to Johnson. ... superb. He was impregnable ... as inaccessible as Mont Blanc.

Those who defend London against charges of racism cite the letter he wrote to the Japanese-American Commercial Weekly in 1913:

> In reply to yours of August 16, 1913. First of all, I should say by stopping the stupid newspaper from always fomenting race prejudice. This of course, being impossible, I would say, next, by educating the people of Japan so that they will be too intelligently tolerant to respond to any call to race prejudice. And, finally, by realizing, in industry and

government, of socialism—which last word is merely a word that stands for the actual application of in the affairs of men of the theory of the Brotherhood of Man.

In the meantime the nations and races are only unruly boys who have not yet grown to the stature of men. So we must expect them to do unruly and boisterous things at times. And, just as boys grow up, so the races of mankind will grow up and laugh when they look back upon their childish quarrels.

In 1996, after the City of Whitehorse, Yukon, renamed a street in honor of London, protests over London's alleged racism forced the city to change the name of "Jack London Boulevard"[failed verification] back to "Two-mile Hill".

Eugenics

London supported eugenics, including forced sterilization of criminals or those deemed feeble minded. His novel Before Adam(1906–07) has been described as having pro-eugenic themes.

London wrote to Frederick H. Robinson of the periodical Medical Review of Reviews, stating, "I believe the future belongs to eugenics, and will be determined by the practice of eugenics."

Works

Short stories

Western writer and historian Dale L. Walker writes:

London's true métier was the short story ... London's true genius lay in the short form, 7,500 words and under, where the flood of images in his teeming brain and the innate power of his narrative gift were at once constrained and freed. His stories that run longer than the magic 7,500 generally—but certainly not always—could have benefited from self-editing.

London's "strength of utterance" is at its height in his stories, and they are painstakingly well-constructed. "To Build a Fire" is the best known of all his stories. Set in the harsh Klondike, it recounts the haphazard trek of a new arrival who has ignored an old-timer's warning about the risks of traveling alone. Falling through the ice into a creek in seventy-five-below weather, the unnamed man is keenly aware that survival depends on his untested skills at quickly building a fire to dry his clothes and warm his extremities. After publishing a tame version of this story—with a sunny outcome—in The Youth's Companion in 1902, London offered a second, more severe take on the man's predicament in The Century Magazine in 1908. Reading both provides an illustration of London's growth and maturation as a writer. As Labor (1994) observes: "To compare the two versions is itself an instructive lesson in what distinguished a great work of literary art from a good children's story."

Other stories from the Klondike period include: "All Gold Canyon", about a battle between a gold prospector and a claim jumper; "The Law of Life", about an aging American Indian man abandoned by his tribe and left to die; "Love of Life", about a trek by a prospector across the Canadian tundra; "To the Man on Trail," which tells the story of a prospector fleeing the Mounted Police in a sled race, and raises the question of the contrast between written law and morality; and "An Odyssey of the North," which raises questions of conditional morality, and paints a sympathetic portrait of a man of mixed White and Aleut ancestry.

London was a boxing fan and an avid amateur boxer. "A Piece of Steak" is a tale about a match between older and younger boxers. It contrasts the differing experiences of youth and age but also raises the social question of the treatment of aging workers. "The Mexican" combines boxing with a social theme, as a young Mexican endures an unfair fight and ethnic prejudice to earn money with which to aid the revolution.

Several of London's stories would today be classified as science fiction. "The Unparalleled Invasion" describes germ warfare against China; "Goliath" is about an irresistible energy weapon; "The Shadow and the Flash" is a tale about two brothers who take different routes to achieving invisibility; "A

Relic of the Pliocene" is a tall tale about an encounter of a modern-day man with a mammoth. "The Red One" is a late story from a period when London was intrigued by the theories of the psychiatrist and writer Jung. It tells of an island tribe held in thrall by an extraterrestrial object.

Some nineteen original collections of short stories were published during London's brief life or shortly after his death. There have been several posthumous anthologies drawn from this pool of stories. Many of these stories were located in the Klondike and the Pacific. A collection of Jack London's San Francisco Stories was published in October 2010 by Sydney Samizdat Press.

Novels

London's most famous novels are The Call of the Wild, White Fang, The Sea-Wolf, The Iron Heel, and Martin Eden.

In a letter dated December 27, 1901, London's Macmillan publisher George Platt Brett, Sr., said "he believed Jack's fiction represented 'the very best kind of work' done in America."

Critic Maxwell Geismar called The Call of the Wild "a beautiful prose poem"; editor Franklin Walker said that it "belongs on a shelf with Walden and Huckleberry Finn"; and novelist E.L. Doctorow called it "a mordant parable ... his masterpiece."

The historian Dale L. Walker commented:

> Jack London was an uncomfortable novelist, that form too long for his natural impatience and the quickness of his mind. His novels, even the best of them, are hugely flawed.

Some critics have said that his novels are episodic and resemble linked short stories. Dale L. Walker writes:

> The Star Rover, that magnificent experiment, is actually a series of short stories connected by a unifying device ... Smoke Bellew is a series of stories bound together in a novel-like form by their reappearing

protagonist, Kit Bellew; and John Barleycorn ... is a synoptic series of short episodes.

Ambrose Bierce said of The Sea-Wolf that "the great thing—and it is among the greatest of things—is that tremendous creation, Wolf Larsen ... the hewing out and setting up of such a figure is enough for a man to do in one lifetime. "However, he noted, "The love element, with its absurd suppressions, and impossible proprieties, is awful."

The Iron Heel is an example of a dystopian novel that anticipates and influenced George Orwell's Nineteen Eighty-Four. London's socialist politics are explicitly on display here. The Iron Heel meets the contemporary definition of soft science fiction. The Star Rover (1915) is also science fiction.

Apocrypha

Jack London Credo

London's literary executor, Irving Shepard, quoted a Jack London Credo in an introduction to a 1956 collection of London stories:

> I would rather be ashes than dust!

> I would rather that my spark should burn out in a brilliant blaze than it should be stifled by dry-rot.

> I would rather be a superb meteor, every atom of me in magnificent glow, than a sleepy and permanent planet.

> The function of man is to live, not to exist.

> I shall not waste my days in trying to prolong them.

> I shall use my time.

The biographer Stasz notes that the passage "has many marks of London's style" but the only line that could be safely attributed to London was the first. The words Shepard quoted were from a story in the San Francisco Bulletin, December 2, 1916, by journalist Ernest J. Hopkins, who visited the ranch just weeks before London's death. Stasz notes, "Even more so than today journalists' quotes were unreliable or even sheer inventions," and says no direct source in London's writings has been found. However, at least one line, according to Stasz, is authentic, being referenced by London and written in his own hand in the autograph book of Australian suffragette Vida Goldstein:

> Dear Miss Goldstein:–
>
> Seven years ago I wrote you that I'd rather be ashes than dust. I still subscribe to that sentiment.
>
> Sincerely yours,
>
> Jack London
>
> Jan. 13, 1909

In his short story "By The Turtles of Tasman", a character, defending her "ne'er-do-well grasshopperish father" to her "antlike uncle", says: "... my father has been a king. He has lived .... Have you lived merely to live? Are you afraid to die? I'd rather sing one wild song and burst my heart with it, than live a thousand years watching my digestion and being afraid of the wet. When you are dust, my father will be ashes."

"The Scab"

A short diatribe on "The Scab" is often quoted within the U.S. labor movement and frequently attributed to London. It opens:

> After God had finished the rattlesnake, the toad, and the vampire, he had some awful substance left with which he made a scab. A scab is a two-legged animal with a corkscrew soul, a water brain, a combination backbone of jelly and glue. Where others have hearts, he carries a tumor of rotten principles. When a scab comes down the street, men turn their backs and Angels weep in Heaven, and the Devil shuts the gates of hell to keep him out....

In 1913 and 1914, a number of newspapers printed the first three sentences with varying terms used instead of "scab", such as "knocker","stool pigeon"or "scandal monger"

842

This passage as given above was the subject of a 1974 Supreme Court case, Letter Carriers v. Austin, in which Justice Thurgood Marshall referred to it as "a well-known piece of trade union literature, generally attributed to author Jack London". A union newsletter had published a "list of scabs," which was granted to be factual and therefore not libelous, but then went on to quote the passage as the "definition of a scab". The case turned on the question of whether the "definition" was defamatory. The court ruled that "Jack London's... 'definition of a scab' is merely rhetorical hyperbole, a lusty and imaginative expression of the contempt felt by union members towards those who refuse to join", and as such was not libelous and was protected under the First Amendment.

Despite being frequently attributed to London, the passage does not appear at all in the extensive collection of his writings at Sonoma State University's website. However, in his book The War of the Classes he published a 1903 speech entitled "The Scab", which gave a much more balanced view of the topic:

> The laborer who gives more time or strength or skill for the same wage than another, or equal time or strength or skill for a less wage, is a scab. The generousness on his part is hurtful to his fellow-laborers, for it compels them to an equal generousness which is not to their liking, and which gives them less of food and shelter. But a word may be said for the scab. Just as his act makes his rivals compulsorily generous, so do they, by fortune of birth and training, make compulsory his act of generousness.
>
> [...]
>
> Nobody desires to scab, to give most for least. The ambition of every individual is quite the opposite, to give least for most; and, as a result, living in a tooth-and-nail society, battle royal is waged by the ambitious individuals. But in its most salient aspect, that of the struggle over the division of the joint product, it is no longer a battle between individuals, but between groups of individuals. Capital and labor apply

themselves to raw material, make something useful out of it, add to its value, and then proceed to quarrel over the division of the added value. Neither cares to give most for least. Each is intent on giving less than the other and on receiving more.

Legacy and honors

Mount London, also known as Boundary Peak 100, on the Alaska-British Columbia boundary, in the Boundary Ranges of the Coast Mountains of British Columbia, is named for him.

Jack London Square on the waterfront of Oakland, California was named for him.

He was honored by the United States Postal Service with a 25¢ Great Americans series postage stamp released on January 11, 1986.

Jack London Lake (Russian), a mountain lake located in the upper reaches of the Kolyma River in Yagodninsky district of Magadan Oblast.

Fictional portrayals of London include Michael O'Shea in the 1943 film Jack London, Jeff East in the 1980 film Klondike Fever, Aaron Ashmore in the Murdoch Mysteries episode "Murdoch of the Klondike" from 2012, and Johnny Simmons in the 2014 miniseries Klondike. (Source: Wikipedia)

NOTABLE WORKS

NOVELS

The Cruise of the Dazzler (1902)

A Daughter of the Snows (1902)

The Call of the Wild (1903)

The Kempton-Wace Letters (1903) (published anonymously, co-authored with Anna Strunsky)

The Sea-Wolf (1904)

The Game (1905)

White Fang (1906)

Before Adam (1907)

The Iron Heel (1908)

Martin Eden (1909)

Burning Daylight (1910)

Adventure (1911)

The Scarlet Plague (1912)

A Son of the Sun (1912)

The Abysmal Brute (1913)

The Valley of the Moon (1913)

The Mutiny of the Elsinore (1914)

The Star Rover (1915) (published in England as The Jacket)

The Little Lady of the Big House (1916)

Jerry of the Islands (1917)

Michael, Brother of Jerry (1917)

Hearts of Three (1920) (novelization of a script by Charles Goddard)

The Assassination Bureau, Ltd (1963) (left half-finished, completed by Robert L. Fish)

SHORT STORIES

"An Old Soldier's Story" (1894)

"Who Believes in Ghosts!" (1895)

"And 'FRISCO Kid Came Back" (1895)

"Night's Swim In Yeddo Bay" (1895)

"One More Unfortunate" (1895)

"Sakaicho, Hona Asi And Hakadaki" (1895)

"A Klondike Christmas" (1897)

"Mahatma's Little Joke" (1897)

"O Haru" (1897)

"Plague Ship" (1897)

"The Strange Experience Of A Misogynist" (1897)

"Two Gold Bricks" (1897)

"The Devil's Dice Box" (1898)

"A Dream Image" (1898)

"The Test: A Clondyke Wooing" (1898)

"To the Man on Trail" (1898)

"In a Far Country" (1899)

"The King of Mazy May" (1899)

"The End Of The Chapter" (1899)

"The Grilling Of Loren Ellery" (1899)

"The Handsome Cabin Boy" (1899)

"In The Time Of Prince Charley" (1899)

"Old Baldy" (1899)

"The Men of Forty Mile" (1899)

"Pluck and Pertinacity" (1899)

"The Rejuvenation of Major Rathbone" (1899)

"The White Silence" (1899)

"A Thousand Deaths" (1899)

"Wisdom of the Trail" (1899)

"An Odyssey of the North" (1900)

"The Son of the Wolf" (1900)

"Even unto Death" (1900)

"The Man with the Gash" (1900)

"A Lesson in Heraldry" (1900)

"A Northland Miracle" (1900)

"Proper "GIRLIE"" (1900)

"Thanksgiving on Slav Creek" (1900)

"Their Alcove" (1900)

"Housekeeping in the Klondike" (1900)

"Dutch Courage" (1900)

"Where the Trail Forks" (1900)

"Hyperborean Brew" (1901)

"A Relic of the Pliocene" (1901)

"The Lost Poacher" (1901)

"The God of His Fathers" (1901)

""FRISCO Kid's" Story" (1901)

"The Law of Life" (1901)

"The Minions of Midas" (1901)

"In the Forests of the North" (1902)

"The "Fuzziness" of Hoockla-Heen" (1902)

"The Story of Keesh" (1902)

"Keesh, Son of Keesh" (1902)

"Nam-Bok, the Unveracious" (1902)

"Li Wan the Fair" (1902)

"Lost Face"

"Master of Mystery" (1902)

"The Sunlanders" (1902)

"The Death of Ligoun" (1902)

"Moon-Face" (1902)

"Diable—A Dog" (1902), renamed Bâtard in 1904

"To Build a Fire" (1902, revised 1908)

"The League of the Old Men" (1902)

"The Dominant Primordial Beast" (1903)

"The One Thousand Dozen" (1903)

"The Marriage of Lit-lit" (1903)

"The Shadow and the Flash" (1903)

"The Leopard Man's Story" (1903)

"Negore the Coward" (1904)

"All Gold Cañon" (1905)

"Love of Life" (1905)

"The Sun-Dog Trail" (1905)

"The Apostate" (1906)

"Up the Slide" (1906)

"Planchette" (1906)

"Brown Wolf" (1906)

"Make Westing" (1907)

"Chased by the Trail" (1907)

"Trust" (1908)

"A Curious Fragment" (1908)

"Aloha Oe" (1908)

"That Spot" (1908)

"The Enemy of All the World" (1908)

"The House of Mapuhi" (1909)

"Good-by, Jack" (1909)

"Samuel" (1909)

"South of the Slot" (1909)

"The Chinago" (1909)

"The Dream of Debs" (1909)

"The Madness of John Harned" (1909)

"The Seed of McCoy" (1909)

"A Piece of Steak" (1909)

"Mauki" (1909)

"The Whale Tooth" (1909)

"Goliath" (1910)

"The Unparalleled Invasion" (1910)

"Told in the Drooling Ward" (1910)

"When the World was Young" (1910)

"The Terrible Solomons" (1910)

"The Inevitable White Man" (1910)

"The Heathen" (1910)

"Yah! Yah! Yah!" (1910)

"By the Turtles of Tasman" (1911)

"The Mexican" (1911)

"War" (1911)

"The Unmasking of the Cad" (1911)

"The Scarlet Plague" (1912)

"The Captain of the Susan Drew" (1912)

"The Sea-Farmer" (1912)

"The Feathers of the Sun" (1912)

"The Prodigal Father" (1912)

"Samuel" (1913)

"The Sea-Gangsters" (1913)

"The Strength of the Strong" (1914)

"Told in the Drooling Ward" (1914)

"The Hussy" (1916)

"Like Argus of the Ancient Times" (1917)

"Jerry of the Islands" (1917)

"The Red One" (1918)

"Shin-Bones" (1918)

"The Bones of Kahekili" (1919)

SHORT STORY COLLECTIONS

Son of the Wolf (1900)

Chris Farrington, Able Seaman (1901)

The God of His Fathers & Other Stories (1901)

Children of the Frost (1902)

The Faith of Men and Other Stories (1904)

Tales of the Fish Patrol (1906)

Moon-Face and Other Stories (1906)

Love of Life and Other Stories (1907)

Lost Face (1910)

South Sea Tales (1911)

When God Laughs and Other Stories (1911)

The House of Pride & Other Tales of Hawaii (1912)

Smoke Bellew (1912)

A Son of the Sun (1912)

The Night Born (1913)

The Strength of the Strong (1914)

The Turtles of Tasman (1916)

The Human Drift (1917)

The Red One (1918)

On the Makaloa Mat (1919)

Dutch Courage and Other Stories (1922)

AUTOBIOGRAPHICAL MEMOIRS

The Road (1907)

The Cruise of the Snark (1911)

John Barleycorn (1913)

NON-FICTION AND ESSAYS

Through the Rapids on the Way to the Klondike (1899)

From Dawson to the Sea (1899)

What Communities Lose by the Competitive System (1900)

The Impossibility of War (1900)

Phenomena of Literary Evolution (1900)

A Letter to Houghton Mifflin Co. (1900)

Husky, Wolf Dog of the North (1900)

Editorial Crimes — A Protest (1901)

Again the Literary Aspirant (1902)

The People of the Abyss (1903)

How I Became a Socialist (1903)

The War of the Classes (1905)

The Story of an Eyewitness (1906)

A Letter to Woman's Home Companion (1906)

Revolution, and other Essays (1910)

Mexico's Army and Ours (1914)

Lawgivers (1914)

Our Adventures in Tampico (1914)

Stalking the Pestilence (1914)

The Red Game of War (1914)

The Trouble Makers of Mexico (1914)

With Funston's Men (1914)

POETRY

A Heart (1899)

Abalone Song (1913)

And Some Night (1914)

Ballade of the False Lover (1914)

Cupid's Deal (1913)

Daybreak (1901)

Effusion (1901)

George Sterling (1913)

Gold (1915)

He Chortled with Glee (1899)

He Never Tried Again (1912)

His Trip to Hades (1913)

Homeland (1914)

Hors de Saison (1913)

If I Were God (1899)

In a Year (1901)

In and Out (1911)

Je Vis en Espoir (1897)

Memory (1913)

Moods (1913)

My Confession (1912)

My Little Palmist (1914)

Of Man of the Future (1915)

Oh You Everybody's Girl (19)

On the Face of the Earth You are the One (1915)

Rainbows End (1914)

Republican Rallying Song (1916)

Sonnet (1901)

The Gift of God (1905)

The Klondyker's Dream (1914)

The Lover's Liturgy (1913)

The Mammon Worshippers (1911)

The Republican Battle-Hymn (1905)

The Return of Ulysses (1915)

The Sea Sprite and the Shooting Star (1916)

The Socialist's Dream (1912)

The Song of the Flames (1903)

The Way of War (1906)

The Worker and the Tramp (1911)

Tick! Tick! Tick! (1915)

Too Late (1912)

Weasel Thieves (1913)

When All the World Shouted my Name (1905)

Where the Rainbow Fell (1902)

Your Kiss (1914)

PLAYS

Theft (1910)

Daughters of the Rich: A One Act Play (1915)

The Acorn Planter: A California Forest Play (1916)